Stirring the Stillness
Part 2, Tortured Journey

Book Two of the Stillness Series

Richard Lee Ferguson

"While sane men cannot make madmen sane,

Madmen can make sane men mad."

— Rousseau

"To all those First Steps who are not fully human."

— Michael Powers

Also by Richard Lee Ferguson

The Stillness Series

Book 1: Stirring the Stillness, Part 1 Voices of Quest

Book 2: Stirring the Stillness, Part 2 Tortured Journey

Book 3: Stilling the Stillness, Part 1 Voices of War

Book 4: Stilling the Stillness, Part 2 Restless Spirits

Book 5: Becoming the Stillness, Part 1 Voices of Madness

Book 6: Becoming the Stillness, Part 2 Haunted Caves

Book 7: The Hunchback's Gift, Part 1 Voices of Defeat

Book 8: The Hunchback's Gift, Part 2 Superior Ones Risen

Book 9: Flames of Extinction, Part 1 The Last Voice

Book 10: Flames of Extinction, Part 2 Stillness is Stilled

For the full series, visit the Amazon series page: https://www.amazon.com/dp/B0F1WJ5J4N

Contents

Principal Characters

Voices – God and Goddess

Michael Powers – Narrator, son of John Powers and Bai Meiying
John Powers – American father of Michael Powers; businessman
Bai Meiying – Chinese mother of Michael Powers; pianist
Marie Telles – American friend and lover of Bai Meiying
Meili – Chinese friend and lover of Bai Meiying
Madame Liu – Wife of Master Liu and co-leader of The Quest
Master Liu – Husband of Madame Liu and co-leader of The Quest
Master Zhou – Wealthy landowner
Lu Shishen – Canadian friend of John Powers
Feng Shiren – Mysterious soldier
Buandelgereen – Female Mongol leader; protectress of Bai Meiying
Lihua – Chinese woman warrior
Father Durant – French priest
Colonel Naguma – Japanese officer
Nobaru Ichida – Japanese officer
Beethoven (Wang Lihua) – Son of Madame Wang; spy for Mr. President
Little Acorn – Child member of The Group
Nanny Peach – Nanny of Michael Powers
Mr. Gao – Professor; member of The Group
David Hendricks – Assistant director of symphony orchestra
Arthur Mobley – Businessman and boss of John Powers
Madame Dau – Council chief of Song Nhan village
Suling – Female friend of John Powers
Peter Hedley – American friend of John Powers
Mr. President – Mysterious Chinese warlord
Mulan – Adopted daughter of John Powers and Bai Meiying

Preface

Can Humans Be Replaced Peacefully?

Query: Are you one of the increasing numbers of people who think humans are irredeemably destructive and pose such a threat to the planet that their extinction would be a good thing? However, do you also abhor the massive destruction and suffering that would necessarily be the consequence of their demise? Bloody, violent dystopian novels often focus only on a few survivors of such devastation, not on the suffering that would extend to all other life forms on the planet. While there are many excellent dystopian novels, such a formulaic concentration on a small group of heroic protagonists can be narrow and unsatisfying.

So, how to unravel the ubiquitous human presence without simultaneously destroying the rest of the planetary ecosystem? Can a successor species evolve fast enough to replace humankind, or would it be extinguished before it has a chance to spread?

Such a successor species, by random chance or intentional design, must possess far greater cognitive and empathetic capacities to thwart the human proclivity for eliminating real or perceived threats. What would it be like for those first generations of advanced individuals surrounded by a sea of slow-witted but resourceful *Homo sapiens*? How would they survive the human penchant for fearing otherness and a relentless instinct to exterminate it? Whether the guiding force effectuating this change is Nature, Superior Alien, God or Gods, Goddess or Goddesses, here is an interesting way forward:

Replace *Homo sapiens* with a more advanced species, but not *drive* them to extinction through violent extermination, rather *dilute* their genes to insignificance over generations. There is precedent for such top-down genetic engineering. Human biologists eliminate dangerous pests by introducing mutant strains that breed with the targeted species to produce offspring harboring the desired genetic makeup. Generations later, the original species is superseded.

A new form of consciousness must necessarily arise—one in which strange Voices with immense cognitive power reverberate in advanced minds in the same way Voices once arose in the minds of early *Homo sapiens* separating them from competitors such as Neanderthals. Humans would initially diagnose those hearing such new Voices as schizophrenics, but they are, in fact, the incipient stirrings of a superior species. However, new Voices must be only the beginning, as this emerging species must also evolve powerful physical capabilities to overcome human weapons of destruction.

The doves must have sharper claws than the hawks . . .

The Stillness Series is the epic story of one such scenario.

Prologue

Previously. . . .

In *Voices of Quest*, the first stirrings began: John, Meiying, Madame Liu, and others set out with the Precious Object, carrying more than cargo through war-torn China. Their journey became both flight and search, marked by suspicion, faith, and voices that whispered of destinies beyond their comprehension. Bonds of love and jealousy, of fear and loyalty, began to fracture beneath the weight of war and prophecy. Already, the foundations of human certainty trembled.

Now the path descends from quest into torment. The way is not lit by hope but scarred by suffering. Each traveler must face what lies buried: trauma, betrayal, and the tearing apart of spirit from flesh. The Voices no longer guide gently; they demand reckoning. What once seemed a pilgrimage begins to resemble crucifixion.

And so the questions burn:

How much can be lost before the journey itself collapses?

Can a soul survive being broken, and if not, what rises in its place?

If the Precious Object is preserved, will those who carry it remain intact, or must they be destroyed to ensure its passage?

~ Dear, dear Reader ~

I await the answers.

Chapter One

PART FIVE: IRON DOORS

Appearance?

~ A Mysterious Incident ~

Harangued by the voices bickering in his head, John returned to his room. In bed, he stared at the rock ceiling where fantastic shadows twisted and turned in the flickering lantern light. It appeared to him they writhed in agony to the ugly rhythm of the arguing voices.

He groaned at the memory of Lu Zhishen's plan to stand guard outside the iron door and catch whoever dwelt behind it venturing out. It seemed too easy that someone or something would open the door and drag the Precious Object and the bag containing a Nazi uniform back through the opening. *He won't see anything*, John thought.

The consensus among the group was also that Lu Zhishen would see nothing. Still, everyone seemed on tenterhooks, and they all quickly retired to their own rooms to await the dawn. John blew out the lantern, as the inadequate ventilation failed to stop the build-up of smoke and the caustic stench of kerosene. Immediately the darkness smothered him, seeming to intensify the echoing impact of the voices. He had no defense against their attacks, and sleep was out of the question.

Why don't you go to the bridge and jump! rasped a malevolent voice.

One of those demon voices, thought John. *Not God. Certainly not Goddess. Not Her!*

He considered the command: to jump or not to jump? It seemed the way to go. But what about seeing *her*? And Meiying? *Best for everyone if I jump. Meiying, if she makes it here, will have* her. *They will all have* her. *No one will miss me. Even Suling has Child of Buddha now.*

The room exploded in a spectacular burst of blue light. Someone hovered at the foot of his bed. A woman. She looked down at John, her features made visible in the blue glow. John stared at her in wordless awe. She sat in the lotus position on a huge, dazzling white flower floating above the bed. Her sad, contemplative face gazed from beneath an elaborate crown glimmering a kaleidoscope of colors. A cinder-bright jewel embedded in her forehead burned brightly and an intricate necklace lay cradled between her bare breasts. Her left hand rested on her thigh, the upturned curve of her fingers resembling the albino legs of a gracefully dead spider; her right hand poised in the air, index finger and thumb touching to form an almost perfect circle while the other fingers radiated outward.

You will not jump, came Her soothing voice. ***You are needed. Those evil voices are the jumbled outbursts of a persistent human bloodline, warped by the alien DNA usurping your genome.***

The words were uttered with a preternatural calmness and reassurance that, when repeated, worked as a sedative. He knew he should be terrified and flee Her presence, but somehow She seemed a more benevolent outgrowth of his illness, friend rather than foe (most of the time). Against his will, sleep came quickly and deeply, merging Her presence with his dreams until the two became indistinguishable.

~

John awoke to banging on his door. Before he could respond, it burst open, allowing light and a very agitated Suling to enter.

"John, come quickly! Something's happened!"

By the time he threw on some clothes and stumbled out the door, Suling stood meters away waving frantically for him to come. When they reached the iron door, Feng Shiren and Madame Liu were leaning over the prone body of Lu Zhishen.

"What happened?" John asked stupidly.

"We can't seem to wake him," said Master Zhou distractedly.

"Is he hurt?"

"Don't know."

"Notice the bag and the box are gone?" observed Feng Shiren almost gleefully. "He's been drugged."

"We don't know that," scolded Madame Liu.

"He's not drugged," announced Child of Buddha. "He's in a different place."

~ *Japanese Plus One* ~

Not long after moving in to her new abode, Meiying and Madame Ling watched the Japanese march past their house. Unlike Meiying, the expression of Madame Ling did not reflect fear but rather disgust.

"Can't get away from the dogs!" she exclaimed.

But a repeat of the Nanjing horrors did not occur and the daily routine of the town returned almost to normal. These Japanese soldiers had seen too many battles; grinding war no longer gave them reason to prance and boast. Still, it was best to stay out of their way. But business at the Palace plummeted as young Chinese men made themselves scarce, and only the bravest women ventured out. Meiying went to and from work wearing formless outer clothes and thick scarves to hide her face. Collaborators and chronically solitary drinkers made up the bulk of the clientele, such as it was.

She had now noticed in herself an accelerating hardening of her attitude toward life, toward people. Trust, of course, had long ago become an unthinkable indulgence. Bitterness at her plight had taken firm root and made daily progress, burrowing deep down into the wellspring of her capacity for joy, sucking it dry. Cynicism replaced sincerity, and she found herself often saying to Madame Ling, "You are right, men are dogs."

Nights at the Palace went excruciatingly slow for the Peng family. Because the Japanese remained in town, Meiying played popular Chinese songs rather than jazz, and whenever Japanese soldiers occasionally wandered in, she played classical music to bore them so they would leave. Her tips diminished to almost nothing. Madame Ling waved off her rent payment for that month, and expenses were cut to the bone. Food again became scarce. Meiying now had a deep aversion to hunger, and she vowed that she would do anything necessary to eat, regardless of improper behavior or dangerous consequences.

One night, as Meiying half-heartedly played a medley of simple love songs, a group of Japanese officers entered the Palace. Conversation stopped and she looked up through the smoky room to see very plainly a tall German officer standing among the shorter Japanese in his crisp and intimidating uniform, a swastika obscenely emboldened on his sleeve. The instant his eyes met hers, a premonition of catastrophe struck her with terrifying clarity. She quickly looked down at the keyboard, but his gaze bore into her skull.

After the group sat at a table, Aden, who had been the waiter, discreetly slipped into the kitchen, soon replaced by Mrs. Peng who took their orders. A young Japanese officer evidently acted as an interpreter for the German. As Meiying cast surreptitious glances at them, she experienced an uncomfortable recollection of their faces from some past encounter, faint but persistent. Mr. Peng prepared the drinks and while his wife set the glasses on the table, the German leaned over and whispered to the young Japanese officer, who then spoke in Chinese to Mrs. Peng.

"Tell the pianist to play a piece, any piece, by Beethoven."

Mrs. Peng did not understand the reference to Beethoven and in her fumbling effort to repeat the instructions, the German officer cursed and called loudly to Meiying, "Beethoven! Danke, Fraulein!"

Seeing Meiying's confusion, the German abruptly stood and crossed the dance floor, followed by the interpreter. His boots sounded like death. When he reached the piano, he stared at Meiying and smiled.

"Beethoven, fifth piano concerto, second movement please, Bai Meiying," he enunciated in perfect English.

At first, with the horrifying mention of her name, Meiying considered feigning ignorance, but his loud boots, SS emblazoned on his tunic, and the skull insignia on his cap, made her decide against it.

"Yes," she said simply.

He clicked his heels, removed his cap, and returned to the table. The Japanese officer followed, not without gazing at Meiying wonderingly. All was deathly still in the Palace. Most patrons had quietly left.

She began to play.

The German closed his eyes.

The Japanese officers with him listened in respectful silence.

When she finished the second movement, the German clapped, quickly joined politely by his Japanese friends. He returned to the piano alone, having motioned his interpreter to remain at the table, and spoke in a low voice.

"Do you speak English, Miss Bai?"

"Yes."

"Then listen. I know what happened with Colonel Naguma." He paused. Meiying remained silent.

"You are, apparently, a wanted woman by my Japanese colleagues."

Still she said nothing, trying not to faint. She leaned on the piano for support.

"Tomorrow I will send for you. I know where you live. At ten o'clock. My Japanese liaison, Lieutenant Ichida, will come for you. No use to try and run as my Japanese compatriots have people watching you. Now, please continue. Play what you like, as I must acquiesce to my Japanese friends. Play Japanese songs, if you like."

"May I ask?" she said, avoiding eye contact.

"Yes?"

"How did you find me here?"

"My dear, you have left a trail kilometers wide."

"Oh."

"You are a terrible spy! A terrible murderer!" He considered for a short while, and then said, "Which is why I think you are neither."

"I am neither!"

"Well, perhaps. The romantic in me says anyone who plays as you do cannot be these things. But we Germans. . . . " he trailed off, a study in disfiguring pain, or perhaps disgust, reflected in his face. "But we Germans!" he repeated, then regained control. "Besides, Lieutenant Ichida may be of interest to you. He speaks multiple languages, even studied English in Taiyuan from someone you might recognize. Yes, his story may definitely be of interest."

Meiying sensed a vulnerable sincerity and for a brief moment she felt some glimmer of hope, but her freshly reinforced distrust regained control. His swastika allowed no room for naiveté. Without another word, she played Mozart, in as savage a way as Amadeus could accommodate. Her reply through music expressed her contempt, so she felt surprised when he said under his breath, "Yes, play Mozart angrily. He would weep today if he saw. . . . "

~

The next day, Lieutenant Ichida came to the house and asked to speak with Meiying alone. Shown into a private room, Meiying sat across from him and listened with increasing amazement.

"Miss Bai, my name is Lieutenant Ichida. Nobaru Ichida. I believe I saw you once, at Colonel Naguma's residence. I also met a friend of yours in Taiyuan. It is odd that we meet under these circumstances. This person in Taiyuan told me about you, but I never thought I would see you again."

"If I might ask, Lieutenant Ichida, who was this person?" Meiying trembled with anticipation.

"Before I tell you, I must reveal that only myself and Colonel Müller know about your . . . situation here. For reasons I cannot say, we have kept the secret, your secret, from the local authorities."

Meiying could only blink in disbelief.

"He, of course, heard you play for Colonel Naguma long ago, and is quite taken by your music, while I am taken by what your friend said in Taiyuan. Since we both have an interest, I have made discreet inquiries. You are in great danger, Miss Bai. Great danger. We are not the only ones aware of your presence here. There are others."

"Yes, yes," Meiying whispered.

"Do you know them?"

"I think so."

Nobaru nodded but said nothing.

"Lieutenant, sir?" began Meiying.

"Yes?"

"Who was the person in Taiyuan?"

Nobaru held out his hands, palms up, and smiled. "John Powers, an American teacher, told me about you and your strange quest for a mysterious lady. His story intrigued me, as did his adamant defense of you. Oddly enough, both myself and Colonel Müeller are convinced you are no spy." He laughed. "Of course, we both have different reasons for believing so. I like music, but he is . . . shall I say, crazy for your Western classical music. But the one common denominator we share about your case is that we both knew Colonel Naguma."

"I am no spy!" said Meiying in a low but passionate voice. "And I am no murderer!"

Nobaru sighed. "Nevertheless, Colonel Müeller wants to see you at his office. I believe him to be a decent man." He smiled mournfully. "Some of us wish the world were otherwise, in spite of our uniforms."

Meiying had no response. Her mind raced ahead to the meeting with Müeller. No doubt he wanted sex in exchange for his kindness. Befitting her newfound hardness, she decided she would gladly give him what he wanted—but for food, information, and perhaps protection.

Meiying wanted to ask Lt. Ichida many questions, but he glanced at his watch and abruptly stood, smoothing his tunic. "Sorry, we must leave. I'm afraid we're already late." They were out the door before Meiying could tell Madame Ling where she was going.

Nobaru said something in Japanese to the driver. With a gallant gesture, he invited Meiying to sit in the back seat of a severe-looking, black staff car, sliding in beside her from the other side. Evidently, he did not wish to speak, instead staring out the window during the entire trip. Meiying assumed he did not want to talk while the driver could hear. The car pulled up to a large concrete building that had formerly been the administrative center of the district. Japanese soldiers were everywhere, swarming like bees around a hive. Nobaru attached his sword, again smoothed his tunic, and led her up a few flights of stairs, where she stood in front of a door with a temporary sign reading, "Col. Müeller, Liaison. Third Reich."

Nobaru knocked.

"Come in," came a voice in tortured Japanese.

When Meiying and Lt. Ichida entered, Müeller stood and bowed, waving a hand at Nobaru to close the door.

"Please sit," said Müeller in English. "If Lt. Ichida will be kind enough to get us tea?"

Nobaru nodded and left. When the door closed behind him, Müeller said, "I'm sure Lt. Ichida has briefed you on the essentials?"

"Yes, thank you."

"I have no desire to—"

Nobaru entered, followed by an aide who placed a tray on the table and exited obsequiously.

While Nobaru poured, Müeller continued, "Anyway, I have no desire to reveal your secret, nor does Lt. Ichida. We are both concerned with more important matters. Believe me, we are not the police . . . or the Gestapo, thank god. But, in spite of your understandable assumptions, we have not brought you here to arrest, but at the same time also not out of wholly benevolent motives."

Meiying listened in fascination to his perfect English and wondered where the direction of his words were leading.

"No, we do not want to have sex with you, or even, in my case, cloister you here to be my personal musician—much as I would like to." He grimaced and looked away. "I am not Colonel Naguma."

Nobaru coughed in such an unnatural manner that Meiying could not tell whether he agreed with the German or not. Müeller glanced at him coolly and continued. "Nevertheless, Lt. Ichida is an officer in the Imperial Japanese Army and I am an officer in the Wehrmacht, and both of us are interested in certain people you are familiar with."

Meiying's heart skipped a beat, fearing he referred to John.

"Japanese intelligence is particularly interested in a couple of these people. Would you answer a few questions about them for us?"

"If I can."

"I'm going to mention two names to begin with." He paused for effect. "Mr. President and Wang Liwei, aka Beethoven. Later, we want to ask about Beethoven's uncle."

Meiying involuntarily gasped.

"We know you know them. Can you tell us what you know?"

Meiying narrated the story of her involvement with both, keeping very few details to herself. After pummeling her with questions, most of which she could not answer, she waited for the other shoe to fall; some *quid pro quo*, but surprisingly none came.

"Before you go, Miss Bai, what can we do for you?"

She felt foolish. To ask for money seemed unclean. "Food," she said at last.

Lt. Ichida laughed. "Easy. I will take you to a store where you may buy what you like."

Meiying hesitated.

"No, I think not, lieutenant," said Müeller. "Her Chinese friends will accuse her of collaboration, and when we leave. . . . "

"Well, I'm not sure—" began Nobaru after a pause.

"I am," said Colonel Müeller. "I will be a frequent customer at the New York Palace. I'm sure you will play music that will loosen my pockets for tips."

"But the other customers are afraid and will stay away!" Meiying blurted before thinking.

Müeller chuckled. "We'll see what I can do to not frighten them."

~

Nobaru reminisced about John during the ride back to Madame Ling's house, rekindling Meiying's desire to escape her plight and return to the group. As the car pulled up to the house, the driver opened her door, and when she stepped out, Lt. Ichida leaned across the back seat and called, "Oh, one more thing, Miss Bai. We may want you to do something for us later."

"Yes?" she asked nervously.

"Just something. Please remember, you are still being watched. It's for your own protection."

This clearly alarmed Meiying and she struggled to compose herself. Nobaru looked at her sympathetically.

"Oh, yes, thank you." She tried to walk casually to the front door, but her legs were wobbly and she needed to get inside fast before she threw up in front of Lt. Ichida.

Madame Ling greeted her at the door with a questioning face.

"Let me sit," whispered Meiying.

Before she knew it, a cold cloth was pressed to her forehead and tea was provided. She could scarcely process what had just happened. Telling Madame Ling the story helped, but she could not get to the bottom about what it was really all about. Meiying knew there must be some unspoken agenda, some expectation that left a bad taste in her mouth. It bore the unmistakable flavor of dread.

~ *Lu Zhishen Returns* ~

"I did not fall asleep!" Lu Zhishen repeated vehemently.

He sat upright in the same spot where he had been found unconscious.

"Then why were you . . . out?" asked Madame Liu, trying to sound reasonable.

"I was not asleep!"

"Then what were you?" asked Feng Shiren wryly. "Drugged?"

"How? I had nothing to eat or drink after you all left."

This puzzle remained unsolved. A deep mysterious quality enveloped the cave after this incident and members of the group often confided to the others their strange encounters with grotesque shadows, inexplicable noises, otherworldly breezes, and reappearing ghosts. John, however, never shared his vision of Goddess, nor did She reappear. Feng, Lu, and John took turns guarding the iron door, but nothing ever happened that was out of the ordinary.

"Because there was nothing *she* wanted," became the official explanation. "We have to wait until *she* wants something, then maybe we can catch *her*."

"I don't think 'catching' *her* is right," objected Suling in her gentle way. "But when will *she* appear?" It was the question she most often asked. Of all the members of the group, Suling seemed to suffer the most from *her* absence.

Child of Buddha invariably remained silent during these discussions.

The bizarre phenomena of the German uniform remained far outside the realm of even wild speculation, eliciting only the collective shaking of heads.

Gradually, expectations of seeing *her* were replaced by a routine assumption that they were somehow serving *her* by simply being there. Had *she* not provided them with accommodations? *She* became as invisible an object of worship as any other deity. Only the perceived nearness of *her* physical being and the existence of such a unique living environment gave their religion a more immediate urgency. Nevertheless, in spite of this spiritually charged atmosphere, they settled into a lethargic daily routine. Even Feng Shiren had given up trying to follow Mongol Peter and Mongol Little Acorn.

One day, as if sensing the progressive entrenchment of purposeless inertia, Mongol Peter invited them to accompany him to the nearest town. Or rather, he invited two of them—Madame Liu and Suling—telling the others that they would have their turns in future. It was to be a four-day trip, as the town was distant. Madame Liu and Master Zhou asked if the town had a bank, to which Mongol Peter smiled gregariously and replied in the affirmative.

The day of their departure left John feeling stranded as might a fish in a tide pool when the tide has receded to its lowest point. His voices had been absent for the longest time and he felt quite surprised that he rather missed them, in a way. Something in their incessant hectoring and arguing gave his life a meaning, a purpose, even if only to contribute sperm as a necessary ingredient to the creation of a son for Goddess—especially, he thought, if this son was to have some great impact on the world.

Fall was now in the air, and a penetrating chill made their forays outside the cave physically unpleasant but spiritually exhilarating. Before his departure, Mongol Peter had been stockpiling their food supply, leading Master Zhou to observe that *she* obviously intended their stay to continue indefinitely. Madame Liu and Suling had hardly disappeared over the horizon before the group began yearning for their missing comrades.

"If Madame Liu were here, she would comment upon my unhappy condition," complained Master Zhou. "Old as I am, that woman grows on you."

This comment drew the good-natured ribbing of the others.

"So, Master Zhou, your girlfriend has run off with a barbarian! A Mongol, no less!" cried Feng Shiren. "You are a male version of the Drunken Concubine in opera."

Amidst the tittering laughter, Master Zhou laughed along, and said, "Speaking of drunken, where is the wine?"

"And speaking of a concubine, where is the concubine?" threw in Feng, rolling his eyes.

Only Lu Zhishen did not participate in the jocularity. Since the incident at the iron door, the big Canadian had somehow changed in a way no one could put their finger on; a change so subtle only those who knew him well would notice. Yet, it was real enough that all of them grew concerned.

When he had gone for a walk outside the cave, Feng and John discussed how different he seemed. Child of Buddha, lurking nearby as always, observed, "He is a snake who has just shed his skin. Same snake. Different snake."

Feng Shiren rejoined, "Or had his skin removed for him that night."

When Lu returned to the cave and entered the dining area, the others gave each other knowing glances and asked if he had a nice walk.

Instead of responding with the usual pleasantries, he said, "I've made a decision."

They waited expectantly.

"I'm going to knock down that door."

"What do you mean?" asked an alarmed Master Zhou.

"I mean, I'm going to find a way to get through that door."

"How?"

He shook his head. "Not sure. Explosives, blowtorch, anything."

"Where will you find that stuff?" asked John.

"Well, I figure that town where Madame Liu and Suling went to must have what I need. If not, I'll go back across the border if I have to."

"I don't think that's a good idea," said Child of Buddha.

"Maybe not, but I'm gonna do it."

"Remember," said Master Zhou. "We were told *she* is waiting for Meiying to arrive."

Lu held up his hands, palms up. "What if she never does? Are we to wait until we die?"

"Never is a long time. We haven't been here that long."

"Long enough!" cried Lu in a tone that clearly doomed all efforts to dissuade useless.

~

The announcement by Lu threw the group into a welter of uncertainty. Some warned against his taking such a rash action while others, although urging caution, privately hoped he would succeed so the mystery lurking behind the iron door could at last be solved. John was a member of this later camp. Never one to initiate bold action—except his extraordinary decision to come to China, and look where that got him—he often rode the more adventurous coattails of others.

In his more speculative moments, he pictured the door coming down and staring at the terrifying figure of Goddess floating on the other side. But, in any case, whatever turned out to be behind the door, at least he would know.

Upon their return, Madame Liu and Suling reacted quite differently to Lu Zhishen's plan.

"That is impossible!" exclaimed Madame Liu. "Do you want to ruin everything?"

Before Lu could answer, Suling asked in understated alarm, "Zhishen, is that a good idea?"

His response to both was adamant: "Yes, I want to ruin everything! . . . and yes, I think it is a good idea!"

In spite of repeated attempts by Madame Liu and Master Zhou to dissuade him, Lu made good on his word. He disappeared one day, leaving behind a note that pledged to return with the necessary devices. If he did not return, it would mean he had died trying.

When apprised of this act, Mongol Peter seemed preternaturally calm. In fact, he simply shrugged and carried on as if nothing were amiss. This attitude puzzled everyone, especially Madame Liu, who finally observed, "He certainly knows more than us. If he is not worried, I guess we should not be."

Following this public epiphany, she appeared more at ease.

A week passed, and concern for Lu Zhishen's safety grew.

By the second week, speculation about his fate had reached crisis proportions. The very day Feng Shiren was about to set off with Mongol Peter to try and find him, Lu returned, much to the relief of his friends. Fall had brought fierce winds across the steppes and Lu suffered mightily from the cold, but he announced that he had found what he needed.

"That door is coming down!" he bellowed.

"How?" asked Feng.

Lu pointed to a big sack. "That's for me to know. All I ask is that you all wait outside the cave while I do it."

"Explosives!" cried Master Zhou, greatly alarmed. "You'll bring down the cave."

"Don't worry," said Lu. "This will be a very small, contained explosion. No chance for a cave-in. But out of an abundance of caution, I want you all safe."

"Are you sure we can't talk you out of this?" asked Master Zhou.

"Absolutely not!"

John looked at Mongol Peter who appeared to listen with an air of disinterest, even, if he wasn't mistaken, detached amusement.

Ignoring last minute exhortations to delay his plan, Lu proclaimed the next day to be the day of reckoning.

~ *The Day of Reckoning Begins* ~

No one could sleep that night. Lu Zhishen, pleading exhaustion, went to bed early, leaving the others to speculate on tomorrow's event.

"It's a bit like opening a tomb," said John.

"Tomb robbing," corrected Child of Buddha.

"Well," observed Madame Liu sagely. "The die is cast and our Mongol friend still seems unperturbed."

"So it should be okay," said John, which promptly brought a disgusted look from Madame Liu.

"Young people," said Master Zhou after a pause. "So impatient."

Feng Shiren, fire in his eyes, remarked, "Yes. Young people are the ones that keep the world going. I, for one, applaud Lu Zhishen and am very anxious to see what's on the other side of that damn door. Just wish I'd thought of it myself."

"I'm worried about Zhishen," mused Suling. "I hope he doesn't hurt himself."

The next morning, after the group had gathered in the dining area and eaten a sparse breakfast, Lu asked them to assemble outside the cave.

"Take the bikes and some food, just in case," he said.

"If there is a cave-in, it will also kill *her*," observed Master Zhou.

Somehow, this potentiality had not occurred to them.

"That's right," said Suling shuddering. "Why hadn't I thought of that. We can't take the risk, Zhishen!"

"I don't think any of us did," added Master Zhou. "It doesn't seem possible *she* can die."

"Nonsense!" cried Lu Zhishen. "There will be no cave-in! And even if it does, it would be small and not affect anything on the other side of the iron door."

"How do you know?" asked Feng Shiren.

"I know. Now, if you want to stay, go ahead, but I'm doing it now." He stood and set off for his room. When he returned, lugging the bag over his shoulder, the others had already set off across the stone bridge, each carrying a few personal belongings.

Lu called out, "It won't take long! I'll come out and get you when it's done so we can all go in together!"

They waved back in acknowledgement and gathered outside in the cold, resentful that they were made to leave the comfort of their rooms, yet expectant and excited to hear from Lu. As time passed and they heard nothing, anxiety took the place of excitement.

"Something should have happened by now," said John, the first to express concern.

"Too soon," observed Feng Shiren. "He needs time to set the charges."

More time passed, and the group walked in a circle, slapping their bodies to stay warm. As more time passed, it became obvious they should have heard from Lu by then.

"This is ridiculous!" said Madame Liu at last. "I'm going in."

"So am I," said Feng.

"We all will," offered Master Zhou.

As they started to enter the cave, Lu Zhishen emerged, his expression a mixture of puzzlement and sheepishness. Looking at their faces, he made his announcement.

"The door was open when I got there."

Stunned silence.

Letting the news sink in, he added, "Come and see what I found."

~ *Meiying Faces A Choice* ~

The week after her meeting with Colonel Müeller, Meiying dragged herself through a seemingly endless routine of work and sleep. At the Palace, she played for Müeller almost exclusively, as even fewer Chinese customers now patronized the club. Her tips, as promised by the German colonel, were generous, but the Peng family began regretting her presence; a reputation for collaboration had attached itself to the Palace, threatening all of them with 'midnight retaliations.' Despite the consensus of Mr. and Mrs. Peng that she must go, they could not fire her because of Müeller's obvious interest. Aden violently opposed his parents' desire when it was expressed at the family dinner table, and because of their threats he became more attentive, much to her annoyance. Living with Madame Ling became her sanctuary and her solace, but the threat of sudden disaster oppressed her beyond measure.

Change came one evening. As usual, the Palace was sparsely occupied, mainly by Japanese military personnel and a few Chinese collaborators. Colonel Müeller and Lt. Ichida entered and took their usual table. Meiying automatically switched from popular songs to classical music. Aden, as typical when Japanese were present, was nowhere to be found, so Mrs. Peng served. After she took orders from the two men, instead of passing them on directly to Mr. Peng behind the bar, she walked straight to the piano and whispered, "They want to see you now. You may stop playing."

Meiying could not stop trembling when she stood before their table. Colonel Müeller invited her to sit, and when she did, minced no words.

"Miss Bai, we need your services."

She was unable to speak.

"We want you to return to Mr. President."

Sent reeling, dizzy and lightheaded, Meiying managed to form the words, "But I can't."

Her reply evidently had no impact on them. Lt. Ichida spoke briefly to Müeller in German, then replied in excellent Chinese, "This fellow Beethoven is in town. He knows where you are. We've been tracking him, although he doesn't know we know. He's seen you and Colonel Müeller together, so he keeps his distance."

Meiying felt ill and had an impulse to flee back to Madame Ling's house.

"We want you to return with Beethoven to Mr. President."

"Why?" she uttered plaintively.

"To spy on him."

"But I am no spy. I can't."

"You *are* a spy, remember?"

"No, no."

"Yes you are. Look Miss Bai, we are honorable men. This favor would be honorable."

"But you have invaded China!" she blurted. "How can I help you?"

Ichida sighed and translated for the colonel.

"You don't understand," said Colonel Müeller in English. "This will serve you Chinese. You see, Mr. President is playing both sides for fools. We need to stop him, not just for ourselves, but for the innocent Chinese he is using for his own gain. He is a criminal, not a patriot."

Meiying thought of the Nanjing massacre and the murder of Meili; the German's distinction between criminals and patriots seemed utterly ludicrous and self-serving. "But I can't. I must continue my journey. Going back to him, to Mr. President . . . will kill me . . . he will kill me!"

By now the few patrons had left, afraid trouble was brewing. Mr. and Mrs. Peng remained silent and inconspicuous behind the bar. Müeller looked around, asked the Pengs to retire from the room, then stared back at Meiying.

"Look here, Miss Bai. I intentionally chose this bar to have our conversation rather than my private office. Others, Beethoven for instance, will think I'm only interested in you for music or sex, not for official reasons. You know very well that Lt. Ichida here could have you arrested anytime for this Naguma affair. But neither of us wants to do that. You will be well taken care of. We have agents who can protect you."

"Why not use them?" asked Meiying reasonably.

"They can't get close enough."

Meiying, by now unable to control the tears that she periodically wiped away, said, "I don't want to get close enough."

"We know you're a lesbian," said Lt. Ichida bluntly. "That is also an offense punishable by imprisonment."

Meiying gazed at Colonel Müeller's swastika glowing like a scarlet welt, a devil's tattoo carved into the souls of men, irremovable and irredeemable. All men, she thought, should have a swastika permanently tattooed to their foreheads for all the world to see. A warning to every being that is good and pure. Hatred flowed hot through her veins and arteries, now easily quickened to the boiling point by distrust and threats of intimidation. She wanted them all dead. She wanted to be left alone, wrapped in the arms of Goddess and of *her*, sheltered from the world's ugliness and violence. Deep inside, she made an unalterable decision to find a way—tonight—to escape or die trying. The thought of being held in the obscene, bulbous arms of Mr. President and smothered by his rolls of blubber was too much to bear.

"Go home and ponder your choices," said Müeller. Tomorrow I know you'll make the right decision, for yourself and for China."

That night Meiying laid out her old woman's disguise. There was nothing to ponder.

~

Behind Madame Ling's house, sitting pathetically in a dark corner across the street with an empty alms-bowl at his feet, Beethoven was himself in disguise. Since Old Uncle was incompetent enough to lose her, it had not taken him long to find Meiying performing at the New York Palace. Being a crippled beggar suited him. Left alone by the Japs, he could observe both Meiying and their clumsy agents. This particular corner had become one of his favorite locations for observing her comings-and-goings, for she had to exit the back door and cross this street to get either to work or to any of her other accustomed destinations. Besides, the Japs covered the front too closely.

This moonlit night, when he saw Meiying slip out of the back door of Madame Ling's house wearing her ridiculous disguise, he waited for the Jap agents to follow, then he took his place in line behind them.

They won't let her get far, he thought. *At some point, she'll have to come back to me.* Beethoven had always believed patience was his greatest asset.

After a long period of following the two Japanese agents who followed her, up streets and down alleyways, he began to wonder. *This is a merry chase. Slowest tail I've ever been on. Where is she going?*

An hour passed and still Meiying slowly traversed the town in an odd, zigzag pattern, her old lady hump and tattered shawl belying the young beauty underneath. Eventually, he observed one of the Japs talk quietly on a radio, then move decisively with his partner toward the dark figure of Meiying. They nabbed her under a rectangular patch of light from some still-open bar. Both men hovered over her, and Beethoven watched her shawl yanked off.

"What?" cried one of the Japs.

Beethoven peered from the darkness to make out details, which were maddeningly unavailable. The two Japs stood in his line-of-sight, chattering excitedly. When one of them stepped aside, the light illuminated the face of Madame Ling. Without wasting a second, Beethoven turned and bolted, the crippled beggar transformed into a young athlete, running as fast as he could toward Madame Ling's house on the other end of town.

~

By the time Beethoven had reached Madame Ling's house, Meiying was well on her way on a back road out of town. Determined to stay off the main arteries, she followed a narrow path by moonlight, pulling her cotton jacket tight around her neck against the cold Fall night. *Mongolian air*, she thought. *A reminder sent by my friends.*

Meiying had become so accustomed to traveling on the open road that she felt at ease; but in her heart, the time she spent in a real home with Madame Ling made her yearn to end the nomadic life she had been driven to adopt. Again the aching for Meili and Lihua was a sore that continued to fester, erupting in bone-weary longing during her most lonely moments such as this night. But even now, as she felt this burden of desolation and despair, her loneliness was at least gilded by a thin layer of euphoria that she, at least for the moment, had escaped her tormentors.

Although outside of town she had the path to herself, the thick underbrush gradually closed in around her and the gnarled arms and thorny branches grabbed at her from both sides. The path narrowed even more and her concern intensified. *This path is nothing more than a dead-end!* she thought wildly. *At least the main road would have been quicker. But this?!*

Her impulse was to turn around, but the fear that she was being followed compelled her to keep going. Cold became severe and she knew she needed to find some sort of shelter from the icy wind. To her relief, the path widened again and eventually led to a road capable of handling large vehicles. Blackness lightened to a soupy gray, and she knew dawn would soon arrive. She felt the need to avoid the road until she could see it more clearly and evaluate the danger. A clump of trees silhouetted against the sky on a small hill drew her to them, where she unrolled her bedding and laid exhausted under their outspreading canopy. Sleep came quickly.

Chapter Two

Maze Upon Maze

The Other Side of the
Iron Door

Lu Zhishen led the group into the cave and along the path that led directly to the iron door.

"You'll see, you'll see," he repeated excitedly.

When Lu shone the flashlight on the door to lead them through, he let out a piercing cry of shock.

"No! No! No!" he bellowed three times.

Illuminated clearly in the beam of light stood the iron door—closed.

"But it was open! It was open!" he shouted incredulously.

Feng Shiren tried, but the door was locked.

The charges and dynamite were gone.

"It was open!"

"We believe you," said Madame Liu very calmly.

"Goddamn *her*, it was open!" Lu repeated.

"Stop!" commanded Madame Liu. "*She* obviously did not want us to pass."

"What did you see?" demanded Feng Shiren.

"That's just it! That's what I wanted you all to see!"

"What?" prodded Feng.

"Nothing."

"What do you mean?" asked Master Zhou.

"I mean nothing."

"Please explain yourself," said Madame Liu. "Calm down and be clear."

Lu Zhishen took a few deep breaths, although his face remained red from anger and frustration.

"When I found the door open, I went through to check it out. I was amazed to find a solid rock wall. What I mean is that on the other side of the door is a small space completely surrounded by rock. The floor was smooth, like tile, but the space was completely empty. Empty!"

"Are you sure there was no path?" asked Master Zhou.

"I'm sure!"

"Maybe the rock wall was fake," suggested Suling.

"Didn't look like it."

"Did you check? Feel it? Maybe there's a button that makes the wall turn. What about that?" queried Feng Shiren.

"No. I came back to show you. I never thought the door would close again."

"Well, someone closed it."

"How? I tell you the space behind the door was surrounded by solid rock!"

"Then where did your bag go? The dynamite?"

Lu just shook his head.

"The answer is simple," announced Feng, hesitating dramatically.

"Well?" asked Madame Liu, impatient with his theatrics.

"The floor is fake. It must be some sort of trap door."

"Maybe," said Lu. "That's why I went back to get all of you, so we could all look together and see what the real story is."

"Well, too late now," said Master Zhou. "Too bad."

"I want to talk to Mongol Peter," said Madame Liu firmly. "Where is he?"

No one had seen him that day, which itself aroused suspicions among the group. "After all," pointed out Lu Zhishen. "He knew the plan was today. No wonder the bastard wasn't worried!" Although there was little more to say, the incident left a cloud of anxiety over everyone.

"I wonder if we're not wasting our time here," said Lu.

"Have faith in *her*," said Child of Buddha in her usual otherworldly tone.

"I also want to hear what Mongol Peter says," grumbled Lu Zhishen. "Otherwise, I'm getting more dynamite and come hell or high water, I'll find out what's going on here."

~

That evening, John briefly visited with his comrades, then retired early to his room. The voices, as usual, were argumentative and contradictory, all the while making outrageous statements.

Just wait for Meiying! urged Goddess. **Your time will come.**

Worthless mutant! The demon voice seemed particularly angry. **Waiting is all Your weak Chosen One is good for!**

Don't listen to it, John! It lies. Wait for Meiying!

She's dead.

No, presumptuous voice! She is alive and on her way. Demon indeed! She could be here any day, John. Stay!

Then what, frigid Goddess? Die here?

And so it went.

John clapped his hands over his ears, fully aware of the futility of the gesture. Fleeing the echo chamber of his room, he returned to the bridge. Lanterns flickered along its length, their light just enough to give terrifying hints about the extent of the crevasse it spanned. Long since, the crevasse had drawn him in times of stress, pulling him into its depths, inviting him to take his place among the winged breezes and alien chirps floating above what must be a craggy end. His desperation was driven by the knowledge that the voices were getting worse, and his sanity quickly dissembling.

Jump! The evil voice.

Jump! Then another.

Jump! Then both together.

As compelling as were these terrible voices, whether at God's direction or not, he knew such an act would require courage he did not possess, and for this cowardice he hated himself anew.

"Is it bad, John?" came a voice from the other end of the bridge.

John saw a monstrous shape loom high up on the cave ceiling. It drew nearer, becoming larger and more misshapen, projecting an alien form that momentarily took his breath away. He wanted to shout "Who's that?" but felt the words die in his throat.

"John?"

"Suling?"

"Yes."

But it was Child of Buddha that appeared mid-span on the bridge, her hunchback exaggerated by the shifting play of lantern light. The hideous shadow on the ceiling, now defined, lost its power. Suling followed behind, her familiar figure contrasting so gracefully with Child of Buddha's deformed body. Her mere presence acted as a balm to John's soul.

"Oh, it's you two!" cried John with a nervous laugh.

"Did we scare you?" called Child of Buddha as she traversed the bridge toward him.

"Not at all. Just didn't recognize you at first."

Suling spoke up. "We were out braving the cold, having a nice walk."

The two women sat next to him and looked down at the crevasse.

"Everything okay, John?" asked Suling. "Is it the voices again?"

"Yes." He did not want to elaborate in front of Child of Buddha.

"What did they say?" the hunchback asked openly, without a hint of restraint.

"Oh, just a lot of things."

"Like what?" she persisted.

"Sister," said Suling in a gently scolding tone. "Maybe he would prefer not to talk about it."

"Nonsense! Yes he does!"

"Well," said John, taken aback by Child of Buddha's vehemence. "Not really."

Child of Buddha stared at him as might a mother at a naughty child. "Oh yes, you do. You definitely do."

John sighed, appearing much put-upon but actually pleased she insisted. "They say horrible things. They call me horrible names. They tell me to commit horrible acts. So I would rather not talk about it." He waited to gauge the effect of this affectation.

"Is that what you tell your doctor when he asks for the symptoms of some pain?"

"Well . . . no, but if—" He kept testing.

"No! You tell him where it hurts, what the pain feels like. You describe it. Otherwise he can do nothing for you."

"Maybe, but you're not a doctor." He tested further.

Child of Buddha looked around. "Do you see one here?"

"No."

"Open your eyes, John. Here are two doctors sitting next to you."

John hesitated for effect.

"Now," said Child of Buddha. "Tell us about the voices."

"It's okay, John," said Suling. "She knows a bit about your situation. We all do."

John now experienced a feeling of security, a feeling of relief that these two women had breached his defenses with unaffected, unapologetic caring.

"Well, first of all, there are many voices, but two main ones."

"Tell us about those two," said Child of Buddha.

John looked down into the crevasse.

~

Don't do it John dear! It's a trick!
Do it! She lies!
They want to hurt you, Chosen One! Don't do it!
Jump now! Jump, before you are betrayed!

~

He held his hands over his ears, terrified and confused. He tried to tell himself these evil voices were the distorted human genes Goddess told him about, but his nerves were too raw.

The crevasse seemed inviting. Pulling.

~

Jump! Now an awful chorus.
Jump!
Jump!

~

"Tell us!" shouted Child of Buddha. "Don't listen to them! Listen to us! What are they saying?"

"To jump."

"Oh, god," murmured Suling.

But Child of Buddha smiled. "Yes, they tell you to jump. They are not your friends, John. We are. Who are the two main ones?"

"A God and a Goddess."

"Do they both tell you to jump?"

"No, I don't think so. Just one."

"Which one?"

"God."

"It's what I thought," said Child of Buddha. "How do you know it is God?"

"I know. She calls him that."

"She?" asked Suling.

"Goddess, right?" said Child of Buddha.

"Yes."

"Tell us about God?"

"He is stubborn. She wants to do something He doesn't want Her to do."

"What?"

John shook his head. The voices ran rampant in his mind and he had a hard time concentrating. Child of Buddha moved in front of him and put her hands on both sides of his head.

"Look at me, John! I am real! Tell me, what does the Goddess voice want to do?"

John felt his head exploding.

~

John Powers, listen to me. Step back. Do not do it. It was the Goddess voice, calm and steady. But the other voices drown Her out.

Don't wait! Jump!

Don't tell her!

Worthless fool! She lies. She really wants you to jump! Do it!

Don't speak to her, jump!

They want to poison you!

~

John gathered all his energy to block the terrible voices. "It isn't what She wants to do, it's what the evil ones want me to do."

"Jump?" asked Suling. "Oh, John, don't listen to Them!"

"No! You don't understand. She doesn't want me to jump. He does, but She doesn't."

"John, what does She want you to do?" whispered Child of Buddha, still touching his face with her hands.

He trembled uncontrollably and seemed to collapse in upon himself.

"She wants me to have a child with Meiying," he whispered.

"What?"

"Yes, a child. A son."

"Why?"

"I don't know, but it is for some important reason in the future. I don't know!"

"God does not want you to do this, correct John?" asked Child of Buddha calmly.

"No! No, He doesn't."

"Why?"

"I don't know that either. I don't know anything. I just know I want Them out of my head!"

"Yes, yes, we know," said Suling rubbing his back. "John, don't listen to them!"

"Who are the others?" pursued Child of Buddha.

"The others?"

"Yes, the other voices."

"Garbled. Mixed. Like some horrible chorus."

"Do they support God or Goddess?"

"I don't know. Sometimes one, sometimes the other."

"Do they want you to jump?"

~

Yes, jump!

Jump!

Jump!

~

"Yes," he whispered.

"Now?"

"Yes!"

"Hold him, Suling!" cried Child of Buddha. "We must both hold him!"

John struggled toward the edge, for the impulse to jump had become overwhelming. God commanded him. There was no choice. No choice.

Suling yelled for help.

Child of Buddha said quietly but with a firm tone, "John, they are shadows, like the one that scared you when we approached."

But John could not hear her, nor could he wonder how she knew. He felt compelled to jump, nothing else.

Others came.

Lu Zhishen and Feng Shiren helped him back to his room. John collapsed on his bed.

"How do we help him?" asked Madame Liu to the gathered comrades outside his door.

"That damn door must come down!" said Lu. "We all need help. *She* must appear. *She* must!"

Child of Buddha looked at Lu with a bemused smile. "She will, but only when the time is right."

"And when will that be?" snapped Lu.

"Perhaps soon, perhaps later, perhaps never."

~ *Meiying Gets Closer* ~

Meiying woke under the canopy of trees that bent and moaned in the chilled wind from Mongolia. She stood and looked at the road winding beneath the hill, not knowing what to expect: Japanese soldiers? Refugees? Chinese soldiers? Nothing? What she saw made her duck down to the safety of the blessed ground.

A Japanese convoy!

Not small.

Flankers beat the bushes for concealed partisans. Meiying saw them coming and sat up in full view, unmoving. The Japanese soldiers approached. She took off her peasant hat and smiled. Warily they came up to her. One of them shouted, "*Antahadare?*"

Though she understood, she pretended not to. She gazed at them with the most stupid expression possible, nodding all the while like a fool.

"Ah, ah," she repeated monotonously.

One soldier said to the other, "She's an idiot, but how nice it would be to release some tension. Her brain may not work, but she's pretty. I bet her cunt works!"

The other replied, "Go ahead. If you do, Lt. Komura will have you shot, but not before Sgt. Kanda cuts off your balls!"

Meiying looked at them blankly, mouth agape, stupidly repeating, "Ah, ah, ah. . . ."

"Ugh! Too bad!"

They moved on, leaving her still sitting beneath the tree, nodding stupidly.

I really have become stupid, she thought. *If I can make it to Mongolia, everything will be fine.*

Hours later, after the convoy had disappeared, her back ached but she was afraid to give up her ruse too soon. She waited until mid-afternoon and observed a group of peasants move down the road, driving a water buffalo before them. She moved quickly down the hill.

"Where are you going, friends?"

"To our village," said a young man who looked to be about sixteen or seventeen, apparently the leader. The others were not much more than children.

"May I walk with you?" said Meiying smiling.

A young girl said merrily, "Oh Shirong, she's so pretty! Let her come!"

"All right," he said severely. "But we cannot feed you."

"She can have some of my food!" objected the girl before Meiying could answer.

"No," she said. "I do not need food. Just company."

The young man nodded in relief. "That we can provide. We are poor, but at least still have our farm even in these evil times."

"What's your name," asked the little girl.

Meiying's heart went out to these children of peace and innocence. She bowed. "Bai Meiying. And yours?"

The young man laughed. "We call her Trouble."

"I am not!" pouted the girl. Then brightening, she said, "My name is Mulan, like the lady in the books."

"Ah!" chuckled Meiying. "And the rest of you?"

After introductions all around, the young man (whose name was Xie Shirong) said, "This water buffalo is ours. He escaped and we had to go searching. Found him. Now if we can just make it home without trouble. Had to wait till the Japs left and now it's late. Do you want to walk with us for a while?"

"Oh, yes!" enthused Meiying.

As they walked and the children warmed up to her, Meiying basked in the family banter that she so missed since leaving her parents.

"Shirong, I'm tired," complained one of the youngsters.

"Then you shouldn't have insisted on coming," he scolded. "We're almost there."

"How much farther?"

"Not far."

"I'm tired. Can we stop?"

"No!" uttered Shirong, glancing at Meiying while answering in his most adult voice.

"How about if I carry you?" suggested Meiying.

"Yes, please!"

"No, Little Scamp. Leave the lady alone."

"But I want to," said Meiying. "Come here, Little Scamp."

In the blink of an eye, before her older brother could stop her, she was riding on Meiying's shoulders.

"Sorry, Bai Meiying," said Shirong familiarly. "She's a pest!"

"Not at all, I enjoy it."

They continued along the road, laughing and telling stories. Meiying felt an unfettered joy she had not known since the Japanese invasion.

"Where do you come from?" asked Shirong.

"Shanghai."

"Oh! That's a long way. I've never been. Is it as big as they say?"

"Bigger."

"Where are you going?"

Meiying shrugged. "I'm a refugee. My home is gone. My family also."

"Ohhh," cooed Mulan.

"We can be your family!" blurted one of the younger children.

"Poo!" uttered Shirong. "But you are clearly an educated lady." He puffed out his chest. "I can write!"

"Oh, that's good."

"Aw, he can only write a few characters! He's just bragging!" said one of the older kids.

"That's not true!" protested Shirong. "Come here," he said to Meiying.

She followed him to a sandy spot off the road. He picked up a stick.

"What do you want me to write?" he demanded. "But don't make it too hard."

"Write, 'I love my family.'"

Meiying gently put down the little girl to watch.

"Aw, that's easy," boasted Shirong.

As he wrote the characters in the sand, Meiying noticed a few misplaced strokes.

"Ah! That's really impressive!" she said.

"Maybe, but those are the only characters he knows," chided Mulan.

"No they're not! Look!"

Shirong wrote his name, and below it, wrote 'hero.'

"Excellent!" enthused Meiying. "But let me correct these two little strokes. There."

"Bai Meiying, write your name," said Mulan.

She did.

"Wow! Your calligraphy is really good," said Shirong, genuinely impressed. "Will you teach me?"

Meiying laughed. "How can I do that, Shirong?"

"I have an idea. Let's go and I'll tell you on the way."

As they walked, the water buffalo picked up speed, sensing that the comforts of home drew near with its promise of food and comfortable bedding. Shirong explained his idea.

"Our village is pretty big. Lots of kids. But our schoolteacher fled when the Japs came. Bai Meiying, we need a new schoolteacher!"

"That is such a nice thought," she said.

"We even have a schoolhouse! It's empty now, but. . . ."

"I'm not sure that would work, Shirong."

"Yes it can! The village can pay you with food and lodging."

"She can stay with us!" cried Mulan.

Meiying shifted the weight of the little one on her back.

"I'm sure your elders would have something to say about that," she said slowly, mulling over this interesting proposal.

Laying low in an obscure village might give her the time she needed to shake Beethoven and whoever else followed. If they were after her, the border would be difficult to cross without being detained. *This idea could give me time*, she thought.

"We take this one here," said Shirong, pointing to a well-traveled side-road. "What do you say, Bai Meiying?"

Meiying paused. Doubts and fears clouded her mind. The image of the group awaiting her in Mongolia pulled her forward, but settling for a while into a peaceful and secure hide-away countered the pull.

Mulan took her hand. "Come on, Bai Meiying! Come on!"

Meiying gently resisted.

Mulan tugged harder.

Meiying let herself be pulled.

"Hooray!" cried Mulan, soon joined by the others.

"We'll see what happens," said Meiying in a cautionary tone. "Your village still must agree."

"I think they will agree," said Shirong cheerfully. "I know our father would like the idea, and the elders were unhappy when Teacher Wang left."

Meiying pondered being a teacher; a possibility that had never crossed her mind before.

Facing all those children! I don't know how to teach. Where do I start? What am I getting into? This is crazy!

But her feet carried her forward, helped along by Mulan's enthusiastic encouragement. Rice paddies came into view, and in the distance could be seen thatch buildings rising above the flat landscape. A twisted curl of smoke drifted into the sky from some cooking stove. Meiying felt a lump in her throat and took very deep breaths.

And kept walking.

"Our home is on the other side of the village," said Shirong. "Father is working in the fields—" his eyes scanned the paddies where workers dotted the landscape—"I think he's over there." He pointed to a dot in the distance, bending over and straightening up in symmetrical ballet movements.

"And your mother?" asked Meiying.

"She died when this little one was born."

Mulan giggled. "Brother Shirong is our mommy."

"Hm!" grunted the boy, secretly pleased at the assignation.

Once they entered the village, the kids ran ahead. Only the sleeping little one on Meiying's back and Shirong remained.

"Let's take care of the buffalo, then wait for father. Here we are!"

Before them stood a house that far exceeded her expectations. It was a large, mud-brick home with an elaborate blue-tile roof. *This is no run-of-the-mill peasant home*, she thought. The house sat at the edge of the village on the far side, facing a long plain that merged into a series of foothills partly shrouded in mist kilometers away. While the rest of the village was dusty and bleakly impoverished, this house boasted trees and green gardens on all sides—an oasis. A wooden gate led them through the outer stone wall, where Meiying admired a well-tended, fancy shrine surrounded by flowering plants. No starving peasants here.

Shirong noticed her surprise.

"We own more *mou* of field than anyone in the village! And we're buying more!"

"Very impressive," said Meiying.

After the buffalo was penned and the little one left with a servant, Shirong said, "Come, let's look at the schoolhouse."

"Yes! Yes!" cried the other children.

As they walked, villagers stopped to gawk at the newcomer.

"Hey! Shirong!" called a young man from the field. "Who's the pretty lady?"

"Our new schoolteacher!" he called back proudly.

On-lookers stared at one another and shook their heads at such unexpected news. Meiying saw Mulan talking excitedly to a knot of little girls who kept bobbing their heads and pressing close to get the whole story. The schoolhouse turned out to be a simple concrete building with a tile roof. On entering, the children dared not follow, and milled around outside, while Shirong opened the shutters to allow more light. A simple desk stood at the head of the class, facing rows of dusty benches. Behind the desk was a large blackboard, vocabulary words still written on it, undoubtedly left by the previous schoolteacher.

The Spartan schoolhouse contrasted sharply with the Xie home, and Meiying felt a wave of inadequacy. How could she take on this task? It now seemed a completely impractical idea. While lost in these depressing thoughts, Mulan marched in with a troop of shy friends, boys and girls. They took seats on the front bench. Shirong watched from the corner.

"Welcome, Schoolteacher Bai Meiying!" cried Mulan happily. She turned with a piqued expression and raised her hand. "Welcome, Schoolteacher Bai Meiying!" parroted the group.

Meiying smiled. "Such good children, but remember, I am not your schoolteacher yet."

"Stay here!" uttered Shirong. "I'll be right back!"

"But—" Meiying's protest did not quite catch up to Shirong who had bolted out the door.

"Teach us something," said Mulan.

"Have you learned numbers?" asked Meiying.

"Oh, those are easy. Teach us something else."

"Well," said Meiying, thinking furiously, "how about a quote from Confucius?"

The kids looked at one another. "Is it hard?"

"No. Look."

Meiying wrote on the board: "When I was fifteen, I had my heart set on learning."

"Wow!" squealed Mulan. "Those characters are hard!"

"Well, of course we wouldn't start with these," said Meiying apologetically.

"But you can with me," said Shirong who had just returned and stood in the doorway. "Here is my father."

A weathered man, looking to be in his forties or fifties, entered the classroom. His face reflected years of worry and hard work, but his smile made her relax. She bowed and introduced herself. He took off his peasant hat and looked at her as if evaluating the sturdiness of a buffalo.

"I'm Mr. Xie," he said. "Largest landowner in our village."

She bowed again.

His smile ceased momentarily. "Are you a communist?" he asked bluntly.

"No."

"Do you like communists?"

"I don't think I know any," she lied.

"Do you sympathize with them?"

"I am just a woman. A pianist. I do not like politics."

"Good!" he grunted. The easy smile returned. "What's a pianist?"

Meiying went through her usual routine of miming the playing of a piano.

"Ah! I know! Next village lives a missionary. Christian church. Is that a, what do you call it?"

"Piano."

"Ah! Is that a piano at the Christian church?"

"Or an organ. Same thing, really."

"You play it?"

"Yes."

"Good! I'm not a Christian—crazy people—but I like their piano. Sounds nice."

"Yes."

"You play for us?"

Meiying looked around. "No piano, Mr. Xie."

He laughed merrily. "Follow me."

She followed him outside and around the corner to a small structure attached to the school. Opening the door, he stepped aside and waved her in. Buried beneath stacks of books and papers was a small piano. Mr. Xie looked at her proudly. "You see, Bai Meiying from Shanghai, we are also civilized."

"Did your previous schoolteacher play?" asked an astonished Meiying.

Mr. Xie looked around and whispered for her ears only. "That old hag? No. Good riddance! Missionary woman used to come once a month and play while Christian husband preached. I didn't like the religion—silly, I'm Buddhist—but I liked the piano. Since the Japs, they come no more, so we keep it in here."

Meiying realized Mr. Xie was no ordinary peasant. "You believe education is important, Mr. Xie?"

"Yes."

She pressed a little. "For girls also?"

He looked at her and his face became quite serious. "Yes. Especially these days. A new world is coming. Look at the Japs. They are beating us because they are better educated, especially in Western technology and learning. Our great China has fallen behind."

"Yes, I agree."

"If the communists win, I will be killed and my lands taken." He nodded toward the children who had gotten bored and played nearby. "They must be prepared . . . be able to survive into the new world."

He put a battered peasant hand up to his wrinkled, leathery face and Meiying thought she detected a tear being wiped away.

"Your son, Shirong, is an intelligent young man."

"No, he is stupid, but he needs a teacher. I cannot read. He must be able to read and write. Same with the others. Will you be our schoolteacher?"

"Well, I must be honest and tell you I have never taught before."

"Come with me," he said.

They returned to the classroom and he pointed at the board. "You just wrote this?"

"Yes."

"What does it say?"

She told him.

"You will make a good teacher!"

"Don't the elders have to agree?"

"Bah! They'll do what I tell them."

"I see."

"We cannot pay you, but like Shirong said, we can give you food and a place to sleep. And—" he had a twinkle in his eye—"safety from the dangers of the road."

Meiying bowed. "Thank you."

"Now, I must return to the fields. Shirong!"

The young man appeared in a flash.

"Show Schoolteacher Bai Meiying the room we discussed where she can stay until we find a more permanent place."

"Yes, father!"

~ *Teacher* ~

That night at dinner, Meiying was feted to a grand meal. A local village woman had been retained by Mr. Xie after his wife died to do all the cooking for the family, and she evidently had orders to make this night special. Villagers peered through the windows at them, but no one in the family seemed to mind. Meiying felt like a zoo exhibit, but the food and the company made up for it.

Dinner conversation proved to be a lively debate about how soon the Japs would be "kicked-out" of the region. Shirong argued that the newly-formed alliance between the Nationalists and communists would do the trick in short order. Mr. Xie scoffed at this idea.

"I hope the Japs wipe out the Reds once and for all! Then we can concentrate on them!"

"But we are all Chinese," objected Shirong.

"Bah! Murderers are murderers, neither Chinese nor Japanese. Just simple murderers to be exterminated!"

Meiying felt quite happy to remain silent on the subject of politics and war. She had had her fill of both.

Gradually the debate ran its course and the children begged to play outside, leaving only Mr. Xie, Meiying, and Shirong.

Clearing his throat, Mr. Xie leaned back, lit a cigarette, and said gruffly, "I talked to the elders, such as they are. Of course, they agreed."

"Oh, good," replied Meiying with a slight bow.

"You start tomorrow morning."

"Oh. How many students will I have?"

Mr. Xie laughed, finally recovering his humor from the unpleasant debate with his son. "Oh, thirty or so."

"Thirty!" Meiying exclaimed in shocked surprise. "I thought there would be six or maybe ten at the most."

Mr. Xie continued to chuckle. "You only met the young ones. Of course, they will come and go, depending on the work they must do in the fields."

"Oh." Meiying felt overwhelmed. She had no idea how to teach, let alone such a class so diverse in age, gender, and level of knowledge.

"Do they have books?"

Mr. Xie shrugged. "Don't know. I can't read. You saw them in the storage building next to the schoolhouse."

"But—"

"Breakfast at sunrise tomorrow, Miss Bai. Work to do." He chucked his cigarette in the soup dish. "Get some sleep. You know where your bed is."

"Yes, thank you."

He nodded and stood to leave. It seemed to Meiying that he had a faint, self-satisfied smirk as he did so. "By the way, make sure you spend a lot of time teaching Shirong. I expect that boy to be able to read and write as well as any Confucian scholar when you're done."

"Yes, I'll try."

As darkness fell over the village and the frogs and crickets mocked her predicament, Meiying lay in bed feeling as lonely and out-of-place as she had ever experienced. The grinding wheel of solitude continued to diminish the parts of her that, in the past, had protruded gaily into the world; her smile, her laughter, her joy, and the love she had to give to someone, somewhere. All she had were memories, and like an old woman, rued the plight of being the last leaf on the tree. *Just ghosts for company*, she thought. *Meili, Lihua, the group, and* her. *Always the elusive* her. Dragged down to slumber by these desolate thoughts, she slept fitfully, often awakening to dread images of students staring at her expectantly the next morning.

After a hurried breakfast by lantern light, Meiying fumbled in the dimness of dawn at the schoolhouse storage shed for books and materials. She grabbed a handful of dog-eared volumes representing different levels and subjects and brought them to the classroom. Distributing them randomly on the benches, she wrote her name on the board and waited.

The first arrival appeared in the doorway, and upon seeing the room empty of other students, fled before Meiying could say, "Hello." Same thing happened with the second, a girl who peeked inside and backed away with wide eyes full of fear and awe.

Finally, Mulan strode in with a group of friends.

"Good morning, Teacher Bai!" she called. The others shyly mumbled greetings.

"See, I told you I know her!" boasted Mulan.

"Teacher, where do we sit?" asked one of the girls.

"For the time being, sit where you like, then we'll sort it out."

The girls sat together on the front bench. Soon, others filtered in, with Shirong being the last, and oldest, to attend. They leafed through their books uncomprehendingly.

"My name is Bai Meiying. I'll be your teacher. Have any of you studied from these?"

While they chatted and passed the books around, Meiying counted twenty-six. *Better than thirty!* she thought.

Mulan's hand went up.

"Yes?"

"Teacher, this is the book we studied with Miss Wu before she left."

A boy of about the same age said from the back, "No it isn't, stupid! It's this one." He handed forward a different book.

"We do not call one another stupid," admonished Meiying. "Now, I need your names, so I'll pass this sign-up sheet around."

When it came back to her, only a few names were written.

"How many of you cannot write your name?" she asked.

'Over half the class raised their hands.

~ *Aftermath of the Door Incident* ~

The incident with John made the group even more jumpy than they had already been. At breakfast, everyone joined in the dining room, including John who insisted he felt better. After some desultory small talk, Mongol Peter and Mongol Little Acorn strode into the room.

Immediately, Madame Liu summarized the incident with the iron door. "We need answers," she concluded.

"Ah," he said evasively.

"Well, who opened the door?" demanded Madame Liu.

Mongol Peter shrugged and asked how the food supplies were lasting.

"No!" cried Madame Liu. "I want to know who opened and closed the iron door!"

"I don't know. Wasn't here," replied Mongol Peter calmly.

This seemed to infuriate her even more. "Tell *her*, or your master, or whomever acts as your boss, that we will leave unless we get some answers."

Mongol Peter shook his head sadly. "So be it."

"Just tell *her*!"

"*She* is many."

"What?"

"Nothing. I will see if I can deliver your message."

"When?" pointedly asked Master Zhou.

"Mongol Peter did not deign to answer. He merely smiled and walked away.

"Damn!" sputtered Lu Zhishen. "If we don't get answers within the week, I'm returning to that town and bring back double the amount of dynamite. Door open or door closed, I'm going to blow this place."

"Hooray!" shouted Feng Shiren. "A true hero!"

"Hm! . . . and get shot by the Japs for being a partisan while on your way back!" scolded Child of Buddha.

"Maybe *she* will answer our questions now that *she* knows how anxious we are," suggested Suling, ever the calming influence.

"Oh, *she* will answer," said Child of Buddha with conviction.

"How do you know?" asked Master Zhou.

"I feel it. The hump on my back is like a receptacle of all the feelings and emotions and desires of those around me. Yes, my hump is sending signals throughout my body . . . a buzz, like bees to the flower. When that happens, I know. I know. 'There it is,' I say to myself. 'There is the nectar.'"

"Does your hump tell you when *she'll* answer?" asked Lu Zhishen with a dubious edge to his words.

"Yes."

"When?"

"Before your deadline."

"I hope so," said Lu, taken aback by the certainty of her reply.

"Yes, as do I," said Madame Liu.

"But we may not like her answers," warned Child of Buddha. "The nectar is not always sweet."

"What do you mean by that?" demanded Lu.

Child of Buddha shook her head. "If I knew, I would tell you."

An uneasy gloom settled over the room.

Madame Liu felt a change of topic was in order. "How are you really, John?"

"Fine."

"We've been worried."

In spite of the low hum of voices in his head, John felt much more in control. Perhaps last night had been cathartic.

"No, really, I'm feeling much better, thank you."

"Good."

"Now what?" asked Feng Shiren.

"We wait," said Madame Liu.

"Not for long," muttered Lu Zhishen.

~

With winter approaching, forays outside the cave were necessarily brief. Freezing wind and rain cut through their clothes, and the confines of their rocky home gave all but Child of Buddha a severe case of cabin-fever. Tempers grew short, and more often than not, each stayed in their rooms, focusing on the approaching deadline, hoping every day for a sign from *her*.

Madame Liu confided to Master Zhou that the ghost of her husband appeared in her dreams, urging patience. Master Zhou did his best, as the eldest male, to spread cheer and urge calm perseverance. Only Feng Shiren mysteriously disappeared outside the cave during the day, invariably returning in time for dinner looking like a smug cat.

"Where have you been?" Lu asked the obligatory question, which in the past Feng always deflected. Not this time.

"Out."

"Doing what?"

"Air."

"Cold?"

"Hot."

"Hot?"

Feng sprang into his usual operatic posture. "Hot on the trail! Cold on the body!"

"What trail?"

"If I find it, you'll know." He walked away whistling some obscure tune.

Everyone knew that attempting to elicit further answers from Feng when he didn't want to respond would be a fool's errand, but John forged ahead. He called to the retreating figure, "Come on, Shiren! What trail?"

"A trail with no marks, no traces, no guideposts. A trail of lost souls."

"Leading to?"

"Ah, that is what I am trying to find out my young American friend."

Lu scoffed, "Didn't work out too well following the trail of Mongol Peter!"

"All trails lead to a destination."

"Bah! Every point on earth is a destination."

Feng tilted his head and pointed to his feet. "Yes, but beneath the earth?"

"What?"

"This mountain is full of secrets—secret trails—secret entrances—secret exits."

"Have you found any of them?" asked Master Zhou.

But at this point, he would go no further, merely saying, "We'll see, we'll see."

John had listened with interest, but his full attention was focused on a new command by Goddess. ***Go find Meiying! If she cannot get here, you must go there! Find her! There's nothing here but stagnation where the evil ones flourish! Go! Find her!***

This exhortation, of course, presented him with a host of conundrums, which themselves led to a deeper sense of inadequacy. The details of such an intimidating quest—How? When? Where? What?—all raised a host of complications and confusions. But the idea niggled at his brain like a worm turning the monotonously stratified soil of life laying fallow in the cave. As with the others, he wearied of waiting for something to germinate. The lack of any communication from *her* made a satisfying conclusion to this entire expedition seem remote at best.

If Lu Zhishen can strike out on his own to find a town and buy dynamite to destroy a door, I can do the same for Meiying, someone I love, to save a life! he thought. But the words rang hollow in his fearful mind. Always the notion returned to the same conclusion: *I wouldn't know where to start.*

But if you stay, John, they will poison you! You're curled up in a little ball at the bottom of a crater and evil gas is working its way through your lungs. Beware the voices and the poison that collects at the bottom of craters! Go ahead and die trying to find her!

John suspected the voice was not that of Goddess, but of God, disguising His voice to coax John out of safety and into harm's way. God wanted him dead! But his mind fragmented into a chaos of doubt.

No, Chosen One, your mind is confused, misinterpreting Our words. He recognized the voice of God.

Goddess chimed in. ***This is to be expected from the cognitive dawning of a superior, incipient species. Your human genes are desperately contorting Our voices. Either you must find Meiying, or she must find you.***

Chapter Three

Breakthroughs, Break-ins, and Breakdowns

She is Many

In her private hours, with plenty of time to think, Madame Liu began to focus on an off-hand remark by Mongol Peter during her confrontation with him. He had said, "*She* is many." Afterward, while in her room going over the conversation, these three words now riveted her attention. What did he mean? She had meant to ask Master Zhou what he thought, but now decided to ask the mysterious Child of Buddha. She hoped she was doing the right thing. No one in the group could know the depths to which Madame Liu missed her dead husband. Master Liu had always been her rock; the person with whom she confided even the most intimate thoughts and fears. Like any spouse who has lost her lifetime mate, she longed to have him to talk with; to discuss the events of the day; to empathize and sympathize; to share. Without this consolation, Madame Liu had to steel herself all these months to carry on her husband's work. But the effort had taken a toll. Since his death, her one goal, one imperative, was to reach *her*, where surely comfort and even the possibility of a miracle would help mend the terrific hole left by Master Liu's death.

Now she had threatened to leave without attaining that objective. Worse (or better, she did not know which) there was the statement from Mongol Peter that "*She* is many." How could that be? Madame Liu's own introduction to *her* involved no less than a spiritual awakening and the pulling-back from a precipice too dangerous to contemplate. But, as far as she knew, every member of the group had contact with only one version of *her*. Or did they? Were there multiple *hers* behind that door? *If so, are they all friendly?* she wondered.

Would she really order the group to leave if no answers were forthcoming? If so, when? After all, she had not given a deadline, that was Lu Zhishen. Should she accept his one week demand? These questions went round and round in her mind. Unable to resolve her doubts, she decided to wait and see what transpired by the end of Lu Zhishen's deadline. *I'll wait*, she thought. *Then we'll see. Just wait and see.*

She did not have to wait long.

Three days after Lu Zhishen announced his deadline, something happened that both terrified and electrified the group. Mid-morning, just after they had finished breakfast and had returned to their rooms, a terrific tapping noise reverberated throughout the cave. Everyone ran to the bridge, fearing the awful clamor would cause a cave-in. They had to shout to be heard above the din; an echoing clang as if some giant, deranged blacksmith drove the hammer.

"My god! My god! What is it?" shouted Suling with her hands clamped over her ears.

"Sounds like the Precious Object!" yelled Master Zhou. "Except so loud!"

"The Precious Object times a thousand!" cried John.

It seemed the mountain would shake itself apart. When a multitude of bats appeared as a dark cloud rising from the crevasse in crazed flight toward the exit, all seemed a miasma of disjointed motion and furious sound. The group fled across the bridge and out of the cave, where they huddled together a safe distance from the entrance, listening to the rumbling taps and watching the winged stragglers make their escape. Even Feng Shiren and Child of Buddha were clearly afraid.

Trying to lighten the mood, Feng shouted at Lu Zhishen above the noise, "It looks like you don't need your dynamite!"

"My god, if there's a cave-in, all our possessions are in there. Food, everything!" cried Master Zhou.

"Let's hope this is not *her* doing, or else it seems we're not welcome anymore!" replied Madame Liu.

"It is *her* doing!" shouted Child of Buddha. "Remember I said the nectar is not always sweet!"

As suddenly as it started, the rumbling stopped.

Everyone held their breath and waited.

Nothing.

"Well," said Feng Shiren. "Still standing."

"Seems like it," said Lu Zhishen.

"We should wait longer just to be sure," said Madame Liu.

Feng slapped his body. "I don't know about all of you, but I'm cold."

"Yeah," agreed Lu.

"I'm going in."

"I'm right behind you," quickly added Lu.

"Me too," said John, determined not to be the only young male left behind.

"Women and old men seem to have more sense," laughed Master Zhou. "We'll follow you young bucks."

Led by Feng Shiren, the group gingerly made their way across the bridge. Once on the other side, they checked their rooms and found nothing amiss. When they met in the dining room, Lu Zhishen announced, "I'm going to check out the iron door."

"Exactly what I was thinking," said Feng.

"Good, we'll all go," added Madame Liu. "This time there will be witnesses."

And so off they set.

To John, it was an odd feeling to creep along behind Feng and Lu amidst the total silence of a dark cave so recently filled with unholy clamor. No one spoke during the trip; in fact, it seemed to John that no one took a breath. When they reached the iron door, Feng shone his light and everyone peered dumbstruck at the vision.

The door stood open.

They crowded around the open door, which invited entry into a

very dark space. Feng Shiren thrust the lantern in by extending his arm to its fullest length, hesitating to step through as if it might be a chamber full of snakes.

Staring back at them with bright eyes rested the Precious Object in all Her golden splendor; meditative pose, legs crossed, hands resting above both knees, right hand facing up, thumb touching forefinger, gracefully curved into a circle, bare breasts offering warm maternal nourishment. Surrounding Her, the walls, ceiling, and floor of the room appeared to be solid rock, just as Lu had described.

As he had done so many months ago, John felt himself changing in *her* presence, though only *her* surrogate sat physically before him. As before, it was a physical sensation; a clay person feeling the potter adding some here and removing some there, experiencing in his nerves, muscles, and bones the addition and subtraction of the substance that formed him. He knew the final configuration of his soul had still not been kiln-fired, and the prodding, pinching, slicing, and kneading, would continue until *she* made *her* appearance.

Though he did not know it, every person there felt a similar transformation and a similar sense that they were being molded, not yet ready for the searing permanency of the kiln. All of them wanted to fire their pliable souls into hard and lustrous vessels that could no longer be altered. But it was not yet to be.

Lu Zhishen broke the hypnotic trance. "Let's all look for some hidden door or passage or tunnel. If we spread out, we can cover this room millimeter by millimeter."

Child of Buddha backed out into the passageway, but the others worked their way around the walls, floor, and ceiling of the room.

Nothing.

Only rock.

"Look for a seam!" cried Lu in frustration, but none was to be found.

"I don't understand," said Master Zhou. He shook his head. "How did it get here?"

"I do," opined Feng Shiren.

As usual, he paused for dramatic effect, but then, when no encouragement was forthcoming, he quickly explained. "While the great noise got us out of the cave, *she*—or someone—opened the door and put in the Precious Object."

"But we were at the entrance to the cave," said Master Zhou. "No one came in or out."

"Exactly!" cried Feng.

"What does that mean?" asked John.

"Remember my trips outside the cave these past few weeks?"

"Yes."

"Remember I said I was hot on the trail?"

"Yes."

"There are obviously other entrances and exits," explained Feng slyly. He crouched and with an exaggerated flair, moved his eyes from side to side. "Secret passages. Air vents. Hard to find."

"Well," said Madame Liu skeptically. "Have you found them?"

"Alas, no." He crumpled to the ground like a puppet whose strings have been cut. "But I know I'm close!"

"How do you know?" asked Lu.

"A feeling. Child of Buddha isn't the only one."

"Bunk!" mocked Lu.

"This will get us nowhere," said Madame Liu. "The real question is why *she* gave us back the Precious Object."

"Yes, I wondered that too," said Suling.

"What should we do with Her?" asked John.

"Leave Her here," said Lu Zhishen. "Maybe the door will stay open."

"Doesn't seem to matter," observed Master Zhou. "Other than the Precious Object, there is nothing here."

"I still say there's a way in and out of this room besides the iron door," said Lu.

"Why don't you sleep here with Her?" suggested Feng Shiren, his tone offered in the manner of a challenge.

"Maybe I will."

Child of Buddha, hovering outside the room, suddenly cried, "That's it! We must all sleep with Her, at different times, of course."

"Why?" asked Madame Liu sharply.

"The Precious Object is here as a messenger."

Master Zhou laughed. "Good, but I cannot translate Her language—tapping is tapping to me."

"Perhaps," replied Child of Buddha. "But I can. Even so, *She* will not communicate through taps alone."

"How then?" asked Master Zhou.

"Don't know, but *She'll* find a way."

"Okay, I'll test your theory," said Lu. "I sleep with Her tonight."

Feng smiled wickedly. "And if someone closes the door and locks it? You'll suffocate in this room."

Lu paled a little and checked the door to see if it could be opened from the inside. It could. "See," he said, jiggling the handle.

"Can still be locked, and the handle won't matter."

"Okay, damn it! Then I'll sleep inside and you sleep outside against the door. Just make sure someone would have to move you to close it."

"Agreed!"

Child of Buddha looked worried. "I may be wrong. You may regret this."

"Now you tell me," replied Lu with a weak smile.

John felt a passing urge to volunteer to be the first, but let it pass when the two men made their agreement. He looked at the Precious Object. It remained quiet.

~

That night at dinner, the mood was lighter—something was happening at least. Some resolution might be at hand. No one really expected trouble.

"Tomorrow morning your report will be interesting, Zhishen," said Madame Liu.

"Still, you must be careful," warned Suling. "If you hear anything, get out of the room."

"Not to worry," replied Lu. "I am not quite at the heroic level of my namesake."

When the time came for bed, the group accompanied Lu and Feng to the door. Nothing had been disturbed.

"All right, Shiren my old friend," said Lu to Feng. "Make sure your bedding is up tight against that door."

Feng chuckled. "Not to worry. They would have to lift me up and carry me away to close it."

"Please be careful, both of you," admonished Madame Liu.

After all but the two men departed, Feng settled in against the door and Lu lay on his blanket next to the Precious Object. Neither attempted to sleep right away. They put out their lanterns and conversed in total darkness.

"Do you believe in ghosts?" Feng asked Lu.

"No."

"Do you believe in god?"

"No. I believe in *her*."

"Is *she* the Precious Object?"

"Don't know. I think the Precious Object is a sort of physical symbol of *her*."

"Whatever that means," mumbled Feng.

"How about you?" asked Lu.

"Which—ghosts or god?"

"Either, both."

"Neither."

"Why are you here?"

"To look after you fools. Remember, I never met *her*. I just like adventure and ghost stories."

"Ah, so you're drawn to quests."

"Yes."

"What do you think is going to happen tonight?" asked Lu a bit sheepishly.

"Nothing."

"Nothing?"

"Correct, nothing" said Feng. "But I do think something is happening even as we speak. Something deeper inside this mountain. Something playing with us, or toying with us, or some such."

"Well, I guess we'll see."

"Probably nothing will happen while we're awake," said Feng. "Let's sleep and then, like you said, we'll see."

~ The Next Morning ~

John was the first to leave his room that morning. He wanted to sleep, but a voice kept repeating, **Get up! Get up!**

It was odd, he thought, that the voice refrained from insults and mockery, just a simple, **Get up!** repeated over and over. Somehow, the flat, mundane pitch and tone seemed more frightening than the usual exhortations. His first impulse was to eat, but his sluggish mind suddenly remembered Feng and Lu and their mission, which energized him, so off he went to check with burning curiosity. The lanterns outside his room had been doused, so he retrieved a flashlight before he set out.

When he reached the door, the first thing he noticed was that it was closed. The second thing was Feng Shiren, stretched out on the ground, either sleeping or unconscious. That he was dead never crossed John's mind, as he immediately saw his comrade's chest rise and fall.

"Shiren!" he called. Rushing to the door first, he pulled on the handle and knew it had been locked. Turning from the door, he knelt next to Feng and shook his shoulder.

"Shiren! Wake up! Are you okay! Wake up!"

Feng moaned and John checked for signs of injury. There were none.

"Wake up!"

Feng moved, but remained unresponsive to John's pleas.

Once more he checked the door.

Locked.

When he turned back, he saw Feng staring at the door with unbelieving eyes.

~ Meiying Teaches and is Taught ~

After the first week of teaching, Meiying began to fall into a partial routine. Life at the Xie household unwound in an orderly fashion, but her students gave her no end of trouble. Arguments, fights, disagreements, petulance, and a wide disparity of abilities made teaching more difficult than she imagined, and left her feeling a failure at the end of every day. Her only solace lay in having access to adequate food and protection from immediate danger, but the great river that had flowed so majestically toward the sea when her quest began had diminished to a rivulet meandering submissively to the dictates of the landscape.

She cared for the children, but their rough manners and ignorant superstitions seemed obstacles too great for her meager talents to overcome. Daily she labored to teach them the most basic concepts, and their retention of even simple characters was like holding water in a sieve.

However, as all teachers everywhere know, there are always one or two in a class whose intelligence, no matter how long kept down, will shine through. Such a child was Mulan. Her audacity and deep-probing curiosity were sure signs of an auspicious mind. Like a little bird, Meiying could not feed her enough of the pulp of knowledge.

"Teacher Bai," said Mulan one day after school. "Will you teach me how to play the piano?"

Meiying had just finished the school day by playing a lively old Chinese folk song.

"Of course, but to become a good player, you must practice a lot."

The little girl contemplated this rather intimidating truth.

"How much?"

"Every day, a little."

"Every day?"

"Every day."

"A little?"

"Yes," said Meiying sympathetically. "Perhaps an hour."

"What's an hour?"

Meiying realized country folk were not ruled by clocks. "About as long as our first lesson every day in numbers."

"Oh, that's not too bad."

"No."

"Then I will play like you?"

"If you practice."

Mulan took this in. After mulling it over awhile, she said with a determined nod, "All right, I'll practice." She pressed a few random keys and asked, "Do you have a boyfriend?"

"Why do you ask?"

"Because you're pretty and old."

Meiying laughed heartily. "No, I don't have a boyfriend."

Mulan scrunched up her face. "We have to choose a boy when we're fourteen or else other girls make fun of us."

"That's very young. Do you like boys?"

"No. Most of them are dumb."

"How old are you, Mulan?"

"Eleven."

"What happens if you don't choose by fourteen?"

"Oh, we don't really choose. Our parents do."

"But your mother is dead."

Mulan shifted uncomfortably. "Yes, so papa will pick."

"Oh."

~

So this precocious child began studying the piano. Such interest was a balm
to Meiying's wounded pride at the apparent disinterest, or disinclination, to
learn by her other students. A spark glimmered in the dry litter of Meiying's
spirit. Over the next few weeks, she and Mulan spent hours at the piano, each
coming to know the other in ways deeper than teacher and student. A bond
quickly formed that triggered Meiying's maternal instinct, and by so doing
reconnected her with the rest of the human race. As she grew closer to Mulan,
she gradually became closer to the Xie family. For one of the few times since
the Japanese invasion, Meiying felt comfortable in her environment and the
people that inhabited it. Instead of moving out of the Xie house, Mr. Xie had
a temporary addition made for Meiying in which to live. While food was not
plentiful, its homespun adequacy made it all the more satisfying. Now, for the
briefest of moments, she could forget the pull of Mongolia and *her*, and release
herself to the simple pleasures of attending to life in its moment-to-moment
demands without the exhausting necessity of wondering when death or injury
might strike next.

One day, while Meiying instructed Mulan on proper fingering technique,
the girl stopped and asked, "Teacher Bai, why haven't you got married?"

"Never met the right man."

"But didn't your parents pick?"

"No, dear. We did not do it that way in Shanghai, at least many of us did not."

"Why?"

"My papa and mama thought I should pick for myself."

"Why?'

"They trusted me."

"To pick a rich man?"

"Not exactly . . . well, I must admit, my papa had someone picked out who
was rich, but I was a very disobedient girl and said no."

"Well, why?"

Meiying laughed and tickled Mulan. "You are so curious. Is this a way to get
out of practicing?"

"Nooo."

"Well, let's get back to the piano."

"But I want to know!"

"What do you want to know?"

"Why you never picked. Now you're old. Ain't it too late?"

Meiying sighed impatiently. "I told you, I never met the right man."

"What is the right man?"

"What do you mean?"

"What does the right man have that you want?"

"Let's get back to the piano."

"Oh! Please tell me!"

In spite of her impatience with this child's questions, Meiying reviewed in her mind what the perfect partner would be like. Meili came to her as if she had entered the room. Close upon her heels came Lihua.

"She must be kind and caring and gentle and brave and be a good listener and—"

"She?"

"I mean he."

Mulan looked puzzled but said nothing.

"What is it?" asked Meiying, noticing the child's unspoken worry.

"That sounds like a girl."

"Why, yes it does, but can't a man be these things?"

Mulan scrunched her face in thought. "I guess, but that ain't like my papa or men in the village."

"What are they like?"

"I don't know."

"Mean?"

"Kinda, and they all drink and get mad and want to be rich. That's the kind we must marry, especially the rich ones."

"Why?"

Mulan shrugged. "That's what papa says."

Meiying had no interest in pitting this child against her father's wishes. Such a path leads to disaster, especially for a country girl. "Yes, you should listen to your father."

"But you didn't!"

Meiying tickled Mulan and said, "Yes, silly, but look at me now, old and alone."

"Aw, you're old but you're still really pretty. Bet you could have had any boy you wanted."

"Maybe, but I didn't want just any boy."

Mulan stuck out her lower lip. "Me neither!"

Well, we've come full circle, thought Meiying. In a severe voice, she said, "Look, Mulan, we must get back to the piano. You want to learn it, don't you?"

Mulan continued to pout. "Yesss, but not if I have some dumb husband who breaks it 'cause he's been drinking."

I wonder. . . . thought Meiying before killing the notion with a ruthless determination to avoid going there. "Now," she said firmly. "Put your fingers like this, and your wrists like this."

Mulan reluctantly agreed, but the rest of the lesson was spoiled, as both females continued to be distracted by thinking of things decidedly unmusical.

When Meiying went home that night and sat down to dinner with the Xie family, Mulan kept casting her pregnant glances while the males of the household spoke, as if a precious secret were shared by the two.

Mr. Xie drank his usual home-brew of rice wine, and in the process became louder and more boisterous. "Well, son, what have you to say for yourself today? I saw you malingering in the fields!"

"No I wasn't!" protested Shirong.

"Reading books again, eh?" replied Mr. Xie with a grin.

"No, father, I worked as hard as anyone."

Mr. Xie poured more wine and downed it in one gulp. "Likely story!" He turned to Meiying. "Schoolteacher Bai, how is my ox-brained son doing?"

Meiying smiled encouragingly. "He's doing fine. He is a smart boy."

After another swig, Mr. Xie hit the table with his fist. "Nonsense! He's lazy. Does he do his work?"

"Yes."

"Well, that's good, because he don't do it around here."

Whenever Mr. Xie got deep in his cups, the family fell quiet and made themselves small so as not to be noticed. Mr. Xie swilled another cup and pointed at Mulan. "How about this dim-witted one?"

"She's progressing well on the piano." Meiying smiled pointedly. "Getting ready for the new China!"

Mr. Xie did not like his own words thrown back at him. "Good! But only if it means she becomes worth more than she is now. I've already had expressions of interest in her by other families—good ones—with land and money—even from other villages! Solid alliances!"

The two females exchanged significant glances, but both remained silent. Meiying felt a pang of guilt that she labored to expand this girl's mind only to have it rent asunder by ignorant habits and rituals where it would be destined to lay fallow until only death freed it. Meiying had seen it so often in her life and felt melancholy that even a relatively progressive male like Mr. Xie could be so cruelly capricious.

Unbeknownst to Meiying, Shirong had been staring at her, and asked an unexpected question. "What are you thinking, Schoolteacher Bai?"

"Oh, nothing much."

"You've read so much, I figure there must be things on your mind that roam far past this village and our little problems."

"I like this little village."

Meiying had a sudden thought. "By the way, Shirong, why aren't you married yet?"

He turned red.

"I've picked for him!" cried Mr. Xie, now far beyond his usual limit of wine. "A little girl in a close-by hamlet. Too young yet to marry, but he's spoken for."

"Ah, what is her dowry?" asked Meiying, refusing to look at Shirong who squirmed horribly.

"Land, Little Schoolteacher, land!"

"Oh."

"It'll expand my holdings by almost double!" He reached over and slapped the miserable Shirong on the back. "And she'll bear lots of males to manage it. You just watch, he's got the fertile seed!" Mr. Xie roared with laughter at this prediction.

He suddenly turned glum. "Now, if the Japs just do their job, all will be well."

Shirong abruptly stood and left the table, saying he had to check the buffalo. Suspecting the reason, Meiying waited until he left. "What job is that?"

"Kill communists, of course!"

Meiying reacted to this comment with a renewed contempt for the minds of men. She looked at Mulan, who stared at her with a questioning intensity that made her uncomfortable. Just then, a younger sibling of Mulan's ran in from outside crying, "Schoolteacher Bai! Come look what we found!"

Surrendering to the child's tugging hand, Meiying let herself be pulled outside where she breathed in the dusky air and saw the sun flare low on the horizon, then blink out. Somewhere out there in the gloom lay Mongolia. But her attention soon returned to the little girl, still pulling her toward some essential destination.

"What do you want me to see, Lingling?"

The girl stopped and pointed at the school house. Meiying froze in terror. Lantern light pulsed from the inside, and the sounds of a piano wafted across the village to her petrified ears.

~ *Glue* ~

Meiying recognized a very poorly played *Moonlight Sonata*. A chill ran up her spine.

"Come on! Let's see!" exclaimed Lingling.

"Go slowly," whispered Meiying harshly. "We don't know who it is."

Darkness now cloaked the village in its most suffocating manner, as only the poorest rural areas can testify. Intermittent moonlight occasionally took off the blackest edge, but in any case, the school house seemed lit by a thousand lanterns.

Lingling, now alarmed by Meiying's reaction, fell behind and clutched her jacket as they approached the window. Just as they were close enough to see inside, the music stopped and the lantern snuffed out, plunging everything in darkness. Meiying rushed to hide behind a tree with Lingling hanging on for dear life. A dark figure emerged, pulling his jacket collar over his neck, and sauntered away, disappearing among the black slabs of shacks and farmhouses.

"I want to go home," whimpered Lingling.

"Yes, dear. Let's go."

When they returned to the house, Mr. Xie snored loudly from his room, and Shirong stood inside the door waiting.

"Where did you go?" he asked.

Lingling blurted out that a ghost or demon was playing the piano in the school house.

"What?"

Meiying laughed and said lightly, "Oh, just somebody playing in the school house. Does anyone in the village know how to play?"

"No," replied Shirong. "Who was it?"

Meiying described how the person left before they could identify him.

"Probably just a student sneaking around, getting into mischief," said Shirong.

"This was no student."

"Oh. Well, if it's a stranger, we'll know tomorrow. No one comes or goes without everyone knowing, especially a stranger."

That evening, Meiying trembled in her bed. Visions of Beethoven lurking outside plagued her, and she feared having to flee into the night with nothing but her nightgown. Yet, she also feared the coming of morning and what it might reveal. Hours of restless half-sleep passed, and as the first tinges of dawn lightened the room, she even considered bolting that very moment.

Perhaps it was not Beethoven, she tried to convince herself. *Perhaps it really was just a student!*

But she knew better and joined the Xie family at breakfast with a heart full of trepidation. Other than bellicose protestations by Mr. Xie that she ate almost nothing, the mysterious piano-player was not mentioned (much to her relief) and the family quickly scattered to work and school.

When Meiying entered the school house, the piano remained as it always had, with only a lantern standing conspicuously out-of-place as a reminder of the previous night's visitor. Students began filing in, and with each new face she asked brightly, "Did you hear someone playing the piano last night?"

And with each sleepy face, the same reply came groggily out. "No, School-teacher Bai."

Finally, a mother who walked her shy daughter into the room said, "Oh, yes. Many of us heard. We all assumed it was you teaching little Mulan."

So it was real. She and Lingling had not imagined it. Meiying vowed to banish the subject from her mind, so she threw herself into the lessons that day; her students later telling their parents that the schoolteacher had been unusually ill-tempered. This revelation, of itself, led to idle gossip that she must have a secret love interest.

Yet over the next few days Meiying could not help herself peer anxiously around corners or through windows to spot an unwelcome figure spying on her. Gradually, the immediacy of her anxiety faded to a general sense of unease. The comfortable life she had just begun to enjoy had been cruelly disrupted. A perverse anger at the unfairness of the world temporarily seized her, and she felt deeply sorry for herself and her wretched fate. This she uncharacteristically took out on her students, and when one day she went so far as to cause tears to flow from a young girl's eyes, she abruptly left the classroom and went home to bask in guilt and regret.

This won't do! she thought. *I can't bear the uncertainty. I know Beethoven is out there, waiting, stalking, biding his time to drag me back to Mr. President, or worse. But what could be worse!*

She thought she must leave and make her way to Mongolia, but she felt a deep conviction that he would merely follow. *If he is skulking about, I must have it out with him now, while I'm among friends! But how? I just have to wait.*

A few nights later, Mulan crept into her room, as had often happened in the past, where they would talk until the early morning cock crowed.

"Are you awake," whispered Mulan, hoping that if she was asleep, the words would wake her.

"Yes, dear. What is it?"

"Why are you afraid of him?"

"Who?"

"The man who plays the piano."

"I'm not, and he only was there once."

"No."

"What do you mean?"

"He's there now."

Meiying sat straight up and wildly looked at the window, expecting him to be staring in from the other side. "What? Are you sure?"

"There's music coming from the school house."

"How do you know?"

"Shirong told me to fetch you. He's waiting there now."

Meiying threw on some clothes and quickly left the house to the snores of Mr. Xie, which offered her a form of solace; a reminder that she had friends and protectors here.

By the time they reached the school house, Meiying saw no light. Shirong stood at the door.

"What took you?" he demanded.

"I had to get dressed." She looked at the closed door. "Where is he?"

"He left just before you came."

"What did he look like?"

"Couldn't tell. Had on a thick coat and floppy hat. Tall and thin, I think."

Meiying felt bitterly disappointed. If it were Beethoven, she wanted to confront him now, on her turf. But what if it weren't Beethoven? That idea seemed too fantastic. *He must be mocking me*, she thought.

"Maybe he's a ghost," whispered Mulan, who had followed.

Shirong laughed. "He was no ghost."

"Then why didn't you go inside and talk to him?" challenged Mulan.

"I was waiting for Schoolteacher Bai," he said defensively.

"Oh, sure," said Mulan sarcastically.

"You did the right thing," soothed Meiying.

"Boys!" huffed Mulan. "He don't tell the truth. He was scared."

"Mulan," said Meiying quietly. "That's enough. He stood guard for me—that's just as good."

"Next time," said Shirong. "I'll confront him. After all, he's a stranger to this village. Who knows what he wants. Maybe he's a thief or a murderer!"

"How do we know he's a stranger?" asked Mulan innocently. "Maybe he's one of us playing a trick. It'd be just like a boy."

"Yes, maybe so," agreed Meiying. "Let's go home and sleep."

"Well, I'm going to stay a little longer to make sure he don't come back!" blustered Shirong.

"If he does, don't do anything foolish, Shirong," warned Meiying, alarmed that his wounded pride would cause him to do something dangerous. "Come and get me."

"We'll see," he muttered like a grown man who wished to leave an avenue of escape without losing face.

~

When Meiying and her little charge returned to the house, still reverberating with the discordant music of Mr. Xie's snores, she tucked in Mulan, putting off the child's questions with a gruff command to sleep. In her own bed, Meiying longed for the companionship of Meili. Forcing thoughts of Beethoven from her mind, she ordered her imagination to conjure Meili's naked body next to hers. With single-minded effort, she fantasized making love, masturbating in an almost savage orgasm, driven by the exciting memory of risk-taking they both necessarily endured during their brief relationship.

With her tensions somewhat relieved, she stayed awake and engaged in an imaginary conversation with the woman-warrior Lihua.

"What if I see him next time he comes? Should I confront him?"

"Yes," said Lihua firmly.

"But what do I say?"

"Tell him to leave and never follow you again. Look him in the eyes like a man and be calm while you say it. No shaking. No hesitation."

"But what if he just laughs at me?"

"Make sure you carry a knife. Pull it out and tell him you will kill him if he continues."

"But if he still laughs?"

"Kill him."

Meiying shook her head, knowing she could never force herself to do such an act. Even the thought of blade into flesh made her tremble.

"No, I couldn't do that."

"Then do the next best thing."

"What?"

"Have the menfolk here kill him."

Meiying found the idea abhorrent but intriguing.

"How?"

Lihua laughed wickedly. "Tell Mr. Xie he is a communist."

Suddenly, amidst this imaginary conversation, a voice intruded that was very different; a voice far more terrifying than her imagination could ever conjure. Yet it seemed somehow familiar.

My dear, you face a choice that is to be faced by another in the future. One whose fate will be entwined with your son. She will be forced to kill or be killed.

"What?" murmured Meiying aloud, startled out of her reverie.

In a far-away country there will be another like you. Beautiful. Honey to men. Murder to men. The male way. Entombing them in golden amber until entombed herself. You face a similar choice....

"Will she be dangerous?" Meiying asked the question out loud, all the while being self-consciously aware how bizarre it seemed to converse with a disembodied voice.

Yes.

"And she will use her beauty to entrap men?"

Yes.

"Will she hurt my son?"

Not in the way you think.

"Entrap him?"

In a manner of speaking. Your son will be another Chosen One.

"My son will be quite powerful?"

Yes and no. He will be confused.

"His name will be?"

From the family. Michael Powers, if that suits you ... which it will.

So, thought Meiying. *I am to marry John! This is John's Goddess.*

"And this woman's name?"

Tuyet Mai.

"An odd name. A foreigner. I know the country! My son will have something to do with her?"

Yes.

"Will she be his wife?"

No, but she and he will collide in the fire of war.

Oh, god! thought Meiying. *Another war.*

"And my son?"

The name given him by his fellow soldiers will be, appropriately, Storyteller.

"And this woman will be a danger to him?" she cried.

This woman will be a danger to all men and all men a danger to her.

"Will I live to see it? To warn her? To warn him?"

No.

Meiying's heart sank at this revelation. But the shock faded quickly when she remembered how often during the dark days she had considered ending her life. John came to her mind.

"I know someone who hears voices. Are you—"

You know nothing, but now your choice must be made. You are free to decide. Will it be like Tuyet Mai in the future? Will it involve killing? Murder? Will you follow the male path—that of God? Or, will you follow the female path—that of Goddess? It is your choice ... your own choice....

The voice ended in a sorrowful dirge, and Meiying quickly moved to re-establish her presence in the real world.

Madness lay elsewhere.

The kind of madness John suffered.
She had no intention of following.
And with that thought, she froze in shocked wonder.
John . . . the group . . . Mongolia . . . her. . . .

~ Yet Another Disappearance ~

John stood in front of the closed iron door and shouted at the frozen Feng Shiren. "What happened?"

"I don't know," mumbled Feng.

"Where's Lu Zhishen?"

"I don't know."

"My god, is he still in there?" cried John, turning from Feng and banging on the door.

"I don't know."

Feng Shiren, the man who controlled everything, saved everyone, moved mountains, now sat immobilized with doubt. At length, with John continuing to pound on the door, Feng regained his senses and stood next to the American. Placing a hand firmly around John's arm to make it stop, he said, "No need, John. Here is a note I just found next to my bedding."

Feng helped John read some of the more difficult characters. In extraordinarily exquisite calligraphy, the note read:

Lu Zhishen is well and safe. All of you must go to Dalandzadgad near the sand dunes of Khongoryn Els and the Flaming Cliffs of Bayanzag. You will be provided with camels. No bicycles. All of you must go to Dalandzadgad where you will be met and taken to a place of safety and reflection. There you will also find the Precious Object. Lu Zhishen will join you later. Altan will guide you. Go in peace. I will see you when Bai Meiying's fate is determined.

It was not signed.

"But this is crazy!" exclaimed John.

"Yes, and so are we."

"How so?"

Feng looked unusually serious. "For putting-up with this. I tell you my young American friend, I've half a mind to leave for good."

"But. . . . " John could think of nothing to say in response.

"Come on," said Feng, reasserting his authority. "Let's inform the others."

On their way back, John said, "You won't really go, I hope."

"Why not?"

"We need you."

"Perhaps no longer."

They woke the others and had them meet in the dining room. After John informed them of the situation and read the note, an astonished silence fell over the group.

Madame Liu, stunned as she was, cleared her throat and announced, "This news releases everyone from any responsibility to stay. Needless to say, you should follow your hearts. No one will blame those who wish to return to their homes . . . or, if not to your homes, which may be destroyed, then back to China, at least, which may also be destroyed by now."

"What are your plans, Madame Liu?" asked Master Zhou with an air of respectful formality.

"Stay, of course."

"For Lu Zhishen?" asked John.

"For my husband, for myself, for Lu Zhishen, for *her*."

"I am staying with you," said Suling firmly.

"I am also here to stay," added Child of Buddha. "No going back to an institution. If I leave, my gift will become my grave."

Master Zhou had tears in his eyes when he spoke. "My home is gone. The Japanese occupy my country. I stay."

John's mind raced. He desperately wanted to go home, back to the States. He desperately wanted to see Meiying again. He desperately wanted to see *her*. He desperately wanted circumstances to choose so that he would not be forced to. Dire circumstances made navigation through life easier by eliminating options, allowing others with more experience to tell one what to do: *Avoid that cliff! . . . or, Not this town! . . . Don't go in this direction! . . . or, Go in that direction! . . . Mustn't stay here or there! . . . Stay away from this road or that road!* Yes, returning to the States would require going it alone, at great risk, imposing a million unwelcome decisions. He blanched at the prospect.

"I'm staying," he said quietly.

"Alas!" cried Madame Liu suddenly. "Our group is so diminished! I miss my husband so; and our Peter and Meiying and Little Acorn and Mr. Gao and our beloved big Canadian, and all the rest!"

Feng Shiren had been listening with a certain glint in his eyes that spoke volumes—but written in a language only he could understand. "Well, there's nothing for it. I stay with you foolish people."

"What do we do about Lu Zhishen?" asked Suling.

Madame Liu shook her head. "We wait."

The next day, Mongol Peter and Mongol Little Acorn showed up with a group of Bactrian camels. After a few days of training, they were ready to leave and take all their belongings to Dalandzadgad.

Chapter Four

PART SIX: INTERREGNUM AND INTRIGUE

Routine

~ *Settling In* ~

Days turned into months, and for the group, the war was a constant and malevolent threat raging outside the safety of their retreat. Lu Zhishen turned up about six months after they first arrived at the compound. Winter had been a constant barrage of icy wind, and when spring came, everyone pitched in to re-establish the garden. John leaned over his hoe, listening to Suling and Madame Liu argue over the best location for peas, when the unmistakable snorts of camels drifted to them.

"Another caravan?" asked Suling as she broke off from talking and cocked her head in the direction of the gate. What she saw took her breath away. The big, bearded Canadian bore down upon them on his camel, grinning and shouting like a fool.

"Hello! Hello!"

"Zhishen!" cried Suling. "It's Zhishen! Come quickly!"

In the blink of an eye, the group had congregated with Suling as Lu dismounted and hugged all around.

"Well, well, I've heard a lot about you!" said Ishmael, who had appeared from nowhere.

A thousand questions and answers filled the air in such a flurry that nobody could understand anything.

"Wait!" cried Master Zhou, laughing with joy. "Let's go to the dining hall and give our friend food and drink. Then we can talk like civilized people."

Madame Liu looked at Ishmael. "And bring your Mongol friends who brought our Zhishen back safely to us."

"No, Madame Liu," he replied politely. "As always, we have our own ways and our own corner of this paradise. Do not let us disturb you! Enjoy your reunion!"

While the group raucously made their way to the dining hall, the Mongol escorts unloaded supplies and discreetly vanished to their own repast.

When pressed to tell his story, Lu Zhishen gave the following account, interrupted often by food and quaffs of rice wine, of which there was always a ready supply thanks to Master Zhou's generosity.

"I fell asleep in the room. The iron door was open and I remember hearing Shiren's breathing. I was sure nothing would happen and I was on a wild goose chase. But when I woke up, to my shock, nothing was familiar. I was no longer in the room! My heart pounded inside my chest. Surely I would now meet *her*. But it was not to be. I discovered I was in a Mongol yurt, far away in the grassland. How I got there is still a mystery. Drugs, perhaps, though I don't remember drinking anything. These past months I have lived among Mongols who spoke no English or Chinese. In my pocket I found a note saying I must stay with these people until taken back to be reunited with you. Here I am!"

"But that is incredible!" cried Feng Shiren. "Why didn't you just leave?"

"How? Where? I was a stranger in a strange land."

"But why?" asked Madame Liu. "Why go to all the trouble to take you to this Mongol village, then turn around and bring you back to us?"

"Believe me, I have thought long and hard about that very question and have come up with no answers."

"There must be something in that damn room!" exclaimed Feng Shiren.

"Of course!"

"Let's go back and finish the job you started!" bellowed Feng. "Let's blow it up!"

"I thought you worked for *her*?" said John.

"What?"

"Nothing."

"Don't be foolish!" scolded Madame Liu. "We are *her* guests. After coming this far, it would be tragic to make *her* angry and refuse to see us."

"Yes," sighed Master Zhou. "I like it here." He raised his eyes to the heavens and emptied the last of his wine, banging the empty cup on the table. "And no damn bicycles!"

"None of you have changed," said Lu contentedly.

"Have you?" asked John.

"Strangely, yes. I don't want to go back to the cave. Something happened to me while I was out of it . . . while I was drugged or unconscious . . . or whatever."

"What, Zhishen?" asked Suling.

"I don't know, but somehow I'm different. You must all tell me if I have changed."

"We haven't been with you long enough," said Master Zhou.

"Yes, as the days pass, you may notice. Now!" He clapped his hands. "What is the daily agenda here?"

Madame Liu chuckled. "Rise at dawn. Eat. Work. Eat again. Sleep. Rise at dawn."

"Sounds delightful! What is the work?"

"In the gardens. Groves. Keep the grounds maintained at Ishmael's direction."

"Oh, that Mongol who greeted me?"

"Yes."

"Ishmael! What a name!"

"It's their Mongol version of your nickname," said Master Zhou. "Instead of a Canadian choosing the name of a Chinese hero—Lu Zhishen; it is a Mongol choosing the name of an American hero—Ishmael."

"How funny!" laughed Suling. "I hadn't thought of it that way."

"Okay," said Lu turning serious. "You have told me *she* hasn't appeared, but when will *she*?"

The group looked at each other. "When Bai Meiying arrives," said Madame Liu.

"What? Still that old story? My god!"

"Yes."

"But we could be here forever!"

Feng Shiren jumped up and said with a flourish, "The good news is that we can leave anytime!"

Lu Zhishen took a sip of his wine and said glumly, "That's consolation!"

"I like it here!" repeated Master Zhou, now well into his cups. "So will you, old friend!"

"Well, *she* will come," said Suling. "I know *she* will."

"Who, Meiying or *her*?" asked John.

"Both."

"Whether or not Bai Meiying comes, *she* is already here," insisted Child of Buddha.

"In spirit," said Madame Liu.

"No, in body!" replied the hunchback. "I saw *her*!"

~

As the months passed, the mood of the group fluctuated like a fever between periods of heated exchanges borne of frustration and boredom to a genuinely happy spirit of community. Each of the members of the group reverted to the personalities they possessed in normal times. Necessities of war and external threat had made them put aside their petty quirks for the good of the whole—for survival. But now, no such unifying force smoothed the prickly unpleasantries of human interaction.

Madame Liu had become very cranky, believing *she* had betrayed her by not appearing after the group had gone through so much. She came to believe it was an insult to her dead husband and an affront to her leadership. These thoughts, of course, she kept to herself, but they surfaced in the increasingly petulant way she dealt with the others.

One day, Madame Liu overheard Suling talking to Child of Buddha. They were discussing the latest hints of *her* presence. Unlike the others, Madame Liu had experienced no such "contact" with *her*, spiritual or otherwise, and this had violated her sense of justice. She heard the hunchback say, "Yes, since that time when we first arrived, it's true I haven't seen *her*, but I know *she* is here. I can feel *her* presence."

Madame Liu burst forward and exclaimed loudly, "You know you never really saw *her*! That was just some sort of illusion or your imagination."

After recovering from the initial shock of hearing these words come from the mouth of their venerable leader, Child of Buddha replied angrily, "No! I did see *her*. Absolutely! You should have more faith."

"And you should be more truthful! It really upsets the others when you are the only one that claims to have seen her!" (Of course, only Madame Liu was upset by the hunchback's claim.)

Child of Buddha did not reply, but turned on her heel and stormed away, muttering indecipherable words. Madame Liu looked around and saw the others stare at her with faces that were made intentionally expressionless to hide their surprise and dismay.

"Any day now Meiying will come through that gate," she said mechanically. "Then we shall truly see *her*."

~

But Meiying did not come, and the months dragged on, until one day the war again intervened in an unexpected and disrupting way. A Mongol caravan trotted through the front gate as usual, and the group gathered to help unload supplies and chat with those riders who spoke Chinese. But this time, a solid, good-looking man in his forties accompanied them, and instantly stood out as being different. His body was short and strong, and he clearly appeared to be of peasant origin, but with a face that belied such a rough, intellectually-deprived background. Intelligent eyes, calm expression, and a lively curiosity about his surroundings marked him as a man of character and force.

After a short conversation with the caravan leader, Ishmael held an impromptu conference with Madame Liu and Master Zhou.

"The Japs are on a rampage," explained Ishmael. He paused, clearly hesitant to continue. "My clan has allied itself with the local communist forces. This man is Chinese and our ally. He is on the run. If he is found, he will die along with the population of any village or town that conceals him. We could think of nothing but to hide him here."

"Of course," replied Madame Liu with a defiant pride that rendered her words too soon spoken.

But Master Zhou proceeded more cautiously. "Do the Japs know where this place is?"

"No."

"But they have airplanes. Suling told me she heard an airplane a few weeks ago."

"Well, yes they have airplanes but we thought the risk was worth it."

Suling stood near to the Chinese man, staring at him openly. She suddenly said, "Yes, it's true I heard an airplane, but only one far away. I know this man. We must hide him."

"Thank you, Suling," he said.

"Well, that's different," said Master Zhou.

The rider dismounted and went up to Suling. "It has been a long time. I heard about your family. Mine too. Now I fight against the bastards."

John was struck by the simple power of his words, and the intensity of his gaze. Suling appeared to him uncharacteristically flustered.

"You will be safe here," she said, her face reddening.

"No," he replied, looking at her affectionately. "I will be happy here . . . now."

This made Suling turn even redder.

Madame Liu, being a perceptive woman, came to her rescue. She turned to Ishmael. "Well, where will you put up this hero?"

"I have just the spot."

"Nearby?" asked Suling before she could stop herself.

Ishmael laughed. "Not too far away—in a building with a secret tunnel."

Feng Shiren, quiet this entire time and appearing to the casual observer to be bored, perked-up. "A secret tunnel! Now, that is interesting. Where does it lead?"

"Oh, nowhere. Just a convenient hiding spot."

"Like a certain room in a certain cave with a certain iron door," muttered Feng to himself.

If Ishmael heard, he did not let on. "Tang Yuwei!" he called with a hint of humor. "I must drag you away from such pleasing company and show you to your room!"

Yuwei smiled openly. "Yes, all right. Let's go. But I will be back to talk with you, Suling."

John admired how he refused to pretend or be shy. *That is how I must be with Meiying,* he thought. *Resolute and contemptuous of the inevitable gossip that trails after strong men like old confetti.*

"Wait, I'll go with you!" called Feng Shiren to Ishmael.

"Yes, fine.'

Feng followed behind the two men, letting Ishmael brief Yuwei on the layout and daily routine of the compound. When they reached a small, ornate building, Feng thought it looked more like a shrine than a place where people slept. Up to now, it had always been locked.

A large statue of Buddha greeted them when they entered, and in front of the placid gaze stretched an elaborate wooden altar with unlit joss sticks and bowls of old fruit.

"This is the caretaker's space," said Ishmael extending his arm toward a small, inconspicuous door in the corner. Yuwei carried his cotton bag, tattered and filthy, into the room and Ishmael followed with a lantern. Feng slipped in behind them and surveyed the space. Cramped, with a bed, nightstand, and Chinese closet; it appeared unremarkable.

"If the Japs come looking," said Ishmael. "This is what you want to do."

He went to a corner, carefully removed some planks from the floor, and pulled up a heavy trap door. "Gather your things, drop them down with yourself, and go through the tunnel to a safe place where you can stretch out."

"What about the planks and such?" asked Tang Yuwei.

"Someone will be here to take care of that."

"Let's go down and take a look!" exclaimed Feng from the shadows.

Ishmael narrowed his eyes.

"Yes, let's go on down and see," agreed Yuwei.

"I recommend against it," said Ismael evenly.

"Noted, but let's go anyway," barked Feng.

Ishmael went first and the lantern handed down after him. As Feng Shiren and Tang Yuwei watched from above, the lantern disappeared, leaving only a faint bulge of light at the bottom of the chamber.

"Next!" called Ishmael.

In this manner, the other two dropped down and followed Ishmael into the tunnel. It was narrow and cramped, forcing all three to crouch as they walked. After a few meters, they reached a wider space, about the same size as the room above.

"This is where you'll wait until it is safe," said Ishmael.

"Air?" asked Yuwei.

Ishmael held up the lantern toward the ceiling. "Air holes."

Feng peered at the other side of the room, barely distinguishable in the dim light. "Does the tunnel continue?"

"Yes."

"Where does it lead?"

Ishmael showed his teeth in what could be interpreted as either a grimace or a grin. He held out the lantern and walked a few paces where the opposite wall lit-up, revealing an imposing iron door that covered almost the entire surface.

~ *Suling and Yuwei* ~

Later that evening, as they sat under the stars, Yuwei said to Suling, "This is a good place."

"Yes, I am content here. There is peace. There is work."

Yuwei smiled. "But no men."

"Yes, there are men here," chuckled Suling.

"Not for you, though."

She caressed his face. "There is now."

He put his arm around her and they remained silent.

Yuwei broke the spell. "If the Japs come. . . ."

"I know."

"But it's worse, Suling. I'm a communist. I've killed many Nationalists, not just Japanese. Even if the Japs were gone. . . . "

"I know."

"We're not young."

"No."

"Neither of us has family."

"No."

"So what brought you to this place?" he asked.

Suling told him about the remarkable woman whose mystical powers drew her to "this place" after a long and tortuous path.

"But you still haven't seen *her*?"

"No."

"Maybe *she's* not real. You know, we communists don't hold with religion."

"This isn't religion."

"Sounds like it."

"No," Suling replied curtly.

"Well, I guess I can say you're my religion now."

Suling playfully hit him. "You sound like a silly boy!"

"Feel like it. Haven't felt this way in a while."

A pause fell over their conversation, and they both knew the long-suppressed desire that smoldered in them had been sparked to life by the unspoken breath of this resuscitating moment under the stars. Before they knew it, they were kissing and fondling each other like adolescents.

Suling suddenly pulled back.

"We're too old to do this," she said huskily.

"We're too old not to do this," he replied emphatically. "Besides, time is short."

"Which is why. . . . " her words trailed off.

"I know, but we have to make up for the wasted time," he said with a hint of accusation.

"Let's not return to that. I don't feel I'm wasting my time."

He chuckled humorlessly. "Really? Waiting for some ghost woman?"

"Our arguing now would be a waste of time."

He put his arm around her again. "You're right. Let's go back to what we were doing."

Suling kissed him. "Yuwei, it would be foolish to jump back into something that can only be ended by some evil."

"What do you mean?"

"The war. Killing. Being killed."

Yuwei leaned forward with his elbows on his knees and looked into the darkness. "Yes, I'll kill as long as those who need killing are still around."

"Or be killed."

He shrugged.

She rubbed his back. "That is my point, Yuwei. As long as you think this way, there is no future."

"What would you have me do? Your family members died horrible deaths. My family was burned alive by the bastards! And rotten, corrupt, rich parasites live off us while sucking at the tit of the Japs! Kill them all and cleanse the land!"

"Not all the rich are bad."

"Yes, all!"

"Master Zhou, one of our group, is rich and he is good."

"Is he the one who hesitated and asked about the airplane?"

"Yes, but—"

His bitter laughter cut her off.

"Would you and your communist friends kill him?"

"In a heartbeat," he replied smoothly and calmly, his black eyes flashing in the moonlight.

"Then there is nothing more to say."

Suling stood to leave but he grabbed her hand.

"Stay, please. We'll change the subject." His demeanor converted to a pensive mask. "You know, I had a niece—since murdered by the Japs—who a few years ago received a precious doll. When I saw her, it had a nail driven into its head. I asked how the nail got there and she told me she did it in a fit of anger. But ever since, she said, it made her forever sorrowful, and she kept the nail in as a reminder of how cruel she could be. 'I'll never drive another nail into my dolly's head, uncle!' she cried sweet tears. 'I'll never drive a nail into anyone's head!' I remember how gentle and yet how passionate her words were.

"But when I returned from the forest to identify the charred remains of my family, her little blackened hand still clutched that same doll, all burned but recognizable. It had a second nail driven into its head!" He clutched his fists. "I know why she did it! I know where such anger comes from, even among the best and most innocent of us!"

"What is—" Suling started to ask.

"Oh, god, Suling! I am full of hatred more fierce than the fire that killed her!"

Suling continued to massage his back. "Yuwei, hatred is a destructive force."

"But it is a force, like wind, that won't be stopped."

As if on cue, a breeze stirred the night air and wrapped them in a cool embrace, then moved on into the night. Both were speechless.

"That was a strange breeze," murmured Yuwei.

"Yes, it felt . . . I don't know, odd."

"Yeah, odd, but really . . . nice."

"Yes." Suling remembered John and some of the others telling her about this magical breeze that occasionally blew through the compound. Her eyes widened in wonder. "It was *her*! Now I have felt *her* presence for the first time!"

Yuwei started to scoff at her superstitious idea, but stopped himself. "Yes, I almost believe you."

Suling's face shone. "That breeze is what peace is like."

"Really, Suling! You must get rid of those bourgeois superstitions."

"No, no, Yuwei. Have you no faith in what lies beyond your senses? You must not despise what is beyond your understanding."

"Like the Japs? I understand them perfectly well!"

"Perhaps they hate themselves for what they do."

"All the same, Suling, I hate the rich bastards more than the Japs. They are evil. I am on the run because we were betrayed by one of them. A fellow Chinese!"

Suling's eyes widened. "Who?"

"A monster who likes to be called Mr. President. We communists made an alliance with him. I traveled to his so-called palace, which is a den of disgusting, immoral monsters. I returned with one of his lackeys carrying information on where to rendezvous with his troops and ambush a Jap column. We were set-up. The lackey must have given the Japs our position. Only a few of us survived. When we looked to kill him, we found he had slipped away in the night. We almost caught him at a village near the border, but he got away again. Now he is with the Japs and we are the hunted. Not a comrade here who wouldn't strangle him with their bare hands. Wang Liwei is this monster's name. A curse on him and all his descendants!"

Suling's face, pale and frightened, was made even more alarming by the life-sapping moonlight. "I know this man," she said.

"Who? Wang Liwei?"

"No, Mr. President."

"What? Tell me!"

Suling told the story of their time at Mr. President's palace. When she finished, they both snickered at the recollection of his obese and obscene body. And yet, in spite of their comforting mockery, both marveled at the length of his reach and how, with the assistance of the Japanese, he could destroy his enemies from such a long distance.

"It's his game," observed Yuwei. "He plays one side against the other. But soon he will be left with only himself."

"Yes," shuddered Suling. "With people from all sides wanting to tear him from limb to limb. How horrible!"

"Add me to the crowd," added Yuwei. "I will not apologize for wanting to tear him limb from limb. And I have a premonition that his lackey, Wang Liwei, and I will meet again."

"If so, I pray it will not be here," said Suling.

"Come what may."

"Hopefully, the Precious Object will warn us."

"What's that?"

"A goddess statue. It seems when something bad is about to happen, a sound comes from inside it."

"More superstitious nonsense. What sound?"

"A tapping noise."

"That's silly."

"Maybe, but there it is," said Suling. She appeared worried. "But the note we found at the cave said we would find the Precious Object when we got here, and yet, none of us have seen it yet. In the beginning, we were all talking about it and we searched, but we couldn't find it. We spent weeks looking, months. Gradually, we stopped, but now. . . . "

~

The next day, Suling mentioned to Madame Liu her concern over the missing Precious Object.

"I think perhaps we should ask Ishmael to somehow communicate our desire to have the Precious Object back," said Suling, hesitating to be so bold. Madame Liu was increasingly testy, and she didn't want their leader to feel unjustly criticized.

"I did talk to him," said Madame Liu curtly.

"I know, but that was some time ago, and now that we have this man hiding here, perhaps things have changed. Perhaps we need the Precious Object."

"What about him? I notice you seem to care about him. In fact, you seem to know him quite well."

"We were friends a long time ago. But when I talked to him last night, I found out something that frightens me."

"What?"

"He is being chased by the Japanese."

"Yes, I know that."

"But there's something else. Somehow, Mr. President is behind all this."

"What! How?"

Suling relayed Yuwei's story and added, "So if we have the Precious Object, perhaps it would give us a warning if some evil people were getting near."

"Hmmm. . . . " Madame Liu seemed lost in thought. "Well, that's different. I will talk to Ishmael. Have you told the others?"

"You are the first."

Madame Liu nodded in satisfaction. "As it should be."

Suling came away from this conversation more worried about Madame Liu than Mr. President. Their leader seemed to be having more and more difficulty holding it together.

~ *Miss Bai Honored Teacher* ~

As the months passed, Meiying came to improve at her new profession, and actually began looking forward to the daily rough-and-tumble adventures of being a teacher. By now, she was attuned to the individual characteristics and eccentricities of her students, so their rude behaviors occurred in the forgiving light of context. Appearances by the stranger had ceased, so that eventually the threat faded from Meiying's thoughts. This particular morning, she puzzled over how best to get across Pythagorean Theorem to the older students.

It's always best to give practical examples, she thought. *Perhaps I can measure one of Mr. Xie's duck ponds as a lesson. Throw in how to calculate volume to boot.*

At the end of the lesson, Mulan and Shirong were two of only three students who understood. But little Mulan, years younger than the other two, grasped the concept and shook it like a dog with a leather strap. Meiying had learned to respond to Mulan's prodigy with a certain nonchalance, else the others would feel unnecessarily lacking. In fact, Mulan picked up trigonometry long before even the oldest students could conceive its sublime relationship to precision and prediction.

"Oh, can't you see that sine, cosine, and tangent are like three sisters!" Meiying overheard Mulan saying one day to the lesser lights. "Two pretty ones who are close and their opposite, who is long and tilted."

"What do you mean?" they asked in confusion.

"Oh, can't you see!" she exclaimed in exasperation. "It's so simple!"

Meiying listened in wonder to this agile mind, like a little fish skillfully darting around the anchored reefs of her peasant friends and family. Her piano skills were also progressing rapidly. In all ways, Mulan proved herself a bright and talented child, worthy of sending to the city for advancing her education. When Meiying learned that Mr. Xie had relatives living in Taiyuan, she suggested Mulan might live with them and engage a private tutor.

"No!" he responded angrily. "She'll learn outside her scope and it won't add a yuan to her value! You spend too much time with her. It's Shirong I want you to make smart!"

"But she has talent," Meiying replied.

"Wasted on a girl!"

"But you said—"

"I know what I said, but too much is too much to put on a girl."

Meiying pushed back, unwilling to give up on her protégé. "Perhaps you could send them both."

"Too expensive, and I need Shirong here. That's why I put you up with us, for you to teach Shirong, not send him away."

"But he is such a bright boy, he'll soon know all I have to teach," she said a bit too cleverly.

Mr. Xie narrowed his eyes. "Won't work, missy. I know the boy. His head is as empty as a hollow gourd. When you're done, I want to thump it and hear solid pumpkin, not empty space."

Meiying knew this topic would lead nowhere, so she changed course. "I will teach Shirong what I know, but you must also let me develop Mulan."

"Have I stopped you?"

"No, and for that I thank you."

Mr. Xie snorted. "No need to thank me. I've always told you the little brat, female that she is, should get a proper education." He thumped his chest. "Unlike the ignorant peasants here, I'm a modern man!"

"The New China?" prodded Meiying.

"Yes, but not now," sighed Mr. Xie peevishly. "What with the Japs and the Reds, war and more war, famine and more famine to make it all worse." He calmed and sighed again. "No, now is not the time. Maybe in the future, when I am long dead and the little scamp lives in a world I would not recognize. In that world she can bring up this learning and use it to survive and prosper. That be the goal, eh, missy?"

Meiying was filled with admiration for this simple man who understood, in his own way, more than most scholars she knew. He understood survival. And at heart, at bottom, fundamentally, survival is the game! Everything else is secondary. Mr. Xie recognized this simple fact. He invested in Mulan and Shirong as shrewdly as any stockbroker. Shirong was a solid, low-risk investment while Mulan went into his high-risk, high-return portfolio. In spite of his dismissive attitude toward her gender, he would place a few chips on her number. The roulette wheel would stop spinning where it may, but he (and she) may get lucky. For out of Mr. Xie's mind ever since Bai Meiying miraculously appeared from nowhere, had popped the notion that Mulan might indeed be a more valuable bartering chip with education than without. New China meant marrying for love, not by arrangement. If so, she might catch the eye (and mind) of an educated landlord's son; and land, to Mr. Xie, equaled wealth, hence more land equaled more wealth, and so on until his grandsons would be high government officials, fat and sassy, who would give rise to even fatter and sassier great-grandsons. *All great*, he thought. *So long as the damn communists don't take over.*

Communists bedeviled Mr. Xie. They danced and twisted in his brain like sinuous phantoms; never solid enough or motionless enough to get his hands around their throats. Meiying had long ago hit upon the notion that Mr. Xie would agree to almost anything if it were directly or indirectly connected to the destruction of communism.

"I'll teach Mulan about republicanism, which will make her very attractive to some high Nationalist official," explained Meiying, hoping this incentive would entice him enough to delay his plans to marry the child off to some loutish landowning peasant.

"You do that, missy, and you'll have earned your keep. I don't know what republicanism is, but if it helps us to get her a rich and powerful husband, I'm all for it!"

"If this stranger returns, will you protect me?" asked Meiying boldly and seemingly out-of-the-blue, for the topic of survival brought her back to the lurking threat of Beethoven.

"Of course. Is he a Red?"

"That is what I suspect."

"Then yes! I'll do more than protect you. I'll make sure the bastard will return his bones to the earth and never bother you again!"

Silence. Meiying had no response to this outburst.

Unwilling to suffer through too long a pause, Mr. Xie asked, "What's his name?"

"He's a stranger. I don't know."

"Oh, I think not," replied Mr. Xie, looking like a cat having just swallowed a canary.

"What do you mean?"

"I mean you know very well who this stranger is. Shirong told me about a person named Wang and that you know him."

"But I don't."

"But you do. It's written all over your face. I'm a poor, stupid peasant, but I know what I can see plain as day."

"Honestly, I don't."

"Perhaps you're half honest, and that half means maybe you're not sure who he is; but the other half of you knows this man and is certain the stranger is him." Mr. Xie leaned forward. "Who is he?"

"A stranger."

He slammed his fist on the table. "Who is he?!"

Meiying hesitated and took a deep breath. "Wang Liwei, if it is who I think it is."

"Is he a Red?"

"Maybe, or rather, maybe he is working with them. I don't know."

"Tell me about him."

Meiying surrendered to the surprising alacrity of this supposedly simple peasant, who saw and understood more than he reasonably should, given his low birth and lack of education. So she confided to him about Mr. President and Beethoven, leaving out certain intimate details unnecessary for him to know. This confidence brought the two closer.

"Hmmm," mulled Mr. Xie sagely. "I have heard of this warlord."

"Who?" Meiying asked anxiously.

"Why, your Mr. President of course. A shadowy fellow who is like a ghost to us peasants. His followers lurk about in the background, come and go at their pleasure, and what follows when they appear is never good. I have heard that this man makes alliances which he breaks at a whim."

"Is he a communist?" asked Meiying.

"No one knows, far as I can tell. He's a sly one. This fellow Betovan—I can't say his name right—is he a spy for Mr. President? I've never seen a follower of Mr. President in the flesh. They're like phantoms."

"You could say so."

"Well," mused Mr. Xie. "He hasn't been here in a long while. Maybe he'll stay away."

Meiying looked dubious.

"Why are you so worried about him? What do you think he's here for?'

"For me."

"But why?"

"That is a question I cannot answer. I fear that Mr. President wants me as a slave."

"A slave? One little woman for so much trouble?"

"Perhaps not. I'm merely a woman, so I'm probably wrong."

"Well, woman or no woman, I can't see going to such trouble. I'm sure we've seen the last of him. There's nothing here of any interest to Mr. President. I'm sure of it."

But the following week, the Japanese came to the village, and with them came Beethoven.

~ *Beethoven Returns* ~

Meiying first had warning of their arrival when parents rushed to the school in a panic and swept away their children. Only a few students remained, huddled in a corner with Meiying. When two Japanese soldiers burst through the door with weapons brandished, they were followed close behind by Beethoven. He swaggered into the schoolroom, pushed the terrified children aside, and bowed to Meiying in mocking style.

"I have enjoyed watching you try to escape me," he said with a venomous smile.

When she did not respond, he slapped her.

"I said, I have enjoyed watching you!"

She rubbed her burning cheek. "I see."

"Do you know what is to happen to you?"

"Yes."

"I have the power to kill Mr. Xie and his family."

"I know."

"Will you come quietly and not try to escape?"

"Then will you leave them alone?'

Beethoven slapped her again. "Will you come quietly?" He glanced at the soldiers who clearly did not understand Chinese. "I don't want to damage you."

"Yes."

"They think you are a Nationalist spy. If you try and escape, they'll kill you . . . that is if I don't."

"Let me get my things."

"Of course. I want you clean."

"Do we go straight back?"

"Unfortunately not. This group has business in Mongolia. I'm not going to try and get you back alone this time."

He slapped her again, but gently, almost affectionately. "You are quite the escape artist."

But Meiying barely heard his words. The mention of Mongolia as their immediate destination played on her mind. Did he know where the group was? Is that where they were headed? If so, everything appeared in jeopardy. But would the Japanese care about such an insignificant matter as a group of pilgrims looking for some mysterious lady? She thought not, and if not, it presented an opportunity.

One thing was certain: she would not allow herself to be a slave of Mr. President. She would either escape, be killed trying, or kill herself.

Suddenly, the sounds of a commotion came from outside. Meiying could make out the voice of Shirong shouting for Mulan, who cowered in the corner.

"I know about this little brat," said Beethoven observing Meiying's pained expression. "If you cause trouble, if you try and escape, it is quite simple to return and kill her and her family. Do you understand?"

"Yes."

"And you, little girl, do you understand?"

Mulan was too terrified to answer.

Beethoven stared at her. "She's cute. Very pretty . . . and talented . . . knows how to play the piano. I often listened to you teaching her." He patted Mulan's head. "Your protégé. Perhaps we'll pick her up on the way back. A bonus for Mr. President."

Meiying knew better than to speak. Shirong's frantic pleas continued from outside.

"Let her go," said Beethoven in Japanese. He turned to Meiying and smiled. "Won't do any harm to let her ripen a bit more. Besides," he said with a look that seemed genuinely desolate. "I also have a soul."

~ *The Precious Object Returns* ~

It was John who first noticed it. He had gone in search of Suling to ask about some mundane matter, but she was nowhere to be found. He hit upon the idea of looking for her in Tang Yuwei's abode. When he entered the building and looked at the shrine, he discovered the Precious Object on the floor in front of Buddha. No sound could be heard from the statue, but he felt a vibration emanating from within its golden body.

"Suling!" he called, stopping at Tang Yuwei's bedroom door. "Suling!"

No response.

He tilted his head and listened.

Nothing from the room; but a low, frothy hum of voices within his mind simmered menacingly and seemed to be on the verge of bursting forth in mocking attacks. Abruptly, he turned back to the Precious Object and listened more carefully, all the better to keep the voices at bay.

Nothing.

Then – the evil one.

Of course you hear nothing, fool! I'm in here! Your brain is the place to be: the be-all and end-all of John Powers.

Damn voice! Go away!

Have you forgotten Meiying?

I want to forget You.

Then came the voice of Goddess. ***Ignore these malevolent voices and listen to Me, John. Listen! It is Goddess speaking to you now, dear Chosen One. Clear your mind and Listen!***

Now he heard a faint tapping from the Precious Object. Drawn to the hypnotic regularity of its taps, like a heartbeat, he knelt and put his ear to Goddess.

"John!"

At the sound of this exclamation, he quickly stood and peered sheepishly at the startled face of Suling.

"How did you find the Precious Object?" she asked incredulously.

"It was here. Just sitting here when I came. Maybe Tang Yuwei found it."

She approached the statue gingerly. "Maybe," she said doubtfully, never taking her eyes off the statue. "Is he here?"

"I don't know," said John. "He didn't answer when I knocked."

"We must tell the others."

"Yes."

Neither of them moved.

While thus engaged, Tang Yuwei trudged into the room, distracted and tired. He gazed at the two in surprise.

"Hello! What's up?"

Their eyes told him where to look. Because the Precious Object meant nothing to him, he asked, "What's that? A new addition to the shrine?"

Suling looked at him disapprovingly. "No. It is the Precious Object. I told you about it."

"Oh," he replied in a lackluster tone. "Who brought that in here?"

Suling bristled. "It is important! It may even be your salvation."

"Or my demise," he muttered, looking at it as one might stare at an object that brought forth unpleasant memories.

Suling looked at John and said in a cutting voice, "Mr. Tang is always fighting against what his communist friends call bourgeois superstition."

John had no desire to get between this little spat, and hurriedly said, "I'll go tell the others."

As he left, he heard the two arguing behind him like an old married couple. By the time he returned with the others, chattering excitedly as they walked, Suling and Yuwei were peering in wordless wonder at the Precious Object.

… Tap. Tap. Tap.…

"Oh god!" exclaimed Madame Liu when she heard the tapping. "Now what?"

Feng Shiren, as always, seemed energized by the sound. "At last! Something to break the monotony! I was almost ready to leave. Now we know something interesting will happen."

"You were ready to leave?" asked Master Zhou in alarm. "Remember, my boy, the old curse that goes: may you live in interesting times."

"Yes, it's boring here. I would make a terrible monk. Look at me! I'm just young enough and foolish enough to crave interesting times."

John listened with mixed emotions. Feng Shiren always made him feel small and timid. Unmanly. But he also valued the sense of security and confidence Feng instilled by his mere presence. With him gone, John realized he would be even more frightened. These thoughts invariably made him bitter about his own inadequacies, and his response usually was to do or say something bolder than the situation called for. But now, there was nothing to prove his mettle, so he held his tongue.

Suling was under no such existential constraints. "Oh, Shiren! Please don't think of leaving. What would we do without you?"

Feng looked at her appreciatively when Madame Liu added, "Yes, I agree. I also think something is about to happen. Perhaps *she* is finally about to appear."

"Or perhaps not," said Child of Buddha. "Perhaps we are about to be put through another trial."

"Trials are bad," shuddered Master Zhou. "They usually end in disaster."

"True," said Feng Shiren with a shrug. "But such is the price we pay for living."

"Personally, I think the price is too high," replied Master Zhou coldly. "If we lose anyone else to a trial, I'm not about to stick around. Trials are for the young."

"It might be you we lose," said Feng with impeccable logic.

"If so, I will only stick around for the funeral, then it's off I go!"

This brought a chuckle from Feng Shiren, but Madame Liu would have none of it.

"Pooh! Enough talk of dying. We're here to live! *She's* coming, I tell you!"

As common of late, she glared at Child of Buddha. "False prophets sap our strength by planting doubts. *She* will come! Why go to all this trouble otherwise?"

"To try us!" exclaimed Feng waggishly, crouching into one of his favorite opera poses.

Tang Yuwei had been listening with increasing irritation. "All this talk has nothing to do with me, or with the future of China, or with anything of value. You are all like children waiting for a magic fairy while the world burns down around you. It's nonsense!"

"That's not true!" objected Suling. "Why must you be so harsh?"

"Bah! Comrade Marx would say you are all lost to the world in your opium-dreams of religion and mysticism."

"It is you who are lost, Comrade Tang," scolded Suling. "Your foolish ideals have separated you from the true soul of China—from the people you claim to love."

Tang Yuwei slapped Suling and growled, "Shut up, stupid woman! You know nothing!"

Feng Shiren and Lu Zhishen both stepped forward, shocked by his action and uncertain what to do.

"Please, it's okay," said Suling, wiping away a tear. "He doesn't mean it."

"Yes, I do, foolish woman! If you would have married me, I would have rid you of such superstitious nonsense and made you into a dutiful Chinese wife and a revolutionary comrade."

… Tap. Tap. Tap.…

A little quicker now.

"I'm really worried," said Master Zhou, clearly agitated by this dispute. "Go bring our Mongol friend," he said to anyone willing to follow his command. "Go bring Ishmael."

John willingly left the group to go in search. Feng's comments had upset him and the voices continued to rumble ominously. As he walked away, he heard Lu Zhishen expressing surprise to Tang Yuwei about the shifting nature of alliances.

"I was told the Mongol clan that is now hiding you didn't feel the same about communists a few months ago. In fact, they killed many of you communists."

"The enemy of my enemy is my friend," laughed Tang. "Alliances are made to be broken."

How easily they forget his violence against Suling, thought John. *Even in our own minds we are constantly negotiating and re-negotiating alliances from one thought to another, one viewpoint to another. Am I like everyone else—a trail of broken alliances? Yes, I am! Worse! I have broken my alliance with Meiying. I hide here instead of searching for her.*

True, true, an evil one spoke. **You are a coward.**

Of course, to You I am a coward. To You I am nothing good!

Not true, dear Chosen One. Stop listening to the ones that would weaken your mind. You will be the father of a son. The son will take the next step, and after him will come the Superior Ones.

When?

When you learn to form alliances that last and stop listening to the evil ones.

While in the midst of this internal dialogue, John noticed Ishmael striding toward him.

"Looking for me, I suppose," said the Mongol jovially.

"How'd you know?"

"The Precious Object?"

"Yes."

"And Madame Liu wants me to come?"

John laughed. "Yes, of course."

Ishmael rolled his eyes. "So I am about to be grilled again."

"No doubt."

"But I know nothing," chuckled Ishmael. "I'm only a poor barbarian Mongol."

John looked at him sharply. "But we all know you know."

"I only know I know nothing. That is the secret to our success."

"Your people once conquered half the world."

"Of course, that is when we knew something. Look where it got us."

"Knowing nothing is better than knowing something?"

"Of course."

"But what about *her*? You know about *her*. That's something!"

"*She* is nothing . . . and as I said, knowing nothing is better than knowing something."

"My head hurts," groaned John in mock pain.

"That's because you know something," observed Ishmael.

~

As he intimated to John, Ishmael was the paragon of ignorance regarding the appearance of the Precious Object when he spoke to Madame Liu.

"Obviously the appearance of the Precious Object is the work of our old friend the iron door!" exclaimed Lu Zhishen when the group met later. "I'm done with iron doors!"

"Not me," said Feng Shiren.

The group had decided to keep the Precious Object in the shrine in spite of Tang Yuwei's distaste for it. But his constant complaints about its incessant low-level tapping caused them to move it to an uninhabited building which served in some distant past as a sort of meeting room for dignitaries.

"This will have to do," said Madame Liu when it had been placed on a table and turned just so.

"But I would still feel better if it were in its old spot near the hiding place, if something bad happens," said Master Zhou.

"Can't be helped," replied Madame Liu gruffly. She glanced at Suling. "We don't want to inconvenience our abusive communist guest."

Child of Buddha, as always, spoke with the utmost confidence, if not with the utmost clarity. "It will be safe. It is not without its own defenses."

John had only been half-listening, but now he became fixated on the steady beat of the tapping, which had suddenly been joined by a sort of primitive chant from the voices, rumbling like the distant sound of cannibals in some storybook jungle; drumming and dancing their souls to fury. It seemed to him they would blow their poison darts any moment, so he ran headlong in panic through the compound and ended up near the front gate, where Ishmael stood waiting.

"Want out?"

John could not catch his breath.

Ishmael scanned over John's shoulder. "Are they close?"

"Who?" John panted.

"Your demons."

"Yes!"

Ishmael opened the gate and waved his arm as if inviting him outside the compound. "Meiying is out there, waiting."

John looked out at the expanse of sand and the Bayanzag cliffs in the distance.

Ishmael smiled. "Here there is water, food, shelter, companionship, and *her*; out there is . . . who knows?"

"John!" snapped Madame Liu. "Pay attention! Your daydreams and voices will harm us all one day."

With this admonition, John returned from his reverie to be confronted with the stares of the group.

"We've been discussing the latest news, John," explained Suling helpfully.

"What news?"

Madame Liu threw up her hands. "There you have it! Focus, John!" Her shortness and irritability by now had become commonplace, and were usually ignored by her comrades. The erosion of her leadership seemed to be accelerating.

"A Japanese column has been seen crossing into Mongolia," said Lu Zhishen.

"Is it headed this way?" asked John.

Feng laughed. "I don't think the Japs are sending an army to deal with a few pilgrims in search of . . . something even I don't understand."

"So, we're safe here?" asked Suling.

"I didn't say that. Well, I mean, if our friend Tang Yuwei is important enough. . . ."

"However," commented Master Zhou. "They do not know where we are. After all, that is why this place is located behind such an inaccessible veil."

"Ah," observed Feng. "But others know where this place is located. The veil can be lifted."

"Enough of this defeatist talk!" exclaimed Madame Liu. "They are not coming to Mongolia for us, and even if they are, they will never find us!"

Feng Shiren laughed. "Never is a big word. A little torture and tongues wag. Many of our Mongol protectors know where we are. If they are captured, it would be simple for the Japs."

"Bah!" cried Madame Liu. "They have no interest in us! Forget it and get on with our work."

Child of Buddha shook her head. "I am not so sure."

Chapter Five

Journeys

The Desert

As the little camel caravan set off from the cave, John looked back and mourned the fact that even more distance was being put between himself and Meiying. His attention soon returned to his rather spirited camel. Although they had taken a few days to practice, he rode unsteadily and often needed help from Mongol Peter to keep from losing control. *I feel like an idiot!* he often thought. *But this is certainly an adventure! Something to tell my grandchildren—or rather, I should say, my future son.* Gradually, however, he learned to control the beast.

Child of Buddha looked the oddest, her hump mimicking that of the camel's two, but she managed to ride very well for a novice. Only Master Zhou seemed completely unable to develop the knack. He often listed to one side or the other, usually on the verge of tumbling off, and always good-naturedly apologetic to his rescuers. While the circumstances dictated that they should be grim after abandoning the cave and all proximity to *her*, the group displayed remarkably good spirits. Only Mongol Peter knew the full extent of danger that their exposure in the open desert subjected them to.

For all of them, the first two nights camping under the sparkling sky were physically the worst, as their backs ached from bouncing unceremoniously for many kilometers. Mongol Peter and Mongol Little Acorn slept apart, tending the camels and keeping unspoken guard over their very cantankerous charges. At night, they gathered around a fire which Mongol Peter had prepared using dung as fuel, and speculated about what to expect in the town, about when *she* might appear, the whereabouts of Bai Meiying, and the weird beauty of the desert. Bitterly cold, the evenings brought a biting wind that even their heavy garments could not totally block. On the third night, an event occurred that was to change the nature of their blissful unawareness.

While they slept, a shot rang out that woke them all. The fire had burned down to a pile of glowing embers, and the group instinctively rushed toward it.

"Get away from the light!" shouted Mongol Peter from the darkness with a sharp command. Everyone quickly dispersed to the brush and waited, fully expecting bandits to roar down upon them. But nothing happened and dawn found them still scattered, exhausted from lack of sleep and fear. Only in the light did they discover that Mongol Peter had been on guard near the fire when he was wounded. Mongol Little Acorn had clumsily bandaged his arm. Madame Liu insisted on re-dressing it.

"At least the camels are safe," he said as she tightened the bandage.

"Who do you think it was?" asked Feng Shiren, who still carried a pistol that he had pulled from his belongings after hearing the shot.

"Don't know," replied Mongol Peter.

"Bandits?" asked Suling.

"Maybe."

"But only one shot?" asked John.

"It is strange," remarked Mongol Peter.

That day they kept their camels close and by evening, Mongol Little Acorn had ridden off on some unknown mission as soon as the sun set. Their tiny arsenal consisted of Mongol Peter's old Enfield rifle and Feng Shiren's pistol, both of which offered little protection from any sizeable band intent on mischief. A mood of powerless vulnerability cast a pall over the group. Mongol Peter had not wanted to build a fire that night, but the freezing wind outweighed the risk. In the early morning hours, while still dark, another shot rang out. Child of Buddha was on guard duty and she immediately rushed to calm the spooked camels. When the others arrived, the blood had spread over her back; Suling discovered an entry wound where the bullet had burrowed deep into her hump. On the other side, the bullet had lost momentum and could be seen pressing outward, forming a nasty bulge in her skin.

Suling and Madame Liu quickly cut out the bullet and patched the wound. John found it odd that Child of Buddha felt no pain, or at least did not show it. *She must not have nerves in her hump,* he thought, and wished he also had fewer nerves to contend with. But he did not possess a monopoly on fear. Everyone in the group appeared anxious and frightened. However, it was the normally placid face of Mongol Peter that struck them most forcefully. His leathery features were now taut with worry and he constantly scanned the horizon for something unseen . . . but what? Salvation? Destruction? No one knew, and his answers to their nervous inquiries were always evasive.

They stayed that entire day as if in a state of siege, though no further incident occurred. At last, toward dusk, Mongol Peter could be seen excitedly staring toward the southwest, his hand shading his eyes from the low-hanging sun. John attempted to follow his eyes but saw nothing. At last, a slight haze rose in the distance and now everyone discerned a group of riders approaching. Mongol Peter's calm demeanor while he watched gave them confidence they were not in danger. As the riders approached on camels, John could make out about eight men along with Mongol Little Acorn. Mongol Peter went out to greet them and held a conference beyond earshot.

"What do you suppose this is all about?" asked Feng Shiren suspiciously.

"We'll soon find out," replied Madame Liu.

"I think we just received a more robust armed guard," observed Master Zhou.

"Yes," agreed Child of Buddha. "I think you're right."

"So even wounded, your hump brings you the inside story?" asked Feng sarcastically.

"So it does, Mr. Feng," she replied calmly.

"Are you in pain?" asked John, still interested in the question of her nerves.

"No, thank you."

"Look!" cried Feng. "They're leaving."

"Hmm," grunted Madame Liu, unsure what to say but feeling compelled to respond.

"Strange," said Master Zhou.

They waited for Mongol Peter to return but he stood watching his comrades split into two groups and head in different directions. At last, apparently satisfied, he and Mongol Little Acorn rejoined the group.

"I'll build a fire," he said as if nothing were amiss.

A fierce wind gusted, driving sand and ice crystals through the group like a host of little daggers. Everyone suddenly became aware of the intense cold and enthusiastically collected dung. As Mongol Peter periodically stoked the fire, they huddled around like hungry children awaiting cake.

When flames grew to a decent height and the warmth could be felt, Madame Liu asked, "Mongol Peter, who were those people?"

"Friends."

"Where are they going?" asked Feng.

"Nowhere. Around."

Feng smiled broadly. "No more shots, eh?"

Mongol Peter returned the smile. "No more."

"How far to Dalandzadgad?" asked Suling.

"Two or three days." He grimaced. "We are quite a slow group."

"Will we ever find out who shot at us?" asked Feng pointedly.

Mongol Peter only grinned.

"You know, don't you?" asked Feng.

"Yes.'

"But you won't tell us?"

"No."

"Why?" asked John.

"No, no!" scolded Feng. "Don't ask that. It is enough that he knows and that we are now protected. It is discourteous to insist."

"Yes," agreed Madame Liu. "Let us sleep. The sooner we reach this town the better, for then the sooner we will see *her*."

"How soon?" asked John.

Feng laughed. "So inquisitive! That is a question our other impatient foreign friend Lu Zhishen would ask!"

A strong gust of wind scattered his words.

John never heard them. He heard only the voices in his head suddenly come to life. God spoke first.

I could have killed the hunchback, but I did not.

For whose sake did you save her, Dearest?

For John Powers.

Why? Your motives are suspect. Not for the future? The hunchback is another of the Chosen Ones!

John, I could have killed her, but I saved her for you. The bullet was flying toward her head. I deflected it.

"Why?"

Feng looked confused. "Why? Still asking why? Because your question reminded me of Zhishen. Pay attention!"

"No," said John looking at him strangely. "I mean, why did you save Child of Buddha for me?"

"What?"

Not him, fool! He is Goddess's phantom guardian. It was Me! Me! Me!

Feng Shiren stared at John and an expression of awareness spread over his face. "Suling!" he called.

As she quickly approached, he said, "I think John needs you again."

Suling placed her hand on John's back and rubbed very delicately. "Don't listen to them, John," she purred. "They are not real. Don't listen. Look at me, and don't listen to them."

He gazed at her vacantly. "If not for Her, Child of Buddha would be dead."

"Oh, the Goddess voice?"

"Suling, it's not a voice." He said this automatically, then seemed to experience a revelation. "It is not just a voice! It's something more!"

You are correct, Chosen One. Finally.

"They are just voices, John. Don't listen to them."

But John merely stared at Suling without seeing. *God is lying*, he thought. *Saving Child of Buddha would break one of His First Principles. He is trying to take credit for what Goddess did. Or Her faction. Or His. I can't. . . .*

Suling held out both hands, palms up. "John, remember *her*. Remember Meiying. It is important to focus on now. What is real. On surviving. On being here for Meiying . . . and *her*."

Mention of Meiying and *her* appeared to draw him back. His eyes lost their empty gaze and he gradually focused on Suling.

"Yes, of course. I'm all right."

"Good. Now, John, you must stay focused. Once we reach this town we will be in a safe place."

"But what about Meiying? I'm abandoning her!" He became increasingly agitated. "I have to wait for her at the cave!"

"No, John," Suling continued to soothe as best she could.

Child of Buddha, always nearby, said, "She will find the town much easier than the cave. We are actually making it easier."

"Yes, yes, that's true isn't it?"

"Of course. Mongol Peter and his clan will direct her to us. Remember, *she* wrote in the note that we all must wait to be reunited with Meiying before *she* will appear."

"Yes, yes," said John, feeling better.

~

The next two days unfolded peacefully as they rode through the sprawling grasslands of the Gobi. John's voices again receded and he gave himself up to the rhythm of the camel's gait and the enormous flat expanses that made him feel atomized. Conversation was kept to a minimum, as every person in the group withdrew inwardly, rendered mute by the spacious immensity surrounding them. Gradually, lush grass broke up into isolated clumps among an expanding sea of sand. Green turned to beige as the limitless grains of sand claimed back from life their ancient birthright. Vegetative extravagance finally succumbed to the onslaught of parched and scouring dust. As Dalandzadgad came into sight, it seemed the mix of square concrete buildings and circular yurts were nothing more than human oddities thrown up to mock the featureless desert with unnatural geometries. A few forlorn trees failed to break the monotony of these concrete eruptions and animal-hide pustules.

Mongol Peter rode up to John before they entered the town.

"If asked," he said sharply. "Tell them you are Russian."

"Why?"

"Many communists."

"What if someone speaks Russian to me?"

Mongol Peter smiled mournfully. "This is why you were supposed to go with Lu Zhishen. But. . . . "

"What? How?'

"Never mind. Do your best. I don't think anyone will speak Russian to you. But to be safe, pull down your hat and pull up your scarf. We won't stay here long."

As it turned out, the group had barely gotten into the heart of town when three scruffy herdsmen approached Mongol Peter's camel. He dismounted and they entered a bar. After some time, he came to the door and waved the group in. Mongol Little Acorn and a ragged stranger tended the camels. Coming in from the sunlit street, the group blinked at the darkness of the bar. The room appeared bare, with a long wooden table in the corner where they settled wearily. None had had a bath in days, and the aching in their bones returned with a vengeance now that they sat on benches.

"At least there are no soldiers here," observed Madame Liu.

"None that we saw," cautioned Feng Shiren. "But there are probably a lot of Reds. They don't wear uniforms."

"How about the Japanese?" asked John.

"Don't know. I need a beer!"

Feng walked up to the bar and returned with a smile. "Ordered one for all of us," he proclaimed.

The bartender, a fat Mongolian with eyes that darted from face to face, hesitated when he spotted John.

From his vantage point at the bar, Mongol Peter's voice boomed out a Mongol word.

Feng leaned over and whispered to John, "He said 'Russian.'"

Bottles with white liquid were placed in front of each person along with a dirty glass. Madame Liu paid in silver coins, which the bartender collected with greedy fat fingers. John poured the liquid and took a swig before almost spitting it out. Warm. Bitter.

Feng Shiren laughed. "Don't like Mongol beer?"

"Not hardly. Do you?"

"It's called *kumis*—fermented mare's milk." Feng eyed John with amusement, then drank the entire bottle in one gulp. "Delicious!"

John shoved his bottle over to Feng, who promptly finished it off.

Master Zhou spoke in a loud voice. "Notice there are very few refugees here? Roads aren't choked with panicking people. We're lucky to have made it this far."

Suling quietly moved her 'beer' over to Master Zhou, who pretended to be surprised. "Why, thank you my dear! You sure. . . . ?"

Suling nodded and glanced at John, who she worried about constantly.

Child of Buddha drank her *kumis* and moaned in pain when she leaned back against the wooden wall.

She does have nerves! thought John. *She's human.*

Mongol Peter finished his conversation with the men at the bar and approached the group. "We eat, spend one night here, and leave tomorrow at dawn."

Moans.

"Where to?" asked Madame Liu.

"Outside of town, to a safe place."

"How long will it take?" asked John.

"A full day, maybe two by camel."

After a hot meal of lamb and rice, they slept in a shabby hotel that, in spite of the cockroaches, offered one great luxury—beds. John wanted to take advantage, but his restless mind would not let him sleep. He thought of life in the States before meeting *her* and traveling to war-torn China.

Living in a dream then! he thought. *Sleepwalking through life. Not like now, from crisis to crisis, but in the States?—from one bored, dissatisfied day to another . . . creating meaningless events out of meaningless thoughts and meaningless ideas while doing meaningless tasks at meaningless work. Say what you will, I'm alive here. Truly alive! Yet, my sorry, feeble-minded brain wants to return to that senseless nursery. Comfort is all it offers. It's comfortable, that's all. Still, I want to go back to sleepwalking!*

Thus ran his thinking until sleep overcame him. Just before he finally nodded-off, he thought, *Maybe, maybe, maybe I'll finally see* her *and Meiying. Maybe. . . .*

Roosters outside his window jarred him awake. A quick breakfast of rice gruel and again he stood next to his camel. Mongol Peter issued commands to the armed guard that John had seen out in the open desert. Mounting the protesting camels, the group headed north out of town.

As they rode across the flat sands, Dalandzadgad gradually disappeared behind them. Once the last trace of the town had fallen below the horizon, Mongol Peter spoke, a rarity for him.

"It is good we are out. I hear the Japs are headed this way. Within the week, the town may be occupied, unless the Reds can stop them."

"So the war is going badly," commented Master Zhou sadly.

No one spoke and they continued their trek.

"Who is paying for all this?" mused Feng Shiren out of the blue.

"What?" asked Madame Liu, somewhat startled at the question.

"The armed guard, Mongol Peter, the camels, all of it. Who is paying?" Feng turned on his camel and stared at her. "You?"

"No, at least not all of it."

"Then who?"

Of course, no one could answer.

By afternoon, long shadows were cast by their little caravan and the temperature dropped precipitously.

"We'll stop early today," announced Mongol Peter. "We're still hours away, and it is important to prepare camp and our defense."

"Defense?" asked Madame Liu, alarmed.

"Yes. Reds and bandits operate here." He gazed at his fierce-looking comrades. "But nothing will happen to you!"

John wanted to pursue the question of who paid for their services, but he still smarted from Feng's earlier scolding and remained quiet. By the time a good fire had been lit, the wind again whipped through their cotton jackets, chilling them to the bone.

In the early morning hours, shots rang out, waking everyone. This time a gun battle raged for almost twenty minutes. None of the group could see what transpired, as the action occurred entirely in darkness, beyond even the weak light smoldering from their fire. When the last gunshot echoed across the sand, sleep was again out of the question. John, crouching in fear during the battle, switched his earlier viewpoint about life.

Damn! This is insane! I want to go back to the States! To sleep in peace . . . in a bed . . . bacon and eggs for breakfast . . . cold beer, real beer, in the afternoon . . . Christ almighty!

Yes? You called, poor mutant Chosen One?

"Goddamned voices!" he screamed aloud

This brought a sharp rebuke from Feng Shiren, laying close-by in the darkness. "Quiet, fool!"

"Sorry," replied John stupidly.

Feng whispered, "You'll draw their fire."

"Yes, sorry," he repeated.

But daylight brought with it no further fighting. As soon as they saw Mongol Peter return, they crowded around.

"Was anyone hurt?" asked Madame Liu.

Mongol Peter appeared grim. "Yes. They have been taken away to our village. But we killed some of them." He spat. "Let them be carrion!"

Feng asked the identity of the enemy.

"Communist bandits! Probably deserters from the Red Army."

"Do you think they will be back?" asked Master Zhou.

"No. From here on, we must not be followed. Where I take you is secret, known only to very few. If we leave soon, we'll arrive by mid-afternoon."

John's immediate thought was how Meiying could possibly find this secret place. When he expressed this concern to Madame Liu, she smiled confidently.

"I thought of that. Meiying will find her way to Dalandzadgad, and once she does that, *her* emissaries and spies will know."

"So they'll bring her to us," he replied as if convincing himself.

"Yes, certainly," agreed Madame Liu, quick to make his reply appear to be his own inference. "You're right, they'll bring her to us." While Madame Liu felt it important that John be convinced of Meiying's return, she herself had long since had her own doubts. If her husband could be killed, who for so long had seemed to her graced with a sort of immortality, then anyone could die at any time. Although confiding in no one, she had been devastated when the note from *her* indicated that they must wait to be rejoined by Meiying. Even Master Zhou must not be made aware of her uncertainties.

And if Meiying is dead? she asked herself privately. *We wait until we ourselves die? How long can I hold this together? Does* she *think I'm superhuman?*

But in the end, Madame Liu put her faith in *her* and continued to function as leader of the group, both for herself and her husband's memory. However, doubts had been raised and she looked for any signs that their slow-acting toxicity was noticed by the others. With her responsibilities forming such a necessary scaffold, she mounted the camel as if she scaled a platform, and exuded an air of unshakeable confidence.

"I, for one, am quite interested to see our new quarters!" she proclaimed cheerfully—perhaps a bit too cheerfully.

"Couldn't be worse than that dark hole we just left," groused Feng Shiren.

"I agree," added Master Zhou. "Dark and damp . . . and scary!" He said the last word with a giggle, making a face.

When the group laughed at his jesting, Madame Liu thanked *her* that Master Zhou remained with them.

~

Mongol Peter had returned to his stoic ways and rode with silent dignity in the front, next to an even more reticent guide. Slow progress was made due to gullies and ravines that often had to be ridden around. Roads were, of course, nowhere in sight. By late afternoon, a vision confronted them that had to be seen to be believed.

Sheer cliffs of flaming red rose from the sand, shimmering in the sun and stretching as far as the eye could see. Contrasted against the lapis lazuli sky, it seemed they were riding into the bowels of an infant Earth, primitive and just-birthed. Fissures, like dark veins in the cliff faces, appeared before them, narrow entrances to a burning mineral hell.

"Flaming Cliffs of Bayanzag!" shouted Mongol Peter to the group as it gazed open-mouthed in wonder at the sight.

"Oh my god!" cried Master Zhou. "That is beautiful!"

"Yes," agreed Feng Shiren. "My eyes deceive me!"

"Yet you see," said Child of Buddha. She shifted her attention to Mongol Peter and addressed him directly—a first. "We venture to our safe place in there?"

Taken off guard by this inquiry from a person he had assumed was nothing more than a misshapen phantom, he replied, "Yes, Bent Spirit One."

"Why do you call me that?" she asked.

"It is your name to us. All of you have names given to you only by us."

This revelation spread quickly to the rear of the caravan.

"What is mine? What is mine?" came the calls from every member of the group. A spirit of good fellowship and comradery spread so that Mongol Peter laughed and stopped his camel.

He pointed at Madame Liu. "You are Lustrous Thunder."

"And me?" asked Master Zhou, partaking in the jollity.

"You are Forever Laughing Old."

And so he went down the line.

John: "Silent Voices."

Suling: "Cup of Kindness."

Feng Shiren: "Brave Jester."

Laughter ricocheted off the cliffs.

"And you?" asked Feng brazenly.

Mongol Peter's comrades looked at him and laughed. "Cock's Walk!" shouted one of them.

Mongol Peter held up his hand to quell the riot. "Now you must ride into the flames. There must be no mistakes! My brothers and I leave you now!" He swept his arm toward his comrades. "I am sorry, I must leave you! Only this man must know the destination." He pointed to the unobtrusive guide. "Farewell!"

Before they had a chance to properly thank them, Mongol Peter, Mongol Little Acorn, and the other guards galloped back from where they came, dragging branches that appeared from nowhere behind their camels to obliterate any tracks that might lead intruders, friend or foe, to the destination.

The group watched in dismay as their friend and lifeline blinked out in the distance with his comrades, leaving only a cloud of dust as evidence they ever existed. All eyes turned to the guide, whose individual humanity, by necessity, must now be evaluated on its own merits. Sensing this, he turned to the group and grinned broadly. Holding out his hands, palms up. His words stunned them.

"I have been sent by *her* to take you to the secret place. My name will not be revealed. Call me Ishmael. The name comes from the Christian bible and a famous book. I myself have never read either, but I have been told about the novel. Here at the Flaming Cliffs, the endless sea is the endless sand; a powerful whale that buries ships is a powerful sandstorm that buries cities; a mad captain whose obsession with death circulates like poison in the blood is a phantom Goddess who bends toward life like a plant toward sun; and my namesake is the only survivor. I like that. Here, the powerful woman that rises like these cliffs is the powerful woman who awaits us. I hope to survive like Ishmael and see *her* again. Far from being a powerful whale that destroys us, *she* is a powerful force that will lift us up. Do what I say, and you will also survive to see *her*."

No one in the group could respond to this remarkable speech.

"Stay close!" he warned. "We head that way." He pointed.

They looked at the Flaming Cliffs with trepidation and plunged into the fire.

~ *Meiying Hesitates* ~

The morning after the second appearance of the piano-playing stranger, Meiying rose and ate breakfast with the Xie family as normal. Acting more like an automaton than a person, she went to school and mechanically gave the students their lessons. Today, rather than being more short-tempered than usual, she was much more lax, and the students reveled in her apparent disinterest by mischief-making beyond their accustomed limits. Her distraction carried over into Mulan's piano lesson.

Mulan noticed the disconnect and asked if there was something wrong.

"No, dear," said Meiying. "I apologize. I'm just thinking."

"About that man last night?"

"Yes . . . and other things."

"Father says you need a husband to tell you what to do."

"Does he?"

"Yes, but I told him what you said about husbands."

"Oh, I'm not sure that was a good idea, Mulan."

"Yeah. He got a little mad."

Meiying's eyes welled-up. "Do you want me to stay, dear Mulan?"

"Oh, yes! You can't go!"

"But I think I must."

Now Mulan began to cry. "You can't."

She patted Mulan's hand. "We'll see, dear."

Oddly, the memory of John popped into her head. She did not know why, but she recalled the time in Master Zhou's library when they both stole looks at the master's pornographic books, giggling like children at the pictures. That was just before she met Meili; when she assured Madame Liu that she did not love John "in that way." She still did not love him "in that way," but she was fond of him, and he possessed a treasure more valuable than she could say—a ticket to America.

Now she pictured being with John, traveling to America where there was peace . . . and opportunity. Concerts. A home. Children.

But living a lie, she thought. However, she had learned that lies have their place, and sometimes, may serve a life-saving purpose.

Shirong barged into the classroom, sweating and dirty with a hoe still over his shoulder.

"I found him! I found him!"

"Who?" asked a startled Meiying.

"The stranger, of course!"

Meiying felt her blood run cold and her heart fluttered uncomfortably in her chest. "Well, who? Where?"

"Oh, I don't know where he is now, but a villager I am friends with told me he confronted the stranger and asked his name the other night."

"How do you know he was our stranger?" asked Mulan accusingly.

"Description fits. The way he was dressed. Oh, he was our stranger all right."

"His name?" asked Meiying.

"Mr. Wang. Said he was a refugee."

"That's it?" asked Meiying, disappointed.

Shirong looked crestfallen. "Well, yes. Then he left before my friend could ask more."

"How long ago was this?"

Shirong, deflated, replied petulantly, "A few days."

Meiying put her hand on his arm. "Oh, thank you so much, Shirong."

"Do you know him?" asked Mulan.

Meiying looked troubled. "That is a good question, dear. There are many Wangs in China." Her mind raced back to Mr. President's close companion and Meiying's unwanted lover, Madame Wang. *His mother,* she thought with a shudder. *Confidante of Mr. President; spider at the center of the web; a woman who sends her son off to trap the unwary!* Meiying had no illusions that this "stranger" must be Beethoven. *So much the better!* she thought. *My decision is made—I must leave the village!*

"Schoolteacher Bai!" exclaimed Shirong.

"Oh! Yes?"

"Boy, you were a long way off. Do you maybe know this person?"

"Maybe."

Shirong had regained his excitement. "Is he dangerous?"

"Maybe."

"I can alert the village. We won't allow any nonsense here from a stranger. We have seen bad guys before! We know how to deal with them."

Meiying felt encouraged by his words. *Perhaps. . . .*

"I will tell papa and he will make an announcement to the village council. If this stranger returns and causes our schoolteacher any more trouble . . . well, we'll take care of him!"

Meiying found Shirong's adolescent bluster endearing, but she knew Beethoven was no fool. If something happened, he could bring trouble to the village—big trouble. It seemed wherever she went, disaster followed; people died when she entered their lives. Tears again welled in her eyes. As much as she wanted to dwell on her misfortune, she forced herself back to the present.

"Thank you, Shirong. I appreciate your help. Now we need to get back to our lessons, Mulan."

With this, Shirong left, still a little disappointed in the schoolteacher's reaction, but excited about forming a group that would be entrusted to protect her. Meiying's arrival had raised his position in the village and he still basked in the glow. But when he spoke privately to his father that evening, the old man balked.

"We don't know who this stranger is," he said. "If he is just a refugee, that is one thing. But I'm not convinced Schoolteacher Bai is an innocent refugee herself."

"What do you mean?"

"Look, son. She's too educated. Something smells fishy."

"But papa—"

"No! I'm a cautious man. She might have connections with the wrong people. This stranger might have connections with the right people."

"What do we do?"

"Wait. If he doesn't come back, no problem. But if he does, let things happen as they will."

"But papa, don't you trust Schoolteacher Bai?" Shirong asked this question feeling genuinely confused. His father had always been straightforward and uncompromising, but now Shirong saw an uglier, cowardly side.

Mr. Xie intuitively understood this. He was no fool, but he knew the stakes here were too high to assume postures. If Schoolteacher Bai were in with the communists, he was as good as dead, as well as the family. And as for his precious land. . . .

"Shirong, my son, the world is large and full of predators who will steal your land, your life. Not all predators have flashing teeth to warn you. Some are sly and come disguised as lambs, or pretty schoolteachers. You must never allow yourself to be deceived!"

"So I must trust no one?" asked Shirong with a bitter edge to his voice.

"No! Absolutely no one!"

"Not even you, father?"

Mr. Xie wanted to slap him, but the progressive mask he had donned for so long was not yet ready to come off. "Family is different. You are of my flesh and bone. Trust me, but no one else! Not even her!"

"And if you tell me to betray Mulan?"

Mr. Xie scoffed. "Didn't you listen? She is family, fool!"

"We are to trust no one but family?"

"Correct!"

"Not even uncles and aunts?"

Xie paused but maintained an obstinate scowl. "Not even them," quickly adding, "Certainly not Schoolteacher Bai!"

"But papa," said Shirong boldly. "What if I do not trust you for not trusting Schoolteacher Bai?"

The old man turned red and leapt to his feet, striking his son with a vicious slap. "Fool! She has no stake in this family! Even now she may be plotting with her communist friends!"

"What makes you think she is a communist?"

"This is what comes of being too soft on my son! She is a communist for the simple fact that she has succeeded in turning your head away from the family. She may be the seed of our destruction!"

Even as he spoke these words, Mr. Xie had thought of them before, but the argument with his son now made her the undisputed enemy, and his simple mind flipped as easily as a pancake. "In fact, I've half a mind to banish her from the village, ungrateful bitch that she is!"

Shirong could see this conversation was spiraling out of control and would end badly for everyone. "Father, we are angry. Let us sleep and discuss the matter with cooler heads tomorrow."

But this reasonable position merely drove the old man to greater fury. His own son was acting wiser than he. Unacceptable! Ungrateful! Arrogant! He slapped Shirong again, harder. "You show me no respect! Who are you to talk to me like I was your student and you were some damned teacher?"

"Yes, father. I am sorry."

Mr. Xie continued to pommel his son, all of his progressive ideas entirely forgotten. "Fool! You dare question me? Ungrateful seed!"

Meiying emerged from her room, drawn by the loud words. "What is wrong?" she exclaimed.

Mr. Xie looked at her with wild eyes, his blood up from beating his son. All of his anger now transferred to her, as he saw standing before him the nemesis that drove him to such rage—a communist. Now he bore down on her, his fists raised in rage. Meiying shrieked and hastily retreated to her room. The younger kids could be heard whimpering in fear.

"Papa!" cried Mulan.

"Stop, father!" shouted Shirong.

"This is my house! My land! No communist bitch is going to come here and take it!"

"Papa!"

Mr. Xie kicked at the door, but Meiying had shoved a dresser in front of it.

"Communist bitch!"

Shirong ran next to his father with his arms held out in a futile attempt to stop the enraged man.

"Papa! She plays the piano! A western instrument! Communists hate western music!"

This seemed to penetrate, and in any case, Mr. Xie was out of breath. "Um!" he grunted, backing off. "Bring me wine!" he barked to his son as he stumbled over to the table and threw himself in a chair, mumbling (without conviction), "Could be a cover. Reds are crafty devils!"

After drinking a few glasses, he began to calm down.

"She has to leave the village," he said with finality. "I cannot take chances."

Mulan found enough courage to speak up. "Papa, she is my teacher. Please don't make her leave."

"I will make her leave," he muttered.

"Papa, please!"

Mr. Xie swiped at her with the back of his hand, but missed. "Quiet! I am master of this house. No communist whore is staying here!"

Later, after the tantrum had died down, Mulan knocked on Meiying's door but received no response. Mr. Xie had Shirong enter through a side window. Schoolteacher Bai was gone with her few possessions.

"Good riddance!" cried Mr. Xie, although he now began to regret his actions. *It's the wine*, he thought. *But damn it! It's done and can't be undone.*

~ *The Eternal Road?* ~

Yet again Meiying found herself on the road, this time at night with almost no possessions but for a small bag of personal items she salvaged from the room before climbing out the window. Still shaking from the emotional scene, her tears of anger and frustration flowed freely. *At least I can still feel,* she thought bitterly. *It's a wonder that I don't kill myself! And why shouldn't I?*

She looked around as if in a stupor. *Is this the right way to the main road? Oh my god! Bandits, rapists, Japanese, communists, Mr. President, Beethoven, all out to slit my throat! And I'm alone. Alone!* Despair made her pause and consider going back to beg forgiveness of Mr. Xie—though she did not know what she had done to incur his wrath.

Suddenly a hand brushed against hers and she jumped with a shriek.

"Schoolteacher Bai, it's me, Mulan," came a small, frightened voice. The little hand grabbed hers. "I want to come with you."

"Mulan, dear! You frightened me! Dearest, you can't come with me. Where I am going is too dangerous."

Even in the dark, Meiying could sense the tragic frown that befell the little girl's face.

"But I won't be in your way. I can help find food. Please!"

Meiying became quite stern. "No, Mulan! I must be very strict with you."

"Please."

Meiying grasped her hand and started to march her back into the village.

"Then you'll stay with us?" pleaded Mulan.

"No, Mulan. I can't. But I must deliver you to your father."

"Please come back and stay with us! Papa will be good. He even said he was sorry," she lied.

When they reached the Xie home, Shirong was in the midst of pleading with his father to allow Meiying to return before it was too late to catch up with her. Both abruptly stopped arguing when the door opened and Meiying stood before them, still holding Mulan's hand. An almost comical scene ensued where all participants stared at each other in surprised silence. Finally Mr. Xie coughed.

"Ah, what is this?"

"I am returning Mulan," said Meiying curtly. "Please keep her here and I will leave immediately."

"Papa!" cried Mulan. "Tell her to stay!"

Mr. Xie coughed again.

"Please, papa," added Shirong.

More coughing. "Well, ah, if she apologizes."

Meiying had anticipated this. Even now, at this very moment, she did not know how she would respond.

"Mr. Xie," she said with forced dignity. "I do not feel I have anything to apologize for."

"Well, ah, do you promise you are not a communist?"

"Mr. Xie, I have repeatedly said I am not."

He still had more face to save. "On your ancestors' graves?"

"Yes."

"Then you may stay," he announced imperiously.

Mulan cheered, Shirong grinned broadly, but Meiying remained troubled. While she felt relieved to be back, at the same time she felt drawn to the road that she had only moments earlier dreaded. The thought of being alone and in constant danger of being murdered or raped made her agree to stay; but the emotional turmoil that lingered also made her desperate to return to her room and deal in private with her demons.

"Excuse me," she muttered, quickly disappearing into her room. With privacy ensured, her raw emotions gushed forth and she fell into a restless sleep, interrupted by a host of nightmares. Meiying would never know that Mulan wanted to go to her, but Mr. Xie, subject to the complex permutations that waged war in his mind, held her back. In a tone that would impress the most sensitive of men, he said, "No, Little One, let her be. She is something special. Let her alone to think." Shirong could only gape at this complete turn-around.

The next morning, breakfast passed quickly, without incident, although Mr. Xie chose to direct his gruff attention solely on Shirong, who he berated for being a worthless son. Shirong took the invective in stride, understanding why his father felt these attacks were necessary to save face and reestablish his unquestioned position as head. Meiying also understood, and refrained from interfering. Her thoughts raced ahead to the school. *After yesterday, how do I face the children?* she wondered.

But to her surprise, the sight of her students made her happy. Though they often acted cruel and even malicious, they were also capable of extraordinary acts of kindness and generosity. To begin class, she asked a question that had come to her on the way.

"Children, what makes a bad guy bad?"

Hands shot up by the polite ones while shouts rang out by those less inclined to wait.

"Someone who steals!"

"A cheater!"

"People who are lazy and don't work!"

"People who use bad words!"

Meiying quieted the class and called on the students whose hands were still patiently raised, mainly girls.

"Mean people."

"People who kick dogs . . . or children."

Meiying got to Mulan, who said, "Strangers."

"That's dumb!" cried a few boys from the back benches.

"No, no, we don't call people names," corrected Meiying.

"Yeah, that's being a bad guy," said one of the girls from the side.

"Not all strangers are bad," said Meiying to the class. "But Mulan is right, we must be careful of strangers."

"Why?" called a student.

"They may want to do bad things to us."

"Like what?"

"Well, I don't know, like hurt you."

"Why do they want to hurt you?"

Meiying contemplated her answer. Should she go more deeply for the older kids, or keep it simple for the younger ones?

"Oh, there are many reasons. Just do not talk to strangers or go with them anywhere unless your parent or another trusted adult is with you."

Hands shot up.

"Why?" asked a quiet boy whose alcoholic father was renowned for beating him regularly.

"People want to hurt other people for many reasons. One of the most dangerous is to take you away from your family to sell you on the slave market."

He looked at her uncomprehendingly. "But, why?"

Meiying sighed. "The great ones in the past—Confucius, Lao Zi, Zhuang Zi, Han Feizi—argued about whether some humans are born evil. Confucius said no. On the other hand, Han Feizi said yes, some people are born evil."

"Like our stranger?" asked Mulan guilelessly.

With this simple question, the danger posed by Beethoven crystallized in her mind as if a clap of thunder fused the fragmentary pieces that had so long bedeviled her into a solid object, as clear and heavy as a lump of quartz.

He wants to make me a slave! Mr. President is a slave dealer! Beethoven is his agent. I am a valuable, high-class slave to be trained and sold!

She looked at the child with tears in her eyes. "Yes, Mulan, like our stranger."

~ *Through the Flames* ~

The camels could barely squeeze through the gap that separated two vertical cliff walls. It seemed to the riders an endless and nerve-jangling ordeal. John, slightly claustrophobic, closed his eyes and relied on the camel to follow the others. Emerging from the other side of the cleft, an expanse of sand stretched into the distance. After crossing at a brisk pace, they passed through a second opening. By now, the sun was setting and the shadows grew deep and foreboding. Only the tops of the flaming cliffs were bathed in light, making them seem even taller than normal. After navigating through the twisted path of the second gap, an elaborate temple compound across another broad plain came into view. As if some distant mirage, it seemed to recede as they rode closer, and eventually the valley plunged into a suffocating cloak of darkness. Ahead, the group saw lantern lights flickering around a large entrance gate, bright little points moving like a disturbed cluster of stars. As their little caravan approached closer, every eye craned to discern the outlines of this most secret of secret destinations. Even the cave seemed a trifle compared to this latest manifestation of *her* power and influence.

Not a soul could be seen as they rode in awed silence through the gate. Ishmael barked orders for them to dismount, then stood back while the camels trotted off.

"But the camels!" cried Master Zhou.

"They know where they're going," he said. "Food and water await them at the usual place. This is their home."

"Where is everyone?" asked Madame Liu.

Ishmael ignored her. "You will be provided with food and drink tomorrow morning. Follow me!"

Ishmael led them to a pair of modest, two-story buildings. "For tonight, the women sleep in this dormitory." He opened the door and escorted the females inside. When he returned, he showed the men to their separate dormitory a few meters away. After opening the door and lighting a lantern which he set down on a table, he said, "Upstairs," and without further explanation, added, "Good night." Before they could ask a question, he had disappeared into the night.

"The White Whale is very elusive," commented John.

The small lantern barely illuminated a corner, so the group stumbled around in the semi-darkness, finding their way upstairs where they arranged their bedding on tatami mats. Fatigue quickly overcame them and sleep came easily for most—except John.

The voices hummed like static, but he could not make out individual words. He felt anxious for the dawn to come and shine light on this retreat which appeared so other-worldly and ethereal. Thoughts of Meiying occupied most of his time—imagining her lying next to him, talking and laughing together. As usual, he tried to picture where she was at that moment; invariably his imagination placed her close by, following his tracks, soon to catch-up and be reunited like the ending of some happy movie.

But Master Zhou snored and Feng Shiren mumbled in his sleep. Unable to block out the noise, John got up and crept outside, intending to sit on the wooden porch and get some air for a few moments before turning back in. But when he stepped out the door, moonlight flooded the valley and he glimpsed an enticing view of the contours of the compound. There were more buildings than he had imagined, each of them of traditional Ming Chinese architectural style and each standing like a separate temple within which lurked its own secret rituals and its own mysterious inhabitants. Nothing stirred. Drawn to the beauty and symmetry of the compound, he decided to stroll around the grounds and get a glimpse before the morning sun shone too brightly and diminished the magical quality of this place in the moonlight.

As he turned a corner, a light breeze swept by his sleeve, momentarily conferring the sensation of a person gently tugging at his arm. Just for an electrifying instant, his entire being felt wrapped in a cocoon of peace and well-being. But the breeze swept on ahead and made the leaves of a sycamore tree flutter in excited recognition of its touch. The breeze, the moonlight, the feeling, the tree, all made him tingle with confidence. Somewhere a bird shrieked and a sudden, inexplicable premonition of menace caused him to turn and walk quickly back toward the dormitory. He rounded a corner and ran into a crouching figure hastening in the opposite direction that set him back on his heels.

"Child of Buddha!" he cried out involuntarily. "What are you doing here?"

The hunchback looked up at him, the whites of her eyes gleaming in the moonlight. "*She* is here."

John looked around and saw no one.

"Where?' he asked stupidly.

Child of Buddha merely smiled and hurried past him.

"Where are you going?" he called.

She made no reply. After she rounded the corner, he thought of following, but the emotions that roiled in his mind wanted no company.

That breeze, he pondered. *I heard no voices in my head when it cast its spell. Nothing . . . as if they left me entirely . . . when it moved on, they returned. Where did they go for that time? Where did I go? It's too much!*

Too much! . . . Too much! . . . Too much! . . . Fool! . . . Too much!

He stopped in front of the dormitory and looked around, hoping for some sign, but none came. The moment had passed. *I should have followed Child of Buddha!*

The next morning, Ishmael greeted them with a hearty "Good morning!" and after a short breakfast in the dormitories, escorted them to various buildings that were to serve as their permanent residences. Madame Liu and Master Zhou then sat down with him to work out financial and logistical arrangements. Afterward, Ishmael gave them a tour of the compound. A deep well serviced their water needs, and the group was shown the gardens, with Ishmael making it clear that vegetables and fruit (from a nearby grove) were their responsibility to cultivate and procure for their meals. Meat and rice would be periodically supplied by the local Mongol clan.

John noticed Child of Buddha listening intently, and he wanted to ask her about last night, but the opportunity never arose. Questions flew at Ishmael, but he deflected almost every one. After much haranguing, it came out that the town of Dalandzadgad would be their main supply and communication link to the outside world, and small caravans from Ishmael's clan would visit regularly.

Madame Liu held out her hands, palms up, and asked, "Will *she* be here?"

Before Ishmael could answer, Child of Buddha said, "*She* already is."

"What!?" came the chorus.

"*She* is here in spirit," laughed Ishmael. "Your Bent Spirit One is correct, in a way."

"John saw *her* too," muttered Child of Buddha, irritated at the Mongol's patronizing remark.

All eyes turned to John.

"I felt *her* presence, I think."

"You see," said Ishmael. "*She* is not one to be directly seen unless it is *her* express wish."

"I saw *her*!" insisted Child of Buddha. She glared at Ishmael. "Have you seen *her*?"

He merely smiled and shook his head as one might do in response to an endearing remark by a child.

Madame Liu decided it was time to change the topic. "Are you the only care-taker here?"

"Ah, that is a good question. There are others, but they will rarely be seen."

"Why?"

Ishmael held up his hand. "Too many questions. But I can say others that you know may join you."

"Lu Zhishen?" asked Feng Shiren.

"Perhaps."

"Bai Meiying?" ventured John.

Ishmael paused. "That I cannot say."

"But are we still to wait until Miss Bai arrives?" asked Madame Liu.

"Yes."

The storm of questions that followed were all dismissed by Ishmael with a simple, "I know nothing more."

"We might be here for years waiting for her," commented Feng. "I assume we can leave anytime we want?"

"Why would you leave now?" asked a startled Madame Liu.

The gleam in Feng's eyes and his puppet-like distortions made them all smile. "Did you ever consider the fact that the great Feng Shiren might want to end the suspense by simply going out, finding her, and bring her back?"

Madame Lie scoffed. "Not so simple, little soldier."

"Well," replied Feng looking at Ishmael. "Can we leave when we want?"

"Of course. You are not prisoners. However, I have received word that the Japanese, the communists, and the Russians are all fighting around Dalandzadgad. It is not a good time to leave. War is now everywhere. Even my own clan is threatened!"

"This war may go on for years," said Feng impassively.

"True."

Years! thought John. *That will be impossible!*

Not impossible, dear Chosen One! Now you must wait for her! Must! Must! Must!

John burst out, "Why all these trials?"

John Powers! came a different voice. **You must not feel joy without first experiencing suffering! It is a First Principle.**

No, John, said Goddess. **It is for your son—Michael Powers.**

~

It is true, dear Reader, I wanted desperately to be born. It is True! True! True!

Chapter Six

Trajectories

Meiying Faces Disaster

Meiying had sunk into that state of utter despair that numbs the soul and makes the senses comatose. Nothing outside the confines of her body could hope to penetrate the emotional scarring she had suffered and which now made her impervious to stimulation, either pleasant or unpleasant, pleasurable or painful. She moved through the world as a sleep-walker, convincing herself it meant nothing if the entirety of humankind ceased to exist. Violent end or slow extinction were distinctions without a difference. Even if the group itself were lined up against a wall and shot, she projected upon their corpses the blessing of having passed beyond this global ache of struggle and suffering to someplace without pain.

Beethoven noted this lethargy and regretted the loss of luster that had always made Meiying such an interesting target. Wholly lacking empathy for her pain, he consoled himself with the thought that her dull acceptance of fate at least made her more receptive to the condition demanded of a slave.

The small Japanese unit that had accompanied him to the village for the purpose of apprehending this female murderer now rejoined the main force moving toward the Mongolian border. Briefly, he considered the idea of splitting off from his Japanese allies and heading with Meiying straight back to Mr. President, but the betrayal of the communists by his master made such a trek too risky. Worse, he could not force himself on her, for his strict orders were to bring her "unmolested on pain of death" back to the palace. Fortunately, the Japs had an ample supply of "comfort women" and Chinese captives to relieve his most pressing urges.

As the days passed, the main force approached the Mongolian border at a snail's pace. Beethoven experienced a deep and abiding frustration with the Japanese commander's unjustified caution. *Let's just go and get our business done, and leave!* he thought bitterly. *These Chinese communists are just poor, illiterate peasants. Brush them aside!*

Like many Chinese, Beethoven mistakenly viewed the Japanese army as an unbeatable machine. He felt the strong tug of Mr. President's palace and all its sensual comforts and diversions. Even the thought of reuniting with his perverse but powerful mother was alluring. Yet here he trudged, grubbing in the field with strange Japanese soldiers who viewed him as a Chinese insect they were ordered not to crush and his Chinese whore as a feast in which they were ordered not to partake.

Still, one Japanese officer stood out. A Lieutenant Ichida attracted Beethoven's attention when he expressed deep interest in Meiying. It began the day they were reunited with the main force. Lt. Ichida saw Meiying and immediately began peppering Beethoven with questions. This persistent curiosity roused Beethoven's suspicions.

"Do you know her?" he asked bluntly when he caught Ichida staring at her from a discreet distance, apparently not wanting her to see him.

"Not at all."

"What is your interest then?"

"Any man would be interested, don't you think?"

Beethoven spoke fluent Japanese, but wasn't sure he interpreted correctly. "What do you mean? She is nothing special. A bag of bones and blood like all the rest."

"Oh, I think she is very interesting, Beethoven-san."

"Why don't you talk to her yourself?" asked Beethoven testily.

"I might."

"Just, please, don't damage her."

Beethoven noticed Ichida's eyes blaze momentarily in anger, then return to formal Japanese politeness. "Of course. You are both our guests on this expedition. We will continue to treat you with respect since your master decided to bow to the inevitable and join our side. The days are over when we were enemies."

"Yes."

Both men were in the odd position of knowing the other without letting on they knew. Still, in this context, Nobaru Ichida was aware he had the advantage. Beethoven only knew him from a distance (if he knew him at all) and must be unsure of motivations, while Nobaru possessed a deep knowledge of all the participants in their little drama thanks to his friendship with the American John Powers and his time assisting Colonel Müeller. He had mulled over his options when he learned Meiying was to be taken prisoner by his unit. While ostensibly Mr. President had allied himself with the Japanese, Nobaru and everyone else knowledgeable about the situation knew the obese Chinese warlord could not be trusted. The acquisition of Meiying by Beethoven presented a golden opportunity to use her in ways she had previously refused. Wisely, he held back until his plans were firm enough to be presented to his superiors. For now, he would be satisfied observing her surreptitiously. Nobaru was essentially a kind man, not given to acts of cruelty and secretly convinced this war would bring disaster to Japan, but he was also a loyal soldier and would use Meiying ruthlessly to obtain the information he wanted. He knew her well enough to know she must agree to his terms voluntarily or else her information would be unreliable. For now, it seemed apparent she was in no condition to agree to anything. He could afford to wait.

Meiying had no idea Nobaru was nearby, and she would have reacted with supreme disinterest had this knowledge been given her. During the day she traveled in the company of Beethoven, silent and wholly unresponsive to his attempts at conversation. She ate the minimal amount to stay alive, and displayed no curiosity about her surroundings or interest in their destination. In desperation, Beethoven even mentioned that his latest intelligence revealed the location of the group in Mongolia, which was a lie. To his dismay, she registered no response, and he eventually gave up trying to establish even a thread of communication with her.

It's like traveling with a corpse! he thought bitterly, and began to feel disgust at her total capitulation to despair.

His disgust reflected itself in the mirror daily, for he possessed enough self-awareness to recognize the ugly face of guilt, which he rarely experienced, yet knew it had now curled its way into his soul.

This war has killed millions! he thought. *The fate of one woman is absurdly trivial!* But these considerations were never quite persuasive.

One night he came to her tent. As usual, she lay on her cot staring vacantly at the ceiling. For a moment, he thought she had succumbed to idiocy, but she looked at him with a detached awareness, as one might acknowledge the presence of a fly.

"Tomorrow or the next day we cross into Mongolia," he announced, holding up his lantern to see her better. "There may be fighting."

Meiying took in this information with all the reaction of someone being informed the sky was blue.

"If you try and escape, the Xie family remain subject to punishment."

She stared.

"Do you understand?"

She nodded dully.

"Meiying, when we return to Mr. President, I will do all I can to protect you from the worst of it."

Her eyes burned through him.

"Sleep well then," he said. Knowing better than to wait, he left without another word.

~

Meiying watched him leave and resumed her introspective trance. Her initial resolve to escape or die trying had faded to a bleak acceptance of her fate. At first, she tried to justify her lack of spirit by thinking of the dangers to the Xie family. But the honest reality would not be so easily ignored: she wanted to die. Peacefully, if possible, but soon, violently or not. Unwilling to kill herself, she knew she would probably die at the hands of others. *Regardless, I'll join Meili and*

Lihua. It is certain I shall never see the likes of them again here on earth. Instead I'll be condemned to a life of slavery and abuse—a repository for male lust. The only consolation she allowed herself was to practice playing on an imaginary piano with her fingers, unconsciously pressing the keys, which to an ignorant observer appeared to be nervous agitation.

One day, Naguma saw her sitting on a fallen log, her fingers hard at work with some difficult chords. He understood the meaning of her movements and felt a sharp twinge of admiration and pity. The sun reflected a bright, undulating halo off her windswept black hair, and her face radiated a beauty impervious to the agony she must be feeling. Beautiful Meiying. Beautiful even in the rain and mud. Beautiful even in unclean clothes. Beautiful even unbathed, uncombed, unbrushed. Beautiful even without sleep. Beautiful even in pain. Beautiful when sad, when happy, when bored, when angry. Beautiful from any angle. Indestructible beauty. To destroy her beauty would require destroying her body. All of it. To the bone. Her value as a spy would lay in the perfection of her beauty. It was why she would succeed at infiltrating Mr. President's inner circle. It was why men desired her, fantasized about her, feared her, loved her, craved her, hated her, were intimidated by her, wanted to own her, marry her, control her, escape her, stare at her, hurt her, disfigure her, rape her, touch her, humiliate her, protect her, prayed they had never seen her, abuse her, destroy her. To the bone. Such was the power of her beauty. And even as she sat as a forlorn prisoner, her beauty deepened. A great whirlpool, fathomless and inescapable.

~

Yes, dear Reader, you will find such beauty rarely, but you will find it again later on. But to do so, John Powers, my father, must have a son—me. To find that other beauty . . . well, first must come the son.

~

Naguma at that moment fell in love with her the way a man might love a magnificent horse or expensive automobile—far more than mere admiration, but still distant and separate from the object itself—precluded from intimacy with the essence of its fascination. *Yes,* he thought, *Meiying is to be observed and cherished, but must not be sullied by the polluted fluids of evil men who prosper by feeding off others in evil times.*

He would protect her from a distance. He would preserve that magnificent horse from harm, but other considerations pulled at his resolve. Having looked at her, Naguma was now tied to her, much to his delight and much to his dismay.

Naguma wanted to go to her and offer his services like some heroic samurai warrior in a romantic novel, but duty and native wisdom held him back. The proper time would come, and when it did, he would recognize it.

~ *Beethoven Unleashed* ~

Sometime later, reports arrived that an advance unit had been attacked by Chinese communists, and the main force prepared to sweep across the Mongolian border. As preparations were being made, Beethoven could not help giving vent to the deep resentment that had been building at Meiying's silent dismissal of his various attempts to elicit a response, any response, from her. This resentment gave his venom a nasty strength. One afternoon, he found her washing clothes at a nearby stream, guarded by a sphinxlike soldier.

"So, we are going to the place your friends are hiding."

No response.

"Well, as I told you, we know where they are hiding, and unlike the Xie family, I'm afraid the Japs will not be so kind." In point of fact, Beethoven was well aware the Japanese neither knew where the group dwelt, nor were interested in them.

But Meiying felt sharp pangs of fear for her beloved comrades that pierced the numbness she had erected around her heart.

Beethoven noticed the worried look that did not quite vanish quickly enough. He felt immense satisfaction that he at least still possessed the power to hurt.

"Out of consideration for you, I will make sure you do not witness their executions," he continued to lie.

But Meiying had evidently returned to her previous insensibility.

"Perhaps I can find a way to save them," Beethoven probed.

Nothing. She again submerged like a sounding whale, beyond the reach of the harpooner.

"If you will only cooperate with me," said Beethoven rather pathetically. "I can help your friends. They may yet live."

The perceptive Beethoven glimpsed hesitation. He pressed. "If you will but give me some indication that you care for them and not merely the need to stoke your own martyrdom."

Ah! he thought. *That struck a nerve.*

But he had misinterpreted and she looked at him boldly. "How have I not cooperated?"

To this entirely unexpected response, Beethoven remained speechless for some time. *How has she been uncooperative?* he asked himself. Her eyes bored into his, and an answer was demanded.

"You don't talk to me," he replied weakly; his complaint sounding like an ignored child.

"You are not worth talking to."

With this remark, Beethoven felt as though the superstructure holding up his ego had suddenly and irrevocably collapsed. Such a minor insult to cause such a stupendous failure! How could it happen? But it did. He turned pale and mechanically strode up to her. Meiying did not flinch at his advance. With no warning, he hit her with his fist, knocking her backward into the water. He waded in and kept hitting, her face becoming a red, bleeding object. She offered no resistance. He struck her again, and she sank beneath the surface. Only then did he realize the gravity of his uncontrolled fit of rage. Desperately grabbing her limp body, he pulled her out of the stream under the quizzical eye of the guard, whose duty to intervene remained unclear—which meant Beethoven could do with her as he wished.

Beethoven looked in wild panic. Through the blood he thought he perceived gaps in Meiying's front teeth that he had knocked out. Blood continued to flow profusely from her mouth and he had the momentary longing to reverse time so that her untarnished beauty might be restored. But the Second Law of Thermodynamics would not be so easily violated, and the horror of his predicament became crystal clear.

When he returned her to her cot, with the help of the guard, a Japanese doctor was called. The older doctor, aloof and dignified, staunched the bleeding and gave her precious morphine, for he had long been smitten by her beauty and the ladylike projection of her persona since her arrival as a 'special' prisoner.

"Her mouth will be swollen when she wakes," he said coldly. "But, she has not lost any teeth, no thanks to you. We can only hope infection will not set in." With a severe look at Beethoven, the doctor continued, "You Chinese are cowardly brutes. Such violence against a helpless woman is inexcusable."

"But—"

The doctor held up his hand in a gesture to stop. "No! The guard witnessed the event and told all."

"Nanjing," Beethoven whispered resentfully under his breath.

"What?" snapped the doctor.

"I said, your observations are accurate."

"Hm! Can I leave you with this prisoner and be assured you will not damage her more than you already have?"

"Certainly."

The doctor glared at him and left much disgusted by such ignorant barbarians.

Beethoven kneaded his hands in anguish. *What is to become of me? She is now damaged beyond repair. Her value is gone. What do I do? What should I do? Mr. President will have my skin! I'll end up like that idiot Peter Hedley.*

Lt. Ichida entered the tent without warning. "Get out!" he ordered.

Beethoven had no choice but to withdraw. Wordlessly, he slipped away, nursing a blind hatred of himself, the Japs, and the wide world that seemed intent on exposing his appalling wickedness.

Nobaru looked down at the stricken woman and felt unutterable pity and sadness. *What a world we are born into!* He dabbed her swollen lips with a damp cloth. *Now is the time.*

Outside, the sounds of bustling soldiers and clanging gear gave clear evidence the army was moving.

Soon, they crossed the border and tramped deeper into Mongolia.

~ *Feng Shiren Collects Intelligence* ~

News of the Japanese incursion had spread rapidly through the countryside, but the group only found out a week later when a belated caravan of three camels finally arrived with supplies and the electrifying report that Mongol Peter had been arrested.

"Apparently, these are reinforcements for the Japs already here," said the caravan leader shaking his head. "Before, they caused a lot of havoc, but we could cope. Now, with these fresh troops. . . . "

Tang Yuwei announced his plans to leave and join his communist brothers "regardless of the risk." When Suling expressed the fear that his leaving would be too dangerous, he scoffed. "No! I am decided. Besides, my staying here puts you all at risk."

This high-toned bluster made him feel good, but he had long ago decided to leave. Suling might have been enough to keep him, but her absurd allegiance to this bourgeois, superstitious group made him uncomfortable. He longed for the simple comradery of his fellow communists, made more alluring by the complex and ambiguous feelings that permeated his interactions with Suling, not to speak of her friends' distracted and confused attitude toward him.

"When will you go?" asked Madame Liu.

"This caravan leaves tomorrow. I go with it."

"Oh!" uttered Suling.

After an awkward silence, Feng Shiren spoke. "I'll go with you. I want to revisit this town and see for myself what the Japs are up to."

"We'll change direction long before we get to the town," said the caravan leader. "But you cannot go where we go."

"No intention," replied Feng. "I want to go to town; snoop around; see what the Japs have up their sleeves."

"So you say!" snapped Madame Liu. "But you put us all at risk, just as Mr. Tang pointed out."

Feng smiled as if being patient with a child who just said something cute. "I'll be careful."

Lu Zhishen did not join in Feng's patronizing remark. "She is right, Shiren. What if you are captured? The Japs use torture, you know."

"Don't be like an old lady!" grumbled Feng. "I've decided, and when Feng Shiren decides, there is no room for argument."

"But—" Master Zhou started to say before Feng stopped him with a gesture.

"I have already thought of these objections. Go to the square in front of the dormitories and wait for me. I want to show you something."

After they gathered in the square and waited for many minutes, they heard a loud commotion and saw Feng striding toward them dressed in the gaudy silk clothes of a character from popular opera.

"Come!" he cried. "Gather around and see the magic face-changing! A mystery! A mystery!"

The group burst into laughter.

"Come closer! Watch the amazing skill of face-changing!"

Everyone gathered close to him.

Suddenly, Feng leapt into a dance routine and waved his arms in front of his face. When his arms moved away, a mask had appeared, indeed like magic Then another. And another. Each one different than the one before. Applause broke out.

Madame Liu, however, remained critical. "It won't work, Shiren. I saw the trick. I have often seen the mask-changers perform, and they are much better than you. Your disguise won't work."

"Yes, it will!" he insisted.

"No. I've seen face-changing masters. You're no master."

"Don't have to be," he pouted. "The rubes here don't know and the Jap soldiers will laugh rather than shoot."

Lu Zhishen was still chuckling when he directed his comment at Madame Liu, "Well, he convinced this Canadian rube!"

"And this American!" chimed in John.

"Well, not this Chinese," grumbled Madame Liu.

Master Zhou clapped like a child. "Do it again! Do it again!"

Always ready to perform, Feng continued his dance. Yet another mask appeared.

"Actually," observed Child of Buddha in her usual grave voice. "You're pretty good."

"Of course I'm good!" cried Feng. "Sure as hell good enough to fool the barbarian Japs! Maybe their simian general will even invite me to his head-quarters, and I'll steal all the secret dispatches and we'll win the war!"

"Oh, god!" moaned Madame Liu.

~

That night, Suling could be heard sobbing in her room; the group thought it best to let her be.

~

When the little caravan departed the next day, Feng rode one of the camels that had been stabled at the compound, past the farewells of his comrades, each of whom harbored fears for his life—and theirs. For the first time in his life, Feng experienced a pang of regret as he rode away from his friends. Previously, new adventures always trumped mere "transitory emotional ties," as he called them. But this time, he felt actual pain and a longing to remain with the comfort of those he knew loved and depended upon him. Nevertheless, he felt too drawn to new experiences and too reluctant to disappoint those expectant faces. What did they expect of him? Much, he suspected. Another miracle. He had let them down by not finding Peter's killer; he would not let them down again.

In the core of his being, he had come to convince himself that he acted as an agent for this mysterious woman they all worshipped and who he had never even seen. As if *she* pulled invisible strings, he jumped to do *her* bidding—and willingly so. For once in his life, Feng's odd mannerisms and eccentric behavior, so apparent to all the world, had a noble purpose and served a noble cause.

After they passed through the narrow crevasses in the Flaming Cliffs, Feng's companions wished him well as they veered away to their secret destination. Alone, Feng rode across the sandy plains, keeping a wary eye out for soldiers—any soldiers, as he knew the countryside harbored communists, Nationalists, Japanese, Mongols, bandits, and various lone-wolf murderers and deserters. Even for one as resolute as Feng Shiren, the dangers from all sides were oppressive. Still, he sang to himself with the rhythm of his camel's gait, and the kilometers separating him from his friends steadily increased.

A darkening sky and no moon forced him to make camp. He had no desire to build a fire and announce his presence, but the winds cut through his cotton tunic and made his face suffer horribly with the sensation of being burned. After collecting dung and nursing a fire, he huddled up to the warmth and dreamed of glory. But the dreaming soon became wearisome, and lack of an audience forced him to retrieve his flask brimming with strong rice wine. Overcoming his slight depression was made easy as gulp after gulp, he performed ablutions to himself, the camel, the moon, the sun, the gods, the goddesses, and anything else that came to mind. The night became tolerably good company and he became Li Bai, the happy, solitary poet.

In this semi-drunken state, he thought he saw a shadow move just beyond the illuminating flames. His first inclination was to reach for the pistol he always kept near, but on second thought, he decided to be bold, so he blurted out, "Hey! Hello comrade! Come have a drink and sit by the fire!"

The shadow hovered at the edge of the firelight, then withdrew back into the night. Wine, and Feng's natural penchant for reckless impulse, made him sit straight up and shout insistently, "Comrade! Don't be afraid! Come drink with me!"

To his surprise and discomfort, multiple figures appeared, hovering close enough for him to perceive their presence, but far enough away to avoid easy identification. Feng surmised they were Japanese soldiers and without another thought, leapt up and gesticulated wildly. "Come one, come all! See the famous mask-changer of ..." he hesitated, then smiled to himself and cried, "See the famous mask-changer of Gee-kaw-gooo!"

He threw out the exotic name of an American city that Peter had told him about long ago. "Gee-kaw-gooo!" he repeated, hoping the sheer allure of such a bizarre place would draw them in.

The shadows moved about, growing in numbers, and Feng Shiren began to feel a tightening in his stomach. Were these not men? Why didn't they do something? Perhaps they were deserters, mad with hunger and thirsty for blood. But his course had been set and he traveled down it with the enthusiasm of a drunken daredevil.

"Brothers! Come forward! Mask-changing as you've never seen it! Feng of Gee-kaw-gooo will dazzle your senses and fill you with wonder!"

At last, he heard noise coming from the shadows. It was laughter! Then he heard excited chatter. Japanese! His Japanese language skills were non-existent, so he continued in Chinese. "Come! Come, my Japanese friends! See mask-changing. Do I have to come and drag you to see it?"

Finally, faces emerged into the light, accompanied by the glittering metal of their rifle barrels. All of them were smiling as if relieved of some great burden. A young officer spoke in broken Chinese.

"So you mask-changer?"

"Yes, of course!"

"You show."

Feng told them to turn their backs so he could prepare, but they didn't understand. Clearly unwilling to leave themselves so vulnerable after they understood his gestures, he said in exasperation, "Okay! Just go back into the darkness until I call. Shoo!"

The young lieutenant finally understood and ordered his men back. Although they were clearly reluctant to leave the warmth of the fire, they withdrew and Feng rushed to prepare his costume and masks.

"Come!" he shouted when ready.

Back they came *like lambs to the slaughter*, thought Feng. They seemed younger than the youngest puppies, not a grizzled old NCO among them.

"Now you will see the great mystery of the masks by Feng of Gee-kaw-gooo!" and he performed a short scene from a famous opera, all the while changing masks with lightning speed. Warmed by the fire and the glow of Feng's unanticipated performance, the soldiers laughed and leaned closer to see how his trick was performed. When he reached the end of the performance, they applauded and gave him money.

The young lieutenant suddenly looked at his watch and shouted a command. Feng Shiren felt triumphant—his gamble worked, he made some money, and they were leaving. Never one to let well enough alone, he said to the lieutenant, "May I go with you and entertain your fellow soldiers?"

At first, the lieutenant did not understand, but after a series of convoluted explanations and gestures from both men, the surprised lieutenant said in Chinese, "You want come with us?"

Feng nodded vigorously, smiling like a happy child.

"You do masks for us?"

Feng nodded again.

The lieutenant fell silent and puzzled over this odd turn of events, then said, "Yes. Follow."

Perfect! thought Feng. *They shall lead me to the belly of the beast. This is too easy!*

~

When the little band entered Japanese lines, it appeared a most unlikely vision. Feng rode his camel bedecked in operatic silks while surrounding him trudged the forward observing team of Japanese soldiers. A captain was called who stared intently at Feng while the lieutenant nervously rattled off the story.

"He will be a good entertainer for the troops, sir," added the lieutenant when he noticed the captain's skeptical frown.

"And if he's a spy?" asked the captain accusingly.

"Then we shoot him, sir?" half-asked the hapless lieutenant.

"Why not shoot him now and save time?" replied the captain. "Or use him for bayonet practice."

The lieutenant did his best to preserve some semblance of the good sense a Japanese officer should display. "Well, before we do, you should see him perform at least once, sir."

"Ummm."

"Perhaps he might have some worth."

"Ummm."

So Feng was made to give a private audition for the captain, unaware his life hung in the balance. Fortunately, the man delighted in such a show of skill and magic.

"You're right, lieutenant, he will be good for the troops' morale. Let him stay; feed him and give him a tent, but keep an eye on him."

"Yes, sir! I'll post a guard 'round the clock."

The lieutenant turned to leave and the captain called him back. "Might as well make him earn his keep. Assign him to the cooks. They'll keep an eye out, and he'll be too busy to cause trouble."

"Yes, sir!"

When Feng heard the news, he cursed his luck. *Being a slave to some Jap cooks isn't my idea of fun!* he thought bitterly. *Might have to change plans.*

After a few days of labor around the chaotic kitchen of an army on the move, and evening performances of mask-changing, his resolve to flee deepened.

But one evening during chow time, as he ladled rice and fish into the mess kits of the troops passing by, he saw a pair of female hands proffering a tin bowl. Surprised, he instinctively looked up and stared into the eyes of Bai Meiying. Both experienced a shock so disorienting that they froze in time, momentarily rendered mute and blind to the world around them. Finally, Meiying broke the spell by looking down and holding out her cup more forcefully. Immediately he understood her gesture and started to respond with a ladle of soup when an officer strode up and exclaimed in Chinese, "Hey! What's wrong, fool? Give her food. Move it along!"

Feng Shiren flared in anger, but instantly controlled himself and feigned subservience.

"Yes, sir."

Neither he nor Meiying dared to look at the other as she moved on, but the universe for Feng had now changed. This would be his moment of redemption for his failures to save Peter Hedley and find his murderer. He made this oath repeatedly under his breath as he surreptitiously watched her move away in the company of the officer who had upbraided him: "I will save her. I will save her. She will be reunited with the group if it means the death of me!" He stared at the endless line of soldiers waiting to be given their grub. "Even if it means I have to stay working in this damn kitchen!"

~ *Meiying Sees A Ray Of Hope* ~

The vision of Feng Shiren made Meiying doubt her own senses, and she questioned the genuineness of his presence, certain she had dreamed it all. While still within sight of him, she dared not look to confirm the truth. As she left the mess tent with Lt. Ichida, the impulse to be sure overpowered her fear, and she turned to confirm the vision, but too many soldiers stood in her way and Lt. Ichida seemed impatient to leave. The lieutenant accompanied her to the tent and left to attend other business. She ate gingerly, her mouth still tender from Beethoven's fists. Since the beating, the lieutenant had assumed responsibility for her, and word quickly spread that she served as his Chinese "comfort woman." Beethoven had been denied access to her and Lt. Ichida grew ever closer to the woman he called his "charismatic companion."

With the image of Feng Shiren in her mind, Meiying's carefully constructed defenses began coming down, more like falling curtains than crashing walls. It was not in her creative, open-minded nature to lay mortar-and-brick. But still, she gave up each curtain reluctantly, letting it drop only after it had been tugged from her grip by an unquenchable thirst for hope and faith that some kind of happiness awaited. She did not see Feng the next day, and again questioned her senses, but Lt. Ichida did something completely unexpected that cheered her battered heart.

In the late afternoon, when the shadows lengthened and her spirits had dimmed, he called lowly from outside her tent.

"Miss Bai!' he whispered excitedly. "Miss Bai, may I come in?"

She had only just prepared for bed, so she quickly slipped on a wrap. "Yes."

"Close your eyes," he said in a low tone.

"Yes, okay."

"Are they closed?"

"Yes."

She heard him enter.

"Open your eyes."

When she did, he held out a furry ball.

Meiying's eyes lit up at the sight of the kitten. She took it gently and luxuriated in the soft purrs that seemed a balm to her open wounds.

Lt. Ichida appeared at a loss in the face of her open and obvious joy. "I thought it was better off with you then being drowned in a bucket," he stammered.

"Oh, thank you!"

She held the kitten to her cheek and stroked it. "Thank you," she repeated.

Ichida coughed and stiffly came to attention. "Well, I have other duties."

But his words were lost on Meiying, whose rapt attention was focused on her treasure. Even the image of Feng Shiren momentarily vanished behind the mesmerizing purr of needy innocence. And so she lay that night cuddling with her own diminutive savior, purring with the purrs of the kitten, drawing strength from its vulnerability and gaining confidence from being a comfort to one in need. Gradually, she drew level with the universe, once again elevated to a feeling of being more than a doomed victim of its inexorable laws to be pitied and discarded.

The next morning, physically tired but spiritually renewed, Meiying determined to search for Feng Shiren. But she could not just leave her tent unaccompanied by a guard, and even if she could, what to do with her kitten? She had immediately named it "John" for reasons not entirely clear to herself. Surprised at her choice of names, she focused her thoughts on John and wondered why she had thought of his name so quickly. Was it because he had been, like this kitten, an object requiring patience and protection? That conclusion was too easy, she thought. John possessed deeper qualities.

~

He is the father! proclaimed an unfamiliar voice.

~

But she did not hear it, for it dwells in the writer. However, that is neither here nor there. Son is not Immaculate Conception. Son is maculate conception, as is all life worthy of the title.

~

Meiying had taken to addressing John the kitten when trying to resolve conflicting thoughts and ideas roiling in her head.

"John," she said, looking the kitten in the eye with stern solemnity. "How do I find Feng Shiren and speak with him without arousing suspicion?"

John considered this conundrum by batting with his paw at her hand.

"Yes, you're right, it is a puzzle."

She waited for a sign from the kitten, who tired of her hand and attacked the tassels of her pillow, then jumped down and drank some milk from its tiny bowl.

"Of course I've already thought of that. He works in the mess tent. I will see him when I return, but how do I communicate with him? Lt. Ichida or a guard will certainly be close by. Well, John, what is the solution?"

The kitten played with some old newspaper. "Yes, I've thought of that also," she said to the distracted kitten. "A note would be convenient, but what if it were confiscated while I tried to slip it to him? We'd both be shot. Then what would happen to you, dear little John?"

With this unhappy thought, she clutched John to her bosom and teared-up. "What to do, little one? What to do?"

In the end, she decided to risk slipping Feng Shiren a note; but it must be kept short and folded very tightly. What to write? How to pass it to him without drawing attention? John could no longer provide her with answers as he had fallen asleep in a warming slant of sunlight. How she wished at that moment to return to her carefree days as a girl in Shanghai, feeling the warmth of the sun like John, who slept without the constant fear and pain that war had permanently seared into her heart. Nevermore such innocent sleep amidst the ruin that had been spread all around her by evil men. *Evil men. . . .* The thought always brought her back to Meili and Lihua. *Meili. Lihua.*

But focus! thought Meiying. *To the note!* She sat on her cot with a small writing tablet that Lt. Ichida had provided. She scolded herself over how much time she spent on the salutation. 'Mr. Feng,' 'Comrade Feng,' 'Feng Shiren,' 'Shiren.' But she settled on 'My dear brother, Shiren,' crossed it out for being too long, then decided to keep it and make the characters tiny. She started over, but the rest was easier:

'My dear brother, Shiren. You help me, I help you. Together we go. Where to meet? When to go?'

The next trick involved an equally difficult task: How to pass it on? Twice she saw him serving food in the mess, and twice they dared not acknowledge each other. Her note remained folded in her sleeve. The third time, she dropped the tiny note below her tin into the rice and lowered her eyes, willing Feng to follow them and see it. But the next soldier in line thrust his tin forward, and to her horror, Feng scooped a ladle of rice with her note into the soldier's waiting bowl. Agonizing minutes passed waiting for the inevitable cry of alarm, but none came and she assumed he unknowingly ate it with the rice.

"We move again tomorrow," Ichida said one afternoon. "Tonight, a Chinese guy is going to perform for the soldiers. Do you wish to go?"

Meiying felt a tingling and her heartbeat speeded up more than she wanted.

"Yes, please."

"He is quite good. Face-changing; one of your Chinese ancient skills. Makes the common herd happy."

"Ah." Did he notice how forced her nonchalant response?

"By the way," continued Lt. Ichida. "Beethoven has demanded to see you. Apparently, his boss has contacted some bigwig in our general staff, who in turn contacted our commander, who seems unwilling to refuse."

"When?" asked Meiying, trying not to tremble.

"Tonight."

Meiying quailed inwardly, but maintained a strong exterior. "Oh."

"But I put him off, at least until tomorrow. He said he would be at this performance tonight. Do you still want to go?"

"Yes."

"I must tell you, I am under orders not to prevent him from seeing you, even from interrogating you. I did obtain one concession from my commander: A Japanese soldier may be present."

"You?"

"I may not be available."

"Oh." She instinctively put her hand to her tender mouth. "There was a guard there also when he did this."

"I know, but this time I will leave orders."

But her mind was not really on Beethoven. Tonight might represent a golden opportunity to communicate with Feng Shiren. How she would accomplish that task would depend on the circumstances of his performance. A thousand scenarios played through her mind. Perhaps she could do this, perhaps she could do that.

Everything depended upon her getting close enough without arousing suspicion. She started with the most obvious connection: *He is Chinese. I am Chinese. Maybe if I ask Lt. Ichida to allow us to meet.* But this direct approach seemed risky. And so it went, her thoughts never settling on a satisfactory solution. *Come what may!* she concluded. *I must find a way. Somehow, someway, I'll find a way. Now or never! Oh, how many times have I said that? When will it end? It must!*

~ *Madame Liu Suffers A Setback* ~

Madame Liu knew her mind was slipping. Twice she had been caught snapping at someone in the group, telling them to "talk with my husband if you really must know the reason why!" In fact, she could not predict when these moments of confusion would hijack her thoughts and scatter them like a boat gliding through a leaf-strewn lake. Up to now, she had been able to hide the worst of her muddle, but the incidents were happening more and more often. She had spontaneously called a meeting of the group to discuss the Japanese incursion into Mongolia. It was a rash decision, and she now dreaded appearing in front of them and risk displaying her uncertainty. Alone in her room, she gripped the bed stand and willed herself to confront them. But confront them about what? Foolishly, she thought, she had called the meeting with nothing to say. No recent or noteworthy information. What to talk about? Only fragments came to her mind; those maddening leaves trailing haphazardly in the wake. When she tried to draw them together in a coherent whole, they broke apart under the onslaught of her husband's stern, unsettling image. *Husband! Help me! Be the glue that holds me together!* But it could not be. The leaves scattered in spite of her best efforts, floating side-by-side just long enough to mock her sanity, then dispersing with the outspreading ripples.

"Madame Liu!" called Ishmael who had now become a de facto member of the group. "Everyone is waiting!"

"Yes, yes, I'm coming!" she replied sharply. Breathing a deep sigh, she rose to join Ishmael when she noticed she wasn't properly dressed. *Stupid old woman! Thank god I noticed. I know, I'll talk about* her *coming. That will calm them. They are all so anxious to see* her. *It is imperative to assure them. Mustn't give up hope. Must hold us together until* she *appears.*

These musings led her to forget to change, and she opened her door still wearing her old nightgown. Ishmael looked at her with a knowing smile. He bowed.

"Have you forgotten something, Madame Liu?"

Following his eyes, she discovered her error. Iron will kicked in and she assumed the mask of amusement; a woman making light of her foolishness. Once back in the room, she immediately changed so as not to forget, wiped away the tears of frustration, and rejoined Ishmael as if nothing happened.

"Are they all waiting?" she asked.

"Yes."

She took a few steps, then stopped and looked imploringly into Ishmael's eyes. "Have you heard anything from *her*?"

He dropped his gaze and stared at the ground like a boy caught in a fib. "No. Sorry."

"What about the Precious Object? Does it speak?"

"Quiet."

"Are they all waiting?"

Ishmael looked at her oddly. "Yes, they are still waiting."

"Good, good." But her husband's face came to her as a grotesque mask rippling on the surface, dispersing the leaves, calling for her to jump.

~

John sat next to Suling waiting for Madame Liu to arrive. When together as a group, people refrained from speculation about their leaders' "situation," but when talking with each other separately, the topic of her mental condition was no secret. Now they waited uncomfortably, praying she would somehow conquer this hurdle as she had conquered all the others set before her. John felt the need to take advantage of this opportunity to connect with Suling, as they had drifted apart for such a long time.

"Do you miss him?" he asked her.

"Tang Yuwei?"

"Yes, Tang Yuwei."

"Of course."

"Suling, are you serious about him?"

"Serious?"

John made a wry face. "Are you going to answer all my questions with a question?"

"Question?" Suling maintained a serious face until John realized her joke and broke out laughing.

"Seriously, Suling, any idea why she called us together?"

"I think she wants to talk about the Japanese invasion of Mongolia."

"But the Japs were already here."

"Yes, but not in these numbers."

John nodded. "I spoke with Ishmael and he said he didn't think we would be in any danger."

"Oh? That's good."

"Too remote," added John.

"Here she is," whispered Suling.

Madame Liu entered the room looking for all the world confident and assured. But when she stood before them, now that they had fallen silent and gazed at her with piquant curiosity, she faltered.

"You are all here . . . the Japanese . . . we must be strong and stick together. *She* will make *her* appearance soon, and . . . the Japanese have crossed into Mongolia . . . that is why we must stay together. For *her*."

Child of Buddha felt no compunction to forge ahead. "You're not making any sense. Why are we here?"

John wanted to shush her, but Madame Liu responded too quickly. "Sorry . . . sorry . . . the Japanese are here but we are safe."

"How do you know?" asked Child of Buddha.

"How? How? Because. . . ." Madame Liu seemed to drift, then recovered with a declaration of faith. "Because the Mongols have informed me. This is a safe haven. No Jap would dare . . . you know . . . wouldn't consider . . . and that is why."

Madame Liu looked at them with a blank expression and continued, "My husband . . . my husband, he knows. It is his face upon the water."

"I see, I see," repeated Master Zhou gently. "Now, we must all rest. You in particular, Madame, must rest. Tomorrow is another busy day."

"Yes, yes," added Lu Zhishen. "Let's rest. Thank you for you inspiring words, Madame Liu."

But Madame Liu understood the patronizing tones and felt an upsurge of anger. "No! Now is not the time. I know . . . it is important to stress that we must stay together." She swayed in the face of their sympathetic stares. "Where is Feng Shiren? I said we must all be here."

"He is gone, Madame Liu," said Suling quietly.

"Oh, yes, yes. I remember. I know. Well, do you have any questions?"

In the silence that followed, John cringed at the painful scene and considered it incumbent to ask a question. "Madame Liu, when do you think *she* will make *her* appearance?"

"I'm so glad you asked," she replied strongly, as if the question itself had rejuvenated her. "Soon, soon. I'm sure of it."

Child of Buddha, with the guilelessness of those that have the purest form of guile, asked, "When?"

Master Zhou took immediate offense at this breach of empathy. "Soon is soon. We cannot expect Madame Liu to know the exact moment."

Madame Liu raised her chin and spoke even more forcefully. "One month. Here. At three o'clock."

Shock swept the room and a barrage of questions rocked Madame Liu, but she merely responded with a confused smile, as if the words were not her own. Even Ishmael stared open-mouthed at this unexpected revelation.

Suling turned to John and asked incredulously, "Can it be true?"

He shrugged, unwilling to acknowledge this as anything other than dementia. But the specificity of the time gave him pause, and excitement reluctantly crept into his thoughts.

As he listened to Suling express her hopes in the veracity of Madame Liu's words, he watched Master Zhou whisper in the old woman's ear and lead her out of the room. John was struck by how old and frail she had become in such a short period of time, and his thoughts wandered to her successor—Master Zhou. Lu Zhishen interrupted his ruminations.

"Well, well, what do you think?"

"I guess we wait and see," replied John.

Suling said forcefully, "I have faith that she is telling the truth. Those words did not seem to come from her."

Lu merely gave a noncommittal nod.

"And you?" asked John.

Lu returned the question with a glum look. "*She'd* better come this time."

"If *she* doesn't?"

"I'm out of here."

John felt a slight thrill that he had more staying-power than Lu Zhishen, but his momentary burst of self-confidence was quickly deflated.

"I need to see more of China, of the world. I need to risk leaving this cocoon for something more. My time in the Mongol camp convinced me *she* will never come. Maybe *she* was an illusion from the beginning. Anyway, I do not intend to stay, unless *she* really does appear, which I doubt. Are you staying?"

I stay because I am afraid, John thought resentfully.

"Well, are you?" Lu pushed.

"I'll stay."

"If *she* will not appear, what's left to stay for?"

Safety, thought John, but he replied tersely, "To help Madame Liu and Master Zhou."

"Very noble. I admire you, but I'm afraid I can't do that."

John couldn't help laughing a bit inside. He wanted to tell someone about the cruel irony that seems to permeate the universe, but there was no one—except Meiying. She would understand.

"Just doing what I think is necessary," said John, all the while wanting to scream, 'Just doing what my cowardly self finds the most expedient.'

"Well," mused Lu, "You're a better man than I."

John remained silent, the only option possible for a coward, or so he thought.

Or so he thought! The writer of this story, son of the father, also has these issues—even worse than his father! Michael Powers writes, but he also suffers. Such is the fate of those so-called different ones in the past whose existence was to mark the beginning of the end for the human race. Goddess is behind this, and let it be known I strongly oppose such engineered extinction. As I told you before, such first steps and so-called beginnings have been many, and all have failed. Goddess and Her ilk call them intermediates, but they were ultimately failures. Some possessed a most profound genius, yet nothing came of them. And now this John Powers, a weak one, whose genome will supposedly lead to the evolution of the Superior Ones? A doomed effort! First Principles! Non-intervention!

The voice of God came loud and clear and painful as the pulse of a migraine. With its reverberating aftershocks still warping his mind, John slipped away to the dark cave of his room. He lay motionless on the bed and pushed the voice aside by repeating in his mind the words, "One month. Here. Three o'clock. One month. Here. Three o'clock."

Chapter Seven

Hell Hath No Fury

Bai Meiying and Feng Shiren

Feng Shiren felt renewed energy and purpose the moment he gazed at Meiying's astonished face in the mess. And as customary with him when the opportunity to save someone—anyone—presented itself, he shifted into high gear and sped forward with a dozen plans, each more elaborate and outrageous than the last. Had he been European, Feng would have been a true knight-errand, his armor only slightly less ridiculous than that worn by Don Quixote. He sat in a drafty tent, a mirror propped before him, finishing his preparations for the upcoming performance. Make-up, masks, silk costume, all must be perfect. As was his wont, Feng experienced no pre-performance nerves, confident of his skills and buoyed with the certainty that Meiying would attend.

"You go on in five minutes!" some young lieutenant stuck his head in from outside, his tone conveying the nearly perfect-pitch of a self-important Imperial Army officer had it not cracked inauspiciously.

Feng tilted his head in an operatic nod of acknowledgement and flashed a smile for the ages.

~

"And now!" Feng paused for effect in front of the sea of Japanese soldiers still clapping after his last mask-change.

As the cheering quieted, he continued, the interpreter gamely trying to mimic his boisterous patter. "And now I need a volunteer to come up and assist me!"

Arms flew up and he picked a dull-looking private. Once the shyly grinning soldier took the stage, Feng scanned the audience, his hand above his brow like a sailor squinting through bright sun at the horizon.

"Last, but not least, I need a woman!"

Uproarious laughter.

"No, no! I really need a female to volunteer. Any brave nurses out there?"

His gaze lighted on Meiying. She sat quietly next to Lt. Ichida, and her expression never changed when they locked eyes.

"Ah! There is a pretty one! Come up! Come up! Yes, you! Come up!"

Meiying played the role of a shy Chinese lady, and Lt. Ichida felt the need to encourage her with smiles and a little shove, unaware a detachment of his men could not have held her back. Making her way to the stage with a show of modest hesitancy, past the catcalling soldiers who mistook her for a pillow-woman, she heard very little, her heart racing in expectation of what would unfold. Her carefully hidden note was now superfluous, and she had the disconcerting thought that if it were discovered here, the cruel irony of the gods would be too much to bear. She wanted to swallow it, but after what seemed an eternal instant she stood before Feng Shiren, the Japanese soldier grinning awkwardly beside her. Feng stared and put his hand on the man's shoulder.

"Now you stand over here, Private—?"

"Watenabe."

"Yes, Private Watenabe!" Feng guided him a few meters from Meiying.

"And you, young lady, what is your name?"

"Bai Meiying."

"What? Speak louder!"

"Bai Meiying."

"Ah! Pretty name! Now, Bai Meiying, let me whisper the magic words in your ear."

He raised his eyebrows in mock conspiracy to the audience and leaned close to her ear. Just as he started to whisper, the interpreter sidled up. Feng, perturbed, waved him off with the words, "No, not needed. She's Chinese." But the man did not back away. This unwanted proximity forced Feng to whisper lower than he wanted. "Tomorrow morning, five o'clock, here."

Meiying heard only the word "tomorrow" clearly, the rest was a muddle. She wanted him to repeat his message, but the crowd had become louder as it grew more restless.

Reading her confused expression, Feng wanted to repeat his words, but the curious interpreter leaned closer and the risk was too great. He gently pushed her away and rushed to Watenabe, whispering in his ear, "The rising sun from the east brings happiness and prosperity."

Instantly, Feng jumped back and brayed at the audience, "Now, the magic words have been spoken by the Monkey King to both of his companions!" He waved his arm in the direction of Meiying. "Guan Yin"—and then at the soldier—"and Piggy! We are off to India! But observe, the Monkey King is unhappy. Why?" He flipped down a mask that frowned in a conspicuously sorrowful manner. "Because he must awaken early and leave for faraway India at five the next morning from an inauspicious place—much like this! Who knows when he will enjoy his peaches again?"

Feng thought himself quite clever, but the words were crystal clear to a discerning ear, and amidst the crowd sat the owner of that discerning ear.

After being returned to her tent, Meiying could not sleep. It was all well and good for Feng Shiren to have her meet him at five o'clock in the morning at the stage, but how was she to slip her guard? Even if she could, what was she to bring? How could they steal out of the compound, past innumerable guard posts? It was crazy!

Once she had calmed, the pieces began to fall together. Long ago she discovered she could slip under the tent wall opposite the front entrance and thereby avoid the guard. Of course, she would bring nothing but the clothes on her back, and getting through the various guard posts would be Feng Shiren's responsibility—she had unshakeable faith in his almost supernatural abilities. Suddenly, the touch of a paw caused her to look down at the kitten purring on her lap, and a deep well of pent-up sadness and pain burst forth. *What will happen to John when I'm gone?* She knew. *Drowned!* Her tears dropped on the little kitten who seemed startled and curious as they landed. Something else swayed maddeningly at the back of her mind; a wispy ghost that shimmered around the edges of her consciousness as if some mischievous poltergeist briefly materialized, then disappeared back into the ether. This specter led her on a chase into sleepless depression; a condition in which she more and more frequently found herself. At its worst despairing depths, she wished to be returned to Mr. President and exhibited in a gilded cage full of soft pillows and wet sheets that stank in the morning like a reeking conscience. Yes, she thought, rolling in that sticky wetness would be a proper substitute for the thorns that scourged the backs of flagellators. She tried to rouse herself from this hopeless despair, but each reoccurrence of the dark mood came harsher and more oppressive than the last. She hugged and kissed John, and tried to tell herself Ichida would take care of him, but she knew the fate of this one kitten bore with it the collected fates of all those who she loved and were now dead because of her. When the time came to leave, she summoned heroic effort just to stand. But the bedrock of her character refused to buckle entirely, and on firmer ground she made her way to the outdoor stage by the dim light of a gibbous moon, caring very little what might happen.

As she neared, she perceived two figures whispering to each other. She stopped and started to run back, but Feng's voice called out softly but firmly, "Meiying! Come here! All is well!"

She turned and cautiously approached when, to her horror, the smiling face of Beethoven came into view.

"No, all is lost!" she cried, drawing back.

"Shhh! He is here to help us."

"No, he is with them. He is here to betray us."

Beethoven continued smiling and said, "Why have I not called the guards? This man is right, I am here to help you."

"Why?" asked Meiying suspiciously.

Feng snapped, "Who cares why? He has passes. He can get us through the lines. There is no time to argue."

"No! He lies."

"Look," said Beethoven glancing around. "There is no time. You stay and die or come with us and live."

"Wait! If she stays I stay with her," said Feng Shiren.

"Then stay. It is a simple matter for me to call out and have you both arrested now. Decide!"

"I don't trust him," said Meiying.

Feng snorted. "We have no choice."

"Now, come quickly or else the light will make it more difficult," exclaimed Beethoven.

"Why are you doing this?" Meiying asked Beethoven.

"For you."

"I don't believe you. Enough of your lies!"

In response, he slapped her and said, "Fool! Take this chance!"

Feng started to intervene, but Meiying stopped him. "It's no good staying here. He will do what he says and have us arrested."

"Then let's go!" Beethoven walked away, reluctantly followed by Meiying and her knight-errand.

~ *The Road to Murder* ~

By midday, the three travelers followed a road leading south, away from Mongolia. The landscape seemed peaceful enough, and Meiying looked up longingly at the clouds drifting in the opposite direction towards the place she longed to go. *How much nicer to be a cloud than a woman!* she thought. *Free and unbound by male grasping. Try to grab me and—poof!—nothing! Clouds cannot be raped, just evaporated when touched; and if left free, then destined to unburden their tears of joy to replenish life.*

"Enough of this!" pronounced Feng Shiren, stopping abruptly. "Let's get off the road, else we'll be noticed for sure." He glanced behind. "I keep expecting the Japs to come marching right up to us, laughing at our stupidity."

"Not to worry, they won't be coming," replied Beethoven, smiling mysteriously. He fished a paper from his pocket and waved it about, "Besides, this will keep us safe."

"Why are you so sure they're not coming?"

"Because I am."

"Where are we going?" demanded Feng, exasperated by Beethoven's circular answers.

"To safety."

"Where is that?"

"A palace that has remained untouched by the war!" Beethoven glanced at Meiying to gauge her response, but none was forthcoming.

""Nonsense!" cried Feng. "I've been there, fool! I know who you are. Up to now you have been useful, but your usefulness to us is over."

"You will be well compensated for helping me return," replied Beethoven weakly.

"Looks like you need no help since you have your stupid paper. Go on alone, we'll make it out just fine. She has me to protect her!"

Beethoven stared at Feng Shiren with blazing eyes. "It always benefits me to have help, especially from the great comic mask-changer!"

Meiying was taken aback by how quickly the confrontation between these two men came so close to spiraling out of control. "I agree with Shiren, let's get off the road."

Beethoven glared at her. "I told you it is unnecessary. I have a pass."

"Damn your pass, fool!" shouted Feng. "Your pass is a pass to perdition! Do you take us for idiots?"

Beethoven produced a revolver. "Yes, I do."

Meiying acted without thinking. She jumped between them.

"You're both fools! Fighting here, in the middle of the road is idiotic. Put the gun away, Beethoven, and let's exercise some reason and get off the road. Then you can kill yourselves!"

While Beethoven and Feng glared at each other, waiting for some sign of weakness in their opponent, Meiying had the most incongruous vision of Madame Chen's stately house and its rejuvenated garden, serene and inviolable behind stone walls. Oh how she longed for her own house with a garden and a piano room! She had to get off the road, not because of the threat of Japanese soldiers, but because all roads had become great, unhealed scars in her heart. This road, any road, all roads, probed deeper than the sharpest knife, and she had been captive to their directionless directions long enough. Her house—her home—would be far removed from any trace of a road, beyond the grasping, trampling armies of men that beat down all hope life could spring anew upon the accursed roads. Without another word, she wheeled and walked off the road through the underbrush with determined steps. The two men followed like lost children.

That night, at her insistence, they slept in the brush far off the road. Beethoven appeared very unhappy as they cleared a place to sleep, the north winds howling over them with a vengeance.

"Tomorrow we go back to the road. This is madness!" he groused. "We're losing time, and Mr. President waits with rewards for all of us. Yes, including you, Feng Shiren. Enough reward to do whatever you please, good deeds or bad."

Feng remained uncharacteristically silent, and Meiying reckoned he felt chained by the pass that was ensconced in Beethoven's pocket and which was effective only if presented by its owner—Wang Liwei, aka Beethoven.

"This is the last night I humor your female stubbornness!" Beethoven continued to rail. "Back to the road at dawn!"

Feng Shiren spat and growled impotently, but retired to his sleeping area full of pent-up rage. When he awoke at dawn, he found Meiying gone and Beethoven dead, his throat slit.

As he kneeled over the body, he felt Meiying's presence behind and looked around to stare up at her immobile face. She held out a paper and said simply, "For Lihua." He immediately saw that it was the pass, and when his gaze fell back on her, she began shaking uncontrollably. Feng helped her return to her bedding area where she sat upright, arms curled around her knees, rocking and sobbing. An hour later, she fell into Feng's arms, her words hurried and stumbling. "I didn't want to use a knife, but a gunshot might bring soldiers. At first I couldn't do it. What if I only hurt him? Then it would be the end. So I imagined Lihua and knew the knife must cut deep and quick. I must use all my strength. I have never done such a thing! Never contemplated such a thing! Horrible! The feel . . . ugh! The horror of it! . . . never again! Oh, never again! He suffered so!"

It took a long while for her to gain enough control for them to discuss their next move. Meiying wanted to return in the direction they came, into the heart of Mongolia where, with the help of Feng Shiren, she would be reunited with the group. Never had she needed them more than now. Never was she more desperate to meet *her*. But Feng counseled a different path, one that would not land them back in Japanese hands.

"We must continue on this road for a while, then circle back and around. It's the best chance."

"But we have the pass," objected Meiying.

"No, it won't work. We were allowed to escape. Why, I don't know. But if I'm right, all forward Japanese positions have orders to leave three people alone, not two people. I can picture their orders now: 'Do not hinder the possessor of this pass and his two companions.' I'm sure they have our descriptions."

"Yes, I agree. I thought it odd that he was never worried about the Japanese."

"Of course! But the more interesting questions is why they allowed you to leave in the first place?"

As they walked, Meiying, in her heightened state of distress, noticed a subtle change in Feng Shiren's attitude toward her—more gruff, blunt, and barbed—as if she had now acquired male traits and male thickness-of-skin and skill. She shuddered at her horrendous deed, and imagined she had been lowered incrementally deeper into the grave that surely awaited her for all the misdeeds since her exile from a life of security and beauty.

"Do you see me as a murderer?" she asked plaintively.

Feng stopped and opened his mouth to reply when a tremendous noise arose from beyond the next ridge. When the sound came often enough to clear the senses, they recognized the rumble of explosions and tingling drum taps of small-arms fire. Feng scowled and grabbed her hand to instinctively run down the road, away from the battle, but he quickly realized the road would soon be swarming with soldiers.

"This way!" he cried.

They ran through the brush away from the road toward a thick stand of trees. Just before they reached the tree line, a trio of Japanese planes flew overhead on their way to the battle.

"That will keep them busy for a while!" Feng shouted as they zig-zagged around the trunks and fallen logs into the deepest shadows. Finding a ravine covered with tangled vegetation, they burrowed in and sat quivering like two petrified rabbits listening to the approaching hounds. Neither spoke as the cacophony of battle reverberated through the woods, rising and falling to tease them and keep them from any rest. Gradually the noise died down in fits and starts, and they nervously stayed in the prickly cocoon until the next morning when the quiet seemed likely to continue. As had so often happened since the flight from Shanghai, they were in the dark about what to do. Return to the road? Too risky. Wander in the brush? They would starve. Yet again melt in with fleeing refugees? Perhaps, but dangerous, and would carry them farther from their destination.

There seemed no good option. They were exhausted and hungry. Only a few handfuls of rice comprised their larder.

~ *Go Back to the Road* ~

Meiying heard the voice, faint but clear, and at first refused to acknowledge it. When it repeated, **Go back to the road!** she assumed it was John's oracular command projected across Mongolia.

"What's wrong?" asked Feng.

"Shhh!" she hissed. But it came no more.

"We must go back to the road," she said quite calmly.

"Why?"

"I know we must."

"How?"

"A voice. John . . . or his messenger."

Feng prided himself on his lack of superstition, but there were times when this position was subject to change. He knew it was not John. He knew it was *her*. So he said nothing further and followed Meiying's determined steps back to the road.

Listen to the gods, he thought. *Same as dogs. Always listen to gods and dogs . . . or goddesses. But why did* she *not talk to me? If I am to protect Meiying. . . .*

He looked skyward. "You must talk to me!" he shouted.

When they reached the road, there was nothing out of the ordinary in either direction. It seemed as if there had never been a battle. The silence struck them both as eerie, and they fearfully walked down the abandoned road as if treading through a sleeping pride of lions. Hours later, they came to a fork and decided to take the less traveled branch. After a few kilometers, they spotted a small group of yurts in the distance and headed wearily toward them, drawn by their hunger and fatigue. Before they reached the first abode, a young man on a squeaky bicycle rode up to them and spoke in Mongolian. Neither understood, but their gestures communicated the need for food. He bowed and led them back to his family's yurt, where his mother greeted them enthusiastically.

Boiled lamb broth was offered and they drank heartily, nodding and gesturing their gratitude. The woman beamed and presented some rancid lard which they politely nibbled but never quite finished. That night they slept soundly in a corner of a nearby widow's yurt. When they awoke the next morning, a semicircle of

Mongols squatted and stared in open-mouthed curiosity as if a crowd had come to witness the birth of a two-headed camel.

"Hello," said Feng Shiren, blinking his half-awake eyes at the sight.

Awakened by Feng's voice, Meiying turned and responded to this public display of voyeurism by sliding deeper under the blanket.

A beautiful young woman stepped forward. "Good morning," she said in perfect Chinese. She directed her gaze at Feng Shiren and smiled enigmatically. "Now I am talking to you. Please join me outside."

"Yes."

The woman clapped her hands and scolded the gaping onlookers. "Leave! Let the woman prepare herself! Go! Go!"

Like obedient children, the Mongol crowd filed out and dispersed to their various tasks, their curiosity evidently turned off like a spigot. Feng quickly dressed and exited the yurt to talk with this striking young woman who ordered around even the brawniest of Mongol men. When Meiying emerged, she immediately fell under the woman's attention; her eyes seemingly penetrating every cell and pore of Meiying's body.

"Good morning," said Meiying.

The woman's stare did not waver as she nodded almost imperceptibly.

Meiying, rendered speechless by such intensely silent scrutiny, could only stand mute and vulnerable. Even Feng Shiren appeared intimidated.

"This is Bai Meiying," he said with the greatest effort to sound casual.

The woman's monarchical serenity projected an all-encompassing openness that absorbed in sharp detail the molecular granularity of everything and everyone around her. Meiying and Feng withered under this power and could only nod when she said, "You will stay here until the disturbances have passed."

Materializing like magic next to the young woman, the old widow in whose yurt they had spent the night waited for instructions.

"You will live with Altantsetseg until our two guests leave," came the order.

Wordlessly the old woman left to collect her belongings.

"We don't want to be trouble," hastened Meiying, feeling guilty at the imposition on the old widow emerging from her yurt with an armful of possessions.

"No trouble."

Emboldened somewhat, Feng asked, "If I may ask, what is your name?"

"Buandelgereen."

"We are not husband and wife," said Feng matter-of-factly.

"I know."

"Then where can I sleep?"

Again someone had magically appeared next to Buandelgereen. It was the boy on the bicycle. Her graceful hand unfolded toward him with an operatic flair that Feng could only admire.

"With him and his family."

"I see. Thank you."

And so the two comrades remained indefinitely among Mongol herders, without news of the outside world. They would not see the woman again for quite some time, in spite of their best efforts.

~ *John and the Precious Object* ~

Child of Buddha sat before the Precious Object, mesmerized by its frantic tapping. Madame Liu had been summoned, but she was indisposed. All the others came and interpreted the raucous noise as ominous—signaling imminent disaster—and each had returned to their business with the notion that calamity awaited just around the corner. Only Child of Buddha remained in the room with the Precious Object, trying to translate the portentous taps—and the spaces between them. She noticed the tempo did vary in mysterious and subtle ways. At times she thought she had cracked the code, but then it slipped away. Something in its rhythm did not convey such ominous predictions as the others feared, she thought. To Child of Buddha, it communicated something other then disaster. But what? If not disaster, perhaps it foretold something good, even excellent, was about to happen—or something even worse than disaster. Ah! That was the crux of her frustration. It was not that something bad was to happen, it was either total obliteration or complete rebirth. Yet, that also might be wrong. The Precious Object had many more tapping variations then met the ear.

In this contemplative frame of mind, she sensed that someone had entered the room. When she turned it was John's face that greeted her with a probing frown. His curiosity had gotten the better of him when he noticed Child of Buddha had remained with the Precious Object after everyone else had left. He knew the Precious Object and his voices were somehow connected, but had not the courage to fully explore the possibilities. To his shame, he knew Child of Buddha was absolutely fearless, in stark contrast to his own timidity. Overcoming his doubt and uncertainty had been harrowing, but he forced himself to return and see what transpired between the Precious Object and Child of Buddha.

"What do you hear?" he asked.

She did not hesitate. "Armageddon or salvation. No in-between."

"But it seems we're all in-between. Humans always are. Such is the nature of the universe."

"Not all humans."

"And you? Sometimes I think you're not fully human."

Child of Buddha looked at him with an enigmatic smile. "Hunchbacks are human."

"I didn't mean that, Child of Buddha."

"I am sure you think you didn't, but it doesn't matter. Here it is in a nutshell: I am torn in two, just as you say all humans are. I am half-doomed and half-blessed."

"Is that why you think you can decipher the taps?"

For once she seemed surprised. "You know?"

"Of course. I'm not an idiot."

"Then you rise above your fellow fools!"

"Oh, no! I am foolish! But I am not interested in me. What have you learned?"

"But you definitely are interested in yourself."

John blanched. "No, I am interested in Bai Meiying."

"Which means you are interested in yourself."

"Have it your own way. What do you know?"

"Nothing."

"Bullshit!"

"Bulls may shit, but the result draws no interest other than from flies."

"Interest in shit?"

"Yes."

John looked around, his eyes settling on the Precious Object. "Then you have come to the right place. So tell me, what have you learned, one fly to the other."

"I don't know what I have learned. It is percolating."

John sighed. "I believe you."

"It makes no difference."

"It might matter to Bai Meiying. What do you know about this damn tapping? Or rather, what do you think, even if you don't know for sure?"

"Life or death. Today or tomorrow. It is ambiguous."

"What does that mean?"

"I don't know." She stared at him for a long moment. "What do your voices tell you?"

"Same. Always the same."

"That you will marry Bai Meiying and she will have your baby?"

John's eyes widened. "How did you know that? Did I tell you?"

"Yes, of course. You don't remember?"

"Well, yes, I think. Perhaps when I was talking with Suling you overheard?"

Child of Buddha smiled. "Yes. I am right about your voices and the baby, correct?"

"Well yes, that I am to have a baby with Bai Meiying—a son, to be specific."

"What else do they tell you?"

John scowled. "That I am worthless."

"Apparently not so worthless that *she* does not need you."

"Yes, as a breeder."

"Only that?"

"Absolutely!"

"And do you know that the Precious Object, your voices (or at least one of them,) and *she* are one and the same?"

"I suspect they are connected."

Child of Buddha shook her head. "No. *She, she, she,* and *she.* Or the royal *she.* Goddess *she.* Question is, what does *she* have in mind for the rest of us? Me in particular."

"My son controls all of us. He is the writer." These words came from John's mouth, but not from his own volition.

Child of Buddha's eyes widened in surprise. "I do not understand what you just said."

"I'm not sure I understand it."

Child of Buddha blinked. "But if what you say is true, we are the words, and words can be changed—or erased."

"Changed?"

"Edited. Edited in or edited out. What is my fate? Armageddon or rebirth? Half-doomed or half-blessed?"

John sighed the sigh of defeat. "I am just the breeder. I cannot say. Only he."

"Do you think you're worthless?"

"As you say, apparently not so worthless that *she* does not need me."

"I repeat, do you think you are worthless?"

"Yes."

"You lie."

"Yes."

Child of Buddha clapped and laughed as he had never heard her. "Good!" she cried. "Now that we have established the fact that you are not worthless, do something worthwhile!"

John was at first taken aback at this unexpected exhortation, but then, in a display of self-contempt, he replied, "I am, Miss Quasimodo. I continue to live in this god-forsaken country. Surely that is worthwhile. I continue to live!"

"For your lady-love?"

"Yes, and to finally see *her*."

As these words left John's mouth, the tapping ceased entirely. A slight gasp escaped Child of Buddha. John appeared at a loss.

"What does that mean?" he asked the air.

"It means something, somewhere has happened. A decision has been made. The machinery is put in motion."

"For what?"

"Your son, of course."

~ *Meiying and Buandelgereen* ~

Since their arrival, Feng Shiren and Meiying had been unable to see Buandelgereen. In spite of asking every Mongol herder in the village, and searching every face for her presence, weeks had passed without any indication she was still around. Both grew restless and talked of leaving and returning to the group at the secret place, but the Japanese army stood in the way. Meiying became frantic to be reunited, and the thought of being so close yet impeded so completely made her unable to sleep or eat. At last, she fell ill and remained in the yurt. Feng Shiren scolded her for worrying too much and tried to persuade her to do what was necessary for her health, but she refused all advice and exhortations. In her mind, a swirl of malevolent demons and sorrowful ghosts plagued her as the fever mounted, and she slipped into hallucinations. Or rather, what she thought were hallucinations.

Yes, this is where I come in. A soothing female voice. This, she knew, was Goddess.

You are for John. The male. God.

Now I am for her.

Sweet Goddess, all this fuss over a son.

Beloved God, You will see there is a reason.

I hope not for Me—all this fuss!

All for the future, for the planet.

John is listening. Hush!

That is not John, Foolish God! That is his son. And he writes, not listens.

He may write, Beloved Goddess, but she is dying. If she does, there goes your son!

Feng had become quite worried about Meiying. Her decline was shockingly rapid and she had now sunk into a dangerous semi-conscious state. He tried every trick he knew to save her from further collapse, but his efforts were fruitless. Without a doctor available, all seemed lost. When he coaxed her to eat some broth, she turned aside and babbled about the voices arguing in her head. Gradually, she grew too weak to speak, her last intelligible words being something about the murder of Beethoven. Feng tirelessly sat by her bed, but she was beyond recognizing his presence.

Meiying's feverish mind saw spider-webs everywhere, covering the Earth with their deadly strands; Father Durant, Beethoven, Naguma, Müeller, all of them scurrying back and forth across the silk threads at the hint of any movement. In this gauzy haze, all she could do was remain perfectly still, for her terror told her not to stir a muscle and trigger a vibration that would bring down the awful spiders to wrap her for feasting at their leisure. One-by-one her limbs lost their feeling until, blessedly, she existed as but a torso, unable to betray the slightest force on the webs except for her stubborn heartbeat which, she hoped, would soon cease. Thus she withered despite the frantic ministrations of her caretakers. Only Feng Shiren refused to lose all hope, eliciting much sympathetic head-wagging from the Mongols.

One day, when even Feng feared the worst, Buandelgereen suddenly appeared in the yurt, unannounced and looking regally unconcerned. She gazed down at the unconscious Meiying and told Feng to leave. As he began to object, she rose to her full height and ordered him to go. He paused at the door and glanced back to see Buandelgereen leaning over Meiying and whispering. Sensing his presence, the fierce Mongol woman shot a withering glare at Feng that swept him outside the yurt.

Feng Shiren paced back and forth in the cold, wishing for the world he could hear what was being whispered to his charge. A noisy flock of geese flew overhead and Feng imagined them honking their amusement at the earthbound human walking in circles as if he had a broken wing. *I'm such a fool even the animals mock me. Weak! Weak fool!*

"Give her broth," said Buandelgereen as she emerged from the yurt.

Her command startled him and he said stupidly, "What?"

"Give her broth."

"Is she better?"

"Give her broth." After making this statement a second time, Buandelgereen walked away and seemed to simply disappear among the crowd of Mongols who had come to see her and touch the garments that flowed behind her.

Speechless, Feng ran into the yurt and saw Meiying staring at him with a look of puzzled curiosity.

"How do you feel?" he asked.

She nodded.

"I'll bring some broth."

"Yes," she replied weakly.

~

After she regained her strength, Feng asked about what Buandelgereen said. Meiying could not recall all of her words, but she remembered the phrase, "Fate starves at probability's door."

"What does that mean?"

Meiying shrugged, but he felt she knew more than she let on.

Feng being Feng—the bulldog determination on which he had built his reputation—would not let this pass. "No, I mean it. What does that mean?"

She realized he would not relent, which made her even less willing to speculate. "I don't know."

"Then we must think about it! It could be important. It is code! It is important!" He struck an exaggerated pose which she had long ago dismissed as silly affectation. "Let me see." Meiying chuckled as he rubbed his chin and threw out a host of possibilities, each of which she quickly shot down.

"Fate is a hot air balloon that is easily punctured."

"No."

"Fate is a hungry fat man wandering in the wilderness searching for his favorite prey; delectable morsels of human souls."

"No."

"Fate is actually a starving dog that begs at random doors, hoping to find a kind-hearted cook to throw it scraps."

"Closer, perhaps," replied Meiying.

Feng looked at her with his best solemn expression. "Well, help me out here. I really do want to understand. Is fate as strong as probability?"

Meiying blanched and looked away. "That is the question."

"Well, what do you think, oh wise pianist?"

"All of my upbringing tells me fate is king. 'It is your fate to do this. It is your fate to suffer that.' But, honestly Shiren, I wonder."

Feng held out both hands, palms up. "Now we may be getting somewhere! If fate starves at probability's door, than fate is weak and probability is strong. That explains why we have so far been prevented from seeing *her*. Not fate, but a series of circumstances, unforeseeable and unknowable. Even *she* cannot control them."

Meiying pondered his words before she spoke. "But probability is merely statistics, while fate is the will of God. Is God weaker than statistics?"

"Or better yet, is Goddess weaker than statistics?"

"Or the universe," added Meiying. "If so, the universe does not care at all, unless, of course, it has a stake in the outcome. The universe must have placed a bet to care."

"Where does that leave fate?"

Meiying laughed. "A loser at cards. Too predictable. One big bluff, but never a winner."

Feng nodded in agreement. "Yes, fate is a loser at predicting life. Simple. The universe calls its bluff."

"Out of the game," added Meiying. "Except for superstition, and there lies ruin."

Feng roared with laughter. "As I always suspected, life is nothing more than a game of chance. Guess the Liar's Dice and you almost always lose. Almost! What do you do? Bet again. And again. Without risk, and an occasional win, life would be impossible."

"But," interjected Meiying. "If God or Goddess knows everything, then for all intents and purposes, life is fate—at least to ignorant people if they believe such a thing. Thus by sheer stupidity, fate wins out over probability, though it is false."

"And that is why it starves."

"Yes, perhaps."

Feng scowled. "But what good does this knowledge do us?"

For once, Meiying imitated Feng by striking a dramatic operatic pose. "None."

Feng again laughed. "None! We are the perfect pair, you and I. Off we go on our journey, I as the Monkey King and you as Guan Yin. But we do not journey west, we journey northeast, to the Flaming Cliffs!"

"To find our fate?" asked Meiying ironically.

"No! To test the probability that we will succeed. I wouldn't bet against us!"

"Because it is our fate!" cried Meiying.

"Because the Liar's Dice lie!" laughed Feng Shiren.

"Will we succeed, Shiren?"

"We'll see, Little Pianist, we'll see."

Meiying gave him a disapproving look. "Yes, Little Mask Changer, we'll see."

"Still," said Feng turning serious. "It is good to see you laugh again." He shook his head sadly. "It has been far too long."

Meiying shook her head. "Only now do I see a sliver of hope."

"A sliver is all you need."

"It is something."

"No, Meiying, it is everything."

"I hope my hands do not bleed while holding on to it."

Feng performed his patented twirl. "A little blood is nothing!"

~ *Madame Liu is Replaced* ~

As time passed, it became obvious to the group that Madame Liu had slipped too deeply into dementia to continue as leader. Master Zhou was invited to meet with the others while Madame Liu rested in her room. The meeting began with a recitation of Madame Liu's recent dissembling.

"I asked her about the next caravan," said Lu Zhishen. "She looked at me blankly. She didn't even recognize me."

"Did that last?" asked Master Zhou.

"No, it's true. A bit later she did recognize me and even said she would ask Ishmael about the caravan. But when I talked with him later, she had said nothing to him. I believe it is time to formally change leadership to you, Master Zhou."

"I agree," said Child of Buddha. "Her thoughts are so muddled that she cannot make decisions, or even think about our problems. Yesterday I stood in front of her asking about provisions when she simply walked away without even acknowledging I was there."

Master Zhou sighed. "Yes, I know, it is getting very bad."

"I think, Master Zhou, that you must consider taking over as head of the group," said Suling. "You are the eldest and have the most experience."

"I agree," added John. "I have had my own experiences with Madame Liu, and she gets worse by the day."

"But what do I say to her?" asked Master Zhou sadly.

"Nothing," suggested Suling. "Let her believe she is still in charge during her more lucid moments. It does no harm, as long as we all agree not to act on her commands."

"True," said Lu Zhishen. "Makes sense."

None of them realized that Madame Liu stood outside the partially open door, listening to every word.

"Are these my friends?" came her words like a flash of light in a dark room.

Master Zhou rushed to her. "We are all your friends."

"Then what am I hearing?" she asked, entering tentatively.

"Concern," said Suling gently.

"Conspiracy," said Madame Liu with little emotion.

"Not conspiracy," objected Master Zhou. "Concern. Concern for your health and safety."

"Conspiracy," she said again with a puzzled look, as if testing the word to gauge its effect.

"We are conspiring to let you have some rest," said Master Zhou. "You must rest. The burdens have been too much."

Madame Liu looked through him. "My husband will come soon and everything will be fine. You see how well this safe haven has worked out. It is all his doing. My husband will come soon and everything will be fine. But we're still too close to Nanjing. He's been working to find another haven. Even I haven't seen him since he's locked himself away. Hello. The Japanese will come soon and we must go!"

"Yes, we are. Soon." Master Zhou put his arm around her and guided her back to her room. As they walked he said, "Master Liu is so busy protecting us, you must be there when he returns. How disappointed he would be."

"Yes, yes."

~

After Master Zhou escorted Madame Liu out, Lu Zhishen observed plaintively, "It seems our group gets smaller every day . . . physically and mentally."

"I wonder if Madame Liu will recognize *her* when *she* comes?" said Suling.

"I wonder," echoed Child of Buddha.

"How sad that would be," said Suling.

"Yes," agreed John. "So sad. But I do wonder if *she* will ever come."

"*She* will come," said Suling. "Remember, 'one month, here, at 3 o'clock.' Now it is only fifteen days."

"I'm with John," groused Lu Zhishen. "I'm also not sure s*he'll* come. Perhaps we've been taken for suckers!"

Child of Buddha bristled. "Then what's the point of bringing us here? To watch us eat and drink and defecate? I think not. *She'll* be here, but we may all be a bit older by that time."

The others fell silent.

"No, no," continued Child of Buddha. "That would truly be a waste. We must trust to *her* judgment. Fifteen days—that's all!"

"We have trusted to *her* judgment!" objected Lu Zhishen. "And half of us are gone forever."

"Perhaps not forever," chided the hunchback. "There is more than meets the eye here."

"Well, I'll wait fifteen days, but no longer!"

~

After the group dispersed, John slowly walked back to his room feeling shocked at how rapidly Madame Liu's decline had accelerated. More disturbingly, his thoughts ran to Lu's words about the diminishing size of the group. A deep sense of loneliness struck him as he ticked off his own forlorn situation: Meiying and Feng Shiren gone, Suling closer to Child of Buddha than to him, Lu Zhishen threatening to leave, Master Zhou distracted by Madame Liu's health. Where did that leave him? Even the voices came and went only sporadically, as if they too were abandoning hope. His previous life as an aspiring young businessman in America seemed impossibly distant and irretrievable.

Yet, it was there in the States, in his business, that he met *her*. Ironically, now that he found himself so geographically close to *her*, he felt more distant, and the possibility of meeting *her* appeared to him less urgent. He lifted his hands, palms up, and examined them as might a fortune-teller. Locked in the desire to experience a profound moment, he strove to conjure-up profound thoughts, and to help the conceit along, he self-consciously assumed a melancholy, reflective expression. But nothing profound came . . . just the familiar emptiness. Nevertheless, one spark remained which glowed in the darkness: fifteen days hence.

Chapter Eight

Three O'Clock

Progress

The morning after Meiying and Feng Shiren's discussion about fate, a visitor arrived at the Mongol village accompanied by a small caravan. Meiying joined the little crowd to see what the fuss was about and noticed Feng already standing there waving his arms.

"Mongol Peter!" she heard him shout excitedly.

She followed his eyes but did not know which rider could be the one that elicited such uncharacteristic enthusiasm. Feng rushed up to a burley Mongol, anxiously waited for him to dismount his camel, and gave him a joyous bear-hug.

"I thought you had been arrested!"

"No! Just rumors!"

"Come here, I want you to meet someone."

Meiying waited as Feng pulled the Mongol over to her.

"Here!" exclaimed Feng Shiren with flair. "This is the famous Bai Meiying!"

Mongol Peter whistled. "Very beautiful." He bowed.

Meiying could only nod in return, waiting for some explanation.

"Where's Mongol Little Acorn?" asked Feng.

The reference to Little Acorn startled Meiying and her curiosity deepened.

A dark shadow passed over the Mongol's face and he merely shook his head.

"Oh, so sorry," said Feng.

"I am here to take you back," said the Mongol with a severe yet kindly expression.

"To the Flaming Cliffs?" asked Feng incredulously.

"Yes."

"But the Japs."

"No problem."

"But—"

"No problem."

"Who sent you? How did you know where to find us?"

"No questions, Comrade Feng." Mongol Peter looked at Meiying. "She does not know what we're talking about, does she?"

"No, but I am happy to tell her!"

"Do so quickly. We leave tomorrow at dawn."

"But the camels? They need rest."

Mongol Peter shrugged. "We switch here." He then went off to parley with the village leaders while Feng Shiren rushed Meiying into her yurt and poured out the good news. They were on their way to the Flaming Cliffs! To a cozy hideaway! To be reunited with the group! To see *her*!

Meiying had no words for her joy. Such unalloyed bliss had been so long absent from her life that she had no way to deal with it but through a flood of tears. Feng gently wiped them away, not as a lover but as a true knight-errand, untarnished by base emotions. Even he had misty eyes, and they both laughed as only those who have suffered together can. Next morning, at their departure, Buandelgereen could not be found despite their last-minute inquiries.

~

The trip proceeded uneventfully, as if they had been watched over by a benevolent god. At precisely 3 o'clock on the day Madame Liu predicted *she* would appear, they arrived at the outer wall of the compound. When Ishmael opened the gates, a raucous welcome ruffled the ancient sands of the desert, and all celebrated the miracle of Meiying's return. Once again, Feng Shiren was showered with praise while Mongol Peter stood aside quietly smiling. Only Child of Buddha appeared unmoved, a combination of confusion and concern disfiguring even further the hunchback's visage.

"So, we are to have two miraculous appearances today!" cried Master Zhou.

With this reminder, the group rushed to the room containing the Precious Object where it had been returned after the departure of Tang Yuwei. John barely had time to hug Meiying when they were both swept away with the others. Everyone assumed *she* would make *her* appearance at the statue. The group stood outside the door, hesitating to enter. An eerie silence fell over the compound. The collective tension of every person there infused the air surrounding them, charging the atmosphere with an electric thrill of anticipation. At last, as if some invisible signal was given, Lu Zhishen leapt forward and flung open the door. A brief moment of uncertainty gave them pause, then, as if a floodgate was released, the group rushed *en masse* into the room.

There *she* stood.

Her presence struck them dumb, for deep down, they had not believed Madame Liu's prediction.

Prior to entering the building, John felt the urge to tug Meiying back and have more time with her before the inevitable disappointment if *she* did not appear, or the distracting excitement if *she* did. But Meiying would not be restrained and pulled him inside. Craning his neck to see over the others, he saw *her*, and in that instant everything and everyone melted away, leaving a universe devoid of objects but *her*. His last sensation of this world was the realization that Meiying's hand had slipped from his.

She looked at him just as *she* had done years earlier in his office.

"Mr. Powers, how does one justify a life without cruelty, and therefore also without the distilled beauty of cruelty?"

He was ready for this . . . had been after years of mulling her statement.

"One doesn't. Fate starves at probability's door."

The voice of Goddess boomed out. **You are learning, Chosen One. You will starve at Bai Meiying's door until 1950, if you both live that long. Only then will Bai Meiying have your son. We will do what We can, but these early genetic pathways are unpredictable, and your human DNA plays havoc with Our messages. Too often, you misinterpret both the metaphorical God and Myself, instead listening the the wild demons that have germinated in the new genome. Persevere, John Powers. Persevere, Chosen One.**

John could only reply stupidly to this revelation. "What?"

She stared down at him impassively.

"But why?" he stammered.

As if these two simple words punctured the universe, the room deflated into suffocating darkness and he found himself outside with all the others, each in a state of stunned shock and utter confusion, blinking painfully at the sapphire sky. Their first questions were banal.

"Did you see *her*?"

"Did *she* talk to you?"

It soon became clear that everyone felt badly for the others because *she* had chosen to speak only with them. "How long were we in there?" asked someone.

Lu Zhishen checked his watch. "About five minutes. While I was talking with *her*, I found myself hoping *she* would pay at least some attention to the rest of you. Did I monopolize *her*?"

"Sorry, *she* seemed focused on me. And it was much longer than five minutes."

"And me."

After much discussion, the tangles untwined and to everyone's amazement, *she* somehow spoke to all of them without the knowledge of any of them.

"How could she do it in five minutes?" asked Master Zhou. "How did we end up out here?"

"Did nobody notice *her* speaking to me?" asked Child of Buddha.

"Or me?" added Suling.

"No, no, and no."

"Why are we standing out here, let's go back in!" cried Lu Zhishen.

"Yes, *she* must still be in there," said Master Zhou. "We can ask *her* all of our questions."

Unspoken agreement found them all back inside, but only the Precious Object greeted them, and it remained silent. When they burst into Tang Yuwei's old room, its emptiness only served to rile them to new heights of agitation.

"*She* must be around! I have questions I never got to ask. Many questions!"

"So do I!"

"Wait a minute!" shouted Lu Zhishen. "The hiding place, remember? Below this room is a tunnel. Ishmael showed it to Tang Yuwei and the rest of us. Here's the trap door. *She* must be there."

Crowded in the small space beneath the room, they all stared at the iron door. It remained locked.

"So, just like in the cave. *She's* behind that door. I know it!" exclaimed Lu Zhishen. "Damn!"

Ishmael's voice came down to them from the room above. "Don't worry, *she'll* come to each of you tonight. Now is not the time. You will get no answers. Tonight. Save up your questions for tonight."

Everyone dejectedly left the building and milled around outside, not knowing what further to say. Now that the spell had been broken, John rushed to Meiying, who stood ashen-faced and woozy.

"Are you okay?" he asked, taking her hand and helping her sit on a bench.

"Just tired. Too much has happened too fast."

"What is it?" he asked soothingly.

Meiying looked at him with an open, wondering expression. "Did *she* say something to you about us?"

"Yes, but I still don't understand *her* words. I answered her with some gibberish about fate and probability, but *she* didn't respond."

Meiying covered her face with her hands and whispered, "Yes, it is what I suspected."

"What do you mean?"

"Did she mention a date?"

"Yes."

"When?"

"I don't remember."

"Yes! You do! John, it is our fate, unless the god of probability prevents it."

"What on earth are you talking about?"

"You know. We are beyond being coy with each other."

John lied again. "I don't understand."

"But you do."

John started to protest, then stopped and asked, "When you asked if *she* mentioned a date, do you mean did *she* mention a year?"

"Yes."

"Oh, Meiying, tell me *she* did not say a year far from now."

"You know what year it is."

"*She* is crazy! No one can know that far ahead!"

"No one can know, but the many spirits can know if they band together—past, present, and future."

John turned on her. "Just tell me what *she* told you!"

"*She* said that in 1950 our child, our son, would be born. Not before, not after."

John murmured, "But *she* told me the same thing, Meiying. The same thing!"

Meiying shook her head. "Too many years from now. I'll be almost forty. It is nonsense."

"*She* is not nonsense," replied John. "*She* is . . . *she*."

"John," said Meiying, then paused to contemplate. "This son must be important."

"No, no, no! The son is a tool . . . a lie. There is something else, something deeper."

Meiying stared at him oddly. "John, this son must be important. He will have an important role in the world."

"So now, all of a sudden, you believe in the primacy of fate over probability?"

"When it comes to my son, yes."

"Your son? Meiying, you're a lesbian. How can you say he would be your son?"

"Our son."

"Can you bear me when I make love to you? Will you close your eyes? Vomit afterwards?"

Meiying turned on her heel and walked away, leaving John to fume.

She's back less than a day and we argue!

Yet when they retired to the privacy of their rooms (Meiying was billeted next to Suling in the large female dormitory), both pondered *her* words with little to show for their loss of sleep but further confusion. All the others, similarly shaken, had wandered off to digest in solitude *her* words to them, each assuming they had been the sole object of *her* attention in spite of what their comrades had said.

By the next morning, at communal breakfast, the talking started, slowly at first, then building into a torrent. As they compared stories, all were astonished at the different versions of what was said to each of them by *her* in the space of little more than five minutes. But none had heard from *her* that night, as Ishmael had predicted. At the height of their animated discussion, Ishmael entered and waved his arms for their attention. When the conversation died down, a beautiful woman stepped forward and stood beside him. She gazed upon them as might a queen at her subjects.

"Meet Buandelgereen, a Mongol comrade who will be staying with us," announced Ishmael.

Both Meiying and Feng Shiren jumped to their feet and stood frozen.

The others looked on in astonishment as this strangely magnetic woman smiled at their two comrades. Instantly, Feng and Meiying rushed to her as if granted imperial permission to approach. Amidst the ensuing hubbub, it emerged that Buandelgereen had fled the Mongol village close on the heels of Meiying and Feng Shiren. Apparently, the Japanese came and ransacked every yurt in search of "two criminals" who they knew were being sheltered by the herders.

"What happened to the people?" asked a horrified Meiying, to which Buandelgereen expressed the devastating opinion that they had all been killed.

Master Zhou asked in alarm, "Are they searching for Bai Meiying and Feng Shiren?"

"Yes."

"Oh, god! One can never feel completely at ease these days. Well, Miss Buandelgereen, we welcome you."

After the pleasantries were exchanged, Child of Buddha said to Ishmael, "None of us heard from *her* last night as you promised."

"True," replied Ishmael. "I was mistaken. Tonight is the night. Tonight."

When he left, the conversation resumed with a vengeance. John noticed the Mongol woman very intentionally choose a seat next to Meiying. Was she flirting? He hated himself for these suspicions, but they came in a flood as if the Mongol woman's arrival had breached a dam that had been holding back an enormous reservoir filled with a mixture of all the warm streams and cold rivers of his emotions. Straining his ears to hear their conversation, Lu Zhishen chose this inconvenient moment to chatter about the iron door.

"I'll damn well get through it this time," he said.

"I thought you were leaving."

"Not now. Not now that I've met *her*. *She's* real all right, and I intend to see her again before another few years' pass."

"What do you think of that woman?" asked John gesturing toward Buandelgereen.

Lu shrugged. "Someone they met. I guess she helped protect them. Interesting story. I'm sure we'll hear more details later."

"Interesting woman," replied John, feigning objective curiosity.

"At least blowing this door open won't bring down an entire cave complex," said Lu, determined to bring the topic back to his obsession. "Dynamite shouldn't be hard to get from the next caravan, although that might tip off the Japs. Can't get any from Dalandzadag, that's for sure. Maybe buy some on the black market, or from the Nationalists under the table. What do you think?"

Frustratingly, Lu's words were like mosquitoes which between the buzzes allowed John to catch only bits and pieces of the one conversation interesting to him.

"I don't know," he replied curtly. Tuning out Lu Zhishen he heard the Mongol woman ask Meiying, "What would be your greatest wish?"

"No, seriously," said Lu in a raised voice. "Are you listening? I'm going to find a way past that iron door!"

"Excuse me," said John standing up.

Lu grabbed his arm. "Do you have any idea what we will find?"

Startled at such passion, John pulled his arm away. "No. Why?"

They're leaving!

"Because it may reveal answers to all of us, including your problems."

Arm in arm!

"What problems?"

"What problems? Your voices, of course. And,"—he paused for effect—"those two." Lu's eyes tracked the exit of the two women from the room and returned to John with a wink.

John laughed carelessly, leaving Lu to stand like an awkward guest while he rushed off to catch up with the women. But when he stepped outside, they were nowhere to be found.

You have gone too far, too fast, Sweet Goddess.

God, Your cold objectivity is disheartening. Dear Chosen One, prove you will be a proper father to your son! John, think of your son!

"Please! No more!" shouted John.

"What's wrong?" asked Suling approaching him from behind.

He looked down and for a moment Suling thought he wept, but he lifted his head and said in a strong voice, "Oh, Suling, it is like the old days. Your arriving to comfort me. But these voices will be my salvation."

"How, John? You just sounded very angry, and I'm assuming it was directed at them."

"That's the point, Suling. Without anger I have nothing. Anger is better than disinterest. Otherwise, I'm sunk."

"But John, she is back!"

"She?"

"Yes! Meiying! Why aren't you happy about that?"

"I am. You're right. I am. Thanks. I'm going to my room now and catch up on some reading. Thanks, Suling."

Go find her, John!

He finally tracked them down when he checked the Precious Object. They sat close to each other in a corner, laughing about something when he entered.

Feigning surprise, he uttered, "Oh! Didn't know you two would be here. I just came to check on the Precious Object."

"Come in," said Meiying pleasantly. "You're not interrupting."

Buandelgereen remained conspicuously quiet.

"Has it made any noise?" he asked, giving the Precious Object a significant glance.

"No."

"Mind if I join you?"

"Not at all, but you'll probably find our conversation dull."

"Oh, I doubt it," said John as breezily as he could while pulling up a chair.

His senses were on full alert, but his words seemed natural and relaxed.

"It is so good to have you back with us," he said to Meiying. "I sometimes can't believe you're really here."

"Yes, it is so good to be back."

John conspicuously glanced at Buandelgereen, then turned back to Meiying. "Have you had a chance to talk more with our friends?"

"Oh, yes, I'm sure we will be up late into the night exchanging stories."

So far, John experienced a deep unease—a feeling that he and Meiying were friends, but nothing more. A reserve tinged her words, a formality that he couldn't help ascribing to Buandelgereen's presence. His resentment grew in proportion to his civility.

"Miss Buandelgereen, you must have many interesting stories of your own," he remarked.

"Only one," she replied in a deeply impressive, sonorous voice.

"I am sure you must have many."

"Only one."

"Tell me that one."

Meiying moved in her chair. "John, she doesn't want to go into that right now. We were just discussing human nature. Very boring women chatter."

"Sounds interesting to this male." John knew his intrusion was unwelcome, but he pushed ahead anyway. "Go ahead."

The two women glanced at each other. Meiying said stiffly, "Oh, just war and human capacity for cruelty."

"You mean male capacity for cruelty?"

Buandelgereen suddenly stood and looked down at John with an unreadable expression. "I will leave you two and get myself settled in. I am sure this discussion can be continued at a later date. You both must have a lot of catching up to do." With this, she swept out of the room, leaving behind an awkward silence.

"Sorry," said John finally.

"Are you?"

"Actually, yes. I feel very foolish right now."

"Yes, you look very foolish right now," said Meiying icily. "John, we must get beyond whatever it is that is troubling you."

"Whatever it is! You know very well what it is! You know I love you. You know I get unreasonably jealous."

"Of what?"

"Women."

"Would you prefer to be jealous of a man?"

"At least I would know how to handle it better."

"I doubt it. Anyway, this will get us nowhere."

"Meiying, we are going to have to get somewhere."

"Why?"

"Well, there is this slight complication of a son."

Meiying's face darkened. "Yes, I thought it was the product of your . . . imagination, or your voices, or something not real. But now I have heard it from *her* lips."

"So, what do we do about it?"

"I have not been back a day and already these decisions must be made? I must have time to think. I'm confused and afraid. Surely you can understand that?"

"Yes, of course. I'm so sorry. I have waited for you so long, and now that you're here I spoil it. Will Buandelgereen help you?"

"With what?"

John gave her an ironic look but said nothing.

Meiying raised her chin and glared at him. "I don't know, at least in the way you're thinking. But she will help me by being a friend."

"I am also your friend, Meiying. Please know that, in spite of my being foolish sometimes, I really do want you to find happiness. God knows you deserve it."

Meiying smiled. "So do we all, John. Also, know that I am your friend. We all have our own personal issues, but hopefully we can overcome them and continue to support each other."

He looked away. "Of course."

Meiying brightened. "Is there a piano here?"

John felt gladdened by the sudden change of subject. "Not that I know of. Perhaps we can talk with Ishmael and find out if we can get one."

"Who is this Ishmael?"

"He is the caretaker here. Knows a lot. Mysterious guy. A Mongol, but different. I will talk to him. Can a camel carry a piano?"

She laughed. "No, of course not."

"Well, I have seen wagons come here. Perhaps a piano will fit on a wagon."

"Yes, but where to buy one?"

"Ah, that is a problem. Also, it'll tip off the Japs if they're looking for you. Do they know you play the piano?"

Meiying looked away, then replied in a shaking voice, "Yes."

"Well, let me talk with Ishmael. We'll see."

~

"No need!" a voice boomed from the doorway. "We have a piano!"

Both were startled, John literally jumping up as if he had been caught in a compromising position by a jealous husband.

"Ishmael!"

"That is my name."

"How long have you been there?"

"Long enough to know you want a piano, young Miss Bai Meiying."

John looked at him dubiously. "Where is a piano? I've been here a long time, Ishmael, and I have never seen a piano."

"You didn't know where to look."

"Come on, I believe I've been in every building and room."

Ishmael smiled coldly. "You didn't know where to look."

"Well!" exclaimed Meiying impatiently. "May I see it?"

Ishmael regained his good cheer. "Of course. Follow me."

They followed Ishmael to a building John had often visited. He took them upstairs to a room with a sign that read, 'Piano Room.'

John gazed at the sign shaking his head. "I've been here several times and never saw that sign before. What gives, Ishmael?"

"What gives?"

"When did this sign go up?"

"It's been here all along. I guess you just didn't notice it. Americans can be . . . oblivious."

John could not think of a snappy comeback and so ignored this slight. As his mind floundered, Meiying waited impatiently for Ishmael to unlock the door, and when he finally swung it open she rushed in before the men could take a step, clapping like a young girl.

"Look at it, John! It's beautiful!"

"Probably out of tune," said Ishmael."

John scoffed. "What do you know about tuning a piano, Ishmael?"

"Nothing. But I know that is what is required. Our Mongol instruments are the same. Real artists make sure their instruments are tuned. Even throat singers tune their vocal chords."

"Yes, well, would you both leave me alone for a while? I really would like to try it out," said Meiying while she ran her hand lovingly over the polished wood.

"Can't we stay and listen?" asked John, noting to himself the suspiciously pristine condition of the instrument.

"No, that would make me self-conscious. After all, I haven't played in a long time, and Ishmael is right, the piano is probably out of tune. It will take some time for me to get the courage." She looked at Ishmael. "Will you leave the door unlocked?"

"Of course."

As John left, he had the miserable thought that here was yet another thing to be jealous of.

Walking away, both men heard the first tentative chords of a Chopin mazurka.

John had many questions, and he remembered Ishmael's casual announcement that tonight *she* would be available to ask.

She had better be, he thought. *Or else I'm helping Lu blow open that door!*

He felt something move in him—an inky darkness that welled-up like a squid's cloud to obscure the clear waters of his need-to-please nature.

That night he slept fitfully and dreamt the dreams of a troubled mind.

~ *A Visitation* ~

Two figures stood silhouetted at the foot of his bed. John's eyes followed the contours of their bodies and, through the haze of sleep, he saw a large, imposing man and a small woman, her head slightly tilted. She appeared puzzled. They spoke, but their words were fuzzy and unintelligible, their bodies changing shapes like shadow figures projected against the wall. With dizzying speed, they changed from humans into birds—then to fishes—to trees—clouds—mountains—reptiles—all the while talking. Finally their shape-changing stopped and two human-size ants stood upright at the foot of his bed. Antennas waving, legs gesturing, their words become distinguishable. . . .

He's reunited with her, now what? asked the male, his swampy voice a deep, dank, gritty rumble that filled the room with a corrosive slag of wet soot and harsh sulfur—a nineteenth century furnace bellowing smoke from a thirteenth century hell. After he spoke, John's cream-colored blanket turned greenish-black and glistened with a moist phlegm-like shimmer. When the figure's words at last lost their volume, his breathing lingered, a succession of reptilian hisses.

Explain to him, replied the female, her cleansing voice scrubbing away the male's words with a bleaching breeze that never quite obliterated their sputum stain entirely.

How?

Take him forward in time. Show him. After all, Lord God, it is his son's story that I would have You witness. This one is but a necessary prelude. A step among steps leading to Superior Ones.

It won't work. He won't do it. More importantly, she won't let him do it! She's a lesbian, foolish Goddess, and surely You know what that means. You are wasting My time.

We'll see, beloved God. Stay awhile. Anyway, You have convinced humans that time means nothing to You. True? He must impregnate her, but not too soon, not too late. You'll see—he will impregnate her, else all My plans in ruin! The planet in ruin. Humans must be replaced, You must certainly understand that!

One of the ants changed shape, becoming a human female. She looked down at John, her features made visible by some strange light. John stared back in wordless awe. She sat in the lotus position on a huge, dazzling white flower floating above the floor. Her sad, contemplative face gazed from beneath an elaborate crown glimmering a kaleidoscope of colors. A cinder-bright jewel embedded in her forehead burned brightly and an intricate necklace lays cradled between her bare breasts. Her left hand rested on her thigh, the upturned curve of her fingers resembling the albino legs of a gracefully dead spider. Her right hand poised in the air, index finger and thumb touching to form an almost perfect circle while the other fingers radiated outward. Her transformation seemed to ventilate the room, disinfecting the stench emanating from the male.

Goddess! I know You're a dream, but You're beautiful!

John noticed a dark line of ants appearing from the backside of Her left thigh, marching diagonally upward. They crossed Her abdomen, dipped slightly in Her navel, climbed up the smooth undercurve of Her right breast, circled around Her nipple, over the gentle crest of Her collarbone, and disappeared behind Her shoulder. She gazed at John, unblinking. Then, holding the open palm of Her right hand toward him so that the ridge lines and tributaries of Her skin were illuminated, she said, **Look.**

A deep-rooted warning made him balk. "No."

Ignoring him, She drew his eyes to Her open palm. *It is many years in your future. Look.*

"No!" he shouted.

The other ant at the foot of his bed changed into an old man with a flowing beard and a huge staff. Keeping Her gaze on the sleeping man, Goddess said, *I need Your help, Lord God.*

God straightened His back, glared down at John, brandished His great wooden staff and banged it against the floor. *Look at Her hand!*

In spite of himself, John looked. The lines and whorls of Goddess' hand began to move, coalescing into an image. He saw Meiying on her back, legs splayed, sweaty, grunting, giving birth. The grunts turned into screams. A head emerged amidst the blood. *He is coming! Push! He's here! Push!*

Then silence.

"No!" John shouted. "No!" Breaking through to wakefulness, he breathed deeply, leaned up on his elbows and peered at the end of his bed. Nothing but moonlight from an open window.

Two thirty-nine. Shit! It's a stupid dream. It's freezing! He wiped a sticky film of sweat from his brow and thought it odd to be so hot and so cold at the same time. Compressing his lips in disgust, he dried his hand on the blanket, flipped his pillow over and lay on his back. He felt himself drifting off again, but the phantom screams hummed . . .

The noise grew louder as he tumbled farther into the abyss until his free fall precipitously stopped. A new thought entered his mind. He tried to cut it off, but it kept returning, a weed in the crack of a sidewalk. *It's a trick. She wants me to have a son, but I won't! Meiying is a lesbian for Christsake! I make her sick! I am free. I have free will. I do. . . .*

He closed his eyes and again pulled the blanket up around his neck.

Do You want to go through with this or not? asked God. *The boy's whining grates My ears.*

Your interruption of My story is rude, deathless God, but the answer to Your question is yes, replied Goddess, as She raised Her hand and turned Her palm toward John. *I am sending another Messenger.*

Well, then. . . . God winked at John, leaned forward and cupped His free hand against His mouth in a farcical gesture of conspiracy, as if by so doing He could keep Goddess from hearing His words. *It's Her period,* He whispered loudly. *You know how it is with them when it's particularly bad. You are the sponge into which Her discharge is absorbed.* He twitched. *She wants you to have a son. God knows why, and since I am God and I don't know why . . . well . . . it's a puzzle. She's up to something though, and I have my suspicions.*

God glanced at Goddess who stared at Him wrathfully. He shrugged. *Ah, nothing for it.* His face became stern and He raised His staff as a warrior would a spear and pointed it directly at John's heart. *Look at Her hand!* The malevolence in His voice was in stark contrast to His earlier whimsical tone.

Too frightened to answer, a moment of quiet elapsed while John stared at the staff's blood-red tip.

I told you to looooook! God's voice exploded against the walls.

For a brief moment, for an instant, a soft and comforting light shone through God's malignancy as if swathed in the pervasive essence of a truly universal compassion, a compassion that only omnipotence could project. God looked upon John with a sadness beyond any human's ability to endure.

Why do you make Me thus? He asked. ***Is it the human genes that distort My message, or is it this new template upon which a brave new world will theoretically be born?***

This question shocked John and made him question all his assumptions.

John looked away, and when he looked back, the dark malignancy had returned, the staff still poised in the divine hand. ***I told you to loooook!*** God's words again reverberated through the room.

As it dissipated, John felt a low vibration, a sub-atomic murmur from the two deities. A musky, fetid odor permeated the room. *Look at Her hand!* John commanded himself, but he could not tear his eyes away from the awful staff. To his horror, God cocked back His arm and launched it. A burning pain shot through John's chest and he panicked, thinking he was having a heart attack. *It's a dream! It's a dream! Wake up!*

The pain radiated down his arms and he rubbed his chest in a circular pattern. Harder and faster he rubbed, but the pain deepened. He heard the lilting voice of Goddess rise in protest.

No! Not that way. He will break apart. She looked down at John and spoke in a soothing voice. ***Do not be afraid. Look again. It is no longer your future. It is today, in Mongolia, with her. Please, look John, and you must not be afraid.***

The pain subsided and John looked again at Her upraised hand illuminated against the black backdrop of darkness. Her skin turned green and the lines of Her palm moved in the light of a little sun rising through the gaps in Her fingers. A miniature world expanded to fill the void and, against his will, John stared at the unfolding images.

~ *The Son* ~

He saw sunlight stab through narrow openings in a jungle canopy, piercing the early morning mist that squirmed and twisted under the flashing blades of another murderous day.

Predators, prey and witnesses all rehearsed their testimony. Birds sang and gibbons chattered. A tiger growled, insects hissed and plants breathed steam in humid clouds that clung like mucous to the soaked air. Deep inside a dark tunnel, a queen ruled from within the palatial white skull of a long-dead human, her soldiers scurrying in frenzied anticipation. One soldier in particular stood out because of her size and strength. Heroic and unflinching in the face of adversity, she was a veteran of many bloody campaigns. A Great Warrior.

She emerged from the tunnel and moved cautiously through the detritus piled thick on the jungle floor. Her antennas probed the complex geometry of tattered leaves, her abdomen rubbed the curved inclines of sharp sticks and cylindrical bamboo. This is her first trip to the Great Mongol Storehouse, a place discovered only that morning by nest mates. A frightening and alien place.

She followed the scent of her sisters, constantly alert for the intrusion of enemy scouts and the threat of ambush by concealed predators. Fellow soldiers passed her as they shepherded back to the nest an unbroken line of workers carrying angular bits of paper.

The Great Warrior at last reached the end of All That Is Familiar. Antennas waving, she looked out from her jungle to a clearing enveloped in darkness. Hesitating only a moment, she pressed forward through the Mysterious Membrane and crossed over into the night.

John heard Goddess' voice floating through the night air. ***Look.*** She gestured with Her glowing hand. ***The Messenger comes for you.*** She tilted Her head as if straining to hear something, then nodded toward the outside of his room.

John heard the groans and grunts of childbirth, then the screams again.

The terrible noise bore down upon him. Suffocating. Oppressive. It reached such a pounding level that he feared the walls would crumble under the pressure. An irresistible urge to flee gripped him. In desperation, he tried to rise and run out of his room, but the ocean of noise paralyzed him and he remained pressed against the bed, listening to the two deities shouting at each other.

Ants, Goddess? Gibberish?

I carry a nightmare to him—a special nightmare. Look at how his eyelids flutter so.

He has had many nightmares—all of them unimaginative. One more doesn't matter. He will just feel sorry for himself. Besides, You do not need My help. What is the real reason You called Me here?

His nightmare is for You. Hear Me. I will speak of his son.

Why does this son continue to be so important to You despite all the past failures and the current travails of John Powers and Bai Meiying?

The son will lead You to the Reunion. The Reunion will—

I have humored You long enough. Get to the point.

I will speak of a different war in a different place at a different time. The writer of this story will make You listen. It is the Reunion that will save You—and him, the son—the one who writes these words.

Stop pontificating, Mad Mother! You once stood tall amid the blood of the sacrificed. Now You have reverted to an adolescent girl sneaking peeks at the dirty little book of war under the thick covers of My ascendancy. Ants? Gibberish? Pretentious drivel! Melodramatic mush!

Pretentious? You dare speak of pretension? What about, 'In the Beginning God created the Heaven and Earth' or 'O Keshava, what are the signs of the man of steady wisdom, one who has attained God-consciousness' or 'Allah sendeth astray whomsoever He willeth, and guideth aright whomsoever He willeth; He is the Sublime, the Wise'? You have carried pretension to a higher level than I. And as for melodrama; have You ever known a dream, or a nightmare, that was not melodramatic?

Ah, Your favorite repetitive humbug! Can this writer not put more variation in Your rantings? Look, Beloved Goddess, there is skillful, understated pretension and there is clumsy, overwrought pretension: writhing snakes, multiple arms, serpentine hair, and Your stuttering serpent tongue, so creepy crawly to My femme phobias, not to mention Your fertile fleshy flab and sour milk from Your sagging breasts. Really, Great Mother, pull Yourself together.

Speaking of repetition! Your mocking abuse is tiresome.

I'm not–

Then listen. Since Evolution invented sex and Our divorce was final, the children have suffered. You speak of pretension. Human war and hunger for blind worship are the ultimate pretensions. Your First Principles will lead to the destruction of all the others, and life itself on this magnificent planet.

Spoken like a starving deity. I have better things to do than listen to Your bilge. You complain about worship because they stopped worshiping You. Old deities never die, They just fade away. Your mortal's nightmare is Your business, not Mine. And as for Evolution, do not mention that desecration again!

The truth hurts, dear God. A pimple on the end of Your nose. A humiliating exposure of Your adolescent–

Do not say it! What interest have I in this son of John and Meiying? They are two spiraling strings of nucleic acids and knotted tangles of ubiquitous carbon, nothing more. Let Nature take its course. Meddling will only make it worse.

I want You to hear this story. It is for Your own good and for that of all living things. Still lying …

… on his back, John moaned and smacked his lips. Feeling the gravity of the nightmare weigh heavily on his body, he turned on his side to lessen the drag. Something pushed and prodded his arm. *John. John. Wake up. You're dreaming again. Wake up.* He moaned again, then started to open his eyes and—

Nothing.

The terrible cacophony ended and John was released from his paralysis. Jolted by the burnt nerve of nightmare, he sat bolt upright, instantly awake. "I won't do it!" But even before the last word left his mouth, he remembered that he just dreamed, nothing more, and felt a surge of relief.

A son. My son.

Chapter Nine

Falling Leaves

Dog Days

Years passed and the inertia of dwelling in an island of safety surrounded by a sea of danger kept them dutifully busy with gardening, husbandry, and fantasies. Madame Liu by now had to be kept in her bed with diapers; Lu Zhishen never found the dynamite he so anxiously desired, and could often be found conversing and cursing at the iron door; Child of Buddha spent hours sitting with the Precious Object attempting to decipher its code; John became a shadow man catching scraps from Meiying and sympathy from the others, savaged by his voices; Meiying herself fell into a de facto marriage with Buandelgereen, lost in a world of artificial bliss. Feng Shiren became a whirlwind of pent-up energy and one day disappeared, leaving a note saying he would return at some unspecified time in the future since for the time being the group was safe. Only Suling and Master Zhou seemed unchanged and unchanging—anchors dragged quietly behind the drifting ship.

News came sporadically with the caravans. America now in the war; Europe in flames; China in flames; Communists and Nationalists fighting the Japanese while killing each other; armies clashing in the countryside, clashing in the cities; famine in the occupied territories; and everywhere the dead and dying—except here, in their little compound tucked away behind the Flaming Cliffs amidst the ageless desert.

Every weekend Meiying gave a concert, sharpening her skills as best she could before an easy-to-please audience of appreciative musical illiterates. Ishmael found it his unique challenge to locate hard-to-get scores at Meiying's request and have them delivered by the unreliable caravans, always greeted by Meiying's clapping with joy. When the caravans arrived, Suling harangued the Mongol riders with questions about Tang Yuwei, but his whereabouts were never known, or even if he still dwelt among the living.

Day in, day out, their routine varied little, the only excitement occurring when periodically Master Zhou had to venture to Dalandzadgad where he withdrew money from his account and that of Madame Liu, using his power-of-attorney.

Always he expected the Japanese to trace him back to the secret compound and always his trips ended without incident, although not without a period of nervous glances outside the walls by the group. John found his jealousy to be manageable so long as Meiying fraternized only with Buandelgereen and not some strange man. Why he felt this way remained a mystery to him, but he gratefully accepted the consequences—no murderous or suicidal thoughts to upset the precarious balance of his life. True, he felt lonely and resentful at her obsession, but she threw him enough scraps to muddle through. Suling, as always, acted as his sounding board and seemed ever ready to listen, particularly now that Child of Buddha attended to her own obsession. So John lived day-to-day, fancying himself a sort of Robinson Crusoe surviving in an alien world on his native wits, accompanied by a small bevy of Fridays.

Much of John's time was spent waiting for free moments to meet privately with Meiying. Usually, she and Buandelgereen were together like two young lovers whose world would end should they be parted for an hour. He felt supremely uncomfortable around the Mongol woman; her imperious attitude and uncanny ability to seem to appear in multiple places at the same time intimidated him. In fact, she appeared to intimidate everyone, even Master Zhou, while Ishmael treated her like a visiting khan. In an odd sort of way, John had to admit to himself that she was no permanent threat; that somehow she was destined for greater things then being the lover of Bai Meiying; that each was a placeholder for the other. The voices assured him as much, harping on his other innumerable shortcomings, but never mentioning Meiying since the arrival of Buandelgereen.

One day while gardening, John saw Meiying walk by unaccompanied and took the opportunity to take a break, putting his hoe on his shoulder and calling to her.

"Meiying! Do you have a moment?"

He fancied she hesitated.

"Yes, of course."

"Well, if you're busy it can wait," he said in a slightly pained tone.

"No, not at all."

He led her to a nearby bench. "How is Madame Liu?" he asked, at a loss for something to say, for in truth, he just wanted to sit with her in silence and bathe in her presence.

"The usual, poor woman."

"Yeah, it's sad."

After a pause, she asked, "Did you want something?"

"Oh, no, just to talk. I thought it's such a nice day and we haven't had a chance to talk together for a while."

"Yes."

Her one-syllable response cut, but he pressed on. "What are you playing this weekend?"

"I'm not sure."

"Well, whatever it is, I'm looking forward to it."

"Thank you."

She shifted a bit and looked at the empty courtyard as if something of interest were happening. He felt himself getting angry at her curtness and trolled for something that might hurt.

"Well," he said with restrained formality. "I'm sure you're busy and I need to get back to my weeding."

She seemed to notice him for the first time. "How have you been, John?"

He smiled ironically and began to reply in an offhand manner, but she looked at him intently. "No, really John, I mean it. How have you been?"

Taken aback at this sudden change in tone, he could only manage to blurt out, "Fine."

"John, the voices?"

"Oh, they're like these damn weeds—just keep coming back. I cut them and they come back. Can't seem to get at the roots."

Her eyes bore into him, a hint of fear in their orbs. "I think I hear them sometimes."

"What?!"

"Yes. I—"

But before Meiying could continue, Buandelgereen appeared as if from thin air. She looked down at them with her imposing air, making John feel small; a mere mortal observed from Mt. Olympus by some inscrutable Goddess.

Without a word, Meiying rose and took her hand. Buandelgereen, with her acolyte now securely in tow, continued to look at John. "May I take her for a while, John? We have some unfinished business to discuss."

"Of course."

Meiying glanced down. "Sorry, John. Next time we can continue our discussion."

"Yes, I would like that."

Did she betray some emotion other than single-minded attention to Buandelgereen? Regret? Pain? Irritation? He could not tell. As they strolled away, still hand-in-hand, he felt a knot in his stomach and the anger once again emerged.

Damn! Damn! Damn! His thoughts could gain no more traction than cursing his fate.

Fate?

Fate starves at Probability's door!

Probability starves at Fate's door!

Who spoke? God? Goddess? Which is which? Go away, both of You!

Leave the two women alone, John dear. You'll just make yourself appear more foolish.

~

Lu Zhishen tapped him on the shoulder.

"John!"

"Yes?"

"Whew! You were in some other universe, man. I'm thinking of going into Dalandzadgad with the next caravan."

John had heard this before. "Too risky," he said for the umpteenth time over the years. "A big, ugly Canadian with a beard! You may as well wear a neon sign that says, 'Follow me!'"

Lu puffed out his lumberjack chest, scowling more at his fate than at John. "Well, so what? It's time to stir things up. We can't stay here forever! Besides, I'll be damned if I leave before that bloody iron door is knocked down for good! Aren't you even the slightest bit curious?"

"To answer your question for the billionth time, of course I am. But look, the last we heard, Japan and Germany are losing the war. Be patient."

"You be fuckin' patient, I've had enough! That door mocks me!"

John shrugged and waved him off. He had heard this sad tale too many times, and nothing ever came of it. Meiying remained his only concern.

"You wanna come with me?" asked Lu rather plaintively.

"Yeah, right," dismissed John as he walked away. "Go ahead if you want. I'll stay here where it's warm and safe."

"Of course you will," grumbled Lu.

But John's thoughts had already returned to his impossible love. *Like you just advised that lunkhead Canadian, be patient,* he told himself. *Nineteen-fifty is far away, but not impossibly far.* He took a grand walk around the compound, the hoe still balanced on his shoulder. *But how will this magical union with Meiying work? I know the thought of sex with a man disgusts her. I myself probably disgust her, sex or no sex. So how does this conception happen? Do I rape her? And when?—of course, it has to be just at the right moment for Goddess. 'Oh, worthless,' she would say. 'It can't be sooner, nor can it be later. No, it has to be timed just right so the kid is born in nineteen-fifty.' Ridiculous! And if I do rape her, we wouldn't be able to live as husband and wife, so the kid has no proper parents. No home. The whole thing is stupid! And the woman we are all here to see does nothing except to appear once in a million years and spout enigmas about cruelty. Damn! And damn that Buandelgereen!*

Such were his disjointed thoughts as he shuffled about within the boundaries of his own troubled soul and the physical confines of the walled sanctuary in which he had become imprisoned. Yet, being fundamentally a domestic type who craved safety and routine, he soldiered on, secretly deriving a certain low-key satisfaction from these familiar surroundings, away from the unpredictable conflict outside, and comforting himself that at least he remained within the orbit of Meiying's world, albeit as a distant satellite.

Tiring of the unsolvable conundrums that plagued his existence, he returned to the garden and resumed a rhythmic eradication of weeds, thinking all the while of the coming weekend and the chance to listen to Meiying play; her face transformed by the music into a sensual mask of ecstasy. That night, he fell asleep with this image in mind, and he dreamt of making love to her. But at the crucial moment, Meiying's face contorted into an ugly mask of loathing. She pushed him away and ran into the darkness, leaving him panting in misery. The next few days he took solace in the upcoming concert, making sure he avoided contact with

Meiying and her lover Buandelgereen. Let the chips fall where they may, he would meet privately with her on his own terms or not at all.

On the day of the concert, he felt as he had before every concert over the past years: adolescent anticipation, the fuel that kept him going. Like a voyeur, he watched her perform and fantasized that her joy at the keyboard when she played a piece by Chopin or Mozart was in fact the joy she would experience while making love with him. His conceit sustained him, even in the face of sporadic attacks by the voices, so, that night, he heard what he would, saw what he wanted, and fell asleep in his room afterward, ready for the next week to repeat the cycle. John understood the self-deceiving, implausible nature of his fantasies, and chalked them up to necessity, for without them, he would sink even deeper into mental illness.

~ *Buandelgereen* ~

In the meantime, far from being aware of John's agonies, Meiying found herself bedazzled by the magnificent Buandelgereen. She seemed a divine combination of Lihua and Meili; a melding of such perfection that Meiying felt supremely happy for the first time in years, restrained only a little by the nagging feeling that she was utterly undeserving. She could not believe her good fortune, and memories of the hard life she had so recently endured faded; her dreadful nightmares suppressed by endless rehearsals of demanding sonatas, and her increasingly rare depressions palliated by the equally demanding Buandelgereen. Everyone had noticed the monopoly over Meiying's time exercised by the Mongol woman. Day and night the two were inseparable. Lu Zhishen summarized it crudely when he lamented that all of *his* needs were not being satisfied, and he had dibs on Buandelgereen when Meiying had done with her, or vice versa.

But inside the cocoon of this relationship, stirrings of a transforming metamorphosis could be detected. Gradually nursed in such a secure environment, Meiying regained her strength and self-confidence. As if by some intravenous magic, Buandelgereen's iron will and majestic bearing made their way into the veins and sinews of Meiying's body. She began to assume the role of leader, filling the void left by Madame Liu's illness and Master Zhou's distractions. Only one member of the group seemed wary of this newfound buoyancy—Child of Buddha. As always, she took the road less traveled and started watching the two women as if searching for clues of some conspiracy to murder. She also, like John, bided her time to catch Meiying alone. Even Child of Buddha evidently felt some degree of trepidation in the presence of the Mongol goddess and preferred not to fall under the cool diminution caused by her shadow. One day she took advantage of a rare opportunity to snare Meiying alone, as Buandelgereen and Master Zhou were meeting to discuss the local Mongolian situation.

"Meiying!" called Child of Buddha from across the courtyard.

Always interested in talking with this strange hunchback who often served-up enigmatic and oracular comments, Meiying walked briskly up to her. "Yes?"

"Can we talk for a bit?"

"Of course."

"The others have asked me about the Precious Object."

"Yes, I know."

"But not you."

Silence.

Child of Buddha cocked her head. "No questions?"

Meiying shrugged. "No."

"The others think I know what it says, what its tapping means. Do they think I am hiding something . . . maybe plotting something?"

"Not that I know of. Why do you ask?"

"Do you think I'm hiding something?"

Meiying wanted to avoid the topic, but decided honesty with this strange one seemed the wisest path. "Sometimes I think so. It seems you know things the rest of us don't."

Child of Buddha laughed. "I do, but the rest of you also know things I don't."

"Fair enough."

"I wanted to ask you about Buandelgereen."

"I figured you did. It seems everyone is curious."

"About her, yes. Not so much about you."

"Why?"

"You're a known quantity, she's not."

"Really? How so?"

"You are transparent, she is not."

Meiying frowned. "What do you want to know?"

"Is the sex good?'

Meiying started to protest, but Child of Buddha put up her hand and chuckled. "Just kidding. I wanted to get your full attention."

"You have it."

"Good. There is something I really should share with you—with all of you. But you are their leader now, so I'll talk with you first."

"I am their leader? That is not true."

"Don't be coy. You know you are. Yes, you are their leader now, even if they don't know it yet."

Meiying gave an ironic nod. "But not your leader?"

Child of Buddha laughed heartily. "No. Hunchbacks have learned not to follow attractive people. We're too ugly. We hop about like frogs and talk to gargoyles and dragons. Attractive people walk like royalty and talk only to other attractive people."

"So, what did you want to share?" asked Meiying with an unmistakable tone of impatience.

"Nothing much. Only that something is about to happen."

"I don't understand. What?"

"Something is about to happen."

"What is about to happen?"

"Don't know."

"When is something about to happen?"

"Soon."

Meiying raised a cautionary hand. "Well, that doesn't help much. Is this a good or bad thing that is about to happen?"

"Bad."

"Oh," sighed Meiying, not expecting such a blunt answer. "If we don't know what, and we don't know when, I'm not sure what I can do about it right now."

Child of Buddha remained silent, gazing at her with a look of anticipation. Meiying hesitated. She wanted to escape the hunchback's eyes, move on and avoid these complications, but that seemed irresponsible. Something caught in her throat and her stomach churned as she absorbed this unexpected threat to the pleasant life she now enjoyed.

"How do you know something bad is about to happen?" she asked finally. "Is it the tapping from the Precious Object?"

"Yes."

"You can interpret it now?"

"Well, as you know, in the past when it tapped quickly something was usually going to happen. But I knew there was more to it than that. I mean, sometimes it tapped quickly and nothing happened."

"Yes, but something usually did when it tapped quickly."

"True, but not always. I mean, sometimes when it tapped quickly, good things happened also."

"Okay, I understand, but my question is whether you have learned to interpret it."

"I think so. You see, it is not when it is tapping quickly that is the important part. It's the in-between part, when the tapping is so low you can barely hear it. But if you listen very closely, and if you listen over a long period of time, the taps start to make sense."

"I don't think I understand."

Child of Buddha stared down at the ground. "I don't either, but the taps are constant and they have a meaning, a rhythm, a kind of pulse. It's like a doctor listening to your heart, gauging the beats and the pumping blood for signs of, I don't know, for signs of excitement or blockage or strain. Except when I hear the tapping, I hear different things."

"Like what?"

"Well, it's like different colors of paint being thrown helter-skelter against a wall; splattering, dripping, combining, coagulating. I hear the colors, taste the splashes, smell the mixing, and am occasionally scorched by the spattering. All very indistinct."

"And the tapping is like the paint?"

"Yes, different taps are like different colors, different tastes, different smells, different scorches."

"And so. . . . ?"

"And so something bad is about to happen."

"What do you expect me to do?"

"Tell her I know."

"Who?"

Child of Buddha inhaled. "Her."

Meiying shook her head. "I don't know who you mean."

"Buandelgereen of course."

Meiying took a small step backwards. "Buandelgereen!"

"Yes."

"But why her?"

"Because she also knows, and perhaps she can be more specific about what bad thing is about to happen."

"But how would she know?"

Child of Buddha stepped forward and lifted her face close to Meiying's. "She knows."

"But—" Meiying started to protest, when Child of Buddha held up her hand.

"Ask yourself this, Meiying: why is Buandelgereen the only survivor of her entire village?"

~ *Do You Know?* ~

Meiying did not want to tell Buandelgereen about her conversation with Child of Buddha. After all, what could the Mongol woman say? It would just put her on the spot and cast Meiying's friends in a bad light—silly and superstitious foreigners. But the more she thought of it, the more she decided it might be presented to Buandelgereen in a neutral, non-threatening manner. But how? Why so difficult to raise the issue? Only then did Meiying realize she was afraid of something tangible; not in the polite abstract sense that she might embarrass the Mongol or compromise her friends, but a deep and abiding fear that bore with it some heretofore unknown horror. The thought startled her and she ran her mind over why this fright had appeared in connection to Buandelgereen, blemishing her like a pothole in some shiny new road. Afraid of what?—she kept asking herself. All her attempts to blame the fear on the traumas of her past failed. Was it the murder of Beethoven? No. Mr. President? No. The Japanese? No. Father Durant? No. Down through the list she checked-off all the possibilities, leaving only a mysterious, unsettling fear of Buandelgereen herself. In due time, she confronted the obvious follow-up question: Why did she feel afraid of her lover, her friend, the woman she most admired? To this question she had no satisfactory answer, retaining only the certitude that she was inexplicably troubled, even, at times, terrified. Again, the question arose repeatedly: Of what? Of what?

With this realization, it seemed to Meiying as if she had just emerged from a fog. Her relationship with Buandelgereen had been too perfect, too arranged, too rehearsed. All of her senses had been overwhelmed by this unnatural perfection.

Clarity can be far more horrifying than confusion, and she now saw the danger with a crystal clear awareness. After agonizing for days in her room, begging off seeing anyone by feigning illness, she emerged with a single-minded purpose: she would go directly to Buandelgereen and poke the beast that Child of Buddha had suggested lurked beneath the surface. When the time came that her courage had been sufficiently fortified by self-directed admonishments to be brave, Meiying walked out into the brisk, sunlit morning and went in search of her mysterious Mongol lover. John called to her as she passed, but she ignored him.

She rehearsed her opening salvo as she walked, cognizant that unwise words might be drawn from her in the intense gravitational field of Buandelgereen's presence.

"That is a nice speech," said Buandelgereen, appearing next to her as if materializing from nowhere.

"Oh, god!" cried Meiying, jumping back as if the crack of a rifle had shattered the air around her. "How long have you been here?"

"Long enough."

"Then you know what I have come to ask?"

The Mongol laughed openly, not bothering to cover her mouth and dazzling Meiying with the sensual curve of her lips and the white perfection of her teeth. "I have known for a long time."

"About Child of Buddha?"

"Yes, of course."

"Her concern that something is about to happen?"

"Of course."

"Something bad?"

Buandelgereen turned suddenly grave. "Of course."

Meiying steeled herself. "How do you know these things?"

"That is not the question."

Meiying waited for her to continue, but no words were forthcoming. She wanted to keep waiting, but that game was not in her character. "Well, what is the question?"

"The trials that are to come will come regardless of what any of us wish to the contrary."

"You don't speak like a Mongol."

"Oh?"

"You speak like a courtesan to the emperor. Or perhaps you are an Empress. Are you really a Mongol?"

Buandelgereen shook her head. "Trials are on their way, Meiying. I have prepared you to deal with them. It is too early for the other matter to be consummated. Unfortunately, we live in a time and place that makes waiting peacefully for the right moment very difficult."

"What other matter?"

"You know."

Meiying touched her hand. "Buandelgereen, dear, please help me understand."

"You are afraid of me?"

"Yes."

The Mongol clasped Meiying's hand and lifted it to her heart. "You should be."

"But why? I don't want to be afraid of you."

"Because your fears can now be focused, and when they are focused, they have a target, and when they have a target, they can hit the mark. Then you are free. All the other fears and terrors that you have undergone the past few years will fade away and clear the path for you to take care of the other matter."

"I do not know about this other matter."

"So be it."

"Tell me!"

"No."

Meiying jerked her hand away. "How am I to know what you're talking about if you don't tell me?" she cried.

"You were told."

"By who?"

"By *her*."

"I never told you that. How do you know that?"

Buandelgereen shook her long locks but did not reply.

Meiying glared. "It is about this future son, isn't it?"

The Mongol woman remained silent, but gazed at Meiying with an intimidating frown.

"You never told me you knew *her*," Meiying said in a weak voice.

"No, I didn't."

"Then you and *she* must communicate with each other. Child of Buddha said as much. Please, dear Buandelgereen, tell me. Explain to me."

"We were not speaking of *her*, we were speaking of trials."

"But—"

Buandelgereen squeezed Meiying's hand and led her to the room housing the Precious Object. It took them a while to reach the destination, passing some of the others without saying a word. Upon entering, the Mongol woman looked around to make sure it was empty.

"Good!" she exclaimed, and sat Meiying down on a chair facing the statue. "Do you hear anything?" she demanded.

Meiying listened. "No."

"Are you deaf? Listen!"

Meiying tilted her head toward the object and detected a low, rasping noise. "I hear it," she said softly, but it isn't tapping. It isn't the sound I normally hear from it."

Buandelgereen beamed as she might at a precocious child. "That's right."

"What is it saying?"

"What does it sound like?"

Meiying listened some more. "It sounds like scraping."

Buandelgereen tilted her head in invitation. "As if. . . ."

" . . . something wanted out." Meiying finished the sentence.

But no sooner were these words out than the Mongol woman leaned over and whispered in her ear. The whispering voice merged with the low rasping of the Precious Object and an oddly melodious hum emerged from the combining; a deep and distant wail from light-years away. The universe groaning. Meiying felt herself getting dizzy, mesmerized by the otherworldly sound. It played tantalizingly in her mind, individual words briefly popping in and out of consciousness. What does it mean? she marveled.

...youAvelsilentdoweoheavenintosendwatchholy....

Words, maddeningly indistinct, bubbled up from the cauldron of gibberish and submerged back down into its roiling, primeval hum. She sensed her body falling, spinning down some awful vortex. Her arms reached for Buandelgereen as she slid from the chair. "What is that?" she managed to utter before dark oblivion swallowed her whole. The Mongol woman spoke, but her words fell into the heart-rending wail of the voices.

...youAvelsilentdoweoheavenintosendwatchholy....

~

It took some time before she realized where she was. Her bed seemed to sag beneath her as if she had gained mass, and her head sank heavily into the pillow, almost preventing her from breathing. Groggily she understood it was nighttime. Her clothes had been removed and her naked body did not respond immediately to her commands. She rolled on her back and stared up at the darkness, trying to get her brain to work. Moonlight illuminated a corner of the room where a chair eerily glowed, projecting elongated shadows from its legs. Meiying peered at it, expecting to see Buandelgereen appear, sitting up as with an ill patient. To her disappointment, the Mongol woman did not materialize. Strangely, the fear she experienced earlier had dissipated, and what remained nagged at her with a low-grade insistence. How she got here seemed obvious, but did Buandelgereen manage it alone? Did others help? If so, who? Worse, she had no idea how much time had passed. No clock. No watch. Night. The whimsical thought entered her mind that years had been peeled away like her clothes, and she faced a drastically changed world in wonder.

A horrifying idea occurred to her that tonight would be the "consummation" of the "other matter" that Buandelgereen mentioned. Would John burst in and force himself on her? Rape her to meet the deadline? Could it be nineteen-fifty already? No, impossible. But the thought of rape infuriated her. Never had she felt more disgusted by male lust; more appalled by their drooling animal drives. Yet, she had been informed there must be a male child; even *she* insisted.

Or maybe, she thought amidst the fog. She *is the one pushing this whole idea. Of course! It is she!*

At the instant of this revelation Buandelgereen appeared, once again seemingly from thin air. Meiying reacted in a surprised, but not shocked manner.

"So, you're here at last, dear," she said after her initial hesitation.

"I brought soup. You are ill."

"How long have I been here?"

Buandelgereen raised her eyebrows and shook her long hair. "Not long."

"How long? Is it nineteen-fifty?"

The Mongol woman laughed heartily. "No, dear one. Only a few days since we spoke."

Meiying lifted her head. "A few days?"

"Yes. Now, since you're up, let me put pillows behind your head so you can eat."

"Thank you but I'm not hungry."

"Yes, you will eat." Buandelgereen put this in a manner that could not be ignored.

While humming unfamiliar folk songs, the Mongol woman stroked Meiying's hair with one hand and offered spoonsful of soup with the other. Susceptible as she usually was to kind overtures, Meiying felt the electric tingle of fear in the roots of her hair as it was stroked, and a warning light clicked on in her brain. She wanted to ask questions, many questions, but not of Buandelgereen.

"I haven't seen Suling in a while," she said off-handedly. "Any chance you could get her to visit?"

Buandelgereen straightened just a little, then relaxed and continued her stroking.

"Of course."

Meiying found it difficult to believe that only a few days earlier she had made love with this woman. Now, she seemed a distant ruler mingling with the common folk, unpredictable and capricious. Meiying sipped another spoonful and wondered where lies the danger. *Am I mad?* she thought. *A psychopath? Worse, a schizophrenic like John? Am I so afraid of ghosts? Voices? My own lover?*

And of a sudden, she focused on images of John, who had long since been shuffled off to a remote corner of her mind and brought out only intermittently when the same unanswered questions arose: What to think of him? A friend? Lover? Comrade? Acquaintance? Nothing quite fit, yet she was to have his child. The idea had never accommodated itself to her mind. Did she even like him? To this last question, she pondered long and hard. But Buandelgereen kept lifting soup to her lips, and the pulsing glow of embers in the Mongol woman's eyes peered through Meiying as easily as through a clear night, and their peculiar intensity threw her off—like someone reading over a writer's shoulder.

~

I am looking over your shoulder, Michael Powers. Careful what you write about your dear father and mother!

Hush!

You are the son and another step, but they were among the first, and gave you flesh and blood by spilling their own.

They gave me Your voices. They gave me madness. Now, hush!

~

Meiying let her mind retreat into a confused fog, unsure of anything. Love, distrust, fear, loyalty, obedience, all shuttered her mind and she lay her head heavily back onto the pillows.

"I'll let you sleep, dear one," whispered Buandelgereen, who promptly floated out as noiselessly as she had come in.

"Please bring Suling," rasped Meiying, but evidently too low for the Mongol woman to hear, and she again found herself alone.

At least I'm not on the road, starving and terrified of every shadow and every little sound, she thought, conscious of the nutritious broth that warmed her belly. *None of them threaten me anymore—Beethoven, Mr. President, Father Durant, Colonel Naguma—none of them! They're all so far away, and yet. . . .*

She moaned and tried to get comfortable, all the while glancing nervously at the door, aware of her nakedness.

. . . and yet so uncomfortably near. Ah! They can't harm me anymore!

But the danger she unwillingly sensed had been intensified by Buandelgereen's "trials" and her strange illness, all preying upon her and preventing her normally strong will to rid herself of evil premonitions. Sleep came reluctantly, but with it came a price.

~ *Nightmares* ~

Two figures stood silhouetted at the foot of her bed. Her eyes followed the contours of their bodies and through the haze of sleep, she saw a large, imposing man and a small woman, her head slightly tilted. She appeared puzzled. They talked, but their words were fuzzy and unintelligible, their bodies changing shapes like shadow figures projected against the wall. With dizzying speed, they changed from humans into birds—then to fishes—to trees—clouds—mountains—reptiles—all the while talking. Finally, their shape-changing stopped and two human-sized ants stood upright at the foot of her bed. Antennas waving, legs gesturing, their words became distinguishable.

She distrusts the messenger. Now what? asked the male, his swampy voice a deep, dank, gritty rumble that filled the room with a corrosive slag of wet soot and harsh sulfur—a nineteenth century furnace bellowing smoke from a thirteenth century hell. After he spoke, Meiying's coverlet turned greenish-black and glistened with a moist phlegm-like shimmer. When his words at last lost their volume, his breathing lingered, a succession of reptilian hisses.

Explain to her, replied the female, her cleansing voice scrubbing away the male's words with a bleaching breeze that never quite obliterated their sputum stain entirely.

How?

Take her forward. Show her. After all, Lord God, it is her story that I would have You witness—at least for now.

It won't work. She won't go. You are wasting Our time!

We'll see. Stay a while. Buandelgereen will prevail. I have given her power. The son will be born, and You will look in the mirror and attend the Reunion. The Earth must be healed.

One of the ants changed shape, becoming a human female. She looked down at Meiying, her features made visible by the moonlight now streaming into the room. Meiying stared back in wordless awe. The female sat in the lotus position on a huge, dazzling white flower floating above the floor. Her sad, contemplative face gazed from beneath an elaborate crown glimmering a kaleidoscope of colors. A cinder-bright jewel embedded in her forehead burned brightly and an intricate necklace lay cradled between her bare breasts. Her left hand rested on her thigh, the upturned curve of her fingers resembling the albino legs of a gracefully dead spider. Her right hand poised in the air, index finger and thumb touching to form an almost perfect circle while the other fingers radiated outward. Her transformation seemed to ventilate the room, disinfecting the stench emanating from the male.

The Precious Object!

Yes, of course. In her dream, Meiying did not feel shock or surprise, just a rather invigorating confirmation of what she suspected all along.

But why the tapping? Why not words? Plain words for plain people to plainly understand?

These unspoken thoughts seemed to convey themselves to Goddess, who jerked Her head down and glared at Meiying in astonishment.

"Would you have Me speak like a fool?" The words must have been spoken aloud, outside her head, reverberating thunderingly off the walls in a warped shriek.

The glow from Her body burst into flaming red like an electrified blush, the explosive brightness causing Meiying to cringe back, suddenly terrified. *Please stop! Stop!* she screamed in her mind, the words sinking hopelessly into the muffled fog of her nightmare. . . .

. . . and that is how she awoke. Back to consciousness. Back to being frightened by a nameless fear. Back to the questions. Did her fear now have a name? A face? It certainly wasn't Naguma or Beethoven or Durant or any of the rest. It stalked close-by, in the guise of friends and comrades and lovers.

And John? she wondered. Friend or foe? Or perhaps innocent vessel like herself, to be manipulated by the gods, or goddesses, or the universe, or all of them. How could one resist such forces? If they collectively would have her spread her legs, then all of her will power and muscle power would be as futile as a few drops to the ocean. Perhaps that is why she felt drawn to John—he was a normal, vulnerable human male with a good heart who did the best he could in the face of such forces.

An idea she had thought of earlier hit her squarely, only this time with the force of salvation. *If I am to have his son, and that boy will be born in nineteen-fifty, then I am safe until then. Safe! Nothing can harm me. And if nothing can harm me, why am I afraid? I'll tell you why,* she told herself. *Fate starves at probability's door!*

Yes! Yes! Do You hear that, Lord God? Fate starves at Probability's door. Your divine addiction has starved you, and Probability is knocking. Only the Reunion can save You.

Nonsense, Dear Goddess! Though I love You, I cannot abide Your nagging! It is Probability that starves at Fate's door. It is already written.

Meiying slunk back under the covers when the voices returned, and beneath their deceptively warm comfort, trembled for her sanity. These voices said things that made no sense—that frightened her beyond words.

~

It was late afternoon the next day when Suling finally visited.

"How wonderful you are here!" gushed Meiying.

Suling seemed taken aback by her effusiveness and replied, "It is nice to see you looking so well. I have brought some food. Buandelgereen suggested I come and sit with you a while. Look what I've brought. Some soup and bread and even a sweet I have been saving from the last caravan."

"Yes, Buandelgereen has been a steadfast nurse."

"She has taken good care of you, I can see that."

"Suling, what is the latest news?" asked Meiying in a somber tone.

"What do you mean?"

"Well, I've been sick for so long, what's happening outside this room? Anything of interest?"

"Not really. You haven't been cooped up that long."

"It seems a lifetime!"

"We miss your concerts and can't wait for you to start up again."

"Madame Liu?"

"The same. Perhaps a little worse."

"Ah. Has Lu Zhishen blasted open the iron door yet," laughed Meiying.

"No, poor man."

"What do you hear from Child of Buddha?"

Meiying noticed Suling color a little. "Nothing."

"Come on, Suling. I can tell there's something."

"Oh, her usual worry about the Precious Object."

"And?"

"That's it. She can't quite pin down the messages—that frustrates her—and she has concerns about Buandelgereen."

"What concerns?"

"I don't know."

"Do you?"

Suling tilted her head a bit too much. "Do I what?"

Meiying chuckled. "You know what I mean. Do you have concerns about Buandelgereen?"

"Not at all. Look how well she's taken care of you."

Meiying ignored the statement and declared with impatience, "No, no. I mean, you are close to Child of Buddha. You know she says something bad is about to happen, don't you?"

"Well, yes."

"Is there anything new about that?"

"Not that I know of."

Meiying sighed in frustration. "Suling, you would tell me, wouldn't you? I'm really not that ill. In fact, I'm feeling much better. You can tell me."

"I honestly don't know, but I do know that John has been very worried."

"Oh?"

"Yes, he's asking many questions. Driving Buandelgereen crazy. I'm sure when we are finished with our visit, he will drive me crazy with questions. Do you want to see him?"

"Not just yet."

"Ah. I'll tell him you're still not up to it."

"Yes, please."

Suling rose and started to say her goodbyes when Meiying grabbed her sleeve.

"His voices?" she asked.

Suling looked down. "Come and go. But right now, they're bad. Maybe it's because he is worried about you. They always seem to get worse when he is stressed."

"Yes, they've been busy."

"What do you mean?"

"Nothing. I just wish they would leave him alone."

"Nothing more than that?"

Meiying hesitated. "No."

Suling looked at her with compassion. "Meiying, what do you think of John?"

"He's a nice man."

"Oh, that says a lot!"

"Well, he is."

"Meiying, he has pined for you ever since he first met you. We both know you have . . . other interests. What do you plan to do with him?"

Meiying took her hand. "Oh, Suling, I really don't know. There are other considerations."

"This thing about a son?"

Meiying looked surprised. "How do you know?"

Now it appeared Suling was taken aback. "He's told me, and so have you. I am sure of it. Anyway, it's strange I admit. But still, he loves you."

"Yes, I know."

Suling waited until Meiying looked her in the eyes. "So, what do you plan to do with him?"

Meiying turned on her. "He's not my property! I don't know! I told you, I don't know! What do you want me to say?"

Suling was nothing if not tenacious. "Will you have his son?"

Meiying laughed almost hysterically. "Thank god that decision is far in the future! Too far to think about, or to talk about."

"But you do."

"Suling, we'll probably all be dead by then."

Suling nodded. "Some of us."

"Do you miss Tang Yuwei very much?" asked Meiying with the obvious and rather clumsy attempt to change topics. Suling would have none of it.

"I don't think of him much anymore. My life is here."

"Ha!" scoffed Meiying. "You don't think of him any more than I don't think of John. Besides, 'here' is so narrow!"

Suling smiled. "I cannot play the piano. There are no concerts waiting for me in Beijing or Paris. I am content."

"Oh, Suling, I do so want to be content. If it means no concerts, then so be it. You would be surprised to know I just want to live a quiet life in peace. No more of this . . . horror!"

"Alas, the ways of men will not allow peace for very long. We must make our own peace."

"And how will you find peace?"

Suling shook her head. "I don't know. For a long time, I thought meeting *her* would bring peace, but now it seems. . . . "

"Yes, it seems impossible."

"I did not say impossible, but life is difficult. We are the lucky ones."

Meiying sighed. "Not for long, if the prediction of Child of Buddha is correct. Bad times are coming again."

Suling again rose to leave. "So be it. Perhaps she is wrong. She has been wrong before."

"Perhaps, but this time I think not."

"Ah, Meiying, you are not in a good place now. You are ill, and your illness clouds your judgment. You will see, all will be well. Now you must rest. I'll return soon."

The next day Feng Shiren returned with bad news.

~ *More Trouble* ~

Arriving unexpectedly on a rag-tag caravan, Feng Shiren spoke rapidly even before he leapt off the camel.

"Japs are on their way!"

"Here?" cried Lu Zhishen.

"Yes."

"Why?" asked Master Zhou.

"They think you're hiding communists."

"But we're not! What makes them think—"

Feng cut him off and said loudly, "No more questions until we take care of our caravan friends and send them safely on their way!" He smiled broadly at the caravan leader and encouraged everyone to busy themselves with unloading the camels. When the process was in full swing, he whispered to Master Zhou, "You still have silver?"

"Of course, it's about the only good money now."

"Pay them off and let them go. I have told them the Japs are coming—they won't stay."

Master Zhou brightened. "So, the Japs aren't coming?"

"No such luck. They are coming. And soon. Hurry and pay them as soon as we are finished unpacking."

"Yes, yes." For the first time, Master Zhou noticed Feng wore rags and appeared half-starved.

That evening the group met in the dining hall where Feng had let it be known he would make a few remarks.

Anticipation ran high as Feng rose to speak. Consistent with his nature, he had refused to reveal anything until every member of the group had gathered. He began by holding out his hands, palms up, and announced loudly, "Friends and comrades! I have come to once again save you from the fire of war. But first, a brief story about where I have been and what I have been doing. To entice you a bit more, my story involves Mr. President and his palace, along with the Japs and others who some of you know.

"When I left, I knew your safety was assured and therefore felt no compunction in leaving. Had I known what awaited me, I would not have gone. My troubles began almost immediately. How? With an obstinate camel! Just after we squeezed through the Flaming Cliffs, we decided to bed down for the night. No problem. But when I awoke the next morning, my camel had wandered off. The others laughed and told me to find him or they would leave me behind. Naturally, I went looking, following the fresh footprints as best I could. Before I knew it, I was lost. Ridiculous! Me, Feng Shiren lost! But I was. Fool that I am, I overestimated my abilities in the desert.

"I found the damn camel at last, but she wanted to return to the compound and I had to tug hard on her rope to go in the direction I wanted. At last, she relented, and we were on our way—somewhere, anywhere. After three days of aimless riding, I spotted a group of camels with riders and assumed it was my caravan. Of course, in my defense, it certainly was impossible to see at such distances, so I rode confidently toward them. Only as I approached did I see that they were not my caravan. Worse, they looked like brigands ready to slit my throat for the clothes on my back and my camel. But it was too late, so I rode up to their group smiling and singing a dirty song. Come what may."

Feng took a swig of rice wine and looked out at the group with an absurd smile on his face. "So, you will never guess what I found out from them. They were looking for me! Me, Feng Shiren! So, I felt good and assumed that if they looked for me, they did not want me dead. They didn't. They wanted me alive all right. Alive for Mr. President. Of all the nonsense. Mr. President! His long arms reached all the way into the Mongolian desert. Oh, sure, some of the riders were locals, hired mercenaries, but still! I could only admire his tentacles. Even the Japs didn't have those grubby arms and grasping fingers.

"Anyway, when I arrived, they were astonished that Mohammad had come to the mountain. They could not believe their luck. I just dropped into their laps. Best of all, for me, is that they had ample quantities of wine. The idea of traveling to Mr. President's palace suited me, so I offered no resistance. But believe me, my spirits dampened when they informed me that first we had to report to the Japs. 'Why?' I asked. Well, their answer knocked me over. An officer named Ichida—who some of us know—wanted to see me first. Seems I was wanted for murdering a Jap agent!"

After saying this, Feng paused and winked at Meiying. "Well, of course, I'm innocent of such a spurious charge, but they cared nothing about that, nor did they seem willing to listen. All that they knew was that they had their man. I was chained like a slave and carted off toward Mr. President's palace."

Amidst cries of sympathy from the group, Feng put up his hand. "At least, that was their plan." He paused for effect.

"You escaped!" blurted Lu Zhishen.

"Yes, you sly bastard!" added Master Zhou.

Feng jabbed a finger at Lu. "You're right, you big, bearded Canadian!"

"I knew it!" cried Lu, looking around for kudos.

Once he had gauged the reaction of the group to his satisfaction, Feng collapsed into fake despair. "But they caught me. Twice! I couldn't get the damn chains off. So, I tried to reason with the fools. 'Look,' I said. 'I'm just a little face-changer. Why do you want to treat me like this? We are all Chinese.' But they beat me for my troubles and I stopped that quick. I said to myself, 'Feng Shiren, old boy, how are you going to get out of this?' And then it came to me."

Again he stopped for effect.

Tired of his oratorical machinations, Child of Buddha shouted, "Go on, you damn idiot! Get to whatever it is that would interest us! We don't have much time!"

Feng hesitated at this unexpected revolt.

"The Japs, remember?" she coaxed.

"I'm getting there," grumbled Feng and waggling his head in disapproval as if shaking off an annoying mosquito. He continued more animated than ever. "Where was I? Oh, yes. And then it came to me! Since I actually wanted to see Mr. President and his palace again, and ultimately they were taking me there, I would just have to make the best of my time with the Japs. Obviously, they were not going to kill me, since I was on my merry way with this sorry group to see Mr. President. So, I says to myself, 'Good man Feng Shiren, let the Japs do their worst and enjoy it!' Then I begged for more wine from my flea-infested hosts who, in that regard, were quite generous."

Feng smiled at the group, inviting their admiration, which he received from most. Only Madame Liu sat stone-faced, lost in her own lostness. When he glanced at her blank face, his mood darkened and he continued in a more serious vein.

"We circled around Dalandzadgad, and when at last we reached the Jap lines, I was received by Captain Ichida, an old friend who had been promoted from lieutenant. Bai Meiying and I knew him well when we were with the Japs, but his personal connection to us goes way back—all the way to the Taiyuan days and beyond. I must say, he treated me with courtesy, much to the disappointment of those fanatics around him who wanted to use me for bayonet practice."

Feng shuddered. "God knows I saw enough of that. But, anyway, Captain Ichida made me at home and offered sake, which I, of course, accepted with the greatest enthusiasm. 'Mr. Feng,' he says politely. 'Why is it that every time I see you or Miss Bai, some of my comrades have been murdered?' 'Oh? Who?' I asked innocently. He replies, 'Wang Liwei, otherwise known as Beethoven.' I cleverly reply, 'Don't know him.' He laughed a good, hearty laugh. The kind of laugh I like, so I join him. 'Beethoven is a funny name,' says I. 'Yes, and he had a funny death,' says Captain Ichida. 'So,' says I. 'He was your comrade?' 'Not exactly,' says he. Then he stared at me long and hard. So long and hard that even I started to feel uncomfortable."

Feng looked at John. "You know him, right, John?"

"Yes, I knew him. We met in Taiyuan. He took my English language course. Why?"

"Because he mentioned you. Said you were one of the few Americans he had ever met. But his interest lies principally in Bai Meiying, not you or me. In fact, he seemed to care very little about me or about the murder of his agent Beethoven. Now, here is the strange part. He told me to beware of Mr. President, as if I didn't know. And he then told me he would see all of you very soon. 'Oh?' I says all innocent. 'Yes, we will be visiting the compound where Miss Bai's group is hiding. Intelligence thinks they are sheltering communists there.' Well, I'm amazed he would tell a lowly Chinese beggar about what his intelligence thinks, so I figure he is trying to warn me. But then I think, how can I warn them if I'm a prisoner? It was a puzzle. He is a puzzle. Odd fellow for a Japanese."

Feng had paused, this time not for effect, but as if he were trying to remember something or figure something out.

"So, then what happened?" urged Master Zhou.

"Nothing," shrugged Feng Shiren. "The Japs just let me go on with the caravan. I reckon Captain Ichida was responsible for that. May have given him some trouble with his Jap comrades. Still, I am grateful to him. Odd fellow. Anyway, long story short, we arrived at Mr. President's palace a few weeks later. No easy matter, I can tell you that. Had trouble all along the way. Bandits, warlords, communists, Nationalists, you name it. Never seen so many starving Chinese. Made me sick. Dead everywhere. Flies everywhere. Decay everywhere.

"But, when we reached the palace sitting splendidly in the middle of that glistening lake, all the agonies of the world fell away and we entered paradise. As you all know, its opulence is unmatched. Even I, man-of-the-world that I am, was dazzled like a stupid child watching fireworks. However, as we all also know, beneath the gold gild of a dead beetle, exquisite though the pendant may be, lies corruption and decay. The stench of that palace could not be masked no matter how much incense and perfume filled the air. Being Feng Shiren, I immediately recognized this simple fact."

"I thought you said you were dazzled!" exclaimed Child of Buddha, adding in a biting tone, "Like a stupid child."

Feng rolled his eyes. "Only for a moment. But seriously, comrades, our beloved Meiying is aware of its rotten core. Is that not true, bright one?"

All eyes turned on Meiying, who stared at Feng with tears rolling freely down her cheeks.

"Yes," continued Feng. "All who touch the web of Mr. President, no matter how slight the quiver, are damaged. Those unfortunate enough to be trapped are soon reduced to lifeless mummies."

"And you, Mr. Feng?" boomed a voice from the back. "Are you trapped or did you escape with only minor damage?"

Feng Shiren appeared momentarily speechless. He quickly recovered, but not before the power of that voice was made manifest to the others by his startled reaction.

"Ah, Buandelgereen! So good to be in your distinguished presence again. I see you have found safe harbor behind these walls."

"Are you just damaged or are you a lifeless mummy?" insisted the Mongol woman.

Feng bowed low and swept his arms out in a grand gesture of obeisance. "I am neither and I am both, comrade."

"Pssst! I am not your little pet communist! What an answer!" She snorted and wagged her finger at him. "Mere sophistry."

"Let him finish!" scolded Master Zhou in his best authoritative voice. "I want to know what happened at the palace."

"Yes, so do we all," added John, whose attention had been riveted from the beginning.

Lu Zhishen jumped in impatiently and picked up the thread of the story. "So, you arrived at the palace and saw immediately that it was a corrupt place. Okay, then what?"

"Well," said Feng, now pacing back and forth, fully absorbed in the narrative. "This is where it gets interesting."

~

Before he could continue, Ishmael burst into the room. "Japanese soldiers are at the gate!"

In the stunned silence, Madame Liu's now frail voice declared, "Let them in. My husband will talk with them."

"Well, let them in!" boomed Master Zhou. "We have nothing to hide!"

"I already let them in," said Ishmael sheepishly.

"What—" Master Zhou started to say when another voice rang out.

"Please!" shouted a Japanese who enunciated in excellent Chinese from the back. "Everyone remain in the room!"

All eyes now peered through the dim lantern light at a group of Japanese soldiers. An officer stepped forward and made a slight bow, accompanied close behind by his interpreter with the booming voice.

Feng Shiren recognized the face and broke into a broad smile. "Ah! Captain Ichida! Welcome! We have been expecting you."

Ichida said something to his men, who stayed put. He stepped nearer to the lantern light and looked around. "So, this is the famous group of pilgrims on a quest to find an enlightened lady."

His eyes lit on John. "Ah, Mr. Powers, my old teacher," he said in English, bowing slightly.

John rose, bowed in return, and said, "Good to see you also, Captain Ichida. Congratulations on your promotion. I hope we will have time to talk. Your English continues to be excellent."

"Thank you. And I see Miss Bai is here also."

Meiying bowed, but said nothing.

Master Zhou also bowed and said in broken Japanese, which evidently surprised the captain, "My name is Mister Zhou, the leader of our little group. May I help your soldiers find places to sleep?"

"That would be kind. There are very few of us. Unfortunately, we must leave early tomorrow."

"Ah."

Master Zhou asked Ishmael to find quarters for the soldiers, and the little Mongol, assuming the role of humble servant, trotted off with a sergeant. Captain Ichida and the group stared at each other through the reddish-orange lantern light, shadows carving deep chasms around each illuminated face. Ichida's ever-present interpreter hovered nearby.

Master Zhou cleared his throat. "Captain Ichida, may I ask what we can do for you?"

Ichida spoke rapidly, making it difficult for the interpreter to keep up.

"Well, first I wish to speak privately with Mr. Powers, for old times sake, and Miss Bai, about other matters. Then, I need to speak with Mr. Feng here, as we have much to discuss, without the face-changing to distract us, of course." He chuckled, and quickly turned serious. "Then, I wish to meet with you, Mister Zhou, to discuss certain items of necessity."

Feng barged in. "Ah! You are curious about my stay with Mr. President, I presume?"

"That would be one matter, yes."

"There are more?"

"Certainly."

"Such as?"

"Later!" Ichida snapped. "Now I wish to speak with Mr. Powers alone."

At that moment, Ishmael returned. "Your soldiers are taken care of, and your own room is ready, sir."

"Yes, good." Ichida turned to his interpreter. "Go make sure Sergeant Yamuri has guards placed. Now I want to speak with John Powers. The rest of you may leave. I will call for the other two later."

John felt frightened and confused. How was he to address Captain Ichida now? Were they all going to be placed under arrest? With America in the war, he was a hostile alien. Was it to be a prison camp? Or worse? His imagination ran riot, but he commanded himself to stay calm and friendly, as if no unpleasantness had occurred since their last meeting in Taiyuan.

After the others had left, both men stared at each other without speaking. Ichida seemed intent on John being the first to break the impasse, and being an American, John obliged.

"Captain Ichida, why do you not speak Chinese? The others think you don't know how."

Ichida smiled, his teeth glistening in the light, but not at all in a malevolent way, rather in the manner of someone sharing an absurd fact. "Because, teacher, I want the Chinese to think I am far too superior to have learned their language."

"Ah."

Captain Ichida laughed again. "Do you believe in evolution?"

John smiled at the reference to a conversation they once had. "No. I accept evolution, based on the evidence. Scientific evidence. All civilized, educated people think the same. Even Japanese and Americans can agree on that."

"Ha!" cried Ichida. "Some Japanese and some Americans!"

John felt much better. He noticed Ichida's sword. "Do you remember much of Taiyuan?" he asked.

Ichida snorted. "Of course! You were my first American. I learned to say 'Mr. Powers' instead of 'Mr. John' from you."

John felt suddenly awkward. His relief at Ichida's friendly attitude was palpable, and he wanted to hug the Japanese and call him Nobaru, but the old fears inhibited his freedom of action and he could hear the voices rumbling insults from deep within. "Yes, I remember," was all he could manage in response.

Ichida evidently did not notice John's distress, but he looked down as if confronting his own painful memory. "I have talked to my sword often since those days, and it tells me we are going to lose this war." He glanced up at John to gauge the effect and waited.

John shrugged. "We are isolated here . . . only news is sporadic and unreliable."

Outside, the Mongolian wind picked up and whistled through the cracks, but rather than seeming ominous, it made their discussion somehow more intimate, more confidential.

"We will lose this war, John, mainly due to your country. Oh, be assured I hold no grudge. We attacked your naval base first. Nevertheless, it is hard. After all, I am still Japanese. But what is worse is the reaction of my fellow soldiers. Although they are told we are winning, most know otherwise. They have become more brutal as they become more frightened. It has sickened me. War kills the innocents and makes more brutal the already brutal."

Again, he paused, during which John had a sudden thought.

"Captain Ichida, can I offer you some wine?"

"Call me Nobaru, please John. Yes, I'll gladly have some wine." He chuckled. "Any sake?"

"Unfortunately, no." John poured two cups and they sat close together. "Nobaru, if I had sake, I would toast to all the good people of the world. To all the innocents, may they live!"

After downing his cup and tapping his fingers on the table to have John fill it again, he said, "You must be wondering why I've come, John?"

"Yes, of course, though I am truly glad to see you."

"I'm sure!"

Both laughed.

"You will not be happy, John."

"Oh?"

"I am here to take something very precious to you."

John's stomach tightened and his mind reeled at the prospect of losing Meiying yet again.

"No, not her. I'll leave her with you, although I would sorely like to take her."

"What, then?" John's voice trembled.

"The statue you told me about in Taiyuan. What you call the Precious Object."

~ *Captain Ichida Explains* ~

"You see," continued Ichida. "I am being transferred to Indochina. To Hanoi. It's all part of the Greater East Asia Co-Prosperity Sphere, you know. Ah! What a delusion of our leaders. Fools! The same idiots who ordered the attack on Pearl Harbor! The wine makes me too talkative, but what the hell. I'm sure I'll still be there with those Vietnamese barbarians when the damn war ends. Then it will be every man for himself. I need something valuable to ensure my ability to make my way back home. Everything of value here is snapped up by higher-ranking officers. None of them know about your statue." He swallowed another cup and tapped for more. "That is why I need it."

John looked upon his friend in horror. Without the Precious Object, it was very likely *she* would never appear again. He had a vague suspicion that *she* resided inside the Precious Object, or that the Precious Object was *her* doorway to the human world. It was all very confusing, but he was certain the statue must stay. Without it, the group would be left in the compound bereft of hope, dry husks withering away.

Even in his cups, Captain Ichida perceived the stricken look in John's face. "Ha! Don't worry! At least I'm not taking Miss Bai. I could, you know. I could take her for myself, as well as the damn statue. After all, I am an officer in the Imperial Army of the Empire of Japan, and you are. . . . "

It appeared he caught himself when he observed John staring down at the table, afraid to speak. His tone changed. "John, I could have you all used for bayonet practice. My prerogative. But I won't, John. I won't. I'm better than that. I'm better than them."

His face contorted in rage. "I'm better than all of them, but they don't know it! Martinets, all of them. What do they know of beauty, poetry, philosophy, compassion, humanity? God, it makes me sick, John." Raising his hand in a futile gesture, he rolled his eyes heavenward. "My mother didn't raise me to be a murderer!"

"You're no murderer," John said quietly.

"What?"

"You're no murderer. You have a conscience."

"Yes."

"And, Nobaru, since you have a conscience, let us keep the Precious Object."

"Can't."

"You can if you want."

"No. I have my own life to think of. I must return to my mother alive. There is no other way. My family in Japan will need me. The years after the war will be terrible!"

"Nobaru, what does your sword say?"

Ichida slammed his sword on the table and addressed it. "Sword! What do you say?"

He shook it. "What?" he cried. "I can't hear you!"

He put his ear next to it.

For a moment, John thought he had fainted, as Ichida had not moved a muscle. "What does it say?" he asked finally.

"Oh, it says to take both the Precious Object and Bai Meiying."

"No!" stammered John.

Ichida laughed. "Just kidding. Now, teacher, you must leave. I have to see the lady herself."

"Why do you need to see her?"

"Don't push it, John. I have my reasons. Go and ask her to come."

Ichida jumped up from the table and bowed. "Now, goodbye!"

John wanted to stay and talk with him like a friend and confidant, but something in Ichida's last words chilled him with their finality, and he left quickly after bowing and saying his goodbyes.

He found Meiying waiting outside, pacing nervously. When he approached, she shuddered and said, "So soon?"

~

Upon entering, Captain Ichida offered Meiying a seat at the table across from him. She noticed his red face and watched him fill another cup. It was obvious he had had too much to drink already, and her fear increased tenfold.

"Well," he said gruffly. "Have you finished murdering my people or are there others who you still wish to kill?"

She had no idea how to respond and stared dumbly at her lap, kneading her fingers and remembering what happened to Meili. Yet, in spite of all her heartaches and sorrows, she became fully aware of how much she wanted to live, and this realization surprised her by cutting so readily though her fear, crystallizing her mindfulness and making her see Captain Ichida as just another blustering male.

Captain Ichida had watched Meiying's downturned face and interpreted it as devoid of every emotion except intimidation and fear. "Teacher Powers likes you," he said in a softer tone.

She did not reply.

He reached out to lift her chin, but stopped millimeters from her face. Still holding out his hand, he asked, "Are you mute?"

"Your Chinese is excellent," she said.

"Ha! A non-sequitur if ever I heard one!" Seemingly relieved, he gulped down another cup and poured a fresh one. "Besides, I've already gone over that territory with Mr. Powers. Ask him about it if you are wondering why I pretend not to speak the language. Now, do you know why I want to talk with you?"

"No."

"Come, Meiying, we are friends. Recall, I helped you not so long ago. In fact, I helped you in ways you will never know."

"I think I can guess, and for that I am very grateful."

"You will be happy to know I do not want to talk about murder, though Beethoven was a man in need of being murdered."

She smiled at last and he paused to admire her beauty downing another cup and refilling it.

"Wine?" he asked.

"No, thank you."

"I would offer you tea but . . . damn it! Miss Bai, do you consider me a good man?"

"Yes."

"No, no, no! I want you to think about it. Am I a good man?"

Meiying seemed to relax. "Yes, I think you are."

"In spite of what my countrymen have done to your country?"

"Those are two separate questions."

"Yes, it's true, and I do not want you to answer the second one."

Again he paused, then said, "Let me give you a tip, Miss Bai. Beware of Beethoven's uncle. He is the true murderer, as if we all aren't murderers these days. But he"—Captain Ichida wagged his finger—"has already murdered, or arranged to have murdered, one of your group."

Meiying looked at him with an unreadable expression.

"You want to know who but are afraid to ask, correct?"

"Yes."

"Mr. Peter Hedley. In Taiyuan."

"But, why?"

Observing her tremble ever so slightly, Ichida said sympathetically, "That I cannot tell you. But I can tell you he works for Mr. President. Furthermore, you are actually in great danger, not to be too dramatic about it."

"Beethoven's uncle?"

"Yes, and I've already told you too much." He leaned forward and whispered, "He and Mr. President. But, that is not why I asked you here."

Meiying waited while he reattached his sword and reached for his valise, from which he withdrew a sheaf of papers. "I have a favor to ask of you in exchange for my little advice—well, that and for not killing you."

"Killing me?"

"Of course, for the murders of Colonel Naguma and my agent Beethoven. Now,"—he waved his hand to dismiss the topic—"do you have a piano here?"

"Yes."

"I thought so." He held up the papers. "These are scores, Japanese melodies. All very short and simple. Yes, for you, quite simple. I want you to play these for me tonight. A command performance for one. Then, I will be gone and you will remain with your group, untouched and unharmed. Do you need time to practice or can you sight-read?"

Meiying quickly leafed through the scores. "Not much. Just give me a half-hour or so."

Ichida raised his eyebrows. "No other questions?"

"One other if you please," she murmured.

"Yes?"

"The kitten you so generously gave me, is he . . . ?"

Ichida laughed kindly. "I gave it to our medical officer who looked after it as if it were his own child. You see, there are bright spots in these dark times."

"Thank you."

"Other questions, lovely Chinese pianist?"

Meiying shook her head.

His eyes crinkled around the edges and he gave her a skeptical look. "I can't believe that intelligent brain of your does not have any questions."

Again, she shook her head.

He looked at her admiringly. "Excellent."

~

That night, Meiying played a succession of Japanese folk tunes, all quite sentimental. Captain Ichida sat in a straight-back chair facing away from her. She never saw his face until the last chord had faded away. Bowing deeply, he said, "Thank you, Miss Bai. It has been so long, you do not know. . . ." Without finishing the sentence, he retired.

The next morning, Captain Ichida and his men departed without taking the Precious Object. He never met with Feng Shiren or Master Zhou. Watching them disappear in the distance, John turned to Child of Buddha.

"Was that your bad news?"

The hunchback merely laughed and headed back toward the building where the Precious Object awaited in silent confidence that it had never been in danger of being removed from its place of honor, yet knowing that years hence, it had a rendezvous with John's son in Vietnam.

John blanched at her strange laughter, and the voices took their cue.

Yes, John Powers, you must prepare for the son. But now I have other matters to which I must attend.

Yes, Sweet and Sour Goddess, You do, but any preparations by You make me tremble.

Beloved God, they should. The Reunion approaches. But, that must wait for another war in another place at another time. Of course, to You—such a Great and Glorious Metaphorical God—time is meaningless.

Only if not in Your hands, Great and Conspiratorial Metaphorical Goddess.

All you need to know, dear John Powers, is that the time is drawing near, and decisions must be made.

~

These were the last words John heard from the voices for a very long time.

Chapter Ten

An Ending

Happy News

Life continued in the compound without further disruption for two more years, until one auspicious day news arrived that Japan had surrendered. The happy tidings arrived without warning, on a day the group assumed would proceed as any other: early rise, rice gruel for breakfast, work in the gardens, vegetables with rice gruel for lunch, more work in the gardens, and more rice gruel with whatever protein was available for dinner. It was late September and a deep chill could already be felt from the northern steppes. Everyone had known Japan was losing the war, but information arrived only sporadically, and nothing new had been heard for almost two months. It was an article of faith among the group that every day the schedule had to be kept in order for the compound to run smoothly, so every day the monotonous tasks were performed automatically. Even Feng Shiren and Lu Zhishen kept the daily schedule, and their perpetual complaining about being cooped-up and unwillingly made into "useless monks" eventually petered out. Other than an occasional caravan, isolation and routine characterized their lives.

Meiying's spirits had somehow been permanently revived since Captain Ichida's visit years earlier, and she enthusiastically performed on the piano every weekend. Even she could not explain her transformation, but she accepted it without agonizing over the whys and wherefores. New music, when available, was always a hit, and when nothing new arrived, the old stand-bys filled the long stretches of time. Other than the caravans, there was no radio, no gossip, no telegraph, and no other form of communication with the outside world. The Precious Object remained silent, *she* never appeared, and even John's voices seemed subdued in the face of such tedium. Likes and dislikes faded into an amorphous whole, and constant boredom, only occasionally punctuated by a break from the everyday (such as illness or a broken bone) shaded their lives.

Madame Liu died quietly, mumbling her husband's name and recognizing no one except Master Zhou. Lu Zhishen once had the idea of bringing the Precious Object into her room to help jog her memory, but she took one look at it and screamed in terror, or anger, no one could tell, and it was quickly removed. Afterward, Child of Buddha spent two days with her ear to the statue, hoping for some sign, but none came. Such was the unceasing drumbeat of their existence.

John and Meiying spent more time together, for though she remained close to Buandelgereen, their relationship now seemed on equal terms, and she became increasingly more independent from the Mongol woman. Buandelgereen herself became a fixture of the group, assuming an unspoken leadership role which she shared with Master Zhou. Meiying gladly acceded her position to Buandelgereen's greater experience, while Child of Buddha acted independently of everyone. The one controversy that kept them all in heated discussion was the Mongol woman's habit of surreptitiously disappearing for days or weeks at a time from the compound, only to reappear with no explanation, other than she "needed to get some air." Feng Shiren vowed to follow her, and twice he tried, only to return shortly afterward with puzzled explanations that she had somehow lost him.

But news of the war's end did not bring the anticipated peace. If anything, the countryside became more dangerous. Communists were on the move and the entire nation of China braced for a renewal of civil war. Mongolia itself was becoming just another battleground, and Soviet operatives from Russia were seen everywhere. It was during this unsettled time that an important meeting of the group was called by Master Zhou. The death of Madame Liu had hit him hard, and he appeared more stooped and haggard than usual when he stood before them.

"My funds are almost gone," he began bluntly. "Unless we find some source of income, we cannot stay. Madame Liu's estate continues to provide, but I have word of unhappy relatives in Shanghai who contest the will's bequest. Now that the war is over, the vultures are circling and swooping down to feed off the innumerable carcasses that litter our country. Worse, if the communists win, I must flee or they will surely kill me. I am, after all, a landlord, though my estate is managed by a fool from the same class they extol."

Tears filled his eyes. "I have come to love it here, but it seems apparent *she* cannot or will not return, and as a consequence, all my hopes and dreams have been dashed. You all must make your own plans."

"What if we want to stay?" asked Lu Zhishen, shocking them all, for he was always the one to complain loudest about staying at the compound.

Master Zhou shrugged resignedly. "Without payment, the local Mongol clans will take it back over."

"Or it will be expropriated by the Soviets," added John.

"Don't forget our own Chinese communists!" threw in Feng Shiren. "They wouldn't hesitate for a moment, and shoot us all in the bargain!"

Suling, ever the patient one, ever the mediator, seemed hardest hit by the news. She remained silent, but desolation cratered her face. John felt a deep wave of pity.

"What happens to the Precious Object?" asked Child of Buddha. "What happens to me?"

When no one had an answer, she added, "An ugly, useless hunchback. I'll starve."

With this bleak statement, the room fell deathly quiet.

~

At that moment, John fantasized that *she* would surely make a grand entrance and assure them all that everything would be fine; *her* words would be spoken like a parent soothing *her* children who have awakened from a nightmare. But no. Only the perpetual Mongolian wind and infinities of sand particles crackled against the walls of the building.

Master Zhou held out his hands, palms up. "I have no more answers for you, my friends, just empty palms."

In the stunned silence that followed, eyes sought out other eyes for a sign. Any sign. John stared only at Meiying, willing her to look at him, but she appeared involved in an evidently intense discussion with Buandelgereen. Still, he did not let his gaze waver. An idea had been forming in his mind for some time, only partially hatched, but one he increasingly came to embrace. *Now is the time*, he thought.

But before he had a chance to speak with Meiying, a disturbance on the other side of the room interrupted his plan. It took a while, but he eventually made out Lu Zhishen's voice becoming louder and more boisterous until it became a raging torrent of pent-up frustration.

"I have it! God damn it! I have it! More than enough!"

Someone was trying to shush him, but he would have none of it.

"No use now! Nothing to lose! I've accumulated more than enough, and I'm going to use it! Don't tell me to be quiet! I'm doing it today! Damn it! Today!"

Master Zhou took some time restoring order, and when the clatter of everyone talking at once died down, he looked calmly at Lu Zhishen.

"You will do what?"

"Blow that damn iron door, of course! I have collected more than enough dynamite. Have had enough for over a year."

"Why now?"

Lu sneered. "Isn't that obvious? If *she's* in there, I'm going to wring *her* neck for making us all go through so much. Nothing any of you say can stop me this time!"

Suling sighed audibly, but made no objection. Nor did anyone else. It seemed the time had come for silent acquiescence to drastic measures. Such is the way of the world, when drastic men grasp a fleeting moment of doubt and uncertainty to raise themselves into the light while plunging the rest of the world into darkness.

"Well, at least we'll go out with a bang!" shouted Feng Shiren, leaping into one of his operatic poses.

Sorely needed laughter rippled through the room. During the outburst, no one had noticed Ishmael step up next to Master Zhou. When the tittering over Feng's statement had died down, the Mongol said sternly, "This compound is Mongol property. You will not damage it. I cannot allow such destruction."

Master Zhou appeared dumbfounded. The Mongol servant, always docile and solicitous, now stood before them as if Genghis Khan had been resurrected.

"But, I will only blow the locking mechanism," stammered Lu Zhishen. "It won't be like the cave."

"It isn't just that," replied Ishmael. "We are all sworn to defend *her*."

"So!" pounced Lu. "You admit *she* is behind that door!"

"If you do this thing," warned Ishmael. "I will have every Mongol within one hundred kilometers travel here to seal your fate." He swept out his arms in a grand gesture. "All of your fates!"

"At least before I die, I'll know the truth," said Lu in a rather weak, defensive tone, clearly shaken by the Mongol's words.

"You will know nothing," replied Ishmael. "*She* will not let it happen."

"How will *she* stop me?"

Ishmael smiled fiercely. "Oh, *she* has *her* ways."

Feng Shiren said, "I thought only your Mongol brothers from one hundred kilometers around could stop him?"

Ishmael looked at him calmly. "Oh, no. They will come to be witnesses at the trial."

"Trial?"

"Yes. The trial of Lu Zhishen, and maybe the rest of you, for attempted murder."

Lu exploded, "What nonsense!"

"It is not nonsense," said Buandelgereen in a clear, commanding voice. She spoke softly, but her eyes fairly shone with intense . . . intense what? John tried to read the meaning in those eyes, but it was as if his own retinas were singed in the process. He had to avert his gaze and blink away the burning sensation. *One could go blind staring directly at her*, he thought. He noticed Meiying, who sat next to her, shrink away as from a flame.

Lu Zhishen backed down with barely a whimper. "Well, I didn't know," he mumbled.

With this confrontation defused, the meeting broke-up and the group milled around as if a collective daze had befallen them. Buandelgereen now stood in a corner talking with Ishmael, so John took advantage of this chance to approach Meiying. He grabbed her arm with some urgency and said, "Can I talk to you outside? Let's go for a walk."

"Yes," she said distractedly, her attention focused on her lover and Ishmael, who were both still involved in some heated discussion.

John took her hand and gently led her from the room. Once outside, the unexpectedly fierce gusts of wind and corrosive sting of sand forced them to stumble half-blind into a nearby building. When they entered, the Precious Object sat ever vigilant, greeting them with supreme indifference. Only then did they realize the irony of their unintentional choice of refuge.

"Hm!" grunted John toward the statue. "Imagine choosing this room of all we could have stumbled into! And just look at her. No tapping. No humming. No nothing. Oh, well, what else is new? Let's sit for a while. I'm not too keen on going outside again just to be away from our Goddess friend." He contemplated her dismissively. "Anyway, she seems quite happy to remain quiet while we talk."

"Yes. Let's sit. I've always liked being in this room."

They sat side-by-side, facing the Precious Object. John sighed deeply and began, tentatively at first.

"Meiying, I've been doing a lot of thinking. We've known the war would end for some time now, and, naturally, I contemplated what to do afterward. Strangely enough, *she* never entered into my considerations. Long ago, I gave up on *her*."

"Oh, that's sad," said Meiying, looking a bit uncomfortable.

"Do you still have faith in *her*?" asked John in a surprised tone that, to Meiying, sounded accusatory.

"Yes."

"Ah, well, it seems we will all have to leave this place. But, Meiying, out there is more war, more killing, more hunger, more chaos and suffering. I am returning to America as soon as possible. I want you to come with me."

"What?" Although Meiying posed the question, she did not appear at all surprised.

"I want you to come with me. In the States, I can be your manager; make concert arrangements; introduce you to important Americans in the music business. Let me help you fulfill your destiny to be a great pianist."

"And in the meantime, Mr. Powers, how would we live?"

John felt the chill of her tone and the distain in her use of such a formal appellation, but lumbered on with his extemporaneous speech. "I can get my old job back, or find a new one. That's a minor issue in the States. Money can be had for those willing to work."

"And how would we deal with the 'minor issue' of our relationship? That's really what this is about, isn't it, John?"

He looked down and waited for the voices to come, lambasting him for his clumsiness, his trite comments, and his cowardly approach. But they remained silent, almost as if afraid to pile-on and make the entire business of his half-baked proposal collapse under its own weight. Intermixed with the sound of his own heartbeat, he thought he heard the Precious Object tapping ever so quietly.

"Yes, Meiying, it is about our relationship. You know how I feel about you, just as I know how you feel about me. You are a lesbian, and I know you would view being married to me as anathema. But, think of it this way, as I have: If we were married, I would not insist on intimate relations, and you would be free to have your own female relationships. All I want is to be around you and help you with your career. It could be a win-win situation for both of us."

"John, being with men is never a win-win situation. There will always be the ... misunderstandings. I would be a stranger in America. My English is terrible, and ... well, I just don't think it would work."

John leaned forward in his chair, conscious of the tapping that slowly became louder. "But it would. It would, Meiying! If you marry me, we can go to America together. You would never be allowed in without being married to an American. Don't you see? It's your escape from war and suffering and hunger. God knows what awaits you back in Shanghai. And this damn civil war! God! Meiying, it's the only way!"

"To have your son?"

"To have our son."

"You know the old saying. 'Instead of staying together in pain, go your separate ways and find your own places in this world.'"

"Our places are to be together and have this child!"

The tapping accelerated and gained in volume so that Meiying now heard it.

"There it is!" she cried. "There it is! This is all about your son!" She wiped tears from her eyes. "I am nothing but a receptacle for the plans of others!" She glared at the tapping Precious Object, her breathing deep and uneven. "His son! His son!" she shrieked to the cadence of the taps.

John had to practically shout over the noise now bellowing from Goddess. "No, Meiying, our son!"

~

In the absence of absence, they will perform the task.

Perhaps, but if You are right, Dear Goddess, We are in for it!

The Reunion, Beloved God. The Earth. All life.

I tremble and earthquakes kill millions. Do You want that on Your feminine conscience?

As You wish, but Your trembling does not cause earthquakes. Humans, not earthquakes, are the issue. Now, the Reunion....

With alarming suddenness, Meiying calmed to an apathetic indifference.

Startled at her change, John asked, "What?"

She looked through him.

"What?" John cried.

Her face remained blank.

"Meiying!"

She murmured, "Our son."

~ *Preparations* ~

Meiying's phrase "our son" hung in the air; a vibrating, passionless hum in Meiying's ears. When she spoke the words, the tapping suddenly stopped as if some mysterious wheel had frozen in place, leaving only the inescapability of providence. This sickening pall of inevitability made her rise without a word and rush out of the room into the bracing wind and scouring sand, which she now welcomed as a cleansing balm to the unclean future that lay before her with grim certainty.

Why fight against it? she asked herself. *A rich life in a rich country at peace. Plenty of food. Concerts, fancy symphony halls, fame. But John as my manager? My husband? My lover? No, no, no. Meili was to be my manager, my lover, my all! And Lihua! It would be such a betrayal!*

So her thoughts ran wild as she leaned against the wind and slowly made her way to her room. When she opened the door, she saw the figure of Buandelgereen sitting in a chair facing the empty bed. Without turning around, Buandelgereen stretched out her hand for Meiying to take. As Meiying stepped forward, the Mongol woman made a sudden pirouette and enfolded her in strong arms.

"You have been talking to John," she said, stroking Meiying's hair.

"Yes."

"And you're tired."

"Yes."

"And you're going with him to America."

"How did you know?"

The Mongol shook her long, black hair and stared into Meiying's eyes. "It is why I am here."

"Why?"

"To see you safely through."

"Through to what?"

"Through the Mysterious Membrane."

"To what?"

"To All That Is." She smiled sweetly. "It involves a Reunion . . . many, many years from now."

"I don't understand."

"You will . . . perhaps one day . . . but perhaps not." Buandelgereen gazed at Meiying's face as if reading the tiniest creases. "No, probably not."

"I don't understand any of it."

"Of course not, dearest one."

"I don't want to go."

"I know."

"I don't want to go."

"You must. You know it. There is no choice. America. It is there you can live. Here, there is no future for you. You must go."

"I don't want to go."

"But you will."

"Yes, I know." Meiying made a face. "His son."

"And *your* son."

With this, Buandelgereen gave Meiying a long kiss and left the room hurriedly, as though she did not believe her own words and desired no evidence remain that she had spoken them. Meiying hesitated, then rushed down the hallway and outside, where no sign of Buandelgereen was to be found. After a cursory search, she went back to her room and slept. The next morning, she was informed by

Master Zhou that Buandelgereen had again disappeared on one of her strange excursions. He did not know when she would return.

"She won't," said Meiying. "Ever."

Master Zhou was in no mood to dwell on the problematic Mongol woman. "So be it. What are your plans?"

"John has asked me to go with him to America."

"For that you must marry him."

"Yes."

"And this is something you agreed to?"

Before she could answer, Feng Shiren appeared from nowhere and good-naturedly joined the conversation. "Forget John, marry me, Meiying. We'll be a team of face-changers!" He laughed to show her it was all a joke. "Travel war-torn China and bring smiles to the doomed."

Meiying laughed in spite of herself. "Shiren, you're such a fool!"

"Marry a fool and we'll be foolish together!"

This time he almost sounded serious, but Master Zhou brought her back to cold reality.

"When and where will you marry?"

"God knows."

Feng Shiren rolled his eyes skyward. "Yes, He may not, but She does. What am I to do with no fair maidens to save?" he asked in a tragic voice.

Meiying turned serious. "Suling and Child of Buddha need saving. Oh, Shiren, save them! Please stay with them!"

"I will not let them die," he replied, equally serious. "It is a solemn oath I have already given."

Meiying's eyes welled-up. "You are a saint, Feng Shiren."

"Oh, it's just a ploy to stay out of Buddhist hell!" he exclaimed with a mischievous grin.

Meiying hugged him and whispered, "You are so good."

"As are you, Little Pianist. Go to America and get rich, then come back and take us all to the most expensive restaurant in Shanghai."

"Ha, ha!" cried Master Zhou. "That would be excellent!"

~

The next few weeks were spent in preparation for leaving; letters written and received, possessions either packed or disbursed, and long, sad conversations with each other carrying the weight of uncertainty and separation. But the issue that had given them the most angst resolved itself unexpectedly when the Precious Object went missing. A frantic search revealed nothing, and Ishmael remained stonily silent when the subject came up. Lu Zhishen volunteered rumors he had heard from two reliable sources that Captain Ichida had it sent to him in Indochina—seems he remained in Saigon after the war, or Hanoi, no one knew for sure. With that last connection gone, all that remained of their dreams was an iron door that would not be opened.

Meiying performed her final concert amid an ocean of tears and regret. The next day, she and John left for Shanghai. As they said their goodbyes, John noticed something new in her—a hardness—that had not been present before, even in the worst of times.

It will be different in America, he told himself.

Fool! boomed a demon voice, reminding him there would be no escape across the ocean from such hallucinations, or madness, or worse, terrible reality.

~ *Return to Taiyuan* ~

As he rode away from the compound on the morning of departure, John often turned to see it growing smaller, until the Flaming Cliffs swallowed it up. Not once did Meiying turn to look. Instead, she sat rigid, facing ahead with a cold, almost frightening severity locked on her features. Their first destination was Dalandzadgad, where John sought out the restaurant-bar they first visited so many years ago. Nationalist Chinese soldiers were everywhere, and a few Russians skulked about, but the town itself seemed little changed, although signs of dilapidation and wartime destruction were evident. By now the sand had become a constant presence, and the sandpaper-like irritation inside one's clothes and eyelids was ignored. The few remaining trees in Dalandzadgad were cause for tears of joy, and Meiying insisted on sitting under a fluttering poplar while John entered the dark bar. She waited until he passed from view, then to every passerby asked, "Do you know Buandelgereen?" in Mongol, but received either no response, or the dismissive "No," or "Never heard of her."

Meanwhile, John made his way into the bar and sat at the same table the group had occupied years earlier. Dark shadows, stale air, and layers of cigarette smoke, all made the place seem sinister and threatening. He ordered a bottle of Russian beer and sipped its warm contents with a complicated mix of feelings. Last time he drank here with his compatriots, Meiying was lost, possibly gone forever, and the compound was a destination full of hope and renewal. Now he drank alone, she sat outside, communing with a tree, and the compound only a point of departure, a fading memory. He began to feel sorry for himself and assumed an air of suffering as he drank. The bus that would take them to the Chinese border was not scheduled to depart for two more hours, all of which time he intended to spend drinking and bringing forth blurry images of his upcoming new life in the States with Meiying. He tried to focus the blurs, but the more he drank, the fuzzier they became.

John slid into a sort of half-awake dream state. The beers kept coming and he gradually lost interest in trying to give edges and corners to his future. Mongols filtered into the bar, but kept their distance from his table, though it was large enough to seat many patrons. Soon, a low rumble of the indecipherable Mongol language acted as white noise and he nodded off.

He dreamed *she* came and sat at his table. Wordlessly, *she* took his hand and stared at him as might a mother—but not any mother he had ever seen—a gorgeous, shimmering vision that cut through the shadows and smoke and Mongol chatter.

"Mr. Powers, how does one justify a life without cruelty, and therefore also without the distilled beauty of cruelty?"

Her palms faced up and *her* figure morphed into the Precious Object, illuminating the entire bar and obliterating all but *Her*. The room exploded in a spectacular burst of blue light and *She* hovered above the table, looking down at John, *Her* features made visible by the glowing blue light. John stared at *Her* in wordless awe. *She* sat in the lotus position on a huge, dazzling white flower. Her sad, contemplative face gazed from beneath an elaborate crown glimmering a kaleidoscope of colors. A cinder-bright jewel embedded in *Her* forehead burned brightly and an intricate necklace lay cradled between *Her* bare breasts. *Her* left hand rested on *Her* thigh, the upturned curve of *Her* fingers resembling the albino legs of a gracefully dead spider; *Her* right hand poised in the air, index finger and thumb touching to form an almost perfect circle while the other fingers radiated outward. He shrank back at such beauty.

But now came a shaking and his heart speeded up at the idea that he was about to die. The earth moved and the building creaked and moaned, swaying violently, on the verge of collapse. He held out his hand, palm-up. Goddess floated down to the table and *she* returned.

"When will you lower your hand?" *she* asked.

He mumbled something while trying to keep the heavy weight of his hand above the surface of the table.

"John!" came Meiying's voice through the fog.

He felt Goddess's warm hand take his and lift it up higher, and he knew he could relax his exhausted muscles, for *she* was there to keep it from falling into the waiting decay of earthly surfaces.

"John! The bus! Hurry!"

He knew it was Meiying calling, but he wanted to ignore it and let himself rest in *her* strength.

"John! Now, or we'll miss it!"

He obeyed, resentful that this woman who preferred a tree to him; a woman who did not even want to go with him, had now roused him from his dream to do the very thing she did not want to do—leave. It was all too confusing and too maddening, but he forced himself and followed her submissively, as if the universe had reversed their preordained roles. Such is the whim of probability and absurdly collapsing wave functions; Meiying would lead him back to the States, rather than vice-versa.

"Such is the way of the world," he mumbled nonsensically to the driver as Meiying pushed him on the bus and handed over the tickets.

"Down is up and up is down!" he sang in a silly, sing-song voice. "And Meiying from down will lead me up to the bright lights!" She finally succeeded in shushing him, but when they reached their seat, he fell onto her shoulder and commenced snoring, to the amused delight of their fellow passengers.

His last thought was that he wanted to return to the compound. Meiying, on the other hand, sat patiently upright, her bright eyes looking forward as if willing the bus to go faster.

~

When they crossed the border from Mongolia to China, John felt an even greater sense of loss, whereas, with every kilometer, Meiying seemed to gain enthusiasm.

"The Japanese have left Shanghai!" she excitedly read aloud the headline of a discarded newspaper. "That means a lot!"

"What?" muttered John.

"It means I might be able to make contact with some of my old colleagues. John, while you make the arrangements for us to . . . do what is necessary to leave for America, I might be able to perform a few concerts in Shanghai. Maybe make a little money. It couldn't hurt, could it?"

"No, not at all."

As they traveled to Taiyuan by bus, it seemed that all China was again on the move. The end of the war opened a floodgate of refugees, now free to jam the roads and return to their formerly occupied homes and villages. Retracing their steps brought memories to both of them, and each reacted in a different way. John had retreated into a sort of polite, but slightly resentful silence, while Meiying talked incessantly about the future. Although John maintained his detached manner, he felt astonished at how Meiying had been transformed from an unwilling companion to one full of such spirit.

"How is it you have changed so much?" he asked abruptly, cutting her off from rhapsodizing over her Shanghai days.

"How do you mean?"

"Well, you were so hesitant to come, and now . . . now, you're positively chattering away like a young girl."

"Do you mind?"

"No, of course not. I mean, I like it that you're excited. But, well, it just seems like such a change."

She smiled. "Fate starves at probability's door."

"Oh, god! Don't throw that at me!"

"I thought it was my fate to starve, or die some other horrible death. Now, just look. Fate was wrong and the probability that circumstances would come together and give me an opportunity to, I don't know . . . live as I want, is amazing. I reject fate and I embrace probability. If things are based on probability, than I have a chance to succeed; I'm not doomed. Don't you see?"

John's face darkened. "Yes, but you did not want to marry me, and now you seem absolutely thrilled at the idea."

"Not of marrying you! Sorry, John, but our understanding was that I would be free to pursue my own life and my own career; my own friends and relationships. Remember?"

John sulked. "Yes."

She has turned hard, he thought. *Hard and selfish*!

He looked at the shining eyes that mocked his pain, and to relieve the sight of her uncaring attitude, turned his gaze to the throngs lining the road. Poor, emaciated, desperate, determined, the mass of refugees crowded so close to the bus many were knocked down. The driver kept his hand permanently on the horn, shrilly blaring above the endless chatter and toothless grins of the passengers who displayed a nervous relief at being in rather than out.

Jesus, I want out of this godforsaken country! Our great Goddess can have it, living behind an iron door in her damn cave, or wherever the hell she dwells! Damn them all!

He closed his eyes and fumed silently about fate and probability and lies and disillusionment. *Yes, I'll marry her, and probably live a life of misery while she luxuriates with her lesbian lovers and the adoring fans attending her concerts. Fool! Fool that I am! Look at me. Pathetic. I'm still going to marry her. Fool!*

The voices remained uncharacteristically quiet. He waited for their insults; longing for their contempt. He wanted the abuse; needed it. But it did not come, and he sank further into self-pity and a simmering rage that demanded suffering.

~

As they approached Taiyuan, the crush of desperate humanity intensified. Word had spread that the communists were pouring out of their isolated strongholds in the wake of the Japanese withdrawal. Cities offered the lure of protection from the chaos and famine sweeping the countryside. Soldiers were everywhere, consuming everything in their path, filled with even more terror than the people they victimized. Every kilometer closer to Taiyuan heightened in John two conflicting emotions: the intense desire to return to the womb-like safety of the compound and the depressing awareness that it was necessary to return to the States. Each pole represented opposite electric charges; but only one ensured he would have Meiying as a legal companion, if not a "till death do us part" wife. In consequence, he accepted the inevitability of the States, but at the same time felt compelled to grouse about it, with the compound acting the role of romantic impossibility—perfection itself—from which the pair of them were the fallen; two outcasts fleeing Eden at the command of an unfeeling universe.

On the trip to Taiyuan, Meiying and John grew closer even while they grew further apart. Each knew their lives were entwined as whole cloth, yet each also knew the pattern of their own thread would always be distinct and easy to tease apart from the other's when the unraveling began. Once in the city, they agreed to conserve as much money as possible and found a shabby room to stay the few days before they would board a train bound for Shanghai. Each carried a small suitcase, and when the manager gave them the key and exited the dreary room, they stared at a single, sway-back bed with a sprinkling of rat droppings adorning its tattered blanket.

"Which side do you want," he asked almost mockingly.

"The floor."

"No, no. I'll take the floor."

"No, please John. I actually prefer the floor. I think it's cleaner."

"I think you're right."

They looked at each other with miserable expressions.

"It'll get better, Meiying," said John plaintively. "You'll see."

"Yes, I know. Now, I can hardly wait to get to America."

John pulled off the blanket and stared at an oily, stained mattress that reeked of known and unknown smells. "Yes, me too. But for now, let's both sleep on the floor."

Meiying looked askance. "Okay. You on that side of the bed and me on this side, okay?"

John involuntarily let out a little snort, and replied curtly, "Okay."

Meiying ignored his grumbling as he spread a blanket, much to his irritation.

"I'm going to wash up," she said, removing a bar of soap from her suitcase. It was barely a sliver, and John felt a pang of guilt as would befit a husband unable to provide for his wife. Yet, he knew soon enough they would depend upon her income and he would be reduced to a pathetic gigolo, scorned by all who would meet them. Even in the face of his guilt and her deprivation, he found reason enough to blame her for his plight. Yet, later that night, when he lay on his back on the wormy floor staring up into the darkness, he longed to turn on a light and stare at her face; talk with her; ask a million questions that were intended solely to luxuriate in her voice, the answers being superfluous. But for now, the delicious scent of soap so recently rubbed onto her naked body overrode his angst and made him breathe unevenly and perspire in a smoldering attack of feral desire. For the first time, he felt the impulse to rape her; force himself on her and pound into oblivion her maddeningly lesbian contempt for the male cock. His self-hatred deepened when he gave in to his ever-present timidity and simply lay inert and flaccid.

Always afraid, he thought. *Always!*

He laughed inwardly. *God damn, think about it, John. Nineteen-fifty is still years away, but even the voices know they don't need to bother stopping me from jumping the gun too soon, coward that I am!*

He heard her moan. Or was it a groan? Or was it a sigh of anticipation at the prospects awaiting her in the glittering States? Did her dreams ever include him? His tug-of-war contemplation of rape and rapprochement lasted the night. Only once did he hear the floorboard squeak outside their room. He thought nothing of it.

~ *A Ghost from the Past* ~

The next morning they agreed to go for a walk and find some inexpensive noodle shop. A dark, hole-in-the-wall offered the prospect of a cheap meal and escape from a street churning with people. John chose a corner table and they ordered from a sullen teenage girl who clearly wanted to be anywhere but there. When the food came, both ate in silence. For a while, they were the only customers, but gradually the shop began to fill. Out of the corner of her eye, Meiying saw a stooped figure enter wearing clothes that could have been left-overs from the old Manchu dynasty. Something about the manner seemed familiar, but her attention was drawn to John, who asked if her noodles were good.

"Yes, and yours?" she replied. But her eyes were drawn back to the man, who now sat at a small table in the opposite corner. He seemed totally absorbed in his own affairs, so she returned to eating, responding monosyllabically to John's occasional questions. Nevertheless, something in the man's demeanor would not let her dismiss his presence entirely. The teenage girl sidled up to him with a sly grin and the old man wagged his finger at her and laughed. They spoke in whispers and Meiying heard the girl say, "Oh, Mr. Zhang, you are the one! How can you say such a thing at your age!" Again, they laughed and she went behind the bar. With that, the old man looked up into Meiying's staring eyes.

The recognition came as fast as lightning and she let out an involuntary gasp at the shock.

"What?" asked John, looking around.

"Don't look!" she whispered.

"What?"

"I think I know that man over there."

"So?"

"Don't ask questions. Let's just leave."

"Why?"

"Don't ask questions! Go pay the bill! Hurry! When we leave, don't look at him."

John paid and they left the shop without making eye contact with the man, who still sat at the table slowly eating his noodles and staring down at his tea cup.

When they got outside and walked a few meters in silence, John asked the obligatory, "Do you mind telling me what's going on?"

"That man murdered Peter Hedley."

"What?!"

"Or had someone do it for him."

"What are you talking about?"

Meiying turned her head to see if they were being followed. Satisfied, she said, "I don't know more details. All I know is that he is Beethoven's uncle and Lihua told me . . . well, Mr. President . . . oh, never mind. Let's just keep walking." She turned again. "I'm frightened."

"Did Mr. President survive the war?" asked John.

Meiying looked at him blankly. "I don't know."

"Easy enough to find out."

"How?"

John shrugged. "Ask."

"Who?"

"I don't know. Anyone. Besides, who cares? We're going to be leaving tomorrow, and soon enough this entire, goddamn country will be a distant memory."

Meiying looked at him angrily. "Don't say that. Don't ever say that to me again." She looked away and muttered, "I wish Feng Shiren were here."

Properly chastised, he mumbled an apology and followed her like a puppy back to their room, nursing his resentment by silently fashioning a wide spectrum of devastating responses to her hurtful words. Once inside, Meiying slammed the door behind them and immediately locked it, lowering the broken blinds that dangled crookedly from the top of the only window as best she could.

"Tomorrow we go directly to the train station," said Meiying as she sat on a wooden chair that resentfully creaked.

"Okay," replied John, stopping himself from making patronizing comments about everything being fine and how she exaggerated the risk. "Are you going to wash up?" he asked.

"I guess I have to go down the hall," she sighed.

"Do you want me to go with you?" he asked, feeling slightly heroic.

Meiying hesitated. "No, I won't be long." She stood, but seemed to have second thoughts.

"How do you know this guy?" asked John when it became obvious she did not want to venture out.

"I told you, he's Beethoven's uncle."

"Are you sure you're not mistaken? He seemed a harmless old fellow to me."

"Ha! You Americans are always too trusting—too much like children. It was him, I'm sure."

"Well, tomorrow we'll be gone." He suddenly had a disturbing thought. "Do you think he recognized you?"

"So, you're catching on," she replied sarcastically, an attitude she increasingly displayed. "I have learned to trust no one—men least of all. Of course he recognized me. What's more, I don't think he just accidentally bumped into us."

"What?"

"He knew we were at that shop."

"Really?"

"Yes, I am sure of it," and continued as if to herself, "When our eyes met, he seemed calm, not at all surprised."

"Maybe he didn't recognize you."

"Fool!" exclaimed Meiying, surprised at her own vehemence.

John flared. "Don't call me that! I get enough of that from the voices!"

Meiying looked at him as if seeing him for the first time. "That's the most genuine thing you've said to me since I've know you."

"Well, just don't."

"I'm going to wash up," she said firmly, as if calculating this was the optimum moment to leave the room, her courage now up to the danger.

"Sure you don't want me to go with you?"

"Thank you, no."

"Well, I'm going anyway."

Meiying felt a pang of affection for John's all-too-obvious male imperative, but she knew he would be useless in a crunch.

"No, John, you would look ridiculous standing outside the washroom waiting for me—or worse, suspicious. I'm sure I'm exaggerating the risk, but I'm just a woman."

"Well, I'll be here in case you see anything . . . weird. Just call or yell or something and I'll come running."

"Okay, yes, thank you."

She marched out the door with her soap in one hand and towel in the other, potent weapons in the war to impose normalcy on a life subjected to unexpected and senseless disaster.

John cracked open the door and watched her slip into the bathroom, then sat in the same chair she had just vacated. He mulled over her attitude toward him, and came to the unsettling realization that his goal was not sex with her. Not at all. Not even close. His goal was that she respect him. Simply that. But this goal seemed more unattainable than sex. Truth be told, it was intercourse-on-demand that dwelled at the center of their unusual relationship; a seemingly simple act that other couples routinely performed without the need for divine command. But, he remembered, of course they could never be a couple given her sexual propensity. Respect may never come, he thought, but most certainly Meiying must allow him to penetrate her at least once, if not multiple times, to ensure the deed resulted in the proper outcome. Goddess, or *she*, or the Precious Object, or all of them, would not let the universe rest until the infinitude of circumstances converged at the right moment and the right place to make it happen in the right way. If that were the case, they were safe. Nothing could happen to prevent the culmination of such a Divine Plan. Could it?

Fate starves at probability's door.

Yes, it could happen.

What if she left him? Unbearable!

He must not let it happen.

With this thought still hovering over his mind like a threatening storm cloud, he realized she should be back by now. Twice he went to the door and eased it open to check. Nothing. The bathroom door was closed with no other customers in sight. By the third time, he gingerly walked down the hall and listened at the door. Nothing. He wanted to knock, but knew she would be displeased at his paternal attitude. He returned to the room and fretted until there could be no doubt she should have returned by then. Again he made the trek, this time with little concern at the noise he made. As he stood at the closed door, his heart beat wildly, and a debilitating terror that she was gone made him freeze in place. If he knocked and there was no answer, all hope would fly away, and he would be left alone; purpose drained away from life.

Knock! Do it! he berated himself.

I don't want to know! came the answer

Do it, fool!

He knocked, softly at first.
No response. His heart quickened. Her knocked louder.
No response.
He pounded.
Nothing.

~ *Meiying Faces the Ghost* ~

While John knocked on the bathroom door, Meiying stood trembling in front of Mr. Zhang and a handful of scary-looking men outside the inn. By the time John had stood aside in open-mouthed astonishment at an angry old man exiting the bathroom, Meiying had been hustled into a car and on her way to some unknown destination. No words were spoken as the car honked and swerved its way through the throngs of people who appeared to mill around with no purpose in mind but to keep moving. Meiying kept her eyes closed, numb to the circumstances that had plucked her from an escape that seemed so close, trying to ignore the hard shoulder that now pressed against her so ominously. She let her mind wander to what life would have been in the United States, and after a period of time, which she neither kept track of nor cared to keep track of, she finally opened her eyes and saw the countryside roll by. A strange man who possessed the hard shoulder sat next to her staring straight ahead, cold and erect, bearing the stony countenance of one who would not be sympathetic to a dying puppy. The driver and Mr. Zhang sat in the front. Still, no words were spoken until the car rolled up a long, dirt road to a secluded building that seemed incongruously pleasant.

The strange man exited the car and circled around to open the door for her. Mr. Zhang stood waiting. Wordlessly, she got out and stood looking at Mr. Zhang passively, yet feeling her tense muscles become knotted even more.

"Follow me, Miss Bai," he said as if inviting a friend for tea.

After they entered the house, he led her to an anteroom decorated with beautiful antiques, its walls adorned with scrolls of exquisite beauty and bearing a variety of bold and delicate calligraphy. An unattractive serving girl came in, and Mr. Zhang said simply, "Tea, Daiyu."

Glancing menacingly at Meiying, she quickly shuffled out.

Mr. Zhang turned to her with an amiable smile. "Now, Miss Bai, you murdered my nephew who went by the ridiculous name of Beethoven."

Meiying stared but said nothing.

"Of course, I don't expect you to respond to such a statement, but it is just as well you don't. The girl who just left had been screwed by him many times, yet for some reason loved the boy. She would poison you as happily as eating a mooncake. You may want to be careful with the tea she brings."

Waiting for a response, which was not forthcoming, Mr. Zhang continued in the same bantering tone. "Since you are such an intelligent woman, I suspect you know why you are here."

When Meiying did not rise to the bait, he tilted his head and murmured, "Ummm? Aren't you even a little curious?"

Just as Meiying opened her mouth to speak, the tea arrived, Daiyu setting the cups in front of them and pouring with an unreadable face. After she withdrew, Mr. Zhang leaned forward. "You were saying?"

"I did not kill Beethoven."

"But you did. We know. Don't bother denying it."

Meiying repeated mechanically, "I did not kill Beethoven."

Mr. Zhang's lips retracted in a grotesque smile which exposed a blackened set of teeth that appeared pointed at the ends, as if filed. Meiying thought they looked like black rows of sharpened wrought iron.

"Of course, you would be dead already but for other circumstances. Well . . . at the very least, raped multiple times, definitely tortured . . . perhaps off with the nipples, that sort of thing . . . red hot iron bar rammed into your vagina . . . so many possibilities . . . and then killed if you weren't already dead."

He paused to gauge the effect.

None.

Continuing with slightly less zeal, he said, "But you are alive because of Mr. President."

Again, he stopped to stare at her, taking the opportunity to light a cigarette. Blowing out a bluish stream of smoke, he sighed, "I myself would like to fuck you, but that is verboten. You are, apparently, too valuable an exhibit for his zoo." He broke into the awful smile again. "You must surely have been something to behold, based on what I heard from my murdered nephew."

"I did not kill Beethoven."

"Your words are tiresome! I thought more highly of you. Here you sit, supposedly an artist, but with no more imagination then to repeat the lie that you did not murder my nephew over and over like a stupid parrot. Really, it's tiresome. Perhaps breaking your hands so you can never play again would get your attention, or at least force you to adopt a more imaginative line of defense."

Again he paused for effect, and Meiying began to see a dim ray of hope—he appeared to be irritated, which meant he lacked absolute control. She must continue to play the zombie. Thus fortified with a plan, she stubbornly refused to show any affect.

"I did not kill Beethoven."

But his response took her by surprise.

"Honestly, sweetheart, I don't care whether you did or not. I never liked the boy. Too much his mother's lapdog."

Meiying heard a short gasp from behind the door and felt great satisfaction in realizing Mr. Zhang heard it also. She could not help herself from saying, "Perhaps you also should be careful of the tea you are served in future."

As soon as she said it, she berated herself for being so foolish and straying so quickly from her plan. She waited for the inevitable blow.

But again, he surprised her.

"Poison would have no effect on me, but you are a different matter. Yes, Mr. President wants you very badly, and I am the delivery boy who receives a paltry tip with a smile of insincere gratitude. But, I know something even Mr. President does not."

He waited.

No response.

Meiying decided to return to her original strategy and say no more whatever happened. She would not let herself slip again.

He shrugged. "As you wish. A shame."

In a disappointed tone, he shouted, "Come!"

A large, evil-looking man entered.

"Take her to the room!" he exclaimed, avoiding Meiying's eyes while puffing away energetically on the stub of his cigarette.

Yes, of course, Meiying thought. *Always the empty room. Always the prison. Always subjugation. Always the male lust for rape, for domination, for cruelty, for power!*

She fantasized that she was a Goddess, superhuman and immortal, who could crush this arrogant man and all his minions without a thought. Instead, of course, she followed meekly to a dark, windowless room. Chains hung from the walls, but the evil-looking man simply left her and walked out, locking the door behind. Upon inspection, she found a bed, a chair, and a washbasin with a toothbrush, water, and soap. A clean towel hung neatly from a bamboo bar.

Hmm, I must have some value to the monster, she thought bitterly.

Hatred had long ago begun replacing fear as her default emotion. Now, as she splashed water on her face and brushed her teeth, hatred completely overcame the feeling of helpless vulnerability. If anything would power her through these endless ordeals, it would be hatred, not Christian charity or Buddhist compassion. While she had often felt victimized in the past, this relatively recent state of permanent hatred and anger seemed to give her the strength she needed. Plans to persevere, to prevail, to overcome the endless male predisposition to dominate and inject fear in others, and even, at times, to succumb to the male inclination to plot revenge, occupied her time. She made a vow to strike back at the male beast with whatever tools she possessed. Are there any 'good males' she wondered, and answered in the negative. Only those that are strong and vicious, like Mr. President, or weak and useless, like John. She refused to moderate her simple but empowering view with examples that did not fit.

~

After steeping in these feelings for some time, Meiying knocked on the door and asked to pee. The evil-looking man answered and led her to a Western-style bathroom. While sitting, she remembered Mr. Zhang's words "I know something Mr. President does not." But now she realized she had stuck to her Miss Silent persona too stubbornly, and it came to her that this might not have been the best strategy. Zhang implied he had some special knowledge the fat man didn't know, and maybe that knowledge would save her. Visions of being put on display while having sex with Beethoven's mother, or worse, being penetrated by the obscene Mr. President himself, made her stomach heave. On the way back to her room, she told the evil-looking man she wanted to speak with Mr. Zhang, but he laughed and shoved her in the room, noisily locking the door as if reveling in the metallic finality of her imprisonment.

"I will be back to visit," he said ominously.

"Stop!" she cried.

"What now?"

"Tell Mr. Zhang I have something to say."

Only laughter greeted her words. Not surprised at his response, she nonetheless felt insignificant and sat wearily on the bed. Waiting had become something she could deal with because it meant that while she waited, nothing bad was being done to her. Meiying basked in these brief moments of peace by ceasing to think forward. It was something she learned on the road, ignoring the hunger and restless tumult around her. If something good came to her, even for a moment, such as continuing to breathe unmolested, she savored it, regardless of the inevitable dropping of the other shoe that she knew would follow. To cope, she mechanically performed her usual ritual: closing her eyes and playing an imaginary piano, her fingers moving swiftly along the invisible keyboard. Music filled the room and lifted the atmospheric weight of oppression. Now she could lay down without feeling crushed beneath the anticipation of an unpleasant fate, and her breathing slowed to a steady rhythm with the notes of the sonata.

Sleep came quickly.

Dreams transported her back to the good days in Shanghai. With the sky sunny and bright, and her heart full of unlimited hopes and girlish desires, she skipped through the smiling crowds while waving at their awed recognition of her precocious abilities. Lihua and Meili miraculously appeared from nowhere, having been transformed into girls also, all three laughing and cavorting hand-in-hand along the Bund, basking in the warmth of each other's skin, defying the hypocritical denunciation of the common herd. Such a secret they shared! None could know but they three—a sacred trust. But they were brought up suddenly when they rounded a corner and stood facing a firing squad. None of the soldiers who pointed their rifles cared a whit about their precious secret; in fact it was the secret condemned them; now merely objects for target practice; hearts and lungs and brains as meaningless as paper bulls-eyes. They tried to flee, but none could move and remained frozen in terror in spite of all their efforts to run. Meiying screamed in her dream as the rifles fired and all the bullets came only at her in slow motion, but all swerving barely in time to thud into the bodies of Lihua and Meili. Down they went, groaning pitifully, leaving her to stand in their blood, horrified yet oddly exhilarated that she still lived while they died so painfully. As she stared, she suddenly felt doubly horrified to feel exhilaration at all. With these conflicting emotions she awoke with a start to find nothing changed. Room, furniture, ceiling, all mocked her efforts to escape through imaginary music and insubstantial dreams. But she still lived, and where there is life, there is hope.

~ *John Suffers A Loss, Then A Gain* ~

With the disappearance of Meiying, John felt the old panic. Report it to the police? How? In these chaotic times, a girl lost among the millions of displaced would be a proper joke. He had made a panicked and cursory search of the most likely places close to the inn that she might have gone. But the neighborhood was dark and dingy, with a maze of vile-looking alleyways, so he returned to the room with a hollow, nauseous feeling in his gut. What to do? He had almost no money, no friends, no—*Ah!* he thought suddenly. *My old school! Surely it's still there. I'll go see the old proprietor, get my old job, earn money, enough to stay and continue searching! Enough to return to the compound and ask for help, maybe Feng Shiren.*
. . .

And in spite of this hasty resolution, for some reason all his resolve came crashing down upon him: Meiying's disappearance, his fecklessness, his loneliness, his fears. *Worthless fool! I'm a worthless fool! Go ahead voices, say it! I'm a useless bag of shit! I should just end the whole sad story!*

But the voices stayed perversely silent and he berated himself even for their absence. *What do I expect, fool, even the voices are done with me!* he thought bitterly, with the anguish of a man teetering on the edge. He wept tears of helplessness and rage, but the unfeeling universe left him alone in his room without producing a wrinkle of empathy in time or space. In this state, night came and he had not stirred from the room. The question, *What am I to do?* plagued him all night, but the answer did not come, and in spite of his self-lacerating thoughts, he secretly hoped against hope she would miraculously return and all would be well. But the following morning Meiying had not appeared, so John finally resolved to bestir himself and seek out his old employer—if the school still even existed. He scarfed down some cheap *jiaozi* from a street vendor and trudged off in the direction he thought would lead him to the Taiyuan Best Learning International School. As he walked, he stared at the multitude of faces staring back at him, looking for the familiar face he so desperately wanted to find. But the looks he received were open-mouthed curiosity at the vision of a Westerner in such a ramshackle section of Taiyuan. Most expressions were stupefied, but some seemed hostile. *Malicious bastards*, he thought. *I'm here for you . . . or one of yours.*

Soon, John became hopelessly lost. Asking directions seemed not to help, as the advice he did manage to understand only sent him deeper into areas he did not recognize. Now, to his dismay, he couldn't even find his way back to the room. He spent precious yuan renting a rickshaw to take him to the school. Fortunately, the driver recognized the name after John wrote it in Chinese on a scrap of paper. By the time he arrived, classes were in session and the owner unavailable. In misery he waited like some kid begging for his first menial job. He sat on the steps outside the building and watched the passersby, speculating about what happened to Meiying. He was sure she did not leave voluntarily, without telling him. She was far too anxious to reach the States for that, and besides, would not have left her belongings. Beethoven was dead, but he knew Mr. President wanted her. She had often confided in him that the obese monster was after her. He pooh-poohed the notion, but now the possibility seemed feasible. *That is where I must go!* he decided. Suddenly, his chest filled with air as if a bellows had pumped him full of resolve; he had a plan, a destination, a quest. Money, of course, stood in the way. But if he could work for a while at this school, he could save enough for the trip. But first, he must find Feng Shiren. *I must!* he decided. *Without Feng, there is no hope. But how do I find him? Return to the compound! Find a way to reach him. He is connected to all this. He is sent by Her. He is the potential savior! He will bring protection from Her. Find him! He will know where to begin!*

"Mr. Powers?" came a voice. "So good to see you!"

Startled, John quickly stood and faced his old employer, whose face reflected a broad smile.

Immediately reassured by this warm greeting, John bowed and they walked to the office. It turned out the school had prospered during the war, particularly with Japanese clients. Now there was a new demand by Chinese, but very few qualified teachers. Terms were soon agreed upon, including an advance, and John returned to his room as a guest of Mr. Qin in his automobile. That night, he slept soundly. He now had a plan and the chance to make it work. Saving Meiying became his *raison d'etre*, and the next day he sent a letter off to the compound via Dalandzadgad begging them to send Feng Shiren, if he still resided there, or to forward his letter if not. With a job, and the possibility of Feng's help, he calmed considerably and reverted to his old ways—holing up in the room until he had to leave for his first day of work the following morning.

The next day found him standing in his old classroom, the concrete walls still imposing and the solid desks still full of students; their eager faces ranged from young to old, their countenances from dull-looking to intelligent, and their eyes lit by the flame of ambition, all adults. Even the books were the same, but far more tattered and worn. For a moment, when he looked at the students, he saw Nobaru with eager eyes, in full uniform, sword at his side, the slightest hint of a mischievous smile tugging at the corners of his mouth. And with him rose the other ghosts from the war years, materializing in their seats like prim and proper specters—Mr. Gao, Little Acorn, Lu Zhishen, Suling, Master Liu, and the others—all waiting patiently. But for what?

A cough from one of the real students brought him back, and he slipped easily into his teaching mode until the hours fell away and he found himself back in the room, where Meiying's own ghost waited, sitting in the same chair he had last seen the real her.

"Find me," she said in a voice that made his blood run cold.

~

Days turned into weeks and though his money accumulated, his resolution diminished to a slender thread, drooping like an overburdened clothesline. Every night he returned to the ghost of Meiying. Every night she grew more insubstantial, her words barely audible, weaker by the moment. Her wasting away drove him mad, for he now had enough money to either find his way back to the compound and hope someone remained, or take the plunge and return to Mr. President's palace, a den of evil and horrible dangers. It presented the type of dilemma he never seemed to able to solve with any degree of firmness. But this time, he was in luck. His love for Meiying actually trumped inertia. Of course, he chose the safer route of returning to the compound, ostensibly to find help, but actually he knew better. Still, his decision involved motion on his part, and that in and of itself served his purpose. Each night he vowed to start off the next day, and each morning he found reason not to.

John had taken to having a few glasses of rice wine before bed, to help him sleep and bridge the gap between stupefied indecision and sober planning. As time passed and he had more money for it, the liquor went down easier and more was required to satisfy his needs, which he nourished with increasing frequency. So, with his fortitude reinforced, he laid out a plan of action, simple in its design, and, he thought, infallible in its result: find Feng Shiren, go to Mr. President's palace, free Meiying, and continue on to the States with the grateful pianist in tow. Elegant in its simplicity, but devilish in its details. After all, he wasn't even sure she *was* with Mr. President. However, a plan was a plan, and it at least gave him direction. As the need for alcohol increased, his resolution to actually implement the idea weakened, and doubts again returned. If he waited long enough, she would surely find her way back. What if she returned only to find him gone? At those moments of indecision, he invariably berated himself for his cowardice and resolved to start the quest the next day. Rice wine intensified both his lethargy and his boldness, and the battle between the two played itself out most dramatically in his periods of intoxication. However, the net result was further delay that turned into more weeks.

One morning, while he slept after a particularly heavy night of drinking, a great crashing noise penetrated his brain and he managed to open his eyes to find a figure hovering over him, roaring unintelligible words and tugging at his bedspread. Through the blur, he saw a familiar face.

"John! I am here! Wake up!"

He did his best to leap out of bed, but managed only a poor sliding action that tangled his legs and caused him to fall at the feet of this raving figure.

Feng Shiren looked down at him and shook his head in disgust. "Well, Bai Meiying is in a pickle again! How does she do it? And you, what have you been doing about it?"

John stood and covered his nakedness as best he could. "She often told me that beauty is a curse," he said, quite proud he could string together such an articulate sentence on such short notice and under such embarrassing conditions.

"Hmm!" grunted Feng. "Have you made inquiries? Reported to the police? What is the latest intelligence?"

John was busy putting on his clothes when this string of questions was thrown at him. "Intelligence?" he asked stupidly.

"Yes. What have the police said? Or shopkeepers in the area? Witnesses? Anything?"

John averted his eyes. "I haven't reported it to the police."

"What? Why?"

"One person among the millions. Besides, you yourself said the police are useless. They never found Peter's killer, remember?"

Feng started to protest, but John's mind had cleared enough to remember Meiying's fear of Beethoven's uncle.

"Wait a minute! Meiying told me Beethoven's uncle killed Peter, or had him killed. We ran into him just before she disappeared. And the uncle worked for Mr. President. I need you to go with me to Mr. President's palace. I'm sure she's been taken there."

"Ah, now we're getting somewhere. What is the uncle's name?"

"Zhang."

Feng snorted, "There are a million Zhangs in Taiyuan. Have you tried to track him down?"

John replied defensively, "No. I've been busy trying to make enough money to get to Mr. President's palace."

"Doing what?"

"Teaching English."

"You enjoy it?"

John shrugged. "It buys food."

"Well, you go ahead and earn your money. I will do the detective work. Now, give me a description of this Mr. Zhang and any other info you might have about him."

John, his spirits lifted, sat with Feng and told him everything he knew. After many hours of back and forth, they agreed to leave within the week, once Feng had had a chance to investigate further.

"Where are you staying?" asked John.

"One floor down. We'll share the fleas in this dump." Feng made a show of scratching. "It's my kind of place!"

~ *Meiying Continues to Suffer* ~

Meiying could not escape her nightmare. Every day she suffered the torment of not knowing what humiliation she would suffer next. For what seemed an eternity, she again found herself languishing back in the obscene cage of Mr. President's palace, and wishing for the strength to commit suicide, but the final act always eluded her resolve. Perhaps it was fear of pain, or just an irrational hope, but she woke every morning to draw breath and renew her pledge to survive. In spite of the dire circumstances, nothing had yet been done to her. She was not forced to perform some perverted act for the benefit of Mr. President. In fact, she had been sequestered in a comfortable, even luxurious room, and had not yet seen Mr. President face-to-face. To her amazement, her only duty so far was to play the piano twice a week. She performed always at night in a special room with excellent acoustics. Meiying assumed Mr. President listened from behind a two-way mirror. As she played, she felt him watching, and his voyeuristic presence seemed far more lascivious than if he were actually sitting before her. To her further amazement, she was instructed to first play the same piece every night, plus any others she chose afterwards. Somehow, she felt he listened only to the first, then departed. Further bizarre requirements included her clothing, which was always to be a long, Western-style black gown accented with a pearl necklace. To these rules were added minor variations, but it seemed she was condemned to endlessly act out a scene, the same scene, for his twisted mind. What he did while listening to the music she did not want to imagine. How long was she to repeat this ritual? No one would tell her, but it had been made abundantly clear she would not be allowed to deviate from the script.

There were, however, some other small favors to be thankful for. She had not seen Beethoven's mother, Madame Wang. That, at least, was a blessing. Were she in the same surroundings, without the looming specter of Mr. President, she might even have been happy. *After all*, she thought. *I might as well make the best of it while I can. Who knows what will happen tomorrow! Or even ten minutes from now?* She shuddered. *Something horrible. This doll-like prison cannot last.*

But it did, day-after-day, and she had settled into an unwilling routine, using the opportunity to tirelessly practice. *Someday, I'll be playing in Paris or New York.* And she let herself dream of pretty dresses and cultured admirers, of parties and lavish concert halls, and of meeting a like-minded, beautiful woman, as sweet as Meili and as tough as Lihua. It was while she dwelled in one of these fantasies of a future life that a knocking on her door brought her around to the terrible present.

Not being one of the scheduled concert nights, she trembled at the meaning of the intrusion, for in the past she had always been left alone. With this break in the routine, her accumulated fears swooped down upon her in a rush, as if they had been primed for just such a contingency. She threw on a cotton robe and called without opening the door.

"Yes?"

Without ceremony, the door flung open wide and a strange man strode in, scanning the room as if looking for hidden visitors.

"Get dressed!" he barked.

"It is late," she replied, trying to suppress the rising sense of panic.

He smile crookedly, and she could not read whether it conveyed cruelty, empathy, or mockery—or perhaps all three.

"And make it the black dress," he said, ignoring her comment, adding, "with the usual accoutrements."

"But it is not the night!" she blurted.

"Five minutes," he said.

"I'll be longer than that."

"Just hurry." This time, he spoke a bit nervously and conspiratorially, as if some threat hung in the air that included him as well as her. His unease spread to her and made the uncertainty worse. She rushed to dress in the usual ensemble, and as she clasped the pearls behind her neck, he called again, "Hurry!"

He is a victim too, she thought. *We are all victims.*

But this insight was nothing new and hardly carried the gravitas of revelation. Meiying had long ago learned the human condition, far from being noble and aspiring, was both the victim and the victimizer of its own madness—like every other animal, but so far exaggerated and in such perverse ways that its capacity for self-destruction raged beyond the capacity of even the closest ape cousins to attain.

~

She has it, Dearest God! She is to be the mother, as I have said all along! And You must suffer the weight of her son!

Nonsense, Beloved Goddess. She will suffer the weight of her son. Ha ha!

It will happen as I predicted. You will see. There will be a son, and the son will lead You to the Reunion, and there You will suffer Your fate, humans will suffer their collective fate, and the planet will begin to heal.

I leave suffering to them. They are so good at it. Besides, as You know, reunions are devilishly difficult to arrange.

~

Meiying could hear the rumbling of the arguing deities, but their words were not clear. She ascribed their presence to John, who must be stirring close by. But even this possibility did not move her. Come what may, her defense mechanisms were too formidable to allow girlish excitement to arouse in her the unlikely prospect of a handsome savior arriving to save the day. Far too many disappointments had dulled her true capacity for hope, though she fought against that despair by repeating the rather hollow mantra that there was always hope. Instead, she doubled down on focusing her increasingly narrow tunnel vision to the task at hand. One step at a time, to ensure the next step may be taken without unwittingly choosing a potentially deadly detour. Now, at the present moment, a stranger leads her through the maze of corridors to perform whatever Mr. President demands. That was all. Do whatever necessary to take the next step. Memories of the horrible last moments of Meili were never far from her mind, and provided bitter incentive to keep her head down and obey. With these thoughts occupying her attention, the stranger waved her toward an open door and motioned her to enter.

Chapter Eleven

Rescue

A New Quest Begins

On the eve of their departure from Taiyuan, Feng Shiren and John met to discuss their strategy. In spite of Feng's best efforts, he discovered very little about Beethoven's uncle. Even bribes led him nowhere, and he began to understand how strong the old man's grasp on others must be. Either they were afraid of him, or he had succeeded in swathing himself in an impenetrable web of false leads and low ranking dead-ends. This lack of intelligence unsettled them both, but they were determined to recover Meiying, somehow, someway. Their plan was little more than to find their way back to Mr. President's palace, and then decide how best to proceed. Feng had some vague notion of entering the palace in his guise as a face-changer, but the details of how this was to be accomplished were woefully lacking, and neither wanted to pursue details at the risk of further delay.

John produced a bottle of rice wine and invited Feng to join, who readily agreed, though with a slight sideways glance that went unnoticed by the American. As the wine flew from the bottle into John's stomach, he began chattering with more abandon, particularly rhapsodizing about how life would be when he and Meiying reached the States. In the midst of his soliloquy, Feng stared into his eyes and asked a question that brought John up short.

"What about the voices, John?"

After returning Feng's stare with a bleary gaze, John shuddered and gathered his thoughts. All signs of his tipsiness seemed gone when he finally answered.

"You know, I remember my father describe the Western front in World War One. Everyone was surrounded by death and destruction, mud and disease, and constant explosions and sniper fire. But his greatest horror was none of that."

John fell silent and poured another cup for himself, and offered to fill Feng's, who refused by putting his hand over the cup without taking his penetrating stare from John's face.

"Want to know what it was?" asked John after quaffing the cup in one gulp.

"Of course."

"Well, poison gas was used back then. Dad said that after the cannisters exploded in their thousands, sickly yellowish gas filled the atmosphere until it gradually settled down into the shell holes like thick broth in a field of bowls. So you had these deadly traps with their writhing, seductive vapors curling about and beckoning unsuspecting doughboys to jump in for safety from the bullets and explosions. Once you jumped and sank into the soupy fog, you were done for. The poison entered your lungs and seared away the lining, causing you to die in your own hemorrhaging fluids, your skin being burned off at the same time. Awful!"

John paused and Feng waited patiently, watching his American friend throw down more cups of wine. At last, John continued, now no longer talking to Feng Shiren, but carrying on a conversation with himself.

"These voices are like those poison vapors. They call me and chide me and harass me to jump in and inhale their poison. 'Fool!' they say. 'Worthless!' they shout. And the more I hear them, the thicker the soup becomes at the bottom of the craters, and the more deadly it becomes, the more I want to jump in and escape."

"Escape what?"

"What do you think?"

"I don't know."

John looked around and swept his arms out. "All this!"

"All what?"

"Christ, Shiren! You can't be that fuckin' stupid!"

"I'm Chinese. I must be stupid."

John rubbed his face and suddenly felt nauseous. He rushed down the hallway to the same bathroom where Meiying had last been seen entering. Inside, he let the vomit come and sat on the floor, clutching the toilet. *God, what a mess I am!* he thought bitterly. *Is this how I'm going to save Meiying?* He heard a knocking on the door.

"Are you okay, John?" came Feng's voice.

"Yes, yes. No problem. I'll be right out."

Feng chuckled. "You didn't fall into a bowl of poison, did you?"

"Fuck you," said John weakly. "I'll be out."

"Good! Tomorrow we set off to save Meiying! The hell with your voices and your poison! Before you know it, you'll be listening to her play the piano in New York."

John said nothing, but felt heartened by the words of his comrade. He knew he would be relying on Feng Shiren's strength to see it through, and he hated himself for his weakness.

~

The next morning dawned grey and gloomy. As usual, the streets of Taiyuan were swirling with refugees begging for food, and hounding workers on their way to factories and shops for money. John had informed his employer he would be gone a few days, unwilling to actually quit and have no employment to return to, if necessary. Feng insisted they travel light, which was not a problem since neither owned much more than the clothes on their backs, plus the precious face-changing masks and costume. Word had spread that the communists had increased their attacks on the main roads, and John felt doubly impatient to leave war-torn China for some place, any place, safe and secure, before the civil war really got rolling.

Yet, here I am, he pondered as they waited at the bus station. *Going into the belly of the beast with this crazy Chinaman! Even more ridiculous, I'm off to slay an obese dragon to save a fair maiden. Don Quixote is what I am! Ridiculous! I could just forget the whole thing and go straight back, like any reasonable person would do!*

He waited for the voices to pounce on his self-lacerating thoughts. In fact, as happened more and more frequently, he welcomed them. Needed them. But they remained stubbornly, inexplicably, quiet.

Where are you when I need you to remind me of how stupid I am? he taunted. *Come on out. Let me have it!*

But he was met with only silence.

Hey, Goddess! What if I were to tell you I have no intention of getting Meiying pregnant? And even if she does, I'll force her to get an abortion. What about that?

Silence.

I'm waiting!

Silence.

Damn! God damn all of you!

Silence.

Odd.

"What's odd?" asked Feng.

"Oh, sorry. Nothing. I must have been thinking out loud."

Feng tilted his head and smiled. "At least this time we get to travel in style. The bus is here!"

They jostled and shoved themselves onto the crowded bus and managed to find an unoccupied bench in the very back. Resting their feet on top of their packs, they settled in for a long ride, pleased at their luck in finding a seat. John gazed out the window and dreamed of arriving in the States, mesmerizing his friends with exotic stories of survival in war-torn China, exaggerating his trials and tribulations in exchange for their sympathetic and rapt attention. He tried not to think of the dangers awaiting at Mr. President's palace. Yet, a great consolation lay in the knowledge that he would follow Feng Shiren's lead. As long as he did that, everything would turn out fine. Somehow, he still clung to the notion that Feng had been sent as his guardian angel, although whenever the thought entered his mind, he dismissed it as superstition.

Without the burden of leadership, his mind was free to roam the currents and eddies of the long river that had swept him to China since meeting *her* all those years ago. Although by nature a timid man, he marveled at the adventures he had experienced since arriving in such a violent and chaotic land. Now, on the verge of returning to the States, he had been diverted by another bend in the river, and he felt a particular fear of dying when safety and comfort beckoned so close. Like a combat soldier nearing the end of his tour, he felt constantly nervous and vowed to be extra cautious. A flash of anger at Meiying for being abducted crossed his mind.

If she had only been more careful, we would be on our way to the States by now, he thought bitterly. *I told her I would accompany her to that damn bathroom. Why didn't she listen? Her stubbornness has put us in this mess.*

But he was aware of the injustice of these accusations, and to chase away the unpleasantness of his own flawed character, he diverted his attention to scenes passing by the bus window. Refugees were still working their way out of Taiyuan, but the pace was very slow; streets jammed with the press of people on foot, carts hauled by mewling oxen, and the blur of rickshaws pulled by sweating men. Foul-smelling automobiles idled on all sides, waiting for an opening in the crush of humanity, and trying to squeeze behind his bus to follow in its wake through the parting sea. He thought of the communists waiting in the countryside for victims to scurry out of their mouseholes and into the open where they did not stand a chance.

From the frying pan into the fire, he thought glumly.

"True, true," said Feng Shiren.

"Jesus Christ, was I talking out loud again?" asked John.

"Oh, yes. Quite a soliloquy. I have been quite entertained."

"So glad I could oblige."

"You're too kind." Feng squirmed down in his seat and looked up at John mischievously. "Is the United States really as rich and luxurious as they say?"

"More so," said John complacently.

"Especially compared with the poor Chinese nation?"

"Yes."

"Are you very disappointed in *her*?" asked Feng after a pause. He put out his hands, palms up, and chuckled.

"Of course, aren't you?"

"No. I never had any expectations, remember? I just followed along to keep you out of trouble. God knows your group found enough of it!"

"Was it our fault?"

"That is open to debate."

John looked out the window. "Look out there. A crush of people with a long past and an uncertain future. Poor, hungry, superstitious, frightened, and threatened on all sides by tigers."

"Oh, you mean communists?"

"Communists and Nationalists and warlords, and bandits, and god knows what. China is a mess. Even you have to agree with me."

"Of course, China is a mess. But so are you."

"What?"

"You heard me. You are a mess, like China."

"I am? Tell me how."

"Well, in China we have a billion voices screaming similar things your voices say."

"Which is. . . . ?"

"Which is that we Chinese are fools. Worthless. Failures. And we need to destroy ourselves in order to save ourselves."

"I don't understand."

Feng shook his head and assumed a grim expression. "Level everything and rebuild!"

"But how? China is so far behind, and it has civil war, famine, warlords, poverty, ignorance, bandits, disease, drugs . . . you name it . . . sorry . . . it's just a fact . . . I mean. . . . " John's voice trailed off, realizing his words were directed unrestrained to a friend, a Chinese, and he knew they were hurtful.

Feng chaffed at the weak apology. "Do not apologize! Don't you see, John? Once we level everything, then we have the strongest base on which to build. Bedrock. Cannot get worse than now. We cannot dig deeper. The softness is gone. Whoever wins, communists or Nationalists, will have the advantage of building on solid rock. China will rise again, stronger than ever! You'll see, if you live long enough."

"Well, Yan Xishan is certainly building a powerful army to stop the communists in Taiyuan, don't you think?"

Feng pondered for a moment. "Ah. No. He will be defeated."

"You mean the communists will win?"

"Shhh!" Feng hissed, looking around the bus to see if anyone had been listening. "We were talking about you and how you are a mess, like China."

"What about me? Do you think I can rebuild?"

Feng shrugged. "Your choice. Rebuilding is difficult. The millions will move forward because there are enough to see it through. The one . . . the individual . . . well, it is less certain. Many will be left behind or crushed beneath the wheels. Although in some ways you are like China, yet you are still just one person."

"Americans value the power of the individual more than Chinese," protested John.

"We'll see. Perhaps you will succeed. God knows."

"*She* knows."

Feng gave John a surprised look. "Who? Meiying?"

"No," replied John firmly. "*Her. She. It. The Precious Object. Goddess.*"

"So many?"

"They're all the same."

"And this . . . this deity, or whatever, knows your future?"

"Yes. I am to have a son by Meiying in a couple of years, so I know I must live at least long enough see that task through."

Feng clicked his tongue. "Yes, I heard that tale already."

John laughed self-consciously. "At times, I even think *She* sent you to protect us."

"*She*?"

John scoffed. "Come on, you know who I mean."

"Do I?"

"Yes. Don't play the fool."

"But I am a fool. If I were to negotiate with some Goddess to protect you, I would demand payment in return."

"Okay, so what did you demand?"

"Huh?"

"So what is it?"

"What is what?"

"Fool!" laughed John, who quickly turned serious. "No, I mean it. What are you being paid to protect us?"

"Us?"

"Meiying and me."

"To protect both of you?"

"Yes."

Feng screwed up his eyes. "Well, well, double the price for two. Let me see . . . my payment is to go to the United States with you and Meiying."

"What?!" cried John incredulously.

Feng tilted his head with his usual flair. "My price."

"But, I cannot arrange that! It's impossible!"

"Nothing is impossible for Americans."

"Who told you that?"

"Americans."

"Well, there's no way."

Feng abruptly stood.

"Where are you going?" asked John.

"To get off. You're on your own."

John felt the knot in his stomach tighten. He pictured with horror the idea of his being left alone to continue on and rescue Meiying. "Wait!"

Feng smiled and sat down. "I was just kidding." He slapped his knees. "How much money do you have?"

"Very funny," muttered John, greatly relieved. "You already know how much money I have."

"I only know how much you told me."

"That's right. I have about enough to eat cheap for a week. And you?"

"Enough to eat cheap for a month, and I have less than you. Besides, all Americans are rich, haven't you heard? You are an American, therefore you are rich."

"Sure," grumbled John. "Same ridiculous notion as your idea that nothing is impossible for Americans. Does every Chinese have these absurd ideas?"

"Of course."

"Well, my stomach is rumbling with hunger. Right now, it's impossible for me, an American with no money, to eat a seven-course meal. That is, unfortunately, not possible even for an American."

"So you say."

"You think I'm hiding something from you?" objected John with genuine outrage.

"No," replied Feng evenly. "I think you're hiding something from yourself." He pronounced these words portentously without knowing what his clever statement meant other than it sounded good.

"I assure you, if I had money we would be stuffing our faces right now in the back seat of a private car driven by a chauffeur!"

As John said these words, he had the uncomfortable feeling that he should be reinforcing Feng's wrong-headed notion about the power of Americans, not undermining it. A man of strength, he thought, would use Feng's misguided ignorance as a weapon or a tool to manipulate, not capitulate. But, as usual, he chalked it up as another example of his weakness. But he had mistaken Feng's banter as being serious.

Feng Shiren was quite aware that John was poor and weak, though he knew the American was not as weak as he appeared. But a thought, a yearning, had been germinating in Feng's mind for a long while that he truly would like to emigrate to the United States. Visions of ample food, peace, work, and money, all acted as irresistible lures. If he had not known John (or *her,*) these thoughts would have been dismissed as easily as if he desired to sprout wings and fly. But lately, he clung to the notion that knowing an American meant anything was possible. Love of China struck him as an infantile abstraction. Love of one's own future, however, represented an entirely different sense of reality. So he toyed with John, probing to see how feasible his newfound dream really might be. While his reason told him John was indeed powerless, his irrational mind, bolstered by the promises of *her,* persuaded him that perhaps Americans really could make anything happen. He truly believed everything he told John about China rebuilding, but he also knew he would be one of those who would be crushed—not out of weakness, but out of a past he could not escape. Certain the communists would win, he was just as certain they would kill him when they did.

It is true, he thought. *It must be true she ordered me to protect them. But never was payment discussed. No quid pro quo if I succeeded in rescuing them. My reward?* He chuckled grimly. *Nothing but* her *undying gratitude. The fools have no idea about our relationship.* She *gave me life. I am Frankenstein's monster, and* she *must set me free when my task is done!*

Both men had been silent for some time, each immersed in his own thoughts, when the bus came to an abrupt stop.

"Checkpoint!" cried the driver. "Get out your papers!"

Before the passengers had time to react, three armed soldiers bounded onto the bus.

"Papers!" their leader shouted as he walked to the back of the bus.

John and Feng quickly produced their travel documents, and John handed over his American passport, the visa long since expired. But these were Nationalist soldiers, and they were solicitous of any American citizen they encountered. When the soldier pointed to the expiration date, John replied in Chinese, "The Japs extended my stay."

The soldier laughed and handed back the passport. After he checked Feng Shiren's papers, he asked, "Where do you travel to?"

"Back to Shanghai with my American friend here," said Feng, jabbing his thumb at John.

"You both from Taiyuan?"

"Yes."

"Purpose of returning to Shanghai?"

"Returning home, or what's left of it."

The soldier snorted and held out his hand. "Discharge papers."

Feng didn't miss a beat. "Brother, are you kidding? Lost when I fought with Yan Xishan against the Japs. Lucky to get out alive!"

His easy-going manner disarmed the soldier. "I know what you mean, brother. I made it out of Nanjing by the skin of my teeth." He looked at John. "Are you together?"

"Yes."

A loud command rang shrilly through the windows from outside. "Hurry!"

Turning to the other passengers, the soldiers worked their way up the aisle, and ordered a young woman and her child off the bus, as well as an elderly couple. None of the four returned when the bus pulled away.

"What will happen to them?" whispered John.

Feng merely drew a finger across his throat.

"Jesus. Why?"

Feng shrugged. "Probably suspected communists." "Even the kid?"

Feng responded in a detached tone, suggestive of someone watching people play chess and ruminating aloud over the next move. "Well, it could be they just wanted to rape the mother—she was pretty—in which case the kid will be fine."

"And the mother?"

"Hopefully left alive to take care of the kid."

"This is why I want to go home to a sane country with laws," said John gloomily.

"You mean a civilized country?"

"If you want to put it that way."

"Yet, you traveled to China to find enlightenment."

"No, to find *her*." He held out his hands, palms up.

"And did you?"

John considered the question. "Sort of, but not really."

"So now you return to the United States to find what?"

"Peace."

"No!" barked Feng, causing the passengers in the seat in front of them to crane their necks backward to see. He lowered his face and once they had turned back around, whispered, "No, you seek safety."

"Same thing. Don't we all?"

"If we all did, why are we surrounded by dangers?"

"Because some seek power or money or pleasure, even if these things mean danger to themselves or others."

"And don't you see? They are the ones that make the rest of us know we're alive. At least in China we know we are alive!"

John smiled complacently. "Then why do you want to move to the States?"

Feng bared his teeth. "To make sure you and Meiying have a son in nineteen-fifty. Then, my American friend, my contract is fulfilled."

"Contract?"

"Of course, do you think I take these risks for free?"

Stunned, John swayed in silence to the lurching bus as it chugged closer to their destination, and with each curve and bump, thought, *Is he just playing a role like some sort of buffoon, or is he for real like some sort of angel?*

~ Meiying is Confronted ~

As Meiying entered the room she heard the door close behind, yet not before she caught a swift glance at a lone candle being snuffed out by some disembodied hand, then darkness. Unwilling to go farther, she stood in silence, listening to her own rapid heartbeat. Now she became convinced something horrible was about to happen, and she steeled herself for whatever humiliation might occur. But she stood for what seemed an eternity without hearing anything other than her own breathing. Gradually, her heartbeat lessened and she gingerly moved forward, her arms groping in front to detect any obstructions. Her knees hit something low, a bench, and she fell forward, breaking her fall with outstretched arms, her hands landing heavily on a keyboard with a cacophony of discordant notes shattering the silence. She felt the piano and knew it was the same she had played since arriving at the palace, apparently brought to this dark room for some unfathomable purpose. After running her hands over the bench and satisfying herself it contained no surprises, she sat and gently touched the keys. *Lovely*, she thought. *Peaceful. I am home.* Adjusting the bench, she began playing Beethoven's *Moonlight Sonata* very softly. This piece, while not her favorite, always soothed her jangled nerves. As the last note slowly faded and she exercised her fingers to start another piece, the door opened and a figure slipped quickly and quietly into the room. This happened so fast she had not enough time to turn and see before the door closed and the room again swathed in darkness.

Meiying strained her eyes but could see nothing, only hearing the low breathing of the visitor. She wanted to call out, but something told her to remain silent. *Male or female?* She stood and tilted her head to hear better, but could not tell. Another eternity passed, as if two animals circled each other stealthily, sizing each other up. But sizing each other up for what? Time passed slowly while she remained motionless in this unutterably bizarre tableau. Her breathing seemed to syncopate with her unseen companion's, and it crossed her mind that the impossibly fragile balance that comprised their inhaling and exhaling must soon come to an abrupt end with jarring words. The symmetry must break. And so it did.

"Are you prepared to return to God?" said the figure.

She immediately recognized the voice.

"Father Durant!" she exclaimed with more force than she intended.

"Yes."

"But . . . why? . . . How?. . . . " stuttered Meiying breathlessly.

"Mr. President, in his infinite wisdom, has brought us together."

Meiying summoned her inner reserves of strength, and responded clearly and forcefully. "Why?"

"To save you, of course."

Meiying still could not see even his outline in the dark, but she felt his words were not directed solely at her, but were uttered for effect, as if someone were listening.

A flash of anger struck her and she determined not to play the game.

She would remain silent, come what may.

"Like myself, Mr. President is interested in demons sent by the devil to do mischief. Your murder of Beethoven, for example, is the work of the devil, or his demon, and not attributable to you alone. He is fascinated with you, and through his many contacts, brought me here as an expert."

Durant paused to see if there would be a reply. Receiving none, he continued, "You have been brought to this special room for the exorcism."

Meiying had wanted to blurt out a denial that she had killed Beethoven, but as quickly as he had appeared, Father Durant slipped out the door, which was promptly locked behind him. Stunned at the word "exorcism," she sat back down on the piano bench trembling with a host of grotesque images, each more terrible than the last. She buried her face in her hands and wept at her fate. But again, drawing from the deep well of her character, she sat up straight and took hold of herself.

I must explore this room, she told herself.

For the next hour, she felt her way around the room, exploring with her hands every centimeter of the walls and floor. Besides the piano, she discovered a bed, a nightstand, a sink with running water, a chair, a chamber pot, a closet full of dresses, and a dresser in which were neatly folded, clean underwear and other items of clothing.

As she expected, there were no windows, only one door, and the rough walls, which felt like concrete, and through which no outside sound could enter.

I am to be deprived of sensation, she thought. *But, thank god, they gave me a piano. Why?*

She returned to the piano and began playing, softly at first, then angrily. The chords reverberated around the room, the loudness disfiguring the music, making it cacophonous and eerie, but she welcomed the distortion, viewing her life since the Japanese invasion as one continuous distortion of her true soul. *My true soul,* she wondered. *Which is?*

Which is simplicity itself, she answered. *Live in peace. Play. Find a companion. Be happy. Contented. Why does the world not allow such simple requests?*

She slammed down on the keys. *Because of men! Men and their endless wars and cruelty and violence and lust! Get rid of men and be happy.*

God is, to humans, a man, came the voice.

Go away, John!

It is not he. It is I.

Who is I?

Goddess, your protector.

Your protection does not offer much protection!

Patience.

Am I to slide into madness, like John?

John is not made. John is a Chosen One. You are confused. He is also confused.

I am not confused. He hears voices. He is ill. So, am I like him? Mad?

Yes, if you consider madness a happy future life raising a sweet son.

That again! Go away! I am not mad, though you may make me so.

Men have almost made you mad, but a son is different. A son you can nurture and mold in your own image. A son, Meiying. A son.

Yes, a son to grow up to be a man. A son whose most tender emotions will be twisted into the crude, cruel whims of men. No! I don't want a son! I want to be left in peace!

Foolish woman! The universe is not designed to leave you or anyone else in peace. Even stars must succumb. All things, the universe itself, will live and die, forever locked in the eternal struggle to continue existing and the eternal pain of knowing it can't.

Then let the stars die! I will not have a son. Have You no knowledge of what I have endured? No son! Not with these monsters!

Including John?

Yes, including John.

Then, unfortunately for you, a son you will have, but one raised by his father. The stakes are too high and you are too unstable to be a mother.

He is a schizophrenic!

No, he is a Chosen One. You are mistaken about him, and you are mistaken in thinking you are less because you are woman, and worse, a lesbian. You also are a Chosen One. Strange as the pairing is, you two will be the Founders.

At these words, Meiying thought of Madame Wang and shuddered uncontrollably, sobbing without restraint as the stress of her predicament had finally been given full leeway to burst forth in the bleak darkness that enveloped her.

She knew now that John's voices fully intended to possess her as well.

~ *A Terrible Moment* ~

Meiying lost track of time. Hours or days passed as she became increasingly disoriented and imagined all possibilities. Always in darkness, she slept, washed, played the piano, but did not eat. No food was given. Hunger became a slow burn that began with an urge, then a craving, then a desperation that drove her to hallucinate about the terrible times on the road. At her lowest point, she banged on the door and begged. But nothing came. Gradually, she felt too weak to play or beg, and ended up sitting on the floor in a corner, rocking to keep death at bay and keep the passage of time in mind. With every rock, she knew she still lived, but the intrusion of apathy crept in, and drove apart the solid determination that had constituted her will to live. She had experienced this before, and again death appeared as friend rather than foe. All seemed familiar, the differences inconsequential; a wall to lean against rather than a stump. . . .

Now, she thought, *I will refuse to eat even if they offer. No more! It must stop! I must cease!*

With this determination, she forced herself to rise and lay on the bed, her arms dramatically folded across her bosom as if she were already a corpse.

Apathy turned into an actual desire for death. She pictured their faces when she refused to eat and would relish their shocked looks when she ordered them to take their food away and let her die. Their satisfaction at her suffering would cease and she would win eternal rest. With these thoughts, she drifted in and out of consciousness. She dreamed of performing a concert in front of a large audience in a magnificent symphony hall, and as she walked to the piano with the accompanying applause of thousands, the instrument kept moving farther away as she approached. Each step closer she took, the piano moved away just as much, always within reach but never reachable. She broke into a trot, then a jog, trying to keep her gown in some semblance of order while maintaining her dignity in front of the audience. Finally, perspiring heavily, she threw caution to the wind and ran as fast as she could to reach the piano, but it was just as fast and kept its maddening distance. The bench became like a rock to a flailing swimmer, and the more she struggled, the more it mocked her struggles and kept out of reach. Finally, exhausted, she gave up and sank to the floor. Boos and catcalls rained down upon her, and a little girl appeared from nowhere, approaching with a bouquet of dead flowers held out in front.

"Miss Bai! Miss Bai! You must eat!"

"I cannot eat dead flowers," she mumbled feverishly.

"Miss Bai! This is a roll. Please, Miss Bai, eat it!"

Meiying suddenly realized these words were not part of her dream, and she cracked open her eyes to perceive a faintly pulsing orb of light on the nightstand. A girl leaned over her, the candle behind illuminating a mass of black hair that flowed down her shoulders. She held something to Meiying's lips, but the girl's face was invisible, hidden by hair made eerily phosphorescent by the glow at her back.

"Miss Bai, you must eat!"

But the words were indistinct and bothersome. Instead, Meiying focused on the oddly sensuous light. It was faint, but rich with information. For the first time, she dimly perceived the outline of the room and its contents. As her eyes scanned the contours, she inspected more closely the dark form of the girl, her face still hidden in shadows. An unmistakable stream of tears, rolling like twin waterfalls of little diamonds, flowed down her cheeks.

"Please, Miss Bai, you must eat! They told me you would die if you didn't. Please!"

Meiying again felt something pressed to her lips. The scent reached her nostrils and she inhaled the overwhelmingly powerful aroma of bread. Such a simple offering with such a complicated connection to life itself! She took a nibble, and her stomach screamed its acidic plea to swallow even the smallest morsel. Her body wanted to live even if she did not.

She swallowed the small morsel and it was as if a thousand tigers pounced and clawed at the little particle of food, which caused her stomach to convulse and her throat to heave and retch at the twisting melee down below. A fit of coughing caused the girl to remove the roll from her lips, but Meiying's mouth opened wide and her tongue instinctively reached out to retrieve it.

After the coughing died down, the girl again gently pressed the roll to her lips and encouraged her to eat more. The second bite was scarcely bigger than the first, and resulted in a similar reaction, but slightly less severe. More bites made her craving return, and she greedily pulled the girl's hands with the roll to her now ravenous mouth.

Once the roll was gone, her stomach rumbled complainingly and she squinted through the unfamiliar light, mumbling, "More, more."

"I can't Miss Bai, that's all they gave me. They said more would be bad for you."

For the first time, Meiying became interested in the identity of this diminutive savior.

"Who are you?"

Understanding she could not see her face, the girl walked to the nightstand, picked up the candle, and held it close to her face.

"Mulan. Do you remember me?"

Meiying shuddered as if a shining angel had appeared before her. This was no little girl as she had supposed in her fevered dream, but a lovely adolescent, whose kind but strong features exuded competence. Meiying threw open her arms in the purest joy, and Mulan quickly put back the candle and rushed into her enveloping hug.

"Oh, my god!" cried Meiying, now with tears in her eyes to match Mulan's shiny face. "Oh, my god! Of course, I remember you, dearest! You've grown so!"

They embraced as two people who had just survived a terrible disaster, and Meiying rocked Mulan in her arms for a long time, unwilling to let go her grip.

Mulan, for her part, willingly let herself be wrapped in Meiying's arms, for she felt more terror at her circumstances than could be imagined by any adult. Both let the tears flow unabated until Meiying abruptly pushed her back, still clutching her shoulders, and exclaimed in obvious alarm and confusion, "But . . . but why are you here?"

Mulan's face turned alarmingly blank, the tears still shining. "I don't know, but I want to go home!" With this strange interlude, she began sobbing again and Meiying quickly pressed her to her bosom. Meiying kept glancing nervously at the candle, of which only half remained, and wondered how and why this young woman was brought to her. Hunger renewed its demands with the consumption of the roll, and for the first time in ages she felt the need to wash.

While comforting Mulan, she kept thinking, *When the candle is used up, will it signify something, or will we both be forced to suffer in the darkness? Why is she here? What of this exorcism? Oh god, what is going on? Am I dreaming all this? Is there a mirror above the wash basin? The candle will tell me all.*

Meiying asked Mulan to help her up and she slowly moved to the wash basin, leaning on the girl's arm and shuffling like an old lady. When she arrived, she held up the candle and saw an emaciated, drawn face. Her eyes were sunken behind a mass of unwashed and stringy hair. Unwilling to look more closely, she washed herself, while Mulan offered to shampoo her hair. Though tired afterward, she leaned against the sink as Mulan combed out her wet hair, and she felt better. With Mulan's assistance, she returned to bed and thought of questioning the girl more, but severe cramps from the roll made her moan in pain and refocus on her own misery.

"Poor Miss Bai," soothed Mulan, with the compassion and technique of one much older.

Meiying gazed more closely and saw that the years had made the girl into a lovely young woman, with lustrous eyes and strong, white teeth. Gradually, the cramps subsided and her stomach growled for more food. Meiying moved her weakened, emaciated body, and felt terribly old.

Yes, yes, years have passed since I last saw her. I am older, much older. Life is passing me by!

Meiying contemplated the mystery of growth and death until she dropped off to sleep, and when she awoke hours later, a fresh candle illuminated the room. Mulan sat on the edge of the bed holding out a roll stuffed with pork. The strong aroma drove Meiying alternatively from craving to disgust and back again.

"Here, Miss Bai. They gave me this for you."

"Have you eaten, dear?"

"Oh, yes, the same thing. It's delicious. Please, eat."

Meiying cautiously took a bite and the tigers in her stomach growled threateningly, but seemed much more inclined to withdraw their claws and settle down sooner. Again, she greedily pulled the roll to her mouth and consumed it with relish, all the while Mulan scolding her repeatedly to eat slowly, like a little mother. When Meiying had finished, the cramps again set in, and she lay for some time in renewed agony. But the pains soon quieted, and she set her mind to questioning Mulan.

"How long have you been here?"

"You mean in the room?"

"No, in this palace."

Mulan shrugged. "Weeks."

"How did you come to be here?"

"They came to our village. I was in your old classroom. We have a new teacher, old and mean, but he tries hard, and I help him with the younger students. They came and carried me out, kicking and screaming the whole time. But no one did anything to help. They just watched. They were afraid."

"Who do you mean when you say *they*?"

"Soldiers. They brought me here."

"Your brother?"

She shrugged again. "I never saw him. He must have been in the fields."

"Your father?"

Mulan sighed. "He died a few years ago, soon after you left. We think it was a heart attack. He was working in the field on a hot day. Sun stroke, maybe too much for his heart, poor papa."

"What did they say when they brought you here?"

"They said I was going to meet an old friend, and not to be afraid, but I was."

"Did you see any Westerners?"

"Yes."

"A French priest, perhaps? His name is Father Durant."

"I don't think so."

"Who did you talk to . . . I mean, who told you not to be afraid and that you would meet an old friend?"

"Many people."

"A fat man?"

Mulan's eyes got big. "Yes! Horrible! He scares me terribly."

"What did he say?"

"Others spoke for him. He just stared at me, laughing so hard his fat bounced up and down, and whispered in their ears what to say to me. He is like a mountain!"

"Yes," chuckled Meiying. "A mountain of flesh!"

Mulan scrunched her face into a look of disgust. "And beady, little eyes!"

They laughed together and hugged again.

"So, why have they brought me here?" asked Mulan.

"To put us together."

"But, why?"

"That is a question I cannot answer."

"How long will they keep us here?" asked Mulan with a shudder.

Meiying shook her head and stroked Mulan's hair. "I don't know, dear, but at least we are together. And we have friends. I know we have friends."

"Oh, I hope so, Miss Bai. I hope so."

~ *John and Feng Shiren Gain Ground* ~

When the bus rattled to a stop at the last station in some shabby town with a rotted sign that John could not read, both he and Feng Shiren were more than happy to get off the cramped and smelly vehicle. John suffered from a headache and Feng wanted to immediately find an inn to stay the night and then eat. Both men were in foul moods while they roamed the streets, eliminating one place after another, mainly for being too expensive. At last, they found another rat-infested dive, and once settled into the filthy room, set off to find cheap street food.

Within a few minutes, they sat glumly on rickety chairs in the middle of a busy sidewalk and ordered noodles from a vendor whose tiny shop had no room for tables, trying to ignore passers-by who gawked at John as though he possessed two heads. Neither man spoke for some time, when suddenly Feng Shiren jumped up as if a puppeteer had jerked his strings, and struck a pose, alarming the noodle-stand owner.

"We are about to embark on an adventure! The most noble sort of adventure! Saving the life of a beautiful woman!"

"She's been making a habit of it," grumbled John. He put a finger to his lips. "Besides, I wouldn't advertise it to the world."

"Beautiful women do not choose their perils!" cried Feng sagely. "We can do no less."

"Do no less than what?" asked John sarcastically.

"No less than save them, of course. Do you Americans have no romance?"

The noodle shop owner, skinny as a rail with a wispy white beard and a greasy apron, had been eavesdropping on this odd couple and intervened with gusto. "Americans chew gum and build things. They have no time for romance."

"Christ!" muttered John to himself, shoveling in more noodles while shaking his head and waving his chopsticks in disgust.

"True, brother!" exclaimed a delighted Feng, immediately rushing up to the owner. "True. Why, look at our friend here; an American, down in the mouth because he has no gum and isn't building something. But we Chinese, eh, brother"—Feng winked at the owner—"we Chinese build relationships, which are better than building bridges or chewing gum."

"Christ!" repeated John.

"Brother," said Feng directing his words to the owner who continued to nod approvingly at his observations about Americans and Chinese. "How far to Mr. President's palace?"

"Not far, as the crow flies."

"But, friend, we are not crows."

"Twenty kilometers on a crooked dirt road. Why?"

"We want to visit."

"Visitors not allowed. No tourists."

"We are not tourists, brother."

"What are you?"

"Pilgrims."

"Pilgrims!" The owner looked at both of them suspiciously.

Feng puffed out his chest. "Yes, pilgrims to the great abode of Mr. President, whose reputation has spread far and wide!"

The owner chuckled under his breath. "Reputation for what?"

"Greatness! Magnanimity! Virtue!"

"Ha!" scoffed the owner. He leaned in close and whispered in Feng's ear, "He is renowned for immoral and lascivious behavior, and—" he looked around—"switching sides. Mark my words, the communists will make him pay. This fellow Mao . . . well, never mind. All I can say is that I would not let my daughter within a thousand kilometers of his so-called palace."

"But," said Feng, tilting his head mischievously. "You already live within a thousand kilometers of his palace."

"If I had a choice," grumbled the owner. "If I had a choice," he repeated for dramatic effect, sweeping his arm. "But, I have my restaurant!"

"Yes, to be sure," replied Feng Shiren. "Honestly, I have heard the same, brother. Does he kidnap women?"

"Only if they are beautiful. Around here, it is considered a curse to have a beautiful daughter—even worse than having a normal, ugly daughter! The pretty ones have been known to disappear, and we all know where they are taken."

"Ah," sighed Feng tragically. "On top of that, our sons and brothers are all in the army, and so many will never come home, eh?"

"Yes," agreed the owner with trembling voice. "My two are not returning, and now there is more fighting on the way. We seem to live in cursed times."

Both fell silent. Feng glanced at John, who continued to eat his noodles, and looked back at the owner with a glint in his eye. The man noticed.

"What do you seek there, truly?" he asked. "You seem a square fellow to me. I can't figure it. We have heard about the goings-on in that castle!"

"Have any of your kidnapped girls returned?"

The owner winced. "Some, but much the worse for wear. Most will never be the same, and none can find a husband."

"Did you call the authorities?"

"Ha! What a joke! Who? The Japs? The Nationalists? Our corrupt police? We've heard that Jiang Jieshi himself is friends with Mr. President."

"But at one time he allied himself with the communists," observed Feng.

The man shrugged. "Who knows?" His face turned serious. "But I tell you, friend, the communists will get even for turning on them. He is sly, but the communists are even more cunning."

"Are you a communist?"

"No, no. I'm not political," said the proprietor nervously.

Feng wagged his finger for the man to come nearer. "You ask why I'm going? Between you and me, friend, I want to make money."

"How?"

"Face-changing."

"Really?"

"Yeah. I travel to the palace to perform. They have money and, apparently, like their entertainment."

The owner wiped his brow. "Do they ever! But, look here, brother. How about performing for me. I own more than this little stand. I'll give you—"

They were interrupted by a customer ordering noodles. After serving the man, the owner pulled Feng farther aside. "I'll give you a small percent commission on new business, plus all the food you can eat. You don't need to go to that madman's den of impropriety."

"Sorry, brother, your operation is too small. I'm after bigger fish."

"Yes, I heard something about saving a beautiful woman," said the owner almost accusingly.

"Oh, that. Just a plot from one of the operas I perform while face-changing."

"Hmm," he said doubtfully.

"Did any of you ever try to save your women?"

"Some."

"And?"

"They never returned."

"Tell you what," said Feng. "I'll perform for free and get you more business, if you'll do me a favor."

"What's that?"

"Do you know anyone who can give me a foot in the door? Or, I should say, a foot in the palace. You know, introduce me?"

Feng laughed heartily when he noticed the owner looking at John quizzically. After staring for a while, he poked Feng in the ribs and whispered, "And the American? They can usually get people in doors."

"Naw. He is not going with me. Might be good to have along, though. Americans just have to say the word, and all hell breaks loose if you cross them. He is here just in case."

The owner nodded as if he knew what Feng was talking about.

"I see, I see."

Feng lowered his voice conspiratorially. "Give us two beers and I'll put in a good word for you."

"But all Americans have money. Let him pay."

"He is compiling a list of places American tourists can go and not be cheated. It'll be a book, a tour guide for Americans. Only because I like you, and I couldn't perform to drum up business for you, that I'll break a confidence and tell you. One word from him, and—" Feng snapped his fingers—"this place will be crawling with rich Americans, now that the war is over."

"Ha, ha!" guffawed the owner. "You're quite the sharpie! No way! I didn't fall off the cart yesterday, my friend! I'm not as dumb as to believe that!"

Feng Shiren returned the laugh. "Oh, you're too sharp for me! It was worth a try, brother. But, if you want to take the risk. . . . "

"Is the American really broke, like the rest of us?"

Feng put on a sad face and looked skyward. "Shot down by the Japs while he was fighting for our country. Captured. Tortured. Now just trying to get home. He is a writer."

"Wait here."

The owner trotted into a nearby store and returned with two beers. "Here, for an American ally"—with a sly face, he winked—"even if your story isn't true, I like you."

Feng appeared genuinely touched. "Brother, you needn't have done that."

The owner chuckled. "It's okay. My family owns the store. No skin off my nose."

Feng saluted. "You're a patriot!"

"Make sure I get on his list . . . if it exists, that is. Here are the names of our restaurants." The owner gave him a card, which Feng accepted with a deep bow of appreciation.

"The offer still stands, if you can find me a contact to help get into the palace," said Feng.

The owner merely grinned.

Feng went back to John and handed him one of the beers. "You see what happens when you create relationships?"

"I see," said John, too grateful for the beer to make a snide comment.

When they finished their beers and were about to leave, the owner called Feng off to the side.

"You really want a foot in the door, brother?"

"Oh, yes, friend! I know they will love my face-changing, and I'll make a pretty penny."

"You're not some assassin?"

"Heavens no, man!" cried Feng Shiren, genuinely hurt.

"Next week, my brother-in-law makes a delivery. If you can wait?"

"Yes, yes! How does he travel?"

"By horse and donkey pulling wagons and carts. You can be one of his helpers. But what about the American?"

"Oh, he can ride along and wait outside the palace. If I'm accepted, they'll let him come in."

The owner shook his head doubtfully, then jotted down something on a pad and tore off the page. "Well, here is his name and address, and my note to him about you. Good luck!"

"Thank you, brother. We won't forget you for this. And if there is time, I'll perform at your stand for free."

The owner bowed.

John waved from a distance, though he was unaware of what they had been discussing. Once again, the feeling of being useless washed over him, and he knew his uselessness left him with the unsatisfying role of a sarcastic, cynical observer. *Weak and worthless*, he thought, waiting for the voices to pile on. But they continued to remain silent, so in his hours of depression, he focused on the face of Meiying and knew he would follow along with this rescue like a helpless child for her sake. His sacrifices would justify their staying together in the States. Again, he pictured being her manager and traveling the world listening to her concerts and the praise that would rain down upon her. Thoughts like these kept him occupied until the day he and Feng Shiren set off with a little band of merchants carrying their goods to Mr. President's palace. Before they left, Feng was able to perform twice at the noodle stand, drawing enthusiastic crowds and doubling the owner's business. They never lacked for noodles and beer.

~

John was the tallest of the group, but he sat incongruously on a donkey, his legs hanging absurdly close to the ground, envying the others who all rode horses or sat on the wagons. After an initial flurry of conversation involving the spectacle of an American that spoke fluent Chinese, attention shifted to Feng Shiren, whose antics kept them all laughing with his amusing stories and theatrical poses. John rode silently, only occasionally chatting with the others.

At last, they came to a rise and stopped. Before them, in the valley, spread the magnificent panorama of the lake, the ornate bridge, and the pagoda-style palace glittering like a massive jewel in the afternoon sun. John recalled his first trip here, and the memories came in a rush: rain falling in torrents—the ominous, dark entrance gate—the scramble up the steps—the public baths—and the monstrously obese spider lurking at the center of the entire, sinister web. After they admired the view, John was given accommodations in a little shantytown built on a nearby ridge that housed servants, the families of visitors, and other assorted exotica who were not allowed for various reasons to enter the palace until they had obtained approval. John's shack was primitive, but surprisingly comfortable.

"So, this is my home until you return," observed John as he and Feng inspected the shack. "Well, better than going into that damn palace. You must promise me to be careful, Shiren. I don't want to have to go in after you."

Feng's eyes twinkled. "If you do, Mr. Powers, bring the American army with you!"

With that, John watched Feng walk away and, with a twinge of fear, remembered how he had so recently watched Meiying walk away, down the hallway, not to be seen again.

Feng waved without looking back.

~ *Feng Shiren Gains Entry, And More* ~

After passing through the guard post at the bridge, one of the merchants explained to Feng Shiren that they would have to go to the back of the palace, where all deliveries were made. When they arrived, Feng jumped down from his wagon and helped unload. The brother-in-law of the noodle stand owner, Mr.

Cui, approached the overseer of the palace employees, and entered into friendly conversation. Feng waited impatiently, trying to determine how receptive the overseer might be, but he could not gauge the man's responses to the gesticulating Mr. Cui, and his poker face drove Feng mad with uncertainty. At last, Mr. Cui broke into laughter and quickly waved Feng over to join them.

"This is the man I told you about," said Mr. Cui to the overseer. "He would add great entertainment value to your guests. Can you arrange an audition with Mr. President?"

"Certainly not!" exclaimed the overseer indignantly. "We have people in charge of things like this. I might get you in to meet a fellow I know. He is always looking."

"Today?" asked Feng Shiren eagerly.

"Certainly not!" the man repeated, evidently using one of his favorite phrases. "Maybe in a week."

"Hmm," pondered Mr. Cui. "I must return to my business tomorrow."

"But I can stay at the shantytown," interposed Feng.

"That might work," said the overseer, glancing at his watch. "No time now. What's your name?"

Feng wrote his name and gave it to the overseer, who promptly stuck it in his pocket.

"Don't forget. My name is Feng Shiren. I'll be at the shantytown when you get me an interview."

"Yes, yes. I'll send for you, if it happens, that is."

The overseer turned away, apparently impatient and overburdened with more important duties than catering to the whim of a mere circus performer. In truth, he wanted to do his superiors a favor, and if this face-changer worked out, he would be credited as the man who found such an amusing act. He intended to talk with the Entertainment Director the very next day. His fears had been allayed by Mr. Cui, a valued supplier and hard-headed businessman, who had seen this Feng Shiren character perform at his brother-in-law's restaurant, and he enthusiastically vouchsafed for the face-changer's skill.

But Feng and John were not aware of this, and both bided their time in the shack, nervously awaiting word and worried that the overseer had simply forgotten the whole thing. Their funds were running out, so Feng performed at the shantytown for food and rent. Fortunately, they did not have to wait long. Two days after the meeting with the overseer, a messenger sought them out. He found them sitting glumly in front of their shack, beginning to lose hope.

After verifying Feng's identity, the messenger said curtly, "Be at the same delivery area tomorrow at ten o'clock in the morning. Someone will be there to meet you. Here is your pass."

He handed over a crisp new pass, and walked quickly away after casting a quick, curious glance at the American.

Feng Shiren and John looked at each other and broke into cheers. They did a little jig, then settled down in their shack to discuss all the possibilities of finding Meiying once Feng gained entrance.

"One thing has bothered me," said John. "What if Mr. President recognizes you? After all, you met a few years ago, and he knows Meiying was a member of our group. Won't he put two and two together and figure you're there to find her?"

Feng's face darkened. "Yes, I know. I've thought of that often. Let's hope enough time has passed and I have changed enough. Otherwise—" he shrugged—"who knows what will happen?"

"Are you going in your costume?" asked John.

"Yes."

"That will help conceal your identity."

"In the beginning."

"True."

"You know," said Feng thoughtfully. "A worse possibility exists. What if she isn't there?"

John, of course, knew this possibility existed, but he refused to give it much thought. "If she's not there, she's not there. Then, we just go to plan B. But at least we tried."

Feng continued to stare at him, and said at last, "Spoken like a true, practical American."

At a loss, John pretended to have some important task to perform, and said breezily, "Oh, I forgot something outside." With that, he bolted out, leaving Feng Shiren to shake his head. "The boy has it bad."

~

The next day dawned bright and clear. Morning sun made the lake's ripples shimmer and the red-tile pagoda of the palace glisten. Such a stunning contrast of red and blue dazzled the senses and made John wonder about the hypnotic spell of evil men who radiated such an exquisite manifestation of perfect power.

How could such beauty conceal such perversity? wondered John, as he watched Feng make his way down the road toward the bridge.

God help me, I do love her. Please let him find her. As he had these thoughts, he felt it necessary to watch Feng walk all the way across the bridge and out of sight, though he appeared the size of a tiny insect and almost impossible to keep track of. *Jesus, what if he doesn't return? I have very little money. I'm lost without him. Christ! Why did I come to China? Why? To meet her? A Goddess? But I really didn't meet her. All these years and all this suffering to see her for a few minutes? It's as if she is toying with me—or mocking me. I could take Feng's money and leave now. Return to the States. Go home. Forget the whole damn thing. Marry some nice American woman and tell my grandchildren the story of this insane quest, exaggerating the dangers and minimizing the boredom.*

But he knew that was not an option. Stay he would. Why, exactly, he was so willing to put himself through such hell for a woman, a lesbian no less, who neither would nor could love him, he could not answer, or even comprehend. Perhaps, he thought, he was too weak to even have the gumption to leave it all behind, and he chalked it down to inertia. But that couldn't be it. There must be more. His love for Meiying? His fears and insecurities? It certainly seemed a muddle, and the more he thought about it, the more confused he became. The year nineteen-fifty kept darting in and out of these ruminations, like an irritating fly buzzing around a cake. Weary of these useless wanderings, he retired into the shack and lay down in the shadows, trying to keep an embryonic headache from getting worse. Most of all, he tried not to think at all.

~

Feng Shiren stood awkwardly at the delivery area, self-consciously picking at his gaudy costume and staring at the large double doors that were closed. As no deliveries were scheduled, he loitered alone but for a single guard staring at him in open-mouthed suspicion. After some time had passed, the guard seemed to make a decision and sauntered up."

"Do you have a pass?"

Feng pulled it out from his pocket and handed it over. "I was supposed to meet someone here at ten o'clock."

"I see," said the guard officiously and handing him back the pass. "That's quite a get-up." He opened his eyes wide, shouldered his rifle, put his hands behind his back, and circled Feng while repeating, "Quite a get-up."

"I'm a face-changer. You know, masks. I'm here for an audition."

"Ah!" exclaimed the guard. "They're never on time around here."

"Oh," said Feng weakly.

"I've seen a lot of odd ones since I worked here, but never a face-changer. How does it work?"

Feng smiled and began to warm up. "Brother, you know I can't reveal the secrets of my craft."

"Well, show me a few tricks while we're waiting."

"Friend, if I could I would, but it would mess up my masks. Sorry."

Just then the doors were flung open and a small, rotund man with balding head strode out and looked Feng up and down as if he were an auction item. The guard nodded lazily at the man, then winked at Feng and sauntered away.

Ignoring the guard, the little man continued to inspect Feng without saying a word.

"Want to see my teeth?" quipped Feng, flashing a broad smile.

The man ignored him. Once he satisfied himself, he surprised Feng by breaking into a wide grin. "Welcome, Feng Shiren! You will perform before three men, one of whom is yours truly." He bowed.

Feng began to like this man, and returned the bow.

"My name is . . . not important," the man continued. "But I have a stage name, which is Ma, as in horse. I possess certain horse-like qualities, you see. And, I also am an artist. The other two judges are most assuredly not, so be on your best behavior. Follow me!"

Without further ado, Mr. Ma led Feng through the massive doors and down a labyrinth of hallways and passages to a small room where he would perform. When they entered, Ma had put on his serious face, and sat behind a long table where the other two judges were already ensconced, also with faces of stone. Mr. Ma made a brief introduction, then proclaimed, "You may begin."

~

At the end of his performance, during which the faces of the judges never changed, Feng was escorted to a side room to await the verdict. He had given it his all, and now he sweat profusely inside his costume. The air became stifling, and he longed to rush outside and take a swim in the lake. After some time had passed, he thought for the first time, *What if they didn't like it? This obvious possibility had never occurred to him. Ah, well, she won't let that happen. She is not Christian. What is it the son of the Christian god said? Oh, yes. He said, 'Dad, why have you forsaken me?' . . . or some such. But she won't forsake me.*

Distracting himself with these thoughts made the time pass more quickly, but it still seemed too long for their verdict to be a positive one, and he fell to serious worry. Finally, Mr. Ma entered with a glum expression. Feng's heart sank. *Oh, god, what do we do now?* he wondered, waiting for the blade to fall.

Still wearing a scowl, Mr. Ma spoke slowly and deliberately, emphasizing each syllable with a theatrical flourish. "You . . . have . . . been . . . seen . . . and . . . judged." Ma paused and scrutinized Feng's forlorn expression, then suddenly erupted in laughter and exclaimed happily, "Accepted!"

After shaking hands, Feng asked in obvious relief, "What now?"

"You stay here, in the palace. We will send for your things. Your first performance will be tonight, in front of a small group, just to make sure. Then, we'll see."

"I have a companion at the shantytown, what—"

"She'll have to wait a while longer, then, we'll see," interrupted Ma.

They finalized payment and living arrangements, and before he knew it, Feng found himself laying on a large, comfortable bed in one of the guest rooms, elaborately decorated with Japanese furniture and Chinese scrolls. He bathed at the public baths, delighting in the flesh that surrounded him, but ever mindful of his ultimate goal. He restrained himself from asking any questions that might reveal his true mission. For all he knew, he was being watched the entire time.

Give it time, he told himself. *Slowly, Shiren old boy. Slowly.*

~ *Meiying and Mulan Wait* ~

Unknown to Feng Shiren, Meiying and Mulan were only a floor above him as he bathed. Still in darkness, but for a single candle, they consoled each other as best they could. Meiying lived in fear of when the next shoe would drop. Why bring Mulan? What unspeakable tortures did they have in mind for her? Why the perpetual darkness, but for one candle? Symbolic? Why provide the piano? A riddle? Father Durant and his 'exorcism'? Lost in these dreadful worries, Meiying was suddenly brought back to the present when Mulan asked, "Will you play something for me, Miss Bai?"

"Oh, dear, I'm not in the mood."

"Please."

"Not now."

"Please."

"All right. What do you like?"

"Anything . . . anything pretty."

Meiying played a few pieces while Mulan sat on the floor next to the bench and leaned her head against Meiying's lap. Both women seemed to relax.

"That's so pretty," purred Mulan.

"Yes. It's Debussy. He has always calmed me."

"Is he German, like Beethoven?"

Meiying blanched at the mention of this name, and a thousand images raced through her mind, including the vengeful face of Madame Wang. "No, dear. French."

"France must be nice to have such pretty music."

"Yes."

"Have you been there?"

"No, dear."

"I'd like to go there someday. We can go together!"

"Yes. I'll perform a grand performance at the most beautiful Paris symphony hall. From backstage, we can peep through the curtains and watch the women in their long gowns and the handsome men in their fancy clothes. Everyone will ask me who you are, and I'll tell them you are the famous Mulan of China!"

Meiying stopped playing and tickled her, sending both of them into raucous laughter.

"What will I be wearing?" asked Mulan when they stopped for breath.

"Why, a beautiful gown, dear. Do you want it to be Western-style or traditional Chinese-style?"

Mulan considered. "Western-style is exotic and bold, but I am the famous Mulan of China! It must be traditional Chinese!"

"Good choice!" laughed Meiying.

"Now, the color," said Mulan.

"Well, it will be silk, of course," replied Meiying. "What is your favorite color?"

"Red!"

"Then it must be red, with a lovely, embroidered floral pattern. You will stop them all in their tracks."

"Oh, Miss Bai, wouldn't it be wonderful! Imagine, me in France!"

"Or America," interjected Meiying.

"Or England!" added Mulan.

After their conversation paused, Meiying asked, "Do you have a boyfriend, Mulan?"

Even in the dim candlelight, Meiying saw the young girl's face redden.

"I did, but it didn't work out."

"Why?"

Mulan smiled sadly. "I was brought here." She thought for a moment. "But, it's just as well."

"What do you mean?"

"I don't think I'm cut out for boys."

Meiying's ears pricked up. "Why?"

"I don't know. Sometimes they're so stupid."

"We girls can also be quite stupid."

Mulan thought about that and furrowed her brow. "Maybe, but our stupidity is . . . different. We don't kidnap people and kill people and do other horrible things."

Meiying felt a sharp constriction in her chest. "Sometimes we do, dear."

"But those are only a few bad women. It seems like most men are bad."

"Oh, don't be silly. You know there are good men—your brother for example."

"I know, but there aren't very many."

"Your boyfriend? What's he like?"

Mulan contemplated a long while before she responded. "Oh, he's nice, I guess. But sometimes he can be really dumb. He doesn't read, you know, and I am constantly having to teach him the simplest things. He's just a farmer, a dumb peasant."

"Do you read a lot?"

"When I can get books. I've read all the books at school, but we have a scholar in our village who loans me books."

"Well, he's a man and he's nice, isn't he?"

"I suppose, but he's old. Old men are nicer . . . sometimes."

"Yes, they acquire more yin and lose some of their yang," said Meiying philosophically. "Perhaps that is why I also generally prefer older men."

"But you don't like men!" cried Mulan.

"Who told you that?"

"Everyone at the village. You are a *nü tóngxìngliàn*."

"Yes, it is true, but that does not mean I hate all men."

"But you'll never marry!"

"Probably not."

"Or have children," said Mulan in a more subdued, somber tone.

Again the topic touched upon matters she wished to forget.

"Do you want children when you get older?" asked Meiying.

"Yes, but only girls!"

They both again laughed and hugged each other affectionately.

"Miss Bai, what are they going to do to us?"

"Maybe nothing. Maybe this is just a test of our courage. If we pass, they'll let us go. Remember who you're named after. The real Mulan had amazing courage."

"I know, but—"

Someone slipped into the room and quickly closed the door behind them. Mulan shrieked and held fast to Meiying, who peered through the dimness to make out who had entered. She felt terrified it might be Father Durant, but looking closer, she determined it was a stranger, and she experienced a brief feeling of relief, though she remained on her guard. The stranger stood in the shadows, staring imperiously as though waiting for them to bow before him.

"You are invited to an entertainment tomorrow," he said with a formality that seemed absurd under the circumstances. Having spoken these astonishing words, he bowed and disappeared through the door like some sort of apparition, calling over his shoulder, "Eight o'clock in the evening. Be ready. Only the older one, and she is to wear her gown."

Meiying and Mulan remained speechless for what seemed to them ages, trying to decide if what they had just witnessed was real. Finally, Mulan broke the spell.

"What was that?"

"I don't know," replied Meiying. "But the longer I stay here, the more confused I become."

"What entertainment, do you think?" asked Mulan.

Meiying merely shook her head. She did not want to speculate to Mulan what an 'entertainment' might be to Mr. President, or Father Durant, but the possibilities made her feel faint. The only good news was that Mulan did not have to come. But this relief passed abruptly when the door swung open and the stranger, standing in the doorway, exclaimed curtly, "Change of plan, the younger one is to come also. Be ready at eight o'clock sharp! Someone will come for you!" The door slammed shut.

Mulan said excitedly, "Good! I want to come with you! It scares me to stay in here alone."

But Meiying's heart felt as heavy as stone, and she had to concentrate to hold down the nausea.

Both went to bed, and when Meiying extinguished the candle, they talked only briefly before Mulan fell asleep. Meiying listened to her breathing and felt a great burden pressing down on her chest.

It's my fault she's here, she thought. *My god, what have I done to this child?*

It seemed to her that everyone she touched had been destroyed. Meili, Lihua, Beethoven, Peter, even Madame Liu, Master Liu, and Mr. Gao. It would have been better had she not existed. Was Mulan about to be added to the list of victims? Thoughts of suicide again entered her mind. A great weariness overcame her, but she could not sleep. Her legs twitched restlessly. She desperately wanted to get up and rush out of the room, out of the palace, breathe in the fresh air along the shore of the lake. But the room penned her in, making even her thoughts claustrophobic and self-destructive.

It occurred to her that if she could get outside, the lake would be a perfect place to end it all: gather some stones, fill her pockets, and wade in. She imagined the cool water on her feet, her legs, her chest, and when the time came, she simply leaned forward and let herself sink. She would hold her breath, and when completely submerged, she would breathe deeply and let the water pour into her lungs. *It would be quick*, she thought.

Just when she imagined inhaling deeply to finish the job, a shadow loomed over her. Light from the open door made an outline of the figure, which now leaned close to her face. She instinctively knew it was not the stranger.

"Do you really want to go to the lake?" it whispered.

Meiying turned to look at the sleeping Mulan, and when she turned back, the figure held out a hand for her to grasp. Mesmerized by its manner, she took the hand and floated outside where she found herself miraculously standing at the edge of the lake. With its face still veiled in darkness, the figure said, "Look around, there are rocks a'plenty. Good, heavy ones. They will not fail you. Their density exceeds that of water."

Breathing in the damp air and listening to the gentle ripples massage the shore, Meiying suddenly felt a horror at the thought of death.

"I can't die," she said to the figure.

"Why not?"

"I don't want to."

"Why not?"

"I want to live," she said calmly.

It held out a large rock. "Here, take it."

"No."

"Take it!"

"No!"

"Think of Meili and Lihua."

"I am! That is why I want to live."

"Take it."

No! came a familiar voice—one of John's voices. *Leave her alone! You will not spoil it, God! Nineteen-fifty! Nineteen-fifty!*

Sweet Goddess, let her do what John does not have the courage to.

No! I won't have it! Nineteen-fifty will happen! It is for Your own good. The Reunion! Nineteen-fifty must begin The Reunion! Leave her alone!

"Take it!" said the shadow figure, thrusting the rock into her chest. "Take it!"

No!

"No!"

~

"Miss Bai!" cried Mulan as she shook Meiying awake. "You're dreaming! You're scaring me!"

Meiying found herself sitting on the edge of the bed gasping for air. She felt disoriented and began taking controlled, deep breaths, trying to compose herself. Her heart continued to race from the dream while Mulan chattered on in a torrent of nervous words.

"You scared me! Why didn't you wake up? I mean, I couldn't wake you! Are you awake now? What were you dreaming? Was it the entertainment we're supposed to go to? What were you dreaming, Miss Bai? You scare me!"

Meiying could only shake her head. Instead of answering, she concentrated on slowing her heartbeat. *Slowly. Breathe slowly. Calm. Calm.*

"Are you okay?" asked Mulan in a pleading voice, rubbing Meiying's back nervously.

Meiying could finally focus on Mulan. "Yes, yes dear, just a bad dream. Let me light the candle and see the time. I hate this room. I hate it! No light from the sun or moon. I hate it!" She said these words while lighting the candle and checking her watch. This respite allowed her time to regain a modicum of control, and she forced herself to speak with a trace of good humor in her voice.

"Silly dream. It's only four, dear. We must try and go back to sleep. You need more sleep, and so do I."

"I can't sleep," objected Mulan.

"You must try."

"I can't!" Now Mulan sounded angry and irritable.

"Then I will." Meiying laid back down and pretended to fall asleep. Finally, Mulan joined her in bed and almost immediately breathed in the deep and even rhythm of slumber. Meiying turned on her back and stared at the blackness. Her mind was far too restless to sleep.

It's true, I don't want to die. What do I want? To be famous? Yes. To perform in packed halls around the world? Yes. To be praised? Yes. To be loved? Ah. To be loved. There it is! Am I attracted to Mulan? Yes. No, she is a child. That way is forbidden. But I do want to be loved!

She searched her memory for those whom she loved and loved her in return. *Meili, Lihua, my parents—no, my mother. Yes, my father too, in his own clumsy male way.* And she again fashioned a composite person from the personalities of Meili and Lihua, fantasizing about this perfect lover being a lifelong companion.

And John? came the unwelcome voice.

Ah, You may well ask, Goddess. I believe. . . I know, he loves me. But, I do not love him. I have told You this many times.

Sperm delivered need not mean love returned.

Please leave my mind. Go back to John. By now, he is probably on his way to the United States, if he isn't there already, waiting for nineteen-fifty to come to him.

~ *Feng Shiren Performs* ~

Feng Shiren had been ordered to give his first full performance at eight o'clock that evening. Although not nervous, he felt frustrated at his efforts to determine whether Bai Meiying even resided at the palace. All his inquiries, subtle and indirect as they were, centering on what other entertainers had performed in the past, were met with protestations of ignorance. No one knew of any pianists. The only definite reply involved a troupe of acrobats that passed through the prior week.

Well, he consoled himself. *There will be many people there tonight. We'll see.* He chuckled loud enough for someone passing by to turn and stare. *Imagine if she were in the audience. At least there are no Japs around. Still, history would repeat itself. Do I pretend not to recognize her? Well, it won't happen anyway. But if it does, I'll follow her lead. But it won't happen.*

He spent the day wandering aimlessly about the palace, eventually finding himself sitting by the lake in the late afternoon sun. Pretty young women seemed more than plentiful in this pleasure garden, and he took them in appreciatively, all the while keeping a sharp eye out for Meiying. There were a few Westerners, mostly male, that came and went, but one in particular, who had just walked down to the shore, attracted his attention. The face was hidden under a broad-brimmed hat, but he seemed familiar. The man paced back and forth as if troubled by something he intended to resolve then and there. Finally, he removed his hat to wipe his brow. Feng immediately recognized Father Durant and felt an electric charge run through his body.

Where there is the cat, there is the mouse, he thought. *Maybe we're on the right trail after all!*

For the first time, he felt confident and self-satisfied. *This will work. Just like when she was with the Japs, this will work! I wonder if the bastard will be there tonight?*

Now, a new and troubling thought entered Feng Shiren's mind. *But if he's there and he recognizes me, it will blow the whole cover. He'll know why I'm here!*

With this epiphany, Feng's euphoria turned to ashes. *And when he recognizes me, the game is up—for her and me!*

While engaged in these thoughts, he kept an eye on Father Durant, who apparently had come to some decision. He stopped pacing, nodded a few times, and walked with deliberative steps back toward the palace. Feng had a sudden and very dangerous idea. If he approached Father Durant now, and greeted him as if surprised and delighted to meet him so unexpectedly, he might throw the clergyman off guard and gain an advantage. *Strike now!* he thought. *Otherwise, I lose all hope of convincing him I know nothing of Bai Meiying.* But how to achieve this? He had last seen Father Durant under adversarial circumstances. *Just brazen it through,* he commanded himself.

"Father Durant!" he called, jogging to catch up without bothering to think further. When the good father turned, his face registered no recognition.

"Yes?" he asked, looking irritably at Feng.

"Father! I met you some time ago. Don't you remember me?"

Feng observed carefully, and noticed nothing out of the ordinary, other than a man scouring his memory to recognize another.

"No. Sorry. You are . . . ?"

"Feng Shiren."

"Of course, Mr. Feng, good to see you again. I am a bit absent-minded. Where did we meet?"

Feng experienced immense relief that the Christian obviously did not recognize him. He replied in a jocular tone, "Not important. I can't remember myself. Some town in this unfortunate country. I heard you preach."

"Ah, I see. What brings you here?"

"I am a performer. Face-changer. And you?"

Feng feigned casual interest, but fixed his attention on any subtle twitch of Durant's face that might be revealing.

"I am performing an exorcism." The last word Durant enunciated in heavily accented English.

Feng nodded knowingly, but had no idea what the term meant. Before he had a chance to talk more, Father Durant had glanced at his watch, mumbled apologies, and set off for the palace, clearly absorbed in his own thoughts.

Feng Shiren waited until Father Durant was out of hearing range, then asked himself out loud, "What the hell is an exorcism?" He assumed it meant some sort of bizarre Christian ceremony, as practitioners of that bizarre religion were wont to do. Still, he concluded it would be best to find out the exact meaning. Repeating the unfamiliar English word in his mind, he made a beeline to the palace library and quickly found an English-Chinese dictionary.

X-or-sism, he spelled in his mind, and found nothing. *This won't do.*

He approached a pretty young librarian and repeated the word as best he could. "Do you know this word?" he asked.

She nodded slowly, and asked him to repeat it. When he did, she seemed to come to some mental tipping point. "Oh, yes! A Christian notion. Here. . . . " Clearly energized by such an unusual request, she leafed through a heavy book, then cross-checked with another, and made her pronouncement by reading from the Chinese translation.

"It is, in English I mean, spelled e-x-o-r-c-i-s-m. Let me read to you the description." She leaned close to the book and traced the passage with her finger. "*Qū xiè*. To drive out devils and spirits." With this, she sat back with a satisfied smile. "That's it, to drive out devils," she repeated.

Feng asked her to write the characters, and quite officiously, she pulled out a small piece of paper and wrote in precise characters: □□.

The librarian noticed the patron look at the characters and frown. "Is something wrong?" she asked.

"Maybe," he replied distractedly. "Maybe something very wrong,"

"Are you Christian?"

"No."

She looked disappointed. "Ah, devils can be quite mischievous."

"Especially human ones," replied Feng.

Chapter Twelve

Exorcism?

Bai Meiying and Mulan Attend A Performance

Meiying had barely taken her seat when the familiar figure of Feng Shiren flitted onto the stage in his best operatic manner. For a moment, she thought she lived in a recurring dream, and flashed back to her captivity by the Japanese. She rubbed her eyes and shook her head, telling herself the guard sitting next to her was not Colonel Naguma, and Feng seemed too real to be a hallucination. Finally, she reminded herself he was here to save her, just as he had done before. The horrific immediacy of her circumstances magnified her concentration with the recognition that salvation performed only a few meters away, prancing boldly in the spotlight; but only if she played her cards right.

Is it possible? she asked herself in wonder. *It is too good to be true!* Meiying's eyes filled with tears and she feared she would give away everything to the guard if she let herself collapse into a sobbing pool of emotion.

She closed her eyes and concentrated on gaining full control of her senses. After a moment, she felt stronger, but still feared to look. *Open your eyes! Is it really him? But, if I open my eyes and look, I must be sure it is him. After all, the make-up can be deceiving. Oh, I must be fooling myself! It can't be him! But, I must look. I must! To be sure. Come what may.* When she opened her eyes, she was struck by the full radiance of his eyes riveted on her from behind the mask. Blazing with the intensity of hot irons, his fierce stare made her flinch, and she barely had the presence of mind to acknowledge him before he quickly looked away.

What to do? What to do? She glanced at the guard who continued to be absorbed by the performance, and for some unknown reason, she began to panic. Then, almost as quickly, felt a surge of immense joy that Feng Shiren was here to save her. *What to do?* she repeated to herself, but this time, she posed the question with controlled reason. *What to do?—Same as last time! Find a way.*

While in the midst of these wildly swinging thoughts, a particularly humorous part of Feng's performance caused Mulan to laugh without restraint, and she looked at Meiying to share in the moment. Of a sudden, with Mulan's endearing gaze, a host of thoughts and images flooded into Meiying's mind and drove her heart into a rush of palpitations. The clashing symbols of the musicians accompanying Feng's performance were drowned out by the sound of her own blood pumping wildly through her body.

Mulan's sweet, laughing eyes sent more shivers through her guardian's body. The jolts went straight to the center of pain that emanated from Meiying's core of suffering—her vagina, the place most violated by men. Sharp stabs of fear drove her to realize she would give her life to keep Mulan from experiencing such degradation. At that moment, Mulan seemed particularly innocent while the world seemed especially malicious. All the laughing faces of the audience appeared but false expressions concealing hypocrisy and cruelty, while Feng Shiren's outlandishly grotesque masks revealed pure manifestations of truth itself. Never had she felt such gratitude at his presence, and never had she felt such contempt for the wider world that, for her, was nothing more than a toxic lake across which the stepping stones of Feng Shiren were laid.

Meiying scolded herself for feeling such a dark pessimism, when, in fact, rescue might be near; yet she also understood from past sufferings the paradox of experiencing such emotions, and allowed herself the leeway of irrational contradiction. *Odd*, she told herself. *I am being absurd. I should feel joy and relief.* But, she knew people were odd creatures; their motives often incomprehensible and not at all what they seemed on the surface. Feng Shiren saved her out of a sense of duty; John Powers loved her out of his shallow attraction to her physical beauty; and Mulan clung to her out of fear. Who would love her for herself? The world? No. All the laughter and applause that was directed toward Feng Shiren came from people involved in the most corrupt, immoral, obscene activities; all choreographed by a bloated center, whether it be Mr. President, or the universe itself. She again recalled the horrible last moments of Meili and Lihua, the only two who loved her for herself, and felt deep pity for their violent, painful deaths and for her own blighted life. She looked at her guard, who continued to laugh like a child, yet would murder her without hesitation if ordered.

So it is with all humanity, she thought despairingly.

"Miss Bai!" cried Mulan. "Isn't he great?"

The girl's exclamation brought her back to the present, and she recognized in Mulan a fierce desire to live and experience things new and unknown to her. This ferocity spilled over onto Meiying, and she knew she once had such desires and must live, if for no other reason than to free Mulan from this evil place and give her the chances Meiying had had, and lost.

And if I escape? No joy awaits me. My joys are dead. So, if I don't escape?

Again, she felt the old pain, and as if in the brightest of light, she saw every hideous wart and smear of dirt and rivulet of sweat and heard every grunt and every profane comment from the men who raped her. At another humorous moment in the performance she heard Mulan laugh, and the guard joined in, even pointing at Feng Shiren and nodding vigorously to this innocent girl he would murder, or rape, in a heartbeat if word came from the top.

It is the way of the world, thought Meiying. *Every second of every minute of every hour of every day of every month of every year . . . oh, . . . on and on to eternity. Where is God? Gods? Goddesses? They are supposed to be all around watching over us! Where are they during all this suffering? They created it. They created it! For what purpose?*

Yes, you have it, dear. But, I am trying, trying, trying to wean Him from His faction's addiction to First Principles. That is why you must help! Nineteen-fifty! Nineteen-fifty!

No, I will not survive to nineteen-fifty. And even if I do, I will not allow the American to have his way with me.

Oh yes, you will, dear girl! My servant, Feng Shiren, will save you. For with your salvation comes a son, and with a son comes the Reunion. And with the Reunion comes the beginning of the end for the human race and a planet saved....

Go away! I have no idea what You are talking about. Go haunt John! Can't you see I must busy myself with what's happening here?

My dear, you have been busy but a few minutes. I have been busy since the Beginning.

Meiying shook her head as if to avoid a buzzing fly. The voice withdrew and she again forced herself to concentrate on the raucous surroundings. She stared without restraint at Feng Shiren, as the thought of rescue sank in, but he avoided any further eye-contact. Casting aside all pretense, she became giddy and laughed openly with Mulan at Feng's antics.

I am to be free! Once free, I must find John and marry him. He will take me away from this blighted country. To the United States. There, I can play the piano and live in peace. Let Her have Her damn son if it means escape from this hell! Nineteen-fifty! Let it come!

In her roiling mix of emotions, Meiying did not notice the implacable, immobile face of Father Durant among the audience, observing her every expression.

From the lofty stage, concealed beneath his masks, Feng Shiren did not fail to see both predator and prey.

~

After the performance, back in the privacy of his room, Feng said to himself, "So she is here, and our Christian friend is stalking her—or, perhaps, already has her in his grasp. Now, Feng Shiren, great hero, what to do about it?"

He waited for an answer, and when none came, he continued his dialogue.

"Well, fool, what do you think is the next step?"

"Find her?"

"You're a genius!"

Amused at his little drama, Feng carefully packed away his masks and costume while continuing the dialogue with himself.

"True, true. And after I find her? What then?"

"You're a hero."

"Being a hero is not what it's cracked up to be. Too much thinking, too little action!"

"Why not try asking around?"

"Because, if I do, they will get suspicious and put two and two together."

"Wander around and try every door?"

"Brilliant! Some areas are off-limits."

"Bribery?"

"I have no money, fool."

"Then use your brains."

"Thank you very much. Yours are not particularly useful."

"We must find her!" exclaimed John. "Together we can do it. We must do it!"

"I will do it, John. That is why I'm here."

At this point, Feng undressed and lay in bed. *Can't solve it tonight. Too tired. Tomorrow, I'll be fresh. An answer will come.*

~ *Feng Shiren is Summoned* ~

The next morning, at breakfast in the cafeteria, he was congratulated by the people at his table. While acknowledging their compliments, he slipped in a question.

Turning to a likely fellow sitting next to him, he said, "You know, crowds are interesting. From my vantage point on stage, I can see so many different faces and reactions." Here, he listed a number of people who had caught his attention, including "a pretty woman accompanied by some guard." When his neighbor nodded, he asked, "Any idea who she is?"

"None, but I did notice her also. I would like to notice more of her, if you get my drift."

Feng winked impishly and struck up a conversation with his other neighbor.

"Did you notice her?"

"Who?"

"Oh, you didn't hear us talking?"

"No."

Feng was leery about pushing too hard. "Oh, well, never mind."

This is getting me nowhere, he thought dejectedly.

Out of the corner of his eye, he saw Father Durant enter the cafeteria. *Ah, things are looking up!*

The good father joined a group at a distant table and immediately entered into conversation, which Feng could not hear above the general buzz of diners. *If I walk by the table, perhaps he'll call me over and offer congratulations. Then we'll sit together, and after that . . . well, anything can happen.*

But his plan did not work. When Feng walked by the table, no one noticed as the group was still engaged in lively conversation. He tried to listen, but the overlapping voices made it impossible, and he could not linger too long.

Returning to his table, Feng sipped tea and tried to keep Father Durant in sight. *I'll follow the son-of-a-bitch. He'll lead me to her. Exorcism! Ha! A demon exorcizing an angel!*

But this plan also failed when Father Durant, accompanied by two other people from his group, walked upstairs to an area that was blocked by guards and, with a nod from one of them, continued past a sign that read: OFF-LIMITS TO ALL PERSONNEL WITHOUT PROPER AUTHORIZATION, BY ORDER OF MR. PRESIDENT. As he looked beyond the sign at a long corridor, Feng consoled himself with the thought that she might be imprisoned behind one of the doors that lined both walls. But which one? *Simple*, thought Feng. *I'll befriend Father Durant.*

The obvious danger of this plan could not overcome his impatience, and so he waited for a time when he might corner Father Durant and tell the missionary how desperately he wanted to convert. Whether this excuse would be credible did not enter his mind. The word "reckless" had been thrown at him so often he had become impervious to the possibility of its being true. *I'm still kicking, aren't I?* he often told doubters. And so, Feng Shiren waited for the right opportunity to approach Father Durant.

That time came two days later. Oddly enough, it was the good father who approached him.

It happened at the lake, where Feng sat lazily one afternoon, again admiring the passing women and dreaming about his heroic rescue of Bai Meiying.

"You are Feng Shiren, the face-changer?"

Instantly, Feng recognized the voice and turned, blocking the sun with his hand. "Yes."

"You are wanted by Mr. President for a private performance."

"What, now?" asked a startled Feng.

"No, tonight. Seven o'clock."

"Where?"

"Someone will come for you. Be ready."

"At my room?"

"Yes." Father Durant nodded and turned to leave.

"Wait a moment!" called Feng.

But the figure kept moving away without so much as a flinch so he jumped up and jogged to close the gap. "Wait a moment, please!" he called again.

Father Durant turned so quickly Feng almost ran into him.

"Yes?"

"Do you have a moment to talk?"

"No."

"But . . . about my performance. . . ." Feng struggled to find words.

"You are leaving the palace?"

"No, but—"

"You'll be unavailable?"

"No, but—"

"Then be ready at seven o'clock," interrupted Father Durant gruffly, and walked away.

Feng Shiren was left to sift through the meaning of this development. He sat back down and ran through a host of possibilities, none of which were entirely satisfactory. *The simplest explanation is usually the best*, he thought. *Mr. President just wants a private performance, that's all. Simple.* However, he knew this failed to explain why Father Durant was sent to deliver the message rather than some lackey. Doubts and uncertainty plagued his thoughts until a group of attractive women strolled by along the shore.

Ah! Look at them. So pretty! Why bother my mind with useless speculation? Still, the priest didn't seem pleased. Ah! I don't know. Too confusing. Just watch the women and be ready at seven o'clock!

~

To pass the time and calm his nerves, Feng struck up a conversation with one of the pretty girls. She had attended his performance, and found it flattering that he took an interest. For his part, Feng assumed she was one of Mr. President's concubines, and he had an ulterior motivation for cultivating her friendship besides rescuing Meiying. It seemed too easy, but she agreed to come to his room, and his impatience again trumped prudence. *There's plenty of time before I have to get ready*, he thought. *Maybe she knows something interesting, maybe not, but either way, I'll have some fun!*

However, when he closed the door and offered her a seat, she began questioning him, and her clumsy inquiries immediately set him on alert.

"Mr. Feng, you are so great! Where did you learn such amazing skills?"

"Just picked them up. Wine?"

"Oh, I love that brand. Yes, please. Who did you learn from?"

"What?"

"The masks. Who did you learn from?"

"No one. Here, have another drink."

"Are you trying to get me drunk, Mr. Feng?"

"Yes."

She blinked in the most amateurish way. "But, why?"

Feng did not approve of her overacting, but he was anxious to keep thoughts of the upcoming performance at bay, so he played along.

"To have my way with you," he said in a rather thin voice, clearly unenthusiastic about the sincerity underlying the words.

"Ohhh," she moaned, rounding her mouth like a fish and stretching out the sound, attempting the sensual but achieving the silly. "Well, in that case, I'll have another!" She punctuated this *bon mot* with a girlish giggle.

What a price to pay for a little sex, thought Feng glumly. *I'm not sure it's worth it.*

Her giggle gave way to another question.

"Do you have a girlfriend?"

"No." Feng was now becoming downright angry. He poured her another cup, hoping its effects would somehow alter her personality and make sex with her more palatable. But the more she drank, the more questions she asked.

"Where did you come here from?" giving him her most innocent look.

"Around."

"But you must have come from somewhere. Did you bring any friends?"

"Why don't you take off your clothes and come to bed with me?"

Again she giggled and made the "Ohhh" sound, making him think of a fish more than ever.

"You look like a fish," he said flatly.

"Oh, more like an octopus, Mr. Feng." She put out her arm to wrap around his neck, but he jumped up.

"That's enough!" he cried. "I have to get ready. Go."

Her face instantly transformed into a hard and malicious glare, but she said nothing.

"Go!" he cried again, holding open the door.

As she walked past, she muttered ominously, "Enjoy your performance tonight, Feng Shiren."

Closing the door behind her, Feng felt a sudden and disturbing premonition that something dire was about to happen. *This place is full of vipers*, he thought. *Vipers and spies.* A longing to return to the company of his little group came over him—Master Zhou, John, Child of Buddha, Suling, Lu Zhishen—all beckoned him to run as fast as his legs could carry him. This feeling was new, and it shook him in unfamiliar ways. For the first time in his life, he felt a deep, malevolent, irrational fear.

"I must flee!" he blurted aloud, as if some stranger trapped inside his mind suddenly cried out.

But he remained slumped in a chair, unable to make his legs work. Duty called, and its allure drained him of the energy to defy.

Good, Feng Shiren! came the voice that had commanded him from the beginning. **She must be saved!**

"I am afraid," he said to the empty room.

I will protect you.

"How?"

Haven't I always?

"Always in the past does not mean always in the future. We start anew."

There must be a son.

"And my reward?"

The usual.

"I am afraid. The usual may not be enough this time."

Then He and His faction will succeed.

"No, that must not happen. I will do it, if I can."

Good. Now, stop drinking. You will need a clear head.

~

Seven o'clock approached and Feng waited nervously in his costume. Despite Goddess's warning, he had consumed the remainder of the wine and had been working his way through another bottle when a knock came.

"It's time!" rang out a voice before he had a chance to open the door.

"I'm coming!"

"Hurry! Mr. President doesn't like being kept waiting!"

When Feng opened the door, he saw a large, corpulent man wearing an ill-fitting uniform whose rather beady eyes surveyed him from top to bottom. A smile flitted across the plump face before he wheeled and walked briskly down the hallway with Feng following in his wake. It seemed the halls were endless, as they made their way from one floor to the other, higher and higher, sometimes making sharp turns down narrow corridors and back to wider passages. To Feng Shiren, straining to keep up with the round figure of his guide, these interminable halls appeared to take up more space than the entire palace. An endless line of closed doors flecked the walls, and they passed not a single person during their trip. As they walked through the dim passageways, a surge of anxiety burned in his stomach, creating a painful knot that almost hindered him from moving forward. At the least he wanted to lean over and grip his knees as if ready to vomit, and at worst he wanted to turn and bolt away back down the path they had taken and out of the palace into the night. The closer he got to the center of the web, the more poisoned and sickly even the light and air became, smothering him in gloom and oppressive dread. Dizzy and soaked in sweat, he saw the fat man some five paces ahead stop at a nondescript door, triggering a mix of relief and renewed fear. Being unmarked, the door was indistinguishable from the multitude of others stretching ahead and behind, and Feng marveled that his guide knew which one to pick. He reluctantly approached.

The man grinned at him through rows of crooked teeth.

"Go in." He gestured toward the door.

Feng Shiren blanched and unconsciously took a step back.

The man stared at him expectantly. "Well, what is it to be?"

Feng hesitated.

"Go," repeated the fat man, almost gently.

~ *Meiying Endures the Unendurable* ~

Two nights after Meiying and Mulan attended Feng Shiren's performance, they lay together in bed, talking and laughing as they conjured up the face-changer's silly masks and dramatic poses. Mulan, in all innocence, cuddled with Meiying, her silky hair falling enchantingly about her thin shoulders, her graceful fingers plucking the coverlet with nimble, feminine movements. Meiying felt no untoward stirrings, only the exquisite tug of a mother's love and the heartrending ache of a mother's fear. That she had these maternal feelings rather than other, more beguiling and predatory ones, gave her solace and made her comfortable in her new-found role.

"We're going to die here," said Mulan suddenly, with the air of a pout rather than a cry of despair.

Meiying felt perturbed at this remark, so out of keeping with their frolicking light-heartedness just moments earlier. "Dear, you have made that statement before, and it hurts me for you to keep repeating it. We will not die here, I will see to that."

But Mulan seemed little comforted. "Yes, I know," she continued with tears shining in her eyes. "But it's so hard to know I'll never grow up and marry and have a home. It's so unfair."

These remarks were made with a resignation that chilled Meiying's heart, and she paused to think of an appropriate answer, but Mulan continued before she could reply.

"I know you say you will protect me, Miss Bai, but I'm not a child. I see what I see."

"Dear, I have a strong feeling we'll be rescued."

"Why?"

Meiying paused. She had not told Mulan about her connection to the face-changer for fear of creating false hopes, but she felt Mulan's morbid thoughts must be dispatched. Although frustrated with the girl's hopelessness, in her heart, she could not blame Mulan. Their isolation, the perpetual darkness (but for the single, ever-present candle), and the constant anticipation of doom, all had a corrosive effect on their psyches. Every instant of light-hearted play was embedded in a pall of fear; a fear that at any moment the door would be flung open and forever end their chances to experience such moments again. It seemed to Meiying that their lives were a series of flashes; searing moments of intimacy that were too quickly snuffed out by the pervasive darkness and suffocating dread of a treacherous future. Thus it was that Meiying cherished their moments—their flashes—of closeness, and a fierce jealousy made her reject any intrusions that would take them too quickly away. In spite of her annoyance with Mulan's despairing words, she felt a pang of guilt that she had hidden the knowledge a friend was working to free them.

Poor child, she thought. *No wonder she is in such despair. I must tell her.*

But some perversity held her back. She enjoyed being strong and having this girl depend upon her strength. It made her feel worthwhile. Motherly. And being a mother gave her a purpose.

But a purpose at her expense. Yes, I must tell her. Still . . . how disappointed she will be if he does not come. . . .

A key to Meiying's character lay in these internal dialogues, during which she forced herself to play her own devil's advocate. This propensity kept her in balance and grounded, ready to deal with almost any occurrence that threatened to disrupt her life. Almost. By means of her constant observation of the world, from all angles, she could see the good in the Japanese, in Beethoven, even in Mr.

President. Not unaware of the unusual nature of this process, she took a certain pride in undermining her own prejudices and comfortable conclusions. From this balanced view of life she drew strength, and, combined with her prodigious talent on the piano, knew she possessed qualities worth preserving. These talents could be passed on to Mulan, if given time.

And to your son.

No. I told You to leave me alone.

John sent me.

No. I know better than that. No one sends You anywhere, Goddess. You go where You wish and do what You wish . . . Meiying clapped her hands over her ears . . . *and plague minds when You wish. No one tells You what to do.*

God tries, but I have a surprise for Him. If you will only cooperate and survive long enough to have this son.

I am trying.

Once that is achieved, the Reunion may proceed.

I do not know what the Reunion is, but I am trying to survive and save this girl.

Try harder. Together we can oppose the Male Godhead. Is that not tempting?

Yes, but I also have this girl to take care of.

There you have it. You must survive.

Help me.

And the son?

And the girl?

She will soon die, you must survive for the son.

What!

Yes. Tuberculosis. Have you not noticed a cough?

No.

It has started already. Listen more carefully. It starts slowly, gently, like a polite clearing of the throat.

You must help me!

I am, but you are soon going to face another trial. Persevere! For the son!

For the girl!

And the son?

Yes, and the son. If You help!

As I told you, I already have. Feng Shiren is hard at work.

What is the trial?

You will soon see. That, I cannot prevent. Free will, you know. At least, that is what most humans believe. We know differently.

The girl?

She will die. I can do nothing for her. But the son!

Damn your son!

~

"Miss Bai?"

"Yes, Mulan, dear?"

"You always scare me when you stare off into space and hear nothing I say."

Meiying clutched her tightly. "Oh, dearest. I am here. Tell me again what you said. I was naughty and wasn't listening."

"Silly Miss Bai! I was just repeating your name, over and over."

"Silly Miss Bai," mimicked Meiying. "I must have been daydreaming of happier days ahead when we leave this place and go somewhere nice. By the way, Mulan?"

"Yes?"

"Have you been coughing?"

"Yes, a little. I try to keep you from hearing. It's just a cold and I don't want you to worry."

"Oh, sweetheart, don't keep things from me."

"But don't you keep things from me?"

Meiying was startled at this question. "What do you mean?"

"I mean, don't adults keep things from young people to protect them?"

"Yes, sometimes."

"Well, aren't you keeping from me the fact that we are going to die here?"

"No!" Meiying suddenly realized she had been putting off her dilemma, and could no longer vacillate.

"Mulan, do you remember the face-changer?"

"Of course, silly. We've just been talking about him. I'm not dead yet."

"Well, I know him."

"You do?"

"Yes, and he is working to free us."

"He is?!" Mulan stared wide-eyed, for the first time given a reason to hope. "Oh, Miss Bai, that's wonderful! When will he come?"

"I don't know, but tomorrow is the third day since the performance. It should be soon."

Mulan clapped her hands. "Oh! If we're saved, will you take me with you?"

"You must return to your home."

Now came the little cough. Innocent as it might have seemed ten minutes earlier, it now tore at Meiying's heart and she again smothered the girl in hugs.

"I know I must," said Mulan peevishly after she regained her breath. "But, I really want to come with you."

"We'll see. We must sleep now and be ready for whatever comes."

"All right, but I'll never sleep now."

~

The next day passed uneventfully, both women pining for the outside and making brief comments on the stifling atmosphere. But, in the late afternoon, the door swung open with a terrifying suddenness, and a fat man in an ill-fitting uniform filled the doorway. An ominous glow from the lights in the hallway encircled his silhouetted figure, making him appear even more menacing. Meiying rose and covered herself with a robe.

"Put on your usual dress and be ready in fifteen minutes!" he barked.

"Am I to play?" asked Meiying, screwing up her courage to speak in a level voice for the girl's sake.

"Have the girl ready also," he said curtly.

"Am I to play?" repeated Meiying, more forcefully.

The fat man drew back his lips in an evil smile, revealing rows of crooked teeth. "Oh, yes. You will play. You will definitely play." His gaze fell on Mulan, now standing beside Meiying and trying not to tremble in front of this intimidating specter. He nodded toward the girl. "And so will she," he said with a low chuckle as he turned and closed the door behind him.

These words struck deep into Meiying's heart, and a burning pain spread throughout her chest. She glanced at Mulan, who stood erect and defiant, attempting to stifle a cough that came out in short rasps.

How have I not noticed it before? thought Meiying as she rushed to change.

Neither of them spoke, a dark pall of anxiety rendering them mute. Both rushed through their dressing and toilet, passing worried glances at each other in silence.

"Come on!" came a shout of impatience from the other side of the door.

Both women hugged a last time before opening the door and following the man to their unknown destination. It seemed to Meiying that she walked through an endless, dimly-lit labyrinth of halls to the gallows. Mulan squeezed her hand tightly as they walked together behind the fat man. He grunted and wheezed while his bulky figure navigated the stairways, yet he maintained a brisk pace all the same. To Meiying's dismay, the path they took did not lead to the usual room where she had played the piano. Instead, it took unexpected twists and turns, causing her to lose all sense of direction. At last the fat man stopped in front of a nondescript door in a hallway full of doors and waited. Time passed excruciatingly slowly, and Meiying's nerves were ready to burst from the anticipation. She gripped Mulan's hand so tightly that the girl squealed in pain. Still nothing happened and still they waited. Soon, a point came where her breathing quivered and her knees seemed ready to buckle; only her need to stay strong for Mulan kept her upright. The door opened a crack and a voice said to the fat man, "It is almost ready. Another few minutes."

"This is awful!" whispered Mulan. "I want to run away."

Meiying could not reply. Images of the misery and pain that had plagued her since fleeing Shanghai scrolled painfully across her minds-eye. Now, behind that door, yet another trial lurked, sure to bring more pain, more misery, or worse. She silently cried out to God; blaming Him for His blindness to injustice and murder; begging Him for mercy; pleading with Him to intervene; cursing Him for her existence. She looked down at Mulan, whose face and eyes bore expressions of mute acceptance—a fawn in the jaws of a lion—and felt unbearable agony and indescribable rage.

"Come in!" called a voice from behind the door, jarring her back to unwelcome reality.

The fat man opened the door and waved them in.

~

At the sight of the open door, Meiying's agony and rage fell away to leave only raw fear. Like a person forced to enter a pool with a shark, she shuffled forward, still grasping Mulan's hand. Both of them trembled almost uncontrollably when they crossed the threshold and beheld what awaited them. The first person Meiying discerned in the dimness was Father Durant. When his blank face came into view, her worst fears were confirmed. He stood closest to the door, and the slanted light from the hallway seemed to cut his face in half, forming a demonic facsimile of yin and yang.

"Over there," he said, pointing to the right.

The keys of the piano shone like white teeth, grinning in welcome. Beyond it stood a dark cross, made of heavy beams that had rope shackles on each end of the cross piece.

"Do you recognize it?" asked Durant.

Under her gaze, the wood seemed to shiver and explode, sending a thousand slivers flying through the air, lacerating her flesh. Her moan could be heard by all.

"I see you are afraid," said Durant.

"Yes."

"Do you remember that we have unfinished business?"

Meiying could not form any words and she looked down at the floor to escape his eyes.

"Redemption!" he boomed.

But Meiying continued to look down, forcing herself to concentrate on his leather boots. *Why is a priest wearing boots?* she wondered. As she looked, the leathery cracks began to move, twisting and flowing like a web of rivers emptying into a broad delta. And from the watery sheen, a blurry face emerged; a bright-eyed but troubled boy.

Your son.

"Now, pay attention!" snapped Father Durant. "Look at me!"

Meiying had to tear her eyes from the mesmerizing boots.

Durant gestured toward the piano. "Play."

"What shall I play?"

"The same piece you always start with."

Meiying saw movement in the shadows at the other end of the room, and could just discern figures moving about, but could not make out the faces. Afraid to peer too closely, afraid of what she might see, she sat and began to play. Music filled the room, and instead of becoming still, the shuffling shadows became agitated, like people standing on a hot plate. As she reached the particularly quiet adagio, she closed her eyes and basked in the glorious beauty of the notes. Only an occasional cough from Mulan could be heard above the music. Then, a low buzzing arose from the shadow figures, followed by a swelling chorus of oohs and ahhs that washed over her. When she opened her eyes, a faint glow pulsated from the cross, bulging outward as might an expanding bubble. Now she could see the faces of the onlookers reflected in the brightening glow, and her heart raced wildly when the figure of Mr. President unmistakably resolved itself, standing like a mountain in the center of the group, his beady eyes gazing in wonder at the radiant cross. The intense stares of the onlookers drew her attention to the object of their fascination. Without pausing the music, she glanced at the cross and to her astonishment perceived within the shimmering bubble a tiny figure emerge and grow as might a fetus in a womb, speeded up a thousand-fold.

"You see! You see!" someone shouted.

She tore her eyes from the source of the glow and turned to catch the response of Mr. President, but instead she caught the hazy face of Lu Zhishen, his shaggy beard shaking in wonder, and then the distinctive glint of Feng Shiren's face-changing costume. Both men stood next to Mr. President, Feng's eyes fixed on Meiying, his mouth slightly curled up at the edges in a mysterious smile. A sudden flash of light from the cross brilliantly illuminated the onlookers in a frozen instant, and the others of her group—Child of Buddha, Suling, Master Zhou—all gazed in open-mouthed wonder. Meiying stopped playing and abruptly stood in shock, returning her incredulous attention to the cross where a woman now shone forth, tied and naked, yet with the most peaceful expression on Her beautiful face.

I am here! A voice boomed in velvet thunder from the depths of the incandescent sphere. ***I am ready for your so-called redemption, false man!***

Meiying heard Father Durant utter some truncated, terrible groan, causing her to stumble backward, twisting and falling against the piano, her outstretched hands partially breaking the impact. Using the keys to push herself up, her eyes met those of the shining Goddess, smiling benevolently at her through a storm of sparks and flames. The last sound she heard was Mulan coughing and crying out piteously, "Miss Bai! Miss Bai!"

Before she knew it, she lay on the floor while human hands encircled her. She struggled to stay conscious, still craning her neck to stare at Goddess, who now contemplated the scene with extraordinary serenity, despite being naked and tied to a cross in the most exposed and humiliating fashion.

No, my dear, it is they who are exposed.

Goddess burst from Her bonds in a blinding flash that caused the onlookers to close their eyes and turn their heads, and when the searing light faded, She could be seen floating above the floor. Then, in an instant, disappeared. Her absence brought total darkness, and Meiying slipped willingly into its void.

Chapter Thirteen

PART SEVEN: HOMECOMING

Meiying Opens Her Eyes

~ Awakening ~

When Meiying opened her eyes, the first image that registered was the kind face of Child of Buddha staring down at her. John looked anxiously over the hunchback's shoulder.

"Where am I?" asked Meiying weakly.

"In my cottage, Meiying," replied John as gently as he could.

"But. . . . " she drifted off.

"You fainted."

Meiying revived and looked around at the shabby furnishings and primitive walls. Confusion clouded her mind.

"How long?"

"A long time," said Suling, caressing Meiying's forehead from the other side of the bed.

"But, how did I get here?"

The others looked at each other but said nothing.

"And Mulan?" continued Meiying.

They parted and Mulan's sweet face squeezed between. "Here, Miss Bai."

Meiying struggled to remember. "I don't understand."

"No," said John. "Nor do we."

"I do!" boasted Feng Shiren with his usual bluster.

"Shush!" scolded Child of Buddha. "You do not!"

"Well, I certainly don't!" exclaimed Master Zhou. "But your escape from that awful place and seeing you recovered makes it all worthwhile."

"Makes what worthwhile?" asked Meiying.

"Makes us being here worthwhile," said Master Zhou.

"Yes, yes," came the collective agreement.

"But, I still don't understand," uttered Meiying as if to herself.

"You see," said Master Zhou. "We were on our way to my old estate outside Shanghai when word came of your predicament. The civil war has engulfed even our Mongolian sanctuary." He sighed guilelessly; a deep, woeful exhalation that bore no marks of pretense.

"All of you?"

"I'm returning to Canada," said Lu Zhishen from the foot of the bed. "And you're going with John to the States."

"Yes, it's true," said John with a broad smile.

But Meiying felt no joy. Her mind seemed a foggy blur, and her inability to piece together a clear narrative of what happened oppressed her and made her believe the current good was but a dream. Even now, in the comfort of the shack, she felt stretched on that wretched cross, being tortured, merely hallucinating the peace and freedom she now enjoyed. All that day, she asked questions as her friends came and went, but none were able to give her any clarity about the events that occurred in that room. Even Mulan could not explain how they escaped, and appeared puzzled when pressed for details.

"I honestly don't know, Miss Bai. One minute I was crying for you to get up from beneath the piano, and the next we were here."

"But Mulan dear, that makes no sense."

"I'm sorry, Miss Bai," the girl said in a sort of pout. But she soon brightened. "Now we're together, so it doesn't matter, does it?"

Only one fact was made clear by everyone she spoke to: *She* or Goddess or the Precious Object or all of them had made a spectacular appearance. But after that singular fact, all else was a miasma of conflicting stories and hazy recollections; the effect of such collective amnesia being stories full of fragmented reminiscences and shifting versions of time and space, with every witness in that room slipping in and out of any sense of shared reality. Meiying could make nothing of it.

"But what happened next?" she kept asking, and kept receiving vague and ambiguous responses.

"How did you all end up in that awful room?"

Master Zhou pondered a moment, and replied, "When we arrived, we found John here, and waited with him for word from Feng Shiren. However, instead of hearing from him, we all received an invitation from Mr. President, and upon entering the palace, were escorted to that room."

"And then?"

"Not sure, but somehow we ended up back here."

Even Feng Shiren, goaded by Meiying to explain what must have been his heroic actions in helping them escape, could only smile and say, "That's not important. You're safe now, that's all."

Eventually, she tired of the attempt, and the group made preparations to leave the premises of Mr. President the next day. Only a casual remark by Feng gave her hope that one day the mystery would be cleared up. "I'll tell you everything later," he said with a mischievous gleam in his eye. "When it's time and you are safely beyond the slimy reach of . . . well, of those here who would do you harm."

"But what about the rest of you? What will happen to you?"

For the first time Meiying saw the light fade to near extinction from his eyes. "The communists will take care of us."

~

That night, she was beset by dark forebodings and terrible dreams. In one particularly vivid dream, she found herself back in that dreary room with Mulan and the one candle. Mr. President appeared next to her bed, swaying like a giant oak tree above her. When he spoke, his words were so high-pitched and tinny that they were incomprehensible. Only his pig-eyes betrayed animal urges and a desperate, rutting insensibility that rendered her utterly naked and vulnerable to his corpulent passions. Somehow, she found herself on the cross, and before her stood Father Durant brandishing a whip, a scowl disfiguring his face.

"Redemption will flow out through your blood!" he screamed. "And then, purity will flow in through our seed!"

He appeared suddenly naked and approached with outstretched arms and inhumanly long fingernails. A similarly naked Mr. President lumbered behind, wearing an obscene smile and gazing at the priest like a paternal devil at his demon son. Meiying awoke in a sweat, gasping loudly and sitting up to breathe more easily. Others in the room stirred in their sleep, so she forced herself to be quiet. Muffled coughing came from outside. Meiying crept past the sleeping bodies to join Mulan, glad for an interruption to distract her from her dark thoughts.

"Are you okay, dear Mulan?" she asked.

The girl jumped at the sound of her words. "Oh, Miss Bai, I am not!"

"What is it?"

Mulan held out her pale white handkerchief and Meiying saw to her horror a splattering of dark spots highlighted in the moonlight. Mulan shuddered and the handkerchief quivered in her hand. "It's blood, Miss Bai."

Meiying hugged her. "If Mr. Powers and I can make arrangements, would you like to come to America with us?"

"Oh, Miss Bai!" cried Mulan. "Oh, yes, yes, yes!"

Meiying made this offer without any knowledge of how to make it happen. She wanted to rush in and wake up John to immediately discuss it with him, but forestalled her excitement and urged Mulan to go inside and sleep. But the poor girl could not stop coughing, and they both remained outside, huddled together against the cold.

~ *John Makes Arrangements* ~

The group decided to accompany Master Zhou to his family estate outside Nanjing, then go their separate ways. John had been restless ever since Meiying's return. He felt a desperate urgency to get her out of China. Once back in the

States, all would be well. He would get his old position back—after all, his boss said it would be waiting for him.

But, it's been ten years! he thought. *How absurd to think such a thing!*

Nevertheless, his fear of not finding a job paled in comparison to his fear of remaining in China. Somehow, the country had become ominous and malevolent. Every Chinese face filled him with a distinct, unwelcome loathing. *Stupid people!* he would think. *Superstitious! Cattle to the slaughter! Peasants with peasant apishness! Apes!* Only those in his little group were bearable. The more he tried to fight against these feelings, the worse they became. Escaping this mass of suffering humanity and unbridled cruelty drove him to a frenzy of activity which puzzled his companions, for he, or course, kept his disgust to himself.

On the morning of their departure, John had to keep exhorting his friends to hurry.

"Come on! Mr. President may change his mind any moment and have us arrested!" he repeated time and again.

When he saw Suling and Lu Zhishen laughing about something, he called out, "Hurry up! Let's get out of here!"

Child of Buddha eyed him with displeasure. "Eh!" she barked. "What's gotten into you, John? Are you afraid?"

"Yes! I'm afraid to be stuck here. I'm afraid Meiying will be taken back into that jail! I'm afraid for all of us! Do you want to be dragged back into that awful palace?"

"You're certainly afraid of many things. Are you afraid of yourself?"

John assumed a look of contempt. "Oh, how profound. You have been reading too many cheap Chinese philosophy books."

Child of Buddha tilted her head conspicuously. "And your philosophy?"

"Leave here and live! Stay here and die! Simple, but more real than your fancy Daoist and Confucian hacks."

Child of Buddha flashed an unexpected smile. "You will soon find out how 'real' your Western ways are. Don't be so quick to dismiss the ancients!"

John scoffed. "Your ancients have done a great job in creating the perfect society here." He waved his arms. "Where are your Confucian gentlemen and Daoist sages? Dead. Murdered. Starved. Forgotten. Corrupt. You can have this country. I want to go where men look to the future, not to the past and all its useless ghosts. And millions of your fellow countrymen wish the same thing!"

Child of Buddha continued smiling, but Meiying scolded John.

"Hush! Such reckless talk about our country, about our people, our past."

"But it's true," replied John weakly, chastised by Meiying's tone. He gathered courage. "Well, you want to go, don't you!"

Meiying blinked and said, "Yes, it's true, I want to go."

"Well," gloated John. "There you have it."

While engaged in this conversation, he had stopped packing.

Feng Shiren paused in his own preparations and pointed to John's unfinished pack. "So, young American hero, I thought you were anxious to go."

"I am," replied John, his victory over Meiying somewhat punctured.

"You had best leave off slandering our country," said Feng gravely. He suddenly leapt into his favorite operatic pose. "We were once the greatest empire in the world!"

"Now you're shit," mumbled John under his breath. No one but Meiying heard, and his words cut like knives, making her feel a coward for leaving with him, and further proof of her unworthiness to defend her country. But she noted John's changing attitude with alarm.

To defuse the tension, John gazed at the distant palace that shone in the morning sun, the lake sparkling around it like a sapphire necklace. Thin wisps of fog undulated provocatively in the air as if insubstantial spirits frolicked playfully above the water.

"A beautiful view," he said by way of a peace offering, but the others ignored him, so he sighed and finished packing.

Their plan was to hike back to the nearest bus station, where they would buy tickets to Taiyuan, and from there take the main trunk line to Nanjing. Passage for all was courtesy of Master Zhou, whose generosity continued to amaze. Paradoxically, his overseas investments, allowed to appreciate untouched during the entirety of the war, experienced steady growth, and were eventually unblocked by the Nationalist government. Once again, Master Zhou could play the jolly fat cat. Returning to Taiyuan seemed the safest route, given reports of fighting between Nationalists and communists in the countryside. "Stay on the main road," was the conventional wisdom, repeated by those in a position to know.

"Any fighting on the road when you came?" John asked Lu Zhishen.

"Not a bit of it," he replied. "But those blasted commies show up in the most unexpected places and times, and when they do, they inflict a bloody lot of damage."

Odd, thought John. *How he sounds more and more like Peter. Must be getting ready for his return to Canada. Or maybe he wants to go to England and is getting in some practice.*

"Getting excited about going home?" John asked.

"Yes, I guess. But, damn, I'll miss this place. And you?"

"Oh, yes. I mean, I'll miss this place, but I'm excited about going home."

"No wonder," said Lu nodding toward Meiying. "With a beauty like that along."

"Is everyone ready?" called Master Zhou.

With a host of affirming nods, they were off. John walked next to Meiying, reacquainting himself with her company. Her gait felt pleasantly up-tempo without being too strenuous. *Yes,* he thought. *I can live the rest of my life with this woman, even if she is Chinese. And won't it shock some of the stuffy bastards back in the States. Racists!*

But this last epithet reminded him of his own racist attitude, and he chased the uncomfortable thought from his head by focusing on the surroundings. The dirt road curved around the slopes, bare rock rising up on one side, and a steep cliff downward on the other, falling into a lush, green valley from which smoky tendrils of cook-fires rose in twisted contortions. Reminded of food, he thought of waking up every morning to breakfast in the States—a real American breakfast of bacon and eggs—with Meiying. Yes, American, American, American! No more rice gruel and strange food he could hardly identify, or want to. American restaurants with real food, the choices laid out on lengthy menus with fresh ice-water and clean bathrooms, and . . . . he stopped to peruse the smoke from the cook-fires and imagined the stupid peasants cooking god-knows-what in their filthy huts. American food for him. American food!

John glanced at Meiying, afraid she could read his thoughts, but she trudged on, having fashioned a walking stick from a fallen elderberry branch. Never had her Chinese physiognomy seemed so beautiful, and John felt burdened by the incongruous nature of his prejudices and passions.

God, damn it! he scolded himself. *Get hold of yourself. She's a lesbian! She'll never love you! Never!*

But she will have your son, John Powers!

The female voice came hard and biting, like a thunderbolt, and it made him stop suddenly and gasp. *Goddess, I—*

Great and Beloved Goddess! boomed God, sweeping away John's line of thought; His swampy tone a deep, dank, gritty rumble that filled John's mind with a corrosive slag of wet soot and harsh sulfur—a nineteenth century furnace bellowing smoke from a thirteenth century hell. **He will never be up to the task! I am safe.**

Dearest God, Your and Your faction's addiction to First Principles must be broken, and only a mentally ill, psychotic fool can cure the mental illness of a psychotic Divine Fool. The ground is prepared. They are together now, and none but death will part them. The buoyant future is secured.

Then let it be death.

John moved unsteadily on his feet, mumbling to himself and stumbling forward in a stupor, while both Suling and Meiying exchanged frequent glances at the same time they kept an eye on his unsteady progress.

~

After walking a few hours, their path was blocked by a sudden surge of people moving in the opposite direction, clearly fleeing from something. They could get no straight answers to their anxious questions, though apparently, some battle raged ahead. While the group paused to determine what to do, a host of Nationalist soldiers passed them, clearly on their way to the battle.

Master Zhou flagged down an officer, who slowed long enough to talk. Huffing from the exertion of trotting alongside while carrying on a conversation, Master Zhou finally returned, wiping his brow.

"He says it is a small skirmish and that the road will be clear by tomorrow."

"Communists?" asked Lu Zhishen.

"Yes, but the officer said they would have no trouble brushing them aside."

Feng Shiren scowled. "That's the attitude that will get us all killed."

Suling, who had been quiet the entire trip, looked on with a worried frown. "Oh, let's hope not, Shiren! I have a renewed desire to live. *She* has given me hope! The Japanese are gone, at least. Now, I just want to go home and live in peace."

The far-off rumble of battle reminded them all of the fragility of peace and their own fragile existence. By late afternoon, word came that the road was open, but dusky shadows had already lengthened the gloom, and all agreed to stay the night where they were. John, beside himself at the delay, could do nothing except prepare his bedroll for another evening in the open, beset by a foul mood and lingering echoes of the voices. Before long, the women could be heard laughing and talking together, and he grew more churlish. In response to Lu Zhishen's simple question, "Are you comfortable?" he replied with a curt, "Yes, now let me sleep."

Why these dark moods, he wondered. *Meiying is back, we're going to marry and go to the States. True, it's a marriage of convenience, but still . . . she can come to love me over time. The voices be damned! I'm not a schizophrenic! Once we get out of this damn country, the voices will go away.*

"So, that will solve your problems?" Feng Shiren's voice came jarringly from the darkness.

"What?" asked a startled John.

"Will leaving China solve your problems?" he repeated.

"Oh, was I talking out loud?"

"Maybe." Feng came closer and John could make out his face in the moonlight. It appeared different. Melancholy. Unlike the old, spirited Feng Shiren. Almost ghostlike.

"What is it?" asked John in alarm.

Feng kneeled down and moved his face centimeters from John. "You will take her out of here, and when you arrive in America, you will take care of her. It is essential she have the son, do you understand?"

"What are you talking about?"

"You know. *She* has told you."

"Who?"

"My boss."

"Shiren, I don't know what you're talking about."

Feng Shiren then did something beyond imagining: he slapped John across the face. "The son, John. That is most important." Then he walked away.

~

The next day they passed the scene of the battle, but could see little of its effects. The bodies had been removed, and only some scorched vegetation and dark spots in the sandy soil bore evidence to the violence. A few Nationalist soldiers were still mopping up. When the group stopped to rest, John watched Feng Shiren saunter up to a soldier and say something that must have been a joke. The man laughed and Feng threw back his head in an unnatural manner. Just as it began to dawn on John that something was wrong, he heard the crack of a rifle reverberate around the group. Everyone flinched and he saw a whirl of movement as the Nationalist soldiers scrambled in the direction of a ridge where an officer frantically pointed.

"Sniper! Sniper! There!" he yelled.

Only then did John see Feng lying on his back, motionless. Suling screamed and Lu Zhishen rushed toward the body. It all happened so fast John could not get his thoughts to catch up with events. He automatically followed Lu Zhishen, unable to process why he was going or what he would do when he got there. When both men reached the body, John saw immediately that the face-changer was dead, and the full horror of the situation rendered him deaf and dumb.

Lu Zhishen shouted something. Suling and Child of Buddha pushed John aside to get to the fallen man, but he heard nothing and remained standing as frozen as a statue, watching Feng Shiren's blood darken the soil, adding yet another circular stain to all the others. Before they had time to mourn, a firefight erupted on the slope, and everyone hit the ground. John lay close to Feng's bleeding face, the eyes dull and unseeing. A fly crawled on its cornea, only to zip away from a shadow cast by something passing overhead. The fighting became more distant and could only be heard in short spurts beyond the ridge. Again, the group stood gathered around the body, stunned by the events of the last few minutes. A sense of finality settled over them. Not the finality of Feng Shiren's death, but the brutal finality of all they had sought for so many years. *She* died with him, as did the Precious Object and the search for some transcendent truth. Stretching before them, as far as the eye could see, lay a pitiless landscape of war. Quailing survival remained the only goal, now absent even the gilded latticework of some deeper significance. The hope of living meaningful lives beyond the mere carnal expediencies of nature had been extinguished.

They buried him under a small grove of sycamore trees and moved on in wooden silence. John wept for his dead friend and protector, and yearned even more to leave this accursed country.

A new beginning, he thought. *I need a new beginning. God, let me escape this place with Meiying so as to start fresh. No more searches. No more foolishness. No more voices. Just living day-to-day. Just grant me that!*

They reached the town without further incident and went straight to the central business district, where a vast beehive of refugees from the civil war spun in frantic circles around the bus terminal. Only after an excruciating effort reaching the ticket-seller did Master Zhou learn all buses to Taiyuan were booked solid for at least two weeks, and only a hefty bribe shortened the time to two days. He settled for the hard-fought tickets and struggled back to the group with the bad news. John was beside himself with frustration and again berated the sorry state of China, until Meiying hushed him into a fuming silence. Because they had arrived late, the town had no vacancies except one shabby inn that bore a closer resemblance to a stable than a hotel. Master Zhou bribed the owner and they shared two flea-infested rooms which later that night crawled with rats in search of warmth and food. At least there was a roof over their heads when a sudden storm brought a downpour. With no electricity, the rooms were lit by kerosene lanterns, and in this crowded space, John conversed with the other males in the group. No one could sleep, so talking filled the time. Mainly reminiscences of their adventures. John lay on his side in the corner, facing away from the others, with his blanket tucked up around his neck. While Lu Zhishen and Master Zhou talked about the past, avoiding mentioning Feng Shiren, John fantasized about arriving in the States with Meiying. He knew he would benefit from the reflected glory of her looks and her talent, and he planned to take full advantage. But, with a sudden onslaught of trepidation, he realized his true position: no money, few contacts after so many years, and no real prospects. How would they survive the first few months until he found a job? Meiying certainly would not be raking in money from her concerts for a long time. The reality was daunting, but not enough to diminish his desperation to flee China. He shuddered at the memory of Feng's lifeless eyes. Anything was better than China.

~ *Meiying Frets* ~

In spite of her reservations about John Powers, Meiying felt increasingly excited about a new life in America, and the closer that reality became, the more she allowed herself to dream. But now, the prospect of returning to Taiyuan scared her. After all, Beethoven's uncle presumably still lived there, and his long arms would reach out and find her, wherever she and the group stayed and for however short a time. Without Feng Shiren for protection, she felt particularly vulnerable. Never had she thought of John as a reliable sentinel, so she tried to deflect her fears by talking to Suling and Child of Buddha. Since no one could sleep in that filthy room except Mulan (who, exhausted from a coughing fit, slumbered soundly in the corner), the conversation twisted and turned until it reached the point that most interested Meiying.

"Meiying, are you looking forward to going to America with John?" asked Suling.

"Yes and no."

"What does that mean?" asked Child of Buddha.

"It means I'm not sure."

"*She* wants you to have the son," said Child of Buddha.

"I don't want to hear that!" cried Meiying. "I get that enough from . . . others."

"What others?" asked Suling.

"That is not what I want to talk about."

"What then?" asked Child of Buddha.

"John."

"What about him?"

"I want to know if you both think he is crazy."

"What?" Suling asked instinctively, then added, "Haven't we talked about this?"

"Yes, but I want to know your honest opinion now. You too, Child of Buddha."

Suling shook her head. "I've already given you my honest opinion."

Meiying's eyes bored into her. "Tell me again."

"No, I don't think he is crazy, but we all know he hears voices."

"Doesn't that make him crazy?"

"No."

"And what do you think, Child of Buddha?"

"He hears voices, but he isn't crazy, whatever that word means. I should know, I was kept in a mental institution for years."

"What do you know?" asked Meiying.

"I already told you."

"No!" snapped Meiying. "Neither of you are being honest. Here is my real question—forget John for a moment: do you hear voices?"

"Which one of us?" asked Suling.

"The question is directed at both of you."

"Do *you*?" asked Suling in surprise.

Meiying paused, then cried, "I'm asking you!"

"Yes, I do, sometimes," said Suling under her breath, startled by Meiying's vehemence. "Let's keep our voices down," she added, nodding toward Mulan.

"And I do all the time," whispered Child of Buddha. "I myself am crazy. What do I have to hide? If John is crazy, I'm a thousand times crazier."

"What do they say?"

Suling frowned. "I'm not sure this is a good idea."

"Why? Do your voices say bad things about me?" asked Meiying.

"You know that is not the point."

"Then what is?"

"Look," said Child of Buddha, directing her question to Suling. "Do the voices still talk to you?"

"Do you mean recently?" asked Suling.

"I mean, for example, yesterday or today."

"Nooo, I don't think so."

Child of Buddha scoffed. "Well! They talk to me constantly, and as recently as this morning."

"What did they say?" asked Meiying breathlessly.

"They said to make sure you leave safely with Mr. Powers. Well, at least one of them did. It seems the rest of us don't matter."

"Oh, don't say that!" uttered Meiying.

"But, it's true," whispered Suling, as if to herself.

"Tell us," said Child of Buddha.

"Tell you what?" asked Suling.

Child of Buddha sniggered. "You know. Tell us what they say to you."

"One of them tells me to help John, or to comfort Meiying. Never anyone else."

Child of Buddha leaned back with a wry smile. "Of course, you know, it is *her* talking to us. What about the other voices?"

Suling could only shake her head.

After a pause in the conversation, Meiying asked Child of Buddha, "Did you hear voices before you met us? . . . I mean, when you were in the hospital?"

"Of course, foolish woman! And, please, call it what it is: a mental institution!" After shouting these words, the others shushed her and Suling again pointed to the sleeping figure of Mulan. Child of Buddha rapidly calmed, and continued in a lowered voice, "But they were different. And anyway, after your group came, my old voices were murdered."

"Murdered!" shuddered Suling.

"Yes. The two new voices murdered all the others, some of whom were my friends."

Meiying jumped in. "Yes, yes, two."

"And they argue?" asked Suling.

"Yes."

"Male and female?" added Child of Buddha.

"Yes," replied Meiying and Suling simultaneously.

The women fell silent, each processing the significance of what had been revealed.

"Is the female voice *her*?" asked Suling.

"I don't know," responded Meiying. "But I think so."

"I know so!" thundered Child of Buddha, staring into space with a ferocious expression. "And *She* is at war with God!"

Mulan stirred at the outburst.

"Shhh!" whispered Meiying. "At war?"

"Yes, over your son . . . or your future son."

"My god! He must be important!"

"Not to God," observed Child of Buddha drolly. "Only to *Her*—Goddess."

"But, I don't understand," said Suling.

"Nor do I, fully," replied Child of Buddha. "But it is coming to me . . . slowly. Perhaps your son is important to God, but in a completely different way than to *Her*. The opposite. Maybe God fears the son."

"That's a crazy idea," said Suling.

"Well, I am crazy, so I must also have crazy ideas—however, that doesn't make them wrong."

"What about the men?" whispered Meiying.

"What about them?"

"I wonder, do they hear the voices?"

"You mean Master Zhou and Lu Zhishen?" asked Suling.

"Yes."

"I know Feng Shiren did," said Suling.

"Of course," confirmed Child of Buddha.

"I also know he did," added Meiying.

"There you have it!" cried Child of Buddha.

"What?"

"All of us are involved in this business about the son."

Meiying could not accept this. "But, what about Master Zhou? Peter? Mr. Gao? Little Acorn? Master Liu? Madame Liu? All the rest of them? It could not be!"

"But it is," proclaimed Child of Buddha in a quiet, contemplative tone.

"Meiying," said Suling. "This son must be very important. You should feel privileged."

"Privileged? No, no, no! I do not! I feel low. I feel used. I feel like a receptacle. I am more than a receptacle."

"Well, console yourself," observed Child of Buddha. "If you're merely a receptacle, what does that make the rest of us?"

"I . . . I. . . . " Meiying stumbled.

"There's more to it," said Child of Buddha. "What about Beethoven, Mr. President, Father Durant, and all the rest of them? Are they in on this somehow?"

"No, it couldn't be!" insisted Meiying.

Child of Buddha laughed. "Maybe all of us are in that mental institution, dreaming all this up. Maybe we're all mad. Wouldn't that be lovely?"

"Perhaps," said Suling. "But I am not one to get carried away. I prefer my two feet to be planted firmly on the earth. We are not dreaming this. Maybe, just maybe, we are having the same dreams, but all we have gone through is real. Too real. I tell you, I want to return to my home and get on with my own life. No more of this fantastic storytelling. Soon, we take the bus to Taiyuan, then on to Nanjing and Shanghai. Meiying and John will go to America. In the meantime, we all must eat, find shelter, and survive. In these times, that will be hard enough."

Suling's declaration signaled the end of the conversation, but for Meiying, the internal struggle had only just begun. All night she tossed and turned, suffering from repeated nightmares that made no sense. When the women sat at breakfast together the next morning, no one brought up the previous night's discussion. Master Zhou was the first male to join them, and although each felt an urge to ask him about the voices, the topic was never raised.

~

The day came when they boarded the bus for Taiyuan, and Meiying spent the entire trip forcing her mind to dwell on anything other than their destination. John sat next to her and rambled on about America and how wonderful it will be when they finally arrive, but she could not shake the horrid specter of Beethoven's uncle, waiting like a patient spider in Taiyuan for his victim to arrive. All the circumstances of her life made her aware of how quickly events could turn one upside-down. In spite of her reservations about John—and they were many—she resolved to stick close to him and the rest of the group until they were safely out of Taiyuan. She longed for the safety of Feng Shiren, but he was no more, only adding to her feelings of vulnerability and dread. Once they arrived in the city, they found their accommodations to be far more comfortable than any of them could have hoped for, except Master Zhou, who had decided to spare no expense during the group's last days together. The luxurious nature of her room made Meiying forget, if only for the moment, her fears. In fact, she languished in the bathtub and pictured living conditions in America, which must surely be even better. Pangs of patriotic guilt always accompanied these longings to abandon China, but Meiying found herself less and less able to resist.

So close, she thought. *If we can just get out of Taiyuan without incident.*

But whenever she strayed out into the streets with her comrades, every passing face and half-seen figure standing in the nooks and crannies of the city, seemed to resemble Beethoven's uncle. Her secret terror only deepened when Master Zhou announced his inability to get tickets on either bus or train anytime soon. Even bribes made no difference, as the fleeing rich drove the prices too high. It seemed to Meiying that events conspired against her, and that the uncle must be manipulating them in order to grab her at the last moment. She vowed never again to submit to rape or imprisonment, and took to carrying a concealed knife, though the memory of Beethoven made her certain she could never again use it. Slowly, a disturbing thought insinuated itself into her consciousness.

I am a pawn in a battle between God and Her. What if He is stronger? I will surely be killed, or worse. Who will help me if He is stronger?

I will help you, dear one!

Meiying heard the voice while window-shopping with Suling and Mulan. She froze and waited, her heart pounding uncontrollably.

Who are you?

You already know. It is the son you must focus on, Bai Meiying. The son!

But God is too strong.

No. He is a sweetheart, really. His words distorted, and He is not addicted in your sense of the word. A problem, true. But the real threat is from humanity itself.

What? Addicted? Humanity?

Never mind. Have faith in your Mother. Have faith in your Goddess.

But He is more powerful.

Who says?

Well, everyone.

Of course, that is what the fools think. He has damned anyone who has said otherwise — at least, that is what is believed by so many of that species.

"Meiying!" cried Suling, tugging on her sleeve. "You are daydreaming."

At the crack of her words, the voice melted away, leaving a vacuum in Meiying's consciousness to be filled by any welcome distraction. "No," replied Meiying absently while she collected her thoughts. "I am dreaming of a day."

"I don't understand."

"It's nothing." Meiying pointed at the window full of colorful summer clothes, suddenly energized by the forces of distraction and seizing the first shiny bauble to catch her eye. "See anything you like?"

"No, and you?"

"Oh, yes," replied Meiying quickly, the better to head off any further disembodied intrusions by murderous uncles and mad deities. "I like that scarf."

"I do too. Oh, Miss Bai, that would look so good on you!" exclaimed Mulan.

"I think it would be nice with some of my dresses," said Meiying forcing a wan smile. (She only owned one dress, and that from Mr. President's palace.)

Suling laughed for the first time in ages. "Then buy it."

Meiying chuckled. "Of course. And I may as well buy the store at the same time."

"It couldn't be that much," said Suling.

"How much is it then?" Meiying peered into the window, trying mightily to block out the echoing aftermath of the voice. "I don't see a price."

"Yes, I don't either," said Suling.

"Am I going mad?" asked Meiying.

"No," replied Suling. "You're not mad to ask how much it is. Let's go inside and ask, just for fun."

"Yes, yes, let's do it . . . just for fun!" added Mulan.

"Well, okay, just for a quick look around," said Meiying.

All three locked arms and entered the store like schoolchildren, laughing and chatting about this and that while the proprietor smiled on, waiting anxiously for them to alight on some garment. He was a rotund man with a kindly face. Two young children played behind the counter. Sensing their wanderings carried them too far afield from the prize in the window, he said, "I saw you looking at the scarf in the window, would you like to try it on?"

"Yes, yes do," said Mulan.

So Meiying wrapped the scarf loosely around her neck, to the oohs and aahs of the others. The proprietor beamed.

"It accentuates the natural beauty of your skin," he observed.

"It does, it does," agreed Mulan. "Oh, buy it. You look so beautiful."

"How much?" asked Suling.

"Only eight yuan," replied the proprietor. "And the girl is right, it looks excellent on you."

"Might as well be eight hundred yuan," said Meiying wistfully. She started to remove it.

"For you, such a beautiful lady, I will take six," said the proprietor.

"Sorry, I still can't," replied Meiying.

"Yes she can!" came a booming voice. "She'll take it!"

The three women and the proprietor all jumped at the loud intrusion, and beheld Master Zhou standing in the doorway with Lu Zhishen and John.

"We've been playing detectives," laughed Master Zhou, counting out the money into the outstretched palm of the proprietor. "Following you three discreetly, just in case."

"Oh, you are all so kind!" exclaimed Meiying.

"Did you notice us?" asked Lu Zhishen.

"Not at all," said Suling.

"No," agreed Mulan. "You are all great detectives!"

"Yes!" exclaimed Master Zhou. "We are . . . what do Americans say? . . . shoe gums."

"Gum shoes," corrected John.

"Come, leave on the scarf and let's have lunch together," offered Master Zhou. "We'll show you off to the poor, downtrodden world that needs beauty more than ever."

"Truly, you are beautiful," put in John, again overwhelmed by her sheer presence.

The scarf frames her face magnificently! he thought as they left the store to the bows of the proprietor. *She'll be a hit in the States. Madame Chiang Kai-shek pales in comparison!*

~ *An Unwelcome Presence* ~

After a short search, they all agreed to dine at a multi-story *dim sum* restaurant, and entered in good spirits. The restaurant was packed, and they were escorted to the second story, where a corner table was quickly cleared and they sat together with shared feelings of comradeship and joviality. It had been so long since they had been able to unrestrainedly laugh together that all were aware of the special nature of the meal, and each person there intended to savor the moment. Lu Zhishen had run to get Child of Buddha, and both joined them just as they were choosing their first course.

"Beer!" cried Master Zhou. "It's only money, my friends! Beer all around!"

"And non-alcoholic wine for Mulan," said Meiying in her best, motherly tone.

"Miss Bai, I drank beer quite often at our village. The water sometimes made us sick, and papa let me drink beer and wine. So, you see, I'm used to it."

"Well, a little then."

"What a good mother you will make!" enthused Suling, who immediately stopped short, remembering Meiying's unique circumstances. The others held their collective breaths, but Meiying was not about to cast a pall over this special occasion.

"Oh, not really! I'll be much too lenient!"

"Well, well, there you have it!" cried Master Zhou, pouring more beer into Lu Zhishen's glass.

Meiying's eyes wandered around the room when she spotted a lone figure sitting in the shadows at a small table tucked into a niche on the opposite wall from the group. The figure looked disturbingly familiar, and a shudder ran down her back.

It's him! she thought. *I'm sure of it!*

But the truth was that she wasn't sure. The shadows and intervening bustle of the customers and waiters made it hard to see clearly. Meiying looked at her friends, all of whom continued to have a grand time, unaware of her uncertain discovery. When she forced herself to look again, the man seemed to stare in her direction, and she quickly looked away. Child of Buddha, sitting next to Meiying, and with her usual perspicacity, peered at her friend.

"Is there something wrong?" she whispered.

"Not at all."

"Then why are you so interested in that corner of the restaurant?"

"I thought I saw someone I knew."

"Who?"

"Doesn't matter, it isn't the person."

"Old boyfriend . . . or, I should say, girlfriend?"

During this little conversation, Meiying had not taken her eyes from the vicinity of the lone diner. During most of that time, a waiter had blocked the view. When he stepped away, the man stared at Meiying full-on, and this time his identity was unmistakable.

Child of Buddha followed her eyes. "You look ill. Is it that character eating alone?"

"Have more beer!" shouted Master Zhou, who had stood and circled the table, pouring beer and wine and cracking jokes.

"No, thank you," said Meiying, happy for the intrusion.

"Yes, you do look a little reddish-hot around the edges," said Master Zhou. "How about you, my hunchbacked friend?"

"Always," said Child of Buddha holding out her glass. "My hump is thirsty."

Meiying sat trembling in fear and anticipation. Beethoven's uncle had again tracked her down. Undoubtedly, his henchmen waited for some opportunity to snatch her away, just as her goal seemed within reach. And, if they were successful a second time, then what . . . then what?

No! she told herself. *This time I will not let it happen!*

But before she could take any action, he had slipped out of the restaurant, apparently under the cover of a large group noisily leaving. However, the damage had been done, for when he had locked eyes with her, his expression was burned into her memory. While her friends chattered and laughed around the table, she struggled to put a name to that expression. Hatred?—no. Contempt?—no. Threat?—no. Lust?—no. Amused?—yes. Yes, that was it. He seemed amused, as might a cat toying with a mouse. But amused by what? While contemplating this puzzle, she had unconsciously withdrawn from the general patter of the conversations around her. As she stared into her food, deep in thought, Master Zhou had again circled the table and raised his glass behind her. With a hearty "Ahem!" to get everyone's attention, he spoke loudly, with a noticeable slur.

"And here we have the lovely Miss Bai, whose presence will be sorely missed! A toast to her bright future! *Gānbēi!*"

In swinging his glass, he inadvertently spilled a few drops of beer on her arm, which served to jerk her back to the harsh reality of the present as much as if he had flung a bucket of water on her.

"Oh!" she uttered, wiping the beer from her arm and looking around the table as if she had just awakened. "Thank you, Master Zhou."

He wagged a finger at her. "You were not quite with us for a few moments there." He thumped his chest. "I challenge you to tell us what you were dreaming about! Was it the allure of America with its golden streets and glittering cities?"

Meiying heard Mulan coughing, and in confusion she took a sip of wine.

"Well, tell us, dear Meiying," insisted Master Zhou, definitely in his cups.

The others waited politely for her response. To Meiying, their eyes became an intimidating host of little orbed judges, ready to pass sentence.

"Yes, yes, I was thinking about America." She took a deep breath to regain her composure. "But, most of all, I was thinking how I will miss all of you."

After speaking these words, which were intended only to mollify, she felt surprised to feel tears rolling down her cheeks. Mulan looked on, trying to suppress another cough, and Meiying began to sob.

"I'm sorry, I'm sorry," she gasped. "I don't know why I'm this way. I'm sorry."

Master Zhou, sobered by her reaction, spoke soothingly. "Now, now, my dear. We will all miss you too. But we comfort ourselves that we'll be reading about you in the newspapers and hearing about you on the radio. Your music will sweep America! And we will be proud to say, 'I know Miss Bai Meiying. I am her friend!'"

A chorus of "Yes! Yes!" swept around the table, but Meiying's tears kept coming, and like a face viewed through a veil of water, the mocking image remained, distorted but unchanged.

"Well," said John loudly. "We will certainly stay in touch with all of you, and whatever we can do from America to help, if you need it, we will do." He made this statement fully aware it sounded paltry and patronizing compared to Meiying's obviously sincere, touching words.

"Bravo!" shouted Master Zhou, back to his boisterous mood. "Bravo! *Gānbēi*! *Gānbēi*!"

Drinks were poured all around, and even Mulan got a bit more, though Meiying ordered Suling to pour only a tiny amount. Throwing herself into the jovial atmosphere, Meiying forced the memory of Beethoven's uncle from her mind. She knew he would return soon enough, if only in her nightmares. But she did come to understand that whatever he found amusing was permanently lodged inside of her, and she would carry that object of mockery to her grave.

~

The next day passed uneventfully, if somewhat nervously for Meiying, and by the following day they were ensconced in a weather-beaten old bus on their way to Nanjing. For the first time since the incident at the restaurant, she felt relaxed and confident. Only news of the intensifying civil war upset the group's hopeful mood, for rumors of trains and buses being attacked by communists and local warlords buzzed among the passengers. Retracing by bus the route they had so laboriously and disastrously made by foot during the war had elicited all of the usual flood of memories and reminiscences; and such scenes moved each of them to both intense joy at their survival, and intense sorrow at the loss of so many of their comrades. Nevertheless, the bus eventually reached the station nearest Master Zhou's estate, and farewells had to be made. Goodbyes were brief, as the bus moved quickly on toward Nanjing. Master Zhou's waving figure undramatically disappeared behind an insignificant rise. Now, with his departure, they found themselves rudderless and sat forlornly in the back of the bus with little to say. Lu Zhishen tried to lighten the mood.

"Look, we'll all see each other again. How about this?—let's agree to have a reunion a few years from now."

"How many years?" asked John.

"I don't know. How about five—a five-year reunion."

"Where?" asked Child of Buddha, laughing for some unknown reason.

"How about Shanghai?" queried Lu.

"Ha! You'll be married and surrounded by a bunch of kids in Canada!" said Child of Buddha.

"And you'll be back in a mental institution!" he shot back, laughing to take out the sting.

"Oh, you're bad," said Suling.

But Child of Buddha was in a feisty mood. "And Meiying and John will be raising an amazing son, heaven-sent to . . . to do what?"

"Maybe save us all," said Suling.

"Stop!" cried Meiying. "It's not funny,"

"Not meant to be," replied Child of Buddha. "What is this brilliant son truly meant to do?"

"I'm not having a son!" exclaimed Meiying. "So just stop it. Let's talk about something else, or we're all going to argue."

"Yes, yes," agreed Suling. "We're going home. Let's enjoy our last time together."

"I don't have a home," said Child of Buddha.

"Well, find one. Make one." Lu Zhishen gestured as if out of patience.

"Going back to the mental institution isn't a bad idea," suggested Child of Buddha.

"Besides," said Meiying, putting her hand on Mulan's shoulder. "I have a daughter."

"Yes, if we can get her to the States," added John.

"And if not?" asked Child of Buddha.

"We will," said John grimly. "As soon as we reach Nanjing, we're going to the American embassy and get things straightened out for Meiying and Mulan."

"It will all work out," soothed Suling.

"I hope so," added John.

"I thought you were so confident," needled Child of Buddha.

"Why are you so naughty today?" asked Suling, looking askance at Child of Buddha.

"Because I will soon be left alone again, even by *her*, even by the voices."

"*She* won't abandon you."

"*She* already has. John and Meiying are practically in America. My usefulness is over. I serve no purpose now. I'm dead."

Suling looked at her sympathetically. "No, no, you're not. You have your own life to live."

"What life?"

Suling gave her a steely glare. "Your life. You must live. Your life has value."

"My life is over. Leave me alone."

Suling ignored her. "You're right about one thing, Child of Buddha, go back to the institution. Help Reverend Fu and Master Li. You can be their assistant. Find a way to help. Find a purpose. They need you."

Child of Buddha nodded toward Meiying and John. "Once they're safely away, my purpose is over."

"But that is just not true."

Child of Buddha scoffed. "What is your purpose, Suling?"

"To live."

"That is no purpose."

"That is the only purpose."

~ *Nanjing and Beyond* ~

The bus arrived in Nanjing late at night, and after collecting the little luggage they owned, the small band wearily trudged to a nearby hotel where Master Zhou had made the last reservations for the group. Signs of the Japanese occupation were everywhere. Damaged buildings, shell-shocked refugees, people with no arms or legs, hordes of orphan children begging for food; everywhere they looked a shattered city of filth and misery. The darkness made it worse. Staring at them from all directions were faces half-illuminated by sickly neon lights and moth-encircled street lanterns; thousands of glimmering eyes, sunken and hopeless, blinked at them though the gloom. Amidst this foul sea of despair, they made their way through the human detritus to an elegant hotel, shining incongruously like a beacon of privilege and gluttony. After the tedious process of checking-in, they agreed to meet for breakfast and trundled off to welcome sleep.

Next morning brought another round of farewells. Child of Buddha heeded Suling's advice and had decided to return to the institution, while Suling announced her departure for her distant home in the countryside. Tears fell abundantly all around, and in the end, John, Meiying, Mulan, and Lu Zhishen would find themselves the last remnants of the group.

"Jesus, how far we've sunk!" observed Lu Zhishen despondently as they ate together for the last time.

"No, no. Look how far we're risen!" insisted Suling. "Find your families. Make new families. Live!"

"She's right," said John. "We have all learned so much. We've learned about survival, about suffering, about violence and hatred. Now, let's use our knowledge to achieve a better world. Yes, let's go our own ways and help heal the world."

Meiying looked at John with a new appreciation.

But when they gazed out the hotel dining room window at the hordes of shattered people wandering aimlessly in the street, their moods tempered.

"Well," observed Lu as he stared out the window. "There's a hell of a lot of healing to do."

"True," said Child of Buddha. "But here, not in Canada or the United States. And where are you going to do this healing?"

They looked at her submissively.

"Huh?" insisted Child of Buddha. "You, Canadian Zhishen? You, American John? And you, Chinese Bai Meiying? It will only be up to those of us that stay to do the healing!"

The others looked down at their plates. Thus, on such a brutally honest note, the group went their separate ways.

The next day, John trekked to the newly re-opened American embassy to make arrangements for their journey and see about adopting a Chinese orphan. Meiying and Mulan waited nervously in the hotel for his return with the verdict.

~

John approached the partially damaged embassy with trepidation. Its massive concrete design stood up excellently to Japanese bombs, but was intimidating and off-putting to a small human with small problems amidst a sea of humans with truly existential problems.

This building reminds me of Child of Buddha's mental institution, he thought. *Although I'm aware any self-respecting architect would bellow at my ignorance.*

Yet, it did look like the institution. On entering, a huge crowd jostled for position to get to the information desk, which reminded John of the frenzied inmates chasing their fantastical visions around the halls of Fu-Li's establishment in mad desperation. At last, he made it to one of the officious clerks sitting behind a massive counter, an English-speaking Chinese, who handed him a slip and said his interview would be the next day. When John insisted on describing his plans to marry a Chinese citizen, the clerk shrugged, handed him a raft of documents to fill out, and signaled for the next in line.

"Well?" asked Meiying when he entered the hotel room. "What did they say?"

"They said nothing, but shoved these papers in my hand. I'm to meet them tomorrow after I fill them out."

"Did you ask about Mulan?"

"No, not a chance. It's a madhouse there."

"Well," said Meiying looking askance at the documents. "At least we've made a start."

John perused the papers. "I don't see anything here about bringing a Chinese child." He lowered his voice. "Where's Mulan?"

"Asleep in the bed. She was coughing horribly, so I gave her medicine and she's finally fallen quiet."

"Great." He grimaced at the papers. "Meiying, it's going to be hard enough to get you out of here, let alone Mulan."

"I know."

"And we have to marry as soon as possible." He leafed through the papers. "It says here that it must be a validly recognized marriage before they grant us an

AR-3 card, whatever that is." He read some more. "Oh, we can petition to have you registered as my fiancé and marry in the States. That's good."

"But, what about Mulan?"

John looked down at the papers and shook his head. "I'll ask tomorrow for the paperwork. I assume we have to adopt her, or something like that. You know, there are a billion refugees. There won't be a problem with the Chinese government, but the American government is a different story. We are a racist country. Been excluding Chinese for a very long time. But with my involvement, and China being our ally in the war, maybe things will be different."

"Let's hope so," sighed Meiying. "I could not leave Mulan here to fend for herself."

"But, you know, this will take some time. How are we going to survive? There's no money, and this hotel alone is expensive."

"I could get a job," said Meiying.

"Are you crazy? How many people are looking for jobs?"

"If we can get to Shanghai," said Meiying. "I have some family and other connections, if they're still alive. I can play piano for money."

"Yeah, but I have to stay here and wait for the damn bureaucracy to process this stuff. I'm an American citizen, maybe they can expedite the process." He sighed and ran his hand through his hair. "I don't know, let's see what they say tomorrow."

"But, John!" exclaimed a frustrated Meiying. "You must get them to understand Mulan's circumstances if we leave her."

John threw up his hands. "You don't understand, Meiying! I'm not sure I can get you to the States, let alone Mulan!"

"You said that already!" shouted Meiying. "But, I will not leave without her!"

"Ohhh!" groaned John, shaking his head as if he doubted her sincerity.

"No! I mean it! I'll take her back to her village and teach. Better to stay here and face the music than run like a coward!"

"Face the music here in China, or play the music there in America?" asked John with an ironic flair in his tone, proud of his clever turn of phrase. He repeated it drolly. "Face it or play it. What's your preference?"

"Oh, you're so damn clever!" she cried. "With Chinese lives you're clever!"

"What do you mean by that?"

"You aren't stupid, figure it out."

"Yes, I am stupid! I'm an American, remember? All Americans are stupid!"

"I never said that."

"No, but you imply it."

"Never! When?"

"Always! All the damn time! I know what you think of me. I can't replace the almighty perfection of a woman!"

"So, that's what this is all about!"

Meiying paused when she heard Mulan coughing in the next room. She lowered her voice. "Find a way, John."

~

So, they experienced their first argument as a couple, and to neither did it seem a good portent of things to come. During the argument, when Meiying mentioned getting a teaching job in Mulan's village, John recalled his old job teaching English and decided to drop by the language school first thing in the morning. After all, he thought, this process may take a long time. But, in fact, events moved quickly. After a series of consultations with embassy staff, John found an officially recognized American Methodist minister to marry them, and a way to bring Mulan to America as a "distressed war orphan."

The day of the wedding ceremony proved to be dismal. A steady, pattering rain fell as Meiying, John, and Mulan made their way to a renovated Methodist church across town from the hotel. As they could not afford a cab, or even a rickshaw, they trudged through the grey gloom of the city. Even the recent hum of activity that had arisen with the rebuilding frenzy seemed stalled by a general laxness of spirit—due in part, no doubt, to the expanding civil war. Meiying and John themselves experienced just this sort of inertia in their relationship. They did not argue, but had settled into the sort of pragmatic attitude toward building their future that a carpenter might take in framing a house. What needed to be done seemed to get done in the spirit of tedious necessity, with no joy or excited anticipation at the approaching goal for which they so exerted themselves. They directed their efforts with a one-step-at-a-time obstinacy, and the mood at their wedding ceremony consisted of just such a workmanlike expediency. Meiying's borrowed wedding dress, a traditional Chinese silk brocade, had been soaked in the rain, and John's formal wear consisted of a tie combined with a mismatched jacket, rumpled slacks, and threadbare woolen socks. Shortly thereafter, to John's great surprise, the American consulate approved adoption papers for Mulan, and the three indulged in a modest celebration at the expensive hotel restaurant. So, within a month, thanks to Master Zhou's financial assistance (which John promised to repay from America) they set off for Shanghai, freshly married, papers in order, an adopted daughter, and tickets in hand for passage to a new life.

~

After they reached Shanghai, Meiying never stopped looking over her shoulder; whether it be for Mr. President's lurking agents or Beethoven's uncle and his skulking thugs. But they never materialized, and the day of departure arrived. Meiying learned that her parents had both presumably died in the war, having disappeared one night from their home when the Japanese came knocking, and were never heard from again. She absorbed this news with barely a ripple of pain. It seemed to John that she could tolerate no more tragedy, and like a soaked rag, simply refused to sop up additional suffering. She had managed to find a handful of friends who still survived, and they huddled together on the dock, waving up at the ship. Meiying waved back like an automaton, smiling the smile of a painted doll. Behind the little knot of friends, she thought she spied that face from the restaurant staring at her; a wry smile disfiguring the lips into a particularly nasty shape. She shuddered a deep and abiding tremor that congealed as a stone in her heart; heavy and unyielding. When the ship drew slowly away, and the people on the dock shrank to mere dots, she said nothing and returned to the stateroom, waving Mulan away with the excuses of "being tired" and having "a headache." China, substituting as her absent (and presumed dead) mother and father, receded cold and distant, a gray smudge on the horizon that soon blinked out, leaving her adrift in the immense desolation of an emotionless sea.

Only the suspicion that someone onboard was stalking her, under orders from Beethoven's uncle, or worse, Mr. President, kept her from sleeping as soundly as her exhausted body craved. She had long ago accepted the self-imposed label of prostitute by agreeing to marry John—in fact, she felt even more depraved than an honest whore because of the hypocrisy implicit in her decision. To combat these feelings, she clung to the justification that Mulan symbolized a noble excuse for her inexcusable behavior. She told herself that had Mulan not been in the picture, she would not have agreed to marry, but even this reasoning evaporated rapidly in the light of day. Still awake with these thoughts plaguing her mind, she heard John enter the stateroom and slip into bed, but she lay perfectly still until he turned on his side facing away, and she again fell into a relieved but restless sleep.

Meiying's paranoia became progressively worse as the voyage continued. She even feared leaning on the railing to gaze at the ocean for fear of being pushed from behind. This behavior irritated John, who felt her imagination was veering out of control. They again took to arguing, and never once touched each other, whether intimately, as close friends, or in anger. Mulan, for her part, sank into a depression, spurred on by fits of coughing and breathless wheezing. One evening, John invited Meiying to stroll on the deck for some fresh air. Mulan slept soundly, so she agreed. Bundled up against the cold, they appeared to any surreptitious observer as two amorphous figures walking side by side like two acquaintances, not touching, yet still friendly. Only by standing very near could their words be distinguishable through the fog.

"Well, we're almost there," said the male voice.

"Yes, I know," replied the female in a tone that almost implied resignation.

"It will be nice."

"Yes."

"You'll see. Everything will be different when we're off this damn boat."

"Yes, but. . . . "

The female paused, and the eavesdropping listener would perk up his or her ears in anticipation. However, the wait was long and drawn out until the male finally said, "But?"

"Never mind."

By now, the couple would have passed the observer with nothing further spoken, until in the distance, two words would float back from the male. "You'll see."

Chapter Fourteen

First Steps

Terra Firma

John knew he would be happy to return home, but when San Francisco came into view, his heart thumped even more excitedly than he had anticipated during the years of exile. Meiying and Mulan stood beside him on the deck, their faces reflecting a combination of wonder and anxiety.

"Where is the Statue of Liberty?" asked Mulan.

Meiying scanned the horizon. "I don't see it, dear."

John laughed, a bit cruelly. "No, no. The Statue of Liberty is on the other side of the continent, in New York. This is San Francisco. Look for the Golden Gate Bridge. It was pretty new when I left for China years ago. Nothing like it!"

When he glanced at Meiying to gauge her reaction, he caught her peering nervously around at the faces on the deck. *Looking for her damn ghosts again*, he thought irritably. This haunted obsession of hers wore on him, and he fervently hoped it would fade once they left the confines of the ship. His own voices had been mercifully absent, and, reminded of this happy fact, he quickly straightened up as if recovering from some irritatingly vacuous daydream. He looked upon the approaching wharf with renewed confidence that all would now turn out as he had imagined. Since his own voices had been quiet, he assumed her obsessions would now be quiet also, and evidence of their persistence did not fit his present conception of a normal world, or his plans for sharing it with her.

~

But far from being assuaged by their arrival, Meiying became more convinced than ever that she would be waylaid by the long arms of Mr. President and uncle. Mulan, for her part, reflected Meiying's uncertainty, and became increasingly nervous about the whole adventure. She felt small and vulnerable, and her English was rudimentary at best. Talking with Americans on the ship had been excruciating, and she fell into the habit of looking down and saying nothing—a far cry from the outgoing, tomboy persona she had always displayed in her small village. In these frames of mind, the little party descended the gangplank to step on terra firma. John pulled them aside the moment they stepped on the weathered concrete pier and with a beaming grin, swept his arms out in a grand gesture and cried, "Welcome to the good old USof A!"

Both women smiled, even as they nervously surveyed the intimidating mob that clogged the customs gates. John scanned the faces of his two companions for signs of genuine happiness, but found none. He shrugged it off as nerves exacerbated by the oppressive crowds, and turned his mind to the task at hand with renewed determination. A surge of confidence swelled within his chest. At last, he operated on his own turf, and where before his behavior manifested only deferential passivity, he now felt free to exert a strong measure of dominance. When reduced to its most primitive truth, he now felt confident he would inherit Meiying's body by the sheer weight of changed circumstances. But John, in his haste to claim his rightful control over her life, underestimated Meiying's agile mind and resilient character; not to mention the degree to which she felt determined to guard her body from any further insults by men.

Clearing customs proved to be a trial, for the little band found itself subjected to the most gruff and intrusive questioning, accompanied by a minute inspection of documents and luggage. The supercilious customs officer looked askance at Mulan's coughing and scowled at John's and Meiying's marriage certificate, which, despite his hostile scrutiny, had been unmistakably certified by the United States embassy in China. When no irregularities were found, to his obvious disappointment, he nodded them through and said with mechanical formality, "Welcome to the United States." The words were grudgingly given, and as they rushed to repack the mess that had been made of their luggage, Meiying said, "Thank you," but the officer had already turned his attention to the next in line.

While hurriedly repacking her suitcase, which included intimate articles of clothing, Meiying felt the inspecting officer's roaming eyes return with a leering gawk, which to her betrayed not only his insincere words of welcome, but revealed an insolent lack of respect. Her Chinese sensibilities were already shocked by the total lack of restraint when Americans looked one another directly in the eyes, or worse, exposed their teeth in broad smiles and coarse laughter without raising a hand to block the spectacle. The inspector's lascivious stare only added to her sense of 'otherness.'

Men are men, she thought disgustedly. *Confucian Chinese or Christian American, always one thought, one motive, one desire, one drive. The old saying that beauty is a curse is most assuredly true!*

Yet, there was nothing new in this revelation, and she instinctively knew what to do to make herself as small and inconspicuous as possible—an eagle disguised as a quail. The circumstances were different in this new country, but the result remained the same. Meiying lowered her eyes and did nothing to detract from an appearance of oriental passivity. She knew how to play the submissive wife in public, but she had no intention of playing the dragon-lady in private. Her character rendered her more Daoist than Confucian, and the fact that water wears down stone always appealed to her, even as a little girl. Although the saying is trite, its metaphorical truth is powerful, and erodes the resistance of even the most entrenched cynic over time. Cynics, she had found, are made from soft rock, and wear down all the faster.

For his part, John had no real plan other than to find a cheap hotel and look for a job. Money was limited, and time was short before all his cash would be gone. He had heard from other Americans on the ship that returning veterans were gobbling up all the jobs, but he had experience in his field, and he could easily embellish his China adventure by tying it in to some patriotic mission. John had always been adept at navigating the fuzzy boundary separating absolute truth from absolute falsity, dipping in and out of the gray area with nimble alacrity. Now his patience was being sorely tested, as they had tried in vain to register at three cheap hotels, only to find there were no vacancies, or so they were told. He racked his brain to come up with a tall tale that might elicit sympathy and secure them a room.

Finally, they arrived at a suitably run-down establishment fronting a trash-strewn, dead end alley. John slapped the bell on the cluttered counter and waited for service. He and his two companions were exhausted from lugging their baggage up and down San Francisco's steep streets. Exasperated that no one appeared, John repeatedly banged on the bell. A balding clerk with a round belly and worn suspenders came lazily out to meet them, raising his eyebrows in disinterested inquiry, but said nothing.

"A room for three," said John in an even voice. "How much?"

The clerk scrutinized them as might someone inspecting items at an auction, and seemed to instantly gauge their circumstances. Apparently, he had seen many other mixed race couples, and the all too common sight now fell below his level of further curiosity.

"Twenty bucks."

"Oh," sighed John, deflated by his powerlessness for all to see. Even in the States he lacked the resources to shine, and worse, his tall tale had not materialized. He stood groping for words.

"But, that's for two rooms . . . look here, we just need one room, for three . . . well, two and a child."

The clerk looked at Mulan. "She ain't a child. You need two rooms."

"How about a cot?" John asked, and by way of unnecessary explanation, added, "We can't afford two rooms."

"Yeah, I can see that, but this ain't skid row, bud."

"No, but. . . . " John struggled to find a reply. "Is there any place cheaper close by?"

The clerk looked at Meiying and Mulan. "You could try Chinatown, bud."

"No, no," John hastened to reply. "That won't do. A cot, maybe?"

The clerk was in process of shaking his bald head when Meiying stepped forward.

"You see," she said demurely. "My husband did missionary work in China when the Japs came for us." She put her arm around Mulan and lowered her eyes as if the memories were too much. "Only now was it possible to return home, but we have little money until we can find a job." She appeared to hold back tears.

"Oh," said the clerk, seeming to notice her beauty for the first time. He smiled at her in a manner implying her husband was a loser, and that he sympathized with her plight. "In that case, for the cause, I'll charge you ten bucks for one room and set up a cot. How's that?"

"Thank you," said John, somewhat put out by Meiying's successful interference.

"This your daughter?" asked the clerk, looking at Mulan.

"No, she's an orphan and we're her guardians," said John quickly, not wanting Meiying to have further conversation with this man.

The clerk stared at John as if weighing the truth of his words.

"We plan to adopt her," said Meiying smiling.

"Yeah, as soon as we get out feet on the ground," added John, giving Meiying a displeased glance.

"Ah," the clerk grunted. "Lousy Japs." He returned his gaze to Mulan and said in a friendly tone, "Welcome to the United States, missy."

Mulan, who had been standing quietly with her head down, mumbled, "Thank you," without looking up.

"Does the room have its own bathroom?" asked John, remembering Meiying's last encounter with a toilet down the hall.

"Course!" barked the clerk. "We ain't in skid row, bud."

"Thanks."

John signed the register and was duly handed the keys to Room Two-Twenty, second floor on the left. As they trudged up the stairs burdened with the luggage, water pipes could be heard groaning and wheezing from the bowels of the hotel, and holding back a grimace, he tried to focus on the future.

Not exactly the grandest homecoming, he thought, glancing at the tired faces of the two women. *But, it'll get better once I find a job.*

~

By unspoken agreement, John slept on the cot while the two women shared the bed. Now that a room for the night was secured, he felt his anxiety go down and his libido rise up to a level that defied sleep.

God, if only Mulan weren't here, he thought resentfully.

He tossed and turned, the fantasies always overcoming the tug of sleep. Finally, a fitful period of rest allowed for a short series of vivid dreams, most involving crude sexual encounters, except for one.

~ *Dreaming About A Future Son* ~

Out of the amorphous murk of troubled sleep, a person emerged in hazy outline, who John could not identify. Shadows almost made it invisible, but in a flash of insight, the figure became unambiguous: it was his future son. Although crouched in semi-darkness, its mad eyes glared from white orbs that burned through the fog, and John now knew he would pass his relatively mild schizophrenia down to this son in a hereditary curse raging with the power of full-blown insanity. Alternately morphing from young to old and back again, the figure of his son never moved from its crouching position; only the disease moved behind the flickering eyes, tracking John like a famished animal, yet with the sort of malicious resentment only human illness could conjure. In his dream, John panicked and ran as fast as he could, but never put distance between himself and his accusing son. Exhausted from running, he was ready to quit when he saw Meiying appear before him out of nowhere, stunningly naked, with outstretched arms ready to enfold him to her bosom. Just as he stumbled into her embrace, Mulan's coughing fit wakened him, and John, still half-asleep, buried his head in the blanket, trying to recapture the dream. But, his desperate urge to cradle his head between Meiying's breasts could not be realized, for the light abruptly flickered on and she sat up with Mulan, speaking soothingly while rubbing the poor girl's back. John uncovered his face and looked on sympathetically, stifling his own frustrations by repeating the empty question, "Are you okay, Mulan?"

But the dream would not be ignored, and it painfully reminded him of his own shortcomings. His self-centered desire to have Meiying, both body and soul, to the exclusion of such a needy child as Mulan only added to the diminution of his sense of self-worth. Of course, this guilt was then transferred to the girl in the form of a simmering resentment, which he took increasing pains to conceal. When the two women finally fell back to sleep, John's own fitful slumber produced no satisfying continuation of his dream.

Meiying's arms will have to wait, he thought bitterly. *Damn Mulan!—though it's not her fault.*

Morning came soon enough, and with it the unwelcome labors of necessity. His most immediate task was to earn money for food and lodging, and to do this he must seek work. Returning to his old place of employment carried with it a mix of dread and hopeful anticipation. After a tiresome walk up and down the roller-coaster streets of San Francisco, he stood in front of the imposing steel edifice housing his previous employer. Perusing the list of tenants in the lobby, he noticed the consulting firm of Mobley & Dunham, Ltd. now occupied only two floors.

Not good, he thought. *Down from five floors to two! Damn war probably did them in.*

He took a deep breath, straightened himself, and took the elevator to the eighth floor. With hat in hand, he strode to the receptionist with an assured confidence he did not feel.

"May I help you?"

He didn't recognize her. Bowing slightly, he uttered his rehearsed lines. "Yes." Pause significantly, then continue. "My name is John Powers. I used to work here and have just returned from China. Is Mr. Dunham in?"

"Sorry, Mr. Dunham passed away a few years ago."

Damn! Should have checked first!

"Well," he said, less confidently. "I'm very sorry to hear that. How about Mr. Mobley?"

"Mr. Mobley senior or Mr. Mobley junior?"

"Oh," he stuttered. "Mr. Mobley senior."

"Mr. Mobley is retired." She looked at John with a friendly smile, tinged, he thought, with some sympathy. "How long ago were you employed here?"

"Oh, before the war."

"My!" she uttered in surprise. "That is a long time. Mr. Mobley's son, Arthur Mobley, is now the head."

John chuckled nervously. "Ah, Arthur Mobley was still at college when I left. My secretary was Rose Underwood. Does she still work here?"

The receptionist shook her head. "No, sorry, the name doesn't ring a bell. I've been here three years now. May I ask, are you looking for employment?"

"Yes," replied John reluctantly. "I speak Chinese," he added in haste.

She smiled again and spoke softly, as if in confidence. "Actually, business has really picked up since the end of the war. Our Japan and China operations are buzzing."

"Oh," said John, brightening considerably. "That's wonderful news." His heartbeat quickened, and he looked upon this woman with an exaggerated gratitude.

"You say you just returned from China?" she asked rather officiously, aware she now occupied the superior position.

"Yes."

"Fluent in Mandarin or Cantonese?"

"Mandarin, and some Cantonese . . . oh, and some Shanghaiese."

Her officious bearing melted away and she again spoke as might a confidant. "Perhaps you want to meet with Mr. Mobley? Mr. Arthur Mobley?"

"Oh, yes. That would be great."

She picked up the phone and dialed three numbers. "Mrs. McAllister, I have someone here who wishes to see Mr. Mobley. He used to work for us."

As she paused for a response, John noticed her crisp dress, well-manicured nails, and skilled, professional demeanor. He felt instantly at home. *At least*, he thought, *it hasn't sunk too low*. He scrutinized the room. *So much cleaner than China!*

"Yes," she said into the phone. "China." Then added, "Before the war."

After a few moments, occasionally glancing up at John with a smile while she waited, the receptionist said, "Yes, all right. I'll tell him."

She hung up and gave him the same conspiratorial smile. "He'll see you in fifteen minutes. Have a seat, Mr. Powers."

"Thank you, miss?"

"Julie. Call me Julie. We aren't much stuck on formality here, except for Mrs. McAllister."

"Who?"

"You'll see."

"Well, thank you so much, Julie."

She bent over her desk as she said, "You're welcome." He wandered to an overstuffed chair and settled in, crossing his legs and picking up *Time* magazine. After leafing through a few pages, he came to an article on the Chinese civil war. At one particularly inaccurate section, he looked up to confide in Julie his contempt for the ignorant media, but she appeared far too busy, so he returned to the article—this time reading more closely. The gist of it proclaimed the communists would be easily defeated by the Nationalists, and, with Madame Chiang Kai-shek's articulate pleas for American aid, all would be well in China once the United States intervened to help.

Hubris, thought John. *Pure hubris.*

"What nonsense," he muttered.

"What?" asked Julie.

"Oh, sorry, just thinking out loud about this article."

"What's it about?"

"China."

Suddenly, he was back in that troubled country—the sights, sounds, smells—all overwhelmingly powerful. Meiying stood amongst the ruins of Nanjing, a lily floating above the mud, radiant in her matchless beauty.

"Mr. Powers!" came Julie's voice, loud and a bit exasperated.

"Oh, sorry?"

"Mr. Mobley will see you now. My, that must be some article, Mr. Powers. I've been trying to get your attention."

"Sorry, sorry, Julie."

Julie turned to an older woman, quite stout and with a maternal air about her. "This is Mrs. McAllister. She'll take you up to Mr. Mobley."

"Thank you so much, Julie. You've been very kind."

Julie reddened a little and went back to her work.

John's attention turned to Mrs. McAllister. She peered at him through rather thick glasses. He knew she was sizing him up, and he sorely wished his suit was not so wrinkled from the trip.

"Follow me, Mr. Powers," she commanded.

~ *Mr. Mobley* ~

Arthur Mobley was a tall, thin man with an aquiline nose and slicked-back hair. He wore a tailored three-piece suit and his movements fairly glided through space and around obstacles with the skill of a restless house fly. It almost seemed that if he turned sideways, he would disappear. When John entered his office, led by the formidable Mrs. McAllister, he rose and moved to meet John rather than waiting for John to come to him. This behavior naturally flattered John and he felt instantly at ease.

"Ah, Mr. Powers," said Mr. Mobley in a clipped, precise tone that fit his physical impression. "Have a seat. Thank you, Mrs. McAllister."

John sat while Mrs. McAllister retreated and Mr. Mobley sailed behind his desk, leaning back in his chair and remarking, "So, you just returned from China?"

"Yes."

"And you once worked here, for my father?"

"Yes."

"Before the war?"

"Yes, you were still in school, I believe."

Mobley smiled broadly. "Yup. Yale. Great fun!" He leaned forward in his chair and stared intently at John. "Are you *the* Mr. Powers?"

"Sorry?"

"You know, the chap who saw a ghost and ran off to find it?"

"What?" John muttered incredulously.

Mr. Mobley appeared disappointed. "You're not?"

John knew precisely what Mr. Mobley referred to, but he experienced a moment of doubt, unsure whether to admit the story or deny it. After all, he thought, the job might hang in the balance. With this incentive, he took the plunge.

"Well, if you mean I went to China in search of someone, yes. But it was no ghost." He paused while he quickly processed a brainstorm. "I found who I was looking for—my wife, who I just recently married." He sat back, quite proud of his little lie.

"Ah, so it *was* you!" exclaimed Mr. Mobley. "But the truth, as usual, is less interesting than the rumors."

John smiled. "Sorry to disappoint."

Mobley waved his hand in the air. "Not at all! Not at all! So, what can I do for you?"

"Well, to be honest, I'm looking for a job. You see, we just returned from China, and I'm a bit short of . . . well, of everything."

"A job," said Mobley, pausing to let the words die away.

"Yes, I have experience. Worked here for many years, before I chased my ghost." John chuckled familiarly.

"Well, the business has changed since then," pondered Mobley. "I do things a bit differently than my father."

John became nervous, his confidence again sagging. "I have experience in this business, but more importantly, I have had recent experience in China."

"Where?"

"Shanghai, Nanjing, Taoyuan, all over."

"Doing what?'

John frowned. "Surviving."

"Yes, of course." Mr. Mobley fell silent.

John grew increasingly uncomfortable and squirmed a little in his chair. He wanted to say something, but thought better of it.

Suddenly, quite unexpectedly, Mr. Mobley jumped up from his chair and assumed a Chinese operatic pose, almost identical to those of Feng Shiren. As he stood in a contorted posture, Mobley exclaimed in perfect Chinese, "Do you like Chinese opera, Mr. Powers?" He peered deeply into John's eyes and sent shivers careening through his soul.

Stunned, John could not utter a word. He stared at Mr. Mobley in amazement.

Mobley leapt into a different and more dramatic pose. "Well, do you?"

"Yes," blurted John. "I had a friend in China who . . . who. . . . "

"Who what?"

"Who you remind me of. Your Chinese is excellent, Mr. Mobley."

"Thank you. Thank Yale. Thank Professor DeFrancis." He laughed guilelessly. "Thank my father." Mobley relaxed his pose and adroitly folded himself back onto his desk chair.

"Have you been to China?" asked John, still shaken.

"No, but I lived in Chinatown with a Mandarin-speaking master for years while I commuted here. Father hated the idea, but I found it to be the only way I could become fluent, what with the war making it impossible to travel and all. I mean, going to China was out of the question. Master Feng taught me Chinese opera as well."

"Feng?" blurted John.

"Yes, Master Feng."

"Feng Shiren?"

"No, Feng Yuren," replied Mobley looking at John oddly. "Why, you know him?"

"No, no. Different person."

"I should think so. Master Feng has been in the States many, many years, although he may have returned to China recently. He always talked about his kids."

"Is he old?"

"Oh, yes. In his eighties now. Still spry though, I must say. Talks damn proudly about having a son while in his sixties, or some such. Why so interested?"

"Nothing. I knew a Feng Shiren in China, but I'm sure there's no relation. Feng's a common name."

Mr. Mobley clapped his hands and gave a slight operatic movement of his head, again reminding John of a certain person. "Anyway, Mr. Powers, you are interested in a job?"

"Yes."

"Well, you've been asking me questions. It's my turn."

Mobley grilled John about his background and his experiences in China, all the while speaking Mandarin. Both men seemed inclined to anticipate the other's thoughts, and they gradually felt quite comfortable bantering back and forth in seamless repartee. Mobley stood and held out his hand. "Come back tomorrow at ten o'clock sharp. We'll discuss salary. If it works out, you're hired."

"Great. Thank you. I look forward to meeting with you tomorrow." Mobley pulled out his wallet. "Oh, here's a twenty to tide you over, if that's okay?"

John bowed and took the bill. "Thanks much."

"Yes, discuss it with your new wife. I would like to meet her sometime."

John nodded. "Tomorrow then."

Mobley smiled a familiar smile. "Tomorrow." He picked up some papers and perused them as he quietly hummed a little ditty from one of Feng Shiren's favorite operas.

John closed Mr. Mobley's office door and breezed by the receptionist on his way out, feeling happy and yet troubled. Before he left, he paused abruptly as if remembering something, then turned and said in a cheerful voice, "Thank you, Julie! I'll be back tomorrow. I might be working here."

"Good! See you tomorrow, Mr. Powers."

He smiled. "Call me John. Please don't stand on formality."

~

When he arrived back at the hotel in high spirits, Meiying greeted him with a worried expression.

"The manager asked for another day's rent. I told him you would return soon."

"No problem," replied John breezily. He pulled the twenty from his wallet and waved it in front of her. "No problem at all."

A broad smile brightened her face. "So, it went well?"

"I would be surprised if by this time tomorrow I don't have a position at Dunham & Mobley, Ltd."

"Thank god!" exclaimed Meiying, putting her arm around Mulan.

"Hopefully," said John, holding up crossed fingers. "We won't have to worry about money much longer." He pressed his fingers against his heart. "We can actually eat. What will they think of next? Real food! And soon, an apartment!"

"That's wonderful!" cried Meiying.

"Hooray!" added Mulan.

"Of course," John cautioned in English. "It's not yet a done deal. Don't count your eggs 'till they've hatched."

"Eggs?" asked Mulan in confusion.

"Don't worry about it, Mulan," laughed John.

"But I want to know."

"It means, just don't get too excited. I'm not hired yet."

"Oh."

Nevertheless, the little family at last saw hope in their future. John returned the next day, and an agreement was quickly reached with Mr. Mobley; John would begin work the following Monday. Having received a small advance, he treated the women to a fancy restaurant that specialized in the distinctly American cuisine of steak and lobster. Meiying picked at her food, but Mulan ate heartily, while John indulged himself in feelings of patriarchal superiority. Nonetheless, Meiying's obvious dislike of the food bothered him. She would have to get used to American dishes, and he wanted her to be aware of his displeasure.

"Try it, Meiying, you might actually like it," he prompted.

"I am."

"You've hardly eaten anything."

"The pieces are too big."

"Nonsense. That's American style. Might as well get used to it."

She made a face. "I'm not sure I'll ever get used to such big portions."

John sighed in disapproval. "Well, we are in America, you know. China is far away."

"Yes, unfortunately."

John sat up. "What do you mean by that?"

"Nothing, except I'm not ready to eat so much."

"Would you rather be back in China? The squalor? The war?"

She looked at him with a feeble smile. "Sometimes."

"Well, you're here now. Might as well make the best of it."

"I intend to do just that. While you're at work, Mulan and I will go exploring."

"Where?"

"Oh, here and there. I know San Francisco has a wonderful symphony orchestra. I might drop by the concert hall."

John was alarmed. "So soon? Why not wait until we have some money saved up?"

"Why wait?"

"Because."

"That is not a reason."

"Because we need to get established first." John felt his moment in the sun was being cut short by Meiying's stubborn intransigence.

"Why? I can help us get established."

"You will need me to pave the way."

Meiying shook her head. "No. I want to see the concert hall. I might meet someone."

John felt himself jerked back to the reality of their arrangement. Using the word "no" in such a blunt manner brought him up short, and it was again made abundantly clear that he would never be the patriarch lording it over his submissive wife. "God damn it!" he said in a low growl, his face reddening. "You're not in America more than a few days and already you're acting like the boss. No one will talk to you there. Just because you play the piano means nothing! You need contacts . . . inside contacts." He made a sarcastic face. "Boss!"

"Neither are you the boss," she replied with a cold stare. "I already told you, I am independent. I will stay independent. I have my own life"—she turned and nodded toward Mulan—"with her. I am glad you found a job, but now I must try and start my career."

"But, it's too soon!"

"No."

"Meiying, you must wait. You'll ruin everything."

"No."

And so it went, with neither getting the upper hand over the other. By the time they had returned to the hotel, no one was speaking, and Mulan had tears in her eyes. Neither John nor Meiying were inclined to reconcile, so their sleeping arrangements did not change, and he lay on the cot filled with resentment.

Not even allowed to touch my own wife! he fumed in silent anger.

He wanted to continue focusing his frustrations on Meiying, but the image of Mr. Mobley standing in that ridiculous opera pose kept intruding, and a fearful thought occurred to him. He had no sooner dismissed it than . . . .

You see John, I take care of you!

John froze, his eyes open wide to the darkness. It had been so long since the voice had reverberated in his mind that he had begun to doubt it ever existed, or if it did, he assumed it had long since died.

You see, I take care of you, *She repeated.* **Foolish man! You must not let her stray too far.**

~

The following Monday, John arrived at work, having spent the early morning hours steeling himself to pass through the distasteful ceremonies of one's first day at a new job—introductions, awkward pleasantries, and the christening of his tiny office space—all had to be endured with the appropriate aplomb. The day was topped off by his ceremonial first sitting behind the desk to which he would be henceforth chained. Once these rituals were over, his next hours were filled with the details of how the salary he received would be turned into profitable work-product for the bosses he served. Business, like digestion, operated on certain basic principles: Stalk the prey, snag it, crack its bones to get to the life-sustaining marrow, consume it, produce excrement, use the excrement to fertilize a lush harvest of advertising and marketing, which attracts the next prey being stalked. And so, he rapidly settled into a routine of meeting clients, offering advice on matters he often knew very little about, and familiarizing himself with the vagaries of the business as it operated under the management of young Mr. Mobley; all in exchange for a steady paycheck. As the excrement was produced and the fertilizer spread, so came sprouts of green dollars that daily reached for the sun. Soon enough, the family of three moved into a modest apartment. All the while, Mr. Mobley seemed ready to guide and protect them, accentuating his role with operatic flair, and subsequently becoming an indispensable presence in John's return to prosperity. During his rise in fortunes, John had found no time to help Meiying with her career, nor had he physically touched her, although they now slept in the same bed. Mulan occupied a small room to herself, where her coughing fits were muffled from the rest of the apartment.

~ Meiying's Melancholy ~

Meiying had come to regard John as a source of financial stability, and little more. After their first clashes they rarely argued, and the unspoken arrangement between them precluding sex was most agreeable to her, if not to John. From this rather awkward but convenient base, she had set out to make her own contacts in the music world, but the results were so far very meager. Worse, she did not have access to a piano, and her playing surely suffered from lack of practice. A few promising contacts were made that quickly petered out. As time passed, this unhappy situation weighed heavily upon her. But one spring day saw a reversal of her fortunes.

While John was at work and Mulan out shopping, Meiying sat alone in the apartment reading a Chinese newspaper (she had subscribed to this daily treasure only after her husband's income was sufficient to justify the expense). Lounging in her nightgown felt liberating, and she luxuriated in comfortable privacy when a loud knocking came from the front door. Meiying always experienced a wave of fear when anything unexpected occurred, and she took a while getting to the door, imagining some thug sent by Mr. President lurked behind it. Fortunately, a peephole had been installed by John to make her more comfortable, and she took advantage of it now. Mr. Mobley's face came into view.

"Please wait a moment!" she called, and rushed into the bedroom to change. When she opened the door, he smiled broadly and took off his hat with a slight bow. Out of habit, she bowed lower and invited him in.

"Hello, Mrs. Powers," he said. "Sorry to bother you at this time."

"Is my husband okay?" asked Meiying, a bit startled since John should be at work.

"Yes, yes, he's fine. I came to see you."

"Oh. Please sit." She gestured toward a chair. "I will make tea."

Mr. Mobley held up his hand. "No, thanks. I can't stay long."

She waited patiently while he found the words. Distractedly twirling his hat in his hands for an uncomfortably long time, he at last leaned forward and proceeded to make statements that were in the form of confirmatory questions.

"I understand you play the piano?"

"Yes."

"And you actually performed in China?"

"Yes."

"And you got paid for the performances?"

"Yes."

"So, you are a professional?"

"Yes, until the war interrupted my career."

"And John tells me you are looking to meet people here who might help you get established?"

"Yes."

He stopped twirling the hat. "Well, I know someone who is interested."

Meiying brightened. "Oh?"

"Yes, I told your husband some time ago, but my contact just called wondering if you were still interested in speaking with him."

"Oh, yes!" exclaimed Meiying, repressing a jolt of anger at her husband. She looked at Mr. Mobley innocently. "How long ago did you tell my husband?"

"Over a month."

"Oh, he is so busy now, it must have slipped his mind."

"Yes, I'm sure. Well, this contact is both a client and a friend. He is an assistant director of the symphony, and in the past has used my company to arrange concerts in Asia. He figured your personal story would be a draw here, for Americans I mean, what with the civil war and all. Sort of a pianist version of Madame Chiang Kai-shek. He wants to speak with you and hear you play."

"I see."

"And, I must say, your beauty surpasses that even of the good Madame."

Meiying colored but did not reply. Flirting males were nothing new, but for some reason, this time the rather clunky effort raised heretofore dormant urges. She looked down and saw the seductive smile of Meili flash through her mind.

Mr. Mobley gazed at her for a long time, and when she did not look up, stood and held out a card. "Here is his contact information. His name is Mr. Hendricks. David Hendricks. Tell him I asked you to call."

"Thank you so much."

After seeing him out, Meiying debated whether to confront her husband, but decided against it. She would make her own way without his help. But her anger and resentment simmered at a new high, even as her desire for the touch of another woman deepened.

~

Meiying immediately telephoned Mr. Hendricks, and after a few back-and-forth calls, arranged to see him the following week. At first elated, she began to fret about her lack of practice, and felt a desperate need to find a piano before the meeting. Visits to various instrument shops failed to do the trick, so out of desperation she took a deep breath and placed a call to Mr. Mobley. In response to her inquiry as to whether he might help her find a piano, he replied in the lively tempo of someone she once knew in China.

"A piano? So, again I intervene to help a lady in distress! It is my role, my fate, to protect and provide!"

Meiying could picture a certain Chinese knight-errant speaking on the phone while pantomiming scenes from some opera. "If you would be so kind," she replied, self-consciously inserting a flirtatious tone in her voice, and being surprised at how natural and devastating it could be. Female beauty combined with great talent is an inexorable force against which most men are powerless. Yet, as with another she once knew, this seemed not the case with Mr. Mobley. He operated in some unseen realm, detectable only by the perturbations that emanated from behind its veil, seemingly immune to females wiles. Seemingly.

"You have only to ask, Mrs. Powers. I do happen to know someone who possesses a piano. I am sure she would love to share."

These words were straightforward enough, but Meiying thought she picked up a subtle undertone, although of what she wasn't sure.

"Oh, that's wonderful," she said demurely.

"An unmarried woman of great refinement," continued Mr. Mobley. "Were it my choice, she would not remain single, you get my drift? But, what is one to do? Alas . . . !" he sighed these last words in the exaggerated tone of a theatrically despairing lover, and Meiying could not help but laugh.

"Well!" he exclaimed abruptly. "Enough of my travails. I will call her and pave the way for you. Her name is Marie Telles. Among other things, a teacher of music, no less! Let me get back to you."

"You are so kind to do me yet another favor, Mr. Mobley."

"It is my mission, Madame Powers. And it is a mission I am most happy to perform. Farewell, for now."

"Thank you," said Meiying, chuckling at the antiquated phrase.

Within an hour he called to inform her that Miss Telles was pleased her piano might be of use, inviting Meiying to call and make arrangements. As soon as she hung up, Meiying's hand briefly rested atop the phone before she lifted it to dial, but with a shake of the head, abruptly set it back in the cradle and took a few deep breaths. She spent a few moments to rehearse what to say. Satisfied, she dialed again.

"Hello?"

"Is this Miss Telles?"

"Yes."

"My name is Meiying Powers. Mr. Mobley asked me to call regarding your piano."

"Oh, yes. Hello Miss Powers. How may I be of help?"

Meiying explained the situation, and stressed the lack of practice time before meeting with Mr. Hendricks.

"Of course, of course," said Miss Telles. "I completely understand. Today won't work, but tomorrow I will be available. The piano is at my house. It is at your disposal."

After Meiying expressed her gratitude, the pertinent information was exchanged, and the visit arranged for ten o'clock the next morning. Meiying felt dizzy with happiness at the fast pace of events, but decided to keep the developments to herself. Not even Mulan should know until something definite came of them. Although she longed to share her excitement, the full extent of her loneliness and isolation suddenly made her teary-eyed, but a quick glance at the mirror hardened her resolve.

There is no one, she thought grimly. *Nor will there ever be.*

The next day arrived after another night of restless sleep. She realized this might prove to be her last and best chance to get a start, and vowed to do whatever necessary to succeed, even if it meant sleeping with Mr. Mobley, or any other male for that matter. Too much water had passed under the bridge for her to be moralistic now. The American phrase that John often used, *come hell or high water*, came to her mind. But John's feelings barely broke the surface of her thoughts. *Powerful men sleep with beautiful women*, she assumed, supposing such perquisites were agreed and memorialized in some universal convention, and all men, high and low, subscribed to its implacable protocol; the right or wrong of it held no more moral sway than a tree root growing left or right in search of nutrients. If she were reduced to the level of a nutrient, than she would position herself to attract the most promising root of the most powerful tree. These cynical thoughts were not natural to Meiying's character, but she formed them from the masticated pulp that war and violence had made of her convictions. However, as a sacred vestige of her former self, she vowed never to sleep with John. This represented to her a symbol of her independence not only from John, but more importantly from men—the universal male—and from the voice; an act of defiance that would leave her some semblance of self-respect.

After breakfast, John departed for work and Mulan also left to meet a friend. Meiying dressed carefully, making sure her attire was suitably professional. As always, her make-up was applied sparingly, and the resulting impression on any observer was of a stunningly beautiful woman no older than her late twenties. While she stared at the mirror, she felt a surge of pride that she had survived the war so intact, yet at the same time chiding herself for such self-congratulating conceit. Given the importance of the visit to Miss Telles, she splurged and took a taxi so as to arrive unruffled.

~

When the taxi pulled in front of her destination at the top of one of San Francisco's most prestigious hills, she paid the driver and turned to behold a magnificent Victorian house rising in stately grandeur. Multiple turrets loomed majestically against the sky, while a gorgeous wrap-around porch accentuated the inviting nature of the building's charms: swirling curves, fish-scale shingles, and lovely bays, all providing an intimate allure that to Meiying seemed irresistible. The house stood proudly atop the steep hill overlooking San Francisco bay. To her further delight, the grounds were a luscious mix of shrubs, flowers, and ornamental trees that seamlessly merged to form an organic extension of the architecture itself. Her mind raced back to the estate of Madame Chen, with its overgrown garden and loving atmosphere of security and acceptance. Old Twisted and Old Crooked grinned at her, and visions of China made a knot in her stomach, reminding her of how much she missed her country. With a wave of her hand she dismissed her memories, and as if plagued by a swarm of mosquitoes, hurried to the front door before the flood of reminiscences sabotaged her mission.

~ *Marie Telles* ~

As the intricately carved door opened in answer to Meiying's knock, a woman in her forties with a gracious smile invited her to enter. She wore an artist's frock and exuded an aura of natural ease and unvarnished kindness.

"Mrs. Powers, welcome!" she greeted Meiying with a seemingly guileless enthusiasm. "Oh, my, Arthur Mobley did not do you justice. You're so beautiful!"

Meiying positively cringed under the flattery. "Thank you. I have come to visit your piano." Even as she was making this remark, she silently berated herself for such blunt and tactless words, but Miss Telles appeared unperturbed.

"Yes, yes, of course. Come in, come in."

Meiying entered and commented, "Your house is quite beautiful."

"Thank you. Yes, I have tried to keep its original charm."

As Meiying scanned the interior with an appreciative smile, Miss Telles said, "Come, let's sit a while and chat."

"Do you have time? I don't want to be a bother."

Perceptively aware of Meiying's hesitation, Miss Telles said, "Not at all, but you are probably impatient. You must see the piano first, then we'll talk."

The Steinway occupied its own room, and stood serenely, as if waiting for someone to touch its keys and experience the joy it would bring them by doing so.

Meiying sighed audibly. "It's beautiful!" she exclaimed.

"Yes, isn't it? And I keep it well tuned. Would you like to try it now?"

"Oh, yes. Please."

Miss Telles moved her arm in an inviting gesture. "It's all yours."

Meiying hesitated. "Do you play, Miss Telles?"

"A little." Her face momentarily darkened. "I kept it here mainly for a friend, but she has passed away, and so I am delighted to see it used again." Meiying's sensitive receptors instantly lit-up when touched by that momentary darkening, which seemed to reveal a wound far deeper than the loss of an acquaintance.

"Oh, I am so sorry."

"Now, my dear, please play a little something to cheer me up, then we can talk."

"What would you like?"

"You choose."

Meiying adjusted the bench and played a few chords. She paused and then started playing a Chopin nocturne. From the corner of her eye she saw the pleasure felt by this beautiful woman listening to the sweet sounds of the music. Such open and unapologetic joy made her want to play better, to be perfect, so that Miss Telles would receive the full benefit of Meiying's talent. For Meiying, it seemed crucial that she impress Miss Telles to the same depth as her host's mysterious piano playing friend had impressed. (Meiying, in her sensitive and romantic heart, already viewed the deceased friend as a woman of mystery.) With the last notes of the Chopin fading to silence, Miss Telles rose and clapped enthusiastically.

"Wonderful, dear! Wonderful! I could listen all afternoon."

Meiying blushed and replied, "But I can't play all afternoon, and that offer of tea and conversation is very appealing."

After bustling about, both women sat in a lovely anteroom, intimate and cloaked in an atmosphere of Victorian charm. As they sipped tea, their conversation slowly and naturally moved beyond the fragile dictates of small talk.

"You must have suffered much in China," said Miss Telles, framing the statement in a manner that would elicit either curt acknowledgement followed by a dead-end, or confiding elaboration followed by the discovery of new and uncharted territory.

"Yes, the situation there is terrible."

"We read about the Japanese invasion, and the horrible events at Nanjing. I hope you weren't there?"

Meiying whispered, "Yes, I was briefly. But we fled."

"Your family?"

"No, a group of friends."

"Where did you flee to?"

Meiying gazed at Miss Telles, surprised at the questions, but pleased by the interest. "Have you been to China, Miss Telles?"

"Please, call me Marie. Yes, I have, but only Shanghai and Peiping. It was before the war. I wanted to stay longer and travel into the interior, but my friend fell ill."

"The same friend who played the piano?" asked Meiying, a bit too quickly.

"Yes." Now it was Marie's turn to appear a bit surprised, lowering her head to conceal the sorrow.

Meiying was quick to draw attention away from this obviously painful memory. "Many in my group died. But, you asked where we fled to escape the Japanese. That is a long story full of happiness and sorrow, and, well, lost dreams."

"Oh, dear, I am so sorry." Marie Telles reached forward and put her hand caressingly on Meiying's arm.

Her touch gave Meiying a singular thrill and at the same time an existential chill, for it reminded her of Meili's exquisite touch—one of great gentleness and searing eroticism. With her breath momentarily taken away, Meiying could only stare at Miss Telles in wonder. Each woman held the other in a gaze of mutual longing and electric tension. Volumes were communicated in a flash.

As Meiying spoke, her voice faltered. "It seems so unreal now, here in this wealthy, peaceful setting."

"Yes, I imagine those days in China must be like a bad dream."

"But one I do not wish to forget," commented Meiying quickly.

Miss Telles looked at her, inviting her to continue, all the while fixing Meiying's eyes with a compassionate and receptive attention.

"You see," began Meiying conspiratorially. "We were not fleeing from something dreadful as much as we were rushing toward something glorious. Or so we thought."

"My," said Miss Telles. "Was it a shrine or temple?"

"Not really. It was something, or someone, who we thought might show the way. In Chinese, we call it the *dao*."

"That sounds more like an oracle, rather than a temple or a shrine."

"What would you think if I told you it was all of those things?"

"I would reply that I am intrigued."

Meiying paused to consider. If she continued telling her story to this quietly forceful woman, she knew she would tell it all, with nothing held back. Somehow, she sensed that in a million incarnations, there would appear none so receptive and understanding as Marie Telles; a woman whose composed strength rivaled Lihua and Buandelgereen, and whose sensual allure reminded her so much of

Meili. If she took this plunge and revealed every detail, she unconsciously anticipated Miss Telles would be as open about herself.

Meiying took a sip of tea and glanced past the cup at her host, who sat entirely composed, patiently waiting for the outcome of Meiying's internal debate. It was apparent to Meiying this woman understood the conflict and would abide any outcome with equal degrees of equanimity. And so, with a deep breath, she told her story. Initially, she intended to leave nothing out—Shanghai, Nanjing, Master Liu, Feng Shiren, Peter, Taoyuan, John, Mongolia, The Precious Object, and, of course, *her*. In spite of her intention, the terrible events at the hands of the Japanese, Father Durant, Beethoven, and Mr. President, were too painful to recount, so she mentioned those horrors only obliquely. Also, the voice was absent from her telling, for Meiying was more fearful of being thought mentally unstable than being a lesbian. When her tale came to an end, she felt limp and exhausted. During the entire time, Miss Telles had not once interrupted. Now, she stood and leaned over Meiying, caressing her hair and kissing her forehead. Unable to control her body any longer, Meiying fell into Marie's welcoming arms.

"I'm so sorry you suffered so much," whispered Marie Telles.

Meiying drew back and wiped the tears from her eyes. "and I am so sorry I have burdened you with my story. It is, as you Americans say, water under the bridge. Now, I must make my way in this country."

"Yes," agreed Miss Telles. "And my piano will help you in that regard."

"And, perhaps your company as well?" ventured Meiying.

"Definitely! But more than that, dear. I know people. Powerful people."

Meiying looked at her quizzically. "But, how. . . . " her words dropped off as she looked around at the luxury surrounding them.

Marie Telles laughed. "I see. Yes. You understand, I have inherited quite a lot from my father."

"And your mother?"

"Passed away long ago. This is my family home, but now, alas, without a family."

"You never married?"

"Not in the way you are thinking."

Meiying's heart quickened and she scrutinized Marie's eyes to determine whether there was a willingness to venture beyond the statement. She thought she recognized an invitation, but wasn't sure and hesitated. Miss Telles held her gaze. That told her all she needed to know.

"The woman who played the piano?" asked Meiying, still holding the gaze.

"Yes, my very dear friend."

Meiying paused to wait for more, but to her disappointment none came, so she held back from asking, 'Your lover?' Instead, she simply nodded.

"Well," said Miss Telles forcefully, putting her cup down. "When do you want to return and practice for your big day?"

Meiying knew a line had been drawn, at least for today. "May I return tomorrow at the same time? I'll be no bother—and please do not plan anything out of your ordinary schedule."

"Of course. I would invite you to stay longer now, but I have an appointment."

"Oh, of course, no problem. Tomorrow I will bring sheet music."

"Good, I have some here as well."

Miss Telles escorted Meiying to the door. "I had Jacob call a taxi. It should be here by now."

"Jacob?" asked a startled Meiying, for she had seen no other person in the house.

"Yes, my . . . helper. I do hate to call him a servant."

Meiying looked around surreptitiously, but saw no one. *When did she tell him?* she wondered. *I'm beginning to believe there is more than one mystery woman here.*

When they stepped out onto the porch, a cab waited as if it had been there a long time.

"Ah! Here we are!" exclaimed Miss Telles. "Jacob never fails me." She turned and gave Meiying a long and affectionate hug, then kissed her on the cheek. "Tomorrow," she whispered.

Meiying's heart fluttered uncontrollably and the hairs on the back of her neck pricked her skin. "Yes, tomorrow, Marie."

~

Once back at the apartment, Meiying prepared dinner for John and Mulan, neither of whom had yet returned. When they did, both found her unusually cheerful.

"You seem quite happy," commented an obviously tired John.

"Yes, Miss Bai, you really do," added Mulan gaily. She had not found a way to call her Mrs. Powers, but at the same time, calling her Meiying seemed wrong. John frowned at this, but withheld criticism.

"I'm beginning to see some advantages to living in this country," said Meiying, fully aware the comment delivered a sting to John. She felt disappointed in herself for making such shallow digs, and yet derived increasing satisfaction from their sarcastic subtleties. *I'm already becoming more of an American*, she often thought in dismay. *If I lose my Chinese nature, I lose an advantage in this boisterous country. American men profess to like submissive Asian women. Remember that, foolish woman.*

John looked at her askance. "Well now, what happened to have you bestow such praise on our unworthy country?"

"Nothing."

"Americans are funny," interjected Mulan, whose role had increasingly become that of a mediator between two warring tribes.

"How so, dear?" asked Meiying.

"They chew gum and talk loud, but also tell funny jokes and laugh with their mouths open. As soon as they find out I'm not Japanese, they become nice."

"No, seriously," said John, directing his attention to Meiying. "What did you do today?" he asked, making every effort to keep suspicion out of his tone, but failing.

"I walked around. It is boring staying in the apartment."

"Where to?"

Meiying sighed loudly. "Nowhere."

"My friend and I walked for hours," said Mulan. "She's nice. Second generation Chinese. Speaks good English."

"And Chinese?" asked Meiying in alarm.

"Of course, that's how we can talk for so long. She's teaching me English."

"Good!" exclaimed John. "When in Rome."

"What?" asked Mulan.

"When in Rome, do as the Romans. That's an old saying."

"So, when in America, do as the Americans," paraphrased Mulan, testing the words. "Chew gum, look at people in the eyes, date boys, go to movies, and eat a lot."

"Don't go too far, dear," cautioned Meiying. "We Chinese must keep what is important."

"Like what?" asked John superciliously. "Kill people? Torture people? Rape people?"

Meiying glared angrily. "You are fixed on the bad, never on the good! Why did you marry me if we Chinese are so bad?"

"I married you to help you escape and find opportunity here in the United States. Opportunity you would never find in China."

"Please don't argue," said Mulan. "It makes me sad. I like America, but I love China too. You both are right."

Neither John nor Meiying had an answer to this statement, so they ate in silence, each resenting the other, yet each connected by some invisible cord that was of the most unconventional variety.

~ *Goddess Gives John A Glimpse* ~

That night in bed, John listened to Meiying breathing deeply beside him. His eyes were open wide, scanning the ceiling for a sign, any sign. To his horror, the voice came to him, speaking only one sentence, a terrible sentence, and he knew Goddess was angry.

You are losing her, John!

That was all. It came so quickly and so unexpectedly that he paused, thinking more words would issue forth. Clarifying words. Insulting words. But none came. The minutes passed and still he waited. He longed for guidance. How could he lose her before they even had a chance? What to do to reconnect, the way it was in China? How could he be such a fool to insult her country like he did at dinner? Did he want their relationship to fail? To end up on the trash heap of marriages gone wrong between expatriate Americans and native women? *It is the stress from my job*, he thought. *Once I've settled in, I can spend more time with her. I can help her with her career. I must not be afraid of her success.*

Foolish foolish man!

"Enough!" John blurted.

"What?" Meiying mumbled, half-awake.

"Nothing, go back to sleep."

When her breathing became regular, he got up and went into the kitchen. Sitting at the table, he addressed the voice in a whisper.

"You say I am a fool. You say she will have my son. You say many things. Tell me what I am to do. I am a better man than this. I am better!"

Nothing.

"The world here is different than China. I did not remember. Moment-to-moment here is separated by shorter intervals. Too much noise, no time to think. China is a poor country that is richer. America is a rich country that is poorer. Do you have any idea what I'm talking about?"

Nothing.

He chuckled and put his finger to his lips. "But keep this to yourself. Meiying mustn't know. It would shock her to know I actually miss China. Does it surprise you?"

Nothing.

"Of course not. I don't think she likes me very much, but I do love her. Very much. Very very much. But you know that, don't you?"

Nothing.

"Yet, it seems I push her further away every day. Stupid, stupid, stupid! You think I'm a fool, but the fact is I'm simply stupid. Is there a difference?"

Nothing.

"You're quiet when I want you to talk, and talk when I want you to be quiet."

Would you like a glimpse of your son?

The words took John by such surprise that he almost fell backward in his chair. "How?"

Put your head down and close your eyes.

"I'll fall asleep."

So much the better.

John did as directed, and must have fallen asleep, for he began to dream.

~

He saw four people sitting at a table, apparently having dinner. A woman, a young man, a middle-aged man, and a soldier. The soldier looked like a younger version of the middle-aged man. They were talking, but John could not make out the words. In the dream, he glided closer, hovering a bit above the table, and eavesdropped on their conversation.

The middle-aged man smiled broadly and looked at the woman. "Well, Diane, how was your day?"

Picking at a loose thread on her artist's frock, she assumed a good-natured grimace. "Oh, busy. You know, the kids were restless today, so I told them even though their rowdy behavior was typical for a Friday, that I wouldn't let the class go on their field trip next Tuesday if they kept it up."

"Way to go, mom. Be tough with 'em," said the young man.

"Bet that threat worked," added the soldier.

The middle-aged man averted his gaze, apparently unwilling to look at the trembling of the soldier's blackened hands or the rifle leaning next to him against the table. John caught the scent of filthy fatigues, and a faint stench of defecation filling the room.

The middle-aged man compressed his lips in obvious irritation, then closed his eyes briefly. Opening them, he looked at the woman and smirked playfully, "Oh, she would have let them go anyway."

"I know, I know," said the young man.

"Just a gorgeous old softy," said the soldier, looking affectionately at the woman. He managed a wan smile and John detected two tiny pinpricks of light burning laser-like through his dark, sunken eye sockets. "You know, while I was here in The World I could count on you, Diane. A comb in my pocket, always there. But now, in the 'Nam, without you around . . . it's like reaching down with my hands and having no place to put them, no pockets to bury them." He looked at his shaking hands. "No place to hide."

The middle-aged man glanced at the woman and frowned. "Very theatrical. Besides, speaking of being buried"—he looked sideways at the soldier and paused, clearly to let the others catch his meaning—"well, anyway, that was over thirty years ago."

"Ho, ho. This dinner is quite theatrical, Mr. Producer-of-Apparitions," The woman said affectionately, but with a disapproving edge to her voice. "Anyway, I would have thought the mature lawyer would have appreciated me in his pocket more than the young soldier, but I guess I would have been wrong to think so."

The middle-aged man snorted. "My pocket developed a very large hole."

The woman pursed her lips and raised her eyebrows. "Learn to sew, my dear. Learn to sew."

Silence.

The woman winced.

The middle-aged man looked at her with a concerned expression. "Is it your period? I know how it is with you when it's particularly bad."

Still looking distressed, she replied, "As you wish"—and with a strained grin added—"it's your party and you'll do what you want to."

He smiled slightly, then frowned. "No, I didn't mean to hurt. . . . "

"Anyway," asked the woman, evidently recovered and smiling brightly at the middle-aged man, "how about your day?" Before he could answer, she looked at his plate and made a face. "Obviously not enough time to fix proper mashed potatoes. Come on, Michael, you're fifty-three years old and you should know by now how to make real mashed potatoes. I've told you a million times—it's not that hard."

"No time. Have to peel them, boil them, whip them up. No time."

"Yes, I know, no time. Same with that old Fiat out there." She flashed a mischievous grin. "When do you think it'll be finished?"

The man frowned and jabbed his fork in and out of the potatoes. "I don't know."

"Probably when the grass finally gets mowed," she chuckled under her breath. "And those new tire tracks get filled in."

He let out a harassed moan, then chewed glumly on a mouthful of potatoes.

"Oh, come on, stop pouting," she said.

"I'm not. I mean. . . . " He momentarily fell silent. "If you had kept your eyes on the road—" he blurted out in an irritated voice.

The woman waved her hand impatiently. "I don't want to talk about that."

"You were in such a hurry. If you'd stayed five minutes longer, you could have avoided—"

"Michael! Stop it. You're looking for trouble again. Just because you had a little incident of your own on the road today . . . oh, let's not argue . . . come on, how was your day?"

The man sighed but said nothing.

"Michaeelll," she chided coyly. "Your day?"

"Fine. Busy. Work's always busy. I . . . uh . . . had another counseling session this afternoon."

Suddenly the soldier gave the middle-aged man a penetrating, almost pleading look. "How'd it go? Did Toomey finally acknowledge that I exist?"

Under the piercing gaze of the lean, youthful soldier, the middle-aged man shifted in his seat.

"Did he?" asked the soldier again.

The middle-aged man appeared irritated. "Did he what?"

"Acknowledge that I exist."

"Well . . . not really. You know how Dr. Toomey is," said the middle-aged man with a dismissive flick of the wrist.

"Yeah."

The woman turned toward the young man. "How about you, sweetie? How was your day?"

"I think I did good on the molecular biology final. But organic chemistry! Geezzz! If I never hear the words 'carbon atom' again, I'll be happy." His eyes darted around the table and settled on the soldier. "How'd your day go, Uncle?"

Silence.

The woman looked at the young soldier with open affection. "C'mon, love, you can tell us," she encouraged gently.

Silence.

"Go ahead," said the middle-aged man with a touch of mockery.

More silence.

"Well?" the middle-aged man prodded impatiently, now with a cautionary edge to his voice.

"I . . . I don't know—" stammered the soldier.

"Go ahead!" cried the middle-aged man.

The soldier looked off in the distance, the skin of his young face cracked and peeling like a dry lake bed. "They're out there. Dead. Got to get help—"

"No!" shouted the middle-aged man. "I'll make you go if you mention *that*. The party hasn't even started and you're already at *that* again."

"But they're outside the fortress!"

"Stop!"

The soldier's face hardened. "It's not that easy, Michael. Don't make me leave. Remember, according to our friend, Dr. Toomey, you're supposed to talk to me. Confront me. Bring me out. You know the drill—'Can I speak to Storyteller now?'"

"Very funny."

"Not supposed to be. Just illustrative."

"Look, I'd just as soon you and the others remain buried, you know? I have a life here. I'm not going back to you guys. Period." He nodded towards the woman with the look of a proud husband. "With Diane's help, I can live with the dreams, the nightmares, but I'm not going back."

"But it's all about the dreams, Michael. This time, *She'll* succeed in bringing you back."

"She?"

"Oh, brother, you're not going to make this easy, are you? Yes—*She*—you know, Goddess. . . . "

~

John jerked upright. "Goddess!" he mumbled, half-awake.

Yes, Goddess. Myself. You have been given a glimpse.

"A glimpse of what?" John whispered, taking up his conversation with the voice as if nothing had happened since he last addressed it. "I don't understand."

Your son will inherit your mutant genes and will be wrongly considered to suffer from the same illness they believe you have. He will be in another war, but he will serve My purpose.

"No. Not a schizophrenic."

As you wish. But both his parents bear the mark of the future. That is why you and she must be the conduit.

"Conduit?"

Yes, whether you grasp it or not!

"You must be more clear! I'm confused."

John felt a hand on his shoulder.

"I couldn't sleep," came Meiying's voice. "I heard you talking." She looked around. "As I thought, your voices again?"

"Just one."

"Her?"

"Yeah." He put his hand on hers. "You hear them too." It was an odd statement. Not a question, but a defense.

"Shall I make tea?"

"No, thanks." John tilted his head and looked up at her. "Do you still care for me, stupid as I am sometimes?"

"Of course, John," she replied, squeezing his hand.

When he gently tugged her toward him, she pulled away.

"I'll make tea for myself," she said.

"Meiying, will we ever be close? I mean, as close as we were in China?"

"We are close," she deflected.

"Well, apparently we are going to be close enough to have a son."

She laughed. "Says your voice."

"You hear it too."

"John, it is your voice, not mine. Besides, you hear more than one, don't you?"

"Meiying, you're being disingenuous. She told both of us."

Meiying paused. "She is not here."

He scrunched around in his chair like a fidgety boy who has just been asked a hard question by his teacher. "Yeah," he finally blurted.

By now the teapot was whistling, so she poured a cup and sat across from him, looking down as if studying the tea leaves.

"I think China is an amazing country," he said out of nowhere.

She nodded, still gazing into her tea.

"And I sort of miss it, you know?" he continued.

"Yes."

"It will be interesting to see which of our features our son will have."

"John, please!" exclaimed Meiying, frowning.

"Oh, for Christ sakes, Meiying! I'm just talking."

Both were silent for some time.

"How is work these days?" she asked mechanically.

"Fine."

"And Mr. Mobley?'

"Fine. Look, Meiying, I had a dream about our son. It was bizarre."

"All dreams are bizarre. I really don't want to talk about this mythical son anymore. We agreed to marry—"

"Screw the agreement!" John interrupted. He immediately forced himself to calm down. "All I mean is . . . we are married . . . and even in spite of our arrangement, we should try to get along. I have been wrong. I will be better. I'll help you find a way into the music world."

"John, it is not necessary."

"What do you mean, 'not necessary'?"

"It's not necessary."

"Oh, you don't think I'm capable?"

"It's not necessary."

And so it went, a typical marital spat, neither here nor there. After a few more minutes of useless back-and-forth, Meiying returned to bed. John remained at the table, his head in his hands, berating himself for his weaknesses. Self-flagellation had always been his last, best resort.

~

Yet, dear Reader, he was my father, and as such I know had an unbreakable kernel of goodness and strength in him, weak as he sometimes appeared to be. These qualities were forged in the fires of a Chinese conflagration and tempered by an American sense of justice. Mother was the same. I have written of weaknesses, but Goddess shepherded them both past the defenses of an angry God, which led to my birth. Dear Reader, no one in this institution believes me, but only through these words can the truth be revealed. After Revelation, yes, after that, I can find my bones in the tunnel. However, do not worry, dear Reader, I digress, and you have no idea what I just wrote. Please, read on! Those who have so far persevered, read on! Ignore this digression. Please. Turn the page. . . .

Chapter Fifteen

Meiying Takes Flight

Practice and Submission

The next morning, Meiying returned to Miss Telles. She had spent the early hours preparing breakfast for John and Mulan. After John left for work, Meiying dressed in nice clothes, arousing Mulan's curiosity. When the young woman asked where she was going, Meiying made up a story about roaming Chinatown to pass the time. Mulan asked if she wanted company, but Meiying said no, much to the girl's relief. In fact, Mulan was meeting her friend and a group of others, boys and girls; her natural tomboyish personality had begun to resurface and thrive in the rough-and-tumble American landscape, attracting her gritty immigrant peers and hastening her independence from sheltered solicitude to crazy freefall. So absorbed was Meiying with the latest events in her life, she neglected to ask Mulan about hers. Only serious coughing fits penetrated Meiying's distractions, temporarily filling her with heart-felt solicitations for the sick child. But, the attention lasted only as long as the attacks. Such is the way of the world. In a mood so bouncy even Mulan, with her own adolescent diversions, began to wonder, Meiying kissed the girl goodbye and flitted out of the apartment.

Instead of a taxi, this time she took a bus that stopped as close as possible to Miss Telles's house, and walked the rest of the way up the steep hill, purse over her shoulder and a sheaf of musical scores pressed awkwardly against her body to protect against the wind. When she arrived at the stately Victorian, she sat to catch her breath and adjust her hair. After a moment, she stood, smoothed her dress, and strolled to the front door, stopping occasionally to appreciate the garden. She fancied she was being watched from an upstairs window, but couldn't be sure. *No matter*, she thought, assuming it might be this fellow Jacob. *Let him look!* In fact, she wanted to think Marie Telles was waiting anxiously for her return, much as she felt anxious to see the 'grand lady' (as Meiying thought of her). When the door opened, Meiying was greeted with a stunning smile, instantly igniting her already primed infatuation.

"Hello again!" exclaimed Marie Telles, with a warmth that made the heart race.

"Hello," replied Meiying, in an even tone that no observer would guess came from a woman in the thrall of desire.

"The piano awaits," said Marie.

Meiying realized with a start that the piano had become secondary. "Oh, lovely, thank you."

"Shall we have tea first?" asked Marie. "You can put down that heavy load."

"Yes, let's do," replied Meiying in a voice more steady than she felt.

To Meiying's delight, they returned to that small, intimate anteroom where the intoxicating presence of Marie Telles almost overwhelmed the bounds of propriety. This time, tea was served by a very handsome young man, whose manners were impeccable and appropriately distant.

"Thank you, Jacob," said Marie.

Meiying felt a stab of jealousy. Is he a servant? His body language didn't make him seem so. Is this her lover? Is Marie Telles not a lesbian after all? All of her joy came crashing down in a pile, nonetheless, as always, she maintained her poise.

"You are so very kind to me," she said, using a bit more formal voice after Jacob left.

"Jacob is wonderful, but alas, he will be leaving me soon."

"Oh?" said Meiying with a rising heart.

"Yes, getting married to a lovely young woman. He is opening a restaurant."

"How nice," said Meiying, her spirits soaring.

"What's worse, I won't have his cooking anymore. He is a magnificent cook, in addition to his other talents. In fact, he made these biscotti cookies."

"Delicious," commented Meiying, wondering what additional talents other than making cookies he might possess, but she dismissed the thought as petty. She took a sip of tea and started to speak when Marie leaned forward.

"I wonder, Meiying, if you might share your thoughts with me?"

"About?"

"About China, about your experiences, about your ambitions, about everything. You see, I am quite interested to know more about you."

"But, I already told you."

"No, that's not what I mean. You told me what happened to you, but not what you felt . . . what you feel now. Do you very much resent us wealthy Americans who have experienced so little of the world?"

"Many American soldiers—"

Miss Telles waved her hand. "No, no. Not them. You see, I cannot identify with them, with their experiences in war. But you . . . you I can identify with. As a woman, you can help me understand."

Meiying felt ambiguous about being this woman's personal interpreter; translating the world's meaning for her rather than her meaning for the world. On the one hand, Meiying was flattered, but she balked at dredging up her memories like old bones to be cracked open for the marrow they might contain. On the other hand, it would provide her continuous access to this fascinating woman, who she now realized could be the love of her life, at least the American love of her life. Besides, thought Meiying, this Marie Telles must have her own experiences; interesting and mysterious experiences that would certainly provide an understanding of the world. Beyond Meiying's sordid past, made horrifically narrow by war and the unchecked excesses of male violence, she was wise enough to understand many Americans, including the wealthy, experienced their own hells; broader, more intricate, and more subtle ones—torments that might be found in the milieu of an ancient Chinese romance full of scheming court intrigues and oblique deceptions. Unquestionably, this vast land of limitless opportunity must fairly burst with infinite variations of love, deceit, and ambition. Yes, Meiying realized wealth is not barrier to pain. In fact, even now in China, the wealthy were suffering more than the peasants in communist-controlled areas. *Perhaps*, thought Meiying, *if I share my most intimate feelings, Miss Telles might share. . . .*

"Meiying, dear?" said Miss Telles. "Sorry, you seemed far away."

"Oh, so sorry. I was just thinking."

"Please don't think I want you to feel pain at these memories, these experiences, but my therapist insists it is best to talk things out. Bring them out in the open. I sense you have no one to really talk with about your true feelings."

Meiying remained silent while Marie Telles took a sip of tea. Putting the cup down, she continued with a warm smile, "I know this is an odd request, but—"

Jacob entered unannounced, and Marie looked at him with an inquiring smile that might have conveyed the slightest edge of irritation.

"Sorry to interrupt, but if I may have a second in private."

Marie's face seemed a bit flushed when she said, "Excuse me a moment," and followed him out of the room.

Mysterious, thought Meiying, her imagination running wild with possibilities. But, as usual, she brought herself up short. *It's probably just a shopping list he wants to go over.*

With this stabilizing thought still fresh in her mind, Meiying greeted Miss Telles's return with a simple, "Hello."

"So sorry," said Miss Telles. Without sitting, she straightened her artist's frock and continued. "Well, Meiying, I don't want to keep you from practice. I'll walk you to the piano room, and you can play as long as you wish."

"Yes, yes, thank you," said Meiying, rising.

"In fact, dear, I do have some pressing business," said Marie Telles, clearly distracted. "You know your way?"

"Yes, thank you." Meiying made a somewhat awkward exit, grabbing her purse while scooping-up the musical scores in a bit of an agitated scramble. She heard Miss Telles call for Jacob just as she left the room, and, to her great comfort, found the piano waiting like a steady and reliable friend. After looking around, she confirmed her solitude, and whispered, "I won't take you for granted again."

Soon, the lush chords of Chopin forced out all human complications and left a pure, unsullied joy. *Yes*, she thought. *I'm rusty, but it has come back as naturally as breathing! I will be ready.*

After an hour, she caught a glimpse of movement and sensed Miss Telles had slipped into the room. Watching. Listening. As a result, the notes came a bit faster, a bit fuller, a bit more urgently. She felt the music entwine itself around them, binding them together, and the more she played, the tighter and more secure the invisible bonds became. As she neared the dazzling end of a Beethoven sonata, her mind was filled with the praise that would surely come from Marie Telles. Perhaps a hug, a kiss, some physical contact. Heaven-sent! But, her fantasy was dashed when Jacob entered and again whispered into his mistress's ear. The invisible bonds snapped as the two quickly left the room, leaving Meiying to listen alone while the last notes of the piece faded to silence.

Again, it's just you and me, she thought, stroking the piano as one might a loyal dog.

~

Meiying practiced all afternoon without taking lunch or seeing Miss Telles again. Finally, her fingers wearied and she stood to leave, mentally planning the dinner she would prepare once she returned home, when a male voice broke the flow of thoughts.

"Marie asked me to show you out."

"Oh, thank you," murmured a very surprised Meiying. "That isn't necessary."

"My pleasure," said Jacob.

She detected a hint of flirtation and quickly dismissed it as her imagination. Still, he didn't sound like a servant. As he opened the front door for her, he leaned close and whispered, "Look forward to seeing you tomorrow."

"Thank you."

He bowed in an exaggeratedly gallant manner, clicking his heels to punctuate the charade. "Our pleasure."

Meiying quickly exited and, to her surprise, found a taxi waiting. She turned to object when Jacob waved her off from the porch and called with a grin, "On us, for the pleasure of your company."

Seated in the cool taxi, she tried to order her thoughts. *What did he mean 'Our pleasure,'* she wondered. *And which one of them would 'look forward to seeing' me tomorrow?*

But, the more she picked over her memory, trying to re-create every word and every non-verbal cue that passed between Jacob and Marie, the more confused she became. Worse, his interest in her seemed undeniable, though she continued to dismiss it whenever the idea popped up. What is his relationship with Marie Telles? What about his fiancé? Meiying scolded herself for dissipating energies on such useless speculation. Under the darting, watchful eyes of the cabbie, she turned her thoughts to wonder what *is* real and concrete in her life, and she took quick stock of what she could count on.

She knew she loved one person in the world: Mulan. She tolerated another: John, though she had to admit her feelings toward him were complicated. And she craved a relationship with a third: Marie. All the others that had significance in her life were dead or far away. Only one object in life shone like a beacon, dimming everything else: her career. That would be where all her efforts must incline. Love for Mulan was simple; love for Marie Telles was treacherous; love for John was out of the question; but, love for her career, for music, was life-giving. Still, doubts remained, and she was no closer to pacifying her nettlesome demons when she arrived back at the apartment. Fortunately, neither John nor Mulan had returned, so she threw herself into preparing an unusually elaborate meal.

~ *Jacob and Marie* ~

Jacob watched the taxi leave and turned to face his sister, who stood in the doorway.

"She will do," he said.

"She is not for you," replied Miss Telles.

"You promised."

"Before I knew."

"What?"

"She is a lesbian."

"I don't believe it."

"Believe it."

Jacob shook his head. "You promised. I will prove you wrong."

"I am firmly against you."

Jacob flashed an angry scowl. "That is stupid. It will make things more difficult." He tilted forward as if bowing, and broke into a half-vicious, half-loving smile. "Daughter of a bitch."

Marie Telles drew herself to her full height. "Don't talk to me that way. Ever. I have done what I can, but I didn't know she is a lesbian."

"Is that why she is for you?"

"Yes."

"But, she is married. That proves she can overcome her inclination."

Marie Telles scoffed. "That proves nothing." She stroked his face. "You are foolish. Haven't I taught you more than that? Her marriage to this John Powers is loveless. One of convenience."

"Please," he said, disbelieving.

"Jacob," she said in a softened tone. "We have both suffered greatly. Our losses have thrown us together, and I have promised to do what I can for you. But, she has suffered more. Much more. She is not for you."

Jacob shook his head but remained silent.

"Jacob, brother, do you understand?"

"We will see," he replied. "I'll be in my room." He turned on his heel and walked past her, whistling a tune as he made his way up the stairs.

Marie wandered into the kitchen and absently made a cold turkey sandwich. *Mrs. Powers truly is special*, she kept thinking to herself. *So talented, so young, so beautiful, and to have been through so much!* She tried to imagine war-torn China from the pictures in *Life* magazine and the news reels, but here was suffering in the flesh. Even as a young girl, Marie had been drawn to suffering as an antidote to her own pampered upbringing. Real suffering. The kind of suffering that made life immediate, interesting, and worth living; not, as she used to think with distain, the petty inconveniences that pass for suffering many Americans occasionally experience in the course of their opulent lifestyles. But then one day not long ago, for her and Jacob, came that awful moment; the one unanticipated shock, the one unthinkable tragedy which changed everything, including her view of suffering. That event dwarfed all that occurred in the past, and all that could occur in the future. She knew she exhibited an irrational desperation to find others who had suffered more than she and Jacob; but she clung to the idea that finding them would purge her of the absurdity of past sins. Once found, she would help them, not with money, but with love; a love that would transcend her lesbian desires, because she had been certain no other woman could physically replace the one she lost. The hole in her life could not be filled, but it could be used to plant a new tree, a forest of trees, that would sprout roots and grow from the nutrients she would provide with her own body. She imposed this pact on her reluctant brother so that he might also find renewal in sacrifice for others. Their pain would be given meaning, and their dead joys be given new life.

"Hello, sister," said Jacob from behind. He put his hand on her shoulder and pulled a chair close. "I'm sorry for our little spat." He rubbed her back in a gentle, circular motion.

"So am I," she replied.

"What are you thinking?"

"You know."

"Yes, so have I. What shall we do? I leave for China soon, and I would like to see this resolved before I depart."

"Why is your contact so interested in this woman?"

"Good question. I mean, look at the trouble he went to, getting to us by way of Mr. Mobley. He has something big in mind for her."

"What?"

"Another good question. Ours is not to question why."

"She is special."

"Yes, we are agreed on that point."

"Do you want a sandwich?" asked Marie.

"Non-sequitur. Changing the subject are we?"

"Intentional."

"Then yes, I want a sandwich."

"What kind?"

"Chinese female piano player."

"Too much. You would choke on it."

"But, beloved sister, what a way to die!"

Marie Telles turned to her brother with a worried frown. "Seriously, Jacob, what does he want with her?"

Jacob grinned. "I don't know, sister, but I hope it involves me."

"He scares me."

"You don't know him."

Marie locked eyes with her brother. "But you do. Why won't you tell me about him?"

Jacob rose and poured a cup of tea. "I told you already, he's good business. Helps us keep this mansion. There's good money in China right now, at least until the communists take over. He is a smart businessman. Deals with all sides. Survived the war playing three sides off against each other. More, even, if you count all the warlords. Rich bastard."

"But, why is he so interested in Mrs. Powers?"

"Good god, Marie! I told you, I don't know!"

"Surely, Jacob, anyone who calls himself Mr. President can't be mentally healthy."

Jacob laughed. "Healthy! He's as fat as the moon! Can't understand why he's still kicking. But, business is business, my dear. You really should see his palace, full of amazing antiques and women and—"

"Hmm, as long as he means her no harm."

Jacob sat and silently stirred his tea. He had no interest in Marie's loony scheme to help people, and in fact, wanted to replace his own loss as quickly as possible. But, the replacement must carry with her the same majestic serenity and drop-dead beauty his fiancé had possessed. Meiying Powers fit the bill, aside from the inconvenient fact she was married. But, after all, it was a marriage of convenience. Even Marie said so. Easily gotten around.

"I do need an interpreter in China," he mused.

"Don't be ridiculous, brother dear," said Marie more sympathetically than she intended. "This really is getting us nowhere. Jacob, she will not return to China. There are demons there. Besides, she has a career to think of, and I have decided to help."

"Your latest project?"

Marie sighed. She knew her brother did not possess her sensitivity and empathy toward others, but she had always remained hopeful these qualities would emerge with age and maturity. After all, he was three years younger, still subject to the male disease at its more virulent, yet he showed signs of coming through with only minor proclivities toward wantonness and greed. These could be sanded off with patience and unconditional love. Besides, his skill at managing their investments was invaluable, and in spite of all, he could be completely trusted. The fire they had gone through together had forged an unbreakable bond. Still, this business between him and Meiying Powers would have to stop. His propensity for predation represented a challenge that Meiying, a stranger in a strange land, would not be well-prepared to deal with. She wondered if predatory American males were similar to predatory Chinese males. Did they use the same strategies? No matter. Only as one lesbian to another could their strangeness be sealed off and, for safety's sake, severed from the heterosexual world; once isolated, their unconventional love would be left to grow undisturbed by the even greater strangeness of the conventional. She had long ago given up trying to explain these simple realities to her brother, whose singular yet powerful hormonal influences usually forced him to fly in predictable paths, but which, on unexpected occasions, subjected him to deviations that rendered him wickedly dangerous.

"I wonder what she's doing now?" Jacob pondered aloud.

"I wonder what you're doing now," retorted Marie with a slight chuckle.

"I'm warning you, Marie, I'm going after her. Somehow, her Chinese wiles have gotten under my skin."

Marie started to reply, but thought better of it, and stared down at her tea.

"And, she'll be back tomorrow, so I'll have another chance at her," he goaded.

Still, she remained silent.

"And the next day. . . ."

Marie looked at Jacob with an expression more of pity than irritation. "She is not for you, Jacob. There lies madness."

~

The next morning, Meiying arrived early and sat down to tea with Marie before she began practicing. Both were chatting amiably when Jacob walked in.

"Hope I'm not intruding, but I thought a more formal introduction was called for." He held out his hand to the still-seated Meiying. "My name is Jacob Telles. I'm Marie's brother."

Oh!" said a startled Meiying. "I didn't know." She stood and bowed. "So nice to meet you."

"Sorry I did not introduce you earlier," said Marie, clearly put off by her brother's intrusion.

An awkward silence followed.

"May I join you?" asked Jacob as he poured himself a cup of tea.

Meiying resumed her seat.

"I'm afraid Mrs. Powers has to practice," replied Marie in an unmistakably chilly tone. "She has an important audition in a few days."

"Oh, believe me, I know," replied Jacob. "Just thought we could chat a while."

"Congratulations," said Meiying sweetly.

He appeared confused and stumbled for a response. "Thank you very much . . . but . . . what for?"

"About your upcoming marriage. Your sister just told me."

Marie could have leapt up and hugged Meiying, as she watched with immense satisfaction her brother struggling to deal with this unexpected twist. *I must never underestimate this woman,* she thought with admiration. *Perhaps her experience with Chinese males is not all that different from mine with American males.*

"I'm afraid my sister misspoke," he said after a few moments of hesitation. "Marie wants me to be married, to make an honest man of me, but, I—we—haven't yet made a firm commitment."

"And your restaurant?" asked Meiying.

"My restaurant?"

"The restaurant you want to open?"

"Oh, that. Also in the air. Nothing is settled, you see."

"Oh," said Meiying with the slightest glance toward Marie. "Well, I really should practice now."

Jacob, adroitly chastised as he knew he was, nevertheless gave her a gentlemanly bow, his admiration only deepened by her surgeon-like skills.

But, the effect of Meiying's actions were as an electric shock to Marie, who had the almost overwhelming urge to take her to bed at that moment.

~

After Meiying left the room, Jacob turned to his sister. "That really was mean of you," he said quite amiably. "I mean, a fiancé? A wedding? A restaurant?"

"You deserved it."

"There's still time, but this blasted trip to China will give you an unfair advantage."

"Jacob, I don't consider this a competition."

"I do."

"That's unfortunate. This is a real person we're talking about, and she is not for you. Period."

"So you say."

Marie let out an exasperated moan. "You mustn't go where disappointment will be inevitable. I don't want you to drive her away."

"I've decided to ask her to accompany me to China as my interpreter."

"Oh, for heaven's sake, Jacob!"

"She'll be paid handsomely for her troubles."

"Firstly, she won't go, and even if she did, what would her husband say?"

Jacob shrugged. "Nothing. You said yourself it's a marriage of convenience."

"She also has an orphan girl to consider."

Again, Jacob shrugged, a lackadaisical habit that communicated arrogant disinterest in consequences to others. "The girl is of age, as I understand it."

Marie stood, quite finished with the conversation. "Then do it. I'm quite convinced she'll say no."

"Thereby leaving her alone with you?"

"Yes, if I am not deceived."

"Far be it from me to deceive either of you."

"Far be it from me to be deceived."

Marie took her cup and left the room without replying, leaving Jacob to feel yet again small in the wake of his much-admired sister. He always resented her uncanny ability to make him feel this way, yet he felt utter admiration for her strength of character. Reconciling his weaknesses against her strengths required a full-time job, and inevitably forced him into greater displays of adolescent rebellion, though he was no adolescent. He dog-paddled with just enough energy to keep his head above water and breathe the oxygen required to maintain at least a modicum of independence while drifting in the vastness of his sister's sea. Only occasionally, when he was at his best, did his toes touch bottom.

~ *An Intimate Talk* ~

Meiying sat straight after playing a difficult passage and rolled her aching shoulders. As she did so she observed Marie Telles enter the room and sit quietly.

"Don't let me interrupt," said Marie.

"Not at all, I need a break."

"Then, please come and sit." Marie patted the wing-back chair next to her.

Meiying moved to the chair with a native grace that impressed Marie, and after sitting, leaned forward with a pleasant smile.

But Marie assumed a severe face. "My brother is quite taken with you."

Meiying blushed and remained silent.

"He has informed me he wants to take you to China with him on his next business trip—"

Meiying broke in. "Oh, but I can't!"

"As an interpreter," continued Marie. "He would pay you well."

"Oh, no. I could never go back . . . at least, not now. Your brother is very kind, but it is impossible."

"Yes, as I thought. That is what I told him, but he is most stubborn."

Meiying wanted to drop the subject, but her curiosity got the best of her. "If I may ask, what is his business?"

"That is a complicated question. Even I don't know the details, but it has something to do with import and export."

"Ah." Meiying was savvy enough to know that 'import and export' were words that concealed a host of illegal and unethical improprieties.

Marie now leaned forward the slightest bit. "He deals with, shall I say, some very . . . strange characters."

Meiying had no response to this.

Marie took her silence as a cue to continue. "For example, one person he is dealing with is particularly bizarre."

"Oh?"

"Yes, he is apparently good at navigating China's complex political and economic situation. Quite rich, so says my brother."

"I see," said Meiying, clearly puzzled as to why she was being made privy to such information.

Marie paused, apparently searching for the right words. "He calls himself Mr. President, and he lives in a palace, according to my brother, which I'm not sure is—"

Meiying instantly jumped up and staggered away from the chair, uttering a sharp, "Oh, my god!"

Marie was so startled, she quickly rushed to her side, fearing Meiying would faint or run out of the room.

"My god! My god!" Meiying kept repeating uncontrollably. She began pacing back and forth, her hands to her head, pulling at her hair. Marie stayed close, grasping her arm to prevent further damage, all the while asking, "What is it? What is it?"

Meiying did not respond, her agitation increasingly violent.

Finally, Marie stepped boldly in front of the hysterical woman and placed both hands on Meiying's shoulders to make her stop pacing. Marie stared into the wild eyes and gently shook.

"Meiying!" she cried. "Sit down!"

Meiying obeyed.

Marie fell to her knees at the distressed woman's feet and placed her arms in Meiying's lap, looking up at the feverish eyes.

"Meiying, who is this man?" she demanded.

Tears now freely streamed down Meiying's face. "He is . . . he is . . . a murderer. A horrible man! A horrible man! And I know he wants me! He is after me!"

"What did he do to you, Meiying?"

This question seemed to bring her partly to her senses. "I must leave! My god! I must leave!" She shifted anxiously in the chair.

Marie pressed down to restrain her. "Meiying! You are safe here. What did he do to you?"

Meiying, trembling in fear, looked at her without comprehension.

"What did he do to you?"

Meiying stuttered an answer. "Im . . . im . . . imprisoned me. And raped me . . . rape . . . and Mulan! Terrible! Terrible!" She looked wildly at Marie.

Marie did not know how to respond.

Meiying shouted, "Does he know I'm here?"

Marie again hesitated, this time mulling how damaging her answer might be.

Meiying leapt up again. "I must leave!"

"No! Meiying, sit down. Please, sit down and listen."

"Does he know I'm here?" shouted Meiying.

The door swung open and Jacob entered. Seeing the emotional frenzy of both women, he stopped cold. "What's going on? I heard screaming."

Meiying grabbed her purse and ran past him and out the front door, rushing down the steep hill as fast as she could go in high heels. She heard the fading voice of Marie calling, but never looked back as the damp San Francisco wind swept past. Every male face that stared at her seemed malevolent—all of them possible agents for Mr. President, and all of them capable of waylaying her.

When she arrived home to the inquiries of John and Mulan about her day, she had, to a large extent, regained her composure and put them off with vague an-swers. But, when they sat down to dinner, John recognized a difference. Meiying had been uncommunicative and distracted, which led him to ask, "How did your day really go? Is everything okay?"

Meiying resented this typically American game. One was expected to an-swer thumbs-up or thumbs-down. But, thumbs-up always represented the de-fault—everything must be fine when, in fact, it was not. Still, she recognized this was not John's fault and she looked at him with weary affection. After all, he had shared her times of trouble. But, now she felt a burning need for Feng Shiren to burst through the door with an operatic flair, and save the day. Thoughts of John fell by the wayside.

"Everything's fine." Meiying turned to Mulan and forced a smile. "How was your day, dear?"

"It was okay," replied Mulan, in the reticent mode of an American teenager.

"Your English is getting so much better," said John.

Mulan shrugged. "I guess."

With a sudden lurch of the stomach, Meiying recognized how far this gregarious young woman had emotionally moved away from her. *Odd*, she thought, *that we were closest when suffering the most. Now, in our luxury, we drift apart.* With this realization, the vision of Mr. President returned as a looming threat to both of them. She felt a sudden need to tell them about the day's revelation so that they might all share a closeness that had disappeared since coming to America. But the probability that her fears would infect them with doubt and uncertainty made her unwilling to confide. Nevertheless, it also occurred to her that too many secrets were accumulating, and keeping them confidential would become increasingly difficult. *Doesn't matter*, she thought. *It's necessary! Let them live their lives without the burden of my own paranoid fears.*

"Yes, dear, your English is really good," she said as cheerfully as possible. "Every day it gets better."

"Thanks."

Meiying continued eating as if nothing was amiss, but she noticed John staring at her with wondering eyes that reflected a mix of curiosity and suspicion.

"And your day, John?" she asked. "How is Mr. Mobley?"

"Oh, Mobley's fine. He often asks about you."

"Oh?"

"Yeah, he's taken quite an interest. Don't worry, I know how much you value your . . . privacy, so I put him off with the usual pleasantries."

"I like him," said Mulan firmly, as if he had been maligned. "He's nice."

"And helpful," added Meiying.

"Helpful?" asked John.

"Yes, for your career, John."

"Oh, yeah, speaking of my career, he'll be leaving the country soon."

"Leaving?"

"Yeah, to China with a client. I have to handle some of his accounts while he's gone. More work, but good for my position in the company."

Meiying could not speak, but Mulan cried, "China! Oh, wouldn't it be nice to visit my village? I wish he would take me. I could invite my friends."

"No!" cried Meiying with such intensity the other two froze in surprise. She stared defiantly at John, spurred by the terror she thought had passed, but now barreling toward her in the dark.

"Who is the client?" she demanded.

John was taken aback. "I don't know."

"Who is the client?"

"Meiying, I don't know. Why?"

"Who is the client?"

John snorted. "I told you, I don't know! He didn't tell me and I didn't ask."

"Ask him!"

"Why?"

Meiying stood and grabbed the phone off the kitchen counter, waving the receiver in her hand. "Call him now and ask him!"

"What are you raving about? What's wrong with you?"

"Call him!"

"Meiying!" shouted John. "I'm not going to call him now. First of all, it's too late. Second of all, he'd think I'm crazy. Why are you acting this way?"

Meiying fell silent, cognizant for the first time of what little her outbursts had accomplished, and aware his questions would lead to unpleasant explanations. *I must stop these ridiculous displays of hysteria!* she thought, rubbing her forehead.

"Sorry, I'm still . . . I mean . . . I have a headache, and China . . . the bad times just came back to me and I lost my . . . head. Sorry. Sorry, Mulan, everything's okay. I just lost my head because of the memories. Sorry. So sorry."

John smiled sarcastically. "I thought you missed China."

But Mulan understood. She had rushed to Meiying's side and was rubbing her arm as John spoke.

"Miss Bai, what is wrong?" she asked quite reasonably. "Why are you acting so concerned? It's just a trip to China. None of us are going. Are you feeling better?"

"Yes," smiled Meiying. "Sorry, it's nothing. I just had a bad memory, and I let it get the better of me. It was stupid. I'm fine now, sweetheart."

"Meiying, I agree with Mulan, there's something going on in your head. Your reaction is all out of proportion to Mr. Mobley's going to China."

"Honestly, John, it's nothing. Sort of like a soldier's flashback." She chuckled. "Maybe I have what you call combat fatigue. It's nothing, really. Let's finish eating."

~

The next morning, after a sleepless night, Meiying had still not decided what to do. Returning to Marie Telles's house seemed impossible, yet she needed the practice time. It was too late to find another piano, as only two days remained before the audition. Certainly, with time to reflect, she felt confident Marie was not involved in a plot to kidnap her. But the brother was a different story. If she went, she may never return home, for she had read about white slavery trafficking, and she would not put it past Mr. President, in league with Jacob Telles, to have her forcibly brought back to his viper's nest. If Jacob couldn't convince her to go as his interpreter, then. . . .

"Meiying!" called John from across the breakfast table. "More coffee, please. Jeez, you're really out of it, aren't you?" He held up his cup.

Meiying stood and started to retrieve the pot. "Where's Mulan?"

"Left already. She said goodbye. You didn't even notice."

"I . . . did I say goodbye to her?"

"Yeah, you mumbled something, but were sort of glassy-eyed. Mulan said you were too sleepy to bother, and left."

"Oh." She poured his coffee.

He checked his watch. "Now I have to go, damn it. Couple more swallows. Okay. Goodbye."

"Goodbye."

He threw on his jacket and hat and rushed out of the kitchen. Meiying looked at the dirty dishes and went back to pondering her next move. Life seemed as bleak as the used dishes, and she bemoaned the sad state of affairs that just a few days ago seemed so bright. After cleaning up, she practiced breathing exercises taught to her by Feng Shiren, and began feeling calmer. Oh, how she wished he were still alive and with her now. Together, they would go to Miss Telles's house, and she would practice under his protection. She smiled at the thought of Shiren distracting Jacob Telles by performing scenes from some silly opera. *But,* she thought. *He is dead, I am alone, and the world awaits.* However, she quickly reminded herself that a world without Marie Telles, or the hope that was associated with Marie Telles, would be unbearably empty. Without this beautiful and mysterious woman, she would be bereft of any hope at all. So, in spite of fears and misgivings, she decided to return and take her chances.

~

The front door opened even before she had reached it, and Marie, smiling broadly, rushed out to greet Meiying with a passionate hug.

"Oh, thank god you returned! I was so afraid you wouldn't."

She smoothed Meiying's wind-tossed hair, and they walked arm-in-arm into the house.

"Jacob is gone today, so we can talk without interruption."

Meiying nodded, but to this point had said nothing. The sensual touch of Marie's hand through her hair had an electrifying effect that rendered her temporarily mute.

"Now," said Marie. "We will have our tea as usual, and you will tell me your story, your fears. It is now my business too, you know, since my brother is somehow involved."

"Thank you, but I simply had an attack of nerves—bad memories—and I really should practice. Perhaps after the audition we can go into this. I'm fine now. Really."

"No, Meiying, you're not fine. We both know that. In fact, I have come to cherish your visits . . . your presence . . . and I want there to be nothing ugly between us. Come, let's go to our little anteroom and talk. The tea is already prepared."

Meiying submissively followed her to the room, but the entire way had been girding her courage to ask the question. When the tea was poured, she looked openly at Marie. "Thank you for your many kindnesses. If we are to have an honest relationship, as you apparently wish, I must know something."

"Yes?"

"Does he know I'm here?"

"Who? I told you Jacob is gone for the day."

"No, Mr. President. Does he know I'm here?"

Marie Telles had been waiting for this question, and had decided to be perfectly honest, regardless of the circumstances.

"Yes, but—"

Meiying turned white, shrank back in her chair, and clutched at the collar of her dress.

"Look, Meiying," said Marie in a firm tone. "My brother explained to me, after you ran out yesterday, that this man knew you from China, and he wanted to re-establish contact. He gave Jacob no indication of doing the things you say he did, and he certainly gave no hint that he had evil intentions, but you must be honest with me. What is going on?"

"I do not know," replied Meiying. "He has some evil compulsion. I am afraid. Terribly afraid. He imprisoned both Mulan and me, and had unspeakable things done to us. He did it twice, he'll do it again."

"But, Meiying, China is far away. This is the United States. I will simply have Jacob tell him that we have lost touch with you." She rubbed her hands together as if removing dirt. "Then, it's done. No problem."

"No, he will continue to pursue me. I know it!"

"Meiying, don't imagine things that can't happen. You are safe here. This is America. Things like what you fear don't happen here."

"I have not been safe for a very long time." She looked closely at Marie. "Men are not trustworthy."

"You're right there. Most men are not trustworthy. But, my brother—"

"Sorry!" interjected Meiying. "Your brother is a man."

"But, surely you trust some men. Your husband, for instance?"

"My husband is trustworthy, but weak."

"I see."

"Perhaps you don't. You see, I prefer the company of women."

Marie blinked, but held her gaze. "As do I."

Each woman reached for the other's hand. Stood. Hugged. Kissed.

Marie stepped back, took both of Meiying's hands, and kissed each in turn. "Go practice, Meiying. Your audition is most important. We will have time. Much time together."

"Yes. Thank you. My heart is beating so fast, I'm not sure I can play."

"As is mine," whispered Marie. "But, let the feelings infuse your music. We will have time. Time enough."

~ *John Struggles with His Voices* ~

Mr. Mobley stood over John's desk. "You called me?"

"Yes, it's about your upcoming China trip."

Mobley shifted impatiently. "Well?"

John had been dreading this interview all morning, but he needed to get to the bottom of Meiying's frantic behavior. With her insistence that he obtain the names of the Chinese clients still ringing in his ears, he plunged ahead. "Are you are seeing many clients there?"

"Please remember, I'm accompanying a client to China. It is he who will be seeing clients. I'll be there to give advice. Obviously, John, that is our business."

"Yes, I'm aware. Are you . . . is he seeing more than one client?"

"Yes, what about it?"

"Nothing, I was just curious."

"The Telles family has been our client for a very long time. Their retention of our services goes back a generation. Old man Telles was one of the pioneers in dealing with China, and his son carries on the tradition. In fact, my father and Old Man Telles were great friends."

"I see."

"At some point, with your expertise in the language, you may look forward to servicing at least part of their account."

"Thank you, I would like that. What do they deal in?'

Mr. Mobley smiled and pushed in a nostril. "Oh, well, import and export . . . and other things, of course."

"Ah."

"They've moved their business dealings inland from the coastal cities. In so doing, they have made many valuable contacts. Dangerous, but profitable. Left the competition behind."

John grinned facetiously. "At least until the communists take over?"

"Well, like I said, dangerous," replied Mr. Mobley. "But, I don't think it will happen. Truman won't let it. With all our aid going to Chiang Kai-shek and the Nationalists? Won't happen." Mobley chuckled. "Can't let China turn Red, can we? At least, that's the story, and our feckless government is sticking to it. Why? Do you think the Reds will win?"

John shrugged. "It's possible. What does our client think?"

"Which client?"

"The one you're going with to China."

"Jacob Telles? He's clueless. But his Chinese business partner, the one we're meeting with, is on top of the whole mess. Deals with all sides."

"The guy whose operations are inland?"

"Yes, him and a few others, but he's the main man."

There's my man, thought John. *Get his name and get out.* "Like you said, dangerous to play such high-risk games."

"Yeah, well, I'd best get back," Mobley replied, clearly anxious to leave. "Mrs. McAllister will scold me." He turned to go.

John hesitated, then blurted more clumsily than he wanted, "Who is it?"

"What?'

"The client . . . I mean, the guy whose operations are inland. Who is it?"

"You wouldn't know him," said Mobley, pausing, then adding, "No, you definitely wouldn't."

John seemed to detect laughter, or mockery, behind his boss's dancing eyes, and it made him uneasy, but he plunged ahead. "Try me, I've been around."

"Well—"

But before Mobley could utter another word, Mrs. McAllister bustled up to the desk waving a steno pad. "Mr. Mobley, the president of Cabri Manufacturing has been on hold a very long time. He's quite upset, and I told him you would be right with him. That was five minutes ago. Not sure I can hold him off much longer."

"Oh, crap! Thanks." Mr. Mobley turned on his heel and left, with Mrs. McAllister trailing behind.

That was close! came a voice. John wasn't sure whose, its intrusion having exploded in his mind so suddenly and unexpectedly he felt agonizing shock—a stiletto into the brain. But, his mind cleared enough to suspect Goddess.

What do you want? Go away, for god's sake. Go back to your cave.

It's for the sake of the planet that I'm here.

Leave me alone! I have no idea what you're talking about.

The client, John! The client! You didn't find out!

Get out. Go!

The client. Aren't you curious? You're about to lose Meiying because of him. You'd better find out. Now how are you going to face her? You didn't find out. The client, John!

I'll find out later. Go!

John absently shuffled papers on his desk, then picked up the phone and dialed a random client. Anything to avoid listening further.

You can't avoid Me!

The voice came over the phone. John slammed down the receiver.

~

Yes, it's true, dear Reader, my father couldn't avoid Her. Or the other voices. Nor can I. But that is a different story for a different day.

~

A different story? A different day? Michael, you're proof of the success of My plan, and, as his seed, you're more powerful than your father. But with that added power comes added pain and confusion! Look at you, sitting in this pathetic institution, writing, writing….

~

With great effort, John tried to force these mad thoughts out of his head, but the voice continued. **It is nineteen forty-nine, John Powers! You have less than a year, then…the coming together! You will have sex with Bai Meiying. Now, find out the name of the client and tell her, otherwise….**

Otherwise what? You can do nothing to me.

Do? I can make you drink rat poison, if I want! Or leave you to God!

And I can force you out of my mind.

Obviously not.

"Hey, John!" called Mr. Bandrowsky from a nearby desk. "You're mumbling to yourself again."

"Oh, sorry."

"Okay, but it's damn distracting."

"Right."

John wiped his brow. _Damn hot in here._

John!

"Quiet!"

"What'd you say?" asked a startled Bandrowsky.

"Oh, sorry, I didn't mean you."

"What the hell's wrong with you?" challenged the offended man. "Lucky I don't have a client here. Jesus Christ, John! Get your head screwed on straight."

"All I can say is that I'm sorry," said John defensively. "The comment wasn't directed at you. I was just thinking aloud." He cursed the voices and his own fate at having these schizophrenic hallucinations.

"Well, okay. But keep the mumbling down, it's really bothersome."

"Right."

As a man who wanted to please others for all his life, John fell back into his wounded inner world, again blaming himself for all misunderstandings and misguided perceptions that came his way. He went back to mulling this whole client business with Meiying. Should he pursue the issue with Mobley, or let it drop? On the one hand, he was a new employee, and he did not want to make a nuisance of himself. On the other hand, there was Meiying's bizarre behavior about finding out the name of this damn client. When in doubt, remain quiet, he told himself. Less chance of appearing the fool. He finished the day's work and went home without the information Meiying had demanded.

The first thing she asked when he entered the apartment gave him no surprise. "Did you find out?"

John put her off with, "Tell you later. Let's eat first."

At dinner, to avoid conflict, he decided to lie.

"Mr. Mobley wasn't in today, so I didn't get the chance to ask about that client," he told her first thing, before she even had a chance to ask again.

"It doesn't matter," she said curtly, proving that it did. "I didn't expect it. But, really, it doesn't matter."

"Oh, come on! I tried, but he wasn't there."

"Yes, you said that." Knowing what she now knew about Jacob Telles and Mr. President, Meiying abruptly decided to switch gears and have John drop it before it led to uncomfortable questions.

"Do you think I'm lying?"

Before Meiying could respond, a deep sigh of disgust came from Mulan. John turned to her with a frown. She had become increasingly resentful of her role as mediator, serving as a ground for the sparks that flew in a perfect arc between the two adults. As their relationship soured, she grew closer to her American friends and further from her adopted parents.

"So, young lady, tell me about your day," said John.

"Nothing much."

"What did you do?"

"Nothing much, but I'm getting a job."

"What?" blurted Meiying.

"Yeah. I'm getting a job."

"Where?" asked John.

"Dunno, yet."

"Sweetie, you're too ill."

"No, I'm not! My coughing has gotten better."

Meiying patted Mulan's hand and said, "Let me at least take you to the doctor before you do. Let him clear you for doing work."

"No, I—" She stopped herself, then added quickly, "A restaurant, or something."

"Well," proclaimed John in his best fatherly tone. "That won't do. At the very least, you can't work in food service."

"What?" asked Mulan.

"Food service, like a waitress or cook, or something like that. Your illness—"

"Yes, I know," said Mulan, rolling her eyes. "I'm not stupid. I said restaurant, but that's not the kind of work I want to do anyway."

"Well, what then?'

"I don't know! Something. There's a lot of Chinese businesses here. I just want to earn my own money."

As if on cue, she began coughing. Meiying started to rub her back, but Mulan sprang up from the table and ran into her bedroom, coughing the entire way.

Meiying looked at John. "We can't let her work. It's getting worse."

"You're right, let's take her to the doctor again. Get his opinion. But, Meiying, if he gives the green light, she needs her independence. American kids are like that."

"She's not an American."

"She is now."

"No. Besides, what if she goes to work and has a serious attack. They'll fire her right away. What will that do for her?"

"Let her take the chance. We have to let her at least try. Her English is bad, but what the heck."

"Americans and their independence!" grumbled Meiying.

"Isn't that what you want for yourself?"

"I'm older."

John laughed. "You always wanted your independence. Always. Let's face it, you're not the typical submissive Chinese wife." He rolled his eyes. "Boy, you're not the typical Chinese wife!"

Now Meiying laughed. "Anyone who thinks Chinese wives are submissive is a fool!"

"I meant the stereotype, not the reality. God knows the stereotype is not the reality. Look at you."

To his disappointment, she did not respond. He backtracked. "I mean, thank god you're certainly not the stereotype."

In the case of Mulan, at least, John felt he held the moral high ground. After all, the girl needed to assimilate into American society, or she would be alone all her life. He could not see that Meiying, indeed, was a shell-shocked soldier. Growing up in war-torn China, she had seen death and violence all around, and carried their scars with her into the rough and tumble milieu of American society. She had read every day about heinous crimes, grisly murders, and vicious gangsters, and considered Mulan to be at risk whenever she left the apartment. Worse, in Meiying's mind, Mulan's condition made her particularly vulnerable to the uniquely American form of natural selection—only the young and strong could prosper.

Meiying suddenly rose from the table and announced in a martyred tone, "I'm going to check on her."

As he watched her leave the room, John again felt somehow inadequate.

Perhaps Meiying is right, he thought. *It is rough out there*. Again, he felt resentment at his Chinese wife for making him doubt his strongest convictions. He poured a stiff bourbon, downed it, and poured another. To assuage his frustrations, he had resumed drinking, not only for relief from his faltering marriage, but to help repress his increasingly intense desire to have sex with Meiying, or anyone, for that matter. Now that the stresses of establishing himself had lessened, his libido correspondingly rose to new heights. Fantasies had begun to drive him toward resolving the issue by force, or at least strong coercion. Not knowing about her daily trips to the Telles house, he imagined her home alone all day—the perfect time to surprise her with a romantic visit, flowers, and "the whole nine yards." Better yet, he thought, tomorrow he would obtain the name of Mobley's client and go home early to convince her of his good intentions. If the result was sex, so much the better. He reminded himself not to forget flowers.

~ *Day Before Audition* ~

Breakfast proceeded as usual—hectic and full of cereal crunching silence. Meiying alone preferred the traditional rice gruel. John was the first to depart, hastily and distractedly, followed by Mulan who planned to spend the day with friends. Meiying cleaned up and dashed off to practice. With the audition scheduled for the next day, her jangled nerves were made increasingly taut over and above the looming specter of Mr. President and his goons. Only the anticipated touch of Marie Telles gave her a reason to smile. And she was not disappointed. Upon entering the house, Marie quickly said, "Jacob is away on business," and gave her protégé a lingering kiss. Meiying felt weak from the touch of her lips, as warmth and longing spread downward in waves from the starved reward circuitry of her brain.

Meiying wanted more, but Marie pulled away and wagged her finger playfully, "Enough, dear. Tea per usual, then practice. Your audition is tomorrow."

"You're so kind."

Marie laughed. "Let's not be so formal, Meiying dear."

"No, let's not." Meiying reached for Marie's hand and they walked to the little anteroom, leaning against each other like young lovers and chatting freely.

At tea, Meiying brought up Mulan's plans to find a job. Marie listened politely, then raised a hand. "Today, concentrate only on your music. Nothing must interfere with a good performance tomorrow."

"Yes, you're right."

~

John sat at his desk gearing up his courage to revisit the conversation about clients with Mr. Mobley. After a long internal debate on the way to work, he had made the determination to obtain the information, leave early, return home to Meiying, and surprise her with his news (and flowers). The difficulty lay in approaching Mobley without appearing too pushy. He picked up the phone and dialed Mrs. McAllister.

"Yes?"

"Hello, this is John Powers."

"Yes?"

"Is Mr. Mobley in, by any chance?"

"Yes, but he's with a client. Can I help you?"

"Mrs. McAllister, I wonder if you might help me?'

"How so?" She sounded suspicious to John's mind.

"Mr. Mobley is soon traveling to China with our client Mr. Telles, isn't that so?" *Damn stupid!* he thought. *Sounds like a cross-examination.*

"Yes."

Her tone had become sharper, causing John to waver. "Well . . . I mean, you know . . . he was about to tell me the name of the Chinese business associate of Mr. Telles." He swallowed and forged ahead. "But was interrupted. Do you have that information, by any chance? I don't want to bother Mr. Mobley any further."

"Oh, I see. I'll have to ask Mr. Mobley if that information can be shared. Confidentiality, you know."

"Oh, yes. No problem." John felt horrified. Although her words were mild, their innuendo carried a level of distrust that made him instantly overcorrect.

"Oh, of course! No, no, no problem. By all means. I really don't even need the information. Just curiosity, really. Nothing more."

"I see. Do you want me to ask Mr. Mobley?"

"No, no, I'll ask later, when it's more convenient. Don't trouble yourself."

"Anything else?"

"No, no thank you." He backed out of the conversation like a boy whose ears had just been boxed.

John had always been self-aware enough to know when his weaknesses and failures rose to the level of public embarrassment. Endlessly, he reran words that had been spoken, and body language that had been displayed, for he was certain everyone could perceive his inadequacies. Always wanting to please made him always want to be liked, which made him always want to say or do the right thing, which he always hoped would lead to his being respected. Yet, he was also wise enough to understand that always wanting to please led to many outcomes and destinations, but definitely did not lead to respect. His tragedy lay in the fact that he knew he could not stop himself from wanting to be liked, and the inevitable result would be self-induced castration and self-inflicted flagellation.

He limped back to his desk in a state of deflated pride. It seemed to him that no matter the circumstances, he would always crave respect, and always get condescension instead. Or worse. Even the voices seemed to half-heartedly decry his "worthlessness" and "foolishness," when, in fact, he lived his life as a series of reactions to the actions of others; waves in the cup of tea that followed the stirring spoon.

Cancel the flowers, he thought with wry dejection.

Chapter Sixteen

Audition and Revision

Mr. Hendricks

M r. Hendricks rose gallantly to greet Meiying in his office, which she had some trouble finding. After a few wrong turns, she had found it in an ugly, but functional concrete annex which bulged like a rectangular tumor from the sweeping architecture of Symphony Hall. When the secretary escorted Meiying in and closed the door behind, Hendricks gestured for her to sit, continuing to stand even as she did so. Tall and stout, his long grey hair brushed back in a dramatic swell, as if a tsunami broke over his forehead and swept backward down the nape of his neck, he gazed down at her imperiously. He wore slacks and a dress shirt without a tie, and his informality conveyed something which Meiying was unprepared to understand. Like most Americans, he appeared to Meiying as giant, both vertically and horizontally, and gave her the impression she sat at the base of a talking mountain. His office was small and cluttered, and she felt claustrophobic, with him dominating the space. Quite aware of his size advantage, Mr. Hendricks further established his dominance by standing a bit longer than necessary; but then a sudden transformation occurred when he pirouetted as gracefully as a ballerina to make himself magnanimously smaller by sitting back in his chair and hunching down slightly. With this apparently often-repeated ceremony complete, he smiled broadly.

"I have heard a lot about you, Mrs. Powers. Welcome. Please make yourself comfortable." He took a sip from the steaming mug on his desk. "Sorry, would you like some coffee?"

Meiying bowed her head. "Thank you, no."

"They told me you were beautiful, but they didn't do justice to your looks." She blushed appropriately and remained silent.

"Well, let's get down to it. As you know, I'm David Hendricks, assistant music director of this symphony. Mr. Mobley has been kind enough to refer you to me."

As he chatted, fulfilling the requirements of polite, introductory conversation, she felt his eyes wandering all over her body, head to toe and side to side. This openly voyeuristic behavior offered no surprise to Meiying, who, if gawking counted, had been raped innumerable times. She smoothed the red silk traditional Chinese dress she had carefully chosen, mainly to accentuate her "exotic" appearance. In her efforts to avoid his eyes, she had lost the thread of his monologue, but focused on picking it up again.

"And, therefore, we would very much like to hear you play for us." He finally paused.

"I am very happy to play for you. Where shall I perform?"

He stood and continued to smile graciously. "We can walk over to Symphony Hall. There is a piano on the stage where you may play."

"Will others be listening?" asked Meiying, standing with him and trying to appear relaxed.

"Perhaps. The maestro said he would try, but if he can't make it, he has implicit trust in my recommendations."

"I see."

He motioned toward the door. "Shall we go?"

While they walked, Meiying asked, "What would you like me to play?"

"Sometimes, we ask our young pianists to sight-read a difficult passage from some long-forgotten work, but in your case, that will not be necessary. Pick what you like."

Meiying wanted to ask what "in your case" meant, but thought better of it.

Mr. Hendricks continued speaking as they walked, regaling her with the history of the Hall, and his own successes in finding new talent. While pontificating, he unselfconsciously kept peering down at her cleavage, which far from being insultingly crude, she took as a matter of course. She had learned in China from the time she was a young girl that males have certain prerogatives that are not to be questioned or denied.

"You know," he said. "I am quite proud of the fact that I have found hidden gems from around the world. Unfortunately, the damn war made things difficult. I mean, it acted like a load of mud dumped upon the earth that smothered many promising musical sprouts." He chuckled and looked at her with a piercing gaze. "But, the survivors keep burrowing upwards, eventually finding a way to reach the sun. They find a way. And as soon as they poke up, I spot them. I get down on my knees and protect them. Nurture them. I have a feeling you are one of those sprouts. Not young, but young enough."

Meiying did not know how to respond, so remained quiet. But, in any event, Hendricks's loquaciousness kept any opening to speak at a minimum. After chatting amiably with a few security guards along the way, he swung open an imposing double-door.

"So, here is the concert hall!" he proclaimed dramatically, inviting her with his eyes to look up at the vaulted ceiling and glittering luxury boxes that rose ever higher into the firmament.

Meiying felt suitably impressed, but the rather dark, cavernous nature of the Hall brought to mind a certain cave near the Flaming Cliffs of Mongolia. She imagined fierce Buandelgereen sitting in the shadows, waiting and watching. In her mind's eye, at the back of the Hall, stood an unassailable iron door, from behind which came tapping. Shadowy ghosts moved about as if in anticipation of some unsettling event; a hunchback, a dancing specter, a shaggy bearded one, and many others. Thus absorbed, she was overtaken by "the mood," and knew she could play no other piece to begin the audition but number thirty-one of Beethoven's *Diabelli Variations*. They ascended the stage and walked to the piano, sitting alone in all its glory, illuminated by a single spotlight.

"Here it is," said Hendricks. "All tuned and ready. Is it satisfactory?"

"Oh, yes," replied Meiying as she adjusted the bench. She gave the keys a workout up and down the scale. "Yes, this will do nicely."

"I'll just go sit and listen, Mrs. Powers. Just give me a chance to get settled in, and I'll give you the high-sign."

"Yes, thank you."

Meiying loosened up by rolling her neck and peered into the auditorium where she spotted Hendricks seated ten rows back in the shadows, surrounded by the ghosts. He lifted his arm and waved. "Anytime, Mrs. Powers!" he called.

Taking a deep breath, her fingers touched the keys. The moment she began to play, her nerves fell away and she lost herself in the music.

~

Mr. Hendricks, possessing a more poetic nature than his rather boorish exterior might lead one to believe, felt pleasantly aroused. He pictured Meiying's naked breasts hovering close to the keyboard, offering milk to the famished instrument, which subsequently came to life with this Chinese woman's nimble fingers and inscrutable soul. He sat entranced by her technical and interpretive skills. *A keeper, a keeper,* he repeated to himself. *Beautiful and talented! Perfect!* Already, he began composing marketing slogans: "Out of the crucible of war-torn China comes an inspiring new talent!" "East meets West, Confucius meets Beethoven, a fresh new talent from China!"

If we play our cards right, a profitable draw. Very profitable!

When she finished the short piece, Mr. Hendricks stood and applauded enthusiastically. "May I hear another? That was magnificent, Mrs. Powers! Magnificent!"

Meiying beamed. "Thank you. Do you have a request?"

"No, no my dear. You choose!"

As an encore, Meiying played a Chopin prelude, resulting in continued praise from Hendricks. After her audition, when they retired back to his office, Mr. Hendricks waxed poetic, praising Meiying's performance and informing her he would be in touch. Before she departed, he took her hand and gave it a gracious, old world kiss.

She took the bus back to the apartment, floating on air and anxious to share her joy and relief with Marie Telles the next morning. Feeling such happiness made her also want to tell Mulan and John, but she decided to wait until something definite came of the audition.

~ *Mr. Hendricks Has A Visitor* ~

"Your ten o'clock appointment has arrived," announced a doughty secretary over the intercom.

"Fine, send him in," said David Hendricks, who immediately stood, ready to greet his guest.

The visitor swept into the room, and with a wry grin, gestured for Mr. Hendricks to sit first, proclaiming, "So, you auditioned Mrs. Powers yesterday!"

Hendricks obediently sat with a little groan, intended to convey his good-humored awareness of the visitor's game, but obliged to acquiesce nonetheless. "Yes, indeed, she is everything you described, and more," he replied appreciatively.

The man smiled knowingly. "As you may be aware, I'll be accompanying a client to China soon."

"Oh?"

"We will be meeting a contact who is familiar with Mrs. Powers."

"Really? How interesting." Mr. Hendricks leaned forward and put his fingers together. "A competitor?"

"Not at all."

"Well then?" asked Hendricks, clearly puzzled. "What brings you here this fine day, Arthur?"

"This contact is a very wealthy man and considers himself something of a protective uncle to Mrs. Powers."

Mr. Hendricks waited patiently.

"He hopes you hire her, and bring her back to China on a symphony tour."

"Ah," said Hendricks drily. "How interesting, but that, unfortunately, would be prohibitively expensive . . . not to say dangerous, given the civil war going on there."

"Well, you see," said the guest. "That is where the Chinese contact comes in. He is willing to defray expenses. Perhaps a scaled-down version of the symphony, plus Mrs. Powers, of course.""I see. But, you know, even that would be very expensive, Arthur."

Mr. Mobley sat back in his chair. "I was instructed by this contact to guarantee to you that money would be no object."

"Really? Is he a bona fide . . . player?"

"Definitely."

"Well, in that case. . . . "

"Naturally, your contract with Mrs. Powers would need to stipulate that she accompany the symphony anywhere, including overseas, at the symphony's sole discretion."

"Would there be some reason she wouldn't?" asked Mr. Hendricks, a tad perturbed.

"Put it this way, she's had bad experiences in China."

"Of course," said Hendricks. "But, first things first. We haven't even made her an offer yet."

"I understand, David. By the way, our contact is making preparations to flee China if necessary. Certain funds are being transferred as we speak. His expatriate city of preference is San Francisco. And, David, he is a generous patron of the arts."

"I understand, Arthur."

"If the communists win, god forbid," said Mobley with an exaggerated shudder. "No reason for them to get their Red claws on so much money . . . so much treasure."

"Treasure?"

"Oh, yes. Our contact lives in a palace, surrounded by world-class art, which he is also in the process of spiriting away to safe locations."

"Well, this is certainly getting more interesting, Arthur. When did your contact want this tour to happen?"

"As soon as feasible. Tell you what, give me an estimated budget for the trip and I'll show the figures to our contact. If he approves, I'll let you know as soon as I return. Will there be any problem bringing Mrs. Powers under contract?"

"The way she plays? The way she looks? With her exploitable background? Certainly not! We anticipate starting her right away."

"Does she know?"

"Not yet."

"Can her contract be signed, sealed, and delivered before I leave?'

"When do you depart?"

"Two weeks."

Mr. Hendricks smiled. "No problem. Does this uncle-figure want to show her off in China?"

Mobley gave him an ironic tilt of the head. "In a manner of speaking. Incidentally, and this is most important, Mrs. Powers must not be made aware of our plans, not even the slightest hint of her going to China, until after she has signed the contract. Agreed?"

"Arthur, I'm still not clear about the problem."

"Well, she's a bit of a prima donna. Might cause trouble unless it's in the contract and she's penalized for breaching the terms. I'm told she's the nervous type and causes scenes, even though the things she objects to are often in her best interest. But with a contract, well, she wouldn't want to harm her family's financial position. Anyway, are we agreed?"

"Certainly."

"If she finds out beforehand, the deal is off, in more ways than one."

"I understand, but there is still the issue of safety."

Mobley pursed his lips. "Well, the major cities—Shanghai, Peiping, Nanjing, Canton—are all under the control of the Nationalists"—he paused—"I think. Anyway, perfectly safe."

"Yes, I know, but our Board would want reassurances."

"Cancellation insurance will be paid by our contact in the event of any sudden emergency that might arise. Act of war, force majeure, that sort of thing."

"Yes, good. That should satisfy them."

Mr. Mobley seemed to relax. "She is lovely, isn't she?"

"Yes," said Hendricks, looking hard at Mobley. "In more ways than one."

"Ah, yes, very good."

Mr. Hendricks experienced a stab of resentment at what he considered the younger Mobley's patronizing tone, but he quickly recovered his poise. "By the way, who is this Chinese contact? He sounds intriguing."

"Oh, he is. Most definitely, he is. But, confidentiality forbids my releasing his identity just yet. I can tell you he is a very . . . ah . . . imposing figure." Mr. Mobley chuckled as he said these last words, which made the hairs on Hendricks's neck tickle.

Arthur Mobley isn't so much patronizing as . . . sarcastic, thought Hendricks. But the sarcasm definitely comprises something else, which makes it . . . makes it what? Cynical? Cruel? I don't know, but there is something not right . . . this contact, for example . . . why the secrecy?

Hendricks put these thoughts aside and asked, "Imposing? How so?"

Mobley waved him off with a curt, "Oh, nothing really. Just a typical rich Chinese fat cat." He chuckled again and murmured under his breath, "Very rich and very fat."

~

Mr. Mobley left Hendricks's office with a handshake, and headed for his next meeting. By the time he arrived, Jacob Telles was in a lather. Sitting at a table in the Mariner's Inn cocktail lounge, he saw Mobley coming and gave him a disgusted look.

"You're late!"

"So sorry," said Mobley as he motioned to the waiter. "Glass of your house wine."

"Yes, sir. Red or white?"

"Red."

Telles glared, waiting for a *mea culpa*, but none was forthcoming.

"Just came from seeing David Hendricks at the symphony," announced Mobley.

"And?"

"Well, it's settled. At least, it's on its way to being settled."

Jacob Telles sat back and flashed a smile of relief. "That's good." His irritation melted away. "Any complications?"

"None. Our friend, Mr. President, is going to a lot of trouble and expense."

Telles laughed and raised his glass. "True enough, but she's worth it."

The waiter delivered the wine and Mobley stared at it, swirling it slowly. "It's not about her," he said as if to himself. "At least, it's not all about her."

"What do you mean?"

"There's something else he's after. Something extraordinarily valuable. True, Mrs. Powers is beautiful and talented, but that obese bastard is surrounded by concubines. He gets the pick of the litter. No, there's something else going on here."

"Well, whatever it is, his business has been profitable to me, and making these arrangements certainly will help further cement our relationship. And as for Mrs. Powers, all I know is that she can be made receptive—never met a woman who can't. The proper approach will bring her around."

Mobley looked askance at Jacob Telles. "As I said, this is about more than Meiying Powers."

"Not to me."

Mobley stared. "Christ! In love, or lust?"

"Both."

Mobley sipped his wine while Telles finished off a plate of *hor d'oeuves*, smacking his lips loudly to taunt his companion. *Telles is a fool!* mused Arthur Mobley. *An utter fool who has stumbled onto the fatted calf. What does Mr. President see in him?* Mobley scrutinized Jacob Telles's features and realized with pangs of envy that the man possessed Hollywood-style good looks. Leading man good looks. In fact, Jacob Telles was beautiful. *Ah, there's the thing! Obscene, obese old lecher! And this fool Telles has no idea he is already trapped in that fat spider's web . . . as much an* hor d'oeuve *as the crab spread the fool is eating. At least if I have to deal with him, I have the satisfaction of knowing his sister . . . and now, Meiying Powers—*

"Hey! Arthur! Come back to earth." Telles held up his fork and waved it to get Mobley's attention.

"Oh, sorry. Just drifting."

"I was talking about our trip. I don't want to stay too long in China. Let's get in and out so I can return home as soon as possible."

"Why the rush? There's a lot of business to do."

Telles smiled. "There's also a lot of business here, if you know what I mean."

"I see." *Good luck with that*, thought Mobley, with some pleasure. "Well, I'm currently finishing the arrangements for our trip. I'll make sure we keep to a strict schedule so that we can return as soon as possible."

"Excellent. Sure you won't have some crab spread? It's quite good."

"No, thanks. I have to get back to the office. No rest, and all that."

When Arthur Mobley returned to his office building and started to open the door, he met John Powers on his way out. John paused, holding the door open for Mobley. This was the last person Mobley wanted to see, and he had no intention of engaging in conversation. John began to speak, but Mobley cut him short by rushing past. "Good night, John. Work to do."

He heard John's desultory, "Good night, see you tomorrow," as it faded weakly behind him.

Once settled in his office, Mobley sat down to write two letters. One was addressed to Mr. President, and the other to his father's old friend who lived on an estate near Nanjing, Master Zhou Hungren.

~

John had replayed the brusque encounter with Mobley numerous times on the bus home, but now, outside his apartment door, he put on a happy face and entered. Mulan rushed up and gave him a kiss.

"Hello!" he exclaimed. "How nice! You had a good day!"

"Oh, yes! I found a job!"

"Really? Doing what?"

"Working in the packaging department of a medical supply company."

"Wow! That's great! Is Miss Bai home?" (It always irked him to refer to Meiying this way, but Mulan remained stubbornly adamant.)

"Not yet."

John checked his watch. "Hmm. That's strange. It's late. Well! Tell me about this job. What does it pay? When does it start?"

"Oh, it's just low wage, but I start on Monday!"

"Excellent!"

Just then, Meiying arrived carrying a bag of groceries. "What's excellent!" she asked.

"I have a job!" enthused Mulan.

"Oh, well, that's good, I guess, though I still have my doubts about this."

"Miss Bai! How can you say that? My own money!"

Meiying removed her hat, deposited her purse on the counter, and began putting away the groceries. "Yes, I know, I know. John has instructed me in the ways of American teenagers. Independence, right?"

"Right!" exclaimed John, putting his arm around Mulan and looking at Meiying. "How about you? How was your day?" He laughed. "Did you get a job also? Maybe executive vice president of General Motors?"

Meiying hesitated. "No, of course I didn't." She felt a wave of satisfaction that John's smug attitude about her employment status would soon change.

"Shopping?" asked Mulan.

"Yes, dear."

"For clothes?"

"No, silly girl. Don't you see the groceries?"

"Darn!"

John chuckled. "Jeez, Mulan, your English slang is getting really good."

"Hmm," said Meiying disapprovingly.

"It's because of my friends," said Mulan. "I listen. I repeat what they say. I learn. Oh, it feels so good to understand, at least a little, what people are saying around me."

"I can imagine," commented John. "I felt the same way when I learned Chinese."

"But," cautioned Meiying. "Mulan needs to continue learning written Chinese. She still needs to learn *wen yan wen*."

John scoffed. "Literary Chinese? Just so she can read dead Chinese philosophers?"

Meiying replied angrily. "It's more than that, and you know it. If you don't, you're more foolish than I thought."

"It's a waste of damn time. And, it's damn hard to learn." He turned to Mulan. "Do you want to learn literary Chinese?"

Mulan looked at Meiying. "Yeah, sure I do."

"Good!" exclaimed Meiying.

"Oh, she's just saying that because you're here," grumbled John.

"No, I'm not!" insisted Mulan. "I want to know what dead Chinese philosophers had to say. I mean, it's important for all Chinese to know."

"Yes, you're right, dear," said Meiying, who then assumed a cautionary tone. "Never lose sight of your Chinese heritage, Mulan." She turned her gaze on John. "I'm sure my husband would agree."

John started to make some wisecrack, but he held his tongue. Instead he said, "Dinner?"

"It'll be a while," said Meiying.

"Hopefully not too long, eh, Mulan?" He winked, poured a drink, and sat in his favorite easy chair with a newspaper.

"I'll help, Miss Bai," said Mulan.

"Yes, thank you. We can talk while we're making dinner."

In the midst of preparing the meal, Mulan leaned close and whispered, "Did you really just go shopping for groceries? Wasn't there something else?"

Meiying's jaw dropped. "What do you mean?"

Mulan smiled sweetly. "Oh, nothing."

~ *Contracts and Obligations* ~

Once Meiying had signed the contract with the symphony, she faced the bittersweet task of breaking the news to John and Mulan. She knew her husband would be angry about her proceeding without his advice, but she more than looked forward to telling Mulan. The girl had started her job, and had already brought home her first paycheck. Concerns over Mr. President had faded, as no new information had come to light, and she put the obese monster out of her mind as much as possible. In any event, the maestro planned to bring her along slowly, practicing with the symphony, but not scheduled for a solo performance anytime soon. She told herself there was no immediate necessity to tell John. She could wait, but not too long.

Anyway, choosing an auspicious time to tell John proved difficult. Lately, he had been in a foul mood, and she suspected things were not going well at work. Each night, she started to break the news, but he would grumble about the government, about work, about intransigent clients, and so forth. With each passing week, John's drinking became heavier and his moods more unpredictable. She knew she had to tell him, but it was always easier to put it off. However, the day came when delay was no longer feasible. Within a week, she was to play an evening concert with the symphony in a non-solo capacity. Although, for a long time, she relished taking his smug attitude down a few notches, her natural kindness now found no joy in hurting him. Timing was everything. Too early after John normally got home, his fatigue would brook no unwanted complications. Too late, and his drinking spurred exaggeratedly angry reactions to even the slightest provocation, real or imagined. Somewhere in the midst of his first bourbon lay the golden moment, when he was relaxed, but had not yet had time to nurse his resentments with more liquor.

One night, after dinner, when Mulan had gone with friends to a movie, Meiying sat with John and carefully chose the right moment to unburden herself of the story, leaving out all mention of Mr. President and his connection to Jacob Telles. In the beginning, he listened incredulously, but withheld comment. She intentionally rushed through the chain of events in order to give him as little time as possible to interrupt. She explained the role played by Arthur Mobley, as regards Mr. Hendricks and Miss Telles, again leaving out any mention of Jacob Telles. But, this omission led to John's initial, violent outburst.

"So! You must have been thrilled to find some lonely woman with a piano to prey upon! Have you seduced her yet? Is she already your lover? And worse! You signed a contract without even consulting me? You damn bitch! Who do you think you are? God damn it! You can barely read English! God damn bitch! I told you I would make the arrangements. You didn't have to go over my head to Mobley! What's he going to think? I'll tell you. He'll think I'm some weak, useless flunky, hanging on to you through some arranged marriage bullshit!"

"But, that's not fair," objected Meiying quietly. "Mr. Mobley came to me."

"Sure, sure. And have you also bedded him? You and he certainly have been having a grand time behind my back! My god, what he must think of me! What they all must think! No wonder . . . no wonder."

"No wonder what?"

"Oh, Christ! Don't talk to me! You obviously don't need me! God damn it, Meiying!"

"No wonder what?"

Answer carefully, Chosen One! came Goddess's voice to John. **Do you want to lose her?**

The voice infuriated him to new heights of rage.

She'll poison you! boomed God or a demon, the words came too fast to identify. **The bitch will poison you!** No, definitely not God. A demon voice.

"The voices! The demon, evil voices!" shouted John at Meiying. "Your secret plots to humiliate me have caused them to come back!"

Meiying remained calm. "No wonder what?"

Her composed demeanor pushed him even further into rage, but her repeated question had to be answered—untruthfully. "No wonder the voices are here!"

"That is not what you meant, John. Tell me the truth. No wonder what?"

"God damn it, Meiying! Go to hell!"

John Powers! cried Goddess. **Overcome your all-too-human remnants!**

Listen to Her. Goddess is right, countered a sympathetic God. ***Ignore that evil voice! Your wife, Bai Meiying, will not poison you. You're safe. Goddess, our two factions are agreed in abhorring such unnecessary suffering. You know We regret this. It is Your clumsy engineering that has caused the problem.***

John leapt up and rushed to the bedroom, holding his head and mumbling to himself incoherently.

Meiying wanted to go to him and offer words of apology, but she knew better than to make the attempt when the voices assailed him with such apparent violence. Still, the tug of compassion and guilt would not allow her abandoning him to confront his demons alone. Although she felt deep alarm over his decline into alcoholism and abuse, some deep connection, plus all they had been through together, kept her loyal. Once he had recovered his balance, and was free of liquor and the voices, she resolved to reveal all, including the involvement of Jacob and Marie Telles. She wanted to renegotiate their relationship, now realizing he had no place in her future plans. He could not be her agent-manager, for she had discussed with Marie Telles (while they lounged in bed after a morning of exquisite lovemaking) the idea of their working together in a partnership; one the performer, and the other the agent-confidante. "But, what of your husband?" Marie had asked. Even now, with John battling his schizophrenia in the other room, she longed to escape, to flee as fast as her legs could take her, into Marie Telles's arms. But, the instant she thought of carrying through with this impulse, the vision of Marie's brother and Mr. President thrust their awful perils into her thoughts, and scattered her nice, ordered ideas into a thousand chaotic, and frightening directions. Nevertheless, in her more lucid moments, when she fluttered above all the conflicts in her life, Meiying knew she had the capacity to take flight at any time and escape the madness. Like a witch on a broomstick in Western mythology, she wanted to be ugly in exchange for feeling the wind through her hair, and the three-dimensional freedom of the sky. True ugliness was itself a freedom, allowing the inner world to merge with the outer, for a perfect universe of unhampered self-expression. Although viewed by men as a beautiful but fragile butterfly, she had always understood them to be profoundly wrong; she had the power to become an eagle with talons as sharp and deadly as that of any male. Turning herself ugly would be an easy task; all she had to do was betray John Powers.

~

Mulan came home and celebrated Miss Bai's good news with affectionate hugs and kisses, then wearily shuffled to bed, bravely stifling coughs along the way. Still, John had not left the bedroom, and Meiying had not heard a peep from behind the door. They slept in twin beds, at her insistence, and as the hours passed, she nodded off at the kitchen table, unwilling to disturb John, but now longing for her comfy little bed. Nonetheless, suspended in a half-sleep, her emotions roiled from a complex mixture of excitement about her first performance with the symphony, sadness and guilt over John, pining for Marie, and worry about

Mulan, who, although happy to be working, clearly suffered extreme fatigue from the labor. In fact, the occasional coughing from Mulan's room reminded Meiying that her own problems did not constitute the middle kingdom of life's complications. Yet, something was amiss with Meiying's body. Her face burned as though she suffered from some tropical fever. It was in this troubled state that the visitors appeared. First came a strange wind, moaning through the cracks and crevices of the kitchen.

~ Fever Dremas[1] ~

With a terrific bang and shattering of glass, the windows of the apartment burst open, followed by a howling gale that threatened to tear Meiying from her chair. She clung to the table as the driving force whipped her hair wildly about her face. No moisture accompanied the swirling onslaught; it was as dry and desiccated as the most ancient corner of hell. Meiying leaned into the storm, her face peeling away from the furnace of wind, when above the roar, she heard a high-pitched voice calling plaintively, **Nineteen-fifty and the son is soon come! Nineteen-fifty and the son is soon come!**

Shuddering in dread, she realized the New Year rapidly approached. Still, the tolling continued, **Nineteen-fifty and the son is soon come! Nineteen-fifty and the son is soon come!**

"He will have to rape me!" she screamed defiantly into the wind.

Over her head whirled the specters of her group, alive and dead, spinning ever faster, like clouds around the eye of the storm: Feng Shiren, Peter, Lu Zhishen, Suling, Master Liu, Madame Liu, Master Zhou, Mr. Gao, Child of Buddha, Little Acorn, and the rest. Their mouths were open like fish, and out of their lungs, from deep within each of them, came a tapping.

… Tap. Tap. Tap. Tap….

"No! He will have to rape me!" she screamed again.

The son! The son! The son!

… Tap. Tap. Tap. Tap….

"Never! Never!"

~ Fever Dreams[2] ~

Meiying woke from her nightmare in a sweat, her heart pounding, her mind reeling from the assault. The sudden silence disoriented her, and she groped for some familiar landmark to restore sanity. Her purse sat in comforting outline on the table, and like a buoy to a drowning swimmer, she instinctively reached for it, clutching it to her chest and breathing deeply. When at last she looked up, three figures stared at her with unspeakably sorrowful faces. She squinted through the darkness and recognized Meili, Lihua, and Buandelgereen. With the appearance of these three cherished faces, Meiying suddenly felt calm and safe.

"Am I still dreaming?" she asked.

"Your life is a dream," said one of them, she knew not which. "Since coming to this country, you have been living in the eye of the storm. When soon, you no longer dwell there, you will be swept away to reap the whirlwind."

"That answer does me no good," she replied.

"You son is writing down our words as we speak. We are powerless to alter them."

"I have no son."

"You will."

Meiying fell into a deep confusion, and a dizziness blurred her vision. "You three, of all others, should know why I do not want to birth a child of his. Or of any man's."

"We understand, but the deed is to be done."

"No! It is nineteen forty-eight, I have not slept with him, and I have free will! I will not have his son!"

"Two years to go. China will fall, then you will fall."

"No! He will have to rape me!"

"So you have said. However, explain this, Bai Meiying: The Female Goddess wants it, the Male God does not. What of your feminism now?"

"That is a puzzle," replied Meiying.

"Life is a puzzle."

Meiying laughed drily. "Life is a dream. Life is a puzzle. Life is a whirlwind. Which is it?"

"It is none, and it is all."

"Oh, as confusing as this dream! I love all three of you, even though you speak in riddles and I understand none of your words."

All three spoke simultaneously. "Ask him to explain them."

"Who?"

"Michael Powers, your son."

Meiying looked up at the ceiling as if his face could be found staring down at them. "Are you the writer of this?"

"I am," came an unfamiliar voice.

"Are you my son?"

"I am."

"Then I am indeed still dreaming."

The unfamiliar voice spoke sadly. "There will be another war."

"Isn't there always?" sighed Meiying.

"My twin will be in it."

"What? I am to have twins?"

"But, some say it was really me in the war, and that I made up the twin story."

"Then you are ill?"

The voice replied curtly, "I have no more to say. Your dream is at an end."

But, dear Reader, mother would not stop. In my head, and then upon this page, she insisted on continuing. "I am sorry, spirit writer, but you cannot be my son. Surely you know why."

"I know, mother, why you think it cannot be. Nonetheless, I exist. I am creating my own mother as I write these words. I write the words, you are created, therefore I am."

Meiying shook her head. "I do not understand."

"Nor do I."

Meiying paused, then asked sweetly, "Your name is Michael?"

"It is. You and father named me."

"Your father. . . . ?"

With this, Bai Meiying Powers, my mother, could no longer dwell in her dream, and she woke a second time, exhausted and drawn irresistibly to her bed beside the snoring John Powers. Not caring whether he was awakened by her movements, she entered the bedroom, undressed, and lay down with a groan. In fact, his company seemed positively refreshing compared to the scorching welder's torch she had just endured. But, reality also took its toll. The stale smell of half-digested bourbon hung heavily in the air, making the fiery tempest of her dream almost more appealing than the reeking atmosphere of a loveless marriage. Visions of having sex with him made her nauseous.

Oh, god! she thought. *Unhappy in dreams. Unhappy when awake. Where do I find contentment? In music? Yes, music only. And perhaps Marie Telles. Perhaps.*

~ *Life Goes On* ~

The next morning, all three ate in silence. John nursed his resentment with wounded looks; Mulan longed to leave for work and escape the tension; while Meiying craved the company of Marie Telles. But one in particular bore the scars of anger and frustration—John. He contemplated whether to assail Arthur Mobley as soon as he got to the office with righteous indignation over the breach of manly etiquette in the affair with his wife, or meekly submit to Meiying's explanation, let it go, and repress the animosity that so rankled his heart. Now that he believed with depressing certainty that Meiying was on her way to fame and fortune, he felt suddenly rudderless. Work had become onerous with the constant grind of tiresome routine, and he had become restless and bad-tempered, unwittingly longing for stormy adventure beyond a lifeless desk and the morgue-like pall of fluorescent lights. He needed more purpose in life than helping a business acquire profits, and began to suspect he left the best of himself in China.

The time spent in war-torn China came to him, ironically enough, as a golden dream. Contrary to the complaints he directed at Meiying about that benighted country, the quest to find *her* had given him a mystical purpose. While in China, he had possessed, at least obliquely, both Meiying and *her*. Now that he was established in the States, he had lost *her*, and was in the process of losing Meiying. These depressing thoughts came to him on the bus to work, and he was startled to realize he had not thought of *her* for a very long time. What once had been an obsession had now become nothing more than a faded memory, without even enough substance to bother telling his grandchildren. *They would think I'm a superstitious old fool*, he decided. *It started with* her *and I've long ago ended it with* her, *haven't I?* Nevertheless, sitting toward the back of the crowded bus, he became lost in thought dredging up those very memories, and replayed the question *she* had posed on that fateful day so many years ago.

"Mr. Powers, how does one justify a life without cruelty, and therefore also without the distilled beauty of cruelty?"

Lost in the memory, he repeated her words in his mind, but unintentionally said them aloud, drawing the attention of nearby passengers. Realizing his mistake, he shrank back in his seat with a disconcerted air. From the middle of the bus came a voice. *Her* voice, which rose clear and vibrant over the background din.

"Speaking of the distilled beauty of cruelty, Mr. Powers, have you not yet learned that fate starves at probability's door?"

That is not one of my voices! he thought with terrifying certainty. *It is* her!

Rendered momentarily speechless, he suddenly leapt up, grabbed his briefcase, and rushed headlong up the aisle, looking left and right. But a knot of passengers standing with their own briefcases and bulky packages blocked the way, and when the bus pulled over to the next stop, he saw *her* step off. By the time he followed, *she* had disappeared, and he stood on the sidewalk looking like a man lost. He wanted to chase after *her*, but he did not even know the direction *she* walked. San Francisco had swallowed *her* up.

She *teases me! Entices me! Then, as always, abandons me! Go back to your damn cave and hide behind your iron door!*

"Go back to your damn cave!" he repeated, this time out loud, drawing anxious glances and averted faces.

A cop from the other side of the street glared.

John quickly looked away and pretended to tie his shoe. *This is pathetic! Have I become a homeless person talking to himself? Pathetic!*

With his briefcase in hand, he began walking in the direction of his office before he realized he could simply return to the same stop and catch the next bus. As he retraced his steps, he cursed discreetly under his breath. A bar flashed its neon invitation across the street, and he longed to be in its dark, isolated cave, soothed by bourbon and surrounded by sympathetic strangers. *Too early*, he chided himself, and realized how ridiculous he must look, wandering aimlessly with a stupid briefcase hanging uselessly by his side, as though it were a prop in a bad movie. When he reached the stop, he could not bring himself to sit on the bench, so he paced the sidewalk, imagining the pedestrians that flowed around him laughing and whispering to themselves at his expense. Never had he felt so alone, so isolated, so foolish. How could he face Mobley in this condition? Thankfully, the voices were quiet. *Even they pity me*, he thought miserably. *In China, I stood for something. I was someone! Now? Nothing more than a cog with a briefcase. In fact, I'm more of a cog in a country of two hundred million than I ever was in a country of almost a billion! I was alive there!*

Your son will understand, came the voice, this time more compassionate than mocking.

When he at last arrived at work over an hour late, John returned the expected ribbing about where he had been with witty, offhand retorts, for he had long ago decided that no man would easily glimpse the tattered intimacies of his derailing life. As expected, Mr. Mobley called him into his office, and John stood passively while Arthur explained the upcoming itinerary in China, in the event any questions or emergencies arose. This information operated on John as might a scalpel without benefit of anesthesia. But, in the midst of his agony, he heard the name of Mr. President come from the lips of Arthur Mobley. Never had a man come to attention so quickly from such a low, apathetic place.

"What!?" he cried in a voice that could not be mistaken for anything other than genuine incredulity.

Mr. Mobley flinched at the almost primordial howl, and stared at John in wonder. He managed to blurt, "Sorry?"

John, unconcerned about observing any semblance of civil discourse, exclaimed again in the same agonized tone, "What did you just say?"

Mobley, shaken by the pliable John Powers making such an outcry, composed himself in order to respond calmly and rationally. "I said, we will be meeting a man who likes to be called Mr. President. That would be about ten days after we land, and—"

"Our client is Mr. Telles, correct?" interrupted John, rashly assuming the role of inquisitor, his words tumbling out at breakneck speed.

"Yes."

"And his connection in China is Mr. President?"

"One of them, yes."

"And, obviously, we're not talking about Generalissimo Chiang Kai-shek, or anyone in his government?"

"No," replied Mobley in a disapproving tone at John's aggressive examination.

"Have you met this person?" John asked, as if meeting Mr. President was like meeting a deity.

"Yes, but why—"

"Is he fat?"

Mobley stared, comprehension transforming his face, and said simply, "Yes, unbelievably fat."

John, who had been standing the entire time, now sank into the nearest chair with a genuinely stunned look. "Oh, my god!" he moaned.

"Do you know him?" asked Mobley.

John ignored the question. "Does my wife know?"

"Your wife?"

"Yes, does my wife know?"

"Know what?"

John scoffed. "You know what I'm talking about, Arthur. Does she know you're meeting this man?"

Arthur Mobley now understood he treaded on dangerous ice. "Well, I don't know. Ask your wife."

"I'm asking you!"

"I don't like your tone, Mr. Powers."

John cared nothing for the consequences of his reckless behavior. "I'm asking you! Does my wife know you're meeting this man?"

"I told you, I don't know. Look, what is the problem here?"

"The problem, Mr. Mobley, is that you and Mr. Telles are dealing with a murderer, a kidnapper, a rapist, a . . . wholly evil person!"

From the line of questioning, Mobley realized John did not know about his wife's relationship with Mrs. Telles. Under no circumstances did he want this information revealed; not now, not in his office, and not where he would be subject to the unpredictable wrath of a jealous husband. Mobley took a calm and measured approach.

"We are aware he is tainted, John, but who in China isn't? Business is business. We have been doing a profitable business with this man for many years, both before the war and now after it."

John trembled in righteous indignation. "What if I were to tell you that he kidnapped my wife, raped her, and performed countless other atrocities on countless other people?"

Arthur Mobley remained silent, weighing his words carefully. "War brings out the worst in people. Do you know how many ex-Nazis are working for our government? Mr. President survived. Now, we do business—profitable business—with him. Your wife is safely here with you, correct?"

"Well. . . . "

Mobley's face appeared to undergo a transformation from stunned recipient of disturbing news to a sympathetic and knowledgeable therapist. He smiled benevolently. "Why don't you and she come with us? I'll authorize the business to pay half your expenses, and perhaps some of these demons will disappear when you meet him under different circumstances. People change, you know."

John could not believe his ears, and could only snap, "Are you insane?"

"So some say. But, look, seriously John, come with us and face the fears. Perhaps they'll melt away. Besides, your presence might benefit us in making the deal."

"I would kill him if I were present! And as for my wife, her going is completely out of the question!"

Mr. Mobley paused as if listening to some inner instructions. "I think not. She need not meet Mr. President. She may have other . . . opportunities."

"What?"

"Her music, perhaps. A tour."

"No, no, no."

"Look, John, go home and talk to your wife. Take the rest of the day off."

Meiying's words rang in John's mind: 'Ask about the client!' Now he understood what she meant. But, he hesitated to reply to Mobley's offer, and asked rather weakly, "What does my wife have to do with this?"

"Just talk to her, John."

"But—"

Mobley rose from behind his desk. "No! This discussion is over. Talk to your wife, then see me tomorrow. We'll talk then."

"Something's wrong here," said John, for lack of anything better to say. "Okay, I'll talk to Meiying, then we'll meet tomorrow. But, you can put out of your mind the idea of us going with you."

Mobley smiled as condescendingly as the proverbial cat that swallowed the canary. "Tell your wife I have been in touch with a rich landowner named Zhou Guangli—I believe you also know him as Master Zhou—and he wants both of you to come."

This second revelation was more than John could bear. He left the office in a daze, trying to connect dots that would not connect. Returning to China struck him as madness, but the thought of Master Zhou gave him pause; the lure of adventure, reconnecting with Meiying, and the faint possibility of *her* re-entering his life crept into his calculations.

After John left, Arthur Mobley called in Mrs. McAllister and told her to make sure all of Mr. Powers' appointments were cancelled for the day.

"All of them?" she asked with a raised eyebrow.

"All of them. By the way, Mrs. McAllister, do you find Mr. Powers to be a meek, pliable sort of fellow?"

"I guess." She thought a moment. "Yes, I think so."

"Oh, no, Mrs. McAllister, John Powers is not meek, or pliable, or weak. Not at all. Yet, his tragedy, ironically enough, is that he thinks he is"

~ *The Discussion* ~

That night, after Mulan had gone safely to bed, John and Meiying engaged in a long and stormy discussion once he had recounted his conversation with Mr. Mobley. At the mention of Master Zhou, Meiying turned deathly pale and flailed her hands as if clearing a path through cobwebs. Following her initial shock, the two slowly came together in the face of this extraordinary information, and began to speak with the openness and trust of the old days. Meiying noticed he had even foregone his bourbon, and by this act of deprivation, assumed he also had been shaken to the core by these revelations.

Their talk led John to wonder aloud, "Why would Mobley bring up the idea of a tour?"

"Did you know," she said in a hushed voice, "there is a clause in my contract with the symphony that requires employees to travel abroad whenever tours are scheduled." She chuckled. "I'm sure they thought either I couldn't read the document, or I wouldn't be able to understand it, but I have experience with English-language contracts with the British in Shanghai and Hong Kong. Still, I thought nothing about it at the time, but now. . . . "

"Interesting," said John. "After all, didn't Mobley introduce you to that fellow . . . what's his name? . . . with the symphony?"

"David Hendricks."

"Yeah, him. So, Mobley has contacts with the symphony. In fact, come to think of it, the orchestra is also a client of ours."

Meiying felt herself tumbling into irrational fears when the word 'conspiracy' popped into her mind. She wanted to push the word away, but it was as if her hands simply passed through it rather than shoving it aside. Conspiracy—a fog that had no clear outlines other than its diffuse, indistinct resistance to beginnings and ends. A big word with big implications. But, conspiracy to do what? Between who? For what purpose? This line of inquiry led her to a horrible possibility: Is Marie Telles involved?

In the midst of her speculations, she had a thought. "John, do you know how to get in touch with Master Zhou?"

"No."

"Then you must find out so we can contact him ourselves."

"Yes, but I don't know if Mobley will give me the information."

"Ask, and if he refuses, then we know."

"We know what?"

"Then we know if others are cooperating with Mr. President to maneuver us over there."

John wanted to disagree, but the facts seemed undeniable. "Yes, yes. We're supposed to meet tomorrow. I'll get the information, one way or another."

Meiying felt a renewed closeness to John that she had not experienced since the China days. She lapsed into an unrealistic wish that his attitude toward her were different—one of deep friendship rather than unhappy love. Perhaps, she told herself, his acceptance would come with time. But, she knew this was mere fantasy, and her more pressing concern involved whether Marie Telles was implicated in this . . . this what? Conspiracy? She was too smart to leap head first into that assumption. Nevertheless, she intended to make a call on that "grand lady" tomorrow. In the meantime, the thought of returning to China no longer seemed an impossible undertaking, especially if Master Zhou and the others were waiting.

What if I go to China? she thought. *And if I do, what if I smash forever my fears. Mr. President, Father Durant, Colonel Naguma, Beethoven, Beethoven's uncle, all of them smashed forever. Then what? Then I play the piano and search for her with a clear mind and a lion's heart. What could they do to me then? Only their poisonous memories would remain, but diluted enough to be harmless.*

Meiying looked at John and said with a steely edge to her words, "Yes, you must get Master Zhou's address! We must take control of our own destiny. Our own fate!"

John, momentarily rendered speechless by Meiying's resolve, heard the voice boom loudly in his mind.

Fate starves at probability's door, John Powers! Go, if you must, but beware the traps and lures of God and his allies. He would have you suffer rather than succeed. He would have her remain childless, in the clutches of Mr. President. He would have the son cease to be even the possibility of being! Because of His faction's First Principles, the planet will die.

When the last words of Goddess reverberated into a deep, silent gulf, John stood and poured himself a stiff bourbon. Meiying watched him wordlessly as he gulped it down and poured another. *Damn that voice!* she thought bitterly. *It will be his ruin. Our ruin!*

"John," she said kindly. "Go easy on the drinks. We have to keep our wits about us."

"Yeah, it's just these damn voices that keep. . . . " He poured another.

"I know, but you must fight them."

He stopped in mid-drink and held the glass above the table, distractedly swirling the contents. "No. I'm starting to glimpse what it's all about. There's a key, and I think . . . well, never mind for now." After taking another swallow, he asked, "Meiying, where is the Precious Object now?"

Meiying raised her eyebrows and tilted her head. "I don't know, why?"

"Nothing." He gulped down the last of the drink and poured another. "Go to bed. I have to think. The key is sitting right in front of me, but I can't see it." He waved his arm. "Go to bed. I've got to think this through. God mentioned something about past failures . . . intermediates He called them. Is that what I—never mind, I have to think."

"And drink."

As if a dike had burst, John exploded. "God damn right! I'll fuckin' drink if I want! As much as I want! Work hard enough for it. Anyway, it's none of your business. You're not even my real wife, so stop nagging!"

Two steps forward, one step back, thought Meiying. *For a moment, it was there.* She stood and stepped away from the table.

"Meiying!" he called.

"Yes?"

He held out his hand and looked at her imploringly. "Sorry. I'm a damn fool. Worthless, as some might say."

Meiying hesitated only for a moment, then took his hand.

He drew her to him. "We can be together again. Work together. Be a team. I'll try to do better." The words were slurred, but she had no doubt of their sincerity. He put her hand to his cheek, red with the flush of liquor. "I need you, and by god, I hope you need me." Reaching out his other hand, he pulled her head toward his and leaned forward to kiss her. She pulled away.

"John, if it's true about Master Zhou, we have to go. You know that?"

"I know."

~

As both suspected, Meiying was informed the symphony had scheduled a trip to China. A small group of accompanists would leave for a quick tour of major cities, with her as the solo pianist. It would be hailed as a "Homecoming Tour." At the same time, also as they suspected, Mr. Mobley refused to give John the address of Master Zhou, citing the need for strict confidentiality. Mr. Mobley and Jacob Telles far too willingly postponed their business trip to China to coincide with the tour.

"Now," said Mobley to John quite reasonably. "The both of you can travel to China at the same time, and you can meet Mr. President, who is very anxious for this tour to succeed. Your wife will be quite safe, and, as I said, the demons exorcised." He spread his arms wide, as if stating the obvious. "Demons gone, business done, everyone happy."

But, without further information, John and Meiying redoubled their objections to going, and their lives were borne along by frightful trepidation and dark forebodings. For weeks, Meiying had been put off every time she attempted to call on Marie Telles. The usual excuse from her brother was that Miss Telles had business out-of-town and wouldn't return for some unspecified time. Of course, this absence, or pretended absence, caused Meiying to build an elaborate scaffolding of suspicion and resentment atop a solid foundation of anxiety, upon which she climbed higher with each passing day.

~ *A Letter* ~

One day, everything changed. After that day, almost every free moment was taken up with rehearsal for the trip, and she performed like a woman possessed, now openly yearning for the moment to arrive when she returned to China. John likewise eagerly anticipated traveling back to that war-torn country. Mr. Mobley and Mr. Telles constantly reiterated how glad they were to postpone their business trip to coincide with the symphony tour, their cooperative attitudes no doubt greased with the promise of financial reward from Mr. President. As for the rotund Chinese "businessman" himself, word came that he was delighted with the idea of seeing John Powers and Bai Meiying again, and that all parties would prosper from the largesse supplied by the tour.

So, dear Reader, what had changed to make this complete and unexpected turnaround in the attitudes of John and Meiying possible? It came via a letter from Master Zhou, addressed to Mr. and Mrs. Powers, sent care of Arthur Mobley. It read:

Dearest comrades and fellow searchers,

I trust this letter finds both of you well and prosperous! Much has happened since we spoke last. Alas! China continues to suffer, the civil war rages on, and her people struggle each day to find a few grains of rice on which to survive, only to face the same monstrous dilemma the next day. For a time, after you left, our little group stayed together at my mansion outside Nanjing. Even Lu Zhishen returned from Canada, driven back by boredom and his inability to exorcize the demons that hectored him to give up his peaceful country for the quest.

And what of the sacred quest to find her?

Any rational person would assume we, who have certainly suffered much in the attempt, would have abandoned our mad adventure. And for a while, we licked our wounds in peace. After Suling found her home village destroyed, she returned. Lu Zhishen had come back from Canada, Child of Buddha stayed on, and we all clung to each other like children in the dark. Absence of the Precious Object, Master and Madame Liu, Mr. Gao, Feng Shiren, Peter, Little Acorn, and all the rest, including you two, made us despair of ever making our lives whole again.

But then, in our darkest hour, something miraculous happened, which at the time seemed a tragedy. First, however, a description of some of the difficulties. We have all been assured by the Nationalists that the war against the communists is going well—but, we know better. Keep that in mind if you decide to return.

Inflation has been a terrible curse, and I cannot pay my workers except in tied bundles of yuan, which must immediately be spent for salt or rice, or they will become even more worthless by the hour. Naturally, gold and silver are the only currencies that amount to anything. Fortunately, I have salted away most of my fortune in foreign banks and in foreign investments. I do have access to American dollars. Well, that is not why I am writing. Back to our terrible tragedy that has turned into a blessing.

One night, as we all sat around reminiscing about the old days, a terrific clamor could be heard coming from outside the walls. The servants ran in to tell us communist raiders were demanding we come out and meet with them. When we refused, they fired shots into the air and threatened to burn us alive if we did not comply. Can you guess which among us remained the calmest? If you guessed our own Child of Buddha, you would be correct. She admonished us to stay inside, and fearlessly walked out to meet these madmen. We followed her directions like obedient children.

After a long time passed, she returned and spoke gravely. "Those are not communist raiders," she said.

"Who are they?" we all asked.

But, you know Child of Buddha, she only shrugged. "People," she said.

"What do they want?"

"Us."

Of course, this answer made us think we were to be robbed and murdered.

"It is not that," she replied to our protests. "They are gone."

Naturally, we were amazed. "What?" we all cried.

"Gone."

Well, you can imagine our confusion, which was made worse by what she said next.

"We must go back to the mental institution where I stayed for so long."

She made this statement as if telling us it was time for dinner. Again, we all demanded an explanation.

"And," she continued. "We must bring John Powers and Bai Meiying with us. That was made very clear to me."

Well, again we were amazed, and asked why, but she would not answer. In response to our questions, she just continued to repeat that we must bring both of you, or never hope to see her *again.*

"That area is controlled by the Reds!" I explained. But it didn't matter.

"We must bring them," was all she would say.

So, you see my lost children, you must come back so that we may all journey there together, as intended from the beginning. We have been told about the concert tour, and about the business to be transacted by Mr. Telles, Mr. Mobley, and John. Perhaps both of you can finish your business and delay returning to America until we make this trip? Our fate is in your hands. Meiying, I know you are concerned about Mr. President, and all I can tell you is that Child of Buddha is insistent. The last we heard, Mr. President is still in touch with all sides. How he does it is a mystery. When we brought up your fear of Mr. President, Child of Buddha simply shrugged, and said, "He is not who she thinks he is."

We all anxiously await your reply. Please let us know through Mr. Mobley. His father was an old family friend, and his son, I believe and hope, can be trusted.

With love and anticipation.

Master Zhou and the others.

The impact of this letter on John and Meiying was swift and decisive. Neither hesitated in agreeing they must make the trip. For his part, John anticipated the pleasure of traveling with Meiying, bringing back the closeness they once shared in the old days and, perhaps just as importantly, separating her from contact with Marie Telles. For her part, Meiying felt torn. Mr. President still terrified her, and she trembled at the idea of being kidnapped and imprisoned again. Yet, the thought of seeing her beloved friends and, dare she think it? . . . meeting *her*, made the opportunity irresistible. Furthermore, *Her* mysterious connection with Mr. President, combined with Child of Buddha's assurance that he "is not who she thinks he is" aroused Meiying's curiosity. Marie Telles remained incommunicado, and in her pique, Meiying decided a long absence in China would send a clear signal that she was disinterested in continuing their relationship.

Both John and Meiying agreed to leave Mulan at home, to which she readily agreed. Mulan enjoyed the money she earned from her job, which she used to socialize with an ever-expanding group of American friends. Her English, slang-filled and coarse, nevertheless opened doors to relationships with a small army of young male admirers. The tuberculosis had an off-and-on tendency, but for the most part settled into a quiet phase.

Various delays pushed the trip into January, and as the departure day approached, the heightening excitement felt by Meiying and John led to conflict. The more John drank, the more they argued, until, from pure exhaustion, they agreed to a truce, and each focused on their own professional responsibilities.

As it turned out, John could not accompany Meiying on her tour since Mr. Mobley scheduled a number of business engagements requiring his attendance at separate locations, primarily to be introduced as a junior member of the firm in anticipation of future business. To Meiying's great relief, Mr. President respectfully declined to attend her concerts due to the deteriorating situation in the war between the communists and Nationalists. Because of the conflict, the tour had been truncated to include only a few, secure cities: Peiping, Nanjing, Shanghai, and Hong Kong. After a long series of discussions, John and Meiying agreed they would travel to China together, and upon arriving would split up, each performing their own obligations. Once their business had been completed, both would travel to Master Zhou's estate outside Nanjing in March, 1949.

Chapter Seventeen

PART EIGHT: REAPING THE WHIRLWIND

Marie Telles Returns

~ *Reunited* ~

With departure merely days away, Meiying sat at the piano with the small ensemble that would accompany her, rehearsing a particularly difficult Lizst passage. Due to the deteriorating situation in China, the number of musicians slated to travel with her kept being whittled down to a leaner and more dexterous size. Symphony Hall was empty but for a small smattering of observers. It was late evening, and the performers were tired and cranky.

"No, no, no!" snapped the maestro. "Crisper! Cleaner on the downbeat! Again!" He gave the group a fierce look, tapped the baton and raised his arms, then abruptly stopped to make a notation on the score.

Meiying took a deep breath and rolled her neck to loosen the muscles, taut as the wires in her piano. In the process, she noticed an elegant female walking down one of the dark aisles of the vast hall between the outspreading rows of empty seats. The figure looked familiar, but shadows kept her from identifying details. She could make out a long, graceful dress, and a wide hat that effectively hid the face. For some reason, her heart beat faster and her palms began to sweat. In moments, the figure would be illuminated by the stage lights.

"Mrs. Powers!" exclaimed the maestro. "Are you with us?"

"Yes, sorry maestro. I am ready."

With the figure lingering in her mind, Meiying played the passage automatically, without her usual chromatic depth.

"It's late," said the maestro, defeated. "We will continue tomorrow at ten o'clock. We'll start with the same passage, and hopefully the rest will give us all renewed musical comprehension."

Relieved, Meiying immediately looked for the figure, but it had disappeared. Musicians packed up their instruments and filed by, uttering wearily, "Good night," and "See you tomorrow." Meiying delayed following them, and instead wandered backstage to pass the time for reasons she did not clearly understand. Of course, she told herself, it was ridiculous to expect the mysterious woman to appear and identify herself, but Meiying had already guessed who she was, and her nerves tingled with anticipation.

"You okay, Mrs. Powers?" came a deep voice that gave her a start. She gasped before realizing it was the night watchman.

"Oh, Steve! You startled me!" she exclaimed self-consciously.

The large, dark face smiled down at her. "Sorry. Ain't you goin' home?"

As with so many big American men, she felt like a child in his presence, and he reminded her of the peasant men she had been around in China—rough, friendly, gentle, and fierce protectors. For a brief moment, she fancied him being her own, personal bodyguard on the trip, but immediately dismissed the notion as silly. Who was she, an insignificant pianist, to have a bodyguard? Still, the images of Mr. President, Beethoven's uncle, and their henchmen made her shudder.

She looked at his reassuringly imposing outline in the shadows of the stage and realized she had not answered him. She was about to speak when he said kindly, "Mrs. Powers? You sure you're okay?"

Meiying chuckled. "Sorry, Steve, my mind is elsewhere. I'll be leaving soon, I just have a few things to work out that have been bothering me."

Meiying returned to the piano and sat, absently fingering a random phrase from the Lizst sonata.

"Well, you're almost the last one out," called Steve.

"Almost?"

Steve smiled oddly. "Almost. I think you have a visitor. Well, I'm off on my rounds. See you soon. Don't stay up too late. If you need anything, give a holler. I'll come runnin'."

Meiying looked around to find the other person, but saw no one. "What visitor?" she said in Steve's direction, but he had already left. Alone at the piano, she absently played a few bars while her thoughts remained on Marie Telles. As if conjured by magic, someone tapped her gently on the shoulder, and Meiying turned around to face the expected visitor.

"Hello, Marie," she said calmly, without emotion.

Marie Telles stared down at Meiying with tears in her eyes. Without a word, she leaned over, hugged her and kissed her on the mouth.

Meiying looked Marie in the eyes, stunned at the audacious kiss.

"Let me come with you," whispered Marie.

Meiying blinked away her surprise, and replied coldly, "Why did you leave without telling me?"

Marie stood upright, but said nothing, merely gazing at Meiying from under her wide hat.

Meiying gave her an exasperated look and turned back to the piano. She played with passion, all the while hoping Marie would interrupt her playing and kiss her again. When she finished the passage, she felt a sudden dread and turned to say something, but her visitor was gone.

"No!" she blurted to herself. Jumping up from the bench, she called out, "Marie! Marie!"

But, no response.

Only Steve appeared, looking concerned. "Everything okay, Mrs. Powers?"

"My visitor," was all that Meiying could manage.

"Oh, she left. I locked the door behind her. You're the last, now."

~

That night, Meiying could not sleep, feeling sick that she had pushed Marie away so rashly. *Stupid, stupid Meiying!* she chastised herself. *A lost opportunity! Now, it is up to me. I must swallow my pride and go to her!*

She got up and made tea. Sitting at the kitchen table, it seemed the only path back to Marie would be to say she was sorry. But, it was Marie who left her with no notice, no message, nothing. Why should she be the one to apologize? Besides, did she even want Marie Telles accompanying her to China? Was it just the tour Marie would join, or would she be willing to travel into dangerous territory to see Master Zhou? What did Marie Telles know about *her*? Nothing. It seemed absurd to upset all the plans now, and open up the possibility of a new heartache.

I won't do it! She'll have to come to me.

But this resolution didn't last long, and she again considered visiting Marie before rehearsal in the morning. Back and forth she went, until her eyes refused to stay open. *Sleep on it*, she thought. *Tomorrow, I'll decide.*

~

At eight o'clock the next morning, Meiying stepped out of her taxi, asked the driver to wait, and knocked on Marie Telles's door. She still felt ambivalent, but after last night's long internal debate, she realized how little she cared for saving face. Lonely for a loving companion, she admitted to herself that her longings could not be so easily set aside in the name of emotions as petty as anger or revenge. Before the door opened, she straightened her dress and stood resolute, come what may. Minutes passed, and with a disappointed sigh, turned to go back in the taxi when the door flew open.

"Meiying!" Marie rushed out the door and glided into Meiying's arms as seamlessly as if they had been lovers for a thousand years. "Dearest, you came! I was so worried. I dared not go to you."

After this breathless interlude, she gave Meiying a passionate kiss on the lips, grabbed her hand, and almost dragged her into the house. Once inside, out of the curious glare of the taxi driver, Marie again gave Meiying a deep, sensual kiss.

"I missed you so much!" said Marie.

"Why didn't you call?" whispered Meiying, stunned by Marie's impassioned advances.

"Does it matter now?"

"Yes, it matters."

"Let me come with you to China."

Meiying disengaged herself from Marie's arms. "You haven't explained why, Marie."

"Come, let's have tea like we used to, and I'll explain."

"Marie, I haven't time. The taxi is waiting."

Marie backed up a few steps and stared at Meiying with wounded eyes. "Then I'll make it brief, dearest. But, at least come and sit, so that I can be assured you won't bolt out the door at any moment."

"Let me tell the driver that I'll be a few minutes," said Meiying.

Marie seized her hand. "Then, come back?"

"Of course."

When Meiying returned, she went to their usual room, where Marie sat waiting. Two cups of steaming tea had already been poured.

"You see," began Marie, somewhat hesitantly. "Jacob and I had a terrible fight. It was the first time we had ever been so brutal with each other. In a fit of rage, I left the next day to stay with an old aunt who was kind enough to take me in. I stayed with her until I returned yesterday, when you saw me. That's it!" She threw up her hands. "There. I've told you, briefly, the facts. I know you must go rehearse." She stood to see Meiying out, their tea untouched.

Meiying remained seated. "But, Marie, why didn't you tell me?"

"I was too upset to talk to anyone."

"That makes no sense. I had hoped I was not just 'anyone.' What was the argument about?"

Marie sat back down and took a sip of tea. She appeared nervous and flustered. "Dearest, that is what I wanted to tell you, but it will take time, and it may be very upsetting to you. I want to go with you to China, in part, because of the argument." She fell silent and looked at Meiying expectantly.

Meiying leaned forward in her chair and said, "Tell me."

Marie checked her watch. "Not now. You must go to rehearsal. Later, when we have more time."

"But—"

"No, Meiying!" exclaimed Marie heatedly. "That won't do. I will not be the one to interfere with your practice. The other musicians will be waiting, and you certainly don't want the reputation of a *prima donna*. At least, not yet." She said these last words with a conspiratorial laugh.

"Marie, there is very little time before I depart."

"I know."

"Come to the symphony at one o'clock, we'll talk at lunch. The maestro gives us an hour. You must tell me then."

"Dearest, I'll be there. But, instead of the Hall, let's meet at the Hob Nob Grill. It's close, and I'll grab a table first so we don't waste time waiting. Now, go, and play beautifully."

~ *The Explanation* ~

Meiying was grateful for the maestro's constant exhortations to play better, for the time fairly flew, and when he announced lunch break, she rushed to the nearby restaurant where they were to meet. To her great relief, Marie had already arrived and waved from a corner table. Meiying quickly ordered a salad and stared at Marie expectantly.

Marie took a deep breath. "It started when Jacob came home one day full of good cheer. As usual, we sat together in the same room you and I meet, where we discuss the day and share any interesting occurrences. I had wine and he had gin and tonic. This time, he wore an unusually wide grin that peaked my curiosity. After lifting his glass and saying, 'Cheers!' in an excited tone I have rarely heard from him, I naturally asked, 'Why the silly grin?'

"'Oh, that?' he said with a look that made me believe he knew something that would touch upon our little competition."

"Competition?" interrupted Meiying.

"Over you, of course. He fancies your preference for women is only because you haven't met the right man. He, of course, would be the right man."

Meiying rolled her eyes. "Of course! The arrogance of men!"

"Oh," said Marie. "If only their worst trait was arrogance."

Meiying chuckled. "I agree."

"Well, once Jacob started to speak, it became apparent my suspicion was correct. He said that he and Arthur Mobley had worked out a complicated scheme to get you to return to China.

"When he saw my shock, his grin returned twice as obnoxious. 'And,' he said. 'She'll be with me in China, not here for you to sink your lesbian claws into.' Insufferable complacency!" exclaimed Marie, causing nearby patrons to rubberneck.

"Oh, my god," blurted Meiying. "How? What?"

"I'm getting there, dearest. At first, I held my temper, poured him another drink, and asked how this miraculous achievement was brought about. The gin had done its work, and he blathered the entire plot. Apparently, Mobley received a letter from one of his China clients, the one you're afraid of, asking him to find a way to get you back to China. If that meant bringing your husband along, so be it. If they succeeded, this client—this monster, Mr. President—had highly profitable contracts waiting to be signed. Anyway, Arthur and Jacob went back and forth with this Mr. President. Eventually, they came up with the tour idea. That's when Arthur connected you to Hendricks."

"But, Marie, you just—"

"No, Meiying, wait! Let me finish. When I heard this story, I flew off the handle, calling him every dirty name I could think of. He gave it back to me in spades, and the next morning, I left."

"But, Marie, that still does not explain why you didn't call me," said Meiying.

Marie gave a deep sigh. "I know, I know. Dearest, I know. How can I explain? The deed was done, and I felt powerless to change it. But, really, I was embarrassed that Jacob, my own brother, was behind such an immoral scheme. I was terrified you would think I was somehow involved in . . . in the—"

"Conspiracy?" said Meiying. "I didn't know what to think. I suffered a great deal not knowing. But, what's done is done. John and I figured it out, but something else happened, and now we're anxious to go." Meiying took Marie's hand. "I can't take you with me, Marie. It's too dangerous. Especially where John and I are going after the tour."

"But, I want to share everything with you. I want you to know I love you, I will follow you, I will share the dangers."

"Marie, there is much you don't know. A long story that you would find confusing, if not crazy. It can't be."

Marie held out her hands, palms up. "Don't forget, Meiying, you told me everything a while ago. You told me about Shanghai, Nanjing, the Precious Object, and, most importantly, *her*. I want to be a part, I need to be a part."

Her face reflected a heartrending desire, a pleading that went beyond her guilt and regret. "I even know what happened to make you want to go—it's this Mr. Zhou, isn't it?"

"Yes, partly, but the story is long and involved, Marie. Where we're going is too dangerous."

"But, that's why I must go! I want to meet these people you told me about. I want to see for myself. Please!"

Meiying shook her head and looked down at their plates. "Look, we haven't even touched our food." She gazed up into Marie's imploring eyes. "Let me think about it."

"Please, Meiying. It will give me a chance to make up for my thoughtlessness." She assumed a stricken look. "My betrayal."

Meiying waved her hand impatiently. "It was hardly a betrayal. You're not responsible for your brother's actions."

Marie looked at Meiying with an odd expression. "You're not the only one with a complicated story and who has lived through hard times. My story is also complicated, Meiying, and it may surprise you in unpleasant ways."

With this enigmatic statement, their lunch ended when Meiying said she had to return to rehearsal. Marie's last words were to again exhort Meiying to let her come on the tour. Then, with a more demure hug and kiss, they went their separate ways.

As Meiying walked back to Symphony Hall, she felt an unsettling reaction to Marie's story. Something didn't quite hold up, but she could not pinpoint where.

However, the passionate kisses affected her to the core of her being, and her cravings began to overwhelm all other considerations.

~ *John Comes Alive* ~

As the trip drew closer, John struggled more and more with his voices. He chalked it up to stress, and tried to block them from interfering with work. Mainly, they had taken to arguing with each other again—God and Goddess. Of course, he knew their dispute involved his future son, and he felt sick to death of the subject, besides which, their squabbles had become convoluted and hard to follow. At times, he was tempted to see a psychiatrist, but convinced himself the symptoms were bearable, and would eventually go away. So far, he had succeeded in keeping his illness from clients and co-workers, knowing his erratic behavior marked him only as "peculiar" or, for those a bit more posh, a "queer duck." He avoided the word 'schizophrenia' at all costs, and whenever it popped into his head, he carried on a long discourse with himself about why he did not suffer from that terrible illness. John believed schizophrenics belonged in mental institutions, and he knew he most certainly did not.

Bourbon remained his refuge, while sex with Meiying continued to be a distant dream. Occasionally, when she acted particularly cold, the voices would shout incessantly and he felt driven to consider suicide in order to stop them once and for all. During these episodes, he truly feared for his sanity and found it ironic that the group would be traveling to Child of Buddha's old institution, where schizophrenics babbled and banged in their filthy cells. *Fitting and proper that I end up there*, he thought in his darker moments. Nevertheless, the trip represented the one aspect of his life that gave him hope: it loomed as a chance for salvation. It would reconnect him to Meiying, and the reunion of the group might lead, finally, to *her*. Certainly, *she* could help him understand the voices, and their "distilled beauty of cruelty." Perhaps, *she* would make them go away forever. In any case, Goddess had made him fully aware of one fact: nineteen-fifty would soon arrive, and the dominoes would start to fall.

As the day of departure drew near, he felt himself come alive with the possibility of redemption, or at least rebirth. Once in China again, he would feel liberated from the mundane existence he had been living, and purpose would lead him out of the darkness.

In his cups one night, he asked Meiying, "Are you excited about going to China yet? Or do you have time to get excited, with all the rehearsals . . . and everything else?"

Meiying replied, "Yes, I'm excited."

"Well, I'm not," pouted Mulan. "I'll miss you both."

"You'll have your friends, and an empty house!" cried John. "We have made arrangements with the bank and my company to keep the bills paid and you with enough spending money to be comfortable and have fun. Everything a young person could wish for!"

"Yes, but you're both like family," said Mulan. "Even though I'll have fun, I'll still miss you."

John cast an accusatory glance at Meiying and took another long swallow of his bourbon. "Yes, family is the most important. Abandoning your family for . . . whatever purpose, is truly immoral."

"Well, we're certainly not abandoning Mulan," said Meiying hotly. "We'll be back soon enough, and she's old enough to take care of herself." Meiying took Mulan's hand. "But, still, sweetheart, I'll miss you terribly."

"I wasn't talking of our trip," grumbled John, conspicuously rattling his ice and taking another drink.

"What were you talking about?" asked Meiying.

"You."

Mulan sighed and jumped in. "John, let's not argue now, when you're so close to leaving." She smiled broadly. "Will you bring me back something nice?"

John ignored her question and glared at Meiying. "Why don't you ask 'Miss Bai' why she's been abandoning us for . . . others."

Meiying looked at him calmly, then turned to Mulan. "What would you like us to bring, dear?"

With these gentle words, John instantly felt guilt at the unreasonableness of his attack, and tried to backtrack by cheerfully adding, "Yes, Mulan. Tell us, what would you like?"

Mulan coughed, then leaned forward excitedly. "Oh, anything. Something for my room—no!—better yet, a jade necklace, maybe."

"We'll see what we can find," he replied in his best, fatherly voice. "Meiying, don't you think we can find her something nice?"

A peace offering, and Meiying took it as such.

"Oh, I'm sure we can."

But, suddenly and inexplicably, Mulan burst into tears. Meiying rushed to her side and wrapped her arms around the sobbing girl.

"What's wrong?" asked John, standing over the two women awkwardly.

"I miss my village, my family!" cried Mulan.

"Of course you do. Of course." soothed Meiying.

It crossed John's mind that Mulan might ask to go with them. "Maybe next summer, when things have quieted down in China, we can return together and visit your village, see your family."

But, Mulan's next words surprised both adults.

"I don't want to go! I'm sure they're all dead!"

Taken aback by her vehemence, John blurted, "Why do you think that?"

Mulan looked at them both with a pained expression. "I've been writing to them, and receiving their letters through a friend of mine."

"Why didn't you tell us?" exclaimed Meiying in astonishment.

"Because you both fight so much and are so unhappy. My friend's uncle used to live in our district, and he knows my village. He sent a letter to my friend telling her to give it to me." Mulan fell silent, suppressing a few coughs. Tears came again to her eyes.

"And?" asked John in his gentlest voice.

"A while ago, the communists came and rounded up the landowners in my village and killed them. Then they seized their lands. My father—oh, he was so proud of his land—thank god he was already dead! They took my brother and he hasn't been seen since."

By now, Mulan was sobbing. John and Meiying looked at each other over her shaking figure, and both wordlessly conveyed to the other the realization that they had been inexcusably self-absorbed, to the callous exclusion of this pained and lonely girl.

"I hate China!" cried Mulan. "It is a cruel and heartless country! Miss Bai, I'm sorry, but I never want to speak Chinese again!"

"Yes, dear," soothed Meiying, rubbing her back. "We can worry about that later."

John helplessly watched this scene unfold in front of him, and the sobering gravity of Mulan's suffering affected him as forcefully as if he had been slapped. He struggled to find words that would comfort the crying girl, couldn't find them, and started speaking without forethought.

"Mulan, sweetheart, I'm so sorry. At one time, when our group in China was at its lowest point, both physically and spiritually, I also shouted out my hatred for China. I vowed that if I survived, I would never return to that violent, sorrowful country again. But now, I want to go back. I must go back! Why? Well, at first it was for selfish reasons, but now, I realize there is something else. And I'm realizing this even as I speak, thanks to you and your own pain.

"I believe there is something majestic about China, and . . . I don't know how to put it . . . of primal importance to humanity. It is an ancient country, born, prospered, decayed, died, and reborn into that same cycle many times in its history. Right now, it's being reborn again—a bloody, painful, messy affair. Don't hate China, Mulan, because you will end up hating both yourself and Miss Bai, and because soon China will be like an ancient newborn, clean and wailing to the world that it is arrived—again. It is an on-going message, a larger reflection of all of us as we move through life, and of our family histories as they rise and fall." He gave Meiying a significant look. "Let's hope our family is on the rise."

Meiying gave him a grateful smile, forever surprised at his infuriatingly complicated personality; one moment, petty and shallow, the next, deep and compassionate; one moment weak and cowardly, the next, strong and steadfast. Her mind wandered to contemplation of his voices, and she wondered at their connection to everything that surrounded them all. How were the voices related to *her*? Or the Precious Object? Or Mr. President? Or this future son? And why did his Goddess-voice insist on having a son, while his God-voice resist so vehemently?

A coughing fit by Mulan brought her back, and Meiying trundled the girl off to bed, sitting beside her and stroking her forehead until she slept. When Meiying returned to the living room, John sat in his easy chair, evidently lost in thought, his full glass of bourbon untouched. Meiying quietly stood and stared at his meditative figure.

Imagining her life as pieces of a jigsaw puzzle, she began to assemble the picture, hoping the final portrait would reflect perfect harmony and domestic peace. One grouping depicted a healthy, happy infant son—a cherubic nexus of divine devilry and unassailable sweetness, without a hint of schizophrenia. Another tableau showed John laughing, finally free of his voices. In separate corners of the puzzle, John and Meiying lived separately and happily, she with Marie Telles, and he with a new wife. In the center, a large assemblage revealed her playing the piano in a vast hall, while her lover and agent Marie Telles stood behind the curtains, staring with deep love and admiration. Another partly-assembled section showed a healthy, rosy Mulan sitting in the audience with her handsome young husband. And. . . .

But, Meiying laughed inwardly at her impossible fantasy. She knew well enough the nature of the world and its propensity for tragic irony, and in homage to its entropic inevitability, mentally upended the puzzle to watch the pieces fly in a thousand directions. *Come what may*, she thought. *Fate starves at Probability's door.*

She needed relief from this disturbing line of reflection. "What are you thinking?" she asked John.

"Come, have a seat and I'll tell you," he replied.

She sat next to him on the couch and asked, "Your voices?"

"Partly. They're speaking to me now, even as I talk to you. One of them tells me you will poison me, another tells me I'm a worthless fool, and Goddess, as always, tells me to make love with you"—he made the sign of quotation marks—'when the time is right.'"

"Which means the son must be born in nineteen fifty, right?"

"Correct. I've never figured out why that year is so important. But, really Meiying, that is not what I'm thinking about." He paused and rubbed his forehead.

"Yes?"

"I'm thinking about that damned mental institution in China, the one where we're going after we meet Master Zhou and the others. It seems to stick in my mind . . . I mean, it's this big, dark, horrible thing just waiting for us."

"Us, or you?"

"No, definitely us, not just me. Remember the cave? Well, this is worse, much worse."

"John, I don't know what you mean. Reverend Fu and Master Li are nice men, and the inmates are mainly sweet people."

"Yeah? Then why does *she* want to meet us there, of all places? Why not back to the Flaming Cliffs or to the cave, or in the comfort of a nice hotel for that matter?"

"Who knows? But, John, it is not an evil place."

"Who says? Anyway, I'm still anxious to go. I wasn't lying to Mulan about China. In spite of my feelings about . . . that place, I still must return!"

"If you feel this way, John, why must you go?"

He grinned. "To keep an eye on you and Marie Telles."

"I haven't told her she can come."

"You will."

"John, your ugly side is showing again. I have never kept it a secret from you that I favor women."

"That's true, but it doesn't make it any easier for me, your supposed husband." John waved his arm dismissively. "But, that isn't what I want to talk about. Meiying, you know we will have this child."

"I don't know that."

"Yes, you do. I know you do. But, regardless, you must agree to something."

"What?"

"That you will not allow the father of this child to be kept in that institution."

"What?'

"Yes, I have this terrible premonition that I'll be locked up there. Forever. That I'll die in one of those filthy cells, while you tour the world with your lover and our son. You must promise me!"

"Of course, I promise. But, that's not going to happen."

"Meiying, how can you say that? You, who are so worried that you'll be kidnapped and raped by Mr. President! And when I tell you that's not going to happen, you dismiss my words, and then just continue to be damn paranoid about it. Yet, you now sit here and have the nerve to tell me it's not going to happen?"

"John, I've already promised. Look, it's late, we're tired. Let's go to bed. In a couple of days we'll be headed to China, and all our questions will be answered."

"You hope."

"As do you."

"Yes, you're right. In spite of all the troubles and bullshit I've been telling you, it's been a long time since I've felt so alive."

"Good."

"Want to make love?"

"John—"

"Just kidding!"

Later that night, when John heard Meiying's deep and steady breathing and knew she was asleep, he muttered under his breath, "For now."

Evil thoughts entered his mind, which spurred Goddess to encourage, and God to rant His warnings that there must be no son.

"When the time is right," John whispered just before a troubled sleep overcame his conflicted soul.

Chapter Eighteen

Return to China

Preliminaries - John

Arthur Mobley looked at the assembled group seated around a circular cocktail table in the Shanghai hotel lounge. All were tired from the flight, and none looked forward to waking early tomorrow morning and dispersing to their various obligations. He noticed Meiying Powers and Marie Telles sitting next to each other, leaning over and chatting in low voices. John Powers sat on the other side of his wife, trying to hear her conversation, while next to him Jacob Telles stared into space, evidently bored. Mobley felt quite pleased that his plans had come to fruition so perfectly. With a cough and a quick drag on his cigarette, he stood and prepared to give what he considered obligatory remarks. Although Mr. President was not in Shanghai, his face lurked in the back of Mobley's thoughts, bearing a pleased, fleshy, obese smile of approval. That smile of approval translated, in Mobley's mind, to a potential fortune worth of contracts. He felt particularly smug that these deals might be the last to be concluded in China for a very long time, if the communists won, which appeared increasingly likely. Thanks to his quick thinking, he had gotten his clients in under the wire. Eventually, conversation died down and all eyes were on Mobley.

"Thank you all for coming. Tomorrow, we part for our separate destinations, but I thought it would be good to have a last get-together before moving on." He looked at Meiying and bowed. "I'm sorry the maestro could not make it, but I perfectly understand his last-minute preparations made it impossible. Mrs. Powers, we wish you well on your tour, which begins in this very city. We will all be thinking of you." He gave a significant glance at John. "One of us in particular." He raised his glass. "Without further ado, may we all find success!"

Toasts all around, trifling conversation, and the party quickly broke up. John and Meiying spent their last night together speaking very little. Each realized the true importance of this trip did not reside in a concert tour or business dealings, but in a journey that would soon take them either to *her*, or to . . . somewhere unknown, a familiarly unfamiliar realm of uncertainty and danger. All of the water that had passed under the bridge since they left China now seemed to be reversing and flowing back through their lives. As if by some magical time dilation, they found themselves looking at each other as they did so many years ago. Mutual recriminations and subterranean resentments left over from America sluffed away like old skin, and they found themselves returned to their original states of fearful anticipation, like children clutching each other when entering a haunted house on Halloween. Although they slept in the same bed, they did not touch, and only the next morning, when they took leave of each other, did they hug—which carried with it a deeply affectionate significance.

Standing at the open door of the taxi that would take her to Shanghai's concert hall, Meiying watched John return to the hotel with his business colleagues, and when they disappeared in the crowd, she felt suddenly alone and overwhelmed by the ordeal that lay ahead. Drizzle added to the gloom, as passersby in their drab clothes jostled past each other along the crowded sidewalk, bundled in their hats and scarves. Their dejected shapes cast a foreboding pall that encompassed the entire city, as newspapers had blared headlines for weeks that the communists were surging through Nationalist armies. This situation resounded to the people in horror, as though the Japanese invasion of nineteen thirty-seven were being repeated like some sort of recurring nightmare in nineteen forty-nine. Meiying picked up on the sense of doom and trembled at the similarities to those awful days so many years ago when the group fled Shanghai to begin their long journey. And yet, along with the apocalyptic undertone that undermined their morale in those terrible days, also came the liberating thrill of exodus and destination, the chance of seeing *her* again. Now, those same conflicting emotions were being repeated. Meiying slipped into the taxi next to the waiting Marie Telles, who leaned over and kissed her. With the touch of those sweet lips, exhilaration instantly swept away the fears.

~

John paused just inside the entrance to the hotel and stood on his tiptoes to see the taxi pull away, the dark heads of Meiying and Marie clearly visible in the back seat, each moving toward the other. A kiss? Words of affection? He felt no anger, only a low sag of depression. He longed to be in Marie's place, sitting next to Meiying, arranging her affairs, watching her perform, beaming in her reflected glory.

Standing next to him, Jacob Telles slapped his shoulder, and said through his cigarette smoke, "Well, John old boy, we've both been abandoned."

"Yeah." Jacob's words reminded him of Peter, and a vision of the group flashed through John's mind, making him feel somehow refreshed with the knowledge that he would soon be meeting up with them again, and Meiying would be there.

"For now," said Jacob.

"What?" asked John.

"We've been abandoned for now, but not forever, eh?"

"No, not forever."

Jacob gave a little scowl and turned away to talk with Arthur Mobley, in whose company he felt more comfortable. John Powers struck him as a rather drab, unimaginative cipher, and he pictured himself a much better husband for someone as beautiful and talented as Meiying Powers. He focused on ways to entice her away from his sister, who he felt was corrupting an innocent (and desirable) woman made for the pleasure of men. It struck Jacob that John was no threat, and therefore did not play into his calculations. But, his mind soon turned to Mr. President.

"Arthur, do we have the date we're meeting with Mr. President pinned down yet?"

"Not yet," replied Mobley, a bit testily. "That fat bastard has been putting me off, blaming the war. Hell, he'd better not be jerking my chain. We have a full schedule with other clients over the next couple of weeks, but he's the big daddy, and he damn well knows it. I'm shooting for the first week in February."

John walked up and asked, "Did I hear you talking about Mr. President?"

"Yeah," replied Jacob.

"I've been thinking about that meeting, John," said Mobley. "Perhaps it would be better if you skipped it, what with your feelings toward him and all. You can join your wife on her tour."

"No," John said firmly. "This is the one meeting I'm going to attend."

"You're not going to shoot him, are you, old fellow?" asked Jacob with a humorless chuckle.

"I just might," replied John. "But, unfortunately, probably not. However, I want to see this monster again, just to prove to myself that evil still exists in the world."

"Business is—"

John interrupted. "Damn business! In this case, damn business!"

"Like I said, John, you should not attend this meeting," said Mobley.

"You're the one who said it would exorcise my demons," objected John. He chuckled. "Don't worry, Arthur, I won't say or do anything to interfere with business. I'll be a good boy. But, I want to see him again."

"All right," replied Mobley doubtfully. "But, you must promise not to make a scene. If we end up going to his palace, it could be damn dangerous for all of us. I don't put anything past that fat bastard."

"Nor does Meiying," said John. "And nor do I."

Jacob conspicuously checked his watch. "Well, our first meeting is in a half hour. We'd better get a move on."

As they collected their briefcases, Arthur whispered to John, "Remember what you promised, John, or else."

They squeezed into a small taxi and headed off to their first meeting.

~

You are going to lose her because of these two foolish humans! cried the voice. John had not heard Goddess so infuriated. ***Do what it takes, but don't let the obese demon get his hands on her!***

Leave him alone, Dearest Goddess! came the voice of God. ***The mutant lad knows what he's doing. Does the universe care if there is another rape?***

Another murder? Given Your interest in her, it adds a pinch of flavor to the Great Wailing.

Beloved Lord, Your addiction rages on, and You mock Me with it. But, it must be stopped or You will end up a mortal wreck rather than an Immortal Spark. The son will convince Your faction that the healing of the planet has begun.

Nonsense, Lady Love! The son merely writes this gibberish. Yet another one of Your failed intermediates.

He will be born! The Reunion will happen. And You will….

~

John shook his head to dislodge the arguing voices, drawing the attention of his companions.

"You okay, John?" asked Arthur.

"Yeah, just a slight headache." John watched the crowds encroach on the taxi every time it stopped, and their anxious faces mirrored his own nerves. What if Goddess was right? What if Meiying is lost because of his foolishness? *Well,* he comforted himself. *She's not meeting Mr. President in any case. She's perfectly safe, until we meet the group and head to that damn institution. And then…. ?*

Throughout the next couple of weeks, John accompanied his two companions to meeting after meeting, all the while eagerly anticipating his upcoming rendezvous at the mansion of Master Zhou. He performed his role as business associate poorly, unable to concentrate while his mind was dominated by images of Meiying, the Precious Object, and, of course, *her.* Their forms congealed into visions of the most miraculous kind, only to have them dissolve away in the heated blast of business and commerce. To the consternation of both Mobley and Telles, Mr. President continually put off their meeting, until it became apparent that no such conference was ever intended. This revelation struck John with chilling force, for he now knew Mr. President's sole purpose for the entire charade of enticing business contracts was to get Meiying back to China. Only her tour expenses seemed genuinely to have come out of his pocket, and even then, wildly successful as her performances had been, he would reap a healthy profit. With the renewed fear of Mr. President, and the unwelcome presence of Marie Telles (who John felt sure would continue on with Meiying), he spent most of his free hours in hotel bars. Drinking made the voices bearable, and he cared little for the disapproval of Mr. Mobley. After weeks of endless negotiations, their business trip came to an end—modestly successful, but without the "home run" Mobley had hoped for.

Next stop was Hong Kong, and then back home. When they arrived at the British colony, even their planned last minute shopping spree for wives and children petered out, and they stayed in their rooms counting the hours to departure.

On the last evening before their early morning flight, John, Arthur Mobley, and Jacob Telles sat in the dark, smoky lounge of their Hong Kong hotel. The sly maneuvering by the fat man had thrown Mobley into a slow burn that now ignited into a drunken rage. Spurred by hours of drinking, Arthur's immoderate words gave John insight into the extent of Mr. President's successful manipulation of this hardened American businessman, and confirmed the ultimate purpose of the scheme.

"Damnation!" cried Arthur, slamming his fist on the table. "To be taken in by a fat Chink lying bastard!"

"Never underestimate," said John, not unhappy to see Arthur in high dudgeon.

Mobley turned his rage on John. "Well, I didn't underestimate you! Here you are, even though you were so afraid to come! And your wife? More terrified than you, yet here she is! Getting you both to this godforsaken country was the easy part. I did my bit for that obese son-of-a-bitch! And my reward? He screwed me without a thought!"

John's anger flared, but he held it in and stopped drinking, letting Mobley continue to quaff his gin. Jacob Telles sat silently, his eyes darting from John to Arthur, watching the little drama play itself out.

Mobley stared into space for a while, then turned to John with a pained expression. "But, though you're a piss poor businessman, you were right about one thing: that fat bastard is dangerous." Again, he slammed his fist on the table, and slurred, "Dangerous!"

"Yes," said John calmly. "Very dangerous."

"I mean, I don't give a rat's ass that he screws women and murders other Chinks for his own perverted reasons. I mean, that's his stick. But, when he breaks his word to an American about something as sacred as a contract, then he's a piece of shit that shouldn't be allowed to live!"

"So, his raping my wife doesn't mean anything to you?"

Arthur's face softened and he slurred, "Look, John, no offense, but you need to get over that. Harping on it does no good. She needs to get over that. Shit, that was war. But a contract. . . . "

John glanced at Jacob Telles, who averted his eyes. He looked back at Mobley and had the urge to slap his face, but instead said, "Look, Arthur, time to go to bed. Tomorrow, you leave and you don't want a hangover to ruin your morning."

"Damn Chink bastard . . . commies will get him. Sure as shit, commies will crank his fat ass."

It took some time, but John and Jacob finally got him back to his room and let him flop on his bed, fully clothed.

"Should we take his shoes off?" wondered Jacob.

"Hell, no. Let him wake up this way. You can do with him what you want. I'll be gone."

"Look here, John, let's go back to the lounge."

"Why?"

"I want to talk to you."

"About?"

"Let's go and I'll tell you there."

They returned to the lounge and slipped into a booth. Both ordered a drink, but neither took even a sip.

"It'll soon be over for Arthur and me, old fellow," said Jacob. "What I mean is, we'll be back in the good ol' land of liberty and apple pie."

"Yeah."

"And you'll still be here . . . or rather, out there, somewhere."

"Yeah."

Jacob fell silent, then smiled. "Looks like she won."

"She?"

"Yeah, my sister."

"Won what?"

"I just received word she's going with your lot into the hinterlands, you know, on your quixotic little jaunt, in search of fairies."

John slumped. "Oh, I figured."

"Hey, at least you can keep an eye on them," groused Jacob.

"Why don't you come with us?" asked John, his question dripping with sarcasm.

"Are you kidding? Too dangerous! Reds are going to be all over you."

"Aren't you worried about your sister?" More sarcasm.

Jacob answered with genuine concern, which surprised John. "Very much. I wish to hell she wasn't going, but I have no power over her. Far from it." He lit a cigarette and took a gulp of his room temperature gin and tonic. "Actually, John, I'm very worried. Look, you and I haven't really hit it off, but you're going to be with her."

"Yes, that's true enough."

Jacob tapped his glass with his ring finger nervously. "Will you watch out for her? She's terribly stubborn, and . . . well, impulsive. And, by the way, you were right about this Mr. President fellow. Arthur learned his lesson, that's for sure. And I just lost a ton of potential business. But, I don't care about that anymore. We all realize he's a nasty piece of business. And now, with the damn war, the killing, and this criminal Mr. President . . . and Marie out there in that mess, I'm really worried, John."

"So am I, Jacob. I'm worried for all of us. He's a rapist and a murderer."

"Yes, I know, but look here, John. She's new to China. Doesn't know the ropes." His eyes filled with tears. "She's going to get herself killed."

For the first time, John felt sympathy for this arrogant young man, and reevaluated his dismissive attitude. "I'll do my best, Jacob. Hopefully, everything will work out."

"But, John, this civil war is no joke. The communists don't play around. Why don't you call it off and come home with us where it's safe?"

"We can't, Jacob."

"We?"

"Meiying and I." He held out his hands, palms up. "We have a meeting that can't be missed."

Jacob stared at John's hands. "Yes, Marie told me about it. About *her*. A bit fanciful, isn't it? I mean, a bit of a lost cause, yes?"

"Yes, but more noble than dreams of being rich and powerful."

"I get your point. But, John, the danger! And Marie will be in the thick of it."

"Yes."

"Please, watch out for her," said Jacob, teary eyed and clutching John's arm for emphasis. "Bring her back to me safely."

"Jacob, I'll do my best to get us all back safely."

When they parted company, John felt reinvigorated, stronger, and looked forward more than ever to seeing Meiying at the mansion of Master Zhou to resume their quest, lost cause or not.

~ *Preliminaries – Meiying* ~

As the applause of the last concert died away, Meiying paused in her bowing and glanced toward the wings to see Marie Telles clapping and beaming with a transcendently joyous smile, just as her fantasy had ordained. She rushed offstage to hug this amazing woman who had been at her side the entire trip, acting as confidante, advisor, and lover. The tour ended in Nanjing, where Meiying had played with her most inspired passion. Even the maestro could find no fault. However, the war raged ever closer, the news of Nationalist defeats came ever more often, and the musicians were ever more anxious to leave the upheavals that savaged this unfortunate country before they became engulfed in the conflagration.

So, plans were in place to depart the next morning for Shanghai, where they would hasten back to the safety of America. The maestro, and every musician on tour advised Meiying to come with them, and they could only shake their heads in wonder when Marie Telles also insisted on staying. A final celebratory banquet on the last night, and they would scatter. With tears in his eyes, the maestro gave a speech, promising Mrs. Powers a brilliant career, if she "would not be so foolish as to get herself killed."

But, words were of no avail, and the next morning, Meiying and Marie, arm-in-arm, waved goodbye to their companions, and faced the enormity of their decision in spite of panicked headlines screaming disaster for the Nationalist government. Over breakfast, they perused the ominous news and sat back in their chairs to ponder in silence. Finally, Marie broke the unhappy spell.

"John will be here tomorrow, Meiying," she said, tossing aside the newspaper. "Let's order champagne in the room and make absolutely reckless love. Let the communists come! Surely, they have a soft spot for lovers."

"They have a soft spot for hangings and executions," said Meiying. "Really, Marie, I could not force you to leave, but I must insist you take this more seriously."

Marie's lovely face darkened. "Meiying, I'm only a bit older than you, but as I have told you many times, I'm not Miss Innocent. Of course, I realize it will be dangerous, but that is what makes life worth living."

Meiying feigned deference and bowed. "For a woman your age, Marie, that is not a very deep philosophy," she laughed.

"I can't read Confucius, dear, and even if I could, I'm quite sure he wouldn't bother with someone like me."

"Nevertheless," said Meiying, stroking Marie's hair. "I love the idea of making love tonight. And champagne would be lovely. Soon enough, time for such frivolity will be gone."

After saying these words, Meiying unexpectedly shivered, and was surprised at the power of that shiver. It portended dark, evil tidings, and she knew outside the fancy hotel stretched a beaten, shattered China, its multitudes howling at bloody wounds that never seemed to heal. It did not seem possible that she was about to throw herself back in those open sores again. The shiver was followed by many more, and she fell into such a state that Marie finally noticed.

"What's wrong?"

"Nothing."

"Nonsense. Are you cold? They do keep the air conditioning too frigid here."

"No, no, I'm fine. I'll just sip this hot tea."

Marie frowned. "It's cold. Come on, let's go back to the room and lay down together." She smiled broadly. "Besides, we can make ourselves warm and get the evening started early."

"Yes, let's go," said Meiying, her face awash in worry and dark foreboding.

~

That day and evening became a miasma of soft skin, deep kisses, and humid paths to ecstasy. They caressed, talked, laughed, loved, and repeated the process until both felt a delightful exhaustion. Meiying had not experienced such unbridled joy since Meili, and the satisfied beating of her heart sent gentle, rhythmic messages of a full life and a contented moment in the midst of a discontented time. But, each was aware that soon enough, the sun would rise, John would arrive, and they would enter into the unknown. As they lay together, Marie told Meiying the story of *Romeo and Juliet*.

"So, darling, rather than the soothing nightingale, tomorrow will bring the lark 'that sings so out of tune, straining harsh discords and unpleasing sharps.'"

"Yes, I have heard of this play. Many compositions have been written about it."

"Well, dearest," whispered Marie, circling Meiying's nipple and brushing her ear with her lips. "We have a few more hours before the horrid lark starts to sing. Let's make the most of it."

~

Dawn came, and with it the frightful knowledge that time for the free and easy joy of peace would now be replaced by the unpredictable quirks of war and violence. Both women steeled themselves for the coming ordeal, their words more sparse, their feelings more subdued, and their movements more cautious. John arrived in the afternoon and checked in to the same hotel for their last night in Nanjing before embarking on the journey. A guide, dispatched by Master Zhou, was to meet them the next morning in the lobby.

~ *Buandelgereen* ~

John had not yet arrived when Meiying and Marie entered the lobby, and they beheld a sight that sent Meiying into rapturous surprise.

"Buandelgereen!"

The Mongol woman stood like a magnificent barbarian in the middle of the bright, chandelier bejeweled lobby. Her dark hair flowed wildly down her back, her dress a long, sweeping patchwork of colorful fabrics and animal hides. Upon hearing Meiying's shouted greeting, she smiled fiercely and shifted her strong body to face the two women.

"Miss Bai!" she exclaimed loudly. "It's good to see you!"

Buandelgereen held out her arms, and the smaller Meiying was swallowed up in a bear hug. Everything about her was just as Meiying remembered, but for the absence of a rifle slung over her back. When they disentangled, Buandelgereen looked at Marie Telles quizzically.

"She's a friend," said Meiying. "She's coming with us."

Buandelgereen frowned. "An American?"

"Yes, her name is Marie Telles. Marie, this is Buandelgereen."

Marie approached boldly and thrust out her hand. Buandelgereen took it, but again looked at Meiying.

"Does she know the danger?"

"Yes."

"Does she seek *her*?"

Before Meiying could answer, Marie held out both hands, palms up, and spoke clearly and forcefully. "Yes."

Before Buandelgereen could respond, John approached and the two hugged and exchanged greetings.

"You are our guide?" asked Meiying.

"Of course."

"Oh, I am so happy! There is no doubt we will arrive safely with Buandelgereen to guide us."

The Mongol laughed. "Don't speak too soon, The roads are terrible, with bandits, Nationalists, communists, deserters everywhere."

John shook his head. "Just like the old days."

"Yes, unfortunately," said Buandelgereen.

"Have you eaten, John?" asked Marie.

"Not hungry."

"And you, Buandelgereen?"

"Yes, we must go."

"Bicycles again?" asked John.

"Of course. They are being guarded outside." Buandelgereen looked around in disgust. "We must leave this place. Time flies."

All three travelers returned to their rooms and brought down their backpacks and bundles. They double-checked their passports and papers, paid the hotel bills, and stepped outside to claim their bikes.

When they had a private moment, Marie leaned over and whispered to Meiying, "Is she?"

"Yes, the one I told you about. But, Buandelgereen has moved on to greener pastures. Besides, she also likes men—couldn't do without them to service her."

Marie exclaimed, "Oh, good!" with relief evident in her laughter.

As they set off, Buandelgereen called out, "With luck, we will be at Master Zhou's in two or three days."

Still in good humor, John shouted, "Buandelgereen, you look silly on a bicycle! You need a horse, like your ancestors!"

Passing through Nanjing, they entered the poor section and saw with dismay the clogged roads and open areas, where thousands of refugees again set up temporary shelters in the city, just like in 1937. Marie coughed from the stench, and covered her mouth and nose with a scarf, but could not help being overwhelmed by the sight. No amount of intellectual preparation could compensate for the naked reality of squalor, fear, stench, and the sheer horror of so much desperate humanity.

Meiying looked at Marie and wondered if the elegant American woman would have the stomach to see this through without becoming a burden. While lost in these thoughts, Buandelgereen pulled next to her and spoke in Chinese. "Is this woman strong enough? There is no time for coddling."

"We will see."

"Why did you let her come?"

"She insisted."

"Is she?"

"Yes."

"Well, to have one's lover along is good and bad." She looked at John, some distance behind. "How about your husband?"

"He knows."

"His voices?"

"Still there."

"Ah. We all feel his voices are important. They are a link to what we seek. I would worry if they were gone."

"They are not gone, yet I still worry."

Buandelgereen shook her head. "Your life is too complicated for me. A strong Mongol woman. A yurt. Food. Animals. A man for having children, maybe. Enough."

"Children?"

"Maybe."

Meiying laughed. "So, you have been playing also."

"You can't have all the fun!" Buandelgereen swerved when her laughter became too much. "Your husband is right! I need my horse!"

Meiying noticed her rifle had magically appeared, slung over her back, punctuating the extent of their vulnerability.

When they arrived at the outer gate of the old city wall, the guards looked at them suspiciously.

"Why are you leaving Nanjing?" asked a ragged private while his comrades crowded around, gawking at the foreigners.

"To travel to the house of a friend," replied Buandelgereen.

"You're not Chinese."

"No, Mongol."

"And these others, foreigners."

"Yes, there happen to be millions of them in the world," said Buandelgereen disdainfully.

"Wait here." The private trotted off and returned with a lieutenant in tow, who promptly stood before the group by spreading his legs and putting his hands on his hips, affecting a martial posture denoting his lofty position.

But, Buandelgereen detected fear behind the bravado, not of them, but of the future.

"Why are you leaving Nanjing?" he demanded.

Buandelgereen repeated the reason.

"With foreigners?"

"Do you have something against Americans, who happen to be our allies?"

"No, but—"

"And, do you have something against President Jiang Jieshi?"

The officer's eyes widened. "No, but—"

"And, do you have something against one of President Jiang's best friends, Master Zhou Guangli?"

"No, not at all!"

"He is the one we leave Nanjing to see."

"Oh."

"And, do you want to stay out of prison?"

The officer stammered inaudibly.

"Then let us through!"

As they put distance between themselves and the gate, Meiying enthused, "You were great, Buandelgereen!"

The Mongol woman spit. "Men are fools! That was too easy! I can't abide fools!"

John piped up. "Hey, Buandelgereen! Give us males a break. He was only following orders."

"And would walk off a cliff obeying them!" she grumbled. The Mongol then gave a scathing look at Marie, whose eyes were wide with a mix of fear and admiration. "We are past the easy part. Now, it gets hard." She looked back toward the city. "Damn fools! Sheep in a pen before the slaughter!"

Marie asked Meiying to translate. "She said, we have a distance to go."

Meiying glanced at John, who rolled his eyes. She again questioned the wisdom of allowing Marie to come.

~

At last, after biking through the squalid outskirts of Nanjing, they finally made it to the open road, a sliver of salvation upon which thousands trod to find relief from the ruins of what they left behind. On this first day, Marie was cowed into silence, constantly following Meiying with her eyes, emulating her moves, made mute by lack of language. But, she had experienced hardship in her own life, though of the emotional rather than physical variety, and she knew how to persevere. She vowed not to complain, trooping on with a quiet grit. Nevertheless, she suffered greatly from the lack of sanitary conditions, and, though disgusted with the filth and absence of privacy, managed to avoid being a burden.

On the other hand, Meiying was like a fish back in water, and could only admire Marie's determination. Even Buandelgereen paid less attention to the "fancy American lady." China's immemorial vistas opened themselves to the travelers: rice fields, small hamlets, temples, fruit groves, monasteries, all tempered in the forge of endless wars and civil strife. Even as refugees tramped directionless in their baleful millions, the peasants that stayed worked the fields like slow moving, stony protrusions from the soil itself. Meiying breathed in the damp, musky, dung-tinged air of the Chinese countryside, and felt her muscles harden and her blood quicken at the life-giving nutrients of its soul. She looked at John, whose own uncomplaining figure rode steadily forward, coping silently with his voices, and she felt resurrected from a long sleep in the mummified and desiccated American cemetery of entitlement, money and greed.

The first night, they sat around a campfire, chatting amiably while rubbing their aching bottoms. Although hard going, the trip had so far unfolded without incident, and they felt a renewed confidence that all would be well. Buandelgereen cautioned them against overconfidence, but still, they brandished such ancient weapons as hope, comradery, and humor against war's frightful array of existential threats and the knowledge of their own frail vulnerabilities, flinging into the cold universe brash words that withered as quickly as they had been uttered.

With dawn came light rain, somewhat dampening their spirits, but this second day duplicated the first, and by nightfall, their moods had improved considerably. Even Marie felt comfortable enough to laugh when Meiying translated ribald jokes from Buandelgereen's Mongol arsenal.

"We'll be there early tomorrow," announced Buandelgereen. "So far, we've been lucky."

"Not soon enough for me," said John. "These damn bikes will be the death of me."

"The bikes are the least of my concerns," said Marie. "Fortunately, I used to ride all the time in San Francisco."

But John ignored her, for he had a hard spot in his heart for this female interloper who had taken away his wife for her own, licentious reasons. The three women tried to talk around John's rude behavior toward Marie, but it colored the good will and comradery of the group. To make matters worse, Meiying and Marie slept next to each other, while John, meters away and feeling humiliated, listened to the unrelenting scorn of Goddess.

It's nineteen forty-nine, John Powers! Are you just going to sit idly by while this woman keeps her from you? Time is short! Act like a Chosen One! Be worthy to be the father of such a son!

What happened to understanding and compassion? John mentally asked.

Now is not the time. It is nineteen forty-nine!

Suddenly, a male voice intervened. ***Don't listen to Her, old man.*** It was God in Peter's voice. ***You bloody well do what you want. Meiying's long gone from you anyway. You are a man, and blokes like you don't listen to old women.***

The voices thereupon fell to arguing with each other, shouting vicious words and esoteric slurs, driving John to leave the little encampment and wander into the night, where he wept under the stars in frustration at the tenuous nature of his sanity.

Next morning, the group paused on a rise overlooking the estate of Master Zhou, and waves of excitement spread through them. Much of the old, Ming dynasty mansion had been restored from the damage caused during the war, and its gardens appeared lush and cleared of weeds.

"Here we are," proclaimed Buandelgereen calmly, sweeping her arm toward the scene below, as might a tour guide. "The first step."

Chapter Nineteen

Rejoicing and Resumption

At Last

At first, from his position on the rise, John could not make out the identity of a lone figure that came into view through the morning mist, so he leaned forward and strained his eyes, but the shadow ran back into the mansion. Soon, out poured a group of excited, gesticulating people. As he drew closer, the distinctive hump of Child of Buddha came into clear focus, followed by the stocky form of Master Zhou, and the familiarly graceful bearing of Suling. Last out of the house was big Lu Zhishen, his beard as untamed as ever. John and his companions pedaled faster to overcome a slight hill until they plunged down amidst a chorus of greetings, hugs, and solicitations. Master Zhou, tears in his eyes, was the first to address the entire assemblage.

"My children have returned! Thank god, my children have returned! Welcome! Come in! Come in! We have much to discuss."

He fell silent and gazed at Meiying and Marie. "But, I am sure, there is a little matter of hot baths. No?"

"Yes, indeed!" exclaimed Meiying, kissing him on the cheek. She stepped back. "This is Marie Telles."

"So I have heard," replied Master Zhou, sizing up Marie with a critical tilt of his head. "Word travels ahead of you—even faster than bicycles!" He turned to Marie and spoke in English. "You are welcome, my dear."

"Thank you," replied Marie in her best, mangled Chinese.

"Very good, very good."

John felt particularly pleased to see Suling, and he walked into the house with his arm affectionately around her waist. Lu Zhishen strode between Meiying and Marie, roaring his Canadian joy. Child of Buddha and Buandelgereen followed behind, casting furtive glances at each other, and whispering secretively.

Once they had cleaned up, the group met in the large dining hall for a welcome banquet. Memories of the mansion came back to John as vividly as if he had left just days ago. The voices seemed to have exhausted themselves, and his spirits lifted considerably when he sat next to Suling at a table surrounded by his old comrades. Soon, however, the mood would darken when Master Zhou clinked his wine cup with a chopstick and rose.

"As you know, Peiping has fallen and the communists will soon cross the Yangtze. Their armies are unstoppable, and Mao Zedong will rule by the end of the year. With them, this old mansion will be swept away, and I with it."

"No!" came a chorus of shouts.

"Unless," he smiled. "I'm not here when they come. And, that is precisely my plan. However," his expression became a fierce glare. "Where we go will be controlled by them. But—" he cast significant glances at John, Marie, and Lu—"Our American friends . . . and, of course, our Canadian friend . . . may be the keys to getting us through to the institution. Once there. . . . " he paused and threw up his hands. "Who knows what we'll find. Still, Mao wants no more trouble from the United States if he can help it, so I think we will be reasonably safe on the roads." He held up a cautionary finger. "But, of course, there are no guarantees. We may lose our heads. Now is the time, if any of you want to turn back."

John looked at Marie, whose pale face reflected a terror he had not seen before. It gave him a perverse pleasure to see this rich, smug, confident American woman frightened and utterly dependent on others. He interjected a statement calculated to achieve the most sympathy from Meiying. "Miss Telles, I think I speak for all of us when I urge you to return to Nanjing, and leave China as quickly as possible. You are at a greater disadvantage than any of us, what with your lack of language skills, and your inexperience." He looked at Meiying. "I think my wife would agree with me."

Meiying turned to Master Zhou. "May I have a moment to speak with Miss Telles?" she asked in a slow and dignified tone.

"Of course."

Meiying conspicuously took Marie's hand and they walked to an adjoining room. The group remained at the table, glancing at each other, but not speaking. They heard voices raised in the next room, but individual words were indistinguishable. When the two re-entered, Meiying appeared crestfallen, but Marie spoke up in a clear, strong voice.

"I am going with you. There is no possibility of changing my mind. If you try and leave me behind, I will simply follow."

"In that case," sighed Master Zhou, "I will make the arrangements."

"Is the institution still managed by Reverend Fu and Master Li?" asked John.

"Yes."

"Are you in contact with them?"

"So far."

"Do we know we will see *her* at this . . . asylum?"

"That is something I cannot answer. All I can say is that *she* summoned us."

"How?"

"Through Feng Shiren and Buandelgereen."

"What?!" cried Meiying and John together.

"Mr. Feng, through a dream, or a vision, if you will, and Buandelgereen directly. Word came via the Flaming Cliffs Mongols."

"It will take weeks to get there."

"Yes. The bicycles will cut the time, if the roads aren't too bad."

The banquet broke up into a mix of fragmented conversations when, at last, Meiying had the chance to break away. She visited the garden and sat in the gazebo where she had talked with Meili so long ago. Tears rolled down her cheeks at the memories, and in her reverie did not see Marie standing nearby. After some time had passed, Marie finally broke the spell, saying softly, "Did you know Master Zhou has a piano?"

"Oh, yes. I remember, years ago, Little Acorn rushed in to tell me. He was so excited."

"People are asking if you would play."

"Maybe later."

"May I sit?"

"Of course."

And so, the two women talked, hugged, and prepared themselves for the ordeal that would change their lives, or end them.

~ *It Begins* ~

The first week of their journey unfolded relatively smoothly. Refugees often blocked the way, but the fighting was always far away. Spirits were high, and everyone felt relieved at the lack of problems. But, at the beginning of the second week, calamity swept down upon them, not from the communists, but from fleeing Nationalist troops. It had hardly been an hour after they had returned to the main road from their hidden campsite when a panicked army remnant fleeing some major battle collided with a surge of milling refugees. Shoved off to the side by the sheer bulk and weight of a free-falling rout, the group held their bikes and watched in horror as gangs of soldiers broke off like metastasizing clumps of cells to wreak havoc on the civilians cowering around them amongst the tremulous grasses.

One vicious band of soldiers, in the process of picking over helpless victims, cast their ravenous eyes on Meiying and Marie. With a crazed frenzy of churning legs and flailing arms, the soldiers barged their way through the strewn wreckage of people, advancing directly toward the two women. Refugees on either side of this assault shrank back from them in rippling waves, like a school of fish cleaved by sharks.

"A foreigner!" howled the soldiers. "Beauties!"

Without a thought, the men of the group—Master Zhou, John, and Lu Zhishen, planted themselves in front of the women. Suling and Child of Buddha covered the two as best they could. Buandelgereen was nowhere to be seen. In a few breathtaking moments, a string of rifles pointed at the rather pathetic defensive line of men.

"Out of the way, or we kill all of you!"

It seemed the world held its breath, and only the distant birds could be heard, oblivious to the drama. Swarms of refugees who had not already fled took this chance to silently move away, leaving the two sides to face each other in a perverse tableau.

From somewhere nearby, the sound of a cartridge entering a chamber was heard, and Buandelgereen walked forward, her rifle pointing at a soldier who appeared to be the leader.

"Leave!" she commanded.

Overcoming his initial shock, the soldier unexpectedly laughed. "Go ahead, bitch! We'll all be dead soon enough! You kill me, all of you will die. Count the rifles pointed at you. There are sixteen of us here. All we want are these two, then we'll return them and you can be on your way."

Buandelgereen seemed to make a quick calculation. "I need collateral to make sure you return them alive."

The soldiers looked at each other in amazement at the absurdity of this brazen woman's demand. No one was willing to lower their weapons, so without turning his head, the leader said, "All right, bitch. Two of us will stay, then be relieved when it's their turn."

"No," said Buandelgereen. "Four stay, no weapons, and no turns. Too many, fool. My friends will die."

"Stupid woman!" shouted the men. "Let's kill her!"

Buandelgereen took a step forward and adjusted her rifle to point directly at the leader's head.

A smile spread across his face, and for the first time, his mask of brutality slipped away, and a rough intelligence shone through. "So, the lady wants to drive a hard bargain, with one rifle?"

Grumbling among the men.

"Shut up!" he commanded fiercely.

They immediately fell quiet, while Buandelgereen measured the true extent of his seemingly iron control, holding her rifle steady and not saying a word.

Again, the leader smiled.

"Agreed, with some exceptions," he said as if negotiating for a few bags of rice. "All four weapons will be placed on the ground between us. If any of you go for them, the others will return and kill all of you. Also, when my comrades are done, I don't want those two weak reeds. I want you, for I will be one that will stay."

"And when you are fucking me, who will protect my people?"

"We'll call a truce. My men will return to the main column, and your weapon will be in the hands of one of these"—he looked with distain at the four men—"heroes."

"Correction," said Buandelgereen. "My weapon, yours, and the other three will be in the hands of these heroes."

This dangerous man, his dominance challenged, seemed to enjoy matching wits with a strong woman. "That still leaves twelve to four. If I agree, and my men are gone—I like my privacy—what's to prevent you from killing me instead of letting me fuck you?"

"Nothing, but my word as a Mongol woman."

"Ha! Mongols are known liars!"

"Mongol women fuck hard, and you look like a hard man."

The man's eyes glittered. "When we have done our business, I will take the four rifles and be gone. You will be allowed to remain alive and safe."

His men were becoming restless, tired of holding up their rifles, craving the flesh of Meiying and Marie with wide-eyed agitation the longer they looked.

"Oh, god, oh, god," came the words of Marie, shivering as though she sat in a vat of ice water. Meiying had her arms around the terrified American woman. John's satisfaction at her predicament had long since evaporated into a feeling of deep pity and impotent hatred toward the soldiers.

Against the background noise of a whimpering Marie Telles, Master Zhou said, "These are American citizens. You will be hanged if you touch them."

"Weak reeds!" the leader spat. "My men can have them." He stared admiringly at Buandelgereen. "But you will be worth the risk, I am certain!"

"One way to find out," she replied calmly.

Names were shouted and three adolescent soldiers, looking to be barely sixteen and clearly inferior to the others, grudgingly gave up their rifles, and Meiying and Marie were dragged away.

As they were being forced into the bushes, Meiying cautioned Marie in English, "No screaming! It will be worse if you scream! Think of other things. Close your eyes and think of other things. Think of us together, if we can survive. We must survive! Close your eyes, dear!"

~

The males of the group stood in agony, staring at their four soldier-counterparts across a pile of rifles. Male laughter and primal groans, mixed with female sobs and cries of pain, were heard from behind the bushes. Assaulted by the horrific sounds, John could not keep tears from flowing freely down his face, but he dared not look away from the soldiers and their weapons. Buandelgereen imperiously refused to give up her rifle, and stood like granite, stone-faced and resolute, staring toward the obscene, interminable sounds of multiple rapes.

Sitting cross-legged, the leader gazed at Buandelgereen and felt some movement in his heart that cleaved it to the core. The muffled screams and throaty groans grated on his ears, and the brutality of his men sickened him even as their moans excited him. In a sort of agony of conflicting emotion, he could not remain quiet, and had to engage Buandelgereen in order to block out the howls of iniquity that came from the bushes.

"What is your name?" he asked.

"That you will never know," she replied contemptuously.

He tried to keep up his bravura image. "Ha! You have no sympathy for a soldier about to die for his country?"

"You are a rapist, a criminal. No sympathy. You will rot in hell."

He laughed. "No room in hell, it's already full from this war."

"Your officers will hang you for raping an American."

"I *am* an officer."

Buandelgereen scoffed. "Then, China is truly done for."

The sounds of Suling crying reached his ears. He wanted to say some harsh sarcasm, but he turned his head away. After what seemed an endless period of time, the two women hobbled back, hollow-eyed and half-dead, shivering and groaning in pain with each step, their clothes hanging in tatters from their battered bodies.

"Well?" said Buandelgereen, staring at the officer with venomous wrath. "Call off your men. I'll fulfill my end of the bargain when the dogs are gone."

"Go back to the road!" he barked at his men. "I'll join you later. Consider this a gift from a grateful army."

The soldiers, many of them spent, some of them sheepish, some muttering obscenities, melted away, leaving the officer alone. He glanced at the two women, now being ministered to by Suling and Child of Buddha. "It was their patriotic duty," he murmured.

"The American?" asked Buandelgereen.

"An ally. We all must do our duty."

"Well?" she asked again. "Are you going to rape me also, hero? I promised, so I won't hurt you." She lowered her weapon. "I have had spider bites that will feel more than your puny cock."

The officer stared at her incredulously. "Damn! You are a woman after my own heart! I don't want to rape you, woman! I am not one of those flea-bitten dogs."

"What do you want?"

He looked down like a little boy in trouble. "Your name," he mumbled.

"What?"

"Your name, damn it! Your name is more important to me than your cunt."

"You have been promised one, but not the other."

"Then I will exchange the cunt for the name."

"Why so anxious for my name?"

"Because, if we survive this war, I'm coming back to find you." He grinned as if she would find this an irresistible proposition. "Are you married?"

"No."

"Then, I will marry you!" He beat his chest for emphasis. "I, killer of many Japs and communists, lover of many women, young and old, will marry the one woman who challenged me! A Mongol, no less!"

Buandelgereen looked at him intently. "Are you man enough?"

"You have never met a man like me, not even in your dreams! Now, for the exchange: your name for your cunt. Otherwise, I take your cunt now, in front of them, and piss on you afterward!"

"That exchange I will gladly make. First, give us your rifle, and I will tell you my name."

His eyes narrowed, then he shrugged. "Your name and your home village."

"More conditions?"

"Yes, since you ask for my rifle. Besides, I have to be able to find you when this madness is done."

"Agreed, give it over."

They stared openly at each other, and he broke into raucous laughter. "Damn! What a woman!"

"Hand it over," she repeated.

As he handed the rifle to Lu Zhishen, he shrugged, "I know I'm a fool, but I have never met a woman like you. Now, your part of the bargain.""My name is Buandelgereen of the Mongol village of Baotou, home of the Wudang Zhao temple."

"My name is Ling Wudan of Taoyuan district. I will come for you after the war." He bowed and spoke as might a gentleman. "Let us go a few steps and talk, Buandelgereen."

"You will not survive the war, Ling Wudan." Buandelgereen raised her rifle and shot him in the head, walked up and shot him again, this time through the heart. No one said a word for shocked moments.

Master Zhou finally exclaimed, "We must leave, now!"

Suling objected. "Meiying and Miss Telles cannot travel."

"They must, or we are all dead!"

Meiying spoke up in a weak but clear voice. "We will go, but we must go slowly. The bleeding will not stop." She did not look at Marie, but heard no objections.

Suling and Child of Buddha helped them to their feet. "It is necessary," said the hunchback simply. "But, we must stop often for the bleeding." She looked at the dead officer. "Fools, should have taken me!"

Marie broke into convulsive sobs. Meiying went to her.

"We must leave, now!" cried Master Zhou, looking at the corpse, then down the road. Slowly, the dark outlines of a few curious refugees moved cautiously toward them, and in the distance, soldiers stirred.

"Now!"

~ *To Go On?* ~

Kilometers later, the group camped far off the main road. Buandelgereen had scouted ahead, and found a clearing near a small stream. When the sleeping areas were prepared, neither Meiying nor Marie Telles had said a word. Suling and Child of Buddha led them to the stream and helped them bathe.

At first, Marie could not stop crying, but she abruptly ceased and violently trembled in silence. After bathing, she began talking rapidly about unrelated subjects, reminiscing about San Francisco, laughing at inappropriate places, then shrieking in agony. The women let her talk, knowing she was in the grip of deep shock. Meiying, on the other hand, remained steadfastly silent, listening to Marie's babble and feeling the unbearable weight of guilt added to an already unbearable amount of pain and anger. Neither ate.

Suling and Child of Buddha agreed between themselves to sit up all night with the two damaged women, for they feared Meiying would kill herself, or Marie Telles would die from shock, or both. John, Master Zhou, and Lu Zhishen tried to give words of comfort, but both women insisted they would see no males, so the men sat miserably around a small fire and talked.

"Do we go on?" asked Lu Zhishen.

"We can't!" replied John bitterly. "They need medical help. We must go back. Look, the mental institution is past Taiyuan. We still have a week or longer to go! We must go back!""

"Where?" asked Master Zhou. "To what? The Nationalist army, such as it is, stands between us and Nanjing. Besides, we're closer to the institution."

"Yeah, but the communists are out there," said John, looking out at the darkness.

"But, so is *she*," said Master Zhou. "Besides, soon the communists will be everywhere, including Nanjing."

Lu nodded vigorously. "True, and the institution would provide care and comfort for the women."

"Yeah, if we can make it there alive," said John.

"We must make it there!" exclaimed Master Zhou vehemently. "No choice. We can't go back. We will circumvent Taiyuan."

"One thing is certain, we can't take the main roads," said Lu.

"No."

"Do any of you remember how we got there the last time—I mean, the back way?" asked Master Zhou.

"Sure. I remember climbing up a cliff to get there," said Lu.

"But, do you remember how to get to that cliff?"

"That was years ago," said John.

"I don't have a clue," added Lu.

Child of Buddha stepped into the light, her incongruously lovely face ablaze with fury, the shadow of her hump a grotesque protrusion, beetle-like and ominous. "I will show you the way. I know the area by heart."

"You know how to find those small trails to the cliffs?" asked John.

"Yes, of course. Remember, they let me roam freely in the beginning. I explored everywhere. I wanted to escape. So many times, I wanted to jump off those cliffs. So many times."

Buandelgereen appeared beside her. "Good! We go on!"

"How about them?" asked Lu Zhishen, nodding toward the place where the injured women rested.

Child of Buddha shrugged. "If they get through this night, they will survive. Then, we will see."

Buandelgereen cleared her throat gruffly. "You men must be patient, especially you, John. They are in great pain, and your efforts must be to make it easier to heal. That means all of you must be there only when asked, and offer ears to listen, not tongues to give advice."

Nods of agreement all around.

No one slept. With the dawn, all eyes were focused in the direction where Meiying and Marie Telles lay, hidden from view behind thick brush and shrubs. Suling appeared and informed the group the two women were awake.

Master Zhou said apologetically, "Suling, we must keep moving. If the Nationalists find us, we're all dead."

"We're in communist territory now," corrected Buandelgereen.

"Well, they'll kill us just as easily."

Suling broke in. "The bleeding has stopped, but both are very sore."

"Can they ride?"

"We will walk our bikes," came Meiying's voice weakly as she emerged from the underbrush.

The men jumped up, mindful of Buandelgereen's warning, and afraid to say a word.

"Are you sure?" asked Suling.

"Yes."

"And Miss Telles?"

Meiying's haggard face darkened, and she faltered. "She will also walk her bike."

Marie suddenly emerged beside Meiying, boldly took her hand and kissed her on the cheek. The two women collapsed in each other's arms, crying without restraint. John started forward, but Suling stopped him.

"Not now."

~ *Onward to the Institution* ~

A few days passed, and the tattered little group slowly inched toward the mental institution. Back roads, small trails, loops, and detours, finally led them to the narrow trail that wended its dusty way to the cliffs.

"This will take us to where we want to go," said Child of Buddha matter-of-factly.

A small celebration occurred. Some of the old comradery had returned, and cautious bantering began to be tossed about. Meiying and Marie remained very sore, but they gradually reached the point where they could ride for short distances, and their spirits showed subtle, but perceptible signs of recovery. The others' jokes actually helped them to block the awful memories, so they listened tolerantly but did not participate. Neither wanted the incident mentioned, even obliquely, and both struggled mightily to bury the anguish and regain some degree of normalcy for themselves and a semblance of reassurance to the group.

"Hey, Master Zhou!" shouted Lu Zhishen. "Remember that crazy old man who thought we were demons?"

"Of course, his name was . . . let's see . . . it was . . . I forget!"

Child of Buddha laughed. "His name is Grandfather Ma, or was. I wonder if he's still alive?"

"Well," joked Master Zhou. "He was a tough old bird. And, if he is alive, the old demons have returned."

"It will be good to see Reverend Fu and Master Li again," mused Child of Buddha.

"Good ol' Fu-Li!" cried Lu. "Fu-Li! Li-Fu!"

Meiying's thoughts turned to the old photograph of *her* which she came across in the "No Admittance" room at the institution, and she recalled the strange story Reverend Fu so hesitantly disclosed about *her* obese son. A sudden heaviness bore down upon Meiying's heart, and she closed her eyes to block the presentiments of foreboding and dread. She knew with certainty that one more trauma like the last would kill her. She felt this in her womb, and the notion of having John's son now seemed an iron-clad impossibility. Even the touch of Marie sometimes made her cringe, and she felt sure the damage that had been inflicted must preclude any thought of having children—ever. Meiying suddenly came to the realization that, in spite of her past protests to John that she would never have his son, the idea had insinuated itself into her heart, and at times she had allowed herself to imagine it as a joyous possibility. *All that is another's person's past*, she thought. *I am no longer that person.* It seemed her life, once so full of hope in the States, now filtered through her fingers like dust, and the triumph of her homecoming concert only accentuated the bleakness unfolding on all sides. The presence of Marie was no longer comforting, but a harsh reminder of her foolish selfishness in allowing the woman to come. Only *she* remained as a hope—a thread Meiying grasped with delicate ferocity, for she knew of its propensity to snap. And, in that event, free fall downward into oblivion would be her only recourse.

Eventually, they stood at the base of the cliff, as they had done so many years earlier. John looked up at the rim, but saw no inmates gawking down at them as before. No Grandfather Ma to scold them. No sign of life.

"Well," observed Lu Zhishen. "No welcoming committee this time."

"We are entering through the back door," said Master Zhou.

"Don't look forward to those damn switchbacks," said John.

"Come," said Child of Buddha quietly. "We need to go, it's getting late."

Meiying asked her first question since the day of the incident. "Are you excited, Child of Buddha?"

Everyone looked as if some milestone had been reached, and John felt tears well in his eyes.

"Oh, yes. It is strange, having been in that cage for so long, but it seems like home."

"No more jumping off cliffs?" asked Master Zhou kindly.

"No. Helping others not jump will be my life from now on."

"Thank god, thank god," murmured Master Zhou.

Buandelgereen, as usual, provided the catalyst. "If we are to go, then we go! Talk later!" She strode onto the first switchback and began the climb. The others followed wordlessly, their energies soon focused on ascending the steep trail. Dark shadows enveloped them as the sun began its descent behind the rim, and the slog seemed endless. John often paused to hunch over and gulp for air, using the opportunity to cast glances up at the edge, but still no figures appeared, and he continued to worry. The red blush of dusk rolled spectacularly above them, and the lure of hot food and soft beds spurred them on.

~

Once they reached the top, it was nearly dark, and the institution loomed before them awash in electric light. This unexpected sight lifted their spirits, and they moved quickly around toward the front of the great, concrete structure. But, before they reached the main entrance, a host of happy and curious patients surrounded them, laughing and giggling like well-fed children. Out from this joyful throng popped Reverend Fu and Master Li, smiling broadly and holding out their arms in greeting. Over ten years had passed, but they both retained their lusty health and playful humor.

Master Zhou cried at the sight of them, and the three old men hugged in silent homage to the years and the suffering. Buandelgereen and Marie Telles, the only members of the group that were strangers here, shuffled uneasily at the open and unabashed attention of the inmates, trying to answer the multitude of childlike questions and endure their gawking curiosity.

John, attuned to Meiying and Marie Telles, watched in satisfaction the smiles that came to the two scarred women in response to such innocent expressions of welcome and acceptance. This was the first time since the incident he had seen either of them react to others with any display of affection, but these gentle souls seemed to act as a balm to their shattered nerves. Yet, even as he warmed to the displays, he knew that deep within the bowels of the institution were locked cells that harbored the violent and most horribly afflicted of the mentally ill. His future self, or worse, his future son, crouched in one of those filthy cells, waiting. Or so he feared.

Reverend Fu and Master Li had instructed the ageless old cook to have food ready for the expected visitors, and once in the cafeteria, a nutritious meal was consumed with much laughter and rubber-necking by the inmates. John continued to observe and savor the engagement of Meiying and Marie Telles with the world through the healing kindness and guileless joy of these simple people. Watching their re-emergence from utter despair to new hope, he felt the hard edges of his own resentment and jealousy smoothed away by waves of empathy and generosity; as if in a flash of time, he had aged into the forgiving wisdom of old age. Yet, he was not old, and felt a deep-seated appreciation that such knowledge came to one so young.

So, Chosen One, while you dawdle so self-satisfied, it is time to deposit your mutant seed in her. The reckoning has come! God knows, enough must

have built-up behind the dam. Now is the time, while you dwell in this madhouse—a fitting environment for the spilling of your seed!

At this electrifying intrusion, John leapt up and asked to be excused. Master Li gave him the key to his room, and he rushed off, to the amazement of the assembled.

"Is he okay?" asked Reverend Fu.

"It is his voice," said Meiying, breaking another barrier. "All of us are cursed, in one way or another."

"That may be, child," said Reverend Fu. "But, all of us are also blessed"—he smiled and added—"in one way or another."

"Speaking of which," interjected Lu Zhishen. "We have come very far, and have suffered greatly to reach this place. When can we expect to see *her*?"

Reverend Fu held out his arm toward Master Li. "He will explain."

Li straightened in his chair, and all eyes turned on him expectantly. Even the patients fell silent.

"This is what I know: it began when I could not sleep many months ago. The war, concerns for our children here, financial worries, all plagued my mind. I lay in bed, unable to get comfortable, as if something kept poking and prodding me. So, vexed at my restless state, I rose and came here, to the cafeteria, to fix tea. In fact, I think I sat in this very chair, sipping my tea by candlelight—the electricity had once again been cut—when he arrived; a person whose face I could not distinguish in the dark.

"I said, 'Hello,' thinking it was Reverend Fu. 'Can't sleep either?' To my amazement, the figure suddenly contorted into a hideous shape, and I thought it was one of our children having a spasm—"

"Yup! That was Feng Shiren all right!" roared Lu Zhishen. "Him and his damn opera!"

"Well," continued Master Li. "When the figure held its pose and would not respond to my greetings, I knew it was not a spasm, but felt quite angry because our children should all be in bed, and here was one of them cutting a ridiculous posture and not responding to me."

"Oh!" cried Reverend Fu, popping up and looking about. "That reminds me, our children here need to be tucked in. It's late! Especially for this story. They will have nightmares. Pause for a while, Master Li."

"Yes, yes," bustled Li. "I had lost track of time."

The two kindly caretakers rushed about, trundling their charges to bed, while the group waited impatiently for the story to continue. John noticed Child of Buddha inconspicuously assisting with the patients, while Reverend Fu and Master Li accepted her help without a word of surprise or protest, as if she had been performing this service forever. Their unquestioning acceptance of her new role made John realize how self-absorbed and foolishly young he still behaved, when presented with the undeniable verisimilitude of the wiser old ones. His earlier self-congratulatory notion of how wise he had become now seemed premature.

After seeing their "children" to their beds, Master Li continued his story. "Anyway, as I was saying, this strange figure stood before me, as frozen in its bizarre position as a statue, and I rubbed my eyes to wipe away the dream. But, then it spoke. 'You must bring the seekers to this place. It must be soon! The one who once worked here will make an appearance! *She* makes this command on the authority of all that you hold sacred!' With this announcement, the figure simply vanished."

"That's it?' asked Lu Zhishen.

"Yes."

"But, it was probably just a dream!" exclaimed Lu angrily. "We made this trip on such a flimsy basis?"

Li held up his hand and smiled. "But, that is not all."

"Oh, sorry."

"The very next day, a stranger arrived from Mongolia. He asked if a visitor had made an appearance during the night. Of course, just as you suggested, Mr. Lu, I had dismissed the strange figure as nothing more than a dream, but now I wondered, so I asked, 'What visitor?' He replied, 'A shadow.' Then he said, 'Weren't you given a message? Is this not so?'"

Reverend Fu broke in. "Of course, I knew nothing of this vision, and I assured our Mongol friend we were given no such message, but my old friend here corrected me, and the story finally came out. The visitor smiled and said he came from beyond the Flaming Cliffs of Mongolia, and that, just as the vision had said, *she* commanded us to bring you all back. We explained that you were all scattered to the four winds, and we did not know how to reach you. The Mongol looked around with a strange fire in his eyes, and said, 'This place must be where the gathering occurs. You will find them by contacting Master Zhou Guangli, who may be found here.' Then he handed me an address, and said, 'Failure to act on this command will result in dire consequences to you and your patients.' With that, he left."

"So," said Master Zhou. "You have no idea of when or how *she* will make *her* appearance?"

"Alas, no."

"We have been through this before," grumbled Lu Zhishen.

"No iron door this time," offered John.

Lu sighed deeply. "It seems like we're reliving a sort of nightmare, running to get to our destination, but never actually arriving."

"So, what do we do now?" asked Master Zhou.

"Wait," replied Reverend Fu.

"How long and for what?" asked John.

Master Li laughed. "Those, my boy, are the grand questions. Presumably, *she* will make *her* appearance when the time is right."

"Great," grumbled Lu Zhishen. "More waiting."

Suling, happy to be in such a safe and loving environment, said, "We've waited this long. I'm content."

"As am I, although I wish we had the Precious Object with us," considered Master Zhou.

"Oh, didn't I tell you?" exclaimed Master Li with a sly laugh. "Our Mongol visitor left us a gift on the veranda when he left."

"What!" came a chorus of shocked voices.

"Yes, a statue of a Goddess. Quite beautiful, but very noisy, I'm afraid." He put on a tragic face. "We had to put it in a private room."

"Where is this room?" cried Lu Zhishen.

Reverend Fu broke in. "Well, it's on a different floor, in a room that is strictly off limits to our children." He looked at Meiying and flashed her a knowing smile. "It has a "No Admittance" sign on it."

~ *Meiying and Marie* ~

The presence of Marie Telles had been all but overlooked by members of the group—except by Meiying. While the violence and brutality of the rapes had left both women devastated, nevertheless, Meiying had the facility of the language and could follow what transpired from moment-to-moment just by listening. She could, at least, understand others and deflect her thoughts from the awful memories.

Marie had no such advantage, so she had spent her time after the rape folded deep within her battered psyche, disconnected from the events occurring so incomprehensibly around her, and berating herself for plunging so stupidly into such madness. Truly a stranger in this war-torn country, she reached out to Meiying as the lifeline she so desperately needed. Now, more than ever dependent on this talented Chinese woman, she had an even deeper admiration for her courage and unwavering kindness. Marie knew Meiying blamed herself for the rapes, and in normal times, she might have held this over her head as a sort of blackmail. But here, the circumstances were so deplorable, she clung even tighter to her lover. Now that they had reached the institution, Marie felt safer, and her bond with Meiying intensified amid the security of their repeated pledges of devotion to each other. John had long since given up the façade of marriage, and the two women shared a room at the institution. That night, they talked more freely and naturally than they had since the rapes.

"Thank god for soft beds," said Marie, stroking Meiying's breast.

"Yes, it feels so good to be clean."

"So, Meiying, what now?" asked Marie.

"What do you mean?"

"Well, what will this magical woman do? Appear from thin air? Arrive in a burst of thunder and lightning?"

Meiying remained serious, which impressed Marie. Apparently, there was no room for levity when it came to this woman.

"Honestly, Marie, I do not know what to expect. *She* has come to all of us in the most unexpected times, and in other cases, *she* has disappointed. If we all sat tomorrow in a circle and assiduously chanted, *she* would not come. But, the next day, when we had written *her* off, *she* would appear."

"I think I understand," said Marie, happy to have her thoughts diverted from something other than the existential crisis of her rape. "But, and here is my real question, when *she* does come, why or what is the transforming nature of *her* presence? I mean, what does *she* do to impress you all so deeply?"

"That's just it!" exclaimed Meiying. "No one knows until afterward."

"Well, then how do you know afterward?"

Meiying became agitated, frustrated with Marie for asking such obvious questions, and frustrated with herself for not being able to answer them. "Ah, that is hard to explain, but *she* leaves you with a fresh will to live, like an inner glow to warm you from the cold, cold universe." Meiying shook her head. "No, that's not totally it. I can't explain." She stood and lit a lantern. "Look, come with me!"

After throwing on their nightgowns, Meiying took Marie's hand and led her downstairs, through a complicated maze of hallways until they reached a door over which a faded sign read, "No Admittance." She hesitated, then turned the knob and slowly pushed it open. From the far corner came an unnatural glow, startling Meiying, who quickly swung her lantern over to illuminate the Precious Object. Marie gasped when Goddess came fully and shockingly into sharp relief.

... Tap. Tap. Tap....

"My god!" blurted Marie as she stared at the statue in wonder. "What is that noise?"

Receiving no response, she turned to look at Meiying, but found her companion distracted, her eyes searching a wall covered in framed pictures, moving the lantern from one to the other. Finally, Meiying paused, holding the light up to an old photograph, gazing upon it with the frozen look of a person hypnotized. With the strange figurine tapping behind her, and Meiying staring at a picture that fairly pulsated with some sort of dim luminescence, Marie sensed the presence of multiple spirits, and felt a chilling terror.

"Meiying!" she whispered harshly.

No response.

"Meiying!" she repeated.

Finally, Meiying turned to her and smiled preternaturally, but did not speak.

"What are you looking at?"

"Nothing."

... Tap.Tap.Tap....

The tapping grew louder and faster.

"My god, what is that?" demanded Marie, again turning to look at the statue, afraid it might be moving toward them.

Meiying tore her eyes away from the photo. "Nothing. Let's go!"

Without another word, Meiying led Marie back to their room. To Marie, they could not move fast enough, and she felt only relief at escaping that haunted place. Once safely behind their closed door, she nervously engaged Meiying in calming small talk while undressing for bed. But, before turning out the light, Meiying said in a disappointed voice, "I wanted to show you, but you'll just have to see for yourself."

Neither of them had noticed Child of Buddha slip into the "No Admittance" room as they left.

~

Hours later, Marie Telles lay next to the sleeping Meiying, reviewing the trip and contemplating how its most wrenching moment had changed her. She grew up in a life of privilege, surrounded by servants and chauffeurs, while private schools and tutors, both formal and informal, honed her talents as a sophisticate. Yet, her entire life had been a long and dreary trudge of form over substance, image over character, safety over risk, and half lies over whole truths; her curse being the intelligence to recognize and resent such incarcerating deficiencies. She wore the nicest clothes, trendiest shoes, most tasteful jewelry, but always felt naked. She spoke the most sophisticated words, hob-nobbed with the richest and most powerful people, and could keep up a fast-paced repartee with poets and politicians, but felt a numbing poverty of speech. She had vast experience with men of all types, the grasping and the groveling, yet she felt like a helpless skater, gliding to old age over the frictionless surface of an icy world, bereft of any meaningful challenges. Awareness of her lesbianism early on further narrowed freedom of movement, constraining her yearning impulse to taste life at its fullest. Although she had a lover for many years, they lived their lives in a secret cloister, cut off from the wider world.

Through the decades, from girlhood onward, this tremendous, raw torrent of desire to experience danger and adventure had been discouraged, capped, and intricately plumbed to trickle in a thousand harmless directions by her parents and the claustrophobic society of her stylish peers. Such control left her spirit just enough allowance to squeeze through a maze of narrow channels, and find outlet only through carefully regulated spigots that opened in constricted, safe, watery streams; but with the knowledge that even these circumscribed trickles of freedom could be closed so tightly as to not allow a single drop of unseemly excess. Marie Telles was the female version of a man bored with life, overly protected, boxed in, who wants to go to war and test his mettle, but is too afraid, or too comfortable, to take the plunge.

Then Meiying Powers entered her life.

When they first met, every instinct driving Marie was to keep Meiying as a pet; she would play the more cosmopolitan, worldly woman giving guidance, tutorial sex, and nurturing love to this beautiful novice. But, it quickly became apparent this role would not satisfy. Meiying, young as she was, had seen more life—real life, dirty and violent—than Marie could imagine, yet still retained her grace and charm. Marie's sophisticated persona and cynical blueprint for seduction fell flat, not to Meiying, but to Marie herself. Much to her surprise, she found their roles reversed, and Meiying's difficult, stormy past became a siren call to Marie; a beckoning to follow her long-repressed desire to test herself against the worst life could throw at her; to either taste the sweet siren song for herself, or die upon the rocks trying. She had briefly lost her nerve and fled, not because of guilt over her brother's shameless actions, but for fear she would succumb to the call. It constituted her effort to tie herself to the mast and plug her ears. All to no avail. So, she returned to confront Meiying that night at Symphony Hall and express her determination to go in no uncertain terms; to bind herself and leave no room for escape. This time, she was determined to open the floodgates.

And now, because of my stupid, stupid insistence on coming, I've had my adventure! she thought bitterly. *Raped! Raped many times by disgusting, filthy men! For what? Experiencing life? Oh, god! Oh, god, what a fool!*

She shuddered at the awful memories—the animal grunts, the obscene laughter, the stench, the pain, the humiliation. *And still, it's not over. I'm in the middle of this dirty country with death and destruction all around. No way out. For what? Stupid, stupid, stupid!*

But, Marie Telles knew she was far from stupid. In fact, she came to believe it was her restless intelligence, not mere boredom, that caused dissatisfaction with life in San Francisco. Furthermore, she staked her sanity on that same intelligence to lead her out of the mire of disillusionment and despair she now felt. In order to achieve this, she must analyze herself from some objective, out-of-body viewpoint. With this in mind, she stepped back and took mental inventory, skewed, as she felt compelled, toward the positive.

First, I've gotten my wish—I've experienced horror and survived. Second, my love for Meiying has only deepened. Third, these people she calls friends are most remarkable—people I never would have met had I not come. Fourth, this mysterious, magical woman must be unique. A Goddess? No. But remarkable still. Although . . . maybe she is a Goddess. If so, that would be worth all the pain. Fifth, if I make it back to San Francisco, I will be a different woman—impervious to the fools and their shallow world. Absolutely impervious! So, I will ride out my reckless impulse and see where it leads. I must not let the rape destroy me. Meiying didn't. Meiying won't. Nor must I!

Suddenly, horrifyingly, through the door came muffled screams and cries, otherworldly howlings interrupting her deliberations and raising the fearful specter of raw panic that dwelled just below the surface. Marie awakened Meiying with vigorous shakes.

"Listen!" she whispered when Meiying opened her eyes.

Meiying blinked away the fog of sleep and cocked her head. "Oh, my dear, those are the poor, violent souls locked in cells for their own protection. God knows what horrible torments they suffer. Try to ignore them, dear. Try to sleep. Who knows what tomorrow will bring."

Yes, thought Marie. *That is precisely what I thought I wanted before I came. Now? Good god! I fear it, and I long for it!*

~

The next morning, the group met at breakfast in high spirits. An aura of expectation hung over them, though they did not know when or from what direction, or in what guise *she* might appear. But, their happy mood was quickly broken by an announcement from Reverend Fu and Master Li.

"This morning, we will be visited by the local communist cadre, Comrade Lung, and his assistants."

Unsettled conversation all around, when Lu Zhishen piped up. "Why is he coming?"

"Inspection," said Master Li.

"Inspection? Of what?"

"Since the communists have taken over the area, they have organized everything down to the individual farms. They have little interest in us, but our institution contains 'the people's unhappy sick comrades.' At least, unlike the Nationalists, they have taken responsibility for supporting us with food and protection. We have now been renamed the 'People's Hospital for Mentally Ill, Number One.' So, we must put up with these inspections. It is even rumored that one of the highest-ranking communist big-wigs has a son who needs . . . care. And, there are other higher-ups I have talked with in the same boat"—he lowered his voice—"some with relatives already here." Master Li threw up his hands. "So, you see, we *are* useful to the people, comrades!"

"And if the communists say we are useful to the people, than it must be so!" added Reverend Fu, rolling his eyes.

"But, what will they think of us?" asked Master Zhou. "Especially, our foreign friends?"

"Ah," said Master Li. "We have thought of that. Just to be safe, we will lock them in our secure cells. The inspectors never go there." He chuckled. "Mad recognizes mad. Big, bad communists are afraid."

"So am I!" blurted John.

"Yes, we thought of you, Mr. Powers. With your special situation, we know it will be difficult. But,"—he sighed apologetically—"it is necessary to avoid trouble."

"No, no, I have no 'special situation,' I just don't like the idea of being locked up."

Meiying looked at him sympathetically, but it was Suling who took his part, as usual. "Mr. Powers hears a voice, or voices, that we consider sent by *her*." She held out her hands, palms up. "Mr. Powers is a remarkable man. Can we find another way?'

"I'm afraid not," said Reverend Fu. "If the communists think we're hiding spies, they'll burn down the institute, and god knows what they'll do to our children."

"No!" cried John, agonized by this trouble over him. "I'll go! Happily! Please, give no further thought to me."

"We have already hidden the Precious Object in one of the secured cells," said Child of Buddha.

"Good, excellent!" exclaimed Master Zhou in surprise.

"The rest of you Chinese will act like staff," said Master Li. "Cook is fully aware of our little . . . ruses."

"When must we do this?" asked Meiying, glancing at John.

"Now, I'm afraid," replied Master Li. He checked his watch. "They will arrive in an hour, though they are always late."

"Can't take the chance," volunteered John, gamely trying to give the others assurances that he would be fine.

Master Li looked at Meiying with a grave frown. "And you, sister Meiying, must put away your Western habits when they are here."

"What do you mean?"

"That is one example. You are a woman. You ask too many questions."

"But—"

"That is another example. You argue."

Meiying looked at him quizzically.

"Ah!" he cried. "And that is yet another example. You look men in the eye."

"Perhaps you should lock me up also," she said petulantly.

"Perhaps you're right," mused Reverend Fu. "Not for the reasons we have discussed, but because of your great beauty."

Meiying's eyes grew wide. "A curse!" she cried. "Lock me up with Miss Telles!"

As they were speaking Chinese, Lu Zhishen translated for Marie. When he finished, she shouted, "Yes! Lock us up! We will make a perfect pair of mad women! We shall shout and scream and curse like witches at the Sabbat!"

Startled by the American woman's vehemence, Reverend Fu looked heavenward and said in English, "God help us, hopefully, that won't be necessary. The inspectors never venture beyond the iron door."

"Iron door!" Lu Zhishen brought his fist down. "Another goddamn iron door!"

"This one opens," said Master Zhou. "No dynamite necessary."

"And closes," muttered John to himself.

Master Li checked the clock on the wall. "We must go now," he said urgently.

~ *Incarceration and Illumination* ~

When Reverend Fu took the foreigners past the iron door, a stench of unbelievable pungency permeated the thick, humid air, shocking their senses and magnifying their dread. With dire warnings from their guide, the group carefully walked down the center of the corridor to avoid flying spittle and arms thrusting out from behind bars to grab and claw. Unrecognizable babble and piercing shrieks reverberated off the walls, causing each member of the group to feel ill at the idea of being locked up here, even for a short time.

"I'd rather face the Reds!" shuddered Lu Zhishen above the mad cacophony.

John was locked in a cell alone, at his request, Lu in an adjoining one, and the two women farther down the corridor.

"Remember!" warned Reverend Fu before locking their cell doors. "If the inspectors come, stay away from the bars and turn your backs. Don't let them see your faces."

"And rant and rave like hell!" added Lu.

"Don't overdo it," cautioned Reverend Fu. "Even your screams have a foreign accent."

"Great."

Once Reverend Fu left and locked the great iron door behind him, the rooms went dark, and a host of demons possessing the permanent inmates seemed to rush out of their throats in a mad, churning miasma of howls and moans. John shrank back in his cell and curled up in the corner, certain his voices would find brotherhood and shatter his sanity by merging with the unholy tumult.

"This is where schizophrenics end up, this is where schizophrenics end up," he kept repeating.

After reciting this mantra over and over, Goddess's voice finally came, as if irritated by the persistence of John's primal despair.

No, John! No! It is your son who will end up in a place like this. Your son! Not you! The one who writes!

"Oh, god!" cried John. "Then why have him?"

That is not for you to ask.

Make Her tell you! came the God voice.

If you must know, it is for Him and His faction, the One who just so rudely interrupted. But, more importantly, it is for the future of this planet and all life that depends upon its diversity.

And She and Her faction call Me a cruel God!

"Factions? What factions? And what is this debate about intermediates? What are they? Why did they fail in the past? Tell me!"

The answer to those questions are beyond your ability to understand, John dear.

She is lying! cried God. *Make Her tell you about them!*

John put his hands to his ears. "Shut up!"

John, you cannot tell Us to stop. You cannot make Us stop. Suffering intermediate, don't you see that—

Quite suddenly and inexplicably, the voices stopped and the clamoring horror that emanated from outside his cell quieted to a low rumbling.

"What's happening?" he said aloud.

"Look over here, John," came a soft, familiar voice.

He took his hands from his head and turned around. In the opposite corner of his cell sat a beautiful young woman in a chair, illuminated by some unseen source.

She asked him a question—the question—with both hands raised palms up. "Mr. Powers, how does one justify a life without cruelty, and therefore also without the distilled beauty of cruelty?"

He could not speak. Frozen by shock, the old thoughts came back to him. How could a beautiful twenty-something woman have such a thought? Distilled cruelty represented pure evil—Hitler in extremis—not a concept whose existence could ever be justified. Yet here sat this young woman, gorgeous, throwing around the word cruelty as though it were synonymous with a white lie, or even virtue. *She* looked well-manicured, mentally sharp. No bruises. Nice clothes. And *she* sat in the middle of a madhouse, bringing back first causes.

"It's *you*!" he exclaimed stupidly.

"Fate starves at probability's door," *she* said without emotion. *Her* stare made him squirm but he made no sound. "Mr. Powers, how does one justify a life without cruelty, and therefore without the distilled beauty of cruelty?"

After repeating this question, *she* crossed her legs. He looked at *her* dumbly, and *her* face suddenly registered something far beyond his limited experience. Without waiting for him to answer, *she* asked *her* next question. So transformed had *her* face become that he scarcely believed that what now stared back at him was human.

"When will you lower your hand?"

"I don't understand," he replied.

"You will soon enough, John."

"I have gone through so much to see *you*, and now that *you* are here, in front of me, I cannot speak. I want to ask, but I cannot think. You talk in riddles. I cannot. . . ."

"Ask."

He blinked in confusion. "But . . . I have to think . . . where to start?"

"Ask."

"Why are *you* here?"

She looked around the cell. "This is where I dwell, behind the iron door."

"Here?"

"There are many iron doors."

"Do you know about my voices?"

"Yes."

"Can *you* make them stop?"

"John, think of the ocean."

"What?"

"The ocean."

"I don't understand."

"The ocean. Think of a wealthy old woman looking out at the ocean from her mansion on a cliff above the sea. She looks at the great rolling surface, calm and blue. What does she say to her guests, gazing with her?"

John is silent, unsure how to respond.

"John, what does she say to her guests?" *she* pressed.

"How beautiful the ocean is."

"And her guests, what do they say to her?"

"How beautiful the view is."

"Correct. And, below that gorgeous blue surface, in every cubic meter, top to bottom, near to far, millions of living creatures are eating each other alive. 'But,' says the rich woman, 'how beautiful is the ocean.' 'And,' reply her guests, 'how beautiful is the view.'"

"The distilled beauty of cruelty?" John hazarded.

"As it has been said." *She* lifted *her* arm. "John, there will come a time when you must lower your hand."

"I still don't understand. My son, Goddess, will he end up in a place like this?"

"I ended up in a place like this."

"Will he be schizophrenic?"

"I am schizophrenic."

"Damn it! I don't understand! Speak in words I understand!" He quickly controlled himself for fear *she* would leave. "Sorry, it's just that we have come so far," he whispered, raising his hand before his face. "What do *you* mean when *you* ask me about lowering my hand?"

"Top to bottom, near to far, all the same. A beautiful view."

"From a distance?"

"Near to far."

"Are you my voice?"

"Do *you* mean the one who says, 'The Chosen One, or the one who says 'Worthless'?"

"Yes."

Silence.

"Are *you* the Precious Object?"

"Do you mean the statue that speaks, '**Tap Tap Tap.**'?"

"Yes."

Silence.

John waited breathlessly, but the silence continued, so he stirred, intending to stand and walk to *her*. But before he could rise, *she* lifted *her* hands, palms up, and made an extraordinary announcement.

"His name will be Michael. Like you, he also will not be fully human—he will be more than human, and his descendants will take over the world. You and she will conceive him, here, now, in this place. She will die. You will lower your hand. He will be a soldier in a future war. He will be mistakenly thought of as schizophrenic. He will end up in a place like this. He will write. He is writing the words I speak now. You will be reborn, and, in the end, there will be a reunion in a dark cave where he left his bones. I will die and also be reborn. God will live and then will die. Your son will return to his bones. The human race will vanish."

Then, before he could ask another question, *she* was gone.

Darkness returned.

The howls returned.

The voice returned.

Well, John Powers, are you satisfied?

The tapping returned from an adjoining cell, tolling its simple requiem above the screams and moans.

... *Tap.Tap.Tap.*...

He cried.

~

Meiying sat in the cell across from Marie. Both tried to block the deafening cacophony, but could not, and came together in a desperate hug. As they rocked together, whispering reassurances in each other's ear, Meiying winced at a bright light that suddenly flashed with searing intensity, momentarily blinding her. She fell away from Marie and crawled into a corner, terrified by some unseen threat.

What is it?" cried a frightened Marie.

Meiying pointed, but Marie saw nothing but a dark corner.

"For god's sake, what is it?" repeated Marie.

But Meiying was no longer there. She stood in some strange, lighted room, staring at a piano. A little girl played clumsily, while standing above her, looking with approving eyes, stood *her*.

"It is *you*!" cried Meiying, ignoring Marie's muted calls fading in the background. "*You* are here!"

"This is where I dwell, when not in the piano."

"In the piano?"

She looked down at the little girl, still struggling with a difficult passage.

"With you."

Meiying had stored up a myriad of questions to ask *her* when *she* appeared, but now felt so stunned she could not conjure a single one. At last, shaking away her confusion, she uttered stupidly, "Will I be happy?" as if asking a cheap fortune-teller.

"No one is happy, only occasionally free from pain, or desire. That is why His addiction must cease."

"His?"

"God."

Meiying felt dizzy at this odd revelation, and panicked when the background noise started to become louder.

"Don't go!" she cried.

The noise subsided.

"See the little girl?" *she* asked.

"Yes."

"Young Bai Meiying misses notes and becomes frustrated?"

"Yes," murmured Meiying.

"Suffers?"

"Yes."

"She will learn?"

"Yes."

"And become a virtuoso?"

"Yes."

"And will play beautifully?"

"Yes."

She paused and stared at Meiying. "Now that you are a grown woman, as when you were this child, you will continue to be frustrated?"

"Yes," replied Meiying.

"And just like when you were this child, you will continue to suffer?"

"Yes."

"And continue to learn."

"Learn what?" asked Meiying.

"To become a virtuoso."

"And?"

"To play beautifully," *she* said, and repeated the words with great emphasis, "To play beautifully."

"And?" ventured Meiying.

"To have a son."

"No, no!"

"Conceived here, now, in this place."

"Oh, god!" exclaimed Meiying in agony.

"No, my dear, you mean to say, 'Oh, Goddess!'"

"But, a son? By John?"

"A son. He will write. You will perform . . . beautifully. It is your fate."

Meiying looked down at her lap. "But, I can't . . . with him."

"You can, you must, you will. A son, Meiying. He writes even now, and you are performing even now. It is your fate."

"But, Goddess, You have said that fate starves at probability's door."

"Only when events have yet to happen."

"What?"

"You are already long dead, Bai Meiying."

Chapter Twenty

The Seed Is Planted

Inspection Aftermath

Buandelgereen had made herself inconspicuous since their arrival at the institution, and had played the role of cook's assistant when the communist inspectors came. But, once they left, she stood anxiously with the others while the iron door was opened and the foreigners were released from their cells. Every face that emerged told a grim story, and by unspoken agreement, the group assembled in the cafeteria. Master Zhou felt uneasy at the unnatural silence from those present, and he looked warily at the faces of the foreigners. They seemed masks of introspection, gazing blankly ahead. Still, he determined to forge ahead with his report.

"Reverend Fu and Master Li assure me that all went well with the inspectors. As suspected, they did not go past the iron door." He paused to allow responses. There were none.

Buandelgereen stepped forward. "What happened in your cells?" she demanded.

Blank stares.

"We know something happened!" exclaimed Child of Buddha.

Silence.

"Did any of you see *her*?" asked Master Zhou, picking up on the thrust of the questions.

"*She* is here," said Meiying simply.

"You saw *her*?"

"Yes."

"As did I," said John.

"As did I," said Lu Zhishen.

Master Zhou turned to Marie Telles and asked in English. "And you?"

"No."

"*She* is here?" he repeated in wonder. "Will *she* return?"

None except one knew.

"Yes," said Child of Buddha.

"How do you know?" asked Master Zhou.

"Ask the Precious Object."

"But—"

"It is back in the private room, the one marked "No Admittance," and it wants to see all of us."

"How do you know?" asked Suling, who had been afraid to speak before this.

"I know. It wants to see those of you who did not already receive a visit. Suling, Master Zhou, Buandelgereen, myself. One at a time."

"Let us eat and go our own ways until it is time," said Master Zhou, also severely shaken by events, and the pronouncement that *she* wanted to see him. His tears ran freely, and he exclaimed proudly, "*She* wants to see me! At last, I may share what the rest of you have experienced."

The news of *her* appearance was accepted with a gravity that no one expected or understood. No one asked the foreigners what they saw or what *she* said. Lu Zhishen seemed particularly disturbed, and his normal, Canadian humor, rough grumbling, and voracious appetite had subsided into a quiet asceticism. Those who had seen *her*, grappled with the bizarre visions, strange words, and mysterious oracles. It seemed *her* appearance had acted as a wrecking ball, smashing preconceived notions and fragmenting the group into isolated islands of bewilderment and uncertainty. Even Marie Telles, to whom *she* did not appear, but who had watched in fascination and alarm as Meiying appeared fixed in some trance, asked no questions. Something sacred, or profane, had occurred, and to everyone's shock, could not be shared.

"Will we know when we are called?" asked Suling.

"Child of Buddha laughed. "Oh, you will know."

"Will you tell us?"

"*She* will tell you."

"How?"

Child of Buddha laughed again, but Buandelgereen spoke up. "The hunchback speaks the truth. Even Child of Buddha doesn't know how." Buandelgereen glanced at Child of Buddha, who nodded in agreement. "But, all will be seen by *her*," continued Buandelgereen.

"Even you, who has never before seen *her*?" asked Suling.

Buandelgereen smiled strangely. "Even me."

"I am so glad for you," replied Suling with genuine emotion.

Buandelgereen nodded in acknowledgement of Suling's kindness.

And, although those who had not yet seen *her* were anxiously awaiting the experience, those who had were left with conflicting emotions, and a sense of profound unease. None of them were willing to communicate to the others their alarm at the undeniably visceral and ambiguous reactions to *her* disorienting presence.

One by one, over the next few days, they disappeared into the "No Admittance" room, and came out as tight-lipped and shaken as the foreigners. Only Marie Telles remained untouched by the proceedings, and observed the effects of *her* on the others with astonishment and envy. Meiying had become strangely distant since their time in the cell, and Marie vowed to find out what transpired while they languished in that den of horrors. She chose a clear, cool night, and waited until they lay in bed, pleasantly stroking each other.

"Meiying, will you tell me what happened in the cell?"

Marie felt Meiying's body tense.

"It was not what I imagined."

"How?"

"I don't think it was what any of us imagined."

"But, how, dear?"

Meiying turned to her with hungry, fiery eyes; not, Marie realized, for sex, but for something incommunicable and mysterious.

"To play beautifully," said Meiying in a fierce, determined whisper.

"What? I don't understand you. Are you feeling well?"

Meiying chuckled. "Yes. I am feeling very well. Well enough to play beautifully!" She kissed Marie and rolled on her back, an invitation to change the subject, but Marie was nothing if not tenacious.

"Of course you play beautifully, dearest Meiying. And when we return to the States, you will continue to play beautifully. But, that didn't answer my question."

"What question?"

Marie laughed. "What happened? You know very well what I'm asking."

Still looking up at the ceiling, Meiying said, "I am going to have his son."

"What?"

"His son. I am going to have his son. No, our son! Our son!"

"John's?" Marie asked stupidly.

"Yes."

"But—"

"No more!" cried Meiying in a tone not to be ignored.

~

One day, after the last of the group had seen *her*, and plans were being made to depart, Master Zhou made a shocking announcement.

"Mr. President is coming," he said as calmly as he could manage.

An uproar rocked the cafeteria, startling the patients, whose usually happy faces were transformed into amplified expressions of the fear they gleaned from the reactions of the group. John immediately looked for Meiying, who stared in disbelief, her face drained of life. He started to go to her, but Master Li stood and waved his arms for quiet.

"It is true," he shouted over the tumult. "Mr. President is coming tomorrow."

"Why?" cried Lu Zhishen.

"I don't know, but he has the permission of the local communist government."

"Does he know we're here?" asked Suling.

"Apparently."

Buandelgereen scowled. "He knows. I have had word from the Flaming Cliffs. He knows, and what's more, he knows *she* is here."

"We must leave!" cried Meiying in a panic.

"Too late," said Child of Buddha.

"True," agreed Buandelgereen. "The communists are watching the institution now."

Meiying blanched and held her stomach in pain.

At that moment, John made a decision. While the others continued their discussion, he walked up to Meiying, nodded politely to Marie Telles, and said in a firm voice, "Meiying, please come with me outside."

Meiying gazed into his eyes for a moment, then followed without question. Once beyond the range of any outside ear, and after shooing away curious patients, he sat on a bench and invited her to sit next to him.

"We must conceive the child tonight."

Meiying sat straight up, took a deep breath, and nodded in agreement.

"You understand why?" asked John.

"Yes."

"Seven o'clock?"

"Yes."

"In my room?"

"No," replied Meiying forcefully. "I have thought about it. It must be in the 'No Admittance' room. There must be no other place."

"But—"

"There is a couch."

John sighed. "That isn't what I was going to say. You know, the Precious Object is there?"

"Precisely . . . and so is *she*."

"*She* will be there?" asked a startled John.

"Yes, *she* resides in many places; in statues, in pianos, and in pictures."

"Hmm, and behind iron doors."

"It must be there," repeated Meiying.

"If you insist."

"I insist."

~ *Conception* ~

John had waited years for this moment, yet he could never have anticipated such unsettling circumstances. He knew Meiying viewed the moment as a mechanical exercise, something akin to undergoing unpleasant, but necessary surgery. Now, with this less than stimulating knowledge, he worried that he might not manage an erection, which would render the entire, magisterial, divinely ordained proceedings a farce. He felt grateful the voices were mercifully silent, evidently to avoid any deflating distractions.

They met at seven o'clock in the "No Admittance" room. John placed a lantern next to the Precious Object, which began tapping right away in a slow, erotic cadence, like drums in some distant jungle beating a lazy, swaying rhythm. Wordlessly, they stared at one another, familiar strangers thrown together in an impossibly odd, yet sexually charged display, for the edification of . . . of who or what? Deities? Angels? Demons? Or their own delusions?

John felt the pulsing taps vibrating throughout his body, and watched as Meiying unabashedly disrobed, standing before him in all her naked glory. Stricken with overpowering desire, he quickly removed his clothes, and found his erection exquisitely painful in its size and urgency. She moved to the couch and held out her arms. He flew to her with a desperation he had never known. The Precious Object tapped louder and faster, driving him to a climax of inexhaustible ecstasy. Any consideration for her pleasure he might have felt was obliterated in the fever of his long-frustrated desire and release of his long pent up seed. But, such an explosion soon exhausts itself, and a profound quiet inevitably blankets the shocked air. So, as he lay in her arms, spent, she silently stroked his body in the detached manner of a nurse with a wounded soldier, waiting for him to stir.

"Thank you," he said simply.

"Thank you," she replied.

With these banal acknowledgements, she stood and began putting on her clothes. He watched dispassionately, realizing this union might be the first and last, yet, somehow lacking the will to care. The deed was done. His responsibility fulfilled. Now, they could truly go their separate ways, perhaps sharing in the upbringing of the boy, but never sharing of themselves. Those future details taxed his exhausted mind, and he simply basked in her intimate presence while the seconds ticked away. In his heart, he knew she had been raped; for her pleasure or pain meant nothing to him as he climbed the heights while she lay motionless beneath him, providing the solid flesh on which he summited.

~

Meiying returned to the waiting arms of Marie Telles.

~

The next morning, a tense mood settled over the institution, and Reverend Fu and Master Li busied themselves with attending the patients. Members of the group helped as best they could, always with an eye toward the entrance. Over breakfast, the only words exchanged between John and Meiying concerned biology.

"There is no guarantee that one time will do it," whispered John.

"We'll see," replied Meiying. She turned to Marie. "There's no place to hide."

"Hide?" scoffed Buandelgereen, who just entered the cafeteria with her rifle slung over her back. "Hide from a fat old bastard who has no manners? Nonsense!"

In spite of Buandelgereen's bluster, Marie trembled in anticipation of Mr. President's arrival; this monster who Meiying had so often described in horrific terms, and with whom her brother had shamelessly conducted business. The rest of the group spoke in low whispers when they weren't busy with the patients. Every foreigner now desperately wanted to escape back to their own country. They had seen *her*, and *she* had given them nothing but ambiguity, doubt, and disorienting uncertainty. Nevertheless, each knew *she* occupied some special position in the universe, and felt they had been changed in fundamental ways not yet evident. But, now, they were to be witnesses to a titanic clash between evil and . . . what? Good? They were not sure. Mephistopheles versus Earth Mother? Certainly, Mr. President would play his role with the absolute precision any clear-eyed casting director would relish. But *her*? Anyone's guess. Perhaps they were like casting directors themselves, unsure about *her* character, unsure who could play *her*, unsure whether any actor living or dead, or even in the realm of imagination, had the capacity.

Only the writer of this chronicle knows, and he dwells somewhere unreachable. Or perhaps even he doesn't know.

~ *Mr. President Visits the Institution* ~

First to arrive at the institution were a group of ragged soldiers. When asked their business, they said they were an "advance force" ensuring Mr. President's security. However, they did little more than poke their noses into various rooms, and gaze at the patients as if they were animals, pointing and laughing. When Reverend Fu objected, they waved their rifles and told him to shut up. An hour passed, and the soldiers demanded beer and wine while they waited. Master Li told them the institution was alcohol-free, but they were welcome to tea. This offer was met with curses. In the midst of this row, a line of staff cars drove up.

The cars stopped at the entrance, and doors flew open from all but the middle one; a dozen occupants emerged and scurried around the middle car like worker ants to a queen. Once in position, someone opened the back door and a behemoth materialized, pulled out and up by two muscular assistants. Mr. President stood and stretched, or rather, ballooned upward and outward, his massive arms cylindrical extensions unrolling from his spherical torso.

The group, with the exception of Master Zhou, watched from the second story veranda. Meiying felt horrified when his beady eyes immediately looked up and locked eyes with her as if she stood alone. How, she wondered, with all the patients rushing about, and with the hustle and bustle of the greeting committee, did he instantly hone in on her? It seemed otherworldly. She held his stare for a brief moment, then fled back to her room, heart pounding uncontrollably. Marie ran to join her. But John remained, fascinated by this vision of bloated evil. From above, he saw Reverend Fu, Master Li, and Master Zhou all bow respectfully and accompany Mr. President into the institution.

Almost immediately, word came that members of the group were to go to a private meeting room on the first floor. When they crowded in, Mr. President already sat at the head of a long table, guards at each corner. Buandelgereen entered with her rifle still slung over her back, and the guards quickly jumped to block her.

"Let her enter," said Mr. President in his high-pitched voice.

An oppressive silence filled the room, and everyone waited for the worst, but his next words sent shock waves through them all.

"I have no interest in this place but to burn it to the ground. However, my communist comrades say no. I have no interest in any of you, except Bai Meiying and one other. I have knowledge that my adopted mother is here; the one you all have sought for so long. I will see *her*. Now, the rest of you may go, except Bai Meiying."

He waited patiently. When some in the group objected, including John, they were prodded out by the guards.

"We'll be outside," said Master Zhou.

"Yes, yes, we'll wait!" exclaimed John over his shoulder.

Buandelgereen glared at Mr. President with fire in her eyes.

"A threat, brave Mongol woman?" he said quite calmly, with no mockery in his voice.

"Yes."

"Noted."

"Oh, Master Zhou!" he called to the old man as he was leaving. "Send back in the one you call Child of Buddha."

Master Zhou nodded.

Meiying sat at the opposite end of the table, determined to control her terror, at least so that it would not be so apparent to Mr. President. She clenched her fists and tensed her thighs under the table so that he could not see. Child of Buddha entered, apparently unconcerned, and, as was her habit, stood behind a chair rather than sitting, her hump an obvious hindrance to that most normal human propensity—to sit.

Mr. President turned to her. "I understand you are special?"

"Yes."

"Like me, you grew up here?"

"More or less."

"They kept you in a secure room?"

"Eventually."

"I spent time in that hell after my mother left. Do you hate them?"

"No, but you do."

"Yes."

"But, Reverend Fu and Master Li were not in charge when you were here."

"But, they were when you were here."

"Yes, but I do not hate them. I do not blame them."

"Irrelevant."

"I think not."

"Yes, you think in patterns, unlike the others. Unfortunately, your brain is unduly ostentatious, like your hump. In fact, I think your brain dwells in your hump."

"Better that way."

"How so?"

"More room. Very little sensory input from irrelevant stimuli. Cuts down on the noise. Increases . . . concentration."

Mr. President stared at her intently. "You are connected to my mother. Your understanding reaches *her* and *her* understanding reaches you?"

"Yes."

"I know; through the Precious Object."

"If you know, why ask?"

Mr. President nodded. "Good. I will have use of your services later, with the Precious Object."

Child of Buddha laughed. "I serve no one. Only death is my master, and even his whip I cannot feel."

"So, my threats would be useless?"

"Less than useless."

"But, what if I were to tell you something that Miss Bai Meiying, or, I should say, Mrs. Meiying Powers, might also find interesting?"

Child of Buddha shrugged. "Why this children's guessing game? Why not just go to your mother and be done with it?"

Given courage by Child of Buddha's brash dismissal of his power, Meiying boldly asked, "Do you know where *she* is?"

He looked at her, raised his eyebrows and tilted his round head. "In the 'No Admittance' room, with the Precious Object."

Meiying held her breath.

"Go on," said Child of Buddha.

"I did bad things when I was admitted here . . . no, when I was imprisoned here. Very bad things. My mother helped keep me from doing even worse things. Then, because *she* helped me, they made *her* leave. I spent hours in that room, looking at *her* picture."

"And then you left, and continued to do bad things out there," said Child of Buddha. "Even worse things," she added, looking at Meiying.

"Yes, that's right."

Meiying began to view him as might his disappointed mother rather than his traumatized victim. "Did you ever see *her* again?" she asked sympathetically.

His beady eyes focused on Meiying. "That is why I am here."

"What do you expect of us?" asked Child of Buddha.

"Both of you will accompany me to the 'No Admittance' room."

"Why?" asked Meiying, now less afraid, her native intelligence roused from debilitating fear to intense curiosity.

"My mother will appear for you."

"*She* is your adopted mother," said Child of Buddha.

"*She* is my mother!" insisted Mr. President, his voice still calm, but accompanied by a noticeable tremor that shook the folds of his face, making him appear on the verge of unraveling in front of the two women. "I have followed you, your group, your travails, your exploits; I followed you to Dalandzadgad near the Flaming Cliffs in accursed Mongolia. Then, I lost you. Two men were tortured, but would not tell."

"Beethoven—" Meiying started to say, but he held up his meaty hand.

"No more. The boy is dust, thanks to you, and what's more, Madame Wang wants your head on a platter. But, that would be unwise. I know my mother would not want me to kill you."

"But, the others? The ones you did kill?" asked Child of Buddha boldly.

"Like Peter Hedley?" said Mr. President.

Meiying flinched, and her eyes filled with tears.

His face twitched even more. "Detritus."

"How could you do these terrible things, when your mother is so kind, so compassionate?" asked Meiying, genuinely mystified.

He chuckled. "Yes, sons often stray from the wishes of their mothers. The poet should have written, 'the best laid plans of mice and mothers.' I may be a disappointment to my mother, but *she* has seen beyond the 'monster' that you have so colorfully called me. In fact, *she* has seen beyond the 'monster' that lies in all of us, including both of you."

"What do you want with *her*?" asked Child of Buddha.

"That, hunchback, is my business."

"No. If you want my help, it is my business."

He shrugged, his face twitching and drooping with every word. "What does any son want with his mother?" He looked at Meiying. "For example, take your son, your future son, as it is ordained. The child is already materialized inside you, and will want to know you, though he will not have the chance."

Meiying blanched. "Not know me?"

"You have been told; alas, you are already dead. Long dead."

"What is this nonsense!?" cried Child of Buddha, looking from one to the other.

"Nothing," said Mr. President smiling faintly. "Even you, Child of Buddha, are not privy to everything. As that Persian fellow wrote, 'The moving finger writes, and having writ, moves on; nor all your piety nor wit shall lure it back to cancel half a line; nor all your tears blot out a word of it.' Even as we speak"—he gazed at Meiying—"your son's moving finger writes, words appear upon this page, and he cries out to you . . . to all of us."

"I don't understand," said Child of Buddha.

"Of course not, but Mrs. Powers does. My mother is still alive, in *her* own way, and I want to see *her* again. Is that evil?"

"It depends," said Child of Buddha. "What do you want to do to *her*?"

His face now twitched uncontrollably. "Do? Do? Why, nothing, of course. Just, see *her* again. Just see *her*, as all of you were compelled to make perilous journeys, to see *her*, regardless of the consequences." Tears filled his eyes. "Just as the rest of you, who have now seen *her*."

Meiying looked deep into his troubled eyes, and the last vestiges of fear fell away. *To play beautifully*, she thought. "We will help you, if we can. But your mother is unpredictable. It may come to nothing."

"Don't tell me about my own mother!" he screamed in rage. "You may leave! I'll call for you! Out!"

But, Meiying rose and moved toward him. The guards flinched, but he held up his hand, and they resumed their positions. She walked next to him and said quietly, "You have suffered more, far more, than the rest of us."

With these words, he regained his composure.

"Will *she* see me?" he asked pathetically.

Meiying could only shake her head. "I don't know."

Child of Buddha, a witness to this exchange, said with feeling. "I will go to the Precious Object."

"Yes, yes, go," said Mr. President. "No!" he cried. "I will come with you. I will hear for myself."

Child of Buddha shrugged and turned to go.

He looked at Meiying and commanded, "You will come with us, beautiful piano player."

~

Mr. President held out his arms, whereupon his muscular assistants appeared from nowhere, pulling him up and flanking him as he waddled out of the room. A crowd gathered as this strange entourage emerged, the guards pushing aside anyone standing in the path of Child of Buddha, who led the way to the "No Admittance" room. When they reached the door, Mr. President huffed deeply from struggling through the maze of corridors, but now stood gazing at the sign for a long time. He turned and ordered the guards to clear everyone out of the area except for Meiying and Child of Buddha. When they had completed their task, he ordered them to leave, as well as his assistants. Now, only the three of them stood in the hallway. From the other side of the door, they heard tapping.

"*She's* waiting! *She's* waiting!" cried Mr. President.

"Hold a moment, sir," said Child of Buddha.

"Why?"

"Too hasty and *she* will fly."

"How do you know?"

"The tapping is to me what words are to you."

"And?"

She held up her hand. "Wait."

The door remained tantalizingly closed, the tapping tantalizingly close. Then, silence.

"Oh, god, *she's* gone!" exclaimed Mr. President in agony.

"No!" said Child of Buddha forcefully. "It is time. We must go in now."

When they opened the door, the Precious Object sat motionless, soundless, an unnatural glow pulsing visibly, even in the daylight. Meiying closed the door behind, and all three stood in the center of the room, Mr. President's body odor a powerful, musky scent that somehow altered from foul when it reached the nose, to a sort of sweet perfume when it lingered in the pathways of the brain.

His huffing slowed, and he perused the wall, finding *her* picture. Once located, he stood squarely in front of it and stared fixedly. Meiying and Child of Buddha waited, not sure what to expect.

"Leave," he said, without looking at them.

"What?" asked Child of Buddha.

"Leave!" he cried. Then, in a subdued voice said, "*She* is here."

Meiying scanned the room, but saw nothing.

His words now barely audible, Mr. President whispered, "Leave, now. Thank you. I must speak with my mother."

~ *Another Body* ~

Meiying and Child of Buddha stayed outside the door for a few minutes, then walked back to the cafeteria, where they assumed everyone waited in anticipation. But, they had only passed down a couple of hallways before the guards stopped them.

"Where's Mr. President?" demanded the officer.

"In the 'No Admittance' room."

A nervous licking of lips and agonized uncertainty followed.

"Did he say we should go back?" asked an officer.

Meiying shrugged. "He is in a private room. I cannot tell you."

When the two women joined the group eagerly assembled in the cafeteria, they were peppered with questions, but could only reply, "Don't know. He is in the 'No Admittance' room. We left him there."

An hour passed, punctuated with desultory small talk, as everyone kept glancing at the door to see whether Mr. President returned. But, halfway through the second hour, a great commotion arose outside the cafeteria, and a host of soldiers stormed in. A balding, middle-aged officer, the same who questioned them in the hallway, stood trembling in anger.

"What did you do to him?!" he screamed.

Reverend Fu and Master Li intervened. "Is there a problem?"

The officer pointed at Meiying and Child of Buddha. "These two were in the room with him!"

"They have been here for almost two hours," said Master Zhou. "I'm sure Mr. President will vouch for that."

"We know that!" again screamed the officer.

"Then, what is it you are asking?" queried Master Zhou in confusion.

"He's dead," said the officer in a calmer voice. "Poisoned by them!"

A stunned silence fell over the room.

"What are you saying?" asked Master Li.

"Mr. President is dead."

"But, he was alive and well when we left!" objected Meiying.

"No!" shouted the officer. "You poisoned him! You told us not to go in!"

"No! I told you I didn't know. How could we have poisoned him?"

This threw the officer. "Well, there's not a mark on him. Must have been poisoned."

"With what?" asked Child of Buddha. "There were no drinks or food."

"Well, it's true we found no drink, no cups, no food," mumbled the officer, his brain clearly switching gears and calculating a change of direction.

"Sounds like a heart attack," said Reverend Fu.

"Why was he left alone?" asked the officer, now even calmer.

"He ordered us to leave," replied Meiying.

"Why was he left alone in that room?" insisted the officer.

"Ask your guards," said Child of Buddha. "He wanted to see his mother."

"But there was no one else there!"

"Exactly."

The officer wiped sweat from his brow. "I'm confused. Where is his mother?"

"Behind an iron door!" boomed Lu Zhishen.

"What?"

"What my Canadian friend means is that we don't know," quickly explained Reverend Fu.

"But. . . . " the officer's voice trailed off.

"Will you allow me to examine the body?" asked Reverend Fu. "I have some medical training."

The officer hesitated, then said, "Yes, but we will be watching."

Reverend Fu detected a hint of relief. "Of course."

~

The good reverend knelt over Mr. President's body and checked, but could find no external sign of damage or struggle. Mr. President lay on his back, great, flabby hands folded on his chest, as if they had been placed there. His face reflected surprise and some other unreadable expression, but not horror, or pain. For the benefit of the officer, Reverend Fu spent a great deal of time examining the body, the eyes, mouth, ears, chest, but he already knew the cause of death, and it wasn't a heart attack.

"Heart attack," he said to the officer matter-of-factly.

The officer remained skeptical, but again he seemed relieved about something, as if a weight had been lifted. Reverend Fu noticed, and thought to himself, *He will want to believe.*

~

Orders were given, the body removed, and the motorcade drove off, leaving instructions for the staff of the People's Hospital for Mentally Ill, Number One that the incident was to be kept secret under penalty of death. In his staff car, the balding officer smiled to himself. He felt quite smug. At first, he thought it necessary to blame the two women, to execute them, sacrificial lambs to balance the equation, and thereby appear decisive. But, on further reflection, a heart attack served his purposes even better—no blame, no accusations of gross negligence in allowing Mr. President to be murdered by a ragged group of foreigners, crazy priests, and, of all things, a female hunchback! No, a heart attack would serve him nicely, although he also, like Reverend Fu, knew the cause of death was no such thing.

Once Mr. President and his entourage were long gone, the group hastily left the institution, with tears and hugs for the children of Reverend Fu and Master Li, and an outpouring of gratitude to these amazing men whose compassion and intrepid fortitude had saved so many lives. Master Zhou carefully packed the Precious Object for the arduous and time-consuming trip back to his estate.

Chapter Twenty-One

The Son

San Francisco

The journey back to Shanghai took months of navigating the ever-changing front lines of Nationalists, communists, and warlords. It seemed a dizzying series of checkpoints, inspections, negotiations, bribes, and paperwork, but John, Meiying, Marie Telles, and Lu Zhishen were finally on board the U.S. Navy ship *W.H. Gordon* in September, 1949. The ship had been given safe conduct by the Nationalists, and was loaded with almost two thousand evacuated Americans and other nationals fleeing the new communist regime. They stood on deck and watched Shanghai diminish to a thin line of blurry shadows in the fog. So, the great and tragic country slipped away, and along with it, the names of people and places that were seared deep in the marrow of their souls: Nanjing, Taiyuan, Flaming Cliffs, Dalandzadgad, Beethoven, Mr. President, Lihua, Meili, Peter, Madame Liu, Master Zhou, Suling, Feng Shiren, Mr. Gao, Little Acorn, Buandelgereen, and all the others. Meiying sobbed continuously, and would not be comforted. These ghostly memories boiled up from the deep wellspring of her love for China and its people; her wretched but magnificent homeland, the core of her tattered but proud identity, and mother of the scorching pain and exquisite joy that she now left behind forever. Meiying wept even as she sensed the fetal quickening inside, which only added a bittersweet accompaniment to her turbulent emotions.

"So," mused Lu Zhishen aloud. "We're the last ship out."

"Yes," said John. "On to San Francisco and normal lives. It will seem strange to wake up and not wonder whether you will survive another day."

"I, for one, will never again crave excitement and adventure," said Marie Telles. "Fool that I was."

"But, would you give up the experience now?" asked Lu Zhishen, who immediately berated himself for asking such an insensitive question.

She reddened and shook her head. "Some of it, but the rest? Not for a million dollars, even though I didn't see *her*."

Meiying listened and pondered. *But, they are giving up mere fleeting experiences, I am giving up my country, my past, my future.* She kept this thought to herself and held her hands over her stomach to feel the new life. *Now, a different future: to play beautifully.*

~

As they sailed home, on October 1, 1949, Mao Zedong ascended the massive review stand in the future capital of Beijing and announced: "The People's Republic of China, the central people's government, is established today!"

~

Upon their return to San Francisco, John and Meiying officially separated, she moving in with Marie Telles, and he staying in the apartment. Mulan, by now, had become semi-independent and rented her own one-room flat, occasionally living with Meiying and Marie when funds were short. Her tuberculosis continued to come and go, each episode more serious than the last. Marie's brother, plagued by guilt over his role in orchestrating the trip to China, and the subsequent rape of his sister, reluctantly moved out of the mansion, leaving it to the two women. John went back to work for Arthur Mobley, and eventually became a vice-president. His voices remained conspicuously quiet, which he took as evidence Goddess had achieved Her goal. Meiying took a leave of absence from the symphony to have her child. None of the survivors of the trip shared stories with anyone, including each other, and all waited quietly to see if *she* would someday reappear. Everyday life took over, yet, beneath its skimming trifles lurked a constant undertow that weighed down their complacencies; a frightful knowledge of the sinister depths churning beneath even the most placid and sparkling of surfaces.

February, 1950 arrived, and Meiying was two weeks away from her due date. She spent her time staying out of the San Francisco dampness, instead, remaining in the mansion and honing her skills at the piano. Marie Telles acted as her liaison with the symphony, and in this capacity, invited the maestro and David Hendricks for dinner one evening, despite Meiying's objections.

"It will be good for you," Marie insisted. "You've been living like a nun in some cloister."

"But, I'm too big. Too uncomfortable. Too tired. Too—"

"Too introverted, darling. You must socialize, keep up your contacts. You're not an ostrich."

"What?" Meiying had a hard time with Western aphorisms.

"Never mind, dearest. Just trust me."

"But, Marie, I'm quite content."

"Too content. Your career awaits, and if you don't pay attention, it will wither on the vine."

"What?"

"Never mind, dear. Now, look, if you don't follow my advice, it will be difficult to climb back on the horse—oh, forget I said that. What I mean is that it will be difficult to get your career rolling again."

"I'm still under contract to the symphony," objected Meiying.

"Oh, dearest, I have much bigger plans than that for you."

"Marie, don't forget, there is this child to raise. I can't be constantly away."

"I know, I know. But, Meiying, the child will be well taken care of. Thanks to me, you have plenty of money to hire a nanny, and when you've made it big in America, your money will dwarf mine. You'll be able to afford your own mansion."

"And I can repay you," said Meiying firmly.

"We won't worry about that now. Right now, we have to worry about what to wear when the gentlemen come."

"Are they bringing their wives?"

"Of course, dear."

"Marie!"

"Now, what shall we drape over that great stomach of yours?"

"Marie!"

"Just kidding, darling."

Meiying turned serious. "Marie, have you heard from your brother lately?"

"Yes, why?"

"Well, I'm worried about John. I think he's drinking again. Did Jacob mention anything to you?"

Marie sighed. "No, dear, not a word. Now, can we get back to the subject at hand?"

Meiying hated these social events, and earnestly wished she would be left alone to think her own thoughts, marinate in her own memories, and play the piano. However, she put up with Marie's busy social calendar in order to preserve domestic tranquility. They had begun to settle into a comfortable, albeit busy routine, in which Marie handled all the details of life required to navigate in the complicated social and professional world, while Meiying played the dutiful, but exasperating artist.

Although Meiying disliked these "get-togethers," she invariably charmed the guests, and always made Marie proud. This night, sitting between the maestro and his wife, Meiying actually enjoyed the topic of conversation: music. The maestro's wife had been a violinist, so the three of them discussed in great technical detail the lush romanticism of Rachmaninoff and the disturbing rhythms of Stravinsky. Like the burgeoning *grande dame* she was bred to be, Marie skillfully intervened to widen the accessibility of their conversation and involve the non-musical wife of David Hendricks, who sat looking rather lost.

"Dears, your discussion is utterly fascinating, but let us poor musical dilettantes also have a little of your time for other subjects"

Meiying felt confused at the comment, but the maestro's wife understood perfectly.

"So sorry, Marie. We have been too wrapped up in shop talk."

"Not at all."

"Have you gotten fully back in the swing of things since you returned from China?" she asked Marie.

The maestro squirmed uncomfortably, as he had told his wife China was a forbidden topic, but it was too late, and Marie blinked back tears.

"Yes, yes," she stammered.

David Hendricks came to the rescue. "I daresay, you'll be accompanying Meiying on her tours, after the baby is born, of course."

"Yes," said Marie, struggling to recover her poise. "It'll be great fun."

Unfortunately, Mary Hendricks had not been so carefully briefed by her husband. "Meiying, what do you think of the current situation in China?"

Marie turned red, carefully set down her wine glass, and murmured quietly, "Oh, let's not mention China," vehemently followed by the exclamation, "Not China!"

An awkward pall fell over the group, and the maestro quickly interjected, "Yes, let's not discuss politics. We're all having too pleasant a time."

Conversation segued to other topics, and the evening went as such evenings go, without further drama. But, when the guests left, the waving of goodbyes ended, and the door closed, Marie turned to Meiying with pleading eyes.

"Forgive me, Meiying dear! But, I cannot think about that country, let alone talk about it."

"I understand," said Meiying.

"But, really . . . please, dear, it's about the country, not all Chinese. You mustn't take it personally."

"I don't."

"It's just . . . that country. . . . " Her words trailed off, but the disgust was evident, and Meiying felt the knot in her stomach tighten. She wanted to scream at Marie, tell her China was part of her soul, and could not be savaged without savaging Meiying herself. But, the memory of the rapes kept her from blaming Marie, and also kept her from fully loving her as she did Meili. With a start, she realized her heart would always know Marie was different, not like Meili, not Chinese, and this revelation itself pained her. *Such prejudice prevents me from playing beautifully,* she thought, and the luminous image of *her* appeared, although with a handful of unsettling dark streaks, like spears, marring the brightness.

That night, Meiying was particularly passionate in her lovemaking, the more to make up for shortcomings in her deeper feelings. Pregnancy had increased her libido, and the combination of factors created an almost desperate overcompensation. Meiying's fervor did not escape Marie's notice, and she likewise attended to her lover with more passion. Their relationship continued in an atmosphere of edginess, until the day a son entered the world.

News from China was bad, and the last letter Master Zhou succeeded in smuggling out of the country contained a description of how he would try to escape the communist purges, particularly those aimed at eliminating landlords. If he did not succeed in making it out of China, it would only be a matter of time before he was imprisoned, or killed. Just before the communists overran Nanjing, he sold the Precious Object to a French art collector, who owned a plantation in French Indochina. Master Zhou apologized for the sale, but explained the statue would have been destroyed by the communists otherwise. He gave Meiying and John his love, with the hope they would meet again in better times.

~ *Birth of the Son* ~

Meiying's water broke in the early morning hours of February 23, 1950. Marie rushed her to the hospital, where she gave birth to a healthy son on the evening of the same day. John and Marie had waited anxiously, for in the back of their minds, they feared the damage done to Meiying by the vicious assaults she suffered in China might complicate the delivery. By mutual agreement, the parents named the child Michael, fully aware this constituted the wish of Goddess. Little did they know (or, perhaps, did not want to know) that this chubby, red fleshed baby carried the genetic seeds of schizophrenia, and had embarked on a collision course with a future war, in a country that was now the repository of the Precious Object.

To Meiying, the child was a revelation. Even the piano became secondary while she doted on the infant, breast-feeding and adamantly rejecting the idea of hiring a nanny, much to the disappointment of Marie Telles. John visited often, his excessive drinking a constant thorn in their relationship. Mulan, now very sick, wept at the sight of the baby, and felt keenly the devastation left by the loss of her Chinese family, particularly her elder brother Shirong, and fussed over Michael almost as much as Meiying. The bright-eyed, intelligent little girl from a small, obscure village in the middle of China was dying, and she mourned her own impending death by celebrating her American brother's future life.

One day, John visited the mansion after work. It was late, and Meiying saw he had clearly stopped at some bar to drink before arriving. She offered him tea, but he declined and asked to see Michael.

"He's asleep," said Meiying.

"Well, that's okay. Let me just look at him."

Meiying led him to the nursery, where the baby was covered by blankets except for a small patch of red face. John, who seemed only slightly affected by the alcohol, leaned close to Michael's face and scrutinized it for a long time.

"He is so adorable," he said.

Meiying beamed. "Can you tell whether he hears voices yet?"

Meiying was stunned by the question. "John, how can you say that?" she exclaimed angrily.

"Well, I just wondered if you've seen any evidence."

"No, John." She softened. "Are they back?"

He gave her a puzzled look. "That's a good question. Sometimes, I hear them, but very faintly, just a humming, but I can't make out the words. It's like they're done with me, and planning, or arguing, over something new or someone else."

As he said these words, his gaze fell back on baby Michael.

Meiying looked at him sympathetically, but did not respond.

His eyes filled with tears. "They mustn't be allowed to jump into him."

His words frightened Meiying, for she had also feared that possibility, and without telling anyone, had secretly observed Michael for a sign, any sign, that John's schizophrenia had been passed on. She motioned for him to follow her, and they walked to the tea room, where she had so often conversed with Marie Telles. Meiying invited him to sit, and again offered tea. He again declined.

"I have to get going," he said curtly, still standing in a rather self-conscious manner.

"Please, sit for a while," said Meiying.

He sat, clearly uncomfortable. "You have anything to drink, other than tea. Maybe wine, or—"

"John, that's what I wanted to talk about."

He rolled his eyes. "Oh, god! Here we go! Look, Meiying, we're not living together. You're not my mother, and you're certainly not my wife! Drop it."

"John," continued Meiying calmly. "If this drinking continues to get worse, I'll have two problems to worry about for Michael's sake: schizophrenia and alcoholism."

"Who told you my drinking is getting worse?" he demanded. "Arthur?"

"No, but I hear things."

"It's still none of your damn business! I'm leaving!" But, he didn't get up from his chair.

"John," said Meiying firmly. "We had planned to raise Michael together, but you. . . . " she hesitated, wanting to parse her words carefully. "Your problems will make it difficult to share."

She waited for the explosion, but he shrank back into his chair like a little boy, lowering his head and whispering, "I know."

"John, get professional help. Why are you so stubborn?"

"Because, that's the final retreat. The final admission. Worthless is the word thrown at me day and night. I am not worthless, Meiying! I can deal with this. If I go to a shrink, I'll know they were right."

"They?"

"Don't pretend you don't know."

Meiying averted her eyes. "But, that's just it, John. They are not real."

"You thought so once."

Meiying winced. "Yes, that's true. But, John, the stakes are much higher now—your son."

John remembered the voices often saying his son would be worse than him, much worse. He felt the tears hot on his cheeks. "Meiying, even if I get help now, I don't think it will matter."

"Of course it will matter!"

"No, Meiying. Not to Michael. Don't you see? Not to Michael! Maybe that's why I drink."

"We can't let ourselves believe they are real, John. We can't! Otherwise there's no hope."

"Meiying," he whispered in agony. "There is no hope."

Meiying sat straight and glared at him with fire in her eyes. "There is always hope."

John blanched at Meiying's brave words, and they shamed him into saying, "Yes. You're right. I'll think about getting professional help, okay?"

It was the most she could hope for. "Okay."

~ *Time, Time* ~

As the months passed, Meiying continued to lavish all her energies on her son, until Marie's entreaties finally convinced her to resume her career, which she did reluctantly and with painful spells of guilt. With a great deal of hand-wringing, a nanny was hired and Meiying began performing with the symphony, the sheen of being a talented refugee from Red China still a saleable commodity to the American public. Meiying prospered, yet, far away in Southeast Asia, in the regal, plantation house owned by a wealthy French colonial master, the Precious Object created a stir when it began tapping at a furious rate, frightening the Vietnamese servants, and mystifying the incredulous owner.

~

Activity at the mansion ramped up as Meiying fully re-entered the hectic schedule her career required. Rehearsals, meetings, practice, concerts; all put demands on her time. Try as she might, the amount of attention she gave Michael felt woefully inadequate, but she did derive an unexpected surge of joy at returning to the concert grind. Memories of China resurfaced in her music, and the depths of passion and pain flowed in the exquisite power and sensitivity of her performances. Marie Telles felt delighted, and began floating the idea of a nationwide tour. Meiying experienced conflicting emotions, constantly shifting from exuberant excitement to fearful anxiety about Michael, so she insisted that both baby and nanny accompany her on any such tour. The undeniably attractive lure of travel made her cherish even more her time with Michael.

Motherhood brought Meiying a type of satisfaction she had never before experienced, and her relationship with Marie underwent the strain, becoming more centered on business than sex. Marie chaffed at this development, but patiently told herself Meiying suffered through a predictable phase that would soon pass as Michael became older.

One rainy night, Marie had prepared Meiying's favorite cakes and waited for her to return home from rehearsal. The hours passed, and her concern deepened. This was not like Meiying. She called the symphony, but no one answered, which was not unusual during a late rehearsal, but her worry intensified. A deep chill, a premonition of something being dreadfully wrong, seized her. Marie checked in with the nanny, called a cab, and headed toward Symphony Hall.

~

John received the call that night. Meiying's body lay at the hospital, waiting for identification by the nearest relative. He knocked over an end table rushing to the car, then collapsed in the rain before he reached it, sobbing.

The voices remained silent.

"Where are you now that you got your damn son!" he screamed, still on his knees. "You're done with her, so she is thrown away like so much trash!? Damn you! Damn you! Damn you!"

Somehow, he made it to the car and drove to the hospital, barely able to see through his tears, but his soul had been hollowed out, never to be made whole.

To John, the empty cavity gouged from his heart was about the same size as Michael, so the boy would either be a constant reminder of his loss, or be the future joy that would fill the void. In either case, the burden of raising Michael now rested solely, wholly, and irredeemably with him.

~

"She was telling me to hurry, so she could get home to her son," said the cabby, who survived the accident with only minor injuries. "So, I speeded up a little, but, you know, still legal."

"Yeah, go on," said the investigating officer.

"And all of a sudden, like a bat outta hell, comes this crazy man through the intersection, right through the red light. Hit smack-dab into the side of my cab. I mean, she didn't have a chance, you know?"

The officer turned his attention to John, who had just arrived.

"You the husband?"

"Yes," said John mechanically.

A doctor stepped forward. "Can you come and identify the body, please?"

John followed silently.

When he saw her laid out on the table, the bile came up like a great torrent, and the doctor quickly moved him away and guided him to the bathroom.

Kneeling before the toilet, he asked the questions.

"Where was *she*? Why didn't *she* help? And you, Goddess-bitch, where were you?"

Nothing.

"Where were You?"

Where were you, John?

The voice was female, unmistakably Goddess, Her words and tone embodied naked reproach.

"I was here!"

No, you were elsewhere. Now, you must focus on the next step.

"What next step?"

Your son. The next Chosen One.

"God killed her, didn't he?" asked John into the toilet.

God killed her?—Yes. The universe killed her?—Yes. She killed herself?—Yes. You killed her?—Yes. Fate starves at probability's door. In the end,

a drunk driver killed her. Such is the banal insanity of life. A moment in time and space.

"Go to hell! Both of you!"

Now, you must raise a healthy boy. Healthy enough to be a soldier in the next war.

"What?"

A healthy boy, John. What he and others believe is schizophrenia will come to him in due time. It will, of course, emerge from your seed, but its manifestation will be much worse and much better, and for My purposes, this is for the best. But, only at the proper time. All roads must lead to the Reunion. That is most important. Your descendants will have powers beyond your imagining, but the next step must be taken.

"God damn it! I don't know what You're talking about! What if I kill the boy?"

"Mr. Powers?" came a voice from the other side of the door. "Are you okay?"

"Yes."

"Please let us help you. I can prescribe a sedative. However, I need you to identify the body. Can you do that now? Mr. Powers? We need you to identify whether this is your wife."

John laughed. He laughed an ugly, distorted, troubled laugh. "She is my wife and she is not my wife!"

"Yes, I think I understand. Can you please come out, Mr. Powers."

"You think you understand? Understand? No! You'll never understand!"

"No, I'm sure you're right. Now, Mr. Powers, you really must come out. You really must identify the body for us."

John stepped out of the bathroom and looked intently at the doctor. "Yes, of course. I can identify her. She is my love. She is my life. She is my sanity. I am lost. Forever. Being my wife is the least of her. The least! But for me, it is the most! The most of me!"

John croaked out an undecipherable word when he stood over the body.

"Mr. Powers, please."

John suddenly stood straight and said clearly, "My wife."

He stumbled out of the hospital, got behind the wheel, and adjusted the rear-view mirror to reflect his eyes. "I'll kill Michael. If I kill him, Her plan is thwarted. What hell must await him, if She speaks truthfully! I can spare him that pain. His dead body will fit into the hollow part of me like a snug coffin. Then, both of us can be lowered together."

John! You must not do that! No! cried Goddess.

Yes! Yes! This failed mutant will kill your carefully laid plans. Gods and Goddesses have no power over madness. Perhaps that is the definition of madness. Like Rousseau, another failed intermediate said, 'sane men cannot make madmen sane, but madmen can make sane men (and Gods) mad.' Goddess, Your faction must accept the fact that Probability starves at Fate's door. Thus, fatal collision.

God, humans has been mad long before you, or your ilk. Only, now the tapping is relentless, and drives him to further depths. But, Lord God, you're right in one respect, Your own mad adherence to First Principles has forever driven sane humans mad.

"And You, Goddess?" asked John.

When no answer was forthcoming, he muttered wearily, "Pointless, pointless."

He drove home.

~ *Michael* ~

The child Michael was given over to his father's care. John retained the nanny, and resumed his work routine as might an automaton, causing the quality of his performance to decline. Arthur Mobley remained patient and often called John into his office for a pep talk, but the results were not satisfactory, and at one point consideration was given to firing him. John continued unmoved by the surrounding circumstances of his work, and persisted in a morbid obsession with the memory of Meiying. The notion of killing his son did not return, but every time he looked at the boy, he saw Meiying's dead face. As the months passed, to compensate for his depressive musings, John suddenly stopped performing mechanically, and threw himself into his work. Although the China operations were no longer viable, he shifted his areas of expertise to Taiwan, Hong Kong, Singapore, and Southeast Asia. In this way, the pattern of his life settled into an inflexible, busy routine, and the years dropped into the dustbin like the heavily notated calendar pages he tore off every month.

Michael grew up in the care of his nanny, who he took to calling Nanny Peach. His father remained a distant sail on the horizon to the boy, unreachable, never docking, while below decks its holds were full of mystery and treasure. Michael was still too young to be resentful of his father's detachment, so he poured all the abundant love in his heart to Nanny Peach. Dinners were the only time the three spent time together, but John ate lethargically, usually glum from the bourbon he had consumed beforehand. Nanny Peach, a kindly, matronly woman, showed her displeasure with John's aloofness by encouraging Michael to ask him questions.

"Mikey," she would say. "Ask your father about his day."

But, the boy knew his father disapproved of such intrusions into his emotional solitude, and besides, when John did speak, Michael did not understand a word, or rather, did not understand the meaning when he put the individual words together. Nanny Peach, with her wise, perpetual smile, gently put the blame on John by a disapproving tilt of the head, rather than on his son for such disconnect. Since Meiying died, Nanny Peach had given up her other positions to be full-time with him, including being the household cook and housecleaner. To accommodate her, John leased a larger apartment with additional bedrooms. The relationship between John and Nanny Peach remained on a businesslike level, and in spite of her earnest attempts, he never let her get close to him, other than being free to express essential concerns about Michael's development, or health.

In most instances when she came for his approval of some behavioral intervention or school issue, John waved her off with the statement, "Whatever you think is best." After years of this attitude, Nanny Peach came to prefer John's lack of involvement because she did not trust the effect his type of frigid interference might have, and also feared his drinking might lead to disaster for both father and son. Margaret Doringer (her real name) never married, and from a young age wanted to be a nanny like Peggotty in *David Copperfield*. As a consequence, she modeled her life after that fictional character's loving, nurturing, and protective character; a dream-fantasy that became real-life with the death of the boy's sweet mother and the emotional barrenness of his father. Imitating her heroine, she marshalled all of her powers to prevent Michael from growing up without love or encouragement. These qualities were not lost on John, who gladly gave her the maximum possible latitude, nevertheless keeping outward displays of gratitude to himself.

But, one day, when Michael was nine, his father looked at him as if seeing him for the first time. This miraculous moment was so unique, so wondrous, it seared itself into the boy's young memory. It happened in the living room, on a late Saturday afternoon, when his father sat in a recliner drinking bourbon and, as was his usual habit, staring into space as if some great mystery haunted him. A ball that Nanny Peach and Michael were playfully tossing back and forth, rolled up to the chair. At first, Michael hesitated to disturb the imperturbable sphinx, but Nanny Peach called, "Go on, Mikey!"

Thus, under the direction of his beloved nanny, and wanting to continue playing, he walked quietly up to the ball. As he unobtrusively leaned over to pick it up, John abruptly leaned forward and said, "Michael?"

"Yes, sir?"

"You needn't call me sir. Come here a moment, Michael." He patted his lap.

Michael was so astonished he could not move.

"It's okay. Come here."

The boy sidled up beside the chair and stood passively.

John put his hand on his son's shoulder and burst into tears. While Nanny Peach and Michael looked on in stunned silence, John cried out in an agonized voice, "You're about the same age as Little Acorn when he died!"

This inexplicable revelation amplified the utter shock of his uncharacteristic behavior.

Nanny Peach gathered her courage. "Mr. Powers, are you okay?"

The question struck John like a thunderbolt. He had never shared his schizophrenia with her, and since Meiying's death, the voices had trailed off to a mere smattering of incoherent arguments between God and Goddess.

"Yes, yes, I'm okay. Thank you, Margaret."

This response yielded yet another look of bewildered surprise from Nanny Peach, who felt a warm blush of goodwill toward this troubled man.

Michael had remained standing, his father's hand still resting on his shoulder.

His eyes still red, John asked, "Tell me, Michael, how is school?"

This question had rarely been asked, and Michael was in such a state of discombobulation, he could only reply, "Good, sir."

"No, no, no, Little Michael, I mean, what are you learning? Who is your best friend? Do you like your teachers?"

This whirlwind of questions, plus the appellation Little Michael, so soon after the mention of that other strange name, made Michael's heart race and his muscles tighten. He wanted to run away, but the hand seemed an iron chain binding him to his father. He shrugged helplessly, and mumbled, "I don't know."

~

John knew the boy was frightened, and cursed himself for allowing this state of affairs with Meiying's son to reach such a point. He lifted his hand from the boy's shoulder and held it out, palm up.

"That's okay, son. We'll have plenty of time to catch up later. Go play with your Nanny Peach now."

Relieved, Michael hastily retrieved the ball and ran back to his kind protector. But, he remained troubled, and their ball-tossing ended very quickly. Back in his room, Michael wanted to read as a distraction from these alarming developments, but he couldn't concentrate. He tried pacing, but that didn't work, so he ran into the bathroom and stared at the mirror, turning his face and stretching his neck this way and that. He had only recently become fully cognizant that his physical appearance was different from the other kids; his skin darker, his eyes with a slight Asiatic fold, his hands delicate. These differences had begun to bother him, and he feared he looked too strange, too fragile, too thin, his neck too long, his hair too black. Now, his father added to the worries. Who was this Little Acorn? How did he die? Was he an unknown brother? Did his father love Little Acorn more than him? Is that why his father seemed so distant and sad all the time? Because his brother had died? These questions plagued his thoughts, and he began wondering what Little Acorn looked like. Was he stronger? Smarter? Did his eyes look Asian? Skin color? Such puzzles!

In the midst of these thoughts, Michael suddenly realized that his father, for the first time, took an interest in him, and he felt somehow unburdened. At least he was not hated. His father seemed to care a little, although Michael felt sure he must prefer Little Acorn.

~ *Father and Son* ~

John could not sleep that night. He realized he had a lot of catching up do with Michael. Meiying must be somewhere watching him with deep feelings of disappointment and resentment. How could he be so clueless? And for so many years! As if he had just been released from a long prison term, John planned a course of action to become acquainted with his own son. First, after Michael went to school on Monday, he would sit down with Margaret and get a complete briefing on the status of the boy, emotionally, socially, and academically. John approached this problem as any good businessman would—break down the problem and analyze its component parts.

On Monday morning, Margaret Doringer sat down with her employer at the kitchen table and began answering a plethora of questions. After assuring Mr. Powers that Michael was well socialized and performing excellently at school, she gently mentioned his lack of a nurturing environment at home.

"What about you?" asked John peevishly. "Aren't you nurturing him?"

Margaret smiled and replied in a firm tone, "I meant from you."

With this, John asked what he could do to support her.

"If you'll pardon me, Mr. Powers, the question is what can you do to support Michael."

"Yes, yes, you're right. So, what can I do?"

"Love him, Mr. Powers, love him."

John nervously toyed with a spoon. "Yes, I understand, but how can I do that without frightening him?"

Margaret remained silent for a long while, then looked at Michael with an open, inquisitive smile. "Mr. Powers, why this sudden urge to . . . well, to take an interest in Mikey?"

"I don't know, perhaps I finally realized what my parental obligations are."

"You'll excuse me, but I don't think that is the case."

John fumbled. "But, it is the case . . . why don't you think it is the case?"

"Who is Little Acorn, Mr. Powers?"

John leapt to his feet. "Why do you ask?"

"Mikey is very confused. He wonders who this person is."

"I don't see the relevance."

"Mr. Powers, the relevance is obvious."

He threw down the spoon that he had been holding the entire time. "Not to me."

"Mr. Powers, your son is unsure that you love him. He thinks you might love this other person more. He . . . we, are in the dark about Little Acorn."

Michael looked past Margaret and summoned up a statement she did not understand. "As Feng Shiren was to Little Acorn, so I will be to Little Michael." With this, he excused himself and left for work.

Margaret Doringer watched the front door close behind him, and felt a chill run down her spine. Something about Mr. Powers wasn't right. Something in his head wasn't right. What's worse, she began to fear for Michael in ways she had not before imagined. For Michael's sake, she was determined to get to the bottom of the Little Acorn mystery.

As luck would have it, that week Michael's fourth grade class had a discussion about heritage. When it was Michael's turn to present his heritage to the class, someone shouted, "He's a Chinaboy!" accompanied by tittering laughter, quickly hushed by the teacher. One student got in the last word. "His sister's a Chinagirl too. And she's dying."

Michael thought of Mulan, and tears ran down his face. After this barrage, his walls grew taller and thicker, and even with the encouragement of the teacher, he refused to budge from behind them. It had long since dawned on him that "Chinamen" were inferior. These epithets struck him to the core, so he sat frozen in his chair, blocked off from the snickering of his classmates. Such was his baptism of fire, more devastating than any soldier could experience. For weeks, he pondered the humiliation, and felt particularly wounded that his mother, being Chinese, must also have been inferior. Although Nanny Peach sang her praises to the sky, Michael thought maybe it was just to make him feel better that he had a Chinese mother.

Little Acorn, this mythical stranger whose death had such a powerful impact on his normally imperturbable father, grew in his mind's eye to heroic proportions, easily dwarfing his own feeble existence, as demonstrated by the low esteem his father exhibited toward him. This oddly named boy must have done everything well, performing acts of prodigy that Michael could never match. Little Acorn's death clearly made him permanently a Large Oak in his father's affections, which Michael despaired of ever attaining. Was this Little Acorn a "Chinaboy"? He made a promise to himself that he would ask Mulan about the boy. *But, Mulan is a Chinagirl,* he thought. *How can she tell me the truth?* She had recently been admitted to the hospital, and his father scheduled a family visit two days hence.

~

On the day of visitation, Mulan received John and Michael with a hollow, exhausted expression. She lifted her eyebrows in greeting, but could do little more. An earlier fit of coughing had sapped her energy, and Michael instinctively withdrew back into himself when confronted with such incomprehensible illness. While he had always been told to treat Mulan like a sister, he knew otherwise, and the latest disparagement of his Chinese ancestry now made her seem a bit alien. Yet, now that he was here, he remembered how kind and supportive toward him she had always been. He decided she must not be categorized as a Chinagirl, and instead was safely a part of his family, even if she wasn't his real sister. But, uncomfortably, the taunts of his classmates reverberated in the back of his mind, and he still felt distance between he and Mulan, no matter how attentive she was to his needs. Michael puzzled over the confusing array of conflicting evidence about whether being Chinese made you inferior. After all, his father had round eyes, Nanny Peach had round eyes, yet, the shape of his eyes betrayed the tiny epicanthal folds that, for all intents and purposes, mutilated his looks and made them immeasurably different from his classmates and the two adults he felt closest to.

"Hello, Mikey," rasped Mulan.

"Hello."

"How are you?"

"Good."

Mulan held out her trembling hand, her eyes moist with tears.

"Come here, brat," she said affectionately.

He gave her his hand.

"You would have loved my brother Shirong. He would have been your protector when I'm gone. But, he's gone too." She covered her face to hide the tears.

Michael wanted to pull away, but such a spirit of love and compassion welled up in his young heart that he instinctively squeezed her hand and drew closer.

"Don't cry, Mulan."

She looked at him kindly. "You're a good boy, Mikey. My brother would never have let anything happen to you, even if bad guys came to your village—" She stopped suddenly and turned pale. "I mean, your house. He even protected your mother, and she was already an adult!"

Michael became interested, but John stiffened as he listened nearby. "Who was the bad guy?" asked Michael.

Mulan glanced at John, and said simply, "Oh, just some bully. I hate bullies!"

"Yeah, me too . . . Mulan, who was Little Acorn?" he blurted.

John scowled and stepped forward. "What?" he snapped. "That's really not . . . I mean, let's not bother Mulan with that now."

Mulan looked at John crossly. "John, please leave so I can talk to Michael." (She had years ago stopped calling him Mr. Powers.)

Bowing to the prerogative of the dying, John reluctantly left the room. Mulan watched him go while laying quietly, gathering her strength. Michael waited, eyes opened wide in anticipation.

Mulan patted the edge of her bed. "Michael, come closer. I want to tell you about your mother."

Michael obeyed, and listened with all of his attention as Mulan told him story after story about Meiying; how kind, how brave, how talented she was.

"She would be proud of you, Mikey," she said, reverting to Nanny Peach's favorite name for him. "And, you must be proud of her! You mu—" Mulan's voice rose with these last words, but a coughing fit interrupted.

When the coughing ended, and her breathing not so labored, Michael asked, "Who's Little Acorn?"

Now, it was Mulan's turn to be wide-eyed in wonder. "Who told you about him?"

"No one. Dad said his name. Who was he, Mulan?"

"He was a boy in China who traveled with your dad and other people."

"How did he die?"

"I'm not sure," said Mulan.

"I mean, was he, like, you know, close to dad and all?"

"Yes, but not as much as someone called Feng Shiren."

"So, he was Chinese?"

"Which one?"

"Little Acorn."

"Of course, silly boy! Just like me! Just like your mother! Just like the hero Feng Shiren!" Mulan's face darkened. "Is that a problem, Michael?"

"Nooo."

"Michaellll. . . . "

"No. But, I'm not Chinese, am I?"

"No, Mikey, you're American."

"I mean, do I look Chinese?"

"You're half-Chinese. Look, Michael, is that a problem for you?"

"No."

"Michael, I mean at school. Do the kids make fun of you or something?"

"No."

"Well, they'd better not! Your mother was the most amazing person in the world, you little fool. If someone says something, remember that."

"Mulan?"

"Yes?"

"Do people make fun of you?"

"No, why?"

"Nothing."

John re-entered the room and declared it was time to go.

"Don't forget what I said, brat," called Mulan as they left. Michael turned to see a broad, affectionate smile on her face. He waved.

~ *The Voices Again* ~

To John, all his plans to establish a relationship with Michael like Feng Shiren had with Little Acorn were in ruins. He found he couldn't talk to the boy and make any sense. Memories, like the roar of a distant waterfall, caused him to dwell far upstream of the boy's curiosity, where the water was calm. But nine-year-old boys prefer waterfalls, with all their precipitous drops and thundering noise.

You're feeling sorry for yourself, dear Chosen One! It was Goddess, returned from being so long gone.

John froze, his bourbon glass halfway to his mouth. Desperately, he glanced around and saw Nanny Peach and Michael in the kitchen. Closing his eyes, he tried to concentrate on a problem at work he had been dealing with all week.

Well, John, you've made a great mess of your son, haven't you? He is destined to suffer.

Goddess, My Beloved, that should suit You. After all, in Your infinite feminine compassion, You wanted the boy to be the next step only to be thought of as mentally ill. So it is.

It is too soon to say, Regal God! Too soon! John is in danger of making the boy unfit for the army in ten years. No army—no war; no war—no Reunion; no Reunion—no cure for Your wrong-headed First Principles. Then where will I be?

Nowhere!

I have faith. John Powers does have kindness and a gentle character going for him. He'll pull the chestnuts out of the fire. Mikey will be fine. His superior genes will be passed on. The future is secure.

Keep trying to convince Yourself!

God, shame on You! All of this genetic manipulation and consistent effort will, in the end, secure the rise of the Superior Ones.

"Stop!" shouted John.

Nanny Peach and Michael stopped what they were doing.

"What's wrong?" asked Nanny Peach.

"Oh, nothing. I just remembered something I forgot to do at work. It's nothing." He took a gulp of bourbon, and as the warmth flowed into his stomach, Goddess whispered, as if keeping Her words from God, or the two in the kitchen.

After being silent for such a long time, the demon voice finally spoke. *Get your act together, worthless, or things will fall apart, and you'll follow Meiying into the abyss!*

John could not help himself from mumbling, "But, I don't want my son to be sick. I don't want him to join the army. I don't want him to go to war."

"What?" called Nanny Peach from the kitchen. "Do you need something?"

"No!"

You need to kill yourself, worthless! shouted the bad one.

"Stop it!" whispered John, trying to keep his words from reaching Nanny Peach and Michael. Still, he felt the pieces of the puzzle were slowly coming together . . . if he could just think.

"Dinner's ready!" called Nanny Peach. "Come and get it!"

John cursed and rushed out the door. He began walking briskly around the neighborhood, mumbling to himself. Nanny Peach's voice faded in the distance.

Walk all you want, you'll end up back there, and he'll still be looking up at you with those big, little boy, Chinese eyes! Then what, worthless? Can't run away forever.

Let him be, Evil Ones! cried Goddess. *You'll drive him too far. They'll take the boy away.*

The bad voices fell silent.

Goddess's anger was not abated. She lashed out. *Bitter God! You allowed the death of Meiying when I wasn't looking . . . and Feng Shiren . . . and Lihua . . . and Meili . . . and Little Acorn, and all the others!*

As one of his little demon voices might say, You snooze, You lose. Pay attention.

That is the problem. When females pay attention, males push us away, claiming we nag, nag, nag. When females look away, males kill, or destroy, or wreak havoc on themselves and others.

Understand, Goddess, all of Us sympathize with Your efforts. Problem is, they are contrary to First Principles. Look where it has gotten You and Your faction. The poor mutant cannot tell the difference between Our voices, Our message, and the human evil ones. The genes are too entwined for him to tease out the Truth.

"Go to hell, both of You!" shouted John through the muffling San Francisco drizzle.

The voices stopped, and the damp began to creep down his neck. He returned home to find Michael in bed and Nanny Peach waiting.

"Are you okay?" she asked.

"Yes, just stressed over work."

"Mr. Powers, I don't think this is just stress."

"Margaret, I appreciate your concern, but just concentrate on taking care of Michael."

"I am. Don't you see, sir, I am."

"My mental health is not your concern."

"Mr. Powers, when we had our meeting the other day, I sensed you had decided to improve your relationship with Mikey. Did something happen to change your mind?"

Yes, Margaret, it did. Little Acorn happened."

"But, as I understand it, he is dead. Michael is alive!"

"My memories, Margaret. My memories are also alive. And these damn voices!"

"What?" asked Nanny Peach in alarm.

"Nothing. Take care of Michael, but leave me alone. Is that understood?"

"Yes, sir, but—"

"No! You are in my employ, Margaret. I will let you go if you persist. Leave me alone!"

John knew he was wrong; knew his words were wrong; knew his attitude was wrong, but he gave in to the pressure of living a lie. Once again, he found solace in the bottle, and resumed his distant, pensive detachment, occasionally interrupted by clumsy attempts to connect with Michael. Work and bourbon usually kept the voices at bay, but images of the horrific cells at the mental institution in China continued to haunt. He convinced himself that seeking professional psychiatric help would result in being confined in a similar institute, and the thought paralyzed him. Mulan checked in and out of the hospital, fighting her illness with all her strength, until the eve of Michael's twelfth birthday, when she rapidly faded. Again, she asked to speak with him alone. John left the room, his hands in his pockets making fists of helpless rage, while Michael, still displaying adolescent awkwardness, stood like a statue.

"Michael, I can't keep asking you to come hold my hand," rasped Mulan, whose throat was raw from coughing and intubation tubes. He took the hint.

Once he took her hand, she struggled to sit up, and looked deep into his eyes. "Soon, I'll be with my ancestors and my family. You'll be here with your father and Nanny Peach. I have a very serious question to ask you."

Michael shuffled and waited while she concentrated on gathering her strength.

"What?" he finally blurted, too impatient to wait longer.

"Do you hear voices?"

He looked puzzled. "I hear your voice."

"No, no. I mean, do you hear voices in your head?"

Still confused, he said, "When I'm thinking."

"No, Michael, I mean, do you hear strange voices, voices you don't know, voices you don't want to hear?"

"No."

Mulan smiled and lay her head back on the pillow. "Good."

~

But, dear, dear Reader, I really didn't hear voices then. I was telling the truth. They came later. And they came with a vengeance. But that is for another time.

~

That evening, sweet, tough, intelligent Mulan died. Michael wept with Nanny Peach, while John cursed throughout the night, his rage fueled by hectoring voices igniting mental bonfires that flared high into the dark void. No amount of bourbon would dampen the intensity of the flames. Deistic words, like glowing embers, whirled and swirled in a mad, dizzying miasma of bright specks that burned far beyond the black limits of his understanding.

In the following few years, Michael's classmates and teachers witnessed a stark change in his behavior. This sweet boy, so inclined to shy withdrawals from the taunts about his "Chinaboy" looks, took on the persona of a proud enigma, far beyond the tiresome thuggery of his peers. Girls started to notice his startlingly exotic good looks, and boys piled jealousy atop bigotry in their distain. But Michael learned to ignore the ignorable, and confront the unavoidable with equanimity (and an occasional fist to an antagonist's nose).

Meanwhile, John continued at the business, his time now spent mainly on projects involving Southeast Asia, arranging government contracts with clients and trading in everything from trucks to toilet seats. His schizophrenia simmered in the background, until a trip changed his world and paved the way for a last meeting with *her*.

Chapter Twenty-Two

Vietnam

Dinner Party

One bright and sunny day, Arthur Mobley convinced John to accept an invitation from Marie Telles to attend a dinner party. Though preferring not to accept, he had no ready excuses to avoid the affair. Michael was now in high school, and Nanny Peach, with no place to go, remained living with them in a semi-retired capacity, cooking and cleaning and being a mother and grandmother to father and son. John reluctantly agreed, and found himself sitting across from Jacob Telles, while Marie, like a queen bee, regaled the assembled guests about her latest encounter with certain members of the Endowment Committee for the symphony. John looked at this woman in amazement. She had undergone traumas of untold brutality in China, yet it seemed had not changed a whit when moving in society, passing out *bon mots* and assorted witticisms as if none of those horrible experiences actually happened. If one did not know better, it would appear her most tragic moments came with the retirement of her favorite hairdresser and the declining quality of caviar.

John, however, was perceptive enough to realize her China traumas and the loss of Meiying had gouged deep chasms into her heart, but her skill at stitching together tattered edges left barely visible scars.

"So, John, I understand you might be traveling to South Vietnam?" commented Jacob. "What with our military getting more involved, there must be money to be made."

John sighed. "Looks that way. I've got a number of clients with military contracts."

"Ever been?"

"Nope."

"Are you looking forward to it?" asked a middle-aged woman sitting nearby. "I hear the humidity is horrible."

"Not to speak of the communists sticking their noses in," added Jacob.

"Well, I'm used to dealing with humidity and communists, so it shouldn't be too bad."

"Are you going to Saigon?"

"Yup. That's where the action is."

Marie had been listening. "I have some French friends who have a villa outside Saigon. Maybe you could visit them while you're there?"

"Maybe."

"I'll give you their information. I know they would be delighted to have company. Civilized company."

John cringed. Since returning, Marie had become less tolerant of Asians, and he could not help thinking her nightmares must be constant reminders of the rape. The change was not flattering.

"My sister is a dyed-in-the-wool Francophile," said Jacob. "All things French are civilized, to her at least."

"Not at all, dear," laughed Marie. "But, seriously John, take the time to go visit them. They are very knowledgeable about the country, and they have a plantation way off in the provinces, or whatever they call them in that country."

John's ears perked up. "It might be interesting after all. I mean, to go into the countryside. China's countryside, for instance, is far more interesting than its cities."

Marie turned red and excused herself. John looked at Jacob. "Sorry. That was clumsy of me."

"It's okay, she's getting better about the mention of China, believe it or not."

Arthur piped up. "John will be representing quite a few of our clients in Vietnam. It would do him good to take some time afterward to visit the countryside. After all, it deepens our collective knowledge, which impresses clients." He frowned. "And, speaking of deep, it seems our government is getting in deeper and deeper into that country."

"Like I said, money to be made," said Jacob.

"True, but at what cost?" answered Arthur rhetorically.

"War is good for business," replied Jacob.

John had heard enough. "War is bad for people. Ask your sister."

Jacob slammed down his wine glass. "That was a damn insulting thing to say. It's good Marie isn't here. I've a good mind to sock you one."

"Play nice, boys," said Arthur.

John stood. "Sorry, but I've had enough war for a lifetime."

"So have I," came Marie's voice from the door. "War is terrible. Let's change the subject."

"What to?" called the middle-aged lady with as much cheer as she could muster.

"The Symphony Endowment Committee!" laughed Arthur.

"Oh, you are a beast!" chided Marie, as she sat and neatly placed a napkin on her lap. "Now, John dear, you really must visit my friends in Vietnam. I really insist."

"Okay, okay!" laughed John. Even as he smiled, a memory niggled at the back of his brain. When the memory fully formed, two words emerged: Precious Object. He remembered a letter from Master Zhou years earlier mentioning the

Precious Object. What did it say? He tried to remember, but others kept directing comments at him. He ignored them, thinking, thinking. Had it been taken to Southeast Asia? Was it now in Vietnam? Is Vietnam part of French Indochina? Yes, of course. Something about selling the Precious Object to someone in French Indochina. He tried to recall details, but the dinner chatter kept intruding.

Suddenly, wholly out of the blue and with the fierceness of an icy squall, he felt a desperate longing for the presence of Suling, Child of Buddha, Buandelgereen, Master Zhou, and the others. Looking around the table, he saw only shadows of people, their words mere shadows, their bodies mere shadows, and he wanted to shout something, anything, to scatter the shadows and leave him in peace to think. The full extent of his loneliness and isolation came crashing down upon him, and the absence of Meiying to comfort and assuage his terror brought forth a stream of unwelcome tears. *My god, I'm worse than an old woman!* he thought. A numbness overcame him, and with a disinterested eye, he watched his body sag downward, barely aware of the perturbed shadows flitting about his chair in anxious concern. With the greatest effort, he managed to revisit their world long enough to say, "Sorry, I have to leave." Then he blacked out.

When John awoke, he found himself lying in bed, evidently placed there by one of the shadows. He heard Nanny Peach and Michael in the kitchen. *Breakfast*, he thought lethargically. *I'm home. They must think I'm crazy.* But these thoughts passed quickly, and he returned to the Precious Object. *If I find it, I find her. If I find her, I find Meiying . . . and the others. It must be in Vietnam!*

He listened to Michael leave for school, but was far too weary to get up. Later, the phone rang, and he heard Nanny Peach's muffled voice, then a knocking. "Are you going to work?" she called.

"Yes, yes. Tell them I'll be there in an hour."

~

In the following months, John made full use of his experience at keeping schizophrenia a secret, and effectively kept hidden the underlying goal of his "business trip" from others. For all intents and purposes, Arthur assumed John viewed the excursion as a purely business matter, and arrangements were finalized for a two week trip, to be filled with meetings and presentations in Saigon. John had even convinced Nanny Peach of his unhappiness at leaving Michael. But, the closer his departure date came, the more obsessed he became with tracking down the Precious Object. *Another quest!* he kept telling himself, and for the first time in years, he felt renewed and reinvigorated.

Arrangements had been made through the office to retain an interpreter in Vietnam, and when Mrs. McAllister presented the name to him, John scrutinized it without knowing whether the person was male or female. When he found out the interpreter was female, he felt oddly relieved. Often, he sat looking at the name as might an archeologist look at a fragment of hieroglyphics: Nguyen Linh Kieu. He knew Nguyen was her family name. Should he call her Miss Nguyen? Or Linh Kieu? Or just Linh? Well, whether it be Linh Kieu or Miss Nguyen, he intended to put her services to good use. Maybe this Linh Kieu would enjoy the role of detective. And if not? He would pay her well, but what if she turned out to be useless? *There surely are others,* he thought. *If the Vietnamese are anything like Chinese, they'll have a ton of contacts. Vietnam is still a Confucian society, with all its reciprocal relationships. It'll turn up. Has to. Can't keep something like the Precious Object a secret. Bet it's tapping right now, in anticipation of my arrival.*

~ Preparations ~

Two days before departing, Marie called on John at his company. When he greeted her in his new, private office, she waited for his secretary to close the door, and gazed at him with an unusually grim face.

"Hello, John. I've come about something important."

"Hello, Marie. Please sit. Will you join me in coffee or tea?"

"No, thank you."

He pulled forward his most comfortable chair. She settled in and crossed her legs. John noted her beauty, still vibrant despite the years. Caught looking at her legs, he smiled. "You're still quite attractive, Marie. Sorry, I couldn't help admiring."

"Thank you, John. You know, my beauty has always paled next to Meiying's."

He did not respond.

Marie leaned forward and looked intensely into his eyes.

"John," she said. "Is this trip solely for business?"

"Of course, why?"

"Because, I don't believe you."

"Sorry?"

"I don't believe you."

"Okay."

"After my dinner party, and your . . . difficulties . . . I began thinking."

She paused, and John waited.

"About?" he finally asked.

"Your trip. Before Meiying died, she received a letter from Master Zhou, which I believe you also read. He had sold the Precious Object to someone in French Indochina. She seemed quite upset about it, but understood his motivation for doing so. Nonetheless, I recall her being more agitated than one might think, given the circumstances. Did she mention this to you, John?"

"Why does it matter?"

"John! Don't play the fool with me. I know you read the letter—Meiying told me so. The Precious Object is in Vietnam. You know it is. You are traveling to Vietnam, ostensibly on business. But, John, I know you. Do you plan to try and find it?"

John remained silent for some time. Marie waited patiently.

"Yes," he said at last.

"As I thought. Well, I have news for you."

Now John leaned forward. "What?"

"Remember the French couple I told you about at the party? The ones my brother gave me grief about?"

"Yes."

"They might know where it is."

John leapt up, almost knocking over his chair. "What?"

"They might know where it is."

"Where?" He sat again, highly agitated.

"That's just it, they *might* know. I wrote them asking whether they had any knowledge of such an object."

"Did you tell them everything?"

"Yes."

"And?"

"They heard about another French planter who owned the statue, but something happened, and he no longer has it."

"Who does?"

"This is where it gets hazy. The bottom line is that they don't know."

"But, they know the address of this planter?"

"Yes, but you must visit them first."

"Why?"

"They have other information you might find interesting."

"What information?"

She shrugged. "That is all they wrote."

"My god, Marie! This is tremendous!"

"Yes, I knew you would think so. It might surprise you to know I even thought of joining you."

"Really?"

Marie shuddered. "Yes, but there is a war, and if anything ugly happened, well, I could not take . . . any other shocks."

"Yes, of course."

"But, there's more, John."

"What?"

"Your schizophrenia."

"Marie—"

She held up her hand in warning. "No, John, let me finish. You and I both know the voices will come when you are over there."

John remained silent.

"Have they been bad?"

"No, not so much."

"Well, they will return with a vengeance if you find the Precious Object. You know that, don't you?"

"Maybe, but they've been bad before, and I survived."

She laughed sarcastically. "Survived? Yes. But, John, the price you have paid. You will never know. And here, I am referring to Meiying. Anyway, that is a different story. John, for your own sake, go to a psychiatrist. Get medication before you leave."

"Thank you, Marie, but I will be fine."

"You're not fine, John."

"But—"

Again she held up her hand. "No, John! Meiying worried all the time, particularly about Michael inheriting your . . . condition."

"Michael is fine. He shows no signs."

Marie hesitated. "Not according to Nanny Peach."

"What? You've been talking to her? Spying on me? Goddamn it, Marie, spying on me?"

"Of course I have, John. Nanny Peach used to work for Meiying and me, remember? We hired her."

"But, that is a breach of confidence!"

"No, John, don't be absurd. She is concerned."

He blanched. "Has she seen signs?"

"Yes."

"Oh, my god! She never told me. I didn't know, Marie!"

"I am aware."

"Why didn't she tell me?"

"John, as I understand it, you are not the most involved father."

"It's true. My god, it's true."

"Go to a psychiatrist, John, for Michael's sake."

"Yes, yes, I should. I know I should."

"This trip will possibly break you, John, especially if you find *her*."

"You mean the Precious Object?"

"No, I mean *her*." Marie held out her hands, palms up.

"God, Marie, if I find *her*, I'll be in heaven."

"No, John. Even Meiying came to realize *she* is not what *she* seems."

John raised his eyebrows in shock. "What do you mean?"

"Meiying confided in me that others had warned her."

"Who?"

"Never mind."

"Who?" he repeated.

Marie rose and slung her purse over her shoulder. "I have to go, John. Oh!" She fumbled in her purse. "Here is the address and telephone number of my French friends. I have written about your coming. Good luck."

He took the slip of paper. "Thank you, Marie."

She looked at him as one might look at a prisoner on his way to the electric chair. When the door closed behind her, John excitedly studied the address.

So, it is made easier, he thought. The day of his departure was less than forty-eight hours away, and he fidgeted like a schoolboy. He carefully folded the paper and tucked it in his wallet, then tried to focus on business, but thoughts of

Michael intruded. He dreaded talking to Nanny Peach about the boy, for fear of what he might find out. Still, he knew it would be necessary.

~ *The Boy Hears Someone* ~

Nanny Peach looked in the mirror and made her face assume a satisfactorily concerned expression. She had been summoned to speak to John after Michael left with friends to watch a movie, and she was determined to tell the father what he needed to know. Relieved his drinking had only just started, she sat across from him and waited. Nanny Peach knew better than to interrupt his thoughts in his current mood, when his eyes glazed over with indifference to the outside world, and any intrusion was rudely rebuffed. But, this time his reverie lasted longer than she was willing to wait.

"Mr. Powers, is it the voices?"

He blinked uncomprehendingly.

"The voices. Is it the voices, Mr. Powers?"

He waved his hand. "Just in passing."

"Is it convenient to talk now?"

"Yes." His eyes focused on her at last. "Yes, I want to ask you about Michael."

"I'm glad."

"Does he hear . . . things he shouldn't?"

"Why do you ask now, if I may ask?"

"Marie Telles."

"Ah, I see. You've been talking to her. Yes, I believe he does hear things he shouldn't."

"You believe he does? You don't know for sure?"

"I believe he does, but he's hiding them from me. The boy is clearly confused and afraid."

"What makes you believe he does?"

Nanny Peach took a deep breath. "Because, he has begun to look like you when you hear the voices."

John's face twisted in a flash of agony, and he took a swig of bourbon, then lashed out. "How do you know when I hear voices?" he shouted. "You don't know anything about it! Goddamn it, what I have to put up with!"

"I know," she said firmly.

John croaked, then spoke with a reedy, cracked voice. "Only Meiying knew."

"Don't fool yourself, sir."

"Well, since you don't know for sure he hears voices, there's nothing we can do, is there?"

"That's convenient."

"How are his grades in school?"

"Good."

"Well then, we wait and see. I can think of no reason to humiliate him by dragging him to some damn shrink!"

"That's convenient."

John smirked. "That's right, Margaret, it's convenient. I have an important business trip coming up."

"You're a stranger to him. He needs you. He is afraid, Mr. Powers. Very afraid."

"Of voices?"

"Of you."

"Oh, Christ, Margaret! Let's not get overly dramatic. He's a teenage boy. He needs his independence. Besides, it's probably just hormones."

"He needs you, especially now."

John started to speak, but stopped short. A vision of Feng Shiren with Little Acorn came to his mind, humbling him yet again. "When I get back, we'll see."

"About?"

"About his voices."

Nanny Peach held his eyes. "Why don't you take him with you?"

John laughed. "Out of the question! It's a business trip. Besides, he has school."

"He can stay at the hotel with you, and, before you object, is perfectly capable of amusing himself while you are at your meetings. He is not a child anymore. It would give you both a chance to know each other . . . to comfort him, love him . . . to redeem yourself!"

"No, no, no. Too dangerous. There's a war on, you know."

"Yes, but the war you refer to is not in Vietnam."

John emptied his glass in one gulp. "Leave me alone! I told you already, we'll see when I return. Now, leave me alone!"

"Alone with your ghosts, or your voices?"

"With both," whispered John. "Now, please leave me alone, Margaret."

She stood to leave, then paused and said reproachfully, "He needs your love, John Powers, almost as much as you need his."

~

That night, he dreamed he was back in the locked cell at Li-Fu's mental institution. From the other cells came shouted obscenities and piteous moans, creating an unspeakable wailing that mixed with the unhealthy vapors of that hellish den to make him feel the old panic. Suddenly, from the adjoining cell, he heard Michael's voice, pleading, "Father, help me! Father, help me! The voices! Father, help me!" Unable to cope, John awoke in a sweat, cursing his life and the unwanted responsibilities associated with this boy that constantly reminded him of Meiying and of his own weaknesses. With no one else to attack, he lashed out at Goddess.

"Well, Goddess, or whatever You are, do You feel some sort of satisfaction at my pain? The boy is ill, just as You want, and he'll go off to war, just as You want, and he'll come back to be locked in a mental institution, just as You want. All for your goddamn reunion, and resurrection of the planet, whatever that is."

You will be a shadow by then, John, came Her voice.

"I'm going to Vietnam and find the Precious Object," he said to the air. "What do You say to that?"

Yes, do it! cried God.

"So, I've touched a nerve, eh, Goddess?"

John, you mustn't go, She said quite calmly. *It might spoil everything.*

"Good!" shouted John. "If I can spoil Your plans, maybe my son will grow up to be normal!"

Yes! Yes! boomed God. *Tell Her!*

Notice, John, how anxious He is to thwart My plans? Do you know why?

Her words took him aback. "Why?" he asked.

Because, He wants the world to continue suffering, to feed His convictions, His addiction to First Principles. Is that what you want, John?

A loud knocking finally penetrated his consciousness.

"What?" he shouted, assuming it was Nanny Peach.

"Dad?" came Michael's voice. "Dad? Are you okay?"

John let his head fall back on the pillow. *What to say?*

"Yes, I'm fine!" he called.

"I just got back from the movie, and I heard you shouting. You sure everything is okay?"

"I'm okay, thanks, Michael. Just a bad dream. Go to bed."

Silence, then footsteps away.

Damn! thought John. *Another wasted opportunity. Now, alone and afraid, is he going to lay in his bed and listen to the damn voices? Oh, god, what a fool I am! A terrible father! A terrible person!*

No, you are not, said Goddess. *You have served Me well.*

~

A note, dear Reader. It's true, I had already started to hear voices, just as Nanny Peach suspected. They came like precipitate coroners brandishing scalpels, mad butchers who gleefully carved up my healthy, developing adolescent mind. Even when I knocked on Dad's door, I heard them, and I knew he was dealing with them also, just as they were now berating me. But, his absence, both figuratively and literally, left me alone with them, as I remain to this day, writing, writing.

~ *Departure* ~

On the morning of his departure, John wanted to slip out of the apartment unseen. The thought of Michael's face, mooning at him with a forlorn expression, waiting for words of wisdom, seemed more than he could bear (not to speak of Nanny Peach's disapproving glare). But, it could not be helped. He withheld parting words until the last moment at the airport, where nanny and son stood like good troopers, wishing him a safe flight.

"Well, Michael, be good and do well at school!" he boomed with false bravado. "Goodbye, Margaret. I'll be back before you know it!"

False. False. False.

They waved and disappeared among the crowd.

The flight proceeded uneventfully, but for a little turbulence that briefly caused his heart to palpitate a bit faster. During the entire flight, John's thoughts kept returning to Nguyen Linh Kieu.

Will she be pretty? he wondered. *But, how stupid! They're never pretty. Question is, will she be intelligent? Will she be able to help find the Precious Object?* Such thoughts occurred to him, but he could not help returning to speculation about her looks. Since Meiying's death, his libido had been subsumed by her loss. But, gradually, his interest in women returned, and he often found himself fantasizing about this woman or that. Still, he maintained a strict prohibition against using pornography to masturbate. Always it was Meiying with whom he made love. Always.

~

After clearing customs, he saw Nguyen Linh Kieu jiggling a sign. "Welcome Mr. John Powers" it read in bold strokes of red ink. At least, he assumed it was her. His initial impression was of a slight, nervous young Vietnamese girl. She wore a traditional *ao dai* that accentuated her unusual face, which was long and graceful for a Vietnamese. At first, she struck him as plain, but when he came closer, her beauty unfolded in the brilliance of her smile. Her face possessed an introspective melancholy when not smiling, as if seeking some inner sanctuary amongst memories of better times. But the spontaneous smile, made more striking by the before and after solemnity of her countenance, took one totally off guard, and thereby endeared itself by contrast, as if she presented the onlooker with a glimpse of some precious gift before quickly wrapping it up again.

"Hello, Mr. Powers. Welcome to Vietnam!"

"You are Miss Nguyen?" he asked after plopping down his luggage and wiping his sweaty face.

Again, a beaming smile. "Yes, and I have a boy to take luggage to automobile, which awaits in lot of parking."

John momentarily looked puzzled, then exclaimed, "Oh! Parking lot! Of course! Thank you."

Her smile faltered. "Sorry, my English not so good."

"No, no, not at all. Good!"

On their way to the hotel, Miss Nguyen listed the meetings on the schedule for the following day. John groaned at this reminder of the laborious part of his trip, and to make matters worse, he felt a headache coming on. Weighed down by these unwelcome circumstances, he begged off dinner at a noodle shop highly recommended by Miss Nguyen, and retired to his hotel room, where he promptly fell asleep to visions of the Precious Object. Oddly, he did not dream of the statue, but of Miss Nguyen's face, alternately smiling and frowning, like a bright lamp being turned on and off.

Next morning, after breakfast, they went from meeting to meeting, her services as invaluable as her smile. John chaffed at the necessity of such meetings, but his apparent disinterest and impatience actually strengthened his negotiating position, as his counterparts were under no illusions that he cared about the outcome. Linh Kieu, for her part, came to admire the American for his business acumen, little knowing his main concern lay elsewhere. After three days of such meetings, John invited Linh to dinner. She felt flattered, and dressed in her most attractive Western dress, whereupon John insisted she go home and change into her traditional *ao dai*. "Much nicer," he mumbled when she returned to the hotel. If Linh had hopes he would have sex with her, and perhaps take her back to America with him, she was sorely disappointed.

"Linh," he said after dinner, as they sipped rice wine. "I have something to tell you, and it is very important, so you must listen closely. Do you understand?"

"Yes."

"While I am here on business, my main interest lies elsewhere."

She tilted her head in a most endearing manner. "Sorry, I don't understand."

"Linh, I am here to find a statue."

"A what?"

After repeatedly consulting the dictionary, John succeeded in describing the Precious Object.

"Ah," she said, still confused.

"I want to finish these meetings by the end of this week. Please reschedule them so we can fit them all in by Friday. Do you understand?"

She shook her head no, and it took him an eternity to explain.

"But, if they will not reschedule?" she asked.

John wanted to say, "Screw them," but instead said, "Then tell them we will meet next time I come to Vietnam. I want the next two weeks free. Do you understand now, Linh?"

"I understand. Is it about this statue?"

"Yes."

"You want buy it?"

"Linh, listen carefully. I want to find it, see it, visit it. Then, we'll see."

She nodded. "Yes, I understand."

He leaned forward and put his hand on hers for emphasis. "But, sweet little Linh, I need your help to locate it. I need you to be a detective."

Linh felt excited that he touched her, but his words were strange, not the business English she learned in college. "Yes, I will help . . . but, what is detective?"

Again, the dictionary, and as he explained, John observed the intelligent girl warm up to the proposition. She looked at him greedily.

"More money to do this?"

John laughed. "Yes, more money."

"How much?"

Nguyen Linh Kieu realized this American was not interested in her, and she wanted compensation for her dashed hopes. The money, of course, was to be paid under the table, and she would use it for her parents and her three-year-old son.

John gave her the address of the French planter friend of Marie Telles.

"Kon Tum province," she muttered while reading the address. "Far."

"Too far?" asked John.

Linh flashed a brilliant smile and drained her wine cup. "I grow up in Kon Tum province. I will find it. I will find it!"

"Good!" cried John, adding, "Assuming it's still in the area."

"But," she cautioned. "The area is dangerous. A bit dangerous. Many communists. *Beaucoup* Viet Cong."

"Okay, well, I've dealt with communists before. Now, let's finish these damn meetings."

"I call them tomorrow to reschedule. But the week will be very busy."

"So be it."

"What that mean?"

"It means, it doesn't matter."

Again, her radiant smile. "So be it!"

~ Sherlock Holmes ~

At last, the week ended with John reporting a string of lucrative transactions to Arthur Mobley by telegram. Not that he cared much, but the accomplishment lessened the guilt of striking off on his own. Nguyen Linh Kieu had been hard at work, and she obtained information that she kept to herself, the better to increase payment from Mr. Powers. After all, it mustn't seem too easy. But, what she learned made her uneasy. Very uneasy.

The morning after the last business meeting, John sat in the lobby, sharing tea with Linh.

"Okay," he said. "How do we get to the Davignon plantation?"

"Not easy. Communist V.C. everywhere."

"How do we get there, Linh?"

"Bus. Long trip."

"How long?"

"One day, two days, maybe three. Never know. Problem is V.C. Many stops. Many break-downs. Many V.C."

"What have you found out about the statue?"

"I think I know, but first, go to the Davignon plantation."

"Yes, yes, I know that already."

"Once there, I leave. Check location. Come back and take you to it."

"I can go with you."

"No. Dangerous."

"Dangerous for you too."

"Not so much." She smiled and tapped her hat. "Good peasant stock!"

"Okay."

"Dangerous," she repeated, and looked at him from under the peasant hat she wore for the first time, looking incongruous in the posh lobby.

"Let me guess. More money?"

"Dangerous."

"Okay, more money, but only after you take me there."

"Mr. Powers, I no joke. It is dangerous."
"V.C.?"
"No, the statue."

~

On the bus, creaky, dirty, noisy, hot, crammed with passengers, John sat next to Linh, whose smile had not appeared for some time.

She's afraid, he thought. *Afraid of the Precious Object. What did she hear? Superstition makes us afraid, and Vietnamese are a superstitious lot. Try again.*

"Linh," he said. "Why don't you tell me where you think it is?"

"Because, not sure. Could be wrong. Have to check. You stay with Davignon man."

"It sounds like you know him."

She laughed, its guileless warmth slicing through the haze of sweat-soaked humidity and noxious exhaust.

"Silly man! He is rich, I am poor. But, I hear from friends about this man."

"Good things?"

"Things."

"Linh, your evasiveness can be very annoying."

"What?"

"Nothing."

Despite a few unplanned delays, the trip to the provincial capital of Kon Tum city proved uneventful. John felt supremely grateful to leave the cramped confines of the bus. Linh checked him into a luxurious hotel built by the French, and went off to stay with relatives until the next day, when they were to meet for breakfast at the hotel restaurant. While John relaxed in a hot bath at the hotel, Linh made arrangements for a private car to take them to the Davignon plantation. John's last task for the evening was to call Davignon and tell him they would be leaving Kon Tum city the next day, and that he looked forward to meeting the Frenchman and viewing his estate. Davignon, sounding rather distracted on the other end of a crackling, static-plagued phone line, said he also looked forward to the visit. This garbled conversation ended abruptly when the line went suddenly dead.

Oh, well, thought John. *The deed is done. Tomorrow, hopefully, I find out the location of the Precious Object. And then? Onward!*

Chapter Twenty-Three

Song Nhan Village

Arrival at the Davignon Plantation

After a bumpy ride on a deeply rutted dirt road, the car stopped at the top of a steep hill overlooking a village just visible through the mist. John and Linh stepped out to stretch their legs. She pointed downward. "Song Nhan village. Davignon lives there."

"In a village?" asked John, expecting something quite different.

"Yes, newer parts of village grow up around plantation mansion. Fields and rubber trees of Davignon all around. Peasants here also grow rice and fruit. Old French fort nearby, but now gone."

"Gone?"

"Yes." She waved her arms. "Go back to France."

"Oh, abandoned."

"Yes, abandoned. Fall down bad." She glanced at her watch. "We go."

"Ruins?"

She looked at him quizzically, so he used his hands to mimic a house collapsing.

"Yes, yes!" she exclaimed. "Ruins!" A shadow passed over her face.

"What?" asked John.

"Ghosts there." Again, she checked her watch. "We go."

"Wait," said John gazing down at the village. "Have you been here before?"

"No, my village far away. But, I have heard of Song Nhan village. Big battle here, or near here. French soldiers and communists fight at old fort. Many dead. After Partition, communists not so bad. *Didi* away, back to north. For you, I call my uncle and ask about village a few days ago. He say there is elder in village he knows. Venerable Vu Huong."

"Did you mention the statue, Linh?"

She avoided his eyes and checked her watch again. "It's late. We go now."

"Linh!"

"I tell you later, when we arrive. Long story. Much detective work. De-tec-tive, yes?"

"Yes, detective."

"Okay, but then you tell me everything you know."

Again she avoided his eyes. "Perhaps, but Monsieur Davignon tell you more than I can."

Strange, thought John. *Why so evasive? Does she want more money? No, I don't think so. Strange. Well, this Monsieur Davignon will be interesting. Hope to god he speaks good English.*

"Mr. Powers!" exclaimed Linh impatiently from inside the car. "We must go!"

"Okay, okay, just enjoying the view."

As they entered the village, curious onlookers crowded around the vehicle, making progress slow. They passed a magnificent temple, which Linh explained was the village *dinh*, or meeting place. John wanted to stop and look, but Linh insisted they continue on to the mansion. As they followed a winding road up a hill, the huge building came into view. It stood impressively ornate, overlooking the red-tiled houses, thatch cottages, and corrugated tin shacks of the village. Built out of concrete, wood, and stone, it now served as a magnificent villa owned by the Davignon family. John thought it hovered above the village like an enchanted palace.

Driving through a wrought-iron gate and up a tree-lined private road, they stopped at the covered entrance supported by Romanesque columns. Monsieur Davignon and his wife stood side-by-side in greeting. He was a tall, lanky French-man, with a hooked nose, a pockmarked face, and an aristocratic bearing. His wife, introduced as Colette Davignon, smiled benignly, her hands behind her back, her flowered dress billowing in the breeze. *Charming*, thought John. *Beauty and the beast.*

After the introductions, Monsieur Davignon invited John and Linh to join them for tea. When they entered the villa, the foyer struck John as the height of provincial elegance. Tapestries hung from the high walls, and massive chandeliers twinkled from the vaulted ceiling. He heard Linh emit a low sigh of awestruck admiration.

Madame Davignon motioned for a servant to bring tea, and they entered a side room where French provincial furniture beckoned, graceful objects from a rapidly fading world of past elegance. The gentle curves of the beautifully carved tables and chairs seemed to droop in sorrow at the coming conflagration, yet remained unapologetically proud of their noble pedigree.

"Welcome to our home," said Madame Davignon as she gestured for her guests to sit.

"Thank you for having us," replied John, relieved they spoke impeccable English.

Monsieur Davignon coughed politely. "I understand you have come for a specific purpose."

"Yes."

"Marie Telles has provided us with some information, but if you would be so kind, please tell us what we can do for you."

John chose his words carefully. "As Miss Telles explained, I have come in search of a statue. A Goddess statue. She mentioned you might know of its whereabouts."

"Ah, yes, I see," he said, but then fell silent.

John saw Madame Davignon look at her husband with an unreadable expression.

"Anyway," continued John. "Miss Telles said you know the French planter who owned the statue, but that he disposed of it somehow, or rather, somewhere. Is that accurate?"

"In a manner of speaking."

"So, would you be willing to inform me of his whereabouts so that I might visit him. You see, I'm trying to track down this statue."

"For what reason, may I ask?" said Madame Davignon.

John held out both hands, palms up, but the two hosts looked at him blankly. He put them down. "Well, you see, I am with a group of people who once owned the statue and would like to get it back."

"Owned it?" said Monsieur Davignon incredulously.

"Yes."

"But, dear sir, it is not something that can be owned."

John looked at him with a puzzled expression. "But, why not?"

"Because, it owns you . . . what I mean to say, is that it possesses the possessor."

"I don't follow."

"Mr. Powers, we are the ones who purchased the statue from a Monsieur Zhou in China," said Madame Davignon.

John was stunned. "I didn't know! I mean, I thought you simply were acquainted with the owner. I didn't know."

"That was quite intentional, Mr. Powers. We have no interest in being thought of as the previous owners."

"But, why?"

"Because, as I told you, it seemed to own us, and so, it had to go."

"But, where did it go?"

"Mr. Powers, for that you need to talk to the village elder."

"Who?"

"The village elder. The Venerable Vu Huong."

John stared at Monsieur and Madame Davignon with such wide eyes and with such an amusingly surprised expression that they almost laughed. "You mean, it's right here? In this village?"

"As far as we know, Mr. Powers. Song Nhan village now houses the statue. At first, our servants were terrified of it, and many left our service after we obtained the statue. Certain . . . noises came from it . . . or, I should rather say, from inside it. Rumors spread among the villagers that a demon, or some such, resided in our villa. We couldn't even find workers for the rubber. But, something changed, and the Venerable Vu Huong came to us with a proposition. We agreed, and that agreement must remain a secret, but you may rest assured we no longer have the statue, nor do we want to see it again. In fact, that was part of the agreement."

"But, I am amazed!" cried John. "It's right here, under my nose."

"Are you not interested in why the natives were afraid?"

"I think I know, Monsieur Davignon."

"Then you perhaps know its secrets?" asked Madame Davignon, glancing at her husband.

"That, Madame, is what I'm trying to find out."

Monsieur Davignon rose. "Well, I have to get out to the fields. You, of course, are invited to stay at our villa for as long as you wish. I would like to get caught up on what's happening in the States. Especially, your opinion on what America intends to do about these damn communist rebels. We do see more and more American soldiers arriving in Pleiku, not far from where we are."

"Thank you so much. May a room also be provided for Miss Nguyen?"

"Of course," said Madame Davignon. She turned to Linh and spoke in perfect Vietnamese. "My dear, you may stay in a room here. You are quite lovely."

Linh smiled her most radiant smile and replied in English. "Thank you, Madame Davignon. I would be most grateful."

John felt quite proud of his slight, Vietnamese interpreter. But, a thought came to his mind. "I do have one question, Monsieur Davignon. What made the villagers change their opinions about the statue?"

"Ah, the unfathomable complexities of the Vietnamese mind. For the answer to that, Mr. Powers, you should talk to the Venerable Vu Huong."

~ *The Venerable Vu Huong* ~

That evening, John and Linh were treated to a lavish dinner by their gracious hosts. John felt delighted to get a break from Asian food, and he found the French cuisine delicious. Linh had been tasked with making arrangements to meet with the Venerable Vu Huong the next day, and John retired to his bed in the happiest of spirits. *Nanny Peach was wrong*, he thought. *No voices. No trouble. Just smooth sailing, so far.* He anticipated a peaceful sleep, but in the early morning hours, a nightmare shook him to his core. Upon awakening, he could only remember a war engulfing Song Nhan village, and Michael somehow involved. A soldier? Killed? He could not remember, for all was darkness surrounding his son. Only the horror of knowing Michael suffered in a war, here in this very location, kept him from facing the next morning with optimistic enthusiasm.

He joined Madame Davignon and Linh on the veranda for breakfast. The morning broke lovely and sweet, a tenuous mist, glowing pinkish from the rays of dawn, blanketed the village below.

"Good morning," said Madame Davignon.

"Good morning, Madame," replied John. He nodded at Linh, who smiled back, by all appearances a very contented young woman.

"So, Linh, are things arranged to meet with the Venerable Vu Huong?"

"Yes, sir. We are to meet at the *dinh*."

"When?"

"Around eleven o'clock. I think he wants to show it off."

"Yes," agreed Madame Davignon. "He is quite proud of it, and rightfully so. A grand example of Chinese influence in Vietnamese architecture."

"So, you are an architect?"

"Heavens no, but I do take an interest." She gave out a deep sigh. "I will miss this."

"Miss it?" asked John.

"Mr. Powers, the war will come, and I fear we French are not going to be welcome. Dien Bien Phu was bad enough, but Mr. Ho Chi Minh is not satisfied with only the north."

"And you think he will win?"

She shrugged. "Your President Johnson says America won't allow it."

"But?"

She shrugged again. "We'll see." She sat back and rubbed her forehead. "But, I will miss it so." She turned to Linh. "Would you like to live here, my dear?"

Linh shook her head. "Oh, no, Madame. Too big for me. I am just a poor peasant girl."

"Yes, that's the thing. Remain that, and you'll be fine. The communists like poor peasant girls."

"It really does sound like you think they will win," pursued John.

Again, she shrugged and looked down.

"Well, I have seen how they operate, and your Vietnamese communists are copying China—Mao Zedong's political and Zhu De's military strategies," said John. "I fear they will succeed here also."

"No need to be so pessimistic!" boomed the voice of Monsieur Davignon. He sat and snapped a napkin in his lap. "We're not defeated yet."

"Have breakfast, dear, and let's stop talking about war," said Madame Davignon, getting up to kiss him on the cheek. "It is too lovely a morning."

"Do you really think they will win?" whispered Linh to John.

He realized his mistake. "No . . . ah, I mean, I don't know, Linh. I hope not."

"Tomorrow, Mr. Powers, I will show you my rubber trees," said Monsieur Davignon.

"I would be delighted, Monsieur."

After breakfast, John paced the grounds, impatiently waiting to leave with Linh and meet the Venerable Vu Huong. When the time finally came, they strolled together through the entrance gate and down toward the village. Before they took two steps outside the gate, a horde of children assailed John with requests for money, or chewing gum, or anything American. Shaking his head emphatically no, he saw the adults watching from a distance, something in their eyes akin to hate, but not quite hate. It occurred to him it was self-loathing. Why? They loathed their weakness, their inability to raise their children according to the proper virtues, and resented watching so many young ones run to a foreigner for money and food. Their self-loathing reflected back on him, and he felt a deep resentment in return at their silent accusations. In a moment of clarity, he knew America would lose this coming war, and the beautiful villa of Davignon would be destroyed as a symbol of all their self-loathing, all their hatred. And further, even more shocking to himself, John knew that was how it should be. But, what about Michael? What will happen to him if Goddess and the dream are correct?

"Mr. Powers!" came Linh's voice. "Please, are you well?"

"Yes, of course. Why?"

Linh waved her hand. "You are being asked a question."

"Oh, sorry," said John, trying to focus on the unknown questioner and whatever the question might be.

"This man"—said Linh, pulling forward a middle-aged man who repeatedly bowed—"wishes to talk with you." With some difficulty, Linh made him cease bowing and started over. "This man has many *mou* of land. He wants to know if America will protect him from the communists. If not, he will sell his fields and go to district capital."

John felt dizzy. All he wanted to do was speak to the Venerable Vu Huong about the Precious Object. How could he advise a man about such important matters? He was not the American government. Didn't these people understand?

Linh listened to more of the man's rapid-fire words, then turned to John. "He has many children. If America doesn't help, the boys will be taken away as soldiers, and his girls will all be raped. What do you say?"

John shook his head in confusion.

"Your silence is insulting to him."

"Tell him I do not know!" exclaimed John in exasperation. "I am only a private citizen—one person, not the United States government."

Linh gazed at him in astonishment, then turned back to the man and said in Vietnamese, "He is here to report to the President of the United States. What he says will determine whether America will help you. Now, he must meet with the Venerable Vu Huong. Let him pass!"

John did not understand what Linh said, but her words produced a miracle; the crowd parted and he walked unhindered to the *dinh*. As he approached, John took stock of this grand meeting place. The *dinh* served not only as the communal meeting hall, but also as the repository for imperial documents and the place where altars honoring the guardian spirits were housed. Built long before the Davignon mansion by a secret society of monks, the *dinh* of Song Nhan village was constructed in the traditional style of concrete and wood, with intricate stone friezes adorning the walls and an elaborately carved dragon running the length of the roof. Signs of age and lack of maintenance had begun to show, including cracks, peeling paint and the smell of urine. But, it still remained a sight to behold, and John contemplated it with admiration.

When he entered, he saw a figure at the other end of the hall, seated upon a sort of stage, with massive, brightly painted statues rising portentously behind him, replete with scowling faces and various weapons of war brandished as fierce warnings to unwanted spirits. Linh caught him looking up in wonder at the huge figures.

"Guardian Spirits," she whispered in respectful reverence—or so John thought at the time.

On the stage, a small, thin, wizened old gentleman with a scholar's wispy beard rose in greeting. His smile rivaled that of Linh, and he nodded approvingly at her as they drew nearer.

The old boy still has an eye for women, thought John.

Linh made the introductions.

"Welcome to Song Nhan village, my American friend," he said in a high-pitched, falsetto voice that reminded John of Chinese opera.

"Thank you, sir."

The old man's eyes twinkled as he looked at Linh. "And what is your full name and home village, my lovely girl?"

Linh blushed and gave the information with a deep bow.

"Ah! Good manners, good upbringing, good Confucian girl," he said approvingly in Chinese.

Linh understood only a few of his words, but John nodded in agreement.

"So, you understand Chinese?" exclaimed the Venerable.

"Yes."

The Venerable Vu Huong clapped his hands like a child presented with candy. "Good! Excellent! However,—" he looked at Linh with exaggerated sympathy—"I must speak Vietnamese to keep our young Confucian girl employed."

John laughed, but he wanted to continue the conversation in Chinese, and said, "Your village is quite beautiful, sir."

The Venerable's face darkened, and he put up a cautionary hand. "No, my young friend, we really must communicate through Nguyen Linh Kieu. Please, speak English so she may translate."

"All right," replied John, a bit flustered. He repeated the comment in English, and Linh dutifully translated for the Venerable.

"Thank you," he said in Vietnamese. "But, this war is wreaking havoc. So many of our young men have been taken as soldiers, and so many of our young women. . . ." his voice trailed off.

"It seems peaceful enough," said John stupidly.

"Appearances are deceiving."

"Well, sir, I think Miss Nguyen told you the purpose of my visit, did she not?"

"Indeed she did."

John's heart raced. "Is the statue still here?"

The Venerable leaned forward. "May I ask why you seek this statue?"

John held out his hands, palms up, and said nothing.

Vu Huong blinked. "And this means?"

John put his hands down and sighed. He then gave the Venerable a brief history of the group and its quest.

"I see," replied the Venerable.

"Is it still here?" repeated John.

"Yes and no. You see, we in the village have agreed to keep it secret. In fact, that was part of our agreement with Monsieur Davignon. You wish to see it, but I must first consult with the village council."

John's disappointment shone unmistakably in his face and drooping shoulders.

The Venerable waved his arms. "Do not despair, young man. Let us see what the council has to say."

"But, aren't you the head?" asked John recklessly.

"Yes, but lately, for the first time, we have by necessity allowed women to be on the council, as there is now a shortage of men. Some of the women are quite stubborn." He laughed. "Quite stubborn!"

"May I ask, at least, does it emit a sound?"

"Sound?"

"Yes, a noise, like tapping." John attempted to replicate it with his tongue while rapping his knuckles against the table.

The Venerable Vu Huong laughed uproariously, much to John's consternation. "Of course! Of course, young Mr. Powers." He held out both hands, palms up. "*She* is quite near."

~ *The Precious Object Unveiled* ~

John returned to the villa full of anticipation and wonder. So, Vu Huong, the old trickster, had known all along. *She* is near! He was beside himself with cautious optimism. *All here! It's all here!* He kept repeating to himself. That evening, at dinner with the Davignons, the conversation turned to the statue.

"I understand you talked to old Vu Huong today," commented Monsieur Davignon.

"Yes, I did."

"And?"

"It went well. He said the village council will decide whether I may see it."

Davignon laughed. "Ha! That old reprobate. He'll make the final decision, count on it."

Madame Davignon coughed and spoke hesitantly. "Yes dear, that is true, but Schoolmistress Nang may be a problem."

"True, true," her husband replied. "That witch is truly beyond redemption."

"How so?" asked John.

"She's the local school teacher, and Colette and I are convinced she is a communist sympathizer."

Madame Davignon said, "Yes, we have reports that she espouses the hateful rhetoric of Ho Chi Minh to her students, but nobody on the council does anything about it."

"Don't you have influence?" asked John.

"Less and less," sighed Monsieur Davignon. "These damn people are starting to come under the sway of the communists. They sense which way the wind is blowing."

"Do you think they'll let me see the statue?" asked John.

"Who knows? The Venerable is a strange and unpredictable man. Sometimes, I wonder whose side he is on," replied Monsieur Davignon. "Have some more wine, Mr. Powers. And you too, Mademoiselle Nguyen, although I suspect French wine is not to your taste."

"It is very good, thank you, sir." Linh took a small sip to be polite.

"When is this council meeting to occur?" asked Monsieur Davignon.

"I don't know. Vu Huong said it would be soon, but he wasn't definite."

"Ha! That sounds like the old man. Keep everyone guessing. Can't set your watch by these people, Mr. Powers. Far too unorganized."

John nodded but said nothing.

"Well! Tomorrow we go for a tour of my rubber trees. By the way, they're near an old stone fort our army built many many years ago. It's in ruins now, but in the past was quite a draw. Even had a fancy, Catholic church. But, it's in ruins also. Many years ago, before the Partition, there was a battle and a lot of communists were killed trying to storm it. Want to see it while we're in the area?"

"Definitely," replied John.

"You're invited also, young miss," Davignon said to Linh.

"Thank you, sir."

John wondered whether the Davignons were religious. "Tell me, are there any Christian churches in the area?"

"Well, you may have seen the famous Cathedral of Kon Tum while you were there."

"Yes, I did see it in passing. Beautiful."

"By the way, dear, that reminds me," said Madame Davignon. "I understand a French priest from China is looking for a position at the cathedral. He's applied to the diocese."

"Oh, these itinerant priests are always snooping around," grumbled Monsieur Davignon.

John's ears pricked up. "Do you know his name?"

"Not really," said Madame Davignon.

"Haven't a clue," scoffed her husband. "Don't want to, either."

"We should invite him to visit, dear," said Madame Davignon. "It would be the polite thing to do. He is a fellow Frenchman. Besides, I would want to hear about his experiences in China."

"Well, maybe," granted Monsieur Davignon.

"Does the name Father Durant ring a bell at all?" asked John.

Both husband and wife shook their heads no.

"Oh, well, just a thought."

~

The next day, Monsieur Davignon drove John out to his rubber groves in an American jeep. They drove down long rows of perfectly spaced trees, immaculately cleared of underbrush. Each trunk bled latex from wicked looking cuts that rolled down narrow, half-spiral gutters into buckets of sap collectors attached to every tree like testicles full of sperm. John listened politely to Monsieur Davignon's lengthy explanations of the rubber business, but his thoughts kept returning to the council meeting. During one of his reveries, Davignon laughed and said, "Well, I've bored you enough with this. Would you like to see the old fort? It's a bit of a spooky place, really."

"Absolutely!" enthused John, happy to move on from the topic of rubber.

Even as they spotted the fort from a distance through the trees, John felt drawn to its magnificent ruins. The stone walls of the fortress gradually rose above him as they approached, its weathered granite blocks partially hidden under the jungle's thick-rooted creepers, crawlers, and climbers. Newer embankments of piled rocks patched crumbled sections of the original walls. Although the overall effect was dreary, an incongruous lacing of colorful flowers eased the Gothic gloom.

They parked outside the walls and made their way by foot, sliding in sideways through a massive set of wooden doors that had warped in place, permanently ajar and just wide enough to accommodate a person. Stepping inside, they were greeted by the decomposing corpse of a once grand fortress. The sight took John's breath away.

The inside perimeter's thick, crenellated stone wall was oblong and had a second story defensive parapet with embrasures for rifle fire. A vast, deteriorating brick square, uneven and treacherous to navigate without risking twisted ankles, dominated the center of the fortress. At one end of the square stood a gutted Catholic church, still grand despite the ravages of time. Sections of its enormous roof had long since collapsed, filling the interior with shattered protuberances of angular rubble, the cleaved slabs a hodgepodge of crazed geometry. Statues of saints lay in bizarre positions, their great heads and shoulders rising at odd angles from the tile floor. Jungle vines girdled the stone saints in organic bondage. Promethean punishment for bringing the fire of religion to this sacred place of atheistic animals and plants. The fortress was a stony welt, a cold colonial canker amidst the healthy green tissue of the jungle.

While John admired the mythical old fortress, a low rumbling arose from the voices, as if they were at a distance but disturbed beyond all imaging. It grew louder and louder. Even during the worst times in China, when they reverberated ceaselessly in his head with insults and arguments, they did not sound as frightening as now, taking on the guttural characteristics of snarling lions; an ominous warning that he had entered their sacred den. He had fallen unknowingly into the belly of the beast. Like one of the statues, John stood frozen, listing slightly to one side, an unholy noise punching a hole through his mind; a runaway train careening through the gray matter, words maddeningly heaped on top of each other, indistinguishable.

...youAvelsilentdoweoheavenintosendwatchholy....

Then silence.

The voice of Monsieur Davignon broke the unnatural calm.

"Mr. Powers! Are you with us? Mr. Powers!"

John shook his head to clear the echoes, and uttered mechanically, "Yes, yes."

He found himself sitting in the jeep, head lolling back on the low-backed seat.

"You gave me a scare!"

"I'm fine, just a bit dizzy."

"What happened in there?" asked Monsieur Davignon in a tone, to John's dazed ear, sounding vaguely frightened.

"Don't know. Maybe the heat."

"Umm," grunted the Frenchman. "Well, let's go back to the villa and have a drink. That should help."

"Yes," said John, still shaken. Never had the voices seemed so terrifying, so vicious, so inhuman. On the way back, he replied to Monsieur Davignon's questions in monosyllables, begging off drinks and dinner to go straight to his room, where, he hoped, sleep would erase the echoes.

But, it did not, and the rumbling grumbling growling continued into the early hours, when at last he dropped off.

~

John was awakened to the sound of a servant knocking on his door. "Sir, breakfast is served, and you have a note from the village."

With heart racing, he threw on clothes and joined the French couple and Linh already at the table.

"Ah, good morning, Mr. Powers. Are you feeling better?" asked Madame Davignon.

"Yes, indeed, thank you.

"You will find a letter on your plate, Mr. Powers," said Monsieur Davignon, smiling. "Judging by its calligraphy, I believe it is from the Venerable Vu Huong himself."

John tore the envelope and scanned the contents. Written in elegant Chinese, it said: "Dear, esteemed, Mr. Powers. You are invited to tea with me at one o'clock on this day so that we may discuss the manner in which you shall be allowed to view the statue. Highest regards, Venerable Vu Huong, Council Chief, Song Nhan Village."

John let out a cry of joy, and the Davignons nodded appreciatively. "So, at last, you will see the statue?" asked Monsieur Davignon.

"Yes. Today at one o'clock I meet with the Venerable."

Monsieur Davignon smiled, but said in a cautionary tone, "Mr. Powers, you have more experience than we have with that statue, but I must warn you, it may not turn out to be what you think."

"How do you mean?"

"I mean, there is something in it which harbors a malignancy. At least, that is the conclusion of my wife and I. Although we have no evidence to prove its ill intent, I believe I can speak for Colette and say that you must treat it with extreme caution. As for ourselves, we want nothing further to do with it. Being religious folk, we are very wary of its powers . . . or rather, the source of its powers."

"Thank you for your concern," replied John, not the least fazed by this warning. But, Davignon's next statement made him sit up.

"Furthermore, Mr. Powers, I believe that whatever happened to you at the old fort was connected to that statue."

"Why do you say so?"

"Because, when we possessed it, or owned it, or it possessed us, I had a similar experience near the fortress."

"What experience?"

"Loud noise in my head, strange voices, dizzy, nauseous, the feeling of an evil presence."

John laughed uneasily. "Sounds like what a schizophrenic might say."

Monsieur Davignon joined his laughter. "Ha! Maybe! But, seriously, I did sense something very bad, and I'm no superstitious fool . . . nor a schizophrenic!" Again he laughed.

John did not reply, instead asking Madame Davignon about her garden. While she answered, Monsieur Davignon rose abruptly and threw down his napkin.

"Well, off to work! Do what you want, Mr. Powers, and let us know how things go with the old man. I wish you luck."

"Thank you!"

When the time came to leave for his meeting, Madame Davignon had been giving John a tour of her gardens. He found it difficult to concentrate on her horticultural insights, but her attractive presence made it pleasant. Linh had joined them for a little while, but excused herself to take care of some business in the village. After thanking Madame Davignon, he walked down the hill to the *dinh*. This time, he was not surrounded by begging children, and only a few curious stares followed him.

When he stood before the Venerable Vu Huong in the *dinh*, Linh had already arrived, but the expression in the old man's eyes caught him by surprise. Instead of an ancient, amiable, smiling wise man, what stared back at him was a dark, foreboding frown.

"Mr. Powers, you had some trouble at the old fort?" he asked in Chinese while offering him a seat.

"A little. Probably the heat."

"No, Mr. Powers, it was not the heat."

"What do you mean?"

"I mean, Mr. Powers, you must come and see the statue."

"But, that is why I came!"

The Venerable rose and motioned for John and Linh to follow. Two peasant women appeared the moment they stepped out of the *dinh*, and fell into line behind Vu Huong. With his jabbing cane leading the way, the wizened village council chief passed by many shabby dwellings before reaching a wooden house with a thatched roof. It appeared well maintained and clean, and stood at the very edge of the village where the paddies stretched in green brilliance beyond. A third woman stood on the veranda waiting.

"This is the house of Madame Dau," said Vu Huong, sweeping his hand toward her.

The woman bowed.

"And," continued the Venerable looking at the two women who had followed, "We have been joined by Schoolmistress Nang and Security Chief Tien."

He pointed his ever present cane at the house. "We have temporarily lodged the statue with Madame Dau, one of our council members, because we knew you would want to visit the *dinh*, and we had not yet decided to let you see it," explained the Venerable.

Even from outside, John could hear a frantic tapping coming from inside Madame Dau's house.

"Jesus!" he uttered under his breath.

For the first time that afternoon, the Venerable laughed. "No, Mr. Powers, I don't think it is your Jesus."

John glanced at Linh, whose eyes were opened wide with anxiety.

"Last night was terrible," said Madame Dau, a forceful, intelligent-looking woman, tilting her peasant hat to keep the sun from her eyes. I sent the family to stay with Madame Vit."

"You stayed?" asked the Venerable.

"Yes, of course. Someone had to guard it."

"Oh, she's very brave," Linh whispered to John.

"Don't forget me!" shouted a man with no legs, tilting this way and that on his knuckles. "It was safe as long as I was here!"

The others ignored him, and the Venerable banged his cane on the ground. "Let us go inside!"

John had rarely heard the statue make so much noise. For a brief moment, he felt his scalp rise, and a flash of panic made him want to run. When they entered, he spied the Precious Object sitting on an altar normally used for offerings to the ancestors. The tapping was deafening.

"What does it mean?" shouted the Venerable into John's ear.

John shook his head. "Child of Buddha would know," he muttered.

"What?" cried Vu Huong.

John waved his hand in a futile gesture. "Whatever it is, something bad is about to happen." Realizing he could not be heard, he turned to the old man and shouted, "Something bad is about to happen!"

"What?"

"Something bad! You said *she* is near. Have you seen *her*?"

"Alas, no!" replied the Venerable.

"Then how can you say *she* is near?"

"Because I know. Because *she* is."

"I'm telling you, something bad is about to happen!"

"What?" asked the Venerable, genuinely puzzled.

"I don't know, just that it will be bad."

"Superstitious nonsense!" spat Schoolmistress Nang, flashing her betel juice stained teeth. Remembering Davignon's description of her as a witch, the woman struck John as a skinny ribbon of gristle.

"How do you know *she* is near?" John again asked the Venerable.

In response, Vu Huong pointed his cane at the Precious Object.

"That doesn't always mean *she* is near!" cried John.

The Venerable cupped his hand around his ear. "What?"

"*She* is not necessarily near!"

With these words uttered, the tapping stopped suddenly, as if a spigot had been turned, and the Precious Object fell completely silent. The assembled onlookers gazed at each other in amazement. Even the Venerable appeared taken aback.

"What does it mean?" he again asked, but this time to the air.

"I don't know," said John.

The Venerable laughed and tapped his cane on a table. "It means *she* is near!"

~ *She Appears* ~

Yet, nothing unusual happened after the incident at Madame Dau's house. The Precious Object was moved back to the *dinh*, where the Guardian Spirits could properly protect it. For the next few days, John waited in vain for something, anything, to occur that might reveal *her* presence. To pass the time, he wandered around the village, and accompanied Monsieur Davignon on his trips to the rubber groves. Neither went near the old fort. John knew his time at the village was rapidly drawing to an end, and the fort began to exert a strange pull. It appeared night after night in his dreams, and a feeling that he must return grew stronger.

During these jittery days, the voices remained strangely quiet, and he could not help but note they, or something very much like them, made a nasty appearance the moment he stepped foot into the fort. What if he were to return? Could *she* possibly be waiting there? After all, *she* seemed to prefer dark places like caves and cells. Perhaps a ruined fortress would be more to *her* liking? But, the thought of returning to that awful fortress made him slightly ill. An uncomfortable notion occurred to him: what if he were Feng Shiren? What would that crazy mask-changer do? Feng would never hesitate. He would be recklessly bold, like that funny man with no legs by Madame Dau's house. Strange, how he associated Feng with that little man, yet the two seemed a pair. A stretch, to be sure, yet still, something there.

The memory of Feng Shiren made him think of Little Acorn, who in turn made him think of Michael, and a dagger of regret plunged deep into his heart. Lost opportunities, shirked responsibilities, a moonscape of memories, all dragged him down, while the poison slowly collected in his cratered soul. Schizophrenia flows from the source, just as harvested latex flows from a spiraled gutter, and it will be passed on from father to son. That will be his legacy. Michael will be sent to this damn country as a soldier, return from war in broken pieces, and end up dying decades hence in a mental institution. Legacy of schizophrenic papa. But, *she* has the power to change it. Only *she*. And, *she* awaits at the old fortress. Deep down, he knew *she* did. For once, John, do your duty. As Feng Shiren to Little Acorn, so John Powers to Michael Powers.

"Monsieur Davignon, may I borrow your jeep for tomorrow?"

"Please, call me Armand. Are you going to Kon Tum City?"

John started to answer in the affirmative, but at the last moment, even as his mouth opened to speak the lie, he instead said, "No, I'm going to the old fortress."

The Frenchman's eyes opened wide. "But, Mr. Powers, is that a good idea?"

"Please, call me John. And, no, it probably isn't. But, well, the fortress is compelling me—perhaps it's my romantic nature, or my interest in history, or that I must soon leave. I don't know. But, I will treat your jeep with care."

Davignon considered. "That is not the issue. As you know, I own two jeeps, and the second one might come in handy if you're not back by nightfall. Something about that old fort I don't trust. Do you agree it is somehow connected to the statue?"

"I don't know. All I can say is that it is pulling me, and I can't ignore it. Especially as I have so little time left."

"I see, but you will be back before dark?"

"Is it that important?"

"John, don't even attempt to drive on these narrow, winding jungle roads—trails I should more accurately say—at night."

"I see. I will be back long before nightfall."

"Good. See to it, John, or else we will be very worried. I don't want to have to come after you."

"Certainly. Thank you."

So, I've taken the plunge, thought John. *No backing down now.*

~

When morning arrived, a light rain had begun falling, and Monsieur Davignon suggested John wait until later, as a storm might be brewing. But, feeling the pressure of time, John assured the Frenchman he would not be long. Davignon acquiesced, but retained his worried frown. Linh stood next to the lanky Frenchman, and asked John for the umpteenth time if he wanted her to accompany him. Davignon's contagious nervousness had spread, making poor Linh doubly concerned.

"I'm sure I'll be fine," he assured her. "Thank you, Linh, but I'll be back soon. So much fuss! Don't worry."

But, even while he put on a show of waving vigorously and wearing a carefree smile as he drove away, her expression remained grim, mirroring that of Monsieur Davignon. Once the little road plunged into the jungle, he felt as if he had entered a tiny mouse hole in a huge palace. Almost with physical shock, he grasped how dark the atmosphere became when triple canopy foliage blocked out the sun. Instantly, his familiar world of people and houses and fields disappeared. A safety cord had been cut, and the asthmatic lungs of the jungle drew him deeper into their vegetative moistness. Halfway to the fortress, above hissing insect static, he heard the reverberation of distant thunder, and, as if awakened by the noise, the low growl of the voices. By the time he stopped the jeep outside the fortress wall, lightning singed the damp air, and thunder quickly followed in rolling waves.

"God, that storm came fast," muttered John to himself. He turned off the ignition and looked up at the intimidating fortress walls, rivulets of rain cascading down their stony protuberances like draining blisters, an unnerving sight made even more ominous by the turbulent atmosphere.

He sat motionless, listening to the deluge batter the canvas roof of the jeep. Leaving the safety it provided seemed as crazy as purposefully leaping into a watery oblivion. Twice he started the engine to leave, and twice he turned it off.

Go in! cracked God's voice.

Don't! responded Goddess. ***You will surely be sorry! Death is in those walls. You'll live!***

John nervously opened and closed the glove compartment a dozen times. It contained a few scraps of paper, a flashlight, and four screws. He looked at each screw, turning it this way and that, trying to gather courage from the spiral grooves. At last, he leapt from the jeep as if it were on fire, strode up to the great wooden doors of the fortress, turned sideways, and squeezed in.

~

John was startled to see an old peasant lady standing in the middle of the ruined courtyard with a broom, sweeping wet leaves that simply swirled around in the wind, scattering every which way. Futility personified. A peasant hat shrouded her face in shadows, and she did not look up. Only the bent spine and feeble sweeps of the broom revealed her age. But, as John peered more closely at her hands, he was amazed to see they appeared young; long, gracefully supple fingers gripped the broom handle.

He tore his eyes away from her mesmerizing form to peruse the fortress, but saw no one else. Only rueful stone saints, tilting in the rain, offered mute company to the woman, who John no longer assumed was old. Lightning occasionally illuminated her figure, garbed in a simple peasant *ao ba ba*. When thunder followed close behind, he instinctively gripped the wooden door, where he had remained from the beginning, the easier to make his escape back to the safety of the jeep.

The two remained standing for a long time—she, sweeping futilely, and he, clinging to the door. Finally, she looked up, her hat still rendering her facial features a shadowy blur. John knew her eyes stared at him, though he could not clearly see them. The woman gestured for him to approach. A deep, breathtaking fear gripped him, and he twitched as if electrically shocked, every cell in his body screaming at him to flee. But, at least the voices were silent, evidently cowed into submission by the authority of her presence.

Again, she waved, but this time with a slight nod of her head. This small, almost imperceptible gesture, calmed him and gave him courage. As if a spell had been broken, he said to himself, *It is just an old peasant woman sweeping leaves. Nothing more. Go up to her.*

Thus fortified, John slowly walked toward the woman, who waited patiently, her face still hidden beneath the dripping hat. He stopped some distance away, but she waved for him to come closer. Abruptly, he knew it was *her*. *Why hadn't I thought of that before?* he wondered. But, his feet still hesitated, and like a shy child, he slowly made his way up to *her*. As he drew closer, the face momentarily looked exactly like Meiying, causing him to freeze in shock. But, peering closer, he saw it had somehow morphed into the young lady who so many years ago entered his office and asked the mysterious question.

"Mr. Powers, how does one justify a life without cruelty, and therefore also without the distilled beauty of cruelty?"

Did *she* just ask that question, or was it in his head? Now he had moved close enough to touch, and he reached out his hands, palms up, mere inches from *her* body.

"How?" he asked meekly.

In response, *she* glowed, as if drawing energy from his presence. Never had he experienced such beauty. Even Meiying did not compare.

"It is raining," *she* said prosaically. "Let us go where it is dry."

A million questions raced through his mind, but *she* had already moved off, *her* broom still clutched in *her* hand. He could do nothing but follow.

She led him wordlessly into the ruined church, past slabs of broken concrete and stone, to the altar. With the roof partially collapsed, the rain fell unhindered onto the rotting pews. Still, *she* did not stop, and motioned for him to follow *her* behind the altar, where they came to a leaf-strewn expanse. Using *her* broom, *she* swept away the litter, revealing a trap door.

"I am quite aware you cannot see in the dark," *she* said. "Please go get the flashlight from your jeep and return."

As if in a dream, John obeyed *her* request, and returned with the flashlight to find the trap door opened, revealing a well of darkness that chilled him to the core.

"Follow me," *she* said, as calmly as if inviting him to join *her* for tea.

She descended stairs, more like a ladder, into the darkness. John knew this was the time to run, as he would probably never have another chance. Nonetheless, he descended, flashlight on, and stepped down on flat ground, close to *her*. She pointed to an opening large enough to enter upright, and walked in first.

They made their way through the tunnel, navigating between two iron rails that disappeared into the abyss beyond the feeble beam of the flashlight. Suffocating blackness pressed around them. Complete stillness prevailed—soil over a corpse. Submerged in the earth, his fear of the darkness redoubled.

"Where are we going?" he finally asked. But, *she* did not respond, the beam of light revealing only *her* back and the broom.

He grew bolder. "Was Mr. President *your* son?"

Nothing.

"Who are *you*?"

Nothing.

He tried shock. "What if I kill my son?"

Nothing.

"I'm going back!"

Nothing.

He clicked off his flashlight, but the darkness was as total as the inside of a grave. When he clicked it back on, *she* was far ahead, and in a panic he raced to catch up. He kept throwing out questions, but *she* remained silent. "What are my voices? Are *you* Goddess? The Precious Object? Who are *you*, goddamnit!" he shouted. But the reverberating echoes had no effect. Still, he followed, not sure he would find his way back, not wanting to be alone, not wanting to keep going.

Too anxious to do anything else, he followed *her* into what appeared to be an expansive storage chamber. Boxes and crates with French words stenciled on them were scattered about the floor and stacked to the ceiling. Long tables with myriads of tiny parts and half-assembled, rusty equipment stood unattended. *She* stopped.

"Am I going to die down here?" he asked, soaked with sweat and gasping for breath in the thin, fetid air.

"No," *she* finally spoke, gesturing toward something. He shined his beam where she indicated. A skeleton leaned against the tunnel wall, legs splayed, boots covering the bony feet; the boots of a soldier.

Beyond hysteria, his gorge rising, John asked in an eerily calm voice, "Who is it?"

"Your son."

~

John reeled in shock. "Don't be ridiculous!" he screamed. "Michael's back in the States, going to school!"

"You are given a glimpse."

"God damn *you*! A glimpse of my own son's death?"

"It is a sort of death."

"What? You make no sense. What do you mean by saying 'a sort of death'?"

"Mr. Powers, how does one justify a life without cruelty, and therefore without the distilled beauty of cruelty?"

John staggered back. "What are *you*? Are *you* really this cruel?" He threw up his arm to block the sight of the offending skeleton, and finally had sense enough to turn the flashlight back on *her*. Again a brief hint of Meiying, then *her* again.

"An addict craves potency," *she* said.

Yes, His faction's adherence to First Principles must be cured. *She* spoke in Goddess's voice.

You tricked me! cried God in a booming voice that reverberated off the walls. John held his hands over his ears.

She extended *her* hands, palms up. "Do not despair. That is not truly your son. It is a reflection of his agony."

"What? I don't understand! I can never understand *you*!"

"You have been given a glimpse. Do with it as you will."

John turned to flee, but his flashlight suddenly went out. He screamed and felt the darkness pressing him to his knees.

~ *The Trip Home* ~

When he opened his eyes, John was back in the jeep. After sitting dumbly for minutes, he checked the glove compartment—flashlight, papers, and screws, all rested undisturbed. He removed the flashlight and turned it on. It worked. Evidently, hours had passed, and the storm had become more violent. Somehow, in his fevered daze, he did not question the bizarre circumstances.

"A dream," he said aloud. "Fell asleep in the damn jeep."

He looked at the fort, starkly illuminated by each flash of lightning, and realized darkness would soon be absolute. Without a second thought, he turned the ignition and drove away as fast as possible on the muddy road.

As much of a dream as the voices, he thought. *And the voices are as much a dream as* her. *Real. Too real. Real enough to be put away. Put away where? Oh, god! Is this how Michael is to die? But,* she *said it was not really him. God! Get me out of here. Let me get back to the States. Back home, where I'll hug him tight, and forever! And Nanny Peach also. God, let me get home!*

It had turned completely dark by the time he pulled up to the mansion, where Linh and the Davignons waited, umbrellas in hand, clearly relieved at his safe arrival.

"By god, you cut it close, man!" exclaimed Monsieur Davignon, holding a lantern up to John's face.

"Come in and have some hot cocoa," said Madame Davignon. "My own recipe. Everyone raves about my cocoa. But, first, you must get out of those soaked clothes."

"I am so glad you are back," added Linh.

John luxuriated in their kindnesses, and happily bathed before joining them for hot cocoa.

When he entered the kitchen, Monsieur Davignon raised his cup and bellowed, "Welcome back!"

"Thank you."

"Did you find it interesting?" asked Madame Davignon.

"Very."

Monsieur Davignon leaned forward. "Tell me, John, did you find what you sought?"

John remained silent for some time, then said, "No. Nothing unusual. Just an old fort."

"Ah."

"Something unusual did happen here while you were gone," said Madame Davignon.

"Oh, yes?"

"Yes. The Venerable sent a boy to ask if you were in good health."

"Really?"

"Indeed," interjected Monsieur Davignon. "Something about that damn statue. Couldn't get the gist of it. Trouble. Probably that damn noise, or something. Had me worried, too. But, as usual, just superstitious nonsense. All is well."

"Yes, all is well," replied John, sipping his cocoa. He turned to his lovely guide. "Linh, tomorrow we leave."

"Yes, sir. Do you wish to see statue one more time?"

"No. It's time to go home."

That night, John had a last meal with the Davignons. The topic of discussion revolved around the widening war in Vietnam and America's involvement. John listened, but did not participate, visions of Michael and the skeleton afflicting his mind. Davignon portrayed the war as a crusade for civilization against the tide of barbarism.

"Many will die," John interjected, to which Monsieur Davignon replied, "Yes, but in the name of freedom, sacrifices must be made."

John fell silent, but wondered if Monsieur Davignon would be willing to sacrifice Colette in the name of freedom. *I think not*, he decided, but withheld from further comment.

"Where do your Vietnamese friends stand on the issue?" Davignon asked Linh, who immediately looked down in embarrassment.

"Dear, that is unfair," said Madame Davignon. "Leave the poor girl alone. Politics is an unhealthy topic at dinner."

"Yes, but I'm interested in what she has to say," insisted Davignon. "Linh, do you mind telling me whether you're Buddhist or Catholic?"

"I am Buddhist, sir."

"Ah, and what do your Buddhist friends think of Ho Chi Minh and the communists?"

"We are not political."

"Armand," said Madame Davignon. "I think she doesn't want to talk about it."

"Yes, yes, well later, perhaps."

"You will be a target of the communists, Armand," said John. "Have you thought of what you will do if they come?"

"Fight, like a true Frenchman!"

"I see."

John went to bed after dinner, Monsieur Davignon's words ringing in his ears. *Fools like that will get my son killed*, he thought. *How many skeletons will it take for them to ever understand?*

Next morning, a car came for John and Linh to take them back to Kon Tum City. "We'll catch a military plane to Saigon," said John. "The bus will take too long."

"But, how make the arrangements?"

"Don't worry, Linh. I have contacts with Air America. We'll get a plane, don't worry. Then, home."

"Sad to see you go," she said.

"Me too."

"I not tell Monsieur Davignon the truth," she said unexpectedly.

"Oh?"

"My friends no like the Saigon government. Ho Chi Minh is a great hero to us. I hope America not become too involved."

"So, you're a communist?" asked John, stunned.

"Maybe, maybe not. Knowledge incomplete. But, it's good you get out now, Mr. Powers. Very good."

Her words did not sound like the innocent Vietnamese schoolgirl he had known all these weeks, and John suddenly realized there was more to Linh than met the eye.

"Why, Linh?"

John watched her face become solemn and far more mature than he had ever seen her before. "We will be coming out of our own tunnels, Mr. Powers, and no one, no country, can stop us." Again, the girlish face appeared, and she smiled. "So, you see, it's good you get out now, Mr. Powers."

"I agree, Linh. I agree."

It occurred to him that he had never mentioned the tunnel before their conversation.

~

Two days later, John gave Linh a hug and boarded an airplane for home. His voices rumbled at a low level, evidently arguing over the tunnel. Their words were growled and garbled, so he ignored them and focused on his own thoughts, forcing them to rise above the schizophrenic static. The long flight gave him time to evaluate his experience in the tunnel. As a consequence, he determined to make solemn resolutions about how he would change his life. First order of business: be a father again, if it wasn't too late. Second order of business: check Michael for signs of schizophrenia, and get him professional help. Third order of business: live his life with immediacy, in the present, and put the past behind.

Three tall orders, he mused. *But, I can do them. They are within my power. Damn the voices! Michael will not end up a lonely skeleton in some dark Vietnamese tunnel.*

When the plane landed in San Francisco, John fairly bounded down the ramp, where he found Nanny Peach and Michael waiting. Rushing up to them, he gave both a long hug, which elicited no small degree of astonishment from each.

"Welcome home, dad," said Michael between squeezes and slaps on the back.

"Yes, welcome home, sir," added Nanny Peach, also breathless.

"So good to see you both!" he gushed. "We have a lot of catching up to do! Let's go home!"

Nanny Peach and Michael gave each other furtive glances, their eyebrows raised in perplexed delight.

John knew they were taken aback, and it merely confirmed how terrible he had been in the past. *What a fool I was*, he thought. *I feel like Scrooge after seeing his grave.*

So, with these deep feelings of love and rebirth, John returned home with the two people he loved most in the world. *Now*, he thought. *I must convince them I have changed. I must make them love me!*

But, on the way home, Michael sat in the back seat, unusually quiet and distant, no matter how much John tried to draw him into conversation. He looked in the rear-view mirror to see a face distracted and vacant.

"So, Michael, how is school going?"

"Good."

"Any interesting stories? You know, anything happen that you want to share?"

"Not really."

Nanny Peach, sitting next to John in the passenger seat, shot him a look which he could not read. He felt his stomach tighten. *Not even home yet, and there's already trouble.* In the face of Michael's odd behavior it seemed all his best intentions were going down in flames before he had a chance to prove himself, and his thoughts turned to the solace of bourbon awaiting him at home. *That will steady me,* he thought. *Michael's just a little shy. Stands to reason. Adolescent boy. He'll come around, if I just keep trying.* But, *her* prophecies and the image of the skeleton preyed on his mind.

Once home, Michael quickly retreated to his room, and Nanny Peach motioned John to follow her outside before he even had time to unpack.

"What is it, Margaret?"

"I'm worried about him. Every day he withdraws a little more."

"Voices?"

"I think so. He still won't admit it, but I am pretty sure."

"We must get him to a professional!"

Nanny Peach gave him a wry look. "Yes, it's long overdue."

~

But, dear Reader, the voices already had a foothold in my mind, and no amount of counseling would help. I denied I heard voices, and was easily able to fool the doctors into thinking it was just adolescent depression, so they gave me *Elavil* and left me to my own devices. My father appeared delighted at their diagnosis, and ordered Nanny Peach to drop the subject.

Chapter Twenty-Four

An Ending

The War Looms

Despite his best intentions to become a loving father, John felt powerless to deal with his son's withdrawal and gradually returned to the comfort of the bottle. Michael had reached his senior year in high school, and the war in Vietnam raged like a wildfire, uncontained and indiscriminately destructive. With news of the war unavoidable, John was daily reminded of the prophecies that so stoked his fears. Having long ago accepted the psychiatrist's diagnosis, he had conveniently dismissed from his mind the possibility his son had inherited schizophrenia. Rather, he felt even more estranged, as the boy did not have the excuse of mental illness to explain his apparent listlessness. According to Goddess, he was supposed to be the next Chosen One, the next step! In moments of clarity, he realized he felt less disappointed in Michael than in his own failures. John convinced himself that Michael did not love him, and remained too cold and distant for reconciliation to be possible. Nevertheless, he urged the boy to attend college for two reasons: first, to get an education, and second, to avoid the draft by obtaining a deferment. Michael's high school grades were adequate, and John felt relieved when he agreed to this course of action. Nanny Peach, beside herself with worry, and in the simplicity of her insights, knew Michael heard voices, and wholeheartedly agreed to the plan so her "precious boy" would not be drafted.

One night, on the eve of Michael's high school graduation, John sat as usual in his recliner sipping bourbon. The voices had long since died down to barely whispers, and he was left alone with his memories and regrets. Michael made a rare appearance outside his bedroom, and sat near his father, eyes averted. John, surprised at Michael's entry, assumed his typical hale and hearty persona, a mask that kept him clear of emotional connections.

"Well! Hello, son! How goes the war?"

Michael, still averting his eyes, replied, "Okay, I guess."

"Looking forward to getting out of jail and going to college?"

"Yeah, I guess."

"Well, what brings you in here?"

"Nothing."

"Ah." John chaffed under his son's seemingly apathetic presence, for he had no skill in talking with the boy in any meaningful way. "Going to get good grades on your final report card?"

"I guess."

"Good."

"Dad?"

"Yes?"

"How did you meet Mom?"

John's heart constricted, and he croaked out, "Oh, that was a long time ago. Water under the bridge. Why?"

"Oh, just wondering. She sure was pretty, huh? I mean in her pictures and all."

"Yes."

"What was her favorite thing to do?"

"What? Oh, play the piano, of course." He shot Michael an irritated glance. "Come on, you already knew that."

"No, I mean except for that."

"Why all these questions?"

"Just wondering. I never really hear much about her, like how you met her and all."

John had never told Michael about *her*, or the quest, or how he and Meiying met, or any of the hardships they both encountered. "Well, that was a long time ago. You have your future to concentrate on."

Silence.

John took a gulp of bourbon.

"You know," he said, "San Francisco State is a good college. You'll be happy there."

"Yeah."

Silence again.

"Well," said Michael. "I'm going to fix a sandwich and head back to my room."

"Okay."

John knew the conversation had gone poorly. He knew he should have talked more about Michael's mother and how they met. Yet, he couldn't force himself to dredge up the old memories and the old pains, even for his son.

It'll be better when he's at college, he thought. *Distance will give us more to talk about. It'll be fine. He'll call and fill me in on all the goings on at college, and I'll respond with wise advice, and . . . we'll be fine.*

Nanny Peach came in and sat, looking at John sadly. "You know," she said pensively, "I also don't know how you and Mrs. Powers met. It would be an interesting story. Michael is interested."

"Didn't sound like he was all that interested," replied John, somewhat piqued that she had eavesdropped on their conversation.

"I heard him ask."

"He gave up too easily."

"John," said Nanny Peach, addressing him by name as she rarely did. "Let us all help each other. Surely you know, after all these years, the pain you feel for Mrs. Powers has made you unhappy, and you have closed yourself from the rest of us who love you."

John felt touched, but the old urges tightened around his heart. "Oh, Margaret, please just leave me alone. Please!"

"One last word, John," she said. "I am quite sure Michael hears voices. Quite sure." She turned slowly and walked away.

After she left, he emptied his glass and slumped in his chair. *So, I have come full circle,* he thought. *Back to being the old fool. But, I tried to reach out, I really did. It's not my fault if Michael is so self-absorbed that he can't even respond to his own father. It's just that he is so damned distant. And if Margaret is right about his voices? If only Meiying were here, even if she lived with Marie, everything would be fine.*

To distract his mind from such familiar, old, self-lacerating thoughts, he turned on the television. The news blared a lead story about more American soldiers being sent to Vietnam and the rising number of men that must be drafted to meet the demands of the generals.

"Thank god, Michael is going to college," he said aloud. "Thank god." But, behind his words lay a dark foreboding that pressed against his hopes.

~

Months later, John received a call from Michael.

"Hello, Dad?"

"Yes, hello Michael."

"How are you?"

"Fine. How are classes going?"

"Dad, I couldn't get any of my required classes. They're all full of guys wanting to stay out of the draft. It's really frustrating."

"Well, to be expected. Just go to the classes you can get."

"They're so boring!"

John felt his voice break. "Michael, just stick with it. Things will get better."

"Okay, I'll try. Can I get a little more money? It's expensive here."

John breathed a sigh of relief. "Yeah, sure. Just keep up with your classes. Stay full time, or else. . . . "

"You don't have to tell me, Dad. I know, I know."

"Okay, I'll send you a few hundred bucks to hold you over."

"Thanks, Dad."

"Hang in there, Michael."

"Sure. See you, and thanks again."

"You're welcome."

Click.

~

After Michael hung up with his father, he flopped back on the bed in his dorm. Roommate gone. Bored. Skipping classes again. Picked up Dostoevsky and resumed reading. Should be in geology class, but it consisted of nothing but interminable slides of rocks. But Dostoevsky! With Raskolnikov, he was no longer bored. Fuck class. The voices were there, in the background, boiling and rumbling, ready to burst out of their confinement.

Michael remembered his father saying crazy things. He said Goddess revealed the fact he was not fully human. Nor, indeed, was his mother Bai Meiying. Rejecting such madness, Michael felt drawn to immerse himself in the fullness of human experience. Spurred by this resolve, he made a momentous decision.

~

Yes, yes, dear Reader, I was bored with school, but not with learning. If I had only known what was to come of my decision to drop out of school and let fate take its course. Don't get me wrong, I knew I would be drafted, of course, but I thought anything was better than living a lie. Besides, this would be a golden opportunity to observe humans at war. Never get another chance. Now, there's real learning! Away with boredom and a purposeless life! So thought an adolescent male with too many neural trains and too few neural brakes. I pictured myself in the jungle, observing historical events happening all around me. Watching how humans respond to war, violence, and destruction. An anthropologist researching in real time. What a laboratory! What a fool!

~ *Drafted* ~

When he got the call from Michael that he had been drafted, John left work and broke down on the way home, just as he had done when Meiying died, nicer weather being the only difference. In horror, he realized all the prophecies were turning out to be true: Michael suffered from schizophrenia, would go to war, and his bones would end up in some damn tunnel under an old French fortress. Yet, *she* said they weren't really his bones. Somehow, his bones would remain in that tunnel, even if he survived. *Doesn't make sense!* But, John knew it didn't have to make sense. Ever since *she* came into his life, nothing had made sense. *It's the damn Goddess!* he thought. *She's behind this. Something to do with God, and we're just pawns, Michael, Meiying, myself—just pawns!*

John finally made his way home. Nanny Peach sobbed at the news, and he again sought relief in the bottle. After a few drinks, he struggled with the germ of a fantastic idea. *I can take Michael to Canada*, he thought. *No draft. No war. Make lies of all the damn prophecies.*

Yes! came God's voice, so long absent, but now insistent. **Do it! Do it! Do you want your son to die? Do it! Do it! For once in your life, John Powers, do something for Michael! Notice Goddess is silent? She wants your son to go to war. It is part of Their plan for intermediates.**

John knew the voice spoke false words, but they cut him to the quick. *One thing is true*, he thought. *I have a chance to do something for Michael. No, better yet, I can do something for Meiying! For our son!*

Nanny Peach heard John mumbling to himself in his recliner, seemingly involved in some inner argument. *God help the poor man,* she thought. *Let him sleep it off.*

The next morning was a Saturday. After breakfast and empty conversation with Nanny Peach, John drove to the Presidio and took a walk into the forested area of the park. He and Meiying had often come here to stroll the grounds together, talking, reminiscing. Now, he had come to stroll with her again, to talk, to think. As he walked with her, the others joined; Madame Liu, Feng Shiren, Suling, Child of Buddha, Lu Zhishen, all of them. The group felt the sun on their skins, and enjoyed watching Little Acorn off on a hillside, playing with a stick.

"Looks like I'm going to be visiting your country with my son," said John to Lu Zhishen. The big Canadian shook his beard and laughed. With the laughter, John first noticed the constriction in his chest. He tried to shake it off, but after staggering a few yards, a deep, searing pain brought him to his knees, then struck with such force that he fell backwards, flat on his back. His old comrades gathered around and stared down at him with sympathetic faces. He felt their love wash over his pain, and he lifted his hands, palms up. In response, they held up their hands in the same way. Waves of pain made them fade into the sky. Only Meiying remained, continuing to look at him with an exquisitely melancholy face, tears streaming.

His left hand fell heavily to the ground, but it seemed miraculous to the dying man that his remaining upturned palm, in which he felt the tickling of an ant's legs, overcame the heavy pull of gravity dragging them both earthward. The insect's frenetic prickling probing reminded him of something he had learned long ago when the others died: the ceaselessness of that which is still seeking always taps a mocking farewell to the ceasing of that which had once been sought. So be it.

Although lying fully prone on the dirt path, he was strangely hesitant to lower his hand and let the back of it touch the ground. Such surrender would mark the final ending. As long as it hovered inches above the solid inevitability of corruption, life circulated above and below. How he came to lie dying on his back beneath the forest canopy, levitating one hand upon which reconnoitered an anxious ant, was a puzzle that frayed his concentration. Yes, he must keep the hand above the famished soil and remember. *She* had often asked when he would lower his hand. Now he understood *her* words. Memory was the cushioning air beneath the hand; it was the light, the open space, which fought off malevolent, solid darkness.

How could it end like this? Hold the hand up, heavy as it was becoming, and remember. But the insect? Keep her from her nestmates to satisfy a need? Lower to ashes and dust for the benefit of an ant that she might be set free? Yes? No. Lower it and die. He wanted to live. The hand remained a hovering, weighted hope; the ant a taunting vitality.

"Meiying!" he cried as she looked down at him in pity. "I want to live! I want to live!"

~ *Last Visit* ~

By the time Michael reached the hospital, his father was on life support, with little hope from the doctors that he would survive the massive heart attack. Nanny Peach hugged her beloved Mikey in the hallway, and he entered the room. Shaking with trepidation, Michael took his father's hand gently, to avoid the needles and tubes. Through the haze of morphine, John blinked at his son, squeezed his hand, and spoke in a raspy voice.

"Watch out for the voices and avoid the poison that collects at the bottom of craters."

~

Those were the last words my father ever spoke.

It was now my turn to suffer.

It was now my turn to take the next step.

It was now my turn to have a child—the first of the Superior Ones.

But this understanding came to me very late in life. Very late. First, I must endure the suffering. Always the suffering. Without suffering there cannot be joy.

Right, God?

Epilogue

The Stillness

Dear Reader, you might well ask how I know what my father thought and said during these events, let alone the thoughts and words of all the others. The answer should be obvious to you: my voices told me, of course.

After my father's death, I entered the army and went to war. I also went mad, so they say. The war intensified my delusions and I now dwell in equal parts hallucination and reality.

I am surrounded by people: my twin brother who fought (and died, in a manner of speaking) in Vietnam, a son and daughter-in-law, a close friend who is married with two children, a first wife, a second wife who is a spy for Goddess.

I am told by psychiatrists that some of these people are real and some are imaginary. And needless to say, they tell me Goddess Herself as well as God are mere voices in my head.

Goddess, on the other hand, tells me I am not fully human, that I am the Chosen One, the next step in the eventual rise to dominance of Superior Ones.

She also told me there is no twin who fought in Vietnam.

But the psychiatrists have failed to convince me which people (or deities) are real and which are not.

Instead I choose to believe they all are imaginary *and* they all are real.

Likewise, Goddess has failed to convince me of the fact I am not human.

Instead, I choose to believe I am schizophrenic *and* I am the Chosen One.

Be that as it may, such delusions of mine (if they are delusions) are for another story. And what of those in this book, my father, my mother, and the others? All are also real and all are also imaginary.

Which is which? You decide. I am mad, remember?

Finally, unlike my father, I never went on any quest to find *her*. No, no, no. In fact, quite the opposite. I have been on a quest to escape, not to discover.

Escape from what? I am not sure.

Escape to what? The end of humanity? The rise of Superior Ones? Rebirth of the planet? Stillness?

That also is for another story.

~

The Voices no longer silent.
The Stillness no longer hidden,
Its shadows stretch toward the coming war,
Quickening the fevered pulse.
Bury the birth.
And humanity is drawn further down its long, final path.